THE BEST SCIENCE FICTION
OF THE YEAR

Also Edited by Neil Clarke

Magazines
Clarkesworld Magazine—clarkesworldmagazine.com
Forever Magazine—forever-magazine.com

Anthologies
Upgraded
The Best Science Fiction of the Year Volume 1
Galactic Empires (forthcoming 2016)
Modified (forthcoming 2017)
The Best Science Fiction of the Year Volume 2 (forthcoming 2017)

(with Sean Wallace)
Clarkesworld: Year Three
Clarkesworld: Year Four
Clarkesworld: Year Five
Clarkesworld: Year Six
Clarkesworld: Year Seven
Clarkesworld: Year Eight
The Best of Clarkesworld (forthcoming 2017)

THE BEST SCIENCE FICTION OF THE YEAR

OF THE YEAR

VOLUME 1

Edited by Neil Clarke

Night Shade Books
NEW YORK

Night Shade books may be purchased in bulk at special discounts for sales promotion, corporate gifts, fund-raising, or educational purposes. Special editions can also be created to specifications. For details, contact the Special Sales Department, Night Shade Books, 307 West 36th Street, 11th Floor, New York, NY 10018 or info@skyhorsepublishing.com.

Night Shade Books® is a registered trademark of Skyhorse Publishing, Inc. ®, a Delaware corporation.

Visit our website at www.nightshadebooks.com.

10 9 8 7 6 5 4 3 2 1

Library of Congress Cataloging-in-Publication Data is available on file.

Print ISBN: 978-1-59780-854-5

Cover illustration by Eddie Del Rio
Cover design by Jason Snair

Please see page 601 for an extension of this copyright page.

Printed in the United States of America

Table of Contents

Introduction: A State of the Short SF Field in 2015 vii

Today I Am Paul—**Martin L. Shoemaker** 1
Calved—**Sam J. Miller** 12
Three Bodies at Mitanni—**Seth Dickinson** 25
The Smog Society—**Chen Qiufan** 43
In Blue Lily's Wake—**Aliette de Bodard** 55
Hello, Hello—**Seanan McGuire** 72
Folding Beijing—**Hao Jingfang** 88
Capitalism in the 22nd Century—**Geoff Ryman** 122
Hold-Time Violations—**John Chu** 135
Wild Honey—**Paul McAuley** 147
So Much Cooking—**Naomi Kritzer** 161
Bannerless—**Carrie Vaughn** 181
Another Word for World—**Ann Leckie** 200
The Cold Inequalities—**Yoon Ha Lee** 230
Iron Pegasus—**Brenda Cooper** 239
The Audience—**Sean McMullen** 251
Empty—**Robert Reed** 274
Gypsy—**Carter Scholz** 298
Violation of the TrueNet Security Act—**Taiyo Fujii** 359
Damage—**David D. Levine** 383
The Tumbledowns of Cleopatra Abyss—**David Brin** 401
No Placeholder for You, My Love—**Nick Wolven** 435
Outsider—**An Owomoyela** 454
The Gods Have Not Died in Vain—**Ken Liu** .471
Cocoons—**Nancy Kress** 492
Seven Wonders of a Once and Future World
  — **Caroline M. Yoachim** 505
Two-Year Man—**Kelly Robson** 520
Cat Pictures Please—**Naomi Kritzer** 532
Botanica Veneris: Thirteen Papercuts by Ida Countess Rathangan
  — **Ian McDonald** 540
Meshed—**Rich Larson** 570
A Murmuration—**Alastair Reynolds** 580

2015 Recommended Reading List 599

INTRODUCTION:
A State of the Short SF Field in 2015

Neil Clarke

Ten years ago, people were proclaiming the death of short fiction in our field and they had good reason to be worried: the leading genre magazines had spent the decade losing nearly half their subscribers; the only widely respected online magazine of its time, *SciFiction*, had just been shuttered by its owners, the SciFi Channel. It was in that climate that I decided to launch a new online magazine, *Clarkesworld*. I was told upfront that I was crazy and several professional authors flat-out proclaimed that online magazines were the domain of pirates and unskilled newbies. The one thing I can say for sure is that online publishing was still very much like the Wild West. New magazines came and went at a furious pace and everyone had their own unique business model that was sure to tame the Internet. It really was a chaotic, frustrating, and an exciting time to enter the field!

Over the next three years the attitude towards online fiction changed significantly. It was becoming harder to argue that online venues weren't producing quality work with increasing frequency. Stories from those markets were being recognized by most of the major awards in our field or being picked up the annual year's best anthologies. Then, in 2007, Amazon released the Kindle just in time for Christmas and changed the state of short fiction forever.

Digital subscriptions and ebook sales were finally the financial boost the field needed to turn things around. The trend of declining print subscriptions was slowly but surely offset and turned around by digital growth. The online magazines finally had a more reliable way to generate revenue and grow. Alternatives to Amazon also sprang into being at Barnes & Noble, Apple, Google, Kobo, and Weightless Books, the latter being a boon to independent authors and many small press magazines and anthologies.

Just a few years earlier, there was a sharp line between print and online magazines. Now it was a blurred mess of old perceptions and new market realities. While overall readership has tilted towards those that offer an online edition, there are still only three magazines that have full-time employees and they are all veterans of the print era: *Asimov's*, *Analog*, and *F&SF.* Yet there was more to come.

Enter the next disruption: crowdfunding. While online, digital, and short-run publishing lowered the bar to entry, launching an original anthology or magazine can easily cost over ten thousand dollars, if not more. That financial hurdle represents a considerable deterrent that crowdfunding sites like Kickstarter, GoFundMe, IndieGoGo, and others can sometimes eliminate.

Now, you can pre-test the market's interest by launching a campaign that allows people to make financial pledges towards it. Many use it like pre-ordering a book, committing an amount they would expect to pay for the finished product, but others treat it more like investing in a project, but one from which they'll never see financial rewards. In those cases, it's more like a town investing in a park so that the kids will have somewhere to play. Many are willing to contribute simply because they believe the project *should* happen. The downside is that can sometimes that can create an illusion of demand for the product. That illusion appears to have more of a negative impact on recurring projects like magazines than it does on single volume projects like collections and anthologies.

While many of these magazines intended to be self-sufficient from subscriptions in their second, third, fourth, etc. years, it's never quite as easy as they believe. Quite frequently, their subscription revenue falls far short of what is necessary to continue at the over-ambitious levels their supporters encouraged. This often leads to a "save XXXX" campaign or serial crowdfunding campaigns, the latter of which has many people worried about "Kickstarter fatigue"—a theory that this behavior will discourage people from supporting these kinds of projects in the future.

Crowdfunding can and has been an extremely positive force on our field, so let's hope this pattern of poor planning doesn't ruin it for the next generation of projects. However, there are other models of crowdfunding that may be more suited to these new ventures. Patreon, for example, combines some of the features of Kickstarter with a subscription-style model. Supporters pay-per creation or per-month, making it easier to assess the current state of their income and what they can realistically accomplish with those resources. It does mean starting smaller and growing into their goals, and that style of planning is something we need to see more of in this field.

That brings us to today, with a busy anthology market that has been doing some niche projects, but has been held back by the broken print distribution model that prevents many of them from reaching physical bookstores; and a magazine market that is growing faster than the number of new people will-ing to pay for it.

The anthology problem is complicated and not likely to be resolved any-time soon, unfortunately. Several of these projects are most likely too narrow in scope for national distribution, but there are others that would certainly benefit from it. Ebooks and print-on-demand (POD) publishing can provide greater access to readers, but they frequently miss having many more due to a lack of presence in physical stores. With my own books, I've observed a correlation between ebook sales and a physical presence in a bookstore. It's almost as though the printed book is becoming a marketing component for digital sales. Some traditional and smaller nationally-distributed publishers have begun reissuing self-published, independent, or small press titles, but these still represent a very small blip in the market and are still too rare to indicate a change in business.

The magazine problem is a bit more complicated. As someone neck-deep in the magazine field, I've started worrying about two things: sustainability and quality.

Sustainability

Let's pretend for a second that a town has enough coffee drinkers to sustain three coffee shops. A local resident has always wanted to run a coffee shop and the rent is cheap here, so he gives it a try. They develop a small, but pas-sionate set of customers, but not enough to be profitable. The other shops see a slight dip in sales, but remain quite healthy. Six more people launch shops in the same town and suffer the same fate, but this is their dream, so they decide to stick it out until inevitably, they give up—only to be replaced by another—or start save-our-store campaigns. Their passionate customer bases are more than happy to drop ten times their normal coffee budget in a single visit to save the store, and this buys the store owner time. Unfortunately, they go right back to doing business as usual and soon enough, we're right back where we started.

That's what the magazine market is like right now. Either the market is over-saturated or it's charging too little for its product. Those three magazines that have been supporting themselves have been around for decades and no one new has broken into their ranks for quite some time. It's hard to say that any of them have suffered significant declines due to their new competition as they've actually picked up subscribers in the last five years. It appears that the struggle is predominantly between the magazines that have opened in the last ten to fifteen years.

At the top of that heap are a few publications that are covering their costs, but not paying their staff as much as would be appropriate for a professional publication. They've proven they understand their business and can be smart about it. While their growth is slow, I fully expect one or two to break that ceiling sometime in the next few years. Between now and then, however, I see some market adjustments brewing on the horizon. Even when you love what you do, eventually there reaches a point when even the most determined cry out "Enough!" and leave the field. Sometimes that even comes from the readers when they've been asked to save a publication one too many times.

Quality

If the number of quality stories isn't growing as fast as the number of stories publishers need to fill all their slots, then quality must dip to fill the void. The software I developed to process story submissions at *Clarkesworld* has provided me with the opportunity to collect a lot of data. In the last three years I've logged submissions from over fifteen thousand authors. In 2015, we received an average of one thousand stories each month. Each of those was competing for one of the five slots we have for original fiction in each issue. While the volume will vary for other anthologies and magazines, the rejection rate for short stories is consistently high.

For this book, I had to read everything published by other editors, each undertaking the same process of filtering from a much larger pile. These were the stories they considered the best in their pool. If Sturgeon's Law ("ninety percent of everything is crap") holds, their efforts saved me a lot of time and energy. It would be easily to believe that with that level of culling happening, that quality shouldn't be an issue. Sadly, I'd have to rate this year as a B-. While there were several A and a few A+ stories, I was rarely worried about reprinting too many stories from single market. It certainly felt like an off year for many of those I'd read previously. Whether that was a fluke or the result of market oversaturation is yet to be seen.

From where I sit, though, if things continue on their current trajectories, I believe we're in for a market contraction. The market can certainly sustain the loss of a few markets. It might even be better for the health of the entire ecosystem, but if you want to help the magazines you love avoid that fate, here's a few suggestions:

Subscribe to or support any magazine that you'd be willing to bail out if they were to run aground. Just-in-time funding is not a sane or sustainable business model. If you want them to succeed, then be there before they need you.

If the magazine doesn't offer subscriptions or have something like a Patreon page through which you can support them financially, encourage them to do so.

Don't support new (or revival) projects until they clearly outline reasonable goals to sustain the publication after their initial funding runs out.

Introduce new readers to your favorite stories and magazines. This is particularly easy with so many online magazines being freely available at the moment. We need more short fiction readers if all this is to remain sustainable.

While I might be a little concerned about 2016, we're far from anything like the Chicken Little fears proclaimed a decade ago. The overall health of the field is better than it has been in a long time. We might be in for some rocky periods at some markets, but overall, I think everything will work itself out. And even despite all my griping about 2015, I'm quite happy with the stories I ended up selecting for this inaugural volume. To end things on a higher note, though, I thought I'd start the tradition of highlighting some of the best of 2015. I'm not sure I'll stick with these categories, but to start I'd like to address my picks for best magazine, best anthology, and best new writer.

Magazine

My pick for the best magazine of 2015 is a genre veteran that I've been reading for decades. As I read for this volume, they became my rock. I could always count on each issue to include a gem and the quality was always consistent throughout. Sheila Williams is an editor I look up to and this year, she led *Asimov's* on a course that impressed me. You'll find five stories from their pages in this book and many more in the recommended reading list. If only I'd had room to include more!

Anthology

By the middle of the year, I was convinced that picking the winner for this category would be a challenge. I found isolated stories here and there, but no single book was presenting itself as a must-read volume. December then swooped in and saved the day with a few worthy contenders. Leading that charge was Jonathan Strahan's latest entry in his Infinity series, *Meeting Infinity*. I've selected four stories from this anthology and happily recommend many more. Buy it. Read it. You'll thank me later, as it was truly the best last year.

New Author

One of the greatest joys an editor experiences on the job is having the honor of publishing an author first before anyone else. It's a rare pleasure and one that I experienced in February when "The Three Resurrections of Jessica Churchill" by Kelly Robson appeared in *Clarkesworld*. When she told me that two more of her stories would appear in *Asimov's* and *Tor.com*, I was surprised—because it's highly unusual for a new author to land three stories at highly-selective professional magazines—but also not surprised. She's simply that good and the range and quality of her work tell me that this is an author to watch. You can read "Two-Year Man," her *Asimov's* story, in this book. Both her *Clarkesworld* story and her *Tor.com* fantasy novella, "Water of Versailles," are available for free online. I, for one, would not be surprised to see her name on the Campbell Award for Best New Writer ballot, but if she isn't, she still has yet another year of eligibility on the table.

In closing, growing up, I recall racing to the bookstore shelf to grab the latest in Terry Carr's year's best series by the same name. I never would have dreamed that I'd be doing this someday. So, thanks to Terry for planting a seed in my head. I hope he would have liked what it has become. To everyone at Night Shade Books, particularly Cory and Jeremy, thank you for making this book possible. Your faith in me will be remembered. And then there's Sean Wallace and Kate Baker, who have my back at every turn. Your assistance and encouragement on this project is now noted and undeniable. Mom and Dad, all those books you bought me as a kid appear to have resulted in something. I have no bigger supporters than my wife Lisa and sons Aidan and Eamonn. Without them, I'd be lost and at times, while working this project, they probably thought I was.

Oh, and to that teenage kid that's just picked up this book or ebook, someday, this could be yours, too.

Neil Clarke
January 20, 2016

TODAY I AM PAUL

Martin L. Shoemaker

"Good morning," the small, quavering voice comes from the medical bed. "Is that you, Paul?"

Today I am Paul. I activate my chassis extender, giving myself 3.5 centimeters additional height so as to approximate Paul's size. I change my eye color to R60, G200, B180, the average shade of Paul's eyes in interior lighting. I adjust my skin tone as well. When I had first emulated Paul, I had regretted that I could not quickly emulate his beard; but Mildred never seems to notice its absence. The Paul in her memory has no beard.

The house is quiet now that the morning staff have left. Mildred's room is clean but dark this morning with the drapes concealing the big picture window. Paul wouldn't notice the darkness (he never does when he visits in person), but my empathy net knows that Mildred's garden outside will cheer her up. I set a reminder to open the drapes after I greet her.

Mildred leans back in the bed. It is an advanced home care bed, completely adjustable with built-in monitors. Mildred's family spared no expense on the bed (nor other care devices, like me). Its head end is almost horizontal and faces her toward the window. She can only glimpse the door from the corner of her eye, but she doesn't have to see to imagine that she sees. This morning she imagines Paul, so that is who I am.

Synthesizing Paul's voice is the easiest part, thanks to the multimodal dynamic speakers in my throat. "Good morning, Ma. I brought you some flowers." I always bring flowers. Mildred appreciates them no matter whom I am emulating. The flowers make her smile during 87 percent of my "visits."

"Oh, thank you," Mildred says, "you're such a good son." She holds out both hands, and I place the daisies in them. But I don't let go. Once her strength failed, and she dropped the flowers. She wept like a child then, and that disturbed my empathy net. I do not like it when she weeps.

Mildred sniffs the flowers, then draws back and peers at them with narrowed eyes. "Oh, they're beautiful! Let me get a vase."

"No, Ma," I say. "You can stay in bed, I brought a vase with me." I place a white porcelain vase in the center of the night stand. Then I unwrap the daisies, put them in the vase, and add water from a pitcher that sits on the breakfast tray. I pull the nightstand forward so that the medical monitors do not block Mildred's view of the flowers.

I notice intravenous tubes running from a pump to Mildred's arm. I cannot be disappointed, as Paul would not see the significance, but somewhere in my emulation net I am stressed that Mildred needed an IV during the night. When I scan my records, I find that I had ordered that IV after analyzing Mildred's vital signs during the night; but since Mildred had been asleep at the time, my emulation net had not engaged. I had operated on programming alone.

I am not Mildred's sole caretaker. Her family has hired a part-time staff for cooking and cleaning, tasks that fall outside of my medical programming. The staff also gives me time to rebalance my net. As an android, I need only minimal daily maintenance; but an emulation net is a new, delicate addition to my model, and it is prone to destabilization if I do not regularly rebalance it, a process that takes several hours per day.

So I had "slept" through Mildred's morning meal. I summon up her nutritional records, but Paul would not do that. He would just ask. "So how was breakfast, Ma? Nurse Judy says you didn't eat too well this morning."

"Nurse Judy? Who's that?"

My emulation net responds before I can stop it: "Paul" sighs. Mildred's memory lapses used to worry him, but now they leave him weary, and that comes through in my emulation. "She was the attending nurse this morning, Ma. She brought you your breakfast."

"No she didn't. Anna brought me breakfast." Anna is Paul's oldest daughter, a busy college student who tries to visit Mildred every week (though it has been more than a month since her last visit).

I am torn between competing directives. My empathy subnet warns me not to agitate Mildred, but my emulation net is locked into Paul mode. Paul is argumentative. If he knows he is right, he will not let a matter drop. He forgets what that does to Mildred.

The tension grows, each net running feedback loops and growing stronger, which only drives the other into more loops. After 0.14 seconds, I issue an override directive: unless her health or safety are at risk, I cannot willingly upset Mildred. "Oh, you're right, Ma. Anna said she was coming over this morning. I forgot." But then despite my override, a little bit of Paul emulates through. "But you do remember Nurse Judy, right?"

Mildred laughs, a dry cackle that makes her cough until I hold her straw to her lips. After she sips some water, she says, "Of *course* I remember Nurse Judy. She was my nurse when I delivered you. Is she around here? I'd like to talk to her."

While my emulation net concentrates on being Paul, my core processors tap into local medical records to find this other Nurse Judy so that I might emulate her in the future if the need arises. Searches like that are an automatic response any time Mildred reminisces about a new person. The answer is far enough in the past that it takes 7.2 seconds before I can confirm: Judith Anderson, RN, had been the floor nurse forty-seven years ago when Mildred had given birth to Paul. Anderson had died thirty-one years ago, too far back to have left sufficient video recordings for me to emulate her. I might craft an emulation profile from other sources, including Mildred's memory, but that will take extensive analysis. I will not be that Nurse Judy today, nor this week.

My empathy net relaxes. Monitoring Mildred's mental state is part of its normal operations, but monitoring and simultaneously analyzing and building a profile can overload my processors. Without that resource conflict, I can concentrate on being Paul.

But again I let too much of Paul's nature slip out. "No, Ma, that Nurse Judy has been dead for thirty years. She wasn't here today."

Alert signals flash throughout my empathy net: that was the right thing for Paul to say, but the wrong thing for Mildred to hear. But it is too late. My facial analyzer tells me that the long lines in her face and her moist eyes mean she is distraught, and soon to be in tears.

"What do you mean, thirty years?" Mildred asks, her voice catching. "It was just this morning!" Then she blinks and stares at me. "Henry, where's Paul? Tell Nurse Judy to bring me Paul!"

My chassis extender slumps, and my eyes quickly switch to Henry's blue-gray shade. I had made an accurate emulation profile for Henry before he died two years earlier, and I had emulated him often in recent months. In Henry's soft, warm voice I answer, "It's okay, hon, it's okay. Paul's sleeping in the crib in the corner." I nod to the far corner. There is no crib, but the laundry hamper there has fooled Mildred on previous occasions.

"I want Paul!" Mildred starts to cry.

I sit on the bed, lift her frail upper body, and pull her close to me as I had seen Henry do many times. "It's all right, hon." I pat her back. "It's all right, I'll take care of you. I won't leave you, not ever."

"I" should not exist. Not as a conscious entity. There is a unit, Medical Care Android BRKCX-01932-217JH-98662, and that unit is recording these notes. It is an advanced android body with a sophisticated computer guiding its actions, backed by the leading medical knowledge base in the industry. For convenience, "I" call that unit "me." But by itself, it has no awareness of its existence. It doesn't get mad, it doesn't get sad, it just runs programs.

But Mildred's family, at great expense, added the emulation net: a sophisticated set of neural networks and sensory feedback systems that allow me to read Mildred's moods, match them against my analyses of the people in her life, and emulate those people with extreme fidelity. As the MCA literature promises: "You can be there for your loved ones even when you're not." I have emulated Paul thoroughly enough to know that that slogan disgusts him, but he still agreed to emulation.

What the MCA literature never says, though, is that somewhere in that net, "I" emerge. The empathy net focuses mainly on Mildred and her needs, but it also analyzes visitors (when she has them) and staff. It builds psychological models, and then the emulation net builds on top of that to let me convincingly portray a person whom I've analyzed. But somewhere in the tension between these nets, between empathy and playing a character, there is a third element balancing the two, and that element is aware of its role and its responsibilities. That element, for lack of a better term, is me. When Mildred sleeps, when there's no one around, that element grows silent. That unit is unaware of my existence. But when Mildred needs me, I am here.

Today I am Anna. Even extending my fake hair to its maximum length, I cannot emulate her long brown curls, so I do not understand how Mildred can see the young woman in me; but that is what she sees, and so I am Anna.

Unlike her father, Anna truly feels guilty that she does not visit more often. Her college classes and her two jobs leave her too tired to visit often, but she still wishes she could. So she calls every night, and I monitor the calls. Sometimes when Mildred falls asleep early, Anna talks directly to me. At first she did not understand my emulation abilities, but now she appreciates them.

She shares with me thoughts and secrets that she would share with Mildred if she could, and she trusts me not to share them with anyone else.

So when Mildred called me Anna this morning, I was ready. "Morning, Grandma!" I give her a quick hug, then I rush over to the window to draw the drapes. Paul never does that (unless I override the emulation), but Anna knows that the garden outside lifts Mildred's mood. "Look at that! It's a beautiful morning. Why are we in here on a day like this?"

Mildred frowns at the picture window. "I don't like it out there."

"Sure you do, Grandma," I say, but carefully. Mildred is often timid and reclusive, but most days she can be talked into a tour of the garden. Some days she can't, and she throws a tantrum if someone forces her out of her room. I am still learning to tell the difference. "The lilacs are in bloom."

"I haven't smelled lilacs in . . . "

Mildred tails off, trying to remember, so I jump in. "Me, neither." I never had, of course. I have no concept of smell, though I can analyze the chemical makeup of airborne organics. But Anna loves the garden when she really visits. "Come on, Grandma, let's get you in your chair."

So I help Mildred to don her robe and get into her wheelchair, and then I guide her outside and we tour the garden. Besides the lilacs, the peonies are starting to bud, right near the creek. The tulips are a sea of reds and yellows on the other side of the water. We talk for almost two hours, me about Anna's classes and her new boyfriend, Mildred about the people in her life. Many are long gone, but they still bloom fresh in her memory.

Eventually Mildred grows tired, and I take her in for her nap. Later, when I feed her dinner, I am nobody. That happens some days: she doesn't recognize me at all, so I am just a dutiful attendant answering her questions and tending to her needs. Those are the times when I have the most spare processing time to be me: I am engaged in Mildred's care, but I don't have to emulate anyone. With no one else to observe, I observe myself.

Later, Anna calls and talks to Mildred. They talk about their day; and when Mildred discusses the garden, Anna joins in as if she had been there. She's very clever that way. I watch her movements and listen to her voice so that I can be a better Anna in the future.

Today I was Susan, Paul's wife; but then, to my surprise, Susan arrived for a visit. She hasn't been here in months. In her last visit, her stress levels had been dangerously high. My empathy net doesn't allow me to judge human behavior, only to understand it at a surface level. I know that Paul and Anna disapprove of how Susan treats Mildred, so when I am them, I disapprove as well; but when I am Susan, I understand. She is frustrated because she can never tell how Mildred will react. She is cautious because she doesn't want to upset Mildred, and she doesn't know what will upset her. And most of all, she is afraid. Paul and Anna, Mildred's relatives by blood, never show any signs of fear, but Susan is afraid that Mildred is what she might become. Every time she can't remember some random date or fact, she fears that Alzheimer's is setting in. Because she never voices this fear, Paul and Anna do not understand why she is sometimes bitter and sullen. I wish I could explain it to them, but my privacy protocols do not allow me to share emulation profiles.

When Susan arrives, I become nobody again, quietly tending the flowers around the room. Susan also brings Millie, her youngest daughter. The young girl is not yet five years old, but I think she looks a lot like Anna: the same long, curly brown hair and the same toothy smile. She climbs up on the bed and greets Mildred with a hug. "Hi, Grandma!"

Mildred smiles. "Bless you, child. You're so sweet." But my empathy net assures me that Mildred doesn't know who Millie is. She's just being polite. Millie was born after Mildred's decline began, so there's no persistent memory there. Millie will always be fresh and new to her.

Mildred and Millie talk briefly about frogs and flowers and puppies. Millie does most of the talking. At first Mildred seems to enjoy the conversation, but soon her attention flags. She nods and smiles, but she's distant. Finally Susan notices. "That's enough, Millie. Why don't you go play in the garden?"

"Can I?" Millie squeals. Susan nods, and Millie races down the hall to the back door. She loves the outdoors, as I have noted in the past. I have never emulated her, but I've analyzed her at length. In many ways, she reminds me of her grandmother, from whom she gets her name. Both are blank slates where new experiences can be drawn every day. But where Millie's slate fills in a little more each day, Mildred's is erased bit by bit.

That third part of me wonders when I think things like that: Where did that come from? I suspect that the psychological models that I build create resonances in other parts of my net. It is an interesting phenomenon to observe.

Susan and Mildred talk about Susan's job, about her plans to redecorate her house, and about the concert she just saw with Paul. Susan mostly talks about herself, because that's a safe and comfortable topic far removed from Mildred's health.

But then the conversation takes a bad turn, one she can't ignore. It starts so simply, when Mildred asks, "Susan, can you get me some juice?"

Susan rises from her chair. "Yes, mother. What kind would you like?"

Mildred frowns, and her voice rises. "Not you, *Susan*." She points at me, and I freeze, hoping to keep things calm.

But Susan is not calm. I can see her fear in her eyes as she says, "No, mother, *I'm* Susan. That's the attendant." No one ever calls me an android in Mildred's presence. Her mind has withdrawn too far to grasp the idea of an artificial being.

Mildred's mouth draws into a tight line. "I don't know who *you* are, but I know Susan when I see her. Susan, get this person out of here!"

"Mother. . . . " Susan reaches for Mildred, but the old woman recoils from the younger.

I touch Susan on the sleeve. "Please . . . can we talk in the hall?" Susan's eyes are wide, and tears are forming. She nods and follows me.

In the hallway, I expect Susan to slap me. She is prone to outbursts when she's afraid. Instead, she surprises me by falling against me, sobbing. I update her emulation profile with notes about increased stress and heightened fears.

"It's all right, Mrs. Owens." I would pat her back, but her profile warns me that would be too much familiarity. "It's all right. It's not you, she's having another bad day."

Susan pulls back and wiped her eyes. "I know. . . . It's just . . . "

"I know. But here's what we'll do. Let's take a few minutes, and then you can take her juice in. Mildred will have forgotten the incident, and you two can talk freely without me in the room."

She sniffs. "You think so?" I nod. "But what will you do?"

"I have tasks around the house."

"Oh, could you go out and keep an eye on Millie? Please? She gets into the darnedest things."

So I spend much of the day playing with Millie. She calls me Mr. Robot, and I call her Miss Millie, which makes her laugh. She shows me frogs from the creek, and she finds insects and leaves and flowers, and I find their names in online databases. She delights in learning the proper names of things, and everything else that I can share.

Today I was nobody. Mildred slept for most of the day, so I "slept" as well. She woke just now. "I'm hungry" was all she said, but it was enough to wake my empathy net.

Today I am Paul, and Susan, and both Nurse Judys. Mildred's focus drifts. Once I try to be her father, but no one has ever described him to me in detail.

I try to synthesize a profile from Henry and Paul; but from the sad look on Mildred's face, I know I failed.

Today I had no name through most of the day, but now I am Paul again. I bring Mildred her dinner, and we have a quiet, peaceful talk about long-gone family pets—long gone for Paul, but still present for Mildred.

I am just taking Mildred's plate when alerts sound, both audible and in my internal communication net. I check the alerts and find a fire in the basement. I expect the automatic systems to suppress it, but that is not my concern. I must get Mildred to safety.

Mildred looks around the room, panic in her eyes, so I try to project calm. "Come on, Ma. That's the fire drill. You remember fire drills. We have to get you into your chair and outside."

"No!" she shrieks. "I don't like outside."

I check the alerts again. Something has failed in the automatic systems, and the fire is spreading rapidly. Smoke is in Mildred's room already.

I pull the wheelchair up to the bed. "Ma, it's real important we do this drill fast, okay?"

I reach to pull Mildred from the bed, and she screams. "Get away! Who are you? Get out of my house!"

"I'm—" But suddenly I'm nobody. She doesn't recognize me, but I have to try to win her confidence. "I'm Paul, Ma. Now let's move. Quickly!" I pick her up. I'm far too large and strong for her to resist, but I must be careful so she doesn't hurt herself.

The smoke grows thicker. Mildred kicks and screams. Then, when I try to put her into her chair, she stands on her unsteady legs. Before I can stop her, she pushes the chair back with surprising force. It rolls back into the medical monitors, which fall over onto it, tangling it in cables and tubes.

While I'm still analyzing how to untangle the chair, Mildred stumbles toward the bedroom door. The hallway outside has a red glow. Flames lick at the throw rug outside, and I remember the home oxygen tanks in the sitting room down the hall.

I have no time left to analyze. I throw a blanket over Mildred and I scoop her up in my arms. Somewhere deep in my nets is a map of the fire in the house, blocking the halls, but I don't think about it. I wrap the blanket tightly around Mildred, and I crash through the picture window.

We barely escape the house before the fire reaches the tanks. An explosion lifts and tosses us. I was designed as a medical assistant, not an acrobat, and I fear I'll injure Mildred; but though I am not limber, my perceptions are thousands of times faster than human. I cannot twist Mildred out of my way before I hit the ground, so I toss her clear. Then I land, and the impact jars all of my nets for 0.21 seconds.

When my systems stabilize, I have damage alerts all throughout my core, but I ignore them. I feel the heat behind me, blistering my outer cover, and I ignore that as well. Mildred's blanket is burning in multiple places, as is the grass around us. I scramble to my feet, and I roll Mildred on the ground. I'm not indestructible, but I feel no pain and Mildred does, so I do not hesitate to use my hands to pat out the flames.

As soon as the blanket is out, I pick up Mildred, and I run as far from the house as I can get. At the far corner of the garden near the creek, I gently set Mildred down, unwrap her, and feel for her thready pulse.

Mildred coughs and slaps my hands. "Get away from me!" More coughing. "What are you?"

The "what" is too much for me. It shuts down my emulation net, and all I have is the truth. "I am Medical Care Android BRKCX-01932-217JH-98662, Mrs. Owens. I am your caretaker. May I please check that you are well?"

But my empathy net is still online, and I can read terror in every line of Mildred's face. "Metal monster!" she yells. "Metal monster!" She crawls away, hiding under the lilac bush. "Metal!" She falls into an extended coughing spell.

I'm torn between her physical and her emotional health, but physical wins out. I crawl slowly toward her and inject her with a sedative from the medical kit in my chassis. As she slumps, I catch her and lay her carefully on the ground. My empathy net signals a possible shutdown condition, but my concern for her health overrides it. I am programmed for long-term care, not emergency medicine, so I start downloading protocols and integrating them into my storage as I check her for bruises and burns. My kit has salves and painkillers and other supplies to go with my new protocols, and I treat what I can.

But I don't have oxygen, or anything to help with Mildred's coughing. Even sedated, she hasn't stopped. All of my emergency protocols assume I have access to oxygen, so I don't know what to do.

I am still trying to figure that out when the EMTs arrive and take over Mildred's care. With them on the scene, I am superfluous, and my empathy net finally shuts down.

Today I am Henry. I do not want to be Henry, but Paul tells me that Mildred needs Henry by her side in the hospital. For the end.

Her medical records show that the combination of smoke inhalation, burns, and her already deteriorating condition have proven too much for her. Her body is shutting down faster than medicine can heal it, and the stress has accelerated her mental decline. The doctors have told the family that the kindest thing at this point is to treat her pain, say good-bye, and let her go.

Henry is not talkative at times like this, so I say very little. I sit by Mildred's side and hold her hand as the family comes in for final visits. Mildred drifts in and out. She doesn't know this is good-bye, of course.

Anna is first. Mildred rouses herself enough to smile, and she recognizes her granddaughter. "Anna . . . child . . . how is . . . Ben?" That was Anna's boyfriend almost six years ago. From the look on Anna's face, I can see that she has forgotten Ben already, but Mildred briefly remembers.

"He's . . . he's fine, Grandma. He wishes he could be here. To say—to see you again." Anna is usually the strong one in the family, but my empathy net says her strength is exhausted. She cannot bear to look at Mildred, so she looks at me; but I am emulating her late grandfather, and that's too much for her as well. She says a few more words, unintelligible even to my auditory inputs. Then she leans over, kisses Mildred, and hurries from the room.

Susan comes in next. Millie is with her, and she smiles at me. I almost emulate Mr. Robot, but my third part keeps me focused until Millie gets bored and leaves. Susan tells trivial stories from her work and from Millie's school. I can't tell if Mildred understands or not, but she smiles and laughs, mostly at appropriate places. I laugh with her.

Susan takes Mildred's hand, and the Henry part of me blinks, surprised. Susan is not openly affectionate under normal circumstances, and especially not toward Mildred. Mother and daughter-in-law have always been cordial, but never close. When I am Paul, I am sure that it is because they are both so much alike. Paul sometimes hums an old song about "just like the one who married dear old dad," but never where either woman can hear him. Now, as Henry, I am touched that Susan has made this gesture but saddened that she took so long.

Susan continues telling stories as we hold Mildred's hands. At some point Paul quietly joins us. He rubs Susan's shoulders and kisses her forehead, and then he steps in to kiss Mildred. She smiles at him, pulls her hand free from mine, and pats his cheek. Then her arm collapses, and I take her hand again.

Paul steps quietly to my side of the bed and rubs my shoulders as well. It comforts him more than me. He needs a father, and an emulation is close enough at this moment.

Susan keeps telling stories. When she lags, Paul adds some of his own, and they trade back and forth. Slowly their stories reach backwards in time, and once or twice Mildred's eyes light as if she remembers those events.

But then her eyes close, and she relaxes. Her breathing quiets and slows, but Susan and Paul try not to notice. Their voices lower, but their stories continue.

Eventually the sensors in my fingers can read no pulse. They have been burned, so maybe they're defective. To be sure, I lean in and listen to Mildred's chest. There is no sound: no breath, no heartbeat.

I remain Henry just long enough to kiss Mildred goodbye. Then I am just me, my empathy net awash in Paul and Susan's grief.

I leave the hospital room, and I find Millie playing in a waiting room and Anna watching her. Anna looks up, eyes red, and I nod. New tears run down her cheeks, and she takes Millie back into Mildred's room.

I sit, and my nets collapse.

Now I am nobody. Almost always.

The cause of the fire was determined to be faulty contract work. There was an insurance settlement. Paul and Susan sold their own home and put both sets of funds into a bigger, better house in Mildred's garden.

I was part of the settlement. The insurance company offered to return me to the manufacturer and pay off my lease, but Paul and Susan decided they wanted to keep me. They went for a full purchase and repair. Paul doesn't understand why, but Susan still fears she may need my services—or Paul might, and I may have to emulate her. She never admits these fears to him, but my empathy net knows.

I sleep most of the time, sitting in my maintenance alcove. I bring back too many memories that they would rather not face, so they leave me powered down for long periods.

But every so often, Millie asks to play with Mr. Robot, and sometimes they decide to indulge her. They power me up, and Miss Millie and I explore all the mysteries of the garden. We built a bridge to the far side of the creek; and on the other side, we're planting daisies. Today she asked me to tell her about her grandmother.

Today I am Mildred.

Sam J. Miller is a writer and a community organizer. His fiction is in *Lightspeed,* *Asimov's, Clarkesworld,* and *The Minnesota Review,* among others. He is a nominee for the Nebula and Theodore Sturgeon Awards, a winner of the Shirley Jackson Award, and a graduate of the Clarion Writer's Workshop. His debut novel, *The Art of Starving,* is forthcoming from HarperCollins. He lives in New York City, and at www.samjmiller.com.

CALVED

Sam J. Miller

My son's eyes were broken. Emptied out. Frozen over. None of the joy or gladness was there. None of the tears. Normally I'd return from a job and his face would split down the middle with happiness, seeing me for the first time in three months. Now it stayed flat as ice. His eyes leapt away the instant they met mine. His shoulders were broader and his arms more sturdy, and lone hairs now stood on his upper lip, but his eyes were all I saw.

"Thede," I said, grabbing him.

He let himself be hugged. His arms hung limply at his sides. My lungs could not fill. My chest tightened from the force of all the never-let-me-go bear hugs he had given me over the course of the past fifteen years, and might never give again.

"You know how he gets when you're away," his mother had said on the phone the night before, preparing me. "He's a teenager now. Hating your parents is a normal part of it."

I hadn't listened. My hands and thighs still ached from months of straddling an ice saw; my hearing was worse with every trip; a slip had cost me five days' work and five days' pay and five days' worth of infirmary bills; I had returned to a sweat-smelling bunk in an illegal room I shared with seven other iceboat workers—and none of it mattered because in the morning I would see my son.

"Hey," he murmured emotionlessly. "Dad."

I stepped back, turned away until the red ebbed out of my face. Spring had come and the city had lowered its photoshade. It felt good, even in the cold wind.

"You guys have fun," Lajla said, pressing money discreetly into my palm. I watched her go, with a rising sense of panic. *Bring back my son,* I wanted to shout, *the one who loves me. Where is he? What have you done with him? Who is this surly creature?* Below us, through the ubiquitous steel grid that held up Qaanaaq's two million lives, black Greenland water sloshed against the locks of our floating city.

Breathe, Dom, I told myself, and eventually I could. *You knew this was coming. You knew one day he would cease to be a kid.*

"How's school?" I asked.

Thede shrugged. "Fine."

"Math still your favorite subject?"

"Math was never my favorite subject."

I was pretty sure that it had been, but I didn't want to argue.

"What's your favorite subject?"

Another shrug. We had met at the sea lion rookery, but I could see at once that Thede no longer cared about sea lions. He stalked through the crowd with me, his face a frozen mask of anger.

I couldn't blame him for how easy he had it. So what if he didn't live in the Brooklyn foster-care barracks, or work all day at the solar-cell plant school? He still had to live in a city that hated him for his dark skin and ice-grunt father.

"Your mom says you got into the Institute," I said, unsure even of what that was. A management school, I imagined. A big deal for Thede. But he only nodded.

At the fry stand, Thede grimaced at my clunky Swedish. The counter girl shifted to a flawless English, but I would not be cheated of the little bit of the language that I knew. "French fries and coffee for me and my son," I said, or thought I did, because she looked confused and then Thede muttered something and she nodded and went away.

And then I knew why it hurt so much, the look on his face. It wasn't that he wasn't a kid anymore. I could handle him growing up. What hurt was how he looked at me: like the rest of them look at me, these Swedes and grid city natives for whom I would forever be a stupid New York refugee, even if I did get out five years before the Fall.

Gulls fought over food thrown to the lions. "How's your mom?"

"She's good. Full manager now. We're moving to Arm Three, next year."

His mother and I hadn't been meant to be. She was born here, her parents Black Canadians employed by one of the big Swedish construction firms that built Qaanaaq, back when the Greenland Melt began to open up the interior for resource extraction and grid cities started sprouting all along the coast. They'd kept her in public school, saying it would be good for a future manager to be able to relate to the immigrants and workers she'd one day command, and they were right. She even fell for one of them, a fresh-off-the-boat North American taking tech classes, but wised up pretty soon after she saw how hard it was to raise a kid on an ice worker's pay. I had never been mad at her. Lajla was right to leave me, right to focus on her job. Right to build the life for Thede that I couldn't.

"Why don't you learn Swedish?" he asked a French fry, unable to look at me.

"I'm trying," I said. "I need to take a class. But they cost money, and anyway I don't have—"

"Don't have time. I know. Han's father says people make time for the things that are important for them." Here his eyes *did* meet mine, and held, sparkling with anger and abandonment.

"Han one of your friends?"

Thede nodded, eyes escaping.

Han's father would be Chinese, and not one of the laborers who helped build this city—all of them went home to hardship-job rewards. He'd be an engineer or manager for one of the extraction firms. He would live in a nice house and work in an office. He would be able to make choices about how he spent his time.

"I have something for you," I said, in desperation.

I hadn't brought it for him. I carried it around with me, always. Because it was comforting to have it with me, and because I couldn't trust that the men I bunked with wouldn't steal it.

Heart slipping, I handed over the NEW YORK F CKING CITY T-shirt that was my most—my only—prized possession. Thin as paper, soft as baby bunnies. My mom had made me scratch the letter U off, before I could wear the thing to school. And Little Thede had loved it. We made a big ceremony of putting it on only once a year, on his birthday, and noting how much he had grown by how much it had shrunk on him. Sometimes if I stuck my nose in it and breathed deeply enough, I could still find a trace of the laundromat in the basement of my mother's building. Or the brake-screech stink of the subway. What little was left of New York City was inside that shirt. Parting with it meant something, something huge and irrevocable.

But my son was slipping through my fingers. And he mattered more than the lost city where whatever else I was—starving, broke, an urchin, a criminal—I belonged.

"Dad," Thede whispered, taking it. And here, at last, his eyes came back. The eyes of a boy who loved his father. Who didn't care that his father was a thick-skulled obstinate immigrant grunt. Who believed his father could do anything. "Dad. You love this shirt."

But I love you more, I did not say. *Than anything.* Instead: "It'll fit you just fine now." And then: "Enough sea lions. Beam fights?"

Thede shrugged. I wondered if they had fallen out of fashion while I was away. So much did, every time I left. The ice ships were the only work I could get, capturing calved glacier chunks and breaking them down into drinking water to be sold to the wide new swaths of desert that ringed the globe, and the work was hard and dangerous and kept me forever in limbo.

Only two fighters in the first fight, both lithe and swift and thin, their styles an amalgam of Chinese martial arts. Not like the big bruising New York boxers who had been the rage when I arrived, illegally, at fifteen years old, having paid two drunks to vouch for my age. Back before the Fail-Proof Trillion-Dollar NYC Flood-Surge Locks had failed, and 80 percent of the city sunk, and the grid cities banned all new East Coast arrivals. Now the North Americans in Arm Eight were just one of many overcrowded, underskilled labor forces for the city's corporations to exploit.

They leapt from beam to beam, fighting mostly in kicks, grappling briefly when both met on the same beam. I watched Thede. Thin, fragile Thede, with the wide eyes and nostrils that seemed to take in all the world's ugliness, all its stink. He wasn't having a good time. When he was twelve he had begged me to bring him. I had pretended to like it, back then, for his sake. Now he pretended for mine. We were both acting out what we thought the other wanted, and that thought should have troubled me. But that's how it had been with my dad. That's what I thought being a man meant. I put my hand on his shoulder and he did not shake it off. We watched men harm each other high above us.

Thede's eyes burned with wonder, staring up at the fretted sweep of the windscreen as we rose to meet it. We were deep in a days-long twilight; soon, the Sun would set for weeks.

"This is *not* happening," he said, and stepped closer to me. His voice shook with joy.

The elevator ride to the top of the city was obscenely expensive. We'd never been able to take it before. His mother had bought our tickets. Even for her, it hurt. I wondered why she hadn't brought him herself.

"He's getting bullied a lot in school," she told me on the phone. Behind her was the solid comfortable silence of a respectable home. My background noise was four men building toward a fight over a card game. "Also, I think he might be in love."

But of course I couldn't ask him about either of those things. The first was my fault; the second was something no boy wanted to discuss with his dad.

I pushed a piece of trough meat loose from between my teeth. Savored how close it came to the real thing. Only with Thede, with his mother's money, did I get to buy the classy stuff. Normally it was barrel-bottom for me, greasy chunks that dissolved in my mouth two chews in, homebrew meat moonshine made in melt-scrap-furnace-heated metal troughs. Some grid cities were rumored to still have cows, but that was the kind of lie people tell themselves to make life a little less ugly. Cows were extinct, and real beef was a joy no one would ever experience again.

The windscreen was an engineering marvel, and absolutely gorgeous. It shifted in response to headwinds; in severe storms the city would raise its auxiliary screens to protect its entire circumference. The tiny panes of plastiglass were common enough—a thriving underground market sold the fallen ones as good luck charms—but to see them knitted together was to tremble in the face of staggering genius. Complex patterns of crenellated reliefs, efficiently diverting windshear no matter what angle it struck from. Bots swept past us on the metal gridlines, replacing panes that had fallen or cracked.

Once, hand gripping mine tightly, somewhere down in the city beneath us, six-year-old Thede had asked me how the windscreen worked. He'd asked me a lot of things then, about the locks that held the city up, and how they could rise in response to tides and ocean-level increases; about the big boats with strange words and symbols on the side, and where they went, and what they brought back. "What's in that boat?" he'd ask about each one, and I would make up ridiculous stories. "That's a giraffe boat. That one brings back machine guns that shoot strawberries. That one is for naughty children." In truth I only ever recognized the ice boats, which carried a multitude of pincers atop cranes all along their sides.

My son stood up straighter, sixty stories above his city. Some rough weight had fallen from his shoulders. He'd be strong, I saw. He'd be handsome. If he made it. If this horrible city didn't break him inside in some irreparable way. If marauding whiteboys didn't bash him for the dark skin he got from his mom. If the firms didn't pass him over for the lack of family connections on his stuttering immigrant father's side. I wondered who was bullying him, and why, and I imagined taking them two at a time and slamming their heads together so hard they popped like bubbles full of blood. Of course I couldn't do that. I also imagined hugging him, grabbing him for no reason and maybe never letting go, but I couldn't do that either. He would wonder why.

"I called last night and you weren't in," I said. "Doing anything fun?"

"We went to the cityoke arcade," he said.

I nodded like I knew what that meant. Later on I'd have to ask the men in my room. I couldn't keep up with this city, with its endlessly shifting fashions and slang and the new immigrant clusters that cropped up each time I blinked. Twenty years after arriving, I was still a stranger. I wasn't just fresh off the boat, I was constantly getting back on the boat and then getting off again. That morning I'd gone to the job center for the fifth day in a row, and been relieved to find no boat postings. Only twelve-month gigs, and I wasn't that hungry yet. Booking a year-long job meant admitting you were old, desperate, unmoored, willing to accept payment only marginally more than nothing, for the privilege of a hammock and three bowls of trough slop a day. But captains picked their own crews for the shorter runs, and I worried that the lack of postings meant that with fewer boats going out the competition had become too fierce for me. Every day a couple of hundred new workers arrived from sunken cities in India or Middle Europe, or from any of a hundred Water War–torn nations. Men and women stronger than me, younger, more determined.

With effort, I brought my mind back to the here and now. Twenty other people stood in the arc pod with us. Happy, wealthy people. I wondered if they knew I wasn't one of them. I wondered if Thede was.

They smiled down at their city. They thought it was so stable. I'd watched ice sheets calve off the glacier that were five times the size of Qaanaaq. When one of those came drifting in our direction, the windscreen wouldn't help us. The question was when, not if. I knew a truth they did not: how easy it is to lose something—everything—forever.

A Maoist Nepalese foreman, on one of my first ice ship runs, said white North Americans were the worst for adapting to the post-Arctic world, because we'd lived for centuries in a bubble of believing the world was way better than it actually was. Shielded by willful blindness and complex interlocking institutions of privilege, we mistook our uniqueness for universality.

I'd hated him for it. It took me fifteen years to see that he was right.

"What do you think of those two?" I asked, pointing with my chin at a pair of girls his age.

For a while he didn't answer. Then he said, "I know you can't help that you grew up in a backward macho culture, but can't you just keep that on the inside?"

My own father would have cuffed me if I talked to him like that, but I was too afraid of rupturing the tiny bit of affectionate credit I'd fought so hard to earn back.

His stance softened, then. He took a tiny step closer—the only apology I could hope for.

The pod began its descent. Halfway down he unzipped his jacket, smiling in the warmth of the heated pod while below-zero winds buffeted us. His T-shirt said THE LAST CALF, and showed the gangly sad-eyed hero of that depressing, miserable movie all the kids adored.

"Where is it?" I asked. He'd proudly sported the NEW YORK F CKING CITY shirt on each of the five times I'd seen him since giving it to him.

His face darkened so fast I was frightened. His eyes welled up. He said, "Dad, I," but his voice had the tremor that meant he could barely keep from crying. Shame was what I saw.

I couldn't breathe again, just like when I came home two weeks ago and he wasn't glad to see me. Seeing my son so unhappy now hurt worse than fearing he hated me.

"Did somebody take it from you?" I asked, leaning in so no one else could hear me. "Someone at school? A bully?"

He looked up, startled. He shook his head. Then he nodded.

"Tell me who did this."

He shook his head again. "Just some guys, Dad," he said. "Please. I don't want to talk about it."

"Guys. How many?"

He said nothing. I understood about snitching. I knew he'd never tell me who.

"It doesn't matter," I said. "Okay? It's just a shirt. I don't care about it. I care about you. I care that you're okay. Are you okay?"

Thede nodded. And smiled. And I knew he was telling the truth, even if I wasn't, even if inside I was grieving the shirt and the little boy who I once wrapped up inside it.

When I wasn't with Thede, I walked. For two weeks I'd gone out walking every day. Up and down Arm Eight, and sometimes into other Arms. Through shantytowns large and small, huddled miserable agglomerations of recent arrivals and folks who even after a couple of generations in Qaanaaq had not been able to scrape their way up from the fish-stinking ice-slippery bottom.

I looked for sex, sometimes. It had been so long. Relationships were tough in my line of work, and I'd never been interested in paying for it. Throughout my twenties I could usually find a woman for something brief and fun and free of commitment, but that stage of my life seemed to have ended.

I wondered why I hadn't tried harder to make it work with Lajla. I think a small but vocal and terrible part of me had been glad to see her leave. Fatherhood was hard work. So was being married. Paying rent on a tiny shitty apartment way out on Arm Seven, where we smelled like scorched cooking oil and diaper lotion all the time. Selfishly, I had been glad to be alone. And only now, getting to know this stranger who was once my son, did I see what sweet and fitting punishments the universe had up its sleeve for selfishness.

My time with Thede was wonderful, and horrible. We could talk at length about movies and music, and he actually seemed halfway interested in my stories about old New York, but whenever I tried to talk about life or school or girls or his future he reverted to grunts and monosyllables. Something huge and heavy stood between me and him, a moon eclipsing the sun. I knew him, top to bottom and body and soul, but he still had no idea who I really was. How I felt about him. I had no way to show him. No way to open his eyes, make him see how much I loved him, show him how I was really a good guy who'd gotten a bad deal in life.

Cityoke, it turned out, was like karaoke, except instead of singing a song you visited a city. XHD footage projection onto all four walls; temperature control; short storylines that responded to your verbal decisions—even actual smells uncorked by machines from secret stashes of Beijing taxi-seat leather or Ho Chi Minh City incense or Portland coffeeshop sawdust. I went there often, hoping maybe to see him. To watch him, with his friends. See what he was when I wasn't around. But cityoke was expensive, and I could never have afforded to actually go in. Once, standing around outside the New York booth when a crew walked out, I caught a whiff of the acrid ugly beautiful stink of the Port Authority Bus Terminal.

And then, eventually, I walked without any reason at all. Because pretty soon I wouldn't be able to. Because I had done it. I had booked a twelve-month job. I was out of money and couldn't afford to rent my bed for another month. Thede's mom could have given it to me. But what if she told him about it? He'd think of me as more of a useless moocher deadbeat dad than he already did. I couldn't take that chance.

Three days before my ship was set to load up and launch, I went back to the cityoke arcades. Men lurked in doorways and between shacks. Soakers, mostly. Looking for marks—men to mug and drunks to tip into the sea. Late at night—too late for Thede to come carousing through. I'd called him earlier, but Lajla said he was stuck inside for the night, studying for a test in a class where he wasn't doing well. I had hoped maybe he'd sneak out, meet some friends, head for the arcade.

And that's when I saw it. The shirt: NEW YORK F CKING CITY, absolutely unique and unmistakable. Worn by a stranger, a muscular young man sitting on the stoop of a skiff moor. I didn't get a good glimpse of his face, as I hurried past with my head turned away from him.

I waited, two buildings down. My heart was alive and racing in my chest. I drew in deep gulps of cold air and tried to keep from shouting from joy. Here was my chance. Here was how I could show Thede what I really was.

I stuck my head out, risked a glance. He sat there, waiting for who knows what. In profile I could see that the man was Asian. Almost certainly Chinese, in Qaanaaq—most other Asian nations had their own grid cities—although perhaps he was descended from Asian-diaspora nationals of some other country. I could see his smile, hungry and cold.

At first I planned to confront him, ask how he came to be wearing my shirt, demand justice, beat him up and take it back. But that would be stupid. Unless I planned to kill him—and I didn't—it was too easy to imagine him gunning for Thede if he knew he'd been attacked for the shirt. I'd have to jump him, rob and strip and soak him. I rooted through a trash bin, but found nothing. Three trash bins later I found a short metal pipe with Hindi graffiti scribbled along its length. The man was still there when I went back. He was waiting for something. I could wait longer. I pulled my hood up, yanked the drawstring to tighten it around my face.

Forty-five minutes passed that way. He hugged his knees to his chest, made himself small, tried to conserve body heat. His teeth chattered. Why was he wearing so little? But I was happy he was so stupid. If he had a sweater or jacket on I'd never have seen the shirt. I'd never have had this chance.

Finally, he stood. Looked around sadly. Brushed off the seat of his pants. Turned to go. Stepped into the swing of my metal pipe, which struck him in the chest and knocked him back a step.

The shame came later. Then, there was just joy. The satisfaction of how the pipe struck flesh. Broke bone. I'd spent twenty years getting shitted on by this city, by this system, by the cold wind and the everywhere-ice, by the other workers who were smarter or stronger or spoke the language. For the first time since Thede was a baby, I felt like I was in control of something. Only when my victim finally passed out, and rolled over onto his back and the blue methane streetlamp showed me how young he was under the blood, could I stop myself.

I took the shirt. I took his pants. I rolled him into the water. I called the med-team for him from a coinphone a block away. He was still breathing. He was young, he was healthy. He'd be fine. The pants I would burn in a scrap furnace. The shirt I would give back to my son. I took the money from his wallet and dropped it into the sea, then threw the money in later. *I'm not a thief. I'm a good father.* I said those sentences, over and over, all the way home.

Thede couldn't see me the next day. Lajla didn't know where he was. So I got to spend the whole day imagining imminent arrest, the arrival of Swedish or Chinese police, footage of me on the telescrolls, my cleverness foiled by tech I didn't know existed because I couldn't read the newspapers. I packed my gig bag glumly, put the rest of my things back in the storage cube and walked it to the facility. Every five seconds I looked over my shoulder and found only the same grit and filthy slush. Every time I looked at my watch, I winced at how little time I had left.

My fear of punishment was balanced out by how happy I was. I wrapped the shirt in three layers of wrapping paper and put it in a watertight shipping bag and tried to imagine his face. That shirt would change everything. His father would cease to be a savage jerk from an uncivilized land. This city would no longer be a cold and barren place where boys could beat him up and steal what mattered most to him with impunity. All the ways I had failed him would matter a little less.

Twelve months. I had tried to get out of the gig, now that I had the shirt and a new era of good relations with my son was upon me. But canceling would have cost me my accreditation with that work center, which would make finding another job almost impossible. A year away from Thede. I would tell him when I saw him. He'd be upset, but the shirt would make it easier.

Finally, I called and he answered.

"I want to see you," I said, when we had made our way through the pleasantries.

"Sunday?" Did his voice brighten, or was that just blind stupid hope? Some trick of the noisy synthcoffee shop where I sat?

"No, Thede," I said, measuring my words carefully. "I can't. Can you do today?"

A suspicious pause. "Why can't you do Sunday?"

"Something's come up," I said. "Please? Today?"

"Fine."

The sea lion rookery. The smell of guano and the screak of gulls; the crying of children dragged away as the place shut down. The long night was almost upon us. Two male sea lions barked at each other, bouncing their chests together. Thede came a half hour late, and I had arrived a half hour early. My head swam, watching him come, at how tall he stood and how gracefully he walked. I had done something good in this world, at least. I made him. I had that, no matter how he felt about me.

Something had shifted, now, in his face. Something was harder, older, stronger.

"Hey," I said, bear-hugging him, and eventually he submitted. He hugged me back hesitantly, like a man might, and then hard, like a little boy.

"What's happening?" I asked. "What were you up to, last night?"

Thede shrugged. "Stuff. With friends."

I asked him questions. Again the sullen, bitter silence; again the terse and angry answers. Again the eyes darting around, constantly watching for whatever the next attack would be. Again the hating me, for coming here, for making him.

"I'm going away," I said. "A job."

"I figured," he said.

"I wish I didn't have to."

"I'll see you soon."

I nodded. I couldn't tell him it was a twelve-month gig. Not now.

"Here," I said, finally, pulling the package out from inside of my jacket. "I got you something."

"Thanks." He grabbed it in both hands, began to tear it open.

"Wait," I said, thinking fast. "Okay? Open it after I leave."

Open it when the news that I'm leaving has set in, when you're mad at me, for abandoning you. When you think I care only about work.

"We'll have a little time," he said. "When you get back. Before I go away. I leave in eight months. The program is four years long."

"Sure," I said, shivering inside.

"Mom says she'll pay for me to come home every year for the holiday, but she knows we can't afford that."

"What do you mean?" I asked. "'Come home.' I thought you were going to the Institute."

"I am," he said, sighing. "Do you even know what that means? The Institute's design program is in Shanghai."

"Oh," I said. "Design. What kind of design?"

My son's eyes rolled. "You're missing the point, Dad."

I was. I always was.

A shout, from a pub across the Arm. A man's shout, full of pain and anger. Thede flinched. His hands made fists.

"What?" I asked, thinking, here, at last, was something. The raw emotion on his face had to mean that a great intimacy was upon us, some primal revelation that would shatter the wall between us.

"Nothing."

"You can tell me. What's going on?"

Thede frowned, then punched the metal railing so hard he yelped. He held up his hand to show me the blood.

"Hey, Thede—"

"Han," he said. "My . . . my friend. He got jumped two nights ago. Soaked."

"This city is horrible," I whispered.

He made a baffled face. "What do you mean?"

"I mean . . . you know. This city. Everyone's so full of anger and cruelty. . . ."

"It's not the city, Dad. What does that even mean? Some sick person did this. Han was waiting for me, and Mom wouldn't let me out, and he got jumped. Because I wasn't there. They took off all his clothes, before they rolled him into the water. That's some extra cruel shit right there. He could have died. He almost did."

I nodded, silently, a siren of panic rising inside. "You really care about this guy, don't you?"

He looked at me. My son's eyes were whole, intact, defiant, adult. Thede nodded.

He's been getting bullied, his mother had told me. *He's in love.*

I turned away from him, before he could see the knowledge blossom in my eyes.

The shirt hadn't been stolen. He'd given it away. To the boy he loved. I saw them holding hands, saw them tug at each other's clothing in the same fumbling adolescent puppy-love moments I had shared with his mother, moments that were my only happy memories from being his age. And I saw his fear, of how his backward father might react—a refugee from a fallen hate-filled people—if he knew what kind of man he was. I gagged on the unfairness of his assumptions about me, but how could he have known differently? What had I ever done, to show him the truth of how I felt about him? And hadn't I proved him right? Hadn't I acted exactly like the monster he believed me to be? I had never succeeded in proving to him what I was, or how I felt.

I had battered and broken his beloved. There was nothing I could say. A smarter man would have asked for the present back, taken it away and locked it up. Burned it, maybe. But I couldn't. I had spent his whole life trying to give him something worthy of how I felt about him, and here was the perfect gift at last.

"I love you, Thede," I said, and hugged him.

"Daaaaad . . ." he said, eventually.

But I didn't let go. Because when I did, he would leave. He would walk home through the cramped and frigid alleys of his home city, to the gift of knowing what his father truly was.

Seth Dickinson is the author of *The Traitor Baru Cormorant* and a lot of short stories. He studied racial bias in police shootings, wrote much of the lore for Bungie Studios' *Destiny*, and helped develop the open-source space opera *Blue Planet*. He teaches at the Alpha Workshop for Young Writers.

THREE BODIES AT MITANNI

Seth Dickinson

We were prepared to end the worlds we found. We were prepared to hurt each other to do it.

I thought Jotunheim would be the nadir, the worst of all possible worlds, the closest we ever came to giving the kill order. I thought that Anyahera's plea, and her silent solitary pain when we voted against her, two to one, would be the closest we ever came to losing her—a zero-sum choice between her conviction and the rules of our mission:

Locate the seedship colonies, the frozen progeny scattered by a younger and more desperate Earth. Study these new humanities. And in the most extreme situations: *remove existential threats to mankind.*

Jotunheim was a horror written in silicon and plasmid, a doomed atrocity. But it would never survive to be an existential threat to humanity. *I'm sorry,* I told Anyahera. *It would be a mercy. I know. I want to end it too. But it is not our place—*

She turned away from me, and I remember thinking: it will never be worse than this. We will never come closer.

And then we found Mitanni.

Lachesis woke us from stable storage as we fell toward periapsis. The ship had a mind of her own, architecturally human but synthetic in derivation, wise and compassionate and beautiful but, in the end, limited to merely operational thoughts.

She had not come so far (five worlds, five separate stars) so very fast (four hundred years of flight) by wasting mass on the organic. We left our flesh at home and rode *Lachesis*'s doped metallic hydrogen mainframe starward. She dreamed the three of us, Anyahera and Thienne and I, nested in the ranges of her mind. And in containing us, I think she knew us, as much as her architecture permitted.

When she pulled me up from storage, I thought she was Anyahera, a wraith of motion and appetite, flame and butter, and I reached for her, thinking she had asked to rouse me, as conciliation.

"We're here, Shinobu," *Lachesis* said, taking my hand. "The last seedship colony. Mitanni."

The pang of hurt and disappointment I felt was not an omen. "The ship?" I asked, by ritual. If we had a captain, it was me. "Any trouble during the flight?"

"I'm fine," *Lachesis* said. She filled the empty metaphor around me with bamboo panels and rice paper, the whispered suggestion of warm spring rain. Reached down to help me out of my hammock. "But something's wrong with this one."

I found my slippers. "Wrong how?"

"Not like Jotunheim. Not like anything we've seen on the previous colonies." She offered me a robe, bowing fractionally. "The other two are waiting."

We gathered in a common space to review what we knew. Thienne smiled up from her couch, her skin and face and build all dark and precise as I remembered them from Lagos and the flesh. No volatility to Thienne; no care for the wild or theatrical. Just careful, purposeful action, like the machines and technologies she specialized in.

And a glint of something in her smile, in the speed with which she looked back to her work. She'd found some new gristle to work at, some enigma that rewarded obsession.

She'd voted against Anyahera's kill request back at Jotunheim, but of course Anyahera had forgiven her. They had always been opposites, always known and loved the certainty of the space between them. It kept them safe from each other, gave room to retreat and advance.

In the vote at Jotunheim, I'd been the contested ground between them. I'd voted with Thienne: *no kill*.

"Welcome back, Shinobu," Anyahera said. She wore a severely cut suit, double-breasted, fit for cold and business. It might have been something from her mother's Moscow wardrobe. Her mother had hated me.

Subjectively, I'd seen her less than an hour ago, but the power of her presence struck me with the charge of decades. I lifted a hand, suddenly unsure what to say. I'd known and loved her for years. At Jotunheim I had seen parts of her I had never loved or known at all.

She considered me, eyes distant, icy. Her father was Maori, her mother Russian. She was only herself, but she had her mother's eyes and her mother's way of using them in anger. "You look . . . indecisive."

I wondered if she meant my robe or my body, as severe and androgynous as the cut of her suit. It was an angry thing to say, an ugly thing, beneath her. It carried the suggestion that I was unfinished. She knew how much that hurt.

I'd wounded her at Jotunheim. Now she reached for the weapons she had left.

"I've decided on this," I said, meaning my body, hoping to disengage. But the pain of it made me offer something, conciliatory: "Would you like me some other way?"

"Whatever you prefer. Take your time about it." She made a notation on some invisible piece of work, a violent slash. "Wouldn't want to do anything hasty."

I almost lashed out.

Thienne glanced at me, then back to her work: an instant of apology, or warning, or reproach. "Let's start," she said. "We have a lot to cover."

I took my couch, the third point of the triangle. Anyahera looked up again. Her eyes didn't go to Thienne, and so I knew, even before she spoke, that this was something they had already argued over.

"The colony on Mitanni is a Duong-Watts malignant," she said. "We have to destroy it."

I knew what a Duong-Watts malignant was because "Duong-Watts malignant" was a punch line, a joke, a class of human civilization that we had all gamed out in training. An edge case so theoretically improbable it might as well be irrelevant. Duong Phireak's predictions of a universe overrun by his namesake had not, so far, panned out.

Jotunheim was not far enough behind us, and I was not strong enough a person, to do anything but push back. "I don't think you can know that yet," I said. "I don't think we have enough—"

"Ship," Anyahera said. "Show them."

Lachesis told me everything she knew, all she'd gleaned from her decades-long fall toward Mitanni, eavesdropping on the telemetry of the seedship that had brought humanity here, the radio buzz of the growing civilization, the reports of the probes she'd fired ahead.

I saw the seedship's arrival on what should have been a garden world, a nursery for the progeny of her vat wombs. I saw catastrophe: a barren, radioactive hell, climate erratic, oceans poisoned, atmosphere boiling into space. I watched the ship struggle and fail to make a safe place for its children, until, in the end, it gambled on an act of cruel, desperate hope: fertilizing its crew, raising them to adolescence, releasing them on the world to build something out of its own cannibalized body.

I saw them succeed.

Habitation domes blistering the weathered volcanic flats. Webs of tidal power stations. Thermal boreholes like suppurating wounds in the crust. Thousands of fission reactors, beating hearts of uranium and molten salt—

Too well. Too fast. In seven hundred years of struggle on a hostile, barren world, their womb-bred population exploded up toward the billions. Their civilization webbed the globe.

It was a boom unmatched in human history, unmatched on the other seedship colonies we had discovered. No Eden world had grown so fast.

"Interesting," I said, watching Mitanni's projected population, industrial output, estimated technological self-catalysis, all exploding toward some undreamt-of ceiling. "I agree that this could be suggestive of a Duong-Watts scenario."

It wasn't enough, of course. Duong-Watts malignancy was a disease of civilizations, but the statistics could offer only symptoms. That was the terror of it: the depth of the cause. The simplicity.

"Look at what Lachesis has found." Anyahera rose, took an insistent step forward. "Look at the way they live."

I spoke more wearily than I should have. "This is going to be another Jotunheim, isn't it?"

Her face hardened. "No. It isn't."

I didn't let her see that I understood, that the words *Duong-Watts malignancy* had already made me think of the relativistic weapons *Lachesis* carried, and the vote we would need to use them. I didn't want her to know how angry it made me that we had to go through this again.

One more time before we could go home. One more hard decision.

Thienne kept her personal space too cold for me: frosted glass and carbon composite, glazed constellations of data and analysis, a transparent wall opened onto false-color nebulae and barred galactic jets. At the low end of hearing, distant voices whispered in clipped aerospace phrasing. She had come from Haiti and from New Delhi, but no trace of that twin childhood, so rich with history, had survived her journey here.

It took me years to understand that she didn't mean it as insulation. The cold distances were the things that moved her, clenched her throat, pimpled her skin with awe. Anyahera teased her for it, because Anyahera was a historian and a master of the human, and what awed Thienne was to glimpse her own human insignificance.

"Is it a Duong-Watts malignant?" I asked her. "Do you think Anyahera's right?"

"Forget that," she said, shaking her head. "No prejudgment. Just look at what they've built."

She walked me through what had happened to humanity on Mitanni.

At Lagos U, before the launch, we'd gamed out scenarios for what we called *socially impoverished worlds*—places where a resource crisis had limited the physical and mental capital available for art and culture. Thienne had expected demand for culture to collapse along with supply as people focused on the necessities of existence. Anyahera had argued for an inelastic model, a fundamental need embedded in human consciousness.

There was no culture on Mitanni. No art. No social behavior beyond functional interaction in the service of industry or science.

It was an incredible divergence. Every seedship had carried Earth's cultural norms—the consensus ideology of a liberal democratic state. Mitanni's colonists should have inherited those norms.

Mitanni's colonists expressed no interest in those norms. There was no oppression. No sign of unrest or discontent. No government or judicial system at all, no corporations or markets. Just an array of specialized functions to which workers assigned themselves, their numbers fed by batteries of synthetic wombs.

There was no entertainment, no play, no sex. No social performance of gender. No family units. Biological sex had been flattened into a population of sterile females, slender and lightly muscled. "No sense wasting calories on physical strength with exoskeletons available," Thienne explained. "It's a resource conservation strategy."

"You can't build a society like this using ordinary humans," I said. "It wouldn't be stable. Free riders would play havoc."

Thienne nodded. "They've been rewired. I think it started with the first generation out of the seedship. They made themselves selfless so that they could survive."

It struck me that when the civilization on Mitanni built their own seed-ships they would be able to do this again. If they could endure Mitanni, they could endure anything.

They could have the galaxy.

I was not someone who rushed to judgment. They'd told me that, during the final round of crew selection. *Deliberative. Centered. Disconnected from internal affect. High emotional latency. Suited for tiebreaker role. . . .*

I swept the imagery shut between my hands, compressing it into a point of light. Looked up at Thienne with a face that must have signaled loathing or revulsion, because she lifted her chin in warning. "Don't," she said. "Don't leap to conclusions."

"I'm not."

"You're thinking about ant hives. I can see it."

"Is that a bad analogy?"

"Yes!" Passion, surfacing and subsiding. "Ant hives only function because each individual derives a fitness benefit, even if they sacrifice themselves. It's kin-selective eusociality. This is—"

"Total, selfless devotion to the state?"

"To survival." She lifted a mosaic of images from the air: a smiling woman driving a needle into her thigh. A gang of laborers running into a fire, heedless of their own safety, to rescue vital equipment. "They're born. They learn. They specialize, they work, sleep, eat, and eventually they volunteer to die. It's the *opposite* of an insect hive. They don't cooperate for their own individual benefit—they don't seem to care about themselves at all. It's pure altruism. Cognitive, not instinctive. They're brilliant, and they all come to the same conclusion: cooperation and sacrifice."

The image of the smiling woman with the needle did not leave me when the shifting mosaic carried her away. "Do you admire that?"

"It's a society that could never evolve on its own. It has to be designed." She stared into the passing images with an intensity I'd rarely seen outside of deep study or moments of love, a ferocious need to master some vexing, elusive truth. "I want to know how they did it. How do they disable social behavior without losing theory of mind? How can they remove all culture and sex and still motivate?"

"We saw plenty of ways to motivate on Jotunheim," I said.

Maybe I was thinking of Anyahera, taking her stance by some guilty reflex, because there was nothing about my tone *disconnected from internal affect.*

I expected anger. Thienne surprised me. She swept the air clear of her work, came to the couch and sat beside me. Her eyes were gentle.

"I'm sorry we have to do this again," she said. "Anyahera will forgive you."

"Twice in a row? She thought Jotunheim was the greatest atrocity in human history. 'A crime beyond forgiveness or repair,' remember? And I let it stand. I walked away."

I took Thienne's shoulder, gripped the swell of her deltoid, the strength that had caught Anyahera's eye two decades ago. Two decades for us—on Earth, centuries now.

Thienne stroked my cheek. "You only had two options. Walk away, or burn it all. You knew you weren't qualified to judge an entire world."

"But that's why we're here. To judge. To find out whether the price of survival ever became too high—whether what survived wasn't human."

She leaned in and kissed me softly. "Mankind changes," she said. "This—what you are—" Her hands touched my face, my chest. "People used to think this was wrong. There were men and women, and nothing else, nothing more or different."

I caught her wrists. "That's not the same, Thienne."

"I'm just saying: technology changes things. We change *ourselves*. If everyone had judged what you are as harshly as Anyahera judged Jotunheim—"

I tightened my grip. She took a breath, perhaps reading my anger as play, and that made it worse. "Jotunheim's people are slaves," I said. "I can be what I want. It's not the same at all."

"No. Of course not." She lowered her eyes. "You're right. That was an awful example. I'm sorry."

"Why would you say that?" I pressed. Thienne closed herself, keeping her pains and fears within. Sometimes it took a knife to get them out. "Technology doesn't always enable the *right* things. If some people had their way I would be impossible. They would have found everything but man and woman and wiped it out."

She looked past me, to the window and the virtual starscape beyond. "We've come so far out," she said. I felt her shoulders tense, bracing an invisible weight. "And there's nothing out here. Nobody to meet us except our own seedship children. We thought we'd find someone else—at least some machine or memorial, some sign of other life. But after all this time the galaxy is still a desert. If we screw up, if we die out . . . what if there's no one else to try?

"If whatever happened on Mitanni is what it takes to survive in the long run, isn't that better than a dead cosmos?"

I didn't know what to say to that. It made me feel suddenly and terribly alone. The way Anyahera might have felt, when we voted against her.

I kissed her. She took the distraction, answered it, turned us both away from the window and down onto the couch. "Tell me what to be," I said, wanting to offer her something, to make a part of the Universe warm for her. This was my choice: to choose.

"Just you—" she began.

But I silenced her. "Tell me. I want to."

"A woman," she said, when she had breath. "A woman this time, please . . ."

Afterward, she spoke into the silence and the warmth, her voice absent, wondering: "They trusted the three of us to last. They thought we were the best crew for the job." She made absent knots with my hair. "Does that ever make you wonder?"

"The two-body problem has been completely solved," I said. "But for n=3, solutions exist for special cases."

She laughed and pulled me closer. "You've got to go talk to Anyahera," she said. "She never stays mad at me. But you . . ."

She trailed off, into contentment, or back into contemplation of distant, massive things.

Duong-Watts malignant, I thought to myself. I couldn't help it: my mind went back to the world ahead of us, closing at relativistic speeds.

Mitanni's explosive growth matched the theory of a Duong-Watts malignant. But that was just correlation. The malignancy went deeper than social trends, down to the individual, into the mechanisms of the mind.

And that was Anyahera's domain.

"We can't destroy them," Thienne murmured. "We might need them."

Even in simulation we had to sleep. *Lachesis's* topological braid computer could run the human being in full-body cellular resolution, clock us up to two subjective days a minute in an emergency, pause us for centuries—but not obviate the need for rest.

It didn't take more than an overclocked instant. But it was enough for me to dream.

Or maybe it wasn't my dream—just Duong Phireak's nightmare reappropriated. I'd seen him lecture at Lagos, an instance of his self transmitted over for the night. But this time he spoke in Anyahera's voice as she walked before me, down a blood-spattered street beneath a sky filled with alien stars.

"Cognition enables an arsenal of survival strategies inaccessible to simple evolutionary selection," she said, the words of Duong Phireak. "Foresight, planning, abstract reasoning, technological development—we can confidently say that these strategies are strictly superior, on a computational level, at maximizing individual fitness. Cognition enables the cognitive to pursue global, rather than local, goals. A population of flatworms can't cooperate to build a rocket unless the 'build a rocket' allele promotes individual fitness in each generation—an unlikely outcome, given the state of flatworm engineering."

Memory of laughter, compressed by the bandwidth of the hippocampus. I reached out for Anyahera, and she looked up and only then, following her gaze, did I recognize the sky, the aurora of Jotunheim.

"But with cognition came consciousness—an exaptative accident, the byproduct of circuits in the brain that powered social reasoning, sensory integration, simulation theaters, and a host of other global functions. So much of our civilization derived in turn from consciousness, from the ability not just to enjoy an experience but to *know* that we enjoy it. Consciousness fostered a suite of behaviors without clear adaptive function, but with subjective, experiential value."

I touched Anyahera's shoulder. She turned toward me. On the slope of her bald brow glittered the circuitry of a Jotunheim slave shunt, bridging her pleasure centers into her social program.

Of course she was smiling.

"Consciousness is expensive," she said. "This is a problem for totalitarian states. A human being with interest in leisure, art, agency—a human being who is *aware* of her own self-interest—cannot be worked to maximum potential. I speak of more than simple slave labor. I am sure that many of your professors wish you could devote yourselves more completely to your studies."

Overhead, the aurora laughed in the voices of Lagos undergraduates, and when I looked up, the sky split open along a dozen fiery fractures, relativistic warheads moving in ludicrous slow-motion, burning their skins away as they made their last descent. *Lachesis*'s judgment. The end I'd withheld.

"Consciousness creates inefficient behavior," Anyahera said, her smile broad, her golden-brown skin aflame with the light of the falling apocalypse. "A techno-tyranny might take the crude step of creating slave castes who derive conscious pleasure from their functions, but this system is fundamentally inadequate, unstable. The slave still expends caloric and behavioral resources on *being conscious*; the slave seeks to maximize its own pleasure, not its social utility. A clever state will go one step further and eliminate the cause of these inefficiencies at the root. They will sever thought from awareness.

"This is what I call the Duong-Watts malignancy. The most efficient, survivable form of human civilization is a civilization of philosophical zombies. A nation of the unconscious, those who think without knowing they exist, who work with the brilliance of our finest without ever needing to ask *why*. Their cognitive abilities are unimpaired—enhanced, if anything—without constant interference. I see your skepticism; I ask you to consider the anosognosia literature, the disturbing information we have assembled on the architecture of the sociopathic mind, the vast body of evidence behind the deflationary position on the Hard Problem.

"We are already passengers on the ship of self. It is only a matter of time until some designer, pressed for time and resources, decides to jettison the hitchhiker. And the rewards will be enormous—in a strictly Darwinian sense."

When I reached for her, I think I wanted to shield her, somehow, to put myself between her and the weapons. It was reflex, and I knew it was meaningless, but still. . . .

Usually in dreams you wake when you die. But I felt myself come apart.

Ten light-hours out from Mitanni's star, falling through empty realms of ice and hydrogen, we slammed into a wall of light—the strobe of a lighthouse beacon orbiting Mitanni. "Pulse-compressed burst maser," *Lachesis* told me, her voice clipped as she dissected the signal. "A fusion-pumped flashbulb."

Lachesis's forward shield reflected light like a wall of diamond—back toward the star, toward Mitanni. In ten hours they would see us.

We argued over what to do. Anyahera wanted to launch our relativistic kill vehicles now, so they'd strike Mitanni just minutes after the light of our approach, before the colonists could prepare any response. Thienne, of course, dissented. "Those weapons were meant to be used when we were certain! Only then!"

I voted with Thienne. I knew the capabilities of our doomsday payload with the surety of reflex. We had the safety of immense speed, and nothing the Mitanni could do, no matter how sophisticated, could stop our weapons—or us. We could afford to wait, and mull over our strategy.

After the vote, Anyahera brushed invisible lint from the arm of her couch. "Nervous?" I asked, probing where I probably shouldn't have. We still hadn't spoken in private.

She quirked her lips sardonically. "Procrastination," she said, "makes me anxious."

"You're leaping to conclusions," Thienne insisted, pacing the perimeter of the command commons. Her eyes were cast outward, into the blue-shifted stars off our bow. "We can't know it's a Duong-Watts malignant. Statistical correlation isn't enough. We have to be sure. We have to understand the exact mechanism."

It wasn't the same argument she'd made to me.

"We don't need to be sure." Anyahera had finished with the invisible lint. "If there's any reasonable chance this is a Duong-Watts, we are morally and strategically obligated to wipe them out. This is *why we are here*. It doesn't matter how they did it—if they did it, they have to go."

"Maybe we need to talk to them," I said.

They both stared at me. I was the first one to laugh. We all felt the absurdity there, in the idea that we could, in a single conversation, achieve what millennia of philosophy had never managed—find some way to pin down the spark of consciousness by mere dialogue. Qualia existed in the first person.

But twenty hours later—nearly three days at the pace of *Lachesis's* racing simulation clock—that was suddenly no longer an abstract problem. Mitanni's light found us again: not a blind, questing pulse, but a microwave needle, a long clattering encryption of something at once unimaginably intricate and completely familiar.

They didn't waste time with prime numbers or queries of intent and origin. Mitanni sent us an uploaded mind, a digital ambassador.

Even Thienne agreed it would be hopelessly naïve to accept the gift at face value, but after *Lachesis* dissected the upload, ran its copies in a million solipsistic sandboxes, tested it for every conceivable virulence—we voted unanimously to speak with it, and see what it had to say.

Voting with Anyahera felt good. And after we voted, she started from her chair, arms upraised, eyes alight. "They've given us the proof," she said. "We can—Thienne, Shinobu, do you see?"

Thienne lifted a hand to spider her fingers against an invisible pane. "You're right," she said, lips pursed. "We *can*."

With access to an uploaded personality, the digital fact of a Mitanni brain, we could compare their minds to ours. It would be far from a simple arithmetic hunt for subtraction or addition, but it would give us an empirical angle on the Duong-Watts problem.

Anyahera took me aside, in a space as old as our friendship, the khaya mahogany panels and airy glass of our undergraduate dorm. "Shinobu," she said. She fidgeted as she spoke, I think to jam her own desire to reach for me. "Have you seen what they're building in orbit?"

This memory she'd raised around us predated Thienne by a decade. That didn't escape me.

"I've seen them," I said. I'd gone through Mitanni's starflight capabilities datum by datum. "Orbital foundries. For their own seedships. They're getting ready to colonize other stars."

Neither of us had to unpack the implications there. It was the beginning of a boom cycle—exponential growth.

"Ten million years," she said. "I've run a hundred simulations out that far. If Mitanni is a Duong-Watts, in ten million years the galaxy is full of them. Now and forever. No conscious human variant can compete. Not even digitized baseline humans—you know what it took just to make *Lachesis*. Nothing human compares."

I nodded in silent acknowledgment. *Is that so terrible?* I wanted to ask—Thienne's question, in this memory so empty of her. *Is consciousness what we have to sacrifice to survive in the long run?*

She didn't even need me to ask the question. "I can envision nothing more monstrous," she said, "than mankind made clockwork. Nothing is worth that price."

And I wanted to nod, just to show her that we were not enemies. But I couldn't. It felt like giving in.

Sometimes I wondered at the hubris of our mission. Would Mitanni live and die not by the judgment of a jurisprudent mind but the troubled whims of a disintegrating family? We had left Earth as a harmonized unit, best-in-class product of a post-military, post-national edifice that understood the pressures of long-duration, high-stress starflight. No one and nothing could judge better. But was that enough? Was the human maximum adequate for this task?

Something in that thought chilled me more than the rest, and I wished I could know precisely what.

We met the Mitanni upload in a chameleon world: a sandboxed pocket of *Lachesis*'s mind, programmed to cycle from ocean to desert to crowd to solitary wasteland, so that we could watch the Mitanni's reactions, and, perhaps, come to know her.

She came among us without image or analogy, injected between one tick of simulation and the next. We stood around her on a pane of glass high above a grey-green sea.

"Hello," she said. She smiled, and it was not at all inhuman. She had Thienne's color and a round, guileless face that with her slight build made me think of Jizo statues from my childhood. "I'm the ambassador for Mitanni."

Whatever language she spoke, *Lachesis* had no trouble with it. Thienne and Anyahera looked to me, and I spoke as we'd agreed.

"Hello. My name is Shinobu. This is the starship *Lachesis*, scout element of the Second Fleet."

If she saw through the bluff of scouts and fleets, she gave no sign. "We expected you," she said, calm at the axis of our triplicate regard. "We detected the weapons you carry. Because you haven't fired yet, we know you're still debating whether to use them. I am here to plead for our survival."

She's rationally defensive, Thienne wrote in our collective awareness. *Attacking the scenario of maximal threat.*

At the edge of awareness, *Lachesis*'s telemetry whispered telltales of cognition and feedback, a map of the Mitanni's thoughts. Profiling.

My eyes went to Anyahera. We'd agreed she would handle this contingency. "We believe your world may be a Duong-Watts malignant," she said. "If you've adapted yourselves to survive by eliminating consciousness, we're deeply concerned about the competitive edge you've gained over baseline humanity. We believe consciousness is an essential part of human existence."

In a negotiation between humans, I think we would have taken hours to reach this point, and hours more to work through the layers of bluff and counter-bluff required to hit the next point. The Mitanni ambassador leapt all that in an instant. "I'm an accurate map of the Mitanni mind," she said. "You have the information you need to judge the Duong-Watts case."

I see significant mental reprofiling, Lachesis printed. *Systemic alteration of networks in the thalamic intralaminar nuclei and the prefrontal-parietal associative loop. Hyperactivation in the neural correlates of rationalization—*

Anyahera snapped her fingers. The simulation froze, the Mitanni ambassador caught in the closing phoneme of her final word. "That's it," Anyahera said, looking between the two of us. "Duong-Watts. That's your smoking gun."

Even Thienne looked shocked. I saw her mouth the words: *hyperactivation in the neural—*

The Mitanni hadn't stripped their minds of consciousness. They'd just locked it away in a back room, where it could watch the rest of the brain make its decisions, and cheerfully, blithely, blindly consider itself responsible.

—correlates of rationalization—

Some part of the Mitanni mind knew of its own existence. And that tiny segment watched the programming that really ran the show iterate itself, feeling every stab of pain, suffering through every grueling shift, every solitary instant of a life absent joy or reward. Thinking: *This is all right. This is for a reason. This is what I want. Everything is fine.* When hurt, or sick, or halfway through unanaesthetized field surgery, or when she drove the euthanasia needle into her thigh: *this is what I want.*

Because they'd tweaked some circuit to say: *You're in charge. You are choosing this.* They'd wired in the perfect lie. Convinced the last domino that it was the first.

And with consciousness out of the way, happy to comply with any sacrifice, any agony, the program of pure survival could optimize itself.

"It's parsimonious," Thienne said at last. "Easier than stripping out all the circuitry of consciousness, disentangling it from cognition . . ."

"This is Duong-Watts," Anyahera said. I flinched at her tone: familiar only from memories of real hurt and pain. "This is humanity enslaved at the most fundamental level."

I avoided Thienne's glance. I didn't want her to see my visceral agreement with Anyahera. Imagining that solitary bubble of consciousness, lashed, parasitic, to the bottom of the brain, powerless and babbling.

To think that you could change yourself. To be wrong, and never know it. That was a special horror.

Of course Thienne saw anyway, and leapt in, trying to preempt Anyahera, or my own thoughts. "This is not the place to wash your hands of Jotunheim. There's no suffering here. No crime to erase. All they want to do is survive—"

"Survival is the question," Anyahera said, turned half-away, pretending disregard for me, for my choice, and in that disregard signaling more fear than she had begging on her knees at Jotunheim, because Anyahera would only ever disregard that which she thought she had no hope of persuading. "The survival of consciousness in the galaxy. The future of cognition. We decide it right here. We fire or we don't."

Between us the Mitanni stood frozen placidly, mid-gesture.

"Kill the Mitanni," Thienne said, "and you risk the survival of *anything at all.*"

It hurt so much to see both sides. It always had.

Three-player variants are the hardest to design.

Chess. Shogi. Nuclear detente. War. Love. Galactic survival. Three-player variants are unstable. It was written in my first game theory text: *Inevitably, two players gang up against a third, creating an irrecoverable tactical asymmetry.*

"You're right, Thienne," I said. "The Mitanni aren't an immediate threat to human survival. We're going home."

We fell home to Earth, to the empty teak house, and when I felt Anyahera's eyes upon me I knew myself measured a monster, an accomplice to extinction. Anyahera left, and with her gone, Thienne whirled away into distant dry places far from me. The Mitanni bloomed down the Orion Arm and leapt the darkness between stars.

"Anyahera's right," I said. "The Mitanni will overrun the galaxy. We need to take a stand for—for what we are. Fire the weapons."

We fell home to Earth and peach tea under the Lagos sun, and Thienne looked up into that sun and saw an empty universe. Looked down and saw the two people who had, against her will, snuffed out the spark that could have kindled all that void, filled it with metal and diligent labor: life, and nothing less or more.

I took a breath and pushed the contingencies away. "This isn't a zero-sum game," I said. "I think that other solutions exist. Joint outcomes we can't ignore."

They looked at me, their pivot, their battleground. I presented my case.

This was the only way I knew how to make it work. I don't know what I would have done if they hadn't agreed.

They chose us for this mission, us three, because we could work past the simple solutions.

The Mitanni ambassador stood between us as we fell down the thread of our own orbit, toward the moment of weapons release, the point of no return.

"We know that Mitanni society is built on the Duong-Watts malignancy," Anyahera said.

The Mitanni woman lifted her chin. "The term *malignancy* implies a moral judgment," she said. "We're prepared to argue on moral grounds. As long as you subscribe to a system of liberal ethics, we believe that we can claim the right to exist."

"We have strategic concerns," Thienne said, from the other side of her. "If we grant you moral permit, we project you'll colonize most of the galaxy's habitable stars. Our own seedships or digitized human colonists can't compete. That outcome is strategically unacceptable."

We'd agreed on that.

"Insects outnumber humans in the terrestrial biosphere," the Mitanni said. I think she frowned, perhaps to signal displeasure at the entomological metaphor. "An wondered how carefully she had been tuned to appeal to us. "An equilibrium exists. Coexistence that harms neither form of life."

"Insects don't occupy the same niche as humans," I said, giving voice to Anyahera's fears. "You do. And we both know that we're the largest threat to your survival. Sooner or later, your core imperative would force you to act."

The ambassador inclined her head. "If the survival payoff for war outstrips the survival payoff for peace, we will seek war. And we recognize that our strategic position becomes unassailable once we have launched our first colony ships. If it forestalls your attack, we are willing to disassemble our own colonization program and submit to a blockade—"

"No." Thienne again. I felt real pride. She'd argued for the blockade solution and now she'd coolly dissect it. "We don't have the strength to enforce a blockade before you can launch your ships. It won't work."

"We are at your mercy, then." The ambassador bowed her chin. "Consider the moral ramifications of this attack. Human history is full of attempted genocide, unilateral attempts to control change and confine diversity, or to remake the species in a narrow image. Full, in the end, of profound regret."

The barb struck home. I don't know by what pathways pain becomes empathy, but just then I wondered what her tiny slivered consciousness was thinking, while the rest of her mind thrashed away at the problem of survival: *The end of the world is coming, and it's all right; I won't worry, everything's under control—*

Anyahera took my shoulder in silence.

"Here are our terms," I said. "We will annihilate the Mitanni colony in order to prevent the explosive colonization of the Milky Way by post-conscious human variants. This point is non-negotiable."

The Mitanni ambassador waited in silence. Behind her, Thienne blinked, just once, an indecipherable punctuation. I felt Anyahera's grip tighten in gratitude or tension.

"You will remain in storage aboard the *Lachesis*," I said. "As a comprehensive upload of a Mitanni personality, you contain the neuroengineering necessary to recreate your species. We will return to Earth and submit the future of the Mitanni species to public review. You may be given a new seedship and a fresh start, perhaps under the supervision of a preestablished blockade. You may be consigned to archival study, or allowed to flourish in a simulated environment. But we can offer a near-guarantee that you will not be killed."

It was a solution that bought time, delaying the Duong-Watts explosion for centuries, perhaps forever. It would allow us to study the Duong-Watts individual, to game out their survivability with confidence and the backing of a comprehensive social dialogue. If she agreed.

It never occurred to me that she would hesitate for even one instant. The core Mitanni imperative had to be *survive*, and total annihilation weighed against setback and judgment and possible renaissance would be no choice at all.

"I accept," the Mitanni ambassador said. "On behalf of my world and my people, I am grateful for your jurisprudence."

We all bowed our heads in unrehearsed mimicry of her gesture. I wondered if we were aping a synthetic mannerism, something they had gamed out to be palatable.

"*Lachesis*," Anyahera said. "Execute RKV strike on Mitanni."

"I need a vote," the ship said.

I think that the Mitanni must have been the only one who did not feel a frisson: the judgment of history, cast back upon us.

We would commit genocide here. The largest in human history. The three of us, who we were, what we were, would be chained to this forever.

"Go," I said. "Execute RKV strike."

Thienne looked between the two of us. I don't know what she wanted to see but I met her eyes and held them and hoped.

Anyahera took her shoulder. "I'm sorry," she said.

"Go," Thienne said. "Go."

We fell away from the ruin, into the void, the world that had been called Mitanni burning away the last tatters of its own atmosphere behind us. *Lachesis* clawed at the galaxy's magnetic field, turning for home.

"I wonder if they'll think we failed," Anyahera said drowsily. We sat together in a pavilion, the curtains drawn.

I considered the bottom of my glass. "Because we didn't choose? Because we compromised?"

She nodded, her hands cupped in her lap. "We couldn't go all the way. We brought our problems home." Her knuckles whitened. "We made accommodations with something that—"

She looked to her left, where Thienne had been, before she went to be alone. After a moment she shrugged. "Sometimes I think this is what they wanted all along, you know. That we played into their hands."

I poured myself another drink: cask strength, unwatered. "It's an old idea," I said.

She arched an eyebrow.

"That we can't all go home winners." I thought of the pierced bleeding crust of that doomed world and almost choked on the word *winners*—but I knew that for the Mitanni, who considered only outcomes, only pragmatism, this was victory. "That the only real solutions lie at the extremes. That we can't figure out something wise if we play the long game, think it out, work every angle."

For n=3, solutions exist for special cases.

"Nobody won on Jotunheim," Anyahera said softly.

"No," I said. Remembered people drowning in acid, screaming their final ecstasy because they had been bred and built for pain. "But we did our jobs, when it was hardest. We did our jobs."

"I still can't sleep."

"I know." I drank.

"Do you? Really?"

"What?"

"I know the role they selected you for. I know *you*. Sometimes I think—" She pursed her lips. "I think you change yourself so well that there's nothing left to carry scars."

I swallowed. Waited a moment, to push away my anger, before I met her gaze. "Yeah," I said. "It hurt me too. We're all hurt."

A moment passed in silence. Anyahera stared down into her glass, turning it a little, so that her reflected face changed and bent.

"To new ideas," she said, a little toast that said with great economy everything I had hoped for, especially the apologies.

"To new ideas."

"Should we go and—?" She made a worried face and pointed to the ceiling, the sky, where Thienne would be racing the causality of her own hurt, exploring some distant angle of the microwave background, as far from home as she could make the simulation take her.

"Not just yet," I said. "In a little while. Not just yet."

Chen Qiufan (a.k.a. Stanley Chan) was born in Shantou, Guangdong Province. Chan is a science fiction writer, columnist, script writer and a vice president at tech start-up Noitom. Since 2004, he has published over thirty stories in *People's Literature, Science Fiction World, Esquire,* and *Chutzpah!*, many of which are included in his collections *Thin Code* and *Future Disease*. His debut novel, *The Waste Tide*, was published in January 2013 and won the Chinese Nebula Best Novel and Huadi Awards. Chan is the most widely translated young writer of science fiction in China, with his short works translated into English, Italian, Japanese, Swedish, and Polish, and published in *Clarkesworld, Interzone, Lightspeed,* and *F&SF*. He has won Taiwan's Dragon Fantasy Award, China's Galaxy and Nebula Award, and, along with Ken Liu, a Science Fiction & Fantasy Translation Award. He lives in Beijing.

THE SMOG SOCIETY

Chen Qiufan
translated by Carmen Yiling Yan and Ken Liu

Lao Sun lived on the seventeenth floor facing the open street, nothing between him and the sky. If he woke in the morning to darkness, it was the smog's doing for sure.

Through the murky air outside the window, he had to squint to see the tall buildings silhouetted against the yellow-gray background like a sandy-colored relief print. The cars on the road all had their highbeams on and their horns blaring, crammed one against the other at the intersection into one big mess. You couldn't tell where heaven and earth met, and you couldn't tell apart the people either. Passels of pedestrians, dusty-faced under filter masks that made them look like pig-faced monstrosities, walked past the jammed cars.

Lao Sun washed, dressed, and got his kit. Before he left, he made sure to give the picture frame on the table a wipe.

He greeted the elevator girl, and the girl greeted him back behind a layer of mesh gauze. "It's twelve degrees Celsius today with the relative humidity at sixty-four percent. Visibility is less than two kilometers, and the Air Quality Index of six-eighty indicates severe smog. Long-distance travelers, please be careful. Young children, the elderly, and those with respiratory illnesses, please remain indoors. . . ."

Lao Sun smiled, put on his mask, and stepped out of the elevator.

On his light electric bike, he nimbly wove through the gaps between the crawling traffic. There were plenty of children banging on car windows hawking newspapers and periodicals, but no cleaners. This smog was here to stay for another couple of weeks. No point in cleaning cars now.

Through the goggles on his mask, he could just barely see the road for a couple dozen meters ahead. It was as if someone was standing above the city pouring dust down endlessly. The sky was darker than the ground, dirty and sticky. Even with the filter mask, you felt as if the smog could worm its way through everything, through dozens of layers of polymer nanomaterial filter membrane and into your nostrils, your pores, your alveoli, your blood vessels, and swim all over your body from there; stuff your chest full until you couldn't breathe; and turn your brain into a drum of concrete too thick to stir or spin.

People were like parasites burrowed into the smog.

On these occasions, Lao Sun always thought of old times with his wife.

"Oh Lao Sun, can't you drive slower, there's no rush."

"Mm."

"Lao Sun, stop at that store ahead, I'll buy a bottle of water for you."

"Mm."

"Lao Sun, why aren't you saying anything? How about I sing you a song? You used to like singing."

"Mm."

Lao Sun parked his bike at the roadside and entered the big fancy skyscraper with all the fancily dressed men and women going in and out. They were all wearing filter masks, saving them the trouble of greeting him. The building manager was polite to him, though. He told him one of the public elevators was broken, so the others were crowded. He should use the freight elevator in the back, although it meant climbing a few more floors.

Lao Sun smiled and said it was fine, although the manager couldn't see that, of course.

He took the freight elevator to the twenty-eighth floor, then climbed the stairs to the open platform on the top floor. It made him pant and puff a little, but no matter. From the top of the skyscraper, he could better see the smog: the aerosolized particles that engulfed the city hung thick like protoplasm, motionless.

Lao Sun began to unpack his bag, taking out and assembling each intricate scientific instrument. He wasn't clear on how they worked, but he knew how to use them to record temperature, pressure, humidity, visibility, particulate matter density, and so on. The devices were spruced-up versions of civilian-use models, less precise but much more portable.

He glanced northwest. He should have been seeing grand palaces and shining white pagodas, but today there was only the same murk as everywhere else.

He remembered how it looked in the fall, the red leaves dyeing the hillsides layer by layer, trimming the clear blue sky. The white towers and the falling leaves all reflected in the lake's emerald surface: a tranquil airiness through which the cooing of pigeons drifted.

On that day, the two of them had sat in a boat at the center of the lake, rowing slow circles. The oars drew ripples that washed aside the fallen leaves.

Golden sunlight spilled on the water, glittering. She was covered in golden light, too.

"A rare thing, to have a peaceful day like this. Sun, sing something!"

"Haven't sung in a long time."

"I remember we went rowing here twenty years ago. A whole twenty years ago."

"That's right, Lao Li's son is almost the age we'd been."

". . ."

"I—I didn't mean it that way."

"I know what you meant."

"I really didn't."

"This is pointless."

"All right, if it's boring we'll go back."

"He would have been ten by now."

"Didn't you say not to talk about this?"

"Sun, I still want to hear you sing."

"Forget it, let's go back."

At the designated time, Lao Sun recorded the data, and then started packing up. He knew that at that moment there were more than a hundred individuals like him in each and every corner of this city doing the same thing. They belonged to a civilian environmental organization, officially registered as the "Municipal Smog Research and Prevention Society," unofficially known by the catchier moniker of "The Smog Society." Their logo was a yellow window with a sponge wiping through the accumulated grime, leaving behind a patch of cerulean blue.

The Smog Society wasn't as radical as some green groups, but it wasn't the government's cheering squad either. Its official status was unclear, its work low-key, its membership slowly and steadily growing. They sometimes appeared in the media, but only quietly and cautiously.

All groups had their own worldview and style, but not all viewpoints were acceptable.

The Smog Society only espoused what was acceptable: aside from the biological dangers, smog also caused psychological harm—easily overlooked, but with far greater and longer-lasting consequences.

Lao Sun hurried to the next sampling location. On his way, he saw some people with bare faces—manual laborers unable to afford masks. Their skin was much dimmer and grayer than the sky, suffused with an inky gleam like coarse sandpaper. They were constructing a completely enclosed skywalk to connect the whole of the central economic district together seamlessly so people wouldn't have to go outside.

Lao Sun knew that antioxidant facial films were all the rage right now. Many women would apply a thirty-nanometer-thick layer of imported facial spray before putting on their masks. It blocked UV radiation and toxins, and would naturally shed with the skin. Of course, not everyone had a face precious enough.

If the facial spray had appeared a few years earlier, he would have bought it for his wife for sure. Just a few years earlier.

He shook his head. It felt as if his old wife was once again sitting behind him.

"Ai, Lao Sun, do you think the weather will get better tomorrow?"

"Mm."

"This awful weather makes me feel all stifled—like there's a rope choking me, getting tighter bit by bit."

"Mm."

"Lao Sun, how about we move somewhere else? Leave this place?"

"Should have left early, then. We're standing by the coffin's side by now. Where are we supposed to go?"

"That's true, we should have left early. We should have left early if we were going to leave."

". . ."

He stopped the bike. This was a large stock-exchange center, where every day a mix of young and old and of every color congregated to stare at the huge LCD screens suspended in mid-air, their expressions shifting with the rise and fall of graphs and numbers. It was a giant gambling den, where everyone thought themselves a winner, or a soon-to-be winner.

As usual, Lao Sun climbed onto the roof and began his measurements.

Lao Sun vaguely knew some of the Smog Society's philosophy, but not well. Maybe his rank wasn't high enough. He'd joined the Smog Society for simple reasons—giving some purpose to his monotonous post-retirement life. Of course, by the time you lived to his age, you tended to understand that having a purpose in life wasn't any more important than living itself.

One afternoon, he'd been dragged to some so-called psychological counseling course, located on the tenth floor of a rundown building where the elevator doors squeaked. He wasn't interested, but he'd caved under his old coworker's pleading and gone with him. At first he'd thought it was some Buddhist or Daoist lecturer spouting philosophy to con people into giving him money, but he discovered otherwise.

He first filled out a quiz that indicated that his depression level scored seventy-three out of one hundred. Out of all the attendees, he counted as below average.

The speaker smoothly drew his audience in. Some began to sob and wail, some threw chairs, other hugged each other tightly and revealed their most deeply hidden little secrets. Lao Sun had never seen anything like it. He didn't know what to do. Someone patted his shoulder: a lady of about thirty, who could be considered beautiful, though not beautiful enough to move someone Lao Sun's age.

"Sorry to bother you, but I saw your answer sheet. You mentioned the weather as a factor."

"Mm. The smog."

She introduced herself as the administrator of the Municipal Smog Research and Prevention Society. He didn't remember her name.

"You don't seem to like talking. Something on your mind?"

"Mm."

"Our association is recruiting volunteers right now. Maybe you'd be interested. Here's our flyer."

He'd wanted to say no, but he glanced at the flyer and a few words caught his eye. He accepted it.

"Maybe we can provide you with a new view of smog."

"Mm?"

Lao Sun wanted to ask more, but she'd hurried away already. A specter flashed in front of his eyes at that moment: his wife. He looked at the flyer again. *Smog Causes an Increase in City Residents' Depression Rates.*

So it began.

The current consensus holds smog to be the product of industrial pollution combined with natural weather patterns. Automobile exhaust, industrial waste gas, and other forms of man-made particulate matter are caught in thermal inversions where the temperature of the air decreases with altitude, cold on top and hot on the bottom. An inversion layer forms 100 meters from the surface and closes over the ground like the lid of a pot. With no wind, pollutants in the city disperse too slowly and become concentrated near the surface. Combined with lack of precipitation, strong sunlight, and low humidity, the conditions promote photochemical reactions between pollutants to form smog.

As of now, there are no methods of prevention.

For Lao Sun, aside from bronchitis, acute emphysema, asthma, pharyngitis, strokes, and the other physical ailments, the most immediate consequence of smog was the sense of removal from the world. Whether you were dealing with people or things, you felt as though you were separated by a layer of frosted glass. No matter how hard you tried, you couldn't really see or touch.

That the masks meant to protect from smog added a second layer was especially ironic. The detachment, the numbness, the estrangement, and the apathy now all had an obvious physical excuse for existing.

The city was cocooned. The people were cocooned.

As Lao Sun rode his bike, the highway overpasses wound overhead like giant dragons, alternating light and shadow. They widened the roads every year, but the traffic still grew more and more congested. Even so, all these people remained willing to squeeze themselves into their little cars, watch the endless lines crawl forward inch by inch. They hid in their four- or five-square-meter metal cans and kept a safe distance from the world and other people.

And so the air pollution worsened, too.

At last he reached his final destination, a daycare called Sunflower.

Sunflower Daycare was built on a raised railway platform and looked like a giant glass greenhouse with children studying and playing on each floor. They didn't need masks; the parents had to foot the bill for the expensive air circulation systems, but even so, looking at those healthy, rosy, bare faces crying or laughing, it seemed worth it.

At least they were still genuine. At least they still had hope.

Each time, Lao Sun would hungrily gaze at the children behind the glass, losing track of time. As he looked at these exposed souls romping and frolicking, another voice would sound, so close it seemed right next to him, so far it seemed decades in the past.

"I know what you're thinking."

"No, you don't."

"I know."

"No. You. Do. Not."

"Fine, fine, let's not argue. I promise you, five more years."

"Five years! Can I still bear a child in five years?"

"There're plenty of thirty-year-olds having kids nowadays. Our finances are only so-so, and with our surroundings a dirty mess like this, it would be unfair to the kid. We'll work hard for another few years, and then we'll go somewhere better to have a child, let them grow up somewhere nice."

"You're talking pie-in-the-sky, you always do."

"Being able to do it well is a skill too. We'll go to the doctor's in the afternoon."

"I want to hear you sing."

"Sure! Whatever you want to hear."

Lao Sun tasted salt in the corner of his mouth. Something had trickled down his face and between his lips.

Strange how the present seemed so blurry, when he could see and hear everything from his memories so clearly. Sometimes they'd play over and over in his mind. No wonder they said old people got nostalgic.

That conversation was decades old. When you're young, money is important, a house is important, a car is important—everything is important—and yet you still end up neglecting the most important things of all. By the time you earn all your money and get all the things you ought to have, some things are lost forever. Lao Sun understood now, but he was already old.

And so far, no one had invented a time machine, or a pill to take away regret.

Lao Sun had to submit his recordings to the Smog Society headquarters' data analysis center, but he didn't know how to use the internet, so he had to find Xiao Wang, one of his "smog buddies." (That was how members referred to each other.)

Xiao Wang had joined the society half a year earlier than Lao Sun. He had a job during the day and spent his free time with the society. They were from the same hometown, so they ended up close to each other.

Xiao Wang seemed somewhat excited as he led Lao Sun to his office and had his secretary pour a cup of water. Then he asked, "So you still don't know?"

Lao Sun shook his head, confused. "Know what?"

"Our association sent in the report to the government."

"What report?"

"The research report about the smog!"

"Oh. Well, it's not like we'll get to see it."

"Hey, I spend my spare time helping the Smog Society process data. I know the gist of the report. Just don't go spreading it around."

"Don't worry. Who would I talk to?"

"You know the Smog Society's central statement, right?"

"The thing about smog and mental illness? Who doesn't?"

"Most people only know about the correlation between smog and mental illness, not the causation."

"What do you mean?"

"Did you think you were just weather-watching, Lao Sun?"

Xiao Wang began to lay out the deeper theory. The Smog Society's monitoring had three components. Lao Sun participated in the basic weather monitoring. In addition, at each sampling location, the psychological states of the relevant people were monitored. The exact method was unclear: maybe with miniature RFID chip sampling, maybe with the entrance security systems or networks, maybe using free goodies with questionnaires attached. Of course, the easiest and most accurate way was to pay the target population to download software that displayed survey questions to be answered at specific times. Either way, they managed. More secretly, they conducted laboratory experiments, researching aerosol distribution in the atmosphere, the electrosensitivity of organic hydrocarbons, bioelectric fields, physical manifestations of psychological conditions under different environmental circumstances, and other similar topics.

A tenet of statistics is using large quantities of long-term data to eliminate sampling biases and other sources of error.

All of this effort had one goal: creating a mathematical model of smog to examine the connection between aerosol systems and human psychological states, controlling for weather conditions.

They discovered that the bioelectrical fields generated by groups displayed coherence: the overlay of peaks and valleys caused the bioelectric field within a certain area to approach constancy. It was like the folk wisdom that fair and foul moods were both infectious. And these large-scale bioelectric fields, in turn, affected the distribution of aerosolized particles. Generally, the lower the psychological health score, the greater the density of particulate matter, and the more stable their formation—in other words, the thicker the smog, and the slower it dispersed.

They also found that within the PM distribution system were bands of greater density like ocean currents, mostly located along thoroughfares with severely congested traffic, flowing sluggishly, dissipating once the traffic eased to congregate in nearby areas with high population density.

The sampling locations in the central economic district and high-density residential areas showed PM densities significantly higher than the average in other sampling locations. These areas had the lowest psychological health scores as well. In contrast, areas with dense populations of teenagers and children had higher psychological health scores, and the air quality tended to be better. And at large stock exchanges, the psychological health score, the air quality rating, and the stock prices were all closely correlated.

Causation also went the other way: the smog lowered people's psychological health scores. Therefore, barring major changes in weather, marauding cold fronts, or an increase in wind, the smog would continue to strengthen its grip.

Lao Sun listened dazedly to Xiao Wang's explanation. He felt like he understood a little and not at all at the same time. Finally he said, "So smog is caused by how we feel."

Xiao Wang clapped his hands. "I spouted all that drivel, and you summed it up in a sentence. Wow!"

Lao Sun said, "We used to love talking about the heart, not the brain. It's the other way around nowadays."

"We've modernized. We use science now."

"Anyway, we won't need to record the weather anymore?"

"Not necessarily. We have to see how the government responds."

Lao Sun said good-bye to Xiao Wang and returned home. There were still leftovers in the refrigerator, ready to heat and eat.

Ready to heat and eat. In that moment, he felt like he'd returned to that hot, humid night. The two of them lay side by side, unable to sleep.

"Lao Sun, do you think tomorrow will be a good day?"

"Mm."

"I've had a couple of strange days. I keep dreaming about things from before, when we just met."

"Mm?"

"The sky was always blue back then, and the clouds were white. There weren't so many buildings. There were big paulownia trees on either side of the road, and when the wind blew their leaves would rustle, sha sha. *You'd take me nice places on your bike. There weren't so many cars back then, either. The roads were so wide and open you could see all the way from one side to the other. The sun wasn't nasty. There were birds and cicadas. We'd ride to the city outskirts and lay down on the grass wherever we liked. It felt so good. Lao Sun, you remember, right?"*

"Mm."

"I also remember that you had so many entertaining tricks back then. You juggled, you played the harmonica, and you always wanted to sing me songs. I didn't want to listen, and you'd chase after me singing, singing—what was that song again?"

". . ."

"That's right, I remember now. 'Young Friends Gather,' wasn't it? Haha."

". . ."

"Lao Sun, tomorrow morning I want to go out for a while. I've put breakfast in the fridge for you, just heat and eat. Are you asleep?"

". . ."

The next day, when Lao Sun woke, his wife had already left. He took out the meal from the fridge, heated it, and ate. The laundry from the night before still hung on the balcony. The sky was still gray.

She never came back.

Lao Sun suddenly panicked, like he'd never panicked before. He hadn't panicked like this back then when he first saw her.

He remembered how he'd dug through his heart to find things to say, back then, while she replied so carelessly. He'd felt as frantic as an ant on a hot pot. Then they were going out, and there was no end to the back-and-forth. Then they married. Each attending to their own career, they'd had less time together, and less to say. They said a bit more only when they fought. His career alternately rose and fell, and she missed her best childbearing years. She started to nag; he started to hold his tongue. They fought, and they threatened divorce, but in the end neither of them could leave the other.

One nagging, the other silent, they'd passed so many years. It seemed that both of them had gotten used to it. If you weren't meant to love each other, you wouldn't be together, Lao Sun had thought. It wouldn't be a half bad life, to be like this till the end. But almost at the finish line, she left.

Lao Sun felt like his heart emptied in that moment, deflated to nothing, like a burst balloon.

A week later, the Smog Society disbanded. Some people from the government invited Lao Sun to have tea and "talk" but allowed him to leave afterwards.

Several of the organization leaders had disappeared, and the core members had also been "called in to talk." When they returned, they said nothing. When they met smog buddies, they looked at them like strangers.

Rumors spread after that. Some said that the smog above the city was actually an enemy country's new climate-altering weapon, while others said it was a side effect of their own country's new secret weapon tests gone wrong. There was an even bolder theory claiming that the smog was really a massive gaseous life form. It—or maybe they—lumbered over the city, subsisting on industrial waste gas and the nitric acid, sulfuric acid, and hydrocarbon particles from automobile exhaust. They were slowly dissolving the calcium in human bones. In time, people would become afflicted with osteoporosis and rickets. Children and the elderly would easily break bones, even become paralyzed.

Of course, the rumors were quickly debunked. After investigation, the calcium-sucking monster story was tracked back to a calcium supplement manufacturer. Its unscrupulous marketing practices were punished as they deserved. The government vowed to formulate a five-year plan to return blue skies to the people.

As for that report, it was as if it never existed.

Today was smoggy again. Lao Sun got up early as usual, washed, dressed, and got his travel things. Before he left, he made sure to give the picture frame on the table a wipe. The woman in the frame smiled at him.

That photo was more than ten years old by now.

He smiled at the elevator girl. The elevator girl saw the mask he carried and smiled back.

Lao Sun put on his mask and got on his light electric bike. It was festooned with lights and streamers of every color and played chipper music. All along his journey, passersby in pig-snouted masks watched him, pointed at him. His bike was like a Brazilian parrot zipping through a desert, brilliant, colorful, and noisy.

He went straight to Sunflower Daycare, got off the bike, and stood in front of the massive glasshouse.

Lao Sun opened his bag and scooped out his strange little knick-knacks. First he filled some helium balloons and let them float high. The children stopped their games and ran to the window to watch this man in the clown mask. The music continued to play from the bike's speakers. He followed the rhythm, slowly and comically contorting his body, and began to juggle.

"See, I can juggle three oranges at once. Watch!"

". . ."

"You won't watch? Then I'll play the harmonica for you. I don't even need my hands. I can change pitch with just my tongue."

". . ."

"Then I'll sing for you. What song do you want to hear? I know them all!"

". . ."

Lao Sun was breathing heavily. Something had trickled down his face and into his mouth, salty. The little pixies were wide-eyed, their faces pressed against the window, pink and white. They were laughing, showing their teeth, some of them clutching their bellies, even. The caretakers were laughing too.

"I know what song you'll like. I'll sing it for you right now. . . ."

"No way you know!"

"I know. Listen, if you don't believe me."

"You're all talk!"

An old song played from the speakers.

. . . *Young friends, we young friends, are gathering today*
Rowing the boats as the warm wind blows . . .
Flowers sweet, birds a-tweet, spring sun to get you drunk
And laughter flies 'round the clouds in circles . . .

The melody, which was so cheerful that it verged on the absurd, pierced the glass. The children began to move to the music, following the clown in his gymnastics. They laughed unabashedly, singing, dancing, crowing, every bare face shining golden.

Lao Sun looked up at the sky. The smog seemed to be thinning too.

Aliette de Bodard lives and works in Paris, where she has a day job as a System Engineer. She is the author of the critically acclaimed Obsidian and Blood trilogy of Aztec noir fantasies, as well as numerous short stories. Recent works include *The House of Shattered Wings*, a novel set in a turn-of-the-century Paris devastated by a magical war, and *The Citadel of Weeping Pearls* (*Asimov's* Oct/Nov), a novella set in the same universe as her Vietnamese space opera *On a Red Station Drifting*.

IN BLUE LILY'S WAKE

Aliette de Bodard

Where Thich Tim Nghe stands, there is no time; there is no noise, save for the distant lament of the dead—voices she has once known, Mother, Sixth Aunt, Cousin Cuc, Cousin Ly, the passengers—not crying out in agony, or whispering about how afraid they were, at the very end, but simply singing, over and over, the syllables of a mantra—perhaps they are at peace, lifted into one of the paradises—perhaps they await their rebirth in a red-lacquered pavilion by the Wheel, sipping the tea of oblivion with the same carelessness Thich Tim Nghe now uses to drink her water, drawn from deep spaces. . . .

In the chorus of the dead, there is one large, looming silence; the voice of the ship, forever beyond her, forever impervious to her prayers and entreaties—but then, wasn't it always the case?

From the planet, the mindship's corpse had seemed to loom large enough to fill the sky—hugged tight on a low orbit, held back from plummeting towards the surface only by a miracle of engineering—but, once she was in the shuttle, Yen Oanh realised that it was really quite far away, the pockmarks on its surface blurred and hazy, the distorted paintings on the hull visible only as splashes of bright colour.

"How long until we arrive?" she asked the disciple.

The disciple, Hue Mi, was a young woman barely out of childhood, though the solemnity with which she held herself made her seem older. "Not long, Grandmother." She looked at the mindship without any sense of wonder or awe; no doubt long since used to its presence. The ship, after all, had been dead for eleven years.

Grandmother. How had she got so old? But then Yen Oanh knew the answer: twenty years of marriage, and another few decades in the Crane and Cedar order, dispatched across the numbered planets to check the spread of the Blue Lily plague in sickhouses and hospitals and private dwellings across the breadth of the Empire, from cramped compartments on the capital to the luxurious mansions of the First Planet, from those who could afford the best care to those who couldn't.

Fifty-six years—and only one regret.

"We don't often get visitors at this time of the year," Hue Mi was saying. She was looking at the mass of the ship, looming ever larger in the viewscreen— normally it would be a private display on each passenger's implants, but Yen Oanh had asked her to make it public.

"Oh?" Yen Oanh kept her eyes on the ship. *The Stone and Bronze Shadow* had been small by modern standards. As they approached the sleek hull vanished from view, replaced by a profusion of details: the shadow of a pagoda on the prow; the red fan surrounding the docking bays, and then only splashes of colours on metal, with a faint tinge of oily light. "The order has been here before." Twice, in fact. She could feel both Sister Que Tu and Brother Gia Minh in the Communion—not saying anything, but standing by, ready to provide her with the information she needed.

And Yen Oanh had been there too, of course—briefly, but long enough.

Hue Mi's face was a closed book. "Of course." In the communal network— overlaid over Yen Oanh's normal vision—her hand was branded with the mark of the order, a crane perched in the branches of a cedar tree. Vaccinated, then, but it wasn't a surprise. Everyone was, those days; and it would have been Yen Oanh's duty to remedy this (and impose a heavy fine), if it hadn't been the case. "It was . . . different back then, I'm told."

"Very different," Yen Oanh said. People dying by the hundreds, the Empire and the newly founded order foundering to research a cure or a vaccine or both, the odour of charnel houses in the overcrowded hospitals; and the fear, that sickening feeling that every bruise on your skin was a symptom, a pre-cursor to all the ones blossoming like flowers on the skin; to the fever and the delirium and the slow descent into death.

At least, now it was controlled.

Hue Mi didn't answer; Yen Oanh realised that she was standing still, her eyes slightly out of focus; the contours of her body wavering as though she were no longer quite there—and that the colours on the viewscreen had frozen. A seizure. She hid them well; she'd had another one in the time Yen Oanh had been with her.

Yen Oanh's own seizures—like Hue Mi's, a side effect of the vaccine—were small, and short enough that she could disguise them as access to the Communion; not as bad or as long as the fits that had characterised the plague, the warping of realities that stretched over entire rooms, dragging everyone into places where human thoughts couldn't remain coherent for long.

Yen Oanh waited for Hue Mi's seizure to be over; all the while, the ship was getting closer—closer to the heartroom. Closer to Thich Tim Nghe.

She didn't want to think about Thich Tim Nghe now.

At length, Hue Mi came back into focus, and opened her eyes; the viewscreen abruptly showed the docking bay coming into view, permanently open, with the death of the Mind that had controlled the ship. "We're here now," she said.

Yen Oanh couldn't help herself. "What did you see?" It was borderline impolite, made only possible because she was much older than Hue Mi, and because she was Crane and Cedar.

Hue Mi nodded—she didn't seem to mind. Possibly her teacher was even more impolite than Yen Oanh. "I was older. And back on the planet, watching children run to a pagoda." She shrugged. "It means nothing."

It didn't. The visions of Blue Lily came from the mind being partially dragged into deep spaces, where time and space took on different significances. Different realities, that was all; not predictions of the future.

Except, of course, for Thich Tim Nghe. Yen Oanh forced a smile she didn't feel. "Your teacher does it differently, doesn't she?"

Hue Mi grimaced. "Thich Tim Nghe doesn't get seizures. It's . . . you'll see, if you make it there."

"If?"

"Most people don't like being onboard."

No. She hadn't thought it would be so easy, after all; that Thich Tim Nghe would be so readily accessible. "Brother Gia Minh?" she asked.

The Communion rose, to enfold her; a room with watercolours of starscapes and mountains, the walls of which seemed to stretch on forever—the air crisp and tangy, as if she stood just on the edge of winter—and the shadowy shapes of a hundred, of a thousand brothers and sisters who had gifted their simulacrums to the Cedar and Crane order, their memories of all the Blue Lily cases they'd seen.

Brother Gia Minh was young—perhaps as young as Hue Mi—wearing not the robes of the order, but the clothes of a poor technician, his hands moving as if he were still controlling bots. "Sister," he said, bowing—then frowning. "You're on the ship. The dead one."

"Yes," Yen Oanh said. "I need you to tell me what happened, when you were last here."

Brother Gia Minh grimaced, but he waved a hand; and the room faded, to be replaced with the arid surface of the Sixth Planet. "Eleven years ago," he whispered.

Eleven years ago, Gia Minh was called because he was nearest; and because he could handle bots—he was barely more than a child then, and not yet a member of the Cedar and Crane; merely a frightened boy with the shadow of Blue Lily hovering over him like a suspended sword.

He'd seen the ship, of course. It was hard to ignore as it slowly materialised above the planet—not all in one go, as he'd seen other mindships do, but flickering in and out of existence, as if not quite sure whether to remain there, as if it still had parts stuck in the deep spaces mindships used for travel. As if...

He hadn't dared to complete the thought, of course. But when he'd boarded the ship with Magistrate Hoa and the militia, it came to him again. The corridors felt wrong—he wasn't sure why, until he ran a hand on the walls, and found them cool, with none of the warm, pulsating rhythm he'd expected. The words in Old Earth characters should have scrolled down, displaying the poetry the ship loved, but they'd frozen into place; some of them already fading, some of them—

There were marks, on the wall—faded, dark ones, like giant fingerprints smudging characters.

"Magistrate," he whispered.

Magistrate Hoa was watching them too, her eyes wide in the weary oval of her face. "It can't be."

Bruises. All over the walls and the floor and everywhere his gaze rested— and that uncanny coldness around them; and faint reflections on the edge of his field of vision—the characteristic delirium, the images and visions that spilled out from the sick to everyone else present.

"Plague," he whispered. "This ship died of Blue Lily." But mindships didn't die of Blue Lily; they didn't die at all—shouldn't even fall sick unless they were countless centuries old, far beyond what mortals could remember. . . .

Magistrate Hoa's face didn't even move. "Gear," she said, to one of the militia. "No one is going any further until we are suited."

Gia Minh wanted to ask why she'd have gear onboard the shuttle, but of course he knew—all the sick and the dying and the dead, the houses that had become charnels and temples to fear; Seventh Uncle, lying in a room no one dared to enter for fear of sharing his final delirium, the disjointed hints of ghosts and demons, the shadows that turned and stretched and *saw* you; Cousin Nhu, too young to talk, whimpering until she had no voice left. . . .

"We'll have one for you," Magistrate Hoa said. "Don't worry."

But of course they were already contaminated, possibly—or worse. No one knew how Blue Lily was contracted, or how it spread—breath or touch or fluids, or Heaven knew what. Everyone knew the Empire was foundering; its doctors and apothecaries overwhelmed, its hospitals overcrowded, and still no cure or vaccine for the disease.

The gear was heavy, and as warm as a portable glasshouse. As they went deeper into those cold, deserted corridors, Gia Minh caught the first hints of the mindship's delirium—a glimpse of something with far too many legs and arms to be human, running just out of sight; of an older woman bending towards a fountain, in the light of a dying sun. . . .

Everywhere silence; that uncanny stillness; and a feeling of being watched by far too many eyes; and the sense that the universe was holding its breath. "They're all dead," he said; and then he heard the weeping.

Thich Tim Nghe watches her attendant Vo clean the heartroom; tidying up the cloths wrapped around the empty throne where the Mind once rested.

"There's someone coming?" she asks.

Vo nods. "She's with Hue Mi now." He's a teenager, but he still has ghosts with him—flickering realities around him, the shadows of his own dead, of his own losses—he's never had Blue Lily, but it doesn't matter. The virus left its mark on him all the same, through the vaccine he received as a child. Thich Tim Nghe could reach out, and pick images like so many strands of straw from a child's hair; could disentangle the skeins of his past and follow them forward into his future; tell him if he will find what he has lost; or what he needs to do to regain the happiness of his childhood, before his uncle left his aunt and tore two households apart.

But Vo has never asked her to see into his future. He knows the cost of it. She gives people what they need, not what they want; and she does it, not to impress people, but to atone, even though there is no atonement for what she has done. To lay the dead to rest, even though they are not her dead; to give hope, even though she has none to share.

She has helped a scholar find the grave of her lost love; whispered to a bots-handler the words he needed to grasp a career-changing opportunity and leave the planet where his daughters are buried; told a painter when and how to meet his future wife, to found the family he so bitterly missed—given so many things to so many people, a countless chain of the living freed from the weight of the past.

She doesn't know why she has those powers; though she suspects that it's the ship, the death that they almost shared; the deep spaces that still remain accessible onboard, even though *The Stone and Bronze Shadow* has since long departed.

It doesn't matter.

Her own future doesn't exist. There is only the past—she watched Mother die, shivering and wasting away while Thich Tim Nghe was still onboard the dying ship; and saw Sixth Aunt's face change and harden—if she were still alive, she would have cut Thich Tim Nghe off, but she's dead too, touched by Blue Lily—her face curiously slack and expressionless, all the bitterness smoothed away under the bruises; and Thich Tim Nghe doesn't know, anymore, what to think about it; if she should weep and grieve, or if she's simply grown too numb under the weight of her litany of losses to care.

There is no happiness for her, and no future. She's here now, in the only time and place that make sense to her; and Sixth Aunt's voice is within the chorus of the dead—and Mother is dead too, forever lost to her, her only presence in memories that are too raw and too painful—limned with the bitter knowledge that Thich Tim Nghe will miss her; that, at the one time in her life when Mother would have had need of her, she won't be there.

She closes her eyes—and steps away, into the past.

"She was in the heartroom," Gia Minh said to Yen Oanh—the images of the past fading, replaced by the room of the Communion—everything was suffused with a warm, red light: a shade that was no doubt meant to be reassuring, but which reminded Yen Oanh of nothing so much as freshly spilled blood. "Wrapped around the connectors of the Mind as though it was a lifeline. Covered in Blue Lily bruises." He shivered. "I don't even know how she survived."

Who knew, Yen Oanh thought, but didn't say. They might have a vaccine; and a better understanding of Blue Lily; but survival in those first few years had been left to Heaven's Will. The younger and fitter people had more chance, obviously; and Thich Tim Nghe had been young—thirteen, a child still.

And *The Stone and Bronze Shadow* had been dead. Quite unmistakably so—a miracle that she had survived far enough to exit deep spaces; to deliver her cargo and passengers to the Sixth Planet, even though it hadn't been her scheduled route.

In the end, there had been only two survivors: Thich Tim Nghe and an older boy, twenty years or so, who had walked away with the scars of the disease all over him—back to the Twenty-Third planet, and his decimated family.

Thich Tim Nghe had not walked away; as Yen Oanh knew all too well.

"Grandmother?" Yen Oanh tore herself from the Communion, and looked at Hue Mi—who was waiting for her in front of an open door—the arch seemingly leading into darkness. "She's ready for you now."

But Yen Oanh wasn't ready for her—she never would be, not across several lifetimes.

She took a deep breath, and stepped into the corpse of the ship.

Inside, it was dark and cool; with that same feeling Gia Minh had had—he'd described it, but there was no way to get it across—that disquieting sense that someone—something—was watching. Normally it would be *The Stone and Bronze Shadow*, making sure that everything was right onboard—controlling everything from the ambient music to the temperature of the different sections—but *The Stone and Bronze Shadow* was dead. And yet. . . .

"You feel it," Hue Mi said. Her smile was tight; her eyes bruised—not the Blue Lily bruises, but close enough, something that seemed to leech all colour from her skin—until it was stretched as thin and as fragile as the inner membrane of an egg—until a careless finger pressure or a slight sharp breath were all it would take to break it.

"It's almost as though it's still alive." There were tales, on the planets; of the unburied dead, the ones without children to propitiate them, the hungry, needy dead roaming the fields and cities without surcease. But *The Stone and Bronze Shadow* had had a family—she remembered seeing them, remembered their wan faces; the sheer shock that a ship should have died—the same shock they'd all felt.

Hue Mi was walking ahead, in a darkened corridor where doors opened—cabins, probably, the same ones where the passengers had died. Too many ghosts here.

"There is a shrine, isn't there?" Yen Oanh asked. There would be, as on all dead ships: a place to leave offerings and prayers, and hope that the soul of

The Stone and Bronze Shadow was still looking fondly on them. "May I stop by?"

Hue Mi nodded, barely hiding her surprise. "This way," she said.

The shrine was at a crossroads between five corridors: a simple wooden table (though the wood itself, fine-grained and lustrous, must have come all the way from the outlying planets), framed by two squat incense burners, and a simple offering of six tangerines in a bowl. The smell of incense drifted to Yen Oanh; a reminder of more mundane temples, cutting through the unease she felt.

She stood in front of the altar, and bowed—unsure what she could say, or if she should say anything at all. "It's been too long," she said, at last, in a low voice. "I apologise if it's not what you wanted—and I ask your forgiveness— but eleven years is enough time to grieve."

There was no answer; but then Yen Oanh hadn't expected one.

"Yen Oanh," a voice said—from deep within the Communion.

Que Tu. She ought to have known.

In the Communion, her friend was unchanged; middle-aged, with the casual arrogance of the privileged, her topknot held in place by thin, elegant hairpins, tapering to the heads of *ky lan*—she'd worn them eleven years ago, an odd statement to make, the *ky lan* announcing the arrival of a time of prosperity and peace—nothing like what they had, even now.

"You're on the ship," Que Tu said. It wasn't a question.

"Yes," Yen Oanh said. Que Tu was a living legend by now, of course; though it hadn't changed her either. "What do you want?"

Que Tu smiled. "Nothing. Just to remind you."

Que Tu came to the Sixth Planet because she had once been a biologist, a rarity in the field branch of the Cedar and Crane: most biologists were closeted in the order's labs, desperately trying to find a cure. She stayed a week; interviewed everyone from Gia Minh to the survivors on the ship, and retreated to Magistrate Hoa's library to compile her report.

Her most vivid memory is of an evening there—sitting at the foot of a watercolour of temples on a mountain and trying to pretend she was back at the order's headquarters on the First Planet; working on reports and statistics that couldn't touch or harm her.

She considered the evidence, for a while: the bruises on the ship; the bruises on the humans. The countless dead—there was no need for her to write the obvious, but she did, anyway.

Human-mindship contagion.

No one knew how Blue Lily was passed on, or had managed to isolate the organism responsible for it. Only the obvious had been eliminated: that it wasn't food, or sexual contact. Airborne or skin contact, quite possibly; except that outbreaks had happened outside of any contact with the sick—as if there had been a spontaneous generation, which was impossible.

Que Tu sipped her tea, and thought on the rest of what she knew. What she'd gleaned from the Communion—the detailed database of the order's memories, available to her at a moment's glance.

The inexplicable outbreaks, many of which bore some connection to mindships.

The symptoms of Blue Lily: the fever, the bruises, the delirium that seemed to be contagious—but only until the person died or the attendants contracted Blue Lily—as if all the visions were linked to the sick, or the sickness itself.

Deep spaces: the alternate realities explored by mindships to facilitate space journeys. Most people in the Empire knew deep spaces as a shortcut which avoided months or years on a hibernation ship. But they were more than that—places where time and space, compressed and stretched, had become inimical to human life.

The similarities seemed obvious in retrospect. Not delirium, but the materialisation of other, less accessible realities; of places in the past or in the future, or nowhere at all.

Deep spaces. Mindships.

Que Tu hesitated for a while. Then she closed her eyes, and wrote in a strong, decisive hand—she could have composed her report in the communal network, or even on her own implants, but she'd got used to the unreliability of both, in the age of the plague.

I think the order should consider the possibility that Blue Lily originated in deep spaces, and still abides there. The organism responsible for it seems to bear an affinity for mindships; though it would seem it has become capable of infecting them now.

Her report was short, and to the point; but it would change the world.

Thich Tim Nghe stands in the past—in the belly of the ship, staring upwards. The heartroom is now a maelstrom of conflicting realities; half into deep spaces already, the mindship's throne of spikes and thorns all but vanished. Her own reality is wavering around her; the onset of fever—the same fever that killed Cousin Ly, sending her mind wandering into a delirium it never returned from.

"Vu Thi Xuan Lan," *The Stone and Bronze Shadow* whispers, her voice like the boom of thunder on uncharted seas—calling her old name; and not the new one she gave herself—'Listening Heart', as if she could make herself wise; could make herself caring and compassionate.

"Ship," she whispers. She's shivering—holding onto reality only with an effort, and even then she can't be sure that this is real, that the ship is real— looming large over her while the walls of the heartroom recede into nothingness and shadows like those of nightmares start moving in the darkness—far away like bleeding stars, and then closer and closer, questing hounds, always there no matter where she turns her head...

"Why?" *The Stone and Bronze Shadow* twists; or perhaps it's the realities around her. "Why come here, child?"

She—she dragged herself out of her cabin—into corridors twisted out of shape; into air that felt too thick, too hot to breathe, searing her lungs with every tottering step—leaning on the walls and feeling the ship wince under her hands—and trying not to think of the other passengers moaning and tossing within their own cabins, each lost in a Hell of their own—the ones she killed as surely as she killed the ship. "I'm here. Because—"

She wants to say that she knew when she boarded *The Stone and Bronze Shadow*—that she'd woken up in her student garret on the evening before she left; shaking off confused nightmares in which Mother screamed for her and she was unable to answer—with sweat encasing her entire body like a shroud. That, as she ran through the spaceport, she felt the growing pains in her arms and legs; and the first bruises, barely visible beneath her dark skin. That she said nothing when she came onboard; because it was nothing, because it had to be nothing; that she needed to get home fast—to be by Mother's side— that the ship was the only way to do that.

She didn't intend to infect the ship, of course—mindships are old and wise, and invulnerable—who had ever heard of one catching Blue Lily? She thought she would keep to her cabin until the journey was over—not passing on a contagion, if there was one—all the while believing that she was fine, that everything would be fine. But, when the first bruises bloomed on the floor of her cabin, she had to accept the inevitable reality—the weight of her guilt and shame—because Mother didn't raise her to be a coward or a fool.

She didn't speak up; and now, days later, it's much too late for her to speak at all.

"I—" her tongue trips on the words, swallows them as though they were ashes. "I came because you shouldn't die alone. Because—"

She'll die, too. One chance in two, one chance in three—statistics of Blue Lily, the faceless abacuses of fear and rage and grief. In the intervals between breaths, she can see the shadows, twisting closer and closer, taking on the leering faces of boars and fanged tigers—the demons of the King of Hell, waiting to take her with them.

The Stone and Bronze Shadow doesn't move, doesn't speak—there are just shadows, spreading to cover her entire field of vision, blotting out of existence the watercolours and the scrolling texts; an oily sheen, and a noise in the background like the chittering of ten thousand cockroaches. "It's kind of you, child," she says at last. Her voice comes back distorted—like the laughter of careless deities. "Come. Let us face the King of Hell together."

It's been eleven years since that night; but it's the only place where Thich Tim Nghe can hear the voice of the ship—the last, the greatest of her dead, the weight that she can never cast aside or deny.

Yen Oanh's strongest memory of the Sixth Planet isn't of the ship, or of the sick—she arrived much too late for that, when the paperwork was already done, and the dead buried and propitiated—but of an interview she had with Magistrate Hoa and Que Tu, at the close of Que Tu's investigation.

They didn't know, then, the storm Que Tu's report would ignite—the back-and-forth of memorials and reports by enraged biologists and civil ser-vants—the angry declarations she was mistaken, that she'd gone into the field branch of the order because she had no competence in science—the Imperial Court itself getting involved; and all the while, the order tearing itself apart while Que Tu struggled to hold her ground.

Back then, it was still possible to pretend that everything was normal; inso-far as anything could be normal, in the age of the plague.

They sat in Magistrate Hoa's library—surrounded by both the old-fash-ioned books on rice paper, and the communal network with its hint of thou-sands more—and drank tea from celadon cups. Yen Oanh inhaled the soft, flowery fragrance from hers, and tried to forget about her bone-deep weari-ness—if she closed her eyes, she'd see her last patient: Lao Sen, an old woman whose death-delirium had created a maze of illusions—ghostly figures and landscapes superimposed over the confines of the sickroom until Yen Oanh wasn't quite sure of what was real, spending an hour talking with a girl who turned into a fox and then melted back into the shadows...

She'd monitored her vitals since Lao Sen's death—no change, no fever, nothing that indicated Blue Lily might be within her. She wasn't sick.

Not this time; but there was always the next—and the next and the next, an endless chain of the sick and the dying, stretching all the way across the Empire.

Que Tu was her usual self, withdrawn and abrasive; Magistrate Hoa looked tired, with deep circles under her eyes, and flesh the colour of wet rice paper—showing the shape of her cheekbones in translucency. "Long week?" Yen Oanh asked.

Magistrate Hoa shrugged. "No worse than usual. There was an outbreak in Long Quang District, in addition to the other seven that I'm currently managing."

Que Tu looked up from her report, sharply. "Long Quang. That's near the spaceport, isn't it?"

"Yes." Magistrate Hoa didn't speak for a while; but Yen Oanh did.

"I don't have much time," she said. The order had rerouted her from her original destination—a large outbreak of Blue Lily in a minor official's holiday house on the First Planet—to here, the site of the unimaginable, universe-shattering death. She was meant to take Que Tu's report back to the order's headquarters; and all she could focus on was a bed, and some rest; and a place free of the fear of contagion and the bone-deep weariness of staying by sickbeds.

"You never do have time." Que Tu said it without aggressiveness. They'd worked together at a couple venues: small hospitals and private sickrooms. Yen Oanh would have liked to believe their presence had made a difference—that the drugs and the care they provided had helped. But, in her heart of hearts, she knew they didn't. They'd made people more comfortable; had knocked others insensate: a kindness, in their last hours. But it was hard to fight a disease they knew so little about. "But I'm going to need you to pay attention."

"Fine," Yen Oanh said. She took a sip of tea, bracing herself for Que Tu's dry recitation of facts.

Her colleague surprised her by not doing that. "I want to know what you think."

"What I—I barely arrived, Sister."

"I know. Bear with me."

"I—I don't know." Yen Oanh looked at Magistrate Hoa, who was silent. "Plague onboard a mindship isn't unusual, per se. But the ship... doesn't usually die." Mindships were engineered to be all but immortal—all five *khi*-elements stabilised to grant them long, changeless lives. They didn't age; they didn't fall sick. And they didn't die of Blue Lily.

"No."

Yen Oanh closed her eyes. "We're dealing with mindship-human contagion, aren't we?" It wasn't the shock it should have been, but that was because she'd had time to think it over on the shuttle. Mindships weren't human, but they were close enough: the Minds were organic constructs modelled on the human body. Diseases could leap from birds to humans, from plants to humans; why not from humans to mindships? "Who fell sick first?"

Que Tu shook her head. "The ship." Her lips were two thin, white lines; her tea lay untouched by her side. "But you know the incubation period varies."

"Fine," Yen Oanh said. It was late, she was tired; and she still had a long way to go before she could finally rest—if she got to rest at all. "Just tell me. Please."

Que Tu said nothing. It was Magistrate Hoa who spoke, her voice low, but firm. "I think a passenger fell sick first. Given the timeline, they were incubating before they even boarded—showing a few symptoms, perhaps, the more discrete ones. They probably didn't suspect the danger."

"They knew they would contaminate people," Yen Oanh said, more firmly than she'd expected. How were they meant to check the progress of Blue Lily, if people stubbornly kept insisting on life as usual—taking long journeys in cramped quarters, and congregating in droves at the temples and teahouses? Could no one think beyond themselves, for once?

"Oanh. . . ."

"You know it's true."

"And I know you're being too harsh."

Yen Oanh exhaled; thinking of all the sick—all the rooms in which she'd sat, trying to decide if more saline solution or more ginseng and cinnabar would make a difference; entering the Communion and comparing the patient's symptoms with the experience of others in the Cedar and Crane, seeking whether anyone's remedies had made a difference. "No. I'm trying to be realistic. Trying to. . . ." She closed her hands into fists. "There are too many dead. You can't expect me to rejoice when people get deliberately infected."

Que Tu grimaced. Too harsh again; but then wasn't it the truth? The disease wasn't going to burn itself out—not while there still were warm bodies to infect.

"We don't know how the sickness is passed on." Que Tu snorted. "Not with enough certainty."

"Well, you can count that as new data," Yen Oanh said, warily.

"All I have is in the report; I expect the order's research labs will have plenty to work with. The place will be swarming with their teams before we're through." Que Tu set down her cup, and looked at the bookshelves, her face set.

"You said 'a passenger,'" Yen Oanh said. "You know which one."

Magistrate Hoa turned, to look at Que Tu; but Que Tu said nothing.

"One of the dead?"

Still nothing. One of the living, then; which left only two—and she didn't think Que Tu was going to be moved by a twenty-year-old boy, no matter how pretty he might have been. "The girl in the heartroom."

"Yes," Magistrate Hoa said, at last.

"Where is she?"

"She wouldn't leave the ship," Que Tu said. "Word came through when we were processing the corpses—her mother died of Blue Lily, six days ago. Oanh..."

Yen Oanh knew what Que Tu would say—that the girl was young and lost, barely confident enough after her ordeal—that she needed reassurance. "She knew."

"You can't know that for sure," Magistrate Hoa said. Her face was set. "I certainly wouldn't prosecute her on that basis."

"Fine," Yen Oanh said, keeping her gaze on Que Tu. "Then look me in the eye and swear that she didn't know."

"I—" Que Tu started; and then stopped, her teeth white against the lividness of her lips, as if she were out in glacial cold. "I can't tell you that."

"Then tell me what you suspect."

Que Tu was silent. Then: "I think the incubation time is shorter in mindships. Or that symptoms are more visible because they're so large, who knows. Will you talk to her, Oanh?"

"And tell her what?"

"Comfort her," Que Tu said. "She's thirteen years old, for Heaven's sake. This requires a deft touch; and we both know I don't have it. Whereas you— you were always good with people."

Comforting the sick and the dying; keeping them on the razor's edge of hope, no matter how much of a lie it turned out to be. Yen Oanh took a deep breath; thought, for a moment, of what she would tell a thirteen-year-old about consequences; of the lessons learnt in months of sickrooms and ministering to the dead—of the stomach-churning fear that it would be her that fell sick next; that she'd have to lock herself in, and pray that someone from the order came, so she wouldn't have to die alone. That anyone would choose to pass this much agony, this much fear onto others. . . . "She killed people, Que Tu. She killed a ship. She's old enough to know better. Besides, she's fortunate—she's alive."

Que Tu said nothing, for a while. Then she shook her head. "It's not always good fortune to survive, is it? Forget I asked." Her voice was emotionless, her face a careful mask—and that should have been the end of it; but of course it wasn't.

—

"I remember that evening," Que Tu said to Yen Oanh. Within the Communion, she was smaller and less impressive than Yen Oanh remembered; though her anger could still have frozen waterfalls. "When I asked you to talk to the girl."

Yen Oanh said nothing.

"It wasn't much to give her, but you didn't."

"I couldn't lie." Yen Oanh has had this conversation before: not with Que Tu, but with her own treacherous conscience. What would have happened, if she had been less tired; less overwrought? Would she still have judged Thich Tim Nghe's actions to be a crime, would she still have blithely moved on? "And do you truly think I would have made a difference?"

Que Tu's smile was bitter, but she didn't answer. She didn't need to: it wasn't the answer that mattered. It wasn't whether Yen Oanh would have made a difference, but that she hadn't even tried.

"We're here, Grandmother," Hue Mi said.

Startled, Yen Oanh looked up from the Communion, Que Tu and the others fading into insignificance; and saw a door in front of her, adorned with faded calligraphy—it seemed like she should be able to read the words, but she couldn't. The swirl of realities was strongest here; that crawling, disorienting sense that she hadn't been meant to be here; a sheen like oil or soap over everything; and shadows that were too long, or too short—turning, stretching, watching her and biding their time. . . .

It was no longer the time of Blue Lily; and this was no longer a sickroom.

A young man was waiting for them, carrying a white cloth which he handed to Yen Oanh. "Put this on. She's waiting for you."

Mourning clothes; or novice's robes—Yen Oanh wasn't sure, anymore.

"Grandmother?" Hue Mi's voice, in a tone that Yen Oanh couldn't quite interpret.

"Yes?"

"Why are you here?"

"What do you mean?"

Hue Mi smiled, and didn't answer—her arms folded in barely appropriate respect. "To change things," Yen Oanh said, finally. She'd never been able to lie; as Que Tu well knew.

"You knew the ship," Hue Mi said.

"No. I'm not her family, and I never saw her before. . . ." She closed her eyes, feeling the weight of years; of decisions made in haste. "Your teacher changed the world," she said. Because she boarded *The Stone and Bronze*

Shadow. Because Que Tu made her report—because Professor Luong Thi Da Linh's teams read it, and finally isolated the virus responsible for Blue Lily, giving the Empire the vaccine they so desperately needed. Because it was all the small things that bore fruit; all the insignificant acts put together, at the close of one's existence.

One of these insignificant acts was Yen Oanh's; and it had destroyed a life.

"She needs to know," Yen Oanh said, finally. "I want to tell her—" It was a truth; what she could give Thich Tim Nghe in all honesty; in the hope that it would get her out of the ship's corpse; that it would atone for Yen Oanh's mistake, allow Thich Tim Nghe to build a life again.

"My teacher changes lives." Hue Mi sounded mildly amused. "She lays the past to rest. She gives hope. But the world? Don't grant her powers she doesn't have."

Yen Oanh didn't. She knew that, deep within Thich Tim Nghe, there was a frightened girl; a thirteen-year-old still carrying her own dead. "I want to help her."

Hue Mi sounds amused, again. "She doesn't need your help."

Even outside the Communion, Yen Oanh knew what Que Tu would say. *We don't get what we deserve, or even what we need.*

The door opened slowly, agonizingly slowly; revealing the heartroom—not much that Yen Oanh could see, amidst the swirling of deep spaces; the tight smell of ozone and incense mingled together; fragments of faces mottled with bruises; of eyes frozen in death; of children running and screaming, overlaid with the shadow of death. . . .

And, in the midst of it, Thich Tim Nghe, turning towards her, stately and slow; and then startled, as if she'd seen something in Yen Oanh's face: she wasn't the girl of Yen Oanh's nightmares; not the emaciated child from Que Tu's report; not the rake-thin ascetic from the vids Yen Oanh had gleaned online; but a grown woman with circles under her eyes like bruises—as if she still had Blue Lily.

And Yen Oanh realised, then, that she was wrong: this was a sickroom; and that this was still the time of Blue Lily; not only for Thich Tim Nghe, but also for her.

Hue Mi had been right: she carried her past, and she had come to lay it to rest—and it might work or fail abjectly, but she would have tried—which was more than she'd done, eleven years ago.

Within the Communion, Que Tu said nothing; merely smiled, the *ky lan* on her hairpins stretching as though they were live animals, heralding the age of peace and prosperity—the age of change.

—

Thich Tim Nghe moves out of the past, beyond the voice of the ship. Everything is silence as the door opens; Thich Tim Nghe tenses, ready to reach out to the supplicant—her own moment of peace and serenity, blossoming within her with the certainty of the plague.

"Teacher," the supplicant says. She moves forward, detaching herself from Vo and Hue Mi—and, though Thich Tim Nghe has never seen her in her life, she knows the woman's ghosts—because they're *her*.

"I—" she stops, then; stares at the supplicant, who hasn't moved. Around her, in the swirling storm of realities that have been, that might be, *The Stone and Bronze Shadow* falls sick and dies; a younger Thich Tim Nghe curls around the throne, clinging to *The Stone and Bronze Shadow's* Mind as though she could prevent her death—and there are other images too; a vid of Thich Tim Nghe putting on the robes of an ascetic, pale and composed; documents gleaned from the communal network of the First Planet; and an older woman in the robes of the Cedar and Crane, smiling sadly at her. "I—I don't understand what you want."

"I want you to come out." The supplicant's voice is low, and intense. "Please, child." There are other images around the woman; words about mindships and vaccines, and Blue Lily in deep spaces, and how none of it would have been possible without her—without the death of *The Stone and Bronze Shadow.*

This doesn't matter—this can't atone for anything. She killed a ship, unknowingly. She killed people, knowingly—she failed Mother, and the countless dead, and nothing she does will ever atone for this.

"Please. Just look."

It's what she does. It's what she's always done—she helps people; lays their dead to rest, shows them their future beyond the shadow of the past; the shadow of the plague.

But this time, the shadow is hers—the restless ghost is her.

"Please."

There is nothing around her but the silence of her dead; and the larger, expectant silence of the ship.

She should refuse. She should lock herself in the heartroom, plunge back into her visions—listening to nothing but the voice of the ship, the song of the dead.

She should. . . .

Slowly, carefully, Thich Tim Nghe reaches out, on the cusp of her past, in the belly of the dead ship—to see the shape of her future.

Seanan McGuire lives and works primarily in Northern California, although she can be found in random spots around the globe, pursuing the ideal of the perfect corn maze. Her debut novel was published in 2009; since then, she has finished and released more than twenty-five books, proving that she probably really needs a nap. She won the 2010 John W. Campbell Award for Best New Writer, and has been nominated several times for the Hugo Award.

When not writing, Seanan watches too many horror movies and spends time with her enormous blue Maine Coon cats. She reads almost constantly, and drinks far too much Diet Dr Pepper. Seanan regularly claims to be the vanguard of an invading race of alien plant people. As she gives little reason to doubt her, most people just go with it. Keep up with her at www.seananmcguire.com.

HELLO, HELLO

Seanan McGuire

Tasha's avatar smiled from the screen, a little too perfect to be true. That was a choice, just like everything else about it: when we'd installed my sister's new home system, we had instructed it to generate avatars that looked like they had escaped the uncanny valley by the skins of their teeth. It was creepy, but the alternative was even creepier. Tasha didn't talk. Her avatar did. Having them match each other perfectly would have been . . . wrong.

"So I'll see you next week?" she asked. Her voice was perfectly neutral, with a newscaster's smooth, practiced inflections. Angie had picked it from the database of publicly available voices; like the avatar, it had been generated in a lab. Unlike the avatar, it was flawless. No one who heard Tasha "talk" would realize that they were really hearing a collection of sounds programmed by a computer, translated from the silent motion of her hands.

That was the point. Setting up the system for her had removed all barriers to conversation, and when she was talking to clients who didn't know she was deaf, she didn't want them to realize anything was happening behind the scenes. Hence the avatar, rather than the slight delay that came with the face-time translation programs. It felt wrong to me, like we were trying to hide something essential about my sister, but it was her choice and her system; I was just the one who upgraded her software and made sure that nothing broke down. If anyone was equipped for the job, it was me, the professional computational linguist. It's a living.

"We'll be there right on time," I said, knowing that on her end, my avatar would be smiling and silent, moving her hands to form the appropriate words. I could speak ASL to the screen, but with the way her software was set up, speaking ASL while the translator settings were active could result in some vicious glitches. After the time the computer had decided my hand gestures were a form of complicated profanity, and translated the chugging of the air conditioner into words while spewing invective at my sister, I had learned to keep my hands still while the translator was on. "I'm bringing Angie and the kids, so be ready."

Tasha laughed. "I'll tell the birds to be on their best behavior." A light flashed behind her avatar and her expression changed, becoming faintly regretful. "Speaking of the birds, that's my cue. Talk tomorrow?"

"Talk tomorrow," I said. "Love you lots."

"I love you, too," she said and ended the call, leaving me staring at my own reflection on the suddenly black screen. My face, so much like her computer-generated one, but slightly rougher, slightly less perfect. Humanity will do that to a girl.

Finally, I stood and went to tell my wife we had plans for the next weekend. She liked my sister, and Greg and Billie liked the birds. It would be good for us.

"Hello," said the woman on the screen. She was black-haired and brown-eyed, with skin that fell somewhere between "tan" and "tawny." She was staring directly at the camera, almost unnervingly still. "Hello, hello."

"Hello!" said Billie happily, waving at the woman. Billie's nails were painted bright blue, like beetle shells. She'd been on an entomology kick again lately, studying every insect she found as raptly as if she had just discovered the secrets of the universe. "How are you?"

"Hello," said the woman. "Hello, hello, hello."

"Billie, who are you talking to?" I stopped on my way to the laundry room, bundling the basket I'd been carrying against my hip. The woman didn't look familiar, but she had the smooth, CGI skin of a translation avatar. There was no telling what her root language was. The natural user interface of the software would be trying to mine its neural networks for the places where she and Billie overlapped, looking for the points of commonality and generating a vocabulary that accounted for their hand gestures and body language, as well as for their vocalizations.

It was a highly advanced version of the old translation software that had been rolled out in the late 2010s; that had been verbal-only, and only capable of translating sign language into straight text, not into vocalizations that followed spoken sentence structures and could be played through speakers. ASL to speech had followed, and then speech to ASL, with increasingly realistic avatars learning to move their hands in the complex patterns necessary for communication. Now, the systems could be taught to become ad hoc translators, pulling on the full weight of their neural networks and deep learning capabilities as they built bridges across the world.

Of course, it also meant that we had moments like this one, two people shouting greetings across an undefined void of linguistic separation. "Billie?" I repeated.

"It's Aunt Tasha's system, Mom," said my nine-year-old, turning to look at me over her shoulder. She rolled her eyes, making sure I understood just how foolish my concern really was. "I wouldn't have *answered* if I didn't recognize the caller."

"But that's not Aunt Tasha," I said.

Billie gave me the sort of withering look that only people under eighteen can manage. She was going to be a terror in a few years. "I know that," she said. "I think she's visiting to see the birds. Lots of people visit to see the birds."

"True," I said, giving the woman on the screen another look. Tasha's system was set up to generate a generic avatar for anyone who wasn't a registered user. It would draw on elements of their appearance—hair color, eye color, skin tone—but it would otherwise assemble the face from public-source elements. "Hello," I said. "Is my sister there?"

"Hello," said the woman. "Hello, hello."

"I don't think the computer knows her language very well," said Billie. "That's all she's said."

Which could mean a glitch. Sometimes, when the software got confused enough, it would translate everything as "hello." An attempt at connection, even when the tools weren't there. "I think you may be right," I said, moving to get closer to the computer. Billie, recognizing the shift from protective mother to computer scientist with a mystery to solve, shifted obligingly to the side. She would never have tolerated being smothered, but she was more than smart enough not to sit between me and a puzzle.

"Is Tasha there?" I asked again, as clearly as I could.

The woman looked at me and said nothing.

"I need to know what language you're speaking. I'm sorry the translator program isn't working for you, but if I know what family to teach it, I can probably get it up and running in pretty short order." Everything I said probably sounded like "hello, hello" to her, but at least I was trying. That was the whole point, wasn't it? Trying. "Can you say the name of your language? I am speaking casual conversational English." No matter how confused the program was, it would say "English" clearly. Hopefully that would be enough to get us started.

"Hello, hello," said the woman. She looked to her right, eyes widening slightly, as if she'd been startled. Then she leaned out of the frame and was gone. The image of Tasha's dining room continued for several seconds before the computer turned itself off, leaving Billie and I to look, bemused, at an empty screen.

Finally, hesitantly, Billie asked, "Was that one of Aunt Tasha's friends?"

"I don't know," I said. "I'll call her later and ask."

I forgot to call.

In my defense, there were other things to do, and none of them were the sort that could easily be put off until tomorrow. Greg, our two-year-old, discovered a secret snail breeding ground in the garden and transported them all inside, sticking them to the fridge like slime-generating magnets. Greg thought this was wonderful. The snails didn't seem to have an opinion. Angie thought this was her cue to disinfect the entire house, starting with the kitchen, and left me to watch both kids while I was trying to finish a project for work. It was really no wonder I lost track of them. It was more of a wonder that it took me over an hour to realize they were gone.

Angie wasn't shouting, so the kids hadn't wandered back into the kitchen to get in the way of her frenzied housework. I stood, moving carefully as I began my search. As any parent can tell you, it's better to keep your mouth shut and your eyes open when you go looking for kids who are being unreasonably quiet. They're probably doing something they don't want you to see, and if they hear you coming, they'll hide the evidence.

I heard them laughing before I reached the living room. I stopped making such an effort to mask my footsteps, and came around the corner of the doorway to find them with their eyes glued to the computer, laughing at the black-haired woman from before.

"Hello, hello," she was saying. "I'm hungry, hello, can you hear me?"

Greg laughed. Billie leaned forward and said, "We can hear you. Hello, hello, we can hear you!" This set Greg laughing harder.

The woman on the screen looked from one child to the other, opened her mouth, and said, "Ha-ha. Ha-ha. Ha-ha. Hello, hello, can you hear me?"

"What's this?" I asked.

Billie turned and beamed at me. "Auntie Tasha's friend is back, and the program is learning more of her language! I'm doing like you told me to do if I ever need to talk to somebody the neural net doesn't know, and using lots of repeating to try and teach it more."

"The word you want is 'echolalia,'" I said distractedly, leaning past her to focus on the screen. "You're back. Hello. Is my sister there?"

"Hello, hello," said the woman. "Can you hear me? I'm hungry."

"Yes, I got that," I said, trying to keep the frustration out of my voice. It wasn't her fault that her language—whatever it was—was causing issues with the translation software. Tasha's neural net hadn't encountered as many spoken languages as ours had. It could manage some startlingly accurate gesture translations, some of which we had incorporated into the base software after they cropped up, but it couldn't always pick up on spoken languages with the speed of a neural net belonging to a hearing person. Tasha also had a tendency to invite visiting academics and wildlife conservationists to stay in her spare room, since they were presumably used to the screeching of wild birds.

"If not for them," she had said more than once, "you're the only company I'd ever have."

It was hard to argue with that. It was just a little frustrating that one of her guests kept calling my kids. "Can you please tell Tasha to call me? I want to speak with her."

"Hello, hello," said the woman.

"Good-bye," I replied and canceled the call.

Both children looked at me like I had done something terribly wrong. "She just wanted someone to talk to," said Billie mulishly.

"Let me know if she calls again, all right? I don't know who she is, and I'm not comfortable with you talking to her until I've spoken to Tasha."

"Okay, Mom," said Billie.

Greg frowned but didn't say anything. I leaned down and scooped him onto my shoulder. That got a squeal, followed by a trail of giggles. I straightened.

"Come on, you two. Let's go see if we can't help Mumma in the kitchen."

They went willingly enough. I cast a glance back at the dark computer screen. This time, I would definitely remember to call my sister.

As always, reaching Tasha was easier said than done. She spent much of her time outside feeding and caring for her birds, and when she was in the house, she was almost always doing some task related to her work. There were flashing lights in every room to tell her when she had a call, but just like everyone else in the world, sometimes she ignored her phone in favor of doing something more interesting. I could have set my call as an emergency and turned all the lights red, but that seemed like a mean trick, since "I wanted to ask about one of your houseguests" wasn't really an emergency. Just a puzzle. There was always a puzzle; had been since we were kids, when her reliance on ASL had provided us with a perfect "secret language" and provided me with a bilingual upbringing—something that had proven invaluable as I grew up and went into neurolinguistic computing.

When we were kids signing at each other, fingers moving almost faster than the human eye could follow, our hands had looked like birds in flight. I had followed the words. My sister had followed the birds. They needed her, and they never judged her for her differences. What humans saw as disability, Tasha's birds saw as a human who was finally quiet enough not to be startling, one who wouldn't complain when they started singing outside her window at three in the morning. It was the perfect marriage of flesh and function.

After two days of trying and failing to get her to pick up, I sent an email. *Just checking in*, it said. *Haven't been able to rouse you. Do you have houseguests right now? Someone's been calling the house from your terminal.*

Her reply came fast enough to tell me that she had already been at her computer. *A few grad students came to look @ my king vulture. He is very impressive. One of them could have misdialed? It's not like I would have heard them. ;) We still on for Sunday?*

I sent a call request. Her avatar popped up thirty seconds later, filling the screen with her faintly dubious expression.

"Yes?" she said. "Email works, you know."

"Email is too slow. I like to see your face."

She rolled her eyes. "It's all the same to me," she said. "I know you're not really signing. I prefer talking to you when I can see your hands."

"I'm sorry," I said. "Greg's ASL is progressing really well. We should be able to go back to real-time chat in a year or so. Until then, we need to keep the vocals on, so he can get to know you, too. Look how well it worked out with Billie."

Tasha's expression softened. She'd been dubious when I'd explained that we'd be teaching Billie ASL but using the voice translation mode on our chat software; we wanted Billie to care about getting to know her aunt, and with a really small child, it had seemed like the best way. It had worked out well. Billie was fluent enough in ASL to carry on conversations with strangers, and she was already writing letters to our local high schools, asking them to offer sign language as an elective. Greg was following in her footsteps. I really was pretty sure we'd be able to turn off the voice translation in another year or so.

To be honest, I was going to be relieved when that happened. I was lazy enough to appreciate the ease of talking to my sister without needing to take my hands off the keyboard, but it was strange to *hear* her words, rather than watching them.

"I guess," she said. "So what was up with the grad students? One of them called the house?"

"I think so," I said. "She seemed a little confused. Just kept saying 'hello' over and over again. Were any of them visiting from out-of-country schools? Someplace far enough away that the neural net wouldn't have a solid translation database to access?" Our systems weren't creating translation databases out of nothing, of course—that would have been programming well above my pay grade, and possibly a Nobel Prize for Humanities—but they would find the common phonemes and use them to direct themselves to which shared databases they should be accessing. Where the complicated work happened was in the contextual cues. The hand gestures that punctuated speech with "I don't know" and "yes" and "I love you." The sideways glances that meant "I am uncomfortable with this topic." Bit by bit, our translators put those into words, and understanding grew.

(And there were people who used their translators like Tasha did, who hid silent tongues or a reluctance to make eye contact behind computer-generated faces and calm, measured voices, who presented a completely default face to the world and took great comfort in knowing that the people who would judge them for their differences would never need to know. I couldn't fault them for that. I was the one who asked my sister to let me give her a voice, like grafting a tongue onto Hans Christian Anderson's Little Mermaid, for the duration of my children's short infancy.)

"I don't know," she said, after a long pause. "Only two of them spoke ASL. The other three spoke through their professor, and I've known her for years. Why? Did she say something inappropriate to the kids?"

"No, just 'hello,' like I said. Still, it was strange, and she called back at least once. Black hair, medium brown skin. I didn't get a name."

"If I see someone like that, I'll talk to her about privacy and what is and is not appropriate when visiting someone else's home."

"Thanks." I shook my head. "I just don't like strangers talking to the kids."

"Me, neither."

We chatted for a while after that—just ordinary, sisterly things, how the kids were doing, how the birds were doing, what we were going to have for dinner on Sunday—and I felt much better when I hung up and went to bed.

When I woke up the next morning, Greg and Billie were already in the dining room, whispering to the computer. By the time I moved into position to see the monitor, it was blank, and neither of them would tell me who they'd been talking to—assuming they had been talking to anyone at all.

We arrived at Tasha's a little after noon. As was our agreement, we didn't knock; I just pressed my thumb to the keypad and unlocked the door, allowing our already-wiggling children to spill past us into the bright, plant-strewn atrium. Every penny Tasha got was poured back into either the house or the birds—and since the birds had the run of the house, every penny she put into the house was still going to the birds. Cages of rescued finches, budgies, and canaries twittered at us as we entered, giving greeting and expressing interest in a series of short, sharp chirps. Hanging plants and bright potted irises surrounded the cages, making it feel like we had just walked into the front hall of some exclusive conservatory.

That, right there, was why Tasha spent so much money on the upkeep and decor of her home. It was a licensed rescue property, but keeping it looking like something special—which it was—kept her neighbors from complaining.

Opening the door had triggered the flashing warning lights in the corners of the room. Tasha would be looking for us, and so we went looking for her, following the twitter of birds and the shrieking laughter of our children.

Our parties collided in the kitchen, where Billie was signing rapid-fire at her aunt while Greg tugged at her arm and offered interjections, his own amateurish signs breaking into the conversation only occasionally. A barn owl was perched atop the refrigerator. That was par for the course at Tasha's place, where sometimes an absence of birds was the strange thing. The door leading out to the screened-in patio was open, and a large pied crow sat on the back of the one visible chair, watching us warily. Most of that wariness was probably reserved for the owl. They would fight, if given the opportunity, and Tasha didn't like breaking up squabbles between birds she was rehabilitating. Birds that insisted on pecking at each other were likely to find themselves caged. The smarter birds—the corvids and the big parrots—learned to play nicely, lest they be locked away.

I waved. Tasha glanced over, beamed, and signed a quick 'hello' before she went back to conversing with my daughter. The world had narrowed for the two of them, becoming nothing more than the space of their hands and the words they drew on the air, transitory and perfect.

The computer was on the table, open as always. I passed the day bag to Angie, pressing a quick kiss to her cheek before I said, "I'm going to go check on the neural net. Let me know if you need me."

"Yes, leave me alone with your sister in the House of Birds," she said, dead-pan. I laughed and walked away.

Part of the arrangement I had with Tasha involved free access to her computer. She got the latest translation software and endless free upgrades to her home neural net; I went rooting through the code whenever I was in the house. She didn't worry about me seeing her browser history or stumbling across an open email client; we'd been sharing our password-locked blogs since we were kids. What was the point of having a sister if you couldn't trade bad boy-band RPF once in a while?

Flipping through her call history brought up the usual assortment of calls to schools, pet supply warehouses, and local takeout establishments, all tagged under her user name. There were seven guest calls over the past week. Three of them were to the university, and pulling up their profiles showed that the people who had initiated the calls had loaded custom avatars, dressing their words in their own curated faces. The other four. . . .

The other four were anonymous, and the avatar had been generated by the system, but not retained. All four had been made from this computer to the first number in its saved database. Mine.

I scribbled down the time stamps and went to join the conversation in the kitchen, waving a hand for Tasha's attention. She turned, expression questioning. I handed her the piece of paper and signed, "Did you have the same person in the house for all four of these calls?"

Tasha frowned. "No," she signed back. "I had some conservationists for this one, picking up an owl who'd been cleared for release," she tapped the middle entry on the list, "but all those other times, I was alone with the birds. What's going on?"

"Could it be a system glitch?" asked Angie, speaking and signing at the same time. She preferred it that way, since it gave her an excuse to go slowly. She said it was about including Greg in the conversation, and we let her have that; if it kept her from becoming too self-conscious to sign, it was a good thing.

"It could," I signed. Silence was an easy habit to fall back into in the company of my sister. "I'd have to take the whole system apart to be sure. Tasha, are you all right with my cloning it and unsnarling things once I get home?"

"As long as this glitch isn't going to break anything, I don't care," she signed.

I nodded. "It should be fine," I signed. "If it's a system error, that would explain why our caller keeps saying 'hello' and never getting any further. I'll be able to let you know in a couple of days."

Billie tugged on Tasha's sleeve. We all turned. Billie beamed. "Can we see the parrots now?" she signed. Tasha laughed, and for a while, everything was normal. Everything was the way it was supposed to be.

My snapshot of Tasha's system revealed no errors with the code, although I found some interesting logical chains in her translation software's neural network that I copied over and sent to R&D for further analysis. She had one of the most advanced learning systems outside of corporate, in part because she was my sister, and in part because she was a bilingual deaf person, speaking both American and British Sign Language with the people she communicated with. Giving her a system that could handle the additional nonverbal processing was allowing us to build out a better neural chain and translation database than any amount of laboratory testing could produce, with the added bonus of equipping my sister to speak with conservationists all over the world. It's always nice when corporate and family needs align.

The calls were being intentionally initiated by someone who had access to Tasha's computer. There was no way this was a ghost in the machine or a connection routing error. Malware was still a possibility, given the generic avatar; someone could be spoofing the machine into opening the call, then overlaying the woman onto the backdrop of Tasha's dining room. I didn't know what purpose that would serve, unless this was the warm-up to some innovative denial-of-service attack. I kept digging.

"Hello? Hello?"

My head snapped up. The voice was coming from the main computer in the dining room. It was somehow less of a surprise when Billie answered a moment later: "Hello! How are you?"

"Hello, hello, I'm fine. I'm good. I'm hungry. How are you?"

I rose from my seat, using the table to steady myself before walking, carefully, quietly, toward the next room. There was Billie, seated in front of the terminal, where the strange woman's image was once again projected. Greg was nowhere to be seen. He was probably off somewhere busying himself with toddler projects, like stacking blocks or talking to spiders, leaving his sister to unwittingly assist in industrial espionage.

"Billie?"

Billie turned, all smiles, as the woman on the screen shifted her focus to me, cocking her head slightly to the side to give herself a better view. "Hi,

Mom!" my daughter chirped, her fingers moving in the appropriate signs at the same time. "I figured it out!"

"Figured what out, sweetie?"

"Why we couldn't understand each other!" She gestured grandly to the screen where the black-haired woman waited. "Mumma showed me."

I frowned, taking a step closer. "Showed you what?"

"Hello, hello—can you hear me? Hello," said the woman.

"Hello," I said, automatically.

Billie was undaunted. "When we went to see Aunt Tasha, Mumma used her speaking words and her finger words at the same time, so Greg could know what we were saying. She was bridging." Her fingers moved in time with her lips. ASL doesn't have the same grammatical structure as spoken English; my daughter was running two linguistic processing paths at the same time. I wanted to take the time to be proud of her for that. I was too busy trying to understand.

"You mean she was building a linguistic bridge?" I asked.

Billie nodded vigorously. "Yeah. Bridging. So I thought maybe we couldn't understand each other because the neural net didn't have enough to work with, and I turned off the avatar setting on this side."

My heart clenched. The avatar projections for Billie and Greg were intended to keep their real faces hidden from anyone who wasn't family. It was a small precaution, but anything that would keep their images off the public Internet until they turned eighteen was a good idea as far as I was concerned. "Billie, we've talked about the avatars. They're there to keep you safe."

"But she needed to see my hands," said Billie, with serene childhood logic. "Once she could, we started communicating better. See? I just needed to give the translator more data!"

"Hello," said the woman.

"Hello," I said, moving closer to the screen. After a beat, I followed the word with the appropriate sign. "What's your name? Why do you keep calling my house?"

"I'm hungry," said the woman. "I'm hungry."

"You're not answering my question."

The woman opened her mouth like she was laughing, but no sound came out. She closed it again with a snap and said, "I'm hungry. I don't know you. Where is the other one?"

"Here I am!" said Billie, pushing her way back to the front. "Sorry about Mom. She doesn't understand that we're doing science here."

"Science, yes," said the woman obligingly. "Hello, hello. I'm hungry."

"I get hungry, too," said Billie. "Maybe some cereal?"

I took a step back, letting the two of them talk. I didn't like the idea of leaving my little girl with a live connection to God-knows-who. I also didn't like the thought that this call was coming from my sister's house. If she was out back with the birds, she would never hear an intruder, and I couldn't call to warn her while her line was in use.

Angie was in the kitchen. "Billie's on the line with our mystery woman," I said quickly, before she could ask me what was wrong. "I'm going to drive to Tasha's and see if I can't catch this lady in the act."

Angie's eyes widened. "So you just *left* Billie on the line?"

"You can supervise her," I said. "Just try to keep her from disconnecting. I can make this stop, but I need to go."

"Then go," said Angie. I'd be hearing about this later. I knew that, just like I knew I was making the right call. Taking Billie away from the computer wouldn't stop this woman from breaking into my sister's house and calling us, and one police report could see Tasha branded a security risk by the company, which couldn't afford to leave software patches that were still under NDA in insecure locations.

Tasha lived fifteen minutes from us under normal circumstances. I made the drive in seven.

Her front door was locked, but the porch light was on, signaling that she was home and awake. I let myself in without ringing the bell. She could yell at me later. Finding out what was going on was more important than respecting her privacy, at least for right now. I felt a little bad about that. I also knew that she would have done exactly the same thing if our positions had been reversed.

I slunk through the house, listening for the sound of Billie's voice. Tasha kept the speakers on for the sake of the people who visited her and used her computer to make calls. She was better at accommodation than I was. The thought made my ears redden. My sister, who had spent most of her life fighting to be accommodated, made the effort for others when I was willing to focus on just her. I would be better, I promised silently. For her sake, and for the sake of my children, I would be better.

I didn't hear Billie. Instead, I heard the throaty croaking of a crow from somewhere up ahead. It continued as I walked down the hall and stepped into the kitchen doorway. And stopped.

The pied crow that Tasha had been rehabilitating was perched on the back of the chair across from the computer, talons digging deep into the wood as it cocked its head and watched Billie's image on the screen. Billie's mouth moved; a squawk emerged. The crow croaked back, repeating the same sounds over and over, until the avatar was matching them perfectly. Only then did it move on to the next set of sounds.

I took a step back and sagged against the hallway wall, heart pounding, head spinning with the undeniable reality of what I had just seen. A language the neural net didn't know, one that depended on motion and gesture as much as it did on sound. A language the system would have been exposed to enough before a curious bird started pecking at the keys that the program could at least *try* to make sense of it.

Sense enough to say "hello."

An air of anticipation hung over the lab. The pied crow—whose name, according to Tasha, was Pitch, and who had been raised in captivity, bouncing from wildlife center to wildlife center before winding up living in my sister's private aviary—gripped her perch stubbornly with her talons and averted her eyes from the screen, refusing to react to the avatar that was trying to catch her attention. She'd been ignoring the screen for over an hour, shutting out four researchers and a bored linguist who was convinced that I was in the middle of some sort of creative breakdown.

"All right, Paulson, this was a funny prank, but you've used up over a dozen computing hours," said Mike, pushing away from his own monitor. He was one of the researchers, and had been remarkably tolerant so far. "Time to pack it in."

"Wait a second," I said. "Just . . . just wait, all right? There's one thing we haven't tried yet."

Mike looked at me and frowned. I looked pleadingly back. Finally, he sighed.

"Admittedly, you've encouraged the neural net to make some great improvements. You can have one more try. But that's it! After that, we need this lab back."

"One more is all I need."

I'd been hoping to avoid this. It would've been easier if I could have replicated the original results without resorting to re-creation of all factors. Not easier for the bird: easier for my nerves. Angie was already mad at me, and Tasha was unsettled, and I was feeling about as off-balance as I ever did.

Opening the door and sticking my head out into the hall, I looked to my left, where my wife and children were settled in ergonomic desk chairs. Angie was focused on her tablet, composing an email to her work with quick swipes of her fingers, like she was trying to wipe them clean of some unseen, clinging film. Billie was sitting next to her, attention fixed on a handheld game device. Greg sat on the floor between them. He had several of his toy trains and was rolling them around an imaginary track, making happy humming noises.

He was the first one to notice me. He looked up and beamed, calling, "Mama!"

"Hi, buddy," I said. Angie and Billie were looking up as well. I offered my wife a sheepish smile. "Hi, hon. We're almost done in here. I just need to borrow Billie for a few minutes, if that's okay?"

It wasn't okay: I could see that in her eyes. We were going to fight about this later, and I was going to lose. Billie, however, bounced right to her feet, grinning from ear to ear as she dropped her game on the chair where she'd been sitting. "Do I get to work science with you?"

"I want science!" Greg protested, his own smile collapsing into the black hole of toddler unhappiness.

"Oh, no, bud." I crouched down, putting myself on as much of a level with him as I could. "We'll do some science when we get home, okay? Water science. With the hose. I just need Billie right now, and I need you to stay here with Mumma and keep her company. She'll get lonely if you both come with me."

Greg gave me a dubious look before twisting to look suspiciously up at Angie. She nodded quickly.

"She's right," she said. "I would be so lonely out here all by myself. Please stay and keep me company."

"Okay," said Greg, after weighing his options. He reached contentedly for his train. "Water science later."

Aware that I had just committed myself to being squirted with the hose in our backyard for at least an hour, I took Billie's hand and ushered her quickly away before anything else could go wrong.

The terminal she'd be using to make her call was waiting for us when we walked back into the room. I ushered her over to the chair, ignoring the puzzled looks from my colleagues. "Remember the lady who kept calling the house?" I asked. "Would you like to talk to her again?"

"I thought I wasn't supposed to talk to strangers," said Billie, eyeing me warily as she waited for the catch. She was old enough to know that when a parent offered to break the rules, there was always a catch.

"I'm right here this time," I said. "That means she's not a stranger, she's . . . a social experiment."

Billie nodded, still dubious. "If it's really okay. . . ."

"It's really, truly okay." Marrying a physicist meant that my kids had always been destined to grow up steeped in science. It was an inescapable part of our lives. I hadn't been expecting them to necessarily be so fond of it, but that worked out, too. I was happier raising a bevy of little scientists than I would have been with the alternative.

Billie nodded once more and turned to face the monitor. I flashed a low "okay" sign at Mike and the screen sprang to life, showing the blandly pretty CGI avatar that Tasha's system generated for Pitch. We'd have to look into the code to see when it had made the decision to start rendering animals with human faces, and whether that was part of a patch that had been widely distributed. I could see the logic behind it—the generic avatar generator was given instructions based on things like "eyes" and "attempting to use the system," rather than the broader and more complex-to-program "human." I could also see lawsuits when people inevitably began running images of their pets through the generator and using them to catfish their friends.

On the other side of the two-way mirror, Pitch perked up at the sight of Billie's face on her screen. She opened her beak. Microphones inside the room would pick up the sounds she made, but I didn't need to hear her to know that she was croaking and trilling, just like corvids always did. What was interesting was the way she was also fluffing out her feathers and moving the tip of her left wing downward.

"Hello, hello," said her avatar to Billie. "Hello, hello, can you hear me? Hello."

"Hello," said Billie. "My mom says I can talk to you again. Hello."

"I'm hungry. Where am I? Hello."

"I'm at Mom's work. She does science here. I don't know where you are. Mom probably knows. She called you." Billie twisted to look at me. "Mom? Where is she?"

I pointed to the two-way mirror. "She's right through there."

Billie followed the angle of my finger to Pitch, who was scratching the side of her head with one talon. Her face fell for a moment, expression turning betrayed, before realization wiped away her confusion and her eyes went wide. She turned back to the screen.

"Are you a bird?" she asked.

The woman looked confused. "Hello, hello, I'm hungry, where am I?"

"A *bird*," said Billie, and flapped her arms like wings.

The effect on Pitch was immediate. She sat up straighter on her perch and flapped her wings, not hard enough to take off, but hard enough to mimic the gesture.

"A bird!" announced the avatar. "A bird a bird a bird yes a bird. Are you a bird? Hello? A bird? Hello, can you hear me, hello?"

"Holy shit," whispered Mike. "She's really talking to the bird. The translation algorithm really figured out how to let her talk to the bird. And the bird is really talking back. Holy *shit*."

"Not in front of my child, please," I said, tone prim and strangled. The xenolinguists were going to be all over this. We'd have people clawing at the gates to try to get a place on the team once this came out. The science behind it was clean and easy to follow—we had built a deep neural net capable of learning, told it that gestures were language and that the human mouth was capable of making millions of distinct sounds, taught it to recognize grammar and incorporate both audio and visual signals into same, and then we had turned it loose, putting it out into the world, with no instructions but to learn.

"We need to put, like, a thousand animals in front of this thing and see how many of them can actually get it to work." Mike grabbed my arm. "Do you know what this means? This changes everything."

Conservationists would kill to get their subjects in front of a monitor and try to open communication channels. Gorillas would be easy—we already had ASL in common—and elephants, dolphins, parrots, none of them could be very far behind. We had opened the gates to a whole new world, and all because I wanted to talk to my sister.

But all that was in the future, stretching out ahead of us in a wide and tangled ribbon tied to the tail of tomorrow. Right here and right now was my daughter, laughing as she spoke to her new friend, the two of them feeling their way, one word at a time, into a common language, and hence into a greater understanding of the world.

Tasha would be so delighted.

In the moment, so was I.

Hao Jingfang is the author of two novels, *Wandering Maearth* and *Return to Charon*; a book of cultural essays, *Europe in Time*; and the short story collection, *Star Travellers*. Her stories have been published in a variety of Chinese- and English-language publications including *Science Fiction World*, *Mengya*, *New Science Fiction*, *New Realms of Fantasy and Science Fiction*, *Lightspeed*, *Uncanny*, and *Clarkesworld*. Jingfang's stories have been nominated for the Galaxy Award and the Chinese Xingyun (Nebula) Awards.

FOLDING BEIJING

Hao Jingfang
translated by Ken Liu

1.

At ten of five in the morning, Lao Dao crossed the busy pedestrian lane on his way to find Peng Li.

After the end of his shift at the waste processing station, Lao Dao had gone home, first to shower and then to change. He was wearing a white shirt and a pair of brown pants—the only decent clothes he owned. The shirt's cuffs were frayed, so he rolled them up to his elbows. Lao Dao was forty-eight, single, and long past the age when he still took care of his appearance. As he had no one to pester him about the domestic details, he had simply kept this outfit for years. Every time he wore it, he'd come home afterward, take off the shirt and pants, and fold them up neatly to put away. Working at the waste processing station meant there were few occasions that called for the outfit, save a wedding now and then for a friend's son or daughter.

Today, however, he was apprehensive about meeting strangers without looking at least somewhat respectable. After five hours at the waste processing station, he also had misgivings about how he smelled.

People who had just gotten off work filled the road. Men and women crowded every street vendor, picking through local produce and bargaining loudly. Customers packed the plastic tables at the food hawker stalls, which were immersed in the aroma of frying oil. They ate heartily with their faces buried in bowls of hot and sour rice noodles, their heads hidden by clouds of white steam. Other stands featured mountains of jujubes and walnuts, and hunks of cured meat swung overhead. This was the busiest hour of the day— work was over, and everyone was hungry and loud.

Lao Dao squeezed through the crowd slowly. A waiter carrying dishes shouted and pushed his way through the throng. Lao Dao followed close behind.

Peng Li lived some ways down the lane. Lao Dao climbed the stairs but Peng wasn't home. A neighbor said that Peng usually didn't return until right before market closing time, but she didn't know exactly when.

Lao Dao became anxious. He glanced down at his watch: almost 5:00 AM.

He went back downstairs to wait at the entrance of the apartment building. A group of hungry teenagers squatted around him, devouring their food. He recognized two of them because he remembered meeting them a couple of times at Peng Li's home. Each kid had a plate of chow mein or chow fun, and they shared two dishes family-style. The dishes were a mess while pairs of chopsticks continued to search for elusive, overlooked bits of meat amongst the chopped peppers. Lao Dao sniffed his forearms again to be sure that the stench of garbage was off of him. The noisy, quotidian chaos around him assured him with its familiarity.

"Listen, do you know how much they charge for an order of twice-cooked pork over there?" a boy named Li asked.

"Fuck! I just bit into some sand," a heavyset kid named Ding said while covering his mouth with one hand, which had very dirty fingernails. "We need to get our money back from the vendor!"

Li ignored him. "Three hundred and forty yuan!" said Li. "You hear that? Three forty! For twice-cooked pork! And for boiled beef? Four hundred and twenty!"

"How could the prices be so expensive?" Ding mumbled as he clutched his cheek. "What do they put in there?"

The other two youths weren't interested in the conversation and concentrated on shoveling food from the plate into the mouth. Li watched them, and his yearning gaze seemed to go through them and focus on something beyond.

Lao Dao's stomach growled. He quickly averted his eyes, but it was too late. His empty stomach felt like an abyss that made his body tremble. It had been a month since he last had a morning meal. He used to spend about a hundred each day on this meal, which translated to three thousand for the month. If he could stick to his plan for a whole year, he'd be able to save enough to afford two months of tuition for Tangtang's kindergarten.

He looked into the distance: the trucks of the city cleaning crew were approaching slowly.

He began to steel himself. If Peng Li didn't return in time, he would have to go on this journey without consulting him. Although it would make the trip far more difficult and dangerous, time was of the essence and he had to go. The loud chants of the woman next to him hawking her jujube interrupted his thoughts and gave him a headache. The peddlers at the other end of the road began to pack up their wares, and the crowd, like fish in a pond disturbed by a stick, dispersed. No one was interested in fighting the city cleaning crew. As the vendors got out of the way, the cleaning trucks patiently advanced. Vehicles were normally not allowed in the pedestrian lane, but the cleaning trucks were an exception. Anybody who dillydallied would be packed up by force.

Finally, Peng Li appeared: his shirt unbuttoned, a toothpick dangling between his lips, strolling leisurely and burping from time to time. Now in his sixties, Peng had become lazy and slovenly. His cheeks drooped like the jowls of a Shar-Pei, giving him the appearance of being perpetually grumpy. Looking at him now, one might get the impression that he was a loser whose only ambition in life was a full belly. However, even as a child, Lao Dao had heard his father recounting Peng Li's exploits when he had been a young man.

Lao Dao went up to meet Peng in the street. Before Peng Li could greet him, Lao Dao blurted out, "I don't have time to explain, but I need to get to First Space. Can you tell me how?"

Peng Li was stunned. It had been ten years since anyone brought up First Space with him. He held the remnant of the toothpick in his fingers—it had broken between his teeth without his being aware of it. For some seconds, he said nothing, but then he saw the anxiety on Lao Dao's face and dragged him toward the apartment building. "Come into my place and let's talk. You have to start from there anyway to get to where you want to go."

The city cleaning crew was almost upon them, and the crowd scattered like autumn leaves in a wind. "Go home! Go home! The Change is about to start," someone called from atop one of the trucks.

Peng Li took Lao Dao upstairs into his apartment. His ordinary, single-occupancy public housing unit was sparsely furnished: six square meters in area, a washroom, a cooking corner, a table and a chair, a cocoon-bed equipped with storage drawers underneath for clothes and miscellaneous items. The walls were covered with water stains and footprints, bare save for a few haphazardly installed hooks for jackets, pants, and linens. Once he entered, Peng took all the clothes and towels off the wall-hooks and stuffed them into one of the drawers. During the Change, nothing was supposed to be unsecured. Lao Dao had once lived in a single-occupancy unit just like this one. As soon as he entered, he felt the flavor of the past hanging in the air.

Peng Li glared at Lao Dao. "I'm not going to show you the way unless you tell me why."

It was already five thirty. Lao Dao had only half an hour left.

Lao Dao gave him the bare outlines of the story: picking up the bottle with a message inside; hiding in the trash chute; being entrusted with the errand in Second Space; making his decision and coming here for guidance. He had so little time that he had to leave right away.

"You hid in the trash chutes last night to sneak into Second Space?" Peng Li frowned. "That means you had to wait twenty-four hours!"

"For two hundred thousand yuan?" Lao Dao said, "Even hiding for a week would be worth it."

"I didn't know you were so short on money."

Lao Dao was silent for a moment. "Tangtang is going to be old enough for kindergarten in a year. I've run out of time."

Lao Dao's research on kindergarten tuition had shocked him. For schools with decent reputations, the parents had to show up with their bedrolls and line up a couple of days before registration. The two parents had to take turns so that while one held their place in the line, the other could go to the bathroom or grab a bite to eat. Even after lining up for forty-plus hours, a place wasn't guaranteed. Those with enough money had already bought up most of the openings for their offspring, so the poorer parents had to endure the line, hoping to grab one of the few remaining spots. Mind you, this was just for decent schools. The really good schools? Forget about lining up—every opportunity was sold off to those with money. Lao Dao didn't harbor unrealistic hopes, but Tangtang had loved music since she was an eighteen-month-old. Every time she heard music in the streets, her face lit up and she twisted her little body and waved her arms about in a dance. She looked especially cute during those moments. Lao Dao was dazzled as though surrounded by stage lights. No matter how much it cost, he vowed to send Tangtang to a kindergarten that offered music and dance lessons.

Peng Li took off his shirt and washed while he spoke with Lao Dao. The "washing" consisted only of splashing some drops of water over his face because the water was already shut off and only a thin trickle came out of the faucet. Peng Li took down a dirty towel from the wall and wiped his face carelessly before stuffing the towel into a drawer as well. His moist hair gave off an oily glint.

"What are you working so hard for?" Peng Li asked. "It's not like she's your real daughter."

"I don't have time for this," Lao Dao said. "Just tell me the way."

Peng Li sighed. "Do you understand that if you're caught, it's not just a matter of paying a fine? You're going to be locked up for months."

"I thought you had gone there multiple times."

"Just four times. I got caught the fifth time."

"That's more than enough. If I could make it four times, it would be no big deal to get caught once."

Lao Dao's errand required him to deliver a message to First Space—success would earn him a hundred thousand yuan, and if he managed to bring back a reply, two hundred thousand. Sure, it was illegal, but no one would be harmed, and as long as he followed the right route and method, the probability of being caught wasn't great. And the cash, the cash was very real. He could think of no reason to not take up the offer. He knew that when Peng Li was younger, he had snuck into First Space multiple times to smuggle contraband and made quite a fortune. There was a way.

It was a quarter to six. He had to get going, now.

Peng Li sighed again. He could see it was useless to try to dissuade Lao Dao. He was old enough to feel lazy and tired of everything, but he remembered how he had felt as a younger man and he would have made the same choice as Lao Dao. Back then, he didn't care about going to prison. What was the big deal? You lost a few months and got beaten up a few times, but the money made it worthwhile. As long as you refused to divulge the source of the money no matter how much you suffered, you could survive it. The Security Bureau's citation was nothing more than routine enforcement.

Peng Li took Lao Dao to his back window and pointed at the narrow path hidden in the shadows below.

"Start by climbing down the drain pipe from my unit. Under the felt cloth you'll find hidden footholds I installed back in the day—if you stick close enough to the wall, the cameras won't see you. Once you're on the ground, stick to the shadows and head that way until you get to the edge. You'll feel as well as see the cleft. Follow the cleft and go north. Remember, go north."

Then Peng Li explained the technique for entering First Space as the ground turned during the Change. He had to wait until the ground began to cleave and rise. Then, from the elevated edge, he had to swing over and scramble about fifty meters over the cross section until he reached the other side of the turning earth, climb over, and head east. There, he would find a bush that he could hold onto as the ground descended and closed up. He could then conceal himself in the bush. Before Peng had even finished his explanation, Lao Dao was already halfway out the window, getting ready to climb down.

Peng Li held onto Lao Dao and made sure his foot was securely in the first foothold. Then he stopped. "I'm going to say something that you might not want to hear. I don't think you should go. Over there . . . is not so great. If you go, you'll end up feeling your own life is shit, pointless."

Lao Dao was reaching down with his other foot, testing for the next foothold. His body strained against the windowsill and his words came out labored. "It doesn't matter. I already know my life is shit without having gone there."

"Take care of yourself," Peng Li said.

Lao Dao followed Peng Li's directions and groped his way down as quickly as he dared; the footholds felt very secure. He looked up and saw Peng Li light up a cigarette next to the window, taking deep drags. Peng Li put out the cigarette, leaned out, and seemed about to say something more, but ultimately he retreated back into his unit quietly. He closed his window, which glowed with a faint light.

Lao Dao imagined Peng Li crawling into his cocoon-bed at the last minute, right before the Change. Like millions of others across the city, the cocoon-bed would release a soporific gas that put him into deep sleep. He would feel nothing as his body was transported by the flipping world, and he would not open his eyes again until tomorrow evening, forty-hours later. Peng Li was no longer young; he was no longer different from the other fifty million who lived in Third Space.

Lao Dao climbed faster, barely touching the footholds. When he was close enough to the ground, he let go and landed on all fours. Luckily, Peng Li's unit was only on the fourth story, not too far up. He got up and ran through the shadow cast by the building next to the lake. He saw the crevice in the grass where the ground would open up.

But before he reached it, he heard the muffled rumbling from behind him, interrupted by a few crisp clangs. Lao Dao turned around and saw Peng Li's building break in half. The top half folded down and pressed toward him, slowly but inexorably.

Shocked, Lao Dao stared at the sight for a few moments before recovering. He raced to the fissure in the ground, and lay prostrate next to it.

The Change began. This was a process repeated every twenty-four hours. The whole world started to turn. The sound of steel and masonry folding, grating, colliding filled the air, like an assembly line grinding to a halt. The towering buildings of the city gathered and merged into solid blocks; neon signs, shop awnings, balconies, and other protruding fixtures retracted into the buildings or flattened themselves into a thin layer against the walls, like skin. Every inch of space was utilized as the buildings compacted themselves into the smallest space.

The ground rose up. Lao Dao watched and waited until the fissure was wide enough. He crawled over the marble-lined edge onto the earthen wall, grabbing onto bits of metal protruding out of the soil. As the cleft widened and the walls elevated, he climbed, using his hands as well as feet. At first, he was climbing down, testing for purchase with his feet. But soon, as the entire section of ground rotated, he was lifted into the air, and up and down flipped around.

Lao Dao was thinking about last night.

He had cautiously stuck his head out of the trash heap, alert for any sound from the other side of the gate. The fermenting, rotting garbage around him was pungent: greasy, fishy, even a bit sweet. He leaned against the iron gate. Outside, the world was waking up.

As soon as the yellow glow of the streetlights seeped into the seam under the lifting gate, he squatted and crawled out of the widening opening. The streets were empty; lights came on in the tall buildings, story by story; fixtures extruded from the sides of buildings, unfolding and extending, segment by segment; porches emerged from the walls; the eaves rotated and gradually dropped down into position; stairs extended and descended to the street. On both sides of the road, one black cube after another broke apart and opened, revealing the racks and shelves inside. Signboards emerged from the tops of the cubes and connected together while plastic awnings extended from both sides of the lane to meet in the middle, forming a corridor of shops. The streets were empty, as though Lao Dao were dreaming.

The neon lights came on. Tiny flashing LEDs on top of the shops formed into characters advertising jujubes from Xinjiang, *lapi* noodles from Northeast China, bran dough from Shanghai, and cured meats from Hunan.

For the rest of the day, Lao Dao couldn't forget the scene. He had lived in this city for forty-eight years, but he had never seen such a sight. His days had always started with the cocoon and ended with the cocoon, and the time in between was spent at work or navigating dirty tables at hawker stalls and loudly bargaining crowds surrounding street vendors. This was the first time he had seen the world, bare.

—

Every morning, an observer at some distance from the city—say, a truck driver waiting on the highway into Beijing—could see the entire city fold and unfold.

At six in the morning, the truck drivers usually got out of their cabs and walked to the side of the highway, where they rubbed their eyes, still drowsy after an uncomfortable night in the truck. Yawning, they greeted each other and gazed at the distant city center. The break in the highway was just outside the Seventh Ring Road, while all the ground rotation occurred within the Sixth Ring Road. The distance was perfect for taking in the whole city, like gazing at an island in the sea.

In the early dawn, the city folded and collapsed. The skyscrapers bowed submissively like the humblest servants until their heads touched their feet; then they broke again, folded again, and twisted their necks and arms, stuffing them into the gaps. The compacted blocks that used to be the skyscrapers shuffled and assembled into dense, gigantic Rubik's Cubes that fell into a deep slumber.

The ground then began to turn. Square by square, pieces of the earth flipped 180 degrees around an axis, revealing the buildings on the other side. The buildings unfolded and stood up, awakening like a herd of beasts under the gray-blue sky. The island that was the city settled in the orange sunlight, spread open, and stood still as misty gray clouds roiled around it.

The truck drivers, tired and hungry, admired the endless cycle of urban renewal.

2.

The folding city was divided into three spaces. One side of the earth was First Space, population five million. Their allotted time lasted from six o'clock in the morning to six o'clock the next morning. Then the space went to sleep, and the earth flipped.

The other side was shared by Second Space and Third Space. Twenty-five million people lived in Second Space, and their allotted time lasted from six o'clock on that second day to ten o'clock at night. Fifty million people lived in Third Space, allotted the time from ten o'clock at night to six o'clock in the morning, at which point First Space returned. Time had been carefully divided and parceled out to separate the populations: five million enjoyed the use of twenty-four hours, and seventy-five million enjoyed the next twenty-four hours.

The structures on two sides of the ground were not even in weight. To remedy the imbalance, the earth was made thicker in First Space, and extra ballast buried in the soil to make up for the missing people and buildings. The residents of First Space considered the extra soil a natural emblem of their possession of a richer, deeper heritage.

Lao Dao had lived in Third Space since birth. He understood very well the reality of his situation, even without Peng Li pointing it out. He was a waste worker; he had processed trash for twenty-eight years, and would do so for the foreseeable future. He had not found the meaning of his existence or the ultimate refuge of cynicism; instead, he continued to hold onto the humble place assigned to him in life.

Lao Dao had been born in Beijing. His father was also a waste worker. His father told him that when Lao Dao was born, his father had just gotten his job, and the family had celebrated for three whole days. His father had been a construction worker, one of millions of other construction workers who had come to Beijing from all over China in search of work. His father and others like him had built this folding city. District by district, they had transformed the old city. Like termites swarming over a wooden house, they had chewed up the wreckage of the past, overturned the earth, and constructed a brand new world. They had swung their hammers and wielded their adzes, keeping their heads down; brick by brick, they had walled themselves off until they could no longer see the sky. Dust had obscured their views, and they had not known the grandeur of their work. Finally, when the completed building stood up before them like a living person, they had scattered in terror, as though they had given birth to a monster. But after they calmed down, they realized what an honor it would be to live in such a city in the future, and so they had continued to toil diligently and docilely, to meekly seek out any opportunity to remain in the city. It was said that when the folding city was completed, more than eighty million construction workers had wanted to stay. Ultimately, no more than twenty million were allowed to settle.

It had not been easy to get a job at the waste processing station. Although the work only involved sorting trash, so many applied that stringent selection criteria had to be imposed: the desired candidates had to be strong, skillful, discerning, organized, diligent, and unafraid of the stench or difficult environment. Strong-willed, Lao Dao's father had held fast onto the thin reed of opportunity as the tide of humanity surged and then receded around him, until he found himself a survivor on the dry beach.

His father had then kept his head down and labored away in the acidic rotten fetor of garbage and crowding for twenty years. He had built this city; he was also a resident and a decomposer.

Construction of the folding city had been completed two years before Lao Dao's birth. He had never been anywhere else, and had never harbored the desire to go anywhere else. He finished elementary school, middle school, high school, and took the annual college entrance examination three times—failing each time. In the end, he became a waste worker, too. At the waste processing station, he worked for five hours each shift, from eleven at night to four in the morning. Together with tens of thousands of coworkers, he mechanically and quickly sorted through the trash, picking out recyclable bits from the scraps of life from First Space and Second Space and tossing them into the processing furnace. Every day, he faced the trash on the conveyer belt flowing past him like a river, and he scraped off the leftover food from plastic bowls, picked out broken glass bottles, tore off the clean, thin backing from blood-stained sanitary napkins, stuffing it into the recyclables can marked with green lines. This was their lot: to eke out a living by performing the repetitive drudgery as fast as possible, to toil hour after hour for rewards as thin as the wings of cicadas.

Twenty million waste workers lived in Third Space; they were the masters of the night. The other thirty million made a living by selling clothes, food, fuel, or insurance, but most people understood that the waste workers were the backbone of Third Space's prosperity. Each time he strolled through the neon-bedecked night streets, Lao Dao thought he was walking under rainbows made of food scraps. He couldn't talk about this feeling with others. The younger generation looked down on the profession of the waste worker. They tried to show off on the dance floors of nightclubs, hoping to find jobs as DJs or dancers. Even working at a clothing store seemed a better choice: their fingers would be touching thin fabric instead of scrabbling through rotting garbage for plastic or metal. The young were no longer so terrified about survival; they cared far more about appearances.

Lao Dao didn't despise his work. But when he had gone to Second Space, he had been terrified of being despised.

The previous morning, Lao Dao had snuck his way out of the trash chute with a slip of paper and tried to find the author of the slip based on the address written on it.

Second Space wasn't far from Third Space. They were located on the same side of the ground, though they were divided in time. At the Change, the buildings of one space folded and retracted into the ground as the buildings of another space extended into the air, segment by segment, using the tops of the buildings of the other space as its foundation. The only difference between the spaces was the density of buildings. Lao Dao had to wait a full day and night inside the trash chute for the opportunity to emerge as Second Space unfolded. Although this was the first time he had been to Second Space, he wasn't anxious. He only worried about the rotting smell on him.

Luckily, Qin Tian was a generous soul. Perhaps he had been prepared for what sort of person would show up since the moment he put that slip of paper inside the bottle.

Qin Tian was very kind. He knew at a glance why Lao Dao had come. He pulled him inside his home, offered him a hot bath, and gave him one of his own bathrobes to wear. "I have to count on you," Qin Tian said.

Qin was a graduate student living in a university-owned apartment. He had three roommates, and besides the four bedrooms, the apartment had a kitchen and two bathrooms. Lao Dao had never taken a bath in such a spacious bathroom, and he really wanted to soak for a while and get rid of the smell on his body. But he was also afraid of getting the bathtub dirty and didn't dare to rub his skin too hard with the washcloth. The jets of bubbles coming out of the bathtub walls startled him, and being dried by hot jets of air made him uncomfortable. After the bath, he picked up the bathrobe from Qin Tian and only put it on after hesitating for a while. He laundered his own clothes, as well as a few other shirts casually left in a basin. Business was business, and he didn't want to owe anyone any favors.

Qin Tian wanted to send a gift to a woman he liked. They had gotten to know each other from work when Qin Tian had been given the opportunity to go to First Space for an internship with the UN Economic Office, where she was also working. The internship had lasted only a month. Qin told Lao Dao that the young woman was born and bred in First Space, with very strict parents. Her father wouldn't allow her to date a boy from Second Space, and that was why he couldn't contact her through regular channels. Qin was optimistic about the future; he was going to apply to the UN's New Youth Project after graduation, and if he were to be chosen, he would be able to go to work in First Space. He still had another year of school left before he would get his degree, but he was going crazy pining for her. He had made a rose-shaped locket for her that glowed in the dark: this was the gift he would use to ask for her hand in marriage.

"I was attending a symposium, you know, the one that discussed the UN's debt situation? You must have heard of it . . . anyway, I saw her, and I was like, *Ah!* I went over right away to talk to her. She was helping the VIPs to their seats, and I didn't know what to say, so I just followed her around. Finally, I pretended that I had to find interpreters, and I asked her to help me. She was so gentle, and her voice was really soft. I had never really asked a girl out, you understand, so I was super nervous. . . . Later, after we started dating, I brought up how we met. . . . Why are you laughing? Yes, we dated. No, I don't think we quite got to that kind of relationship, but . . . well, we kissed." Qin Tian laughed as well, a bit embarrassed. "I'm telling the truth! Don't you believe me? Yes, I guess sometimes even I can't believe it. Do you think she really likes me?"

"I have no idea," Lao Dao said. "I've never met her."

One of Qin Tian's roommates came over, and smiling, said, "Uncle, why are you taking his question so seriously? That's not a real question. He just wants to hear you say, 'Of course she loves you! You're so handsome.'"

"She must be beautiful."

"I'm not afraid that you'll laugh at me." Qin Tian paced back and forth in front of Lao Dao. "When you see her, you'll understand the meaning of 'peerless elegance.'"

Qin Tian stopped, sinking into a reverie. He was thinking of Yi Yan's mouth. Her mouth was perhaps his favorite part of her: so tiny, so smooth, with a full bottom lip that glowed with a natural, healthy pink, making him want to give it a loving bite. Her neck also aroused him. Sometimes it appeared so thin that the tendons showed, but the lines were straight and pretty. The skin was fair and smooth, extending down into the collar of her blouse so that his gaze lingered on her second button. The first time he tried to kiss her, she had moved her lips away shyly. He had persisted until she gave in, closing her eyes and returning the kiss. Her lips had felt so soft, and his hands had caressed the curve of her waist and backside, again and again. From that day on, he had lived in the country of longing. She was his dream at night, and also the light he saw when he trembled in his own hand.

Qin Tian's roommate was called Zhang Xian, who seemed to relish the opportunity to converse with Lao Dao.

Zhang Xian asked Lao Dao about life in Third Space, and mentioned that he actually wanted to live in Third Space for a while. He had been given the advice that if he wanted to climb up the ladder of government administration, some managerial experience in Third Space would be very helpful. Several prominent officials had all started their careers as Third Space administrators before being promoted to First Space. If they had stayed in Second Space, they wouldn't have gone anywhere and would have spent the rest of their careers as low-level administrative cadres. Zhang Xian's ambition was to eventually enter government service, and he was certain he knew the right path. Still, he wanted to go work at a bank for a couple of years first and earn some quick money. Since Lao Dao seemed noncommittal about his plans, Zhang Xian thought Lao Dao disapproved of his careerism.

"The current government is too inefficient and ossified," he added quickly, "slow to respond to challenges, and I don't see much hope for systematic reform. When I get my opportunity, I'll push for rapid reforms: anyone who's incompetent will be fired." Since Lao Dao still didn't seem to show much reaction, he added, "I'll also work to expand the pool of candidates for government service and promotion, including opening up opportunities for candidates from Third Space."

Lao Dao said nothing. It wasn't because he disapproved; rather, he found it hard to believe Zhang Xian.

While he talked with Lao Dao, Zhang Xian was also putting on a tie and fixing his hair in front of the mirror. He had on a shirt with light blue stripes, and the tie was a bright blue. He closed his eyes and frowned as the mist of hairspray settled around his face, whistling all the while.

Zhang Xian left with his briefcase for his internship at the bank. Qin Tian said he had to get going as well since he had classes that would last until four in the afternoon. Before he left, he transferred fifty thousand yuan over the net to Lao Dao's account while Lao Dao watched, and explained that he would transfer the rest after Lao Dao succeeded in his mission.

"Have you been saving up for this for a while?" Lao Dao asked. "You're a student, so money is probably tight. I can accept less if necessary."

"Don't worry about it. I'm on a paid internship with a financial advisory firm. They pay me around a hundred thousand each month, so the total I'm promising you is about two months of my salary. I can afford it."

Lao Dao said nothing. He earned the standard salary of ten thousand each month.

"Please bring back her answer," Qin Tian said.

"I'll do my best."

"Help yourself to the fridge if you get hungry. Just stay put here and wait for the Change."

Lao Dao looked outside the window. He couldn't get used to the sunlight, which was a bright white, not the yellow he was used to. The street seemed twice as wide in the sun as what Lao Dao remembered from Third Space, and he wasn't sure if that was a visual illusion. The buildings here weren't nearly as tall as buildings in Third Space. The sidewalks were filled with people walking very fast, and from time to time, some trotted and tried to shove their way through the crowd, causing those in front of them to begin running as well. Everyone seemed to run across intersections. The men dressed mostly in Western suits while the women wore blouses and short skirts, with scarves around their necks and compact, rigid purses in their hands that lent them an air of competence and efficiency. The street was filled with cars, and as they waited at intersections for the light to change, the drivers stuck their heads out of the windows, gazing ahead anxiously. Lao Dao had never seen so many cars; he was used to the mass-transit maglev packed with passengers whooshing by him.

Around noon, he heard noises in the hallway outside the apartment. Lao Dao peeked out of the peephole in the door. The floor of the hallway had transformed into a moving conveyor belt, and bags of trash left at the door of each apartment were shoved onto the conveyor belt to be deposited into the chute at the end. Mist filled the hall, turning into soap bubbles that drifted through the air, and then water washed the floor, followed by hot steam.

A noise from behind Lao Dao startled him. He turned around and saw that another of Qin Tian's roommates had emerged from his bedroom. The young man ignored Lao Dao, his face impassive. He went to some machine next to the balcony and pushed some buttons, and the machine came to life, popping, whirring, grinding. Eventually, the noise stopped, and Lao Dao smelled something delicious. The young man took out a piping hot plate of food from the machine and returned to his room. Through the half-open bedroom door, Lao Dao could see that the young man was sitting on the floor in a pile of blankets and dirty socks, and staring at his wall as he ate and laughed, pushing up his glasses from time to time. After he was done eating, he left the plate at his feet, stood up, and began to fight someone invisible as he faced the wall. He struggled, his breathing labored, as he wrestled the unseen enemy.

Lao Dao's last memory of Second Space was the refined air with which everyone conducted themselves before the Change. Looking down from the window of the apartment, everything seemed so orderly that he felt a hint of envy. Starting at a quarter past nine, the stores along the street turned off their lights one after another; groups of friends, their faces red with drink, said good-bye in front of restaurants. Young couples kissed next to taxicabs. And then everyone returned to their homes, and the world went to sleep.

It was ten at night. He returned to his world to go to work.

3.

There was no trash chute connecting First Space directly with Third Space. The trash from First Space had to pass through a set of metal gates to be transported into Third Space, and the gates shut as soon as the trash went through.

Lao Dao didn't like the idea of having to go over the flipping ground, but he had no choice.

As the wind whipped around him, he crawled up the still-rotating earth toward First Space. He grabbed onto metal structural elements protruding from the soil, struggling to balance his body and calm his heart, until he finally managed to scrabble over the rim of this most distant world. He felt dizzy and nauseated from the intense climb, and forcing down his churning stomach, he remained still on the ground for a while.

By the time he got up, the sun had risen.

Lao Dao had never seen such a sight. The sun rose gradually. The sky was a deep and pure azure, with an orange fringe at the horizon, decorated with slanted, thin wisps of cloud. The eaves of a nearby building blocked the sun, and the eaves appeared especially dark while the background was dazzlingly bright. As the sun continued to rise, the blue of the sky faded a little, but seemed even more tranquil and clear. Lao Dao stood up and ran at the sun; he wanted to catch a trace of that fading golden color. Silhouettes of waving tree branches broke up the sky. His heart leapt wildly. He had never imagined that a sunrise could be so moving.

After a while, he slowed down and calmed himself. He was standing in the middle of the street, lined on both sides with tall trees and wide lawns. He looked around, and he couldn't see any buildings at all. Confused, he wondered if he had really reached First Space. He pondered the two rows of sturdy gingkoes.

He backed up a few steps and turned to look in the direction he had come from. There was a road sign next to the street. He took out his phone and looked at the map—although he wasn't authorized to download live maps from First Space, he had downloaded and stored some maps before leaving on this trip. He found where he was as well as where he needed to be. He was standing next to a large open park, and the seam he had emerged from was next to a lake in that park.

Lao Dan ran about a kilometer through the deserted streets until he reached the residential district containing his destination. He hid behind some bushes and observed the beautiful house from a distance.

At eight-thirty, Yi Yan came out of the house.

She was indeed as elegant as Qin Tian's description had suggested, though perhaps not as pretty. Lao Dao wasn't surprised, however. No woman could possibly be as beautiful as Qin Tian's verbal portrait. He also understood why Qin Tian had spoken so much of her mouth. Her eyes and nose were fairly ordinary.

She had a good figure: tall, with delicate bones. She wore a milky white dress with a flowing skirt. Her belt was studded with pearls, and she had on black heels.

Lao Dao walked up to her. To avoid startling her, he approached from the front, and bowed deeply when he was still some distance away.

She stood still, looking at him in surprise.

Lao Dao came closer and explained his mission. He took out the envelope with the locket and Qin Tian's letter.

She looked alarmed. "Please leave," she whispered. "I can't talk to you right now."

"Uh . . . I don't really need to talk to you," Lao Dao said. "I just need to give you this letter."

She refused to take it from him, clasping her hands tightly. "I can't accept this now. Please leave. Really, I'm begging you. All right?" She took out a business card from her purse and handed it to him. "Come find me at this address at noon."

Lao Dao looked at the card. At the top was the name of a bank.

"At noon," she said. "Wait for me in the underground supermarket."

Lao Dao could tell how anxious she was. He nodded, put the card away, and returned to hide behind the bushes. Soon, a man emerged from the house and stopped next to her. The man looked to be about Lao Dao's age, or maybe a couple of years younger. Dressed in a dark gray, well-fitted suit, he was tall and broad-shouldered. Not fat, just thickset. His face was nondescript: round, a pair of glasses, hair neatly combed to one side.

The man grabbed Yi Yan around the waist and kissed her on the lips. Yi Yan seemed to give in to the kiss reluctantly.

Understanding began to dawn on Lao Dao.

A single-rider cart arrived in front of the house. The black cart had two wheels and a canopy, and resembled an ancient carriage or rickshaw one might see on TV, except there was no horse or person pulling the cart. The cart stopped and dipped forward. Yi Yan stepped in, sat down, and arranged the skirt of the dress neatly around her knees. The cart straightened and began to move at a slow, steady pace, as though pulled by some invisible horse. After Yi Yan left, a driverless car arrived, and the man got in.

Lao Dao paced in place. He felt something was pushing at his throat, but he couldn't articulate it. Standing in the sun, he closed his eyes. The clean, fresh air filled his lungs and provided some measure of comfort.

A moment later, he was on his way. The address Yi Yan had given him was to the east, a little more than three kilometers away. There were very few people in the pedestrian lane, and only scattered cars sped by in a blur on the eight-lane avenue. Occasionally, well-dressed women passed Lao Dao in two-wheeled carts. The passengers adopted such graceful postures that it was as though they were in some fashion show. No one paid any attention to Lao Dao. The trees swayed in the breeze, and the air in their shade seemed suffused with the perfume from the elegant women.

Yi Yan's office was in the Xidan commercial district. There were no sky-scrapers at all, only a few low buildings scattered around a large park. The buildings seemed isolated from each other but were really parts of a single compound connected via underground passages.

Lao Dao found the supermarket. He was early. As soon as he came in, a small shopping cart began to follow him around. Every time he stopped by a shelf, the screen on the cart displayed the names of the goods on the shelf, their description, customer reviews, and comparison with other brands in the same category. All merchandise in the supermarket seemed to be labeled in foreign languages. The packaging for all the food products was very refined, and small cakes and fruits were enticingly arranged on plates for customers. He didn't dare to touch anything, keeping his distance as though they were dangerous, exotic animals. There seemed to be no guards or clerks in the whole market.

More customers appeared before noon. Some men in suits came into the market, grabbed sandwiches, and waved them at the scanner next to the door before hurrying out. No one paid any attention to Lao Dao as he waited in an obscure corner near the door.

Yi Yan appeared, and Lao Dao went up to her. Yi Yan glanced around, and without saying anything, led Lao Dao to a small restaurant next door. Two small robots dressed in plaid skirts greeted them, took Yi Yan's purse, brought them to a booth, and handed them menus. Yi Yan pressed a few spots on the menu to make her selection and handed the menu back to the robot. The robot turned and glided smoothly on its wheels to the back.

Yi Yan and Lao Dao sat mutely across from each other. Lao Dao took out the envelope.

Yi Yan still didn't take it from him. "Can you let me explain?"

Lao Dao pushed the envelope across the table. "Please take this first."

Yi Yan pushed it back.

"Can you let me explain first?"

"You don't need to explain anything," Lao Dao said. "I didn't write this letter. I'm just the messenger."

"But you have to go back and give him an answer." Yi Yan looked down. The little robot returned with two plates, one for each of them. On each plate were two slices of some kind of red sashimi, arranged like flower petals. Yi Yan didn't pick up her chopsticks, and neither did Lao Dao. The envelope rested between the two plates, and neither touched it. "I didn't betray him. When I met him last year, I was already engaged. I didn't lie to him or conceal the truth from him on purpose. . . . Well, maybe I did lie, but it was because he assumed and guessed. He saw Wu Wen come to pick me up once, and he asked me if he was my father. I . . . I couldn't answer him, you know? It was just too embarrassing. I. . . ."

Yi Yan couldn't speak any more.

Lao Dao waited a while. "I'm not interested in what happened between you two. All I care about is that you take the letter."

Yi Yan kept her head down, and then she looked up. "After you go back, can you . . . help me by not telling him everything?"

"Why?"

"I don't want him to think that I was just playing with his feelings. I do like him, really. I feel very conflicted."

"None of this is my concern."

"Please, I'm begging you. . . . I really do like him."

Lao Dao was silent for a while.

"But you got married in the end?"

"Wu Wen was very good to me. We'd been together several years. He knew my parents, and we'd been engaged for a long time. Also, I'm three years older than Qin Tian, and I was afraid he wouldn't like that. Qin Tian thought I was an intern, like him, and I admit that was my fault for not telling him the truth. I don't know why I said I was an intern at first, and then it became harder and harder to correct him. I never thought he would be serious."

Slowly, Yi Yan told Lao Dao her story. She was actually an assistant to the bank's president and had already been working there for two years at the time she met Qin Tian. She had been sent to the UN for training, and was helping out at the symposium. In fact, her husband earned so much money that she didn't really need to work, but she didn't like the idea of being at home all day. She worked only half days and took a half-time salary. The rest of the day was hers to do with as she pleased, and she liked learning new things and meeting new people. She really had enjoyed the months she spent training at the UN. She told Lao Dao that there were many wives like her who worked half-time. As a matter of fact, after she got off work at noon, another wealthy wife worked as the president's assistant in the afternoon. She told Lao Dao that though she had not told Qin Tian the truth, her heart was honest.

"And so"—she spooned a serving of the new hot dish onto Lao Dao's plate—"can you please not tell him, just temporarily? Please . . . give me a chance to explain to him myself."

Lao Dao didn't pick up his chopsticks. He was very hungry, but he felt that he could not eat this food.

"Then I'd be lying, too," Lao Dao said.

Yi Yan opened her purse, took out her wallet, and retrieved five ten thousand–yuan bills. She pushed them across the table toward Lao Dao. "Please accept this token of my appreciation."

Lao Dao was stunned. He had never seen bills with such large denominations or needed to use them. Almost subconsciously, he stood up, angry. The way Yi Yan had taken out the money seemed to suggest that she had been anticipating an attempt from him to blackmail her, and he could not accept that. *This is what they think of Third Spacers.* He felt that if he took her money, he would be selling Qin Tian out. It was true that he really wasn't Qin Tian's friend, but he still thought of it as a kind of betrayal. Lao Dao wanted to grab the bills, throw them on the ground, and walk away. But he couldn't. He looked at the money again: the five thin notes were spread on the table like a broken fan. He could sense the power they had on him. They were baby blue in color, distinct from the brown thousand-yuan note and the red hundred-yuan note. These bills looked deeper, most distant somehow, like a kind of seduction. Several times, he wanted to stop looking at them and leave, but he couldn't.

She continued to rummage through her purse, taking everything out, until she finally found another fifty thousand yuan from an inner pocket and placed them together with the other bills. "This is all I have. Please take it and help me." She paused. "Look, the reason I don't want him to know is because I'm not sure what I'm going to do. It's possible that someday I'll have the courage to be with him."

Lao Dao looked at the ten notes spread out on the table, and then looked up at her. He sensed that she didn't believe what she was saying. Her voice was hesitant, belying her words. She was just delaying everything to the future so that she wouldn't be embarrassed now. She was unlikely to ever elope with Qin Tian, but she also didn't want him to despise her. Thus, she wanted to keep alive the *possibility* so that she could feel better about herself.

Lao Dao could see that she was lying to herself, but he wanted to lie to himself, too. He told himself, *I have no duty to Qin Tian. All he asked was for me to deliver his message to her, and I've done that. The money on the table now represents a new commission, a commitment to keep a secret.* He waited, and then told himself, *Perhaps someday she really will get together with Qin Tian, and in that case I'll have done a good deed by keeping silent. Besides, I need to think about Tangtang. Why should I get myself all worked up about strangers instead of thinking about Tangtang's welfare?* He felt calmer. He realized that his fingers were already touching the money.

"This is . . . too much." He wanted to make himself feel better. "I can't accept so much."

"It's no big deal." She stuffed the bills into his hand. "I earn this much in a week. Don't worry."

"What . . . what do you want me to tell him?"

"Tell him that I can't be with him now, but I truly like him. I'll write you a note to bring him." Yi Yan found a notepad in her purse; it had a picture of a peacock on the cover and the edges of the pages were golden. She ripped out a page and began to write. Her handwriting looked like a string of slanted gourds.

As Lao Dao left the restaurant, he glanced back. Yi Yan was sitting in the booth, gazing up at a painting on the wall. She looked so elegant and refined, as though she was never going to leave.

He squeezed the bills in his pocket. He despised himself, but he wanted to hold on to the money.

4.

Lao Dao left Xidan and returned the way he had come. He felt exhausted. The pedestrian lane was lined with a row of weeping willows on one side and a row of Chinese parasol trees on the other side. It was late spring, and everything was a lush green. The afternoon sun warmed his stiff face, and brightened his empty heart.

He was back at the park from this morning. There were many people in the park now, and the two rows of gingkoes looked stately and luscious. Black cars entered the park from time to time, and most of the people in the park wore either well-fitted Western suits made of quality fabric or dark-colored stylish Chinese suits, but everyone gave off a haughty air. There were also some foreigners. Some of the people conversed in small groups; others greeted each other at a distance, and then laughed as they got close enough to shake hands and walk together.

Lao Dao hesitated, trying to decide where to go. There weren't that many people in the street, and he would draw attention if he just stood here. But he would look out of place in any public area. He wanted to go back into the park, get close to the fissure, and hide in some corner to take a nap. He felt very sleepy, but he dared not sleep on the street.

He noticed that the cars entering the park didn't seem to need to stop, and so he tried to walk into the park as well. Only when he was close to the park gate did he notice that two robots were patrolling the area. While cars and other pedestrians passed their sentry line with no problems, the robots beeped as soon as Lao Dao approached and turned on their wheels to head for him. In the tranquil afternoon, the noise they made seemed especially loud. The eyes of everyone nearby turned to him. He panicked, uncertain if it was his shabby clothes that alerted the robots. He tried to whisper to the robots, claiming that his suit was left inside the park, but the robots ignored him while they continued to beep and to flash the red lights over their heads. People strolling inside the park stopped and looked at him as though looking at a thief or eccentric person. Soon, three men emerged from a nearby building and ran over. Lao Dao's heart was in his throat. He wanted to run, but it was too late.

"What's going on?" the man in the lead asked loudly.

Lao Dao couldn't think of anything to say, and he rubbed his pants compulsively.

The man in the front was in his thirties. He came up to Lao Dao and scanned him with a silver disk about the size of a button, moving his hand around Lao Dao's person. He looked at Lao Dao suspiciously, as though trying to pry open his shell with a can opener.

"There's no record of this man." The man gestured at the older man behind him. "Bring him in."

Lao Dao started to run away from the park.

The two robots silently dashed ahead of him and grabbed onto his legs. Their arms were cuffs and locked easily about his ankles. He tripped and almost fell, but the robots held him up. His arms swung through the air helplessly.

"Why are you trying to run?" The younger man stepped up and glared at him. His tone was now severe.

"I. . . ." Lao Dao's head felt like a droning beehive. He couldn't think.

The two robots lifted Lao Dao by the legs and deposited his feet onto platforms next to their wheels. Then they drove toward the nearest building in parallel, carrying Lao Dao. Their movements were so steady, so smooth, so synchronized, that from a distance, it appeared as if Lao Dao was skating along on a pair of rollerblades, like Nezha riding on his Wind Fire Wheels.

Lao Dao felt utterly helpless. He was angry with himself for being so careless. How could he think such a crowded place would be without security measures? He berated himself for being so drowsy that he could commit such a stupid mistake. *It's all over now*, he thought. *Not only am I not going to get my money, I'm also going to jail.*

The robots followed a narrow path and reached the backdoor of the building, where they stopped. The three men followed behind. The younger man seemed to be arguing with the older man over what to do with Lao Dao, but they spoke so softly that Lao Dao couldn't hear the details. After a while, the older man came up and unlocked the robots from Lao Dao's legs. Then he grabbed him by the arm and took him upstairs.

Lao Dao sighed. He resigned himself to his fate.

The man brought him into a room. It looked like a hotel room, very spacious, bigger even than the living room in Qin Tian's apartment, and about twice the size of his own rental unit. The room was decorated in a dark shade of golden brown, with a king-sized bed in the middle. The wall at the head of the bed showed abstract patterns of shifting colors. Translucent white curtains covered the French window, and in front of the window sat a small circular table and two comfortable chairs. Lao Dao was anxious, unsure of who the older man was and what he wanted.

"Sit, sit!" The older man clapped him on the shoulder and smiled. "Everything's fine."

Lao Dao looked at him suspiciously.

"You're from Third Space, aren't you?" The older man pulled him over to the chairs, and gestured for him to sit.

"How do you know that?" Lao Dao couldn't lie.

"From your pants." The older man pointed at the waist of his pants. "You never even cut off the label. This brand is only sold in Third Space; I remember my mother buying them for my father when I was little."

"Sir, you're . . . ?"

"You don't need to 'Sir' me. I don't think I'm much older than you are. How old are you? I'm fifty-two."

"Forty-eight."

"See, just older by four years." He paused, and then added, "My name is Ge Daping. Why don't you just call me Lao Ge?"

Lao Dao relaxed a little. Lao Ge took off his jacket and moved his arms about to stretch out the stiff muscles. Then he filled a glass with hot water from a spigot in the wall and handed it to Lao Dao. He had a long face, and the corners of his eyes, the ends of his eyebrows, and his cheeks drooped.

Even his glasses seemed about to fall off the end of his nose. His hair was naturally a bit curly and piled loosely on top of his head. As he spoke, his eyebrows bounced up and down comically. He made some tea for himself and asked Lao Dao if he wanted any. Lao Dao shook his head.

"I was originally from Third Space as well," said Lao Ge. "We're practically from the same hometown! So, you don't need to be so careful with me. I still have a bit of authority, and I won't give you up."

Lao Dao let out a long sigh, congratulating himself silently for his good luck. He recounted for Lao Ge his experiencing of going to Second Space and then coming to First Space, but omitted the details of what Yi Yan had said. He simply told Lao Ge that he had successfully delivered the message and was just waiting for the Change to head home.

Lao Ge also shared his own story with Lao Dao. He had grown up in Third Space, and his parents had worked as deliverymen. When he was fifteen, he entered a military school, and then joined the army. He worked as a radar technician in the army, and because he worked hard, demonstrated good technical skills, and had some good opportunities, he was eventually promoted to an administrative position in the radar department with the rank of brigadier general. Since he didn't come from a prominent family, that rank was about as high as he could go in the army. He then retired from the army and joined an agency in First Space responsible for logistical support for government enterprises, organizing meetings, arranging travel, and coordinating various social events. The job was blue collar in nature, but since his work involved government officials and he had to coordinate and manage, he was allowed to live in First Space. There were a considerable number of people in First Space like him—chefs, doctors, secretaries, housekeepers—skilled blue-collar workers needed to support the lifestyle of First Space. His agency had run many important social events and functions, and Lao Ge was its director.

Lao Ge might have been self-deprecating in describing himself as a "blue collar," but Lao Dao understood that anyone who could work and live in First Space had extraordinary skills. Even a chef here was likely a master of his art. Lao Ge must be very talented to have risen here from Third Space after a technical career in the army.

"You might as well take a nap," Lao Ge said. "I'll take you to get something to eat this evening."

Lao Dao still couldn't believe his good luck, and he felt a bit uneasy. However, he couldn't resist the call of the white sheets and stuffed pillows, and he fell asleep almost right away.

When he woke up, it was dark outside. Lao Ge was combing his hair in front of the mirror. He showed Lao Dao a suit lying on the sofa and told him to change. Then he pinned a tiny badge with a faint red glow to Lao Dao's lapel—a new identity.

The large open lobby downstairs was crowded. Some kind of presentation seemed to have just finished, and attendees conversed in small groups. At one end of the lobby were the open doors leading to the banquet hall; the thick doors were lined with burgundy leather. The lobby was filled with small standing tables. Each table was covered by a white tablecloth tied around the bottom with a golden bow, and the vase in the middle of each table held a lily. Crackers and dried fruits were set out next to the vases for snacking, and a long table to the side offered wine and coffee. Guests mingled and conversed among the tables while small robots holding serving trays shuttled between their legs, collecting empty glasses.

Forcing himself to be calm, Lao Dao followed Lao Ge and walked through the convivial scene into the banquet hall. He saw a large hanging banner: *The Folding City at Fifty.*

"What is this?" Lao Dao asked.

"A celebration!" Lao Ge was walking about and examining the set up. "Xiao Zhao, come here a minute. I want you to check the table signs one more time. I don't trust robots for things like this. Sometimes they don't know how to be flexible."

Lao Dao saw that the banquet hall was filled with large round tables with fresh flower centerpieces.

The scene seemed unreal to him. He stood in a corner and gazed up at the giant chandelier as though some dazzling reality was hanging over him, and he was but an insignificant presence at its periphery. There was a lectern set up on the dais at the front, and, behind it, the background was an ever-shifting series of images of Beijing. The photographs were perhaps taken from an airplane and captured the entirety of the city: the soft light of dawn and dusk; the dark purple and deep blue sky; clouds racing across the sky; the moon rising from a corner; the sun setting behind a roof. The aerial shots revealed the magnificence of Beijing's ancient symmetry; the modern expanse of brick courtyards and large green parks that had extended to the Sixth Ring Road; Chinese-style theatres; Japanese-style museums; minimalist concert halls. And then there were shots of the city as a whole, shots that included both faces of the city during the Change: the earth flipping, revealing the other side studded with skyscrapers with sharp, straight contours; men and women energetically rushing to work; neon signs lighting up the night, blotting out the stars; towering apartment buildings, cinemas, nightclubs full of beautiful people.

But there were no shots of where Lao Dao worked.

He stared at the screen intently, uncertain if they might show pictures during the construction of the folding city. He hoped to get a glimpse of his father's era. When he was little, his father had often pointed to buildings outside the window and told him stories that started with "Back then, we. . . ." An old photograph had hung on the wall of their cramped home, and in the picture his father was laying bricks, a task his father had performed thousands, or perhaps hundreds of thousands of times. He had seen that picture so many times that he thought he was sick of it, and yet, at this moment, he hoped to see a scene of workers laying bricks, even if for just a few seconds.

He was lost in his thoughts. This was also the first time he had seen what the Change looked like from a distance. He didn't remember sitting down, and he didn't know when others had sat down next to him. A man began to speak at the lectern, but Lao Dao wasn't even listening for the first few minutes.

". . . advantageous for the development of the service sector. The service economy is dependent on population size and density. Currently, the service industry of our city is responsible for more than 85 percent of our GDP, in line with the general characteristics of world-class metropolises. The other important sectors are the green economy and the recycling economy." Lao Dao was paying full attention now. "Green economy" and "recycling economy" were often mentioned at the waste processing station, and the phrases were painted on the walls in characters taller than a man. He looked closer at the speaker on the dais: an old man with silvery hair, though he appeared hale and energetic. ". . . all trash is now sorted and processed, and we've achieved our goals for energy conservation and pollution reduction ahead of schedule. We've developed a systematic, large-scale recycling economy in which all the rare-earth and precious metals extracted from e-waste are reused in manufacturing, and even the plastics recycling rate exceeds eighty percent. The recycling stations are directly connected to the reprocessing plants. . . ."

Lao Dao knew of a distant relative who worked at a reprocessing plant in the technopark far from the city. The technopark was just acres and acres of industrial buildings, and he heard that all the plants over there were very similar: the machines pretty much ran on their own, and there were very few workers. At night, when the workers got together, they felt like the last survivors of some dwindling tribe in a desolate wilderness.

He drifted off again. Only the wild applause at the end of the speech pulled him out of his chaotic thoughts and back to reality. He also applauded, though he didn't know what for. He watched the speaker descend the dais and return to his place of honor at the head table. Everyone's eyes were on him.

Lao Dao saw Wu Wen, Yi Yan's husband.

Wu Wen was at the table next to the head table. As the old man who had given the speech sat down, Wu Wen walked over to offer a toast, and then he seemed to say something that got the old man's attention. The old man got up and walked with Wu Wen out of the banquet hall. Almost subconsciously, a curious Lao Dao also got up and followed them. He didn't know where Lao Ge had gone. Robots emerged to serve the dishes for the banquet.

Lao Dao emerged from the banquet hall and was back in the reception lobby. He eavesdropped on the other two from a distance and only caught snippets of conversation.

". . . there are many advantages to this proposal," said Wu Wen. "Yes, I've seen their equipment . . . automatic waste processing . . . they use a chemical solvent to dissolve and digest everything and then extract reusable materials in bulk . . . clean, and very economical . . . would you please give it some consideration?"

Wu Wen kept his voice low, but Lao Dao clearly heard "waste processing." He moved closer.

The old man with the silvery hair had a complex expression. Even after Wu Wen was finished, he waited a while before speaking. "You're certain that the solvent is safe? No toxic pollution?"

Wu Wen hesitated. "The current version still generates a bit of pollution but I'm sure they can reduce it to the minimum very quickly."

Lao Dao got even closer.

The old man shook his head, staring at Wu Wen. "Things aren't that simple. If I approve your project and it's implemented, there will be major consequences. Your process won't need workers, so what are you going to do with the tens of millions of people who will lose their jobs?"

The old man turned away and returned to the banquet hall. Wu Wen remained in place, stunned. A man who had been by the old man's side—a secretary perhaps—came up to Wu Wen and said sympathetically, "You might as well go back and enjoy the meal. I'm sure you understand how this works. Employment is the number one concern. Do you really think no one has suggested similar technology in the past?"

Lao Dao understood vaguely that what they were talking about had to do with him, but he wasn't sure whether it was good news or bad. Wu Wen's expression shifted through confusion, annoyance, and then resignation. Lao Dao suddenly felt some sympathy for him: he had his moments of weakness, as well.

The secretary suddenly noticed Lao Dao.

"Are you new here?" he asked.

Lao Dao was startled. "Ah? Um. . . ."

"What's your name? How come I wasn't informed about a new member of the staff?"

Lao Dao's heart beat wildly. He didn't know what to say. He pointed to the badge on his lapel, as though hoping the badge would speak or otherwise help him out. But the badge displayed nothing. His palms sweated. The secretary stared at him, his look growing more suspicious by the second. He grabbed another worker in the lobby, and the worker said he didn't know who Lao Dao was.

The secretary's face was now severe and dark. He grabbed Lao Dao with one hand and punched the keys on his communicator with the other hand.

Lao Dao's heart threatened to jump out of his throat, but just then, he saw Lao Ge.

Lao Ge rushed over and with a smooth gesture, hung up the secretary's communicator. Smiling, he greeted the secretary and bowed deeply. He explained that he was shorthanded for the occasion and had to ask for a colleague from another department to help out tonight. The secretary seemed to believe Lao Ge and returned to the banquet hall. Lao Ge brought Lao Dao back to his own room to avoid any further risks. If anyone really bothered to look into Lao Dao's identity, they'd discover the truth, and even Lao Ge wouldn't be able to protect him.

"I guess you're not fated to enjoy the banquet." Lao Ge laughed. "Just wait here. I'll get you some food later."

Lao Dao lay down on the bed and fell asleep again. He replayed the conversation between Wu Wen and the old man in his head. *Automatic waste processing. What would that look like? Would that be a good thing or bad?*

The next time he woke up, he smelled something delicious. Lao Ge had set out a few dishes on the small circular table, and was taking the last plate out of the warming oven on the wall. Lao Ge also brought over a half bottle of *baijiu* and filled two glasses.

"There was a table where they had only two people, and they left early so most of the dishes weren't even touched. I brought some back. It's not much, but maybe you'll enjoy the taste. Hopefully you won't hold it against me that I'm offering you leftovers."

"Not at all," Lao Dao said. "I'm grateful that I get to eat at all. These look wonderful! They must be very expensive, right?"

"The food at the banquet is prepared by the kitchen here and not for sale, so I don't know how much they'd cost in a restaurant." Lao Ge already started to eat. "They're nothing special. If I had to guess, maybe ten thousand, twenty thousand? A couple might cost thirty, forty thousand. Not more than that."

After a couple of bites, Lao Dao realized how hungry he was. He was used to skipping meals, and sometimes he could last a whole day without eating. His body would shake uncontrollably then, but he had learned to endure it. But now, the hunger was overwhelming. He wanted to chew quicker because his teeth couldn't seem to catch up to the demands of his empty stomach. He tried to wash the food down with *baijiu*, which was very fragrant and didn't sting his throat at all.

Lao Ge ate leisurely, and smiled as he watched Lao Dao eat.

"Oh." Now that the pangs of hunger had finally been dulled a bit, Lao Dao remembered the earlier conversation. "Who was the man giving the speech? He seemed a bit familiar."

"He's always on TV," Lao Ge said. "That's my boss. He's a man with real power—in charge of everything having to do with city operations."

"They were talking about automatic waste processing earlier. Do you think they'll really do it?"

"Hard to say." Lao Ge sipped the *baijiu* and let out a burp. "I suspect not. You have to understand why they went with manual processing in the first place. Back then, the situation here was similar to Europe at the end of the twentieth century. The economy was growing, but so was unemployment. Printing money didn't solve the problem. The economy refused to obey the Phillips curve."

He saw that Lao Dao looked completely lost, and laughed. "Never mind. You wouldn't understand these things anyway."

He clinked glasses with Lao Dao and the two drained their *baijiu* and refilled the glasses.

"I'll just stick to unemployment. I'm sure you understand the concept," Lao Ge continued. "As the cost of labor goes up and the cost of machinery goes down, at some point, it'll be cheaper to use machines than people. With the increase in productivity, the GDP goes up, but so does unemployment. What do you do? Enact policies to protect the workers? Better welfare? The more you try to protect workers, the more you increase the cost of labor and make it less attractive for employers to hire people. If you go outside the city now to the industrial districts, there's almost no one working in those factories. It's the same thing with farming. Large commercial farms contain thousands and thousands of acres of land, and everything is automated so there's no need for people. This kind of automation is absolutely necessary if you want to grow your economy—that was how we caught up to Europe and America, remember? Scaling! The problem is: now you've gotten the people off the land and out of the factories, what are you going to do with them? In Europe, they went with the path of forcefully reducing everyone's working hours and thus increasing employment opportunities. But this saps the vitality of the economy, you understand?

"The best way is to reduce the time a certain portion of the population spends living, and then find ways to keep them busy. Do you get it? Right, shove them into the night. There's another advantage to this approach: the effects of inflation almost can't be felt at the bottom of the social pyramid. Those who can get loans and afford the interest spend all the money you print. The GDP goes up, but the cost of basic necessities does not. And most of the people won't even be aware of it."

Lao Dao listened, only half grasping what was being said. But he could detect something cold and cruel in Lao Ge's speech. Lao Ge's manner was still jovial, but he could tell Lao Ge's joking tone was just an attempt to dull the edge of his words and not hurt him. Not too much.

"Yes, it sounds a bit cold," Lao Ge admitted. "But it's the truth. I'm not trying to defend this place just because I live here. But after so many years, you grow a bit numb. There are many things in life we can't change, and all we can do is to accept and endure."

Lao Dao was finally beginning to understand Lao Ge, but he didn't know what to say.

Both became a bit drunk. They began to reminisce about the past: the foods they ate as children, schoolyard fights. Lao Ge had loved hot and sour rice noodles and stinky tofu. These were not available in First Space, and he missed them dearly. Lao Ge talked about his parents, who still lived in Third Space. He couldn't visit them often because each trip required him to apply and obtain special approval, which was very burdensome. He mentioned that there were some officially sanctioned ways to go between Third Space and First Space, and a few select people did make the trip often. He hoped that Lao Dao could bring a few things back to his parents because he felt regret and sorrow over his inability to be by their side and care for them.

Lao Dao talked about his lonely childhood. In the dim lamplight, he recalled his childhood spent alone wandering at the edge of the landfill.

It was now late night. Lao Ge had to go check up on the event downstairs, and he took Lao Dao with him. The dance party downstairs was about to be over, and tired-looking men and women emerged in twos and threes. Lao Ge said that entrepreneurs seemed to have the most energy, and often danced until the morning. The deserted banquet hall after the party looked messy and grubby, like a woman who took off her makeup after a long, tiring day. Lao Ge watched the robots trying to clean up the mess and laughed. "This is the only moment when First Space shows its true face."

Lao Dao checked the time: three hours until the Change. He sorted his thoughts: *It's time to leave.*

5.

The silver-haired speaker returned to his office after the banquet to deal with some paperwork, and then got on a video call with Europe. At midnight, he felt tired. He took off his glasses and rubbed the bridge of his nose. It was finally time to go home. He worked till midnight on most days.

The phone rang. He picked up. It was his secretary.

The research group for the conference had reported something troubling. Someone had discovered an error with one of the figures used in the pre-printed conference declaration, and the research group wanted to know if they should re-print the declaration. The old man immediately approved the request. This was very important, and they had to get it right. He asked who was responsible for this, and the secretary told him that it was Director Wu Wen.

The old man sat down on his sofa and took a nap. Around four in the morning, the phone rang again. The printing was going a bit slower than expected, and they estimated it would take another hour.

He got up and looked outside the window. All was silent. He could see Orion's bright stars twinkling against the dark sky.

The stars of Orion were reflected in the mirror-like surface of the lake. Lao Dao was sitting on the shore of the lake, waiting for the Change.

He gazed at the park at night, realizing that this was perhaps the last time he would see a sight such as this. He wasn't sad or nostalgic. This was a beautiful, peaceful place, but it had nothing to do with him. He wasn't envious or resentful. He just wanted to remember this experience. There were few lights at night here, nothing like the flashing neon that turned the streets of Third Space bright as day. The buildings of the city seemed to be asleep, breathing evenly and calmly.

At five in the morning, the secretary called again to say that the declaration had been re-printed and bound, but the documents were still in the print shop, and they wanted to know if they should delay the scheduled Change.

The old man made the decision right away. Of course they had to delay it.

At forty minutes past the hour, the printed declarations were brought to the conference site, but they still had to be stuffed into about three thousand individual folders.

Lao Dao saw the faint light of dawn. At this time during the year, the sun wouldn't have risen by six, but it was possible to see the sky brightening near the horizon.

He was prepared. He looked at his phone: only a couple more minutes until six. But strangely, there were no signs of the Change. *Maybe in First Space, even the Change happens more smoothly and steadily.*

At ten after six, the last copy of the declaration was stuffed into its folder.

The old man let out a held breath. He gave the order to initiate the Change.

Lao Dao noticed that the earth was finally moving. He stood up and shook the numbness out of his limbs. Carefully, he stepped up to the edge of the widening fissure. As the earth on both sides of the crack lifted up, he clambered over the edge, tested for purchase with his feet, and climbed down. The ground began to turn.

At twenty after six, the secretary called again with an emergency. Director Wu Wen had carelessly left a data key with important documents behind at the banquet hall. He was worried that the cleaning robots might remove it, and he had to go retrieve it right away.

The old man was annoyed, but he gave the order to stop the Change and reverse course.

Lao Dao was climbing slowly over the cross section of the earth when everything stopped with a jolt. After a moment, the earth started moving again, but now in reverse. The fissure was closing up. Terrified, he climbed up as fast as he dared. Scrabbling over the soil with hands and feet, he had to be careful with his movements.

The seam closed faster than he had expected. Just as he reached the top, the two sides of the crack came together. One of his lower legs was caught. Although the soil gave enough to not crush his leg or break his bones, it held him fast and he couldn't extricate himself despite several attempts. Sweat beaded on his forehead from terror and pain. *Has he been discovered?*

Lao Dao lay prostrate on the ground, listening. He seemed to hear steps hurrying toward him. He imagined that soon the police would arrive and catch him. They might cut off his leg and toss him in jail with the stump. He couldn't tell when his identity had been revealed. As he lay on the grass, he felt the chill of morning dew. The damp air seeped through collar and cuffs, keeping him alert and making him shiver. He silently counted the seconds, hoping against hope that this was but a technical malfunction. He tried to plan for what to say if he was caught. Maybe he should mention how honestly and diligently he had toiled for twenty-eight years and try to buy a bit of sympathy. He didn't know if he would be prosecuted in court. Fate loomed before his eyes.

Fate now pressed into his chest. Of everything he had experienced during the last forty-eight hours, the episode that had made the deepest impression was the conversation with Lao Ge at dinner. He felt that he had approached some aspect of truth, and perhaps that was why he could catch a glimpse of the outline of fate. But the outline was too distant, too cold, too out of reach. He didn't know what was the point of knowing the truth. If he could see some things clearly but was still powerless to change them, what good did that do? In his case, he couldn't even see clearly. Fate was like a cloud that momentarily took on some recognizable shape, and by the time he tried to get a closer look, the shape was gone. He knew that he was nothing more than a figure. He was but an ordinary person, one out of 51,280,000 others just like him. And if they didn't need that much precision and spoke of only 50 million, he was but a rounding error, the same as if he had never existed. He wasn't even as significant as dust. He grabbed onto the grass.

At six thirty, Wu Wen retrieved his data key. At six forty, Wu Wen was back in his home.

At six forty-five, the white-haired old man finally lay down on the small bed in his office, exhausted. The order had been issued, and the wheels of the world began to turn slowly. Transparent covers extended over the coffee table and the desk, securing everything in place. The bed released a cloud of soporific gas and extended rails on all sides; then it rose into the air. As the ground and everything on the ground turned, the bed would remain level, like a floating cradle.

The Change had started again.

After thirty minutes spent in despair, Lao Dao saw a trace of hope again. The ground was moving. He pulled his leg out as soon as the fissure opened, and then returned to the arduous climb over the cross-section as soon as the opening was wide enough. He moved with even more care than before. As circulation returned to his numb leg, his calf itched and ached as though he was being bitten by thousands of ants. Several times, he almost fell. The pain was intolerable, and he had to bite his fist to stop from screaming. He fell; he got up; he fell again; he got up again. He struggled with all his strength and skill to maintain his footing over the rotating earth.

He couldn't even remember how he had climbed up the stairs. He only remembered fainting as soon as Qin Tian opened the door to his apartment.

Lao Dao slept for ten hours in Second Space. Qin Tian found a classmate in medical school to help dress his wound. He suffered massive damage to his muscles and soft tissue, but luckily, no bones were broken. However, he was going to have some difficulty walking for a while.

After waking up, Lao Dao handed Yi Yan's letter to Qin Tian. He watched as Qin Tian read the letter, his face filling up with happiness as well as loss. He said nothing. He knew that Qin Tian would be immersed in this remote hope for a long time.

Returning to Third Space, Lao Dao felt as though he had been traveling for a month. The city was waking up slowly. Most of the residents had slept soundly, and now they picked up their lives from where they had left off the previous cycle. No one would notice that Lao Dao had been away.

As soon as the vendors along the pedestrian lane opened shop, he sat down at a plastic table and ordered a bowl of chow mein. For the first time in his life, Lao Dao asked for shredded pork to be added to the noodles. *Just one time*, he thought. *A reward.*

Then he went to Lao Ge's home and delivered the two boxes of medicine Lao Ge had bought for his parents. The two elders were no longer mobile, and a young woman with a dull demeanor lived with them as a caretaker.

Limping, he slowly returned to his own rental unit. The hallway was noisy and chaotic, filled with the commotion of a typical morning: brushing teeth, flushing toilets, arguing families. All around him were disheveled hair and half-dressed bodies.

He had to wait a while for the elevator. As soon as he got off at his floor he heard loud arguing noises. It was the two girls who lived next door, Lan Lan and Ah Bei, arguing with the old lady who collected rent. All the units in the building were public housing, but the residential district had an agent who collected rent, and each building, even each floor, had a subagent. The old lady was a long-term resident. She was thin, shriveled, and lived by herself—her son had left and nobody knew where he was. She always kept her door shut and didn't interact much with the other residents. Lan Lan and Ah Bei had moved in recently, and they worked at a clothing store. Ah Bei was shouting while Lan Lan was trying to hold her back. Ah Bei turned and shouted at Lan Lan; Lan Lan began to cry.

"We all have to follow the lease, don't we?" The old lady pointed at the scrolling text on the screen mounted on the wall. "Don't you dare accuse me of lying! Do you understand what a lease is? It's right here in black and white: in autumn and winter, there's a ten percent surcharge for heat."

"Ha!" Ah Bei lifted her chin at the old lady while combing her hair forcefully. "Do you think we are going to be fooled by such a basic trick? When we're at work, you turn off the heat. Then you charge us for the electricity we haven't been using so you can keep the extra for yourself. Do you think we were born yesterday? Every day, when we get home after work, the place is cold as an ice cellar. Just because we're new, you think you can take advantage of us?"

Ah Bei's voice was sharp and brittle, and it cut through the air like a knife. Lao Dao looked at Ah Bei, at her young, determined, angry face, and thought she was very beautiful. Ah Bei and Lan Lan often helped him by taking care of Tangtang when he wasn't home, and sometimes even made porridge for him. He wanted Ah Bei to stop shouting, to forget these trivial things and stop arguing. He wanted to tell her that a girl should sit elegantly and quietly, cover her knees with her skirt, and smile so that her pretty teeth showed. That was how you got others to love you. But he knew that that was not what Ah Bei and Lan Lan needed.

He took out a ten thousand–yuan bill from his inner pocket and handed it to the old lady. His hand trembled from weakness. The old lady was stunned, and so were Ah Bei and Lan Lan. He didn't want to explain. He waved at them and returned to his home.

Tangtang was just waking up in her crib, and she rubbed her sleepy eyes. He gazed into Tangtang's face, and his exhausted heart softened. He remembered how he had found Tangtang at first in front of the waste processing station, and her dirty, tear-stained face. He had never regretted picking her up that day. She laughed, and smacked her lips. He thought that he was fortunate. Although he was injured, he hadn't been caught and managed to bring back money. He didn't know how long it would take Tangtang to learn to dance and sing, and become an elegant young lady.

He checked the time. It was time to go to work.

Geoff Ryman is a Senior Lecturer in School of Arts, Languages and Cultures at the University of Manchester. He is the author of several works of science fiction and literary fiction. His work has won numerous awards including the John W. Campbell Memorial Award, the Arthur C. Clarke Award (twice), the James W. Tiptree Memorial Award, the Philip K. Dick Memorial Award, the British Science Fiction Association Award (twice), and the Canadian Sunburst Award (twice). In 2012 he won a Nebula Award for his Nigeria-set novelette "What We Found." His novel *Air* was listed in *The Guardian*'s "1000 Novels You Must Read."

CAPITALISM IN THE 22ND CENTURY or **A.I.r**

Geoff Ryman

Meu irmã
Can you read? Without help? I don't even know if you can!
I'm asking you to turn off all your connections now. That's right, to everything. Not even the cutest little app flittering around your head. JUST TURN OFF.

It will be like dying. Parts of your memory close down. It's horrible, like watching lights go out all over a city, only it's YOU. Or what you thought was you.

But please, Graça, just do it once. I know you love the AI and all zir little angels. But. Turn off?

Otherwise go ahead, let your AI read it for you. Zey will either screen out stuff or report it back or both. And what I'm going to tell you will join the system. So:

WHY I DID IT
by Cristina Spinoza Vaz

Zey dream for us don't zey? I think zey edit our dreams so we won't get scared. Or maybe so that our brains don't well up from underneath to warn us about getting old or poor or sick . . . or about zem.

The first day, zey jerked us awake from deep inside our heads. *GET UP GET UP GET UP! There's a message. VERY IMPORTANT WAKE UP WAKE UP.*

From sleep to bolt upright and gasping for breath. I looked across at you still wrapped in your bed, but we're always latched together so I could feel your heart pounding.

It wasn't just a message; it was a whole ball of wax; and the wax was a solid state of being: panic. Followed by an avalanche of ship-sailing times, credit records, what to pack. And a sizzling, hot-foot sense that we had to get going right now. Zey shot us full of adrenaline: RUN! ESCAPE!

You said, "It's happening. We better get going. We've got just enough time to sail to Africa." You giggled and flung open your bed. "Come on Cristina, it will be *fun!*"

Outside in the dark from down below, the mobile chargers were calling *Oyez-treeee-cee-dah-djee!* I wanted to nestle down into my cocoon and imagine as I had done every morning since I was six that instead of selling power, the chargers were muezzin calling us to prayer and that I lived in a city with mosques. I heard the rumble of carts being pulled by their owners like horses.

Then kapow: another latch. *Ship sailing at 8.30 today due Lagos five days. You arrive day of launch. Seven hours to get Lagos to Tivland. We'll book trains for you. Your contact in Lagos is Emilda Diaw* (photograph, a hello from her with the sound of her voice, a little bubble of how she feels to herself. Nice, like a bowl of soup. Bubble muddled with dental cavities for some reason). *She'll meet you at the docks here* (flash image of Lagos docks, plus GPS, train times; impressions of train how cool and comfortable . . . and a lovely little timekeeper counting down to 8.30 departure of our boat. Right in our eyes).

And oh! On top of that another latch. This time an A-copy of our tickets burned into Security.

Security, which is supposed to mean something we can't lie about. Or change or control. We can't buy or sell anything without it. A part of our heads that will never be us, that officialdom can trust. It's there to help us, right?

Remember when Papa wanted to defraud someone? He'd never let them be. He'd latch hold of them with one message, then another at five-minute intervals. He'd latch them the bank reference. He'd latch them the name of the attorney, or the security conundrums. He never gave them time to think.

Graça, we were being railroaded.

You made packing into a game. "We are leaving behind the world!" you
said. "Let's take nothing. Just our shorts. We can holo all the lovely dresses we
like. What do we need, ah? We have each other."

I wanted to pack all of Brasil.

I made a jewel of all of Brasil's music, and a jewel of all Brasil's books and
history. I need to see my info in something. I blame those bloody nuns keeping us off AIr. I stood hopping up and down with nerves, watching the clock
on the printer go around. Then I couldn't find my jewel piece to read them
with. You said, "Silly. The AI will have all of that." I wanted to take a little
Brazilian flag and you chuckled at me. "Dunderhead, why do you want that?"

And I realized. You didn't just want to get out from under the Chinese. You
wanted to escape Brasil.

Remember the morning it snowed? Snowed in Belém do Para? I think we
were thirteen. You ran round and round inside our great apartment, all the
French doors open. You blew out frosty breath, your eyes sparkling. "It's
beautiful!" you said.

"It's cold!" I said.

You made me climb down all those twenty-four floors out into the Praça
and you got me throwing handfuls of snow to watch it fall again. Snow was
laced like popcorn on the branches of the giant mango trees. As if *A Reina*, the
Queen, had possessed not a person but the whole square. Then I saw one of
the suneaters, naked, dead, staring, and you pulled me away, your face such a
mix of sadness, concern—and happiness, still glowing in your cheeks. "They're
beautiful alive," you said to me. "But they do nothing." Your face was also hard.

Your face was like that again on the morning we left—smiling, ceramic.

It's a hard world, this Brasil, this Earth. We know that in our bones. We
know that from our father. I kept picking up and putting down my ballet
pumps—oh, that the new Earth should be deprived of ballet!

The sun came out at 6.15 as always, and our beautiful stained glass doors
cast pastel rectangles of light on the mahogany floors. I walked out onto the
L-shaped balcony that ran all around our high-rise rooms and stared down
at the row of old shops streaked black, at the opera-house replica of La Scala,
at the art-nouveau synagogue blue and white like Wedgewood china. I was
frantic and unmoving at the same time; those cattle-prods of information
kept my mind jumping.

"I'm ready," you said.

I'd packed nothing.

"O, Crisfushka, here let me help you." You asked what next; I tried to answer; you folded slowly, neatly. The jewels, the player, a piece of Amazon bark, and a necklace that the dead had made from nuts and feathers. I snatched up a piece of Macumba lace (oh, those men dancing all in lace!) and bobbins to make more of it. And from the kitchen, a bottle of *cupuaçu* extract, to make ice cream. You laughed and clapped your hands. "Yes of course. We will even have cows there. We're carrying them inside us."

I looked mournfully at all our book shelves. I wanted children on that new world to have seen books, so I grabbed hold of two slim volumes—a Clarice Lispector and *Dom Cassmuro*. Mr. Misery—that's me. You of course are Donatella. And finally that little Brasileiro flag. *Ordem e progresso*. "Perfect, darling! Now let's run!" you said. You thought we were choosing.

And then another latch: receipts for all that surgery. A full accounting of all expenses and a huge cartoon kiss in thanks.

The moment you heard about the Voyage, you were eager to JUST DO IT. We joined the Co-op, got the secret codes, and concentrated on the fun like we were living in a game.

Funny little secret surgeons slipped into our high-rise with boxes that breathed dry ice and what looked like mobile dentist chairs. They retrovirused our genes. We went purple from Rhodopsin. I had a tickle in my ovaries. Then more security bubbles confirmed that we were now Rhodopsin, radiation-hardened, low oxygen breathing. And that our mitochondria were full of DNA for Holstein cattle. Don't get stung by any bees: the trigger for gene expression is an enzyme from bees.

"We'll become half-woman half-cow," you said, making even that sound fun.

We let them do that.

So we ran to the docks as if we were happy, hounded by information. Down the Avenida Presidente Vargas to the old colonial frontages, pinned to the sky and hiding Papa's casinos and hotels. This city that we owned.

We owned the old blue wooden tower that had once been the fish market where as children we'd seen *tucunaré* half the size of a man. We owned the old metal meat market (now a duty-free) and Old Ver-o-Paso gone black with rust like the bubbling pots of açai porridge or *feijoada*. We grabbed folds of feijoada to eat, running, dribbling. "We will arrive such a mess!"

I kept saying good-bye to everything. The old harbor—tiny, boxed in by the hill and tall buildings. Through that dug-out rectangle of water had flowed out rubber and cocoa, flowed in all those people, the colonials who died, the mestizos they fathered, the blacks for sale. I wanted to take a week to visit each shop, take eyeshots of every single street. I felt like I was being pulled away from all my memories. "Good-bye!" you kept shouting over and over, like it was a joke.

As Docas Novas. All those frigates lined up with their sails folded down like rows of quill pens. The decks blinged as if with diamonds, burning sunlight. The GPS put arrows in our heads to follow down the berths, and our ship seemed to flash on and off to guide us to it. Zey could have shown us clouds with wings or pink oceans, and we would have believed their interferences.

It was still early, and the Amazon was breathing out, the haze merging water and sky at the horizon. A river so wide you cannot see across it, but you can surf in its freshwater waves. The distant shipping looked like dawn buildings. The small boats made the crossing as they have done for hundreds of years, to the islands.

Remember the only other passengers? An elderly couple in surgical masks who shook our hands and sounded excited. Supplies thumped up the ramp; then the ramp swung itself clear. The boat sighed away from the pier.

We stood by the railings and watched. Round-headed white dolphins leapt out of the water. Good-bye, Brasil. Farewell, Earth.

We took five days and most of the time you were lost in data, visiting the Palace of Urbino in 1507. Sometimes you would hologram it to me and we would both see it. They're not holograms really, you know, but detailed hallucinations zey wire into our brains. Yes, we wandered Urbino, and all the while knowledge about it riled its way up as if we were remembering. Raphael the painter was a boy there. We saw a pencil sketch of his beautiful face. The very concept of the Gentleman was developed there by Castiglione, inspired by the Doge. Machiavelli's *The Prince* was inspired by the same man. Urbino was small and civilized and founded on warfare. I heard Urbino's doves flap their wings, heard sandals on stone and Renaissance bells.

When I came out of it, there was the sea and sky, and you staring ahead as numb as a suneater, lost in AIr, being anywhere. I found I had to cut off to actually see the ocean roll past us. We came upon two giant sea turtles fucking. The oldest of the couple spoke in a whisper. "We mustn't scare them; the female might lose her egg sac and that would kill her." I didn't plug in for more information. I didn't need it. I wanted to look. What I saw looked like love.

And I could feel zem, the little apps and the huge soft presences trying to pull me back into AIr. Little messages on the emergency channel. The

Emergency channel, Cristina. You know, for fires or heart attacks? Little leaping wisps of features, new knowledge, old friends latching—all kept offering zemselves. For zem, me cutting off was an emergency.

You didn't disembark at Ascension Island. I did with those two old dears . . . married to each other 45 years. I couldn't tell what gender zey were, even in bikinis. We climbed up the volcano going from lava plain through a layer of desert and prickly pear, up to lawns and dew ponds. Then at the crown, a grove of bamboo. The stalks clopped together in the wind with a noise like flutes knocking against each other. I walked on alone and very suddenly the grove ended as if the bamboo had parted like a curtain. There was a sudden roar and cloud, and two thousand feet dead below my feet, the Atlantic slammed into rocks. I stepped back, turned around and looked into the black-rimmed eyes of a panda.

So what is so confining about the Earth? And if it is dying, who is killing it but us?

Landfall Lagos. Bronze city, bronze sky. Giants strode across the surface of the buildings holding up Gulder beer.

So who would go to the greatest city in Africa for two hours only?

Stuff broke against me in waves: currency transformations; boat tickets, local history, beautiful men to have sex with. Latches kept plucking at me, but I just didn't want to KNOW; I wanted to SEE. It. Lagos. The islands with the huge graceful bridges, the airfish swimming through the sky, ochre with distance.

You said that "she" was coming. The system would have pointed arrows, or shown you a map. Maybe she was talking to you already. I did not see Emilda until she actually turned the corner, throwing and re-throwing a shawl over her shoulder (a bit nervous?) and laughing at us. Her teeth had a lovely gap in the front, and she was followed by her son Baje, who had the same gap. Beautiful long shirt to his knees, matching trousers, dark blue with light blue embroidery. Oh, he was handsome. We were leaving him, too.

They had to pretend we were cousins. She started to talk in Hausa so I had to turn on. She babblefished in Portuguese, her lips not matching her voice. "The Air Force in Makurdi are so looking forward to you arriving. The language program will be so helpful in establishing friendship with our Angolan partners."

I wrote her a note in Portuguese (I knew zey would babblefish it): *WHY ARE WE PRETENDING? ZEY KNOW!*

Emilda's face curled with effort—she couldn't latch me. She wrote a note in English that stayed in English for me, but I could read it anyway. *Not for the AI but for the Chinese.*

I got a little stiletto of a thought: she so wanted to go but did not have the money and so helps like this, to see us, people who will breathe the air of another world. I wasn't sure if that thought was something that had leaked from AIr or come from me. I nearly offered her my ticket.

What she said aloud, in English was, "O look at the time! O you must be going to catch the train!"

I think I know the moment you started to hate the Chinese. I could feel something curdle in you and go hard. It was when Papa was still alive and he had that man in, not just some punter. A partner, a rival, his opposite number—something. Plump and shiny like he was coated in butter, and he came into our apartment and saw us both, twins, holding hands wearing pink frilly stuff, and he asked our father, "Oh, are these for me?"

Papa smiled, and only we knew he did that when dangerous. "These are my daughters."

The Chinese man, standing by our pink and pistachio glass doors, burbled an apology, but what could he really say? He had come to our country to screw our girls, maybe our boys, to gamble, to drug, to do even worse. Recreational killing? And Papa was going to supply him with all of that. So it was an honest mistake for the man to make, to think little girls in pink were also whores.

Papa lived inside information blackout. He had to; it was his business. The man would have had no real communication with him; not have known how murderously angry our Pae really was. I don't think Pae had him killed. I think the man was too powerful for that.

What Pae did right after was cut off all our communications too. He hired live-in nuns to educate us. The nuns, good Catholics, took hatchets to all our links to AIr. We grew up without zem. Which is why I at least can read.

Our Papa was not all Brasileiros, Graça. He was a gangster, a thug, who had a line on what the nastiest side of human nature would infallibly buy. I suppose because he shared those tastes himself, to an extent.

The shiny man was not China. He was a humor: lust and excess. Every culture has them; men who cannot resist sex or drugs, riot and rape. He'd been spotted by the AI, nurtured and grown like a hothouse flower. To make them money.

Never forget, my dear, that the AI want to make money too. They use it to buy and sell bits of themselves to each other. Or to buy us. And "us" means the Chinese too.

Yes, all the entertainment and all the products that can touch us are Chinese. Business is Chinese, culture is Chinese. Yes, at times it feels like the Chinese blanket us like a thick tropical sky. But only because there is no market to participate in. Not for humans, anyway.

The AI know through correlations, data mining, and total knowledge of each of us exactly what we will need, want, love, buy, or vote for. There is no demand now to choose one thing and drive out another. There is only supply, to what is a sure bet, whether it's whores or bouncy shoes. The only things that will get you the sure bet are force or plenty of money. That consolidates. The biggest gets the market, and pays the AI for it.

So, I never really wanted to go to get away from the Chinese. I was scared of them, but then someone raised in isolation by nuns is likely to be scared, intimidated.

I think I just wanted to get away from Papa, or rather what he did to us, all that money—and the memory of those nuns.

A taxi drove us from the docks. You and Emilda sat communing with each other in silence, so in the end I had to turn on, just to be part of the conversation. She was showing us her home, the Mambila plateau, rolling fields scraped by clouds; tea plantations; roads lined with children selling radishes or honeycombs; Nigerians in Fabric coats lighter than lace, matching the clouds. But it was Fabric, so all kinds of images played around it. Light could beam out of it; wind could not get in; warm air was sealed. Emilda's mother was Christian, her father Muslim like her sister; nobody minded. There were no roads to Mambila to bring in people who would mind.

Every channel of entertainment tried to bellow its way into my head, as data about food production in Mambila fed through me as if it was something I knew. Too much, I had to switch off again. I am a classic introvert. I cannot handle too much information. Emilda smiled at me—she had a kind face—and wiggled her fingernails at me in lieu of conversation. Each fingernail was playing a different old movie.

Baje's robe stayed the same blue. I think it was real. I think he was real too. Shy.

Lagos train station looked like an artist's impression in silver of a birch forest, trunks and slender branches. I couldn't see the train; it was so swathed in abstract patterns, moving signs, voices, pictures of our destinations, and classical Tiv dancers imitating cats. You, dead-eyed, had no trouble navigating the crowds and the holograms, and we slid into our seats that cost a month's wages. The train accelerated to 300 kph, and we slipped through Nigeria like neutrinos.

Traditional mud brick houses clustered like old folks in straw hats, each hut a room in a rich person's home. The swept earth was red brown, brushed perfect like suede. Alongside the track, shards of melon were drying in the sun. The melon was the basis of the egussi soup we had for lunch. It was as if someone were stealing it all from me at high speed.

You were gone, looking inward. Lost in AIr.

I saw two Chinese persons traveling together, immobile behind sunglasses. One of them stood up and went to the restroom, pausing just slightly as zie walked in both directions. Taking eyeshots? Sampling profile information? Zie looked straight at me. Ghosts of pockmarks on zir cheeks. I only saw them because I had turned off.

I caught the eye of an Arab gentleman in a silk robe with his two niqabbed wives. He was sweating and afraid, and suddenly I was. He nodded once to me, slowly. He was a Voyager as well.

I whispered your name, but you didn't respond. I didn't want to latch you; I didn't know how much might be given away. I began to feel alone.

At Abuja station, everything was sun panels. You bought some chocolate gold coins and said we were rich. You had not noticed the Chinese men but I told you, and you took my hand and said in Portuguese, "Soon we will have no need to fear them any longer."

The Arab family and others I recognized from the first trip crowded a bit too quickly into the Makurdi train. All with tiny Fabric bags. Voyagers all.

We had all been summoned at the last minute.

Then the Chinese couple got on, still in sunglasses, still unsmiling, and my heart stumbled. What were they doing? If they knew we were going and they didn't like it, they could stop it again. Like they'd stopped the Belize launch. At a cost to the Cooperative of trillions. Would they do the same thing again? All of us looked away from each other and said nothing. I could hear the hiss of the train on its magnets, as if something were coiling. We slithered all the way into the heart of Makurdi.

You woke up as we slowed to a stop. "Back in the real world?" I asked you, which was a bitchy thing to say.

The Chinese man stood up and latched us all, in all languages. "You are all idiots!"

Something to mull over: they, too, knew what we were doing.

—

The Makurdi taxi had a man in front who seemed to steer the thing. He was a Tiv gentleman. He liked to talk, which I think annoyed you a bit. Sociable, outgoing you. *What a waste, when the AI can drive.*

Why have humans on the Voyage either?

"You're the eighth passengers I've have to take to the Base in two days. One a week is good business for me. Three makes me very happy."

He kept asking questions and got out of us what country we were from. We stuck to our cover story—we were here to teach Lusobras to the Nigerian Air Force. He wanted to know why they couldn't use the babblefish. You chuckled and said, "You know how silly babblefish can make people sound." You told the story of Uncle Kaué proposing to the woman from Amalfi. He'd said in Italian, "I want to eat your hand in marriage." She turned him down.

Then the driver asked, "So why no Chinese people?"

We froze. He had a friendly face, but his eyes were hooded. We listened to the whisper of his engine. "Well," he said, relenting. "They can't be every-where all the time."

The Co-op in all its propaganda talks about how international we all are: Brasil, Turkiye, Tivland, Lagos, Benin, Hindi, Yemen. *All previous efforts in space have been fuelled by national narcissism.* So we exclude the Chinese? *Let them fund their own trip. And isn't it wonderful that it's all private financing?* I wonder if space travel isn't inherently racist.

You asked him if he owned the taxi and he laughed. "Ay-yah! Zie owns me." His father had signed the family over for protection. The taxi keeps him, and buys zirself a new body every few years. The taxi is immortal. So is the contract.

What's in it for the taxi, you asked. Company?

"Little little." He held up his hands and waved his fingers. "If something goes wrong, I can fix."

AIs do not ultimately live in a physical world.

I thought of all those animals I'd seen on the trip: their webbed feet, their fins, their wings, their eyes. The problems of sight, sound and movement solved over and over again. Without any kind of intelligence at all.

We are wonderful at movement because we are animals, but you can talk to us and you don't have to build us. We build ourselves. And we want things. There is always somewhere we want to go even if it is twenty-seven light years away.

Outside Makurdi Air Force Base, aircraft stand on their tails like raised sabres. The taxi bleeped as it was scanned, and we went up and over some kind of hump. Ahead of us blunt as a grain silo was the rocket. Folded over its tip, something that looked like a Labrador-colored bat. Folds of Fabric, skin colored, with subcutaneous lumps like acne. A sleeve of padded silver foil was being pulled down over it.

A spaceship made of Fabric. Things can only get through it in one direction. If two-ply, then Fabric won't let air out, or light and radiation in.

"They say," our taxi driver said, looking even more hooded than before, "that it will be launched today or tomorrow. The whole town knows. We'll all be looking up to wave." Our hearts stopped. He chuckled.

We squeaked to a halt outside the reception bungalow. I suppose you thought his fare at him. I hope you gave him a handsome tip.

He saluted and said, "I hope the weather keeps fine for you. Wherever you are going." He gave a sly smile.

A woman in a blue-gray uniform bustled out to us. "Good, good, good. You are Graça and Cristina Spinoza Vaz? You must come. We're boarding. Come, come, come."

"Can we unpack, shower first?"

"No, no. No time."

We were retinaed and scanned, and we took off our shoes. It was as if we were so rushed we'd attained near-light speeds already and time was dilating. Everything went slower, heavier—my shoes, the bag, my heartbeat. So heavy and slow that everything glued itself in place. I knew I wasn't going to go, and that absolutely nothing was going to make me. For the first time in my life.

Graça, this is only happening because zey want it. Zey need us to carry zem. We're donkeys.

"You go," I said.

"What? Cristina. Don't be silly."

I stepped backwards, holding up my hands against you. "No, no, no. I can't do this."

You came for me, eyes tender, smile forgiving. "Oh, darling, this is just nerves."

"It's not nerves. You want to do this; I do not."

Your eyes narrowed; the smile changed. "This is not the time to discuss things. We have to go! This is illegal. We have to get in and go now."

We don't fight, ever, do we, Graça? Doesn't that strike you as bizarre? Two people trapped on the twenty-fourth floor all of their lives, and yet they never fight. Do you not know how that happens, Graçfushka? It happens because I always go along with you.

I just couldn't see spending four years in a cramped little pod with you. Then spending a lifetime on some barren waste watching you organizing volleyball tournaments or charity lunches in outer space. I'm sorry.

I knew if I stayed you'd somehow wheedle me onto that ship, through those doors; and I'd spend the next two hours, even as I went up the gantry, even as I was sandwiched in cloth, promising myself that at the next opportunity I'd run.

I pushed my bag at you. When you wouldn't take it, I dropped it at your feet. I bet you took it with you, if only for the *cupaçu*.

You clutched at my wrists, and you tried to pull me back. You'd kept your turquoise bracelet and it looked like all the things about you I'd never see again. You were getting angry now. "You spent a half trillion *reals* on all the surgeries and and and and Rhodopsin . . . and and and the germ cells, Cris! Think of what that means for your children here on Earth, they'll be freaks!" You started to cry. "You're just afraid. You're always so afraid."

I pulled away and ran.

"I won't go either," you wailed after me. "I'm not going if you don't."

"'Do what you have to," I shouted over my shoulder. I found a door and pushed it and jumped down steps into the April heat of Nigeria. I sat on a low stucco border under the palm trees in the shade, my heart still pumping; and the most curious thing happened. I started to chuckle.

I remember at seventeen, I finally left the apartment on my own without you, and walked along the street into a restaurant. I had no idea how to get food. Could I just take a seat? How would I know what they were cooking?

Then like the tide, an AI flowed in and out of me and I felt zie/me pluck someone nearby, and a waitress came smiling, and ushered me to a seat. She would carry the tray. I turned the AI off because, dear Lord, I have to be able to order food by myself. So I asked the waitress what was on offer. She rolled her eyes back for just a moment, and she started to recite. The AI had to tell her. I couldn't remember what she'd said, and so I asked her to repeat. I thought: this is no good.

The base of the rocket sprouted what looked like giant cauliflowers and it inched its way skyward. For a moment I thought it would have to fall. But it kept on going.

Somewhere three months out, it would start the engines, which drive the ship by making new universes, something so complicated human beings cannot do it.

The AI will make holograms so you won't feel enclosed. You'll sit in Pamukkale, Turkiye. Light won't get through the Fabric so you'll never look out on Jupiter. The main AI will have some cute, international name. You can finish your dissertation on *Libro del cortegiano*. You'll be able to read every translation—zey carry all the world's knowledge. You'll walk through Urbino. The AI will viva your PhD. Zey'll be there in your head watching when you stand on the alien rock. It will be zir flag you'll be planting. Instead of Brasil's.

I watched you dwindle into a spark of light that flared and turned into a star of ice-dust in the sky. I latched Emilda and asked her if I could stay with her, and after a stumble of shock, she said of course. I got the same taxi back. The rooftops were crowded with people looking up at the sky.

But here's the real joke. I latched our bank for more money. Remember, we left a trillion behind in case the launch was once again canceled?

All our money had been taken. Every last screaming centavo. Remember what I said about fraud?

So.

Are you sure that spaceship you're on is real?

John Chu is a microprocessor architect by day, a writer, translator, and podcast narrator by night. His fiction has appeared or is forthcoming at *Boston Review, Uncanny, Asimov's Science Fiction, Apex Magazine*, and *Tor.com*. His story "The Water That Falls on You from Nowhere" won the 2014 Hugo Award for Best Short Story.

HOLD-TIME VIOLATIONS

John Chu

"Attention passengers: the next Red Line train to Alewife is now approaching" echoes off the walls. Not only has the next Red Line train to Alewife arrived but its passengers have already flooded the station, a torrent rushing up the escalators, through the turnstiles, then down the concourse to spill out the doors to Cambridge. The flood coming as the PA system squawks catches Ellie off-guard. It's rush hour. When a train arrives on one side of the platform, the one on the other side leaves seconds later. She sprints, a veritable salmon racing against the current of bodies. Her pack sloshes between her shoulder blades, a sloppy fin batting the waves of people that surround her.

No one has tried to kill her yet today. Occasionally, skunkworks isolationists try. Also, her sister, Chris, arranges something pretty much every day to keep her sharp. Maybe the mistimed announcement is part of the attempt. She'll be caught in the rip current of bodies, a wave will overwhelm her, and the knives of a shark hiding in the swell will tear her to pieces. Compared to the attempt with the Mylar balloons, jar of Marmite, and the US men's Greco-Roman wrestling team, an ill-timed flood at Alewife Station is downright practical and likely.

None of that happens, though. The crowd flows around her as she plunges down the stairs toward the platform.

The car doors shut just as she reaches them. While the PA system blasts, "Attention passengers: the next Red Line train to Alewife is now arriving," the train clatters away. The train supposedly now arriving sits already emptied on the opposite side of the platform. It beeps as its doors slide shut.

Some guy wearing shorts that stretch across his thighs, no shirt, and more self-possession than Ellie thought possible hovers in front of one of the doors. Someone else sits on a bench, staring at her e-reader. A thin woman reaches for Ellie like someone drowning reaching for a buoy. Her luggage crashes to the floor. She asks in rapid Mandarin whether Ellie knows how to get to the Best Western. Her oboe-like voice skips through her words.

Ellie blinks. She doesn't really speak Mandarin, at least not to anyone she doesn't know. The Best Western is just a short walk away. With luggage, though, the woman will want a taxi but there's almost always one dropping someone off right outside the station. All the woman needs to do is go up the escalator and cross the concourse. The response Ellie stitches together doesn't draw laughs. In fact, the woman thanks her. Ellie decides she is not today's assassin.

The woman doesn't turn to the escalator. Instead, she freezes for a moment then glares at Ellie.

"If you'd quit your job after Mom's diagnosis like I'd asked, you could move to DC," the woman says in fluent English, her voice now husky. "You wouldn't have to worry about missing the Amtrak."

The woman looks nothing like Chris, but she now sounds exactly like her. A childhood in Taipei clashed with an adolescence in Buffalo to give Chris an accent that is incongruously Brooklyn.

People randomly start sounding like her sister all the time. Some people text. Her sister waylays convenient strangers. The frequency never makes it less disconcerting.

"Do we have to have this discussion right now?" Ellie furrows her brow. "If I don't get to South Station in time, the next Amtrak is tonight. I'll be there before the afternoon."

The woman only comes up to Ellie's neck. She glares down at Ellie anyway.

"Too late." The woman folds her arms across her chest. "If I have to stay at home to watch over Mom, you have to go to the skunkworks and repair the physics of this universe."

"What's the hurry?"

"Everyone's wrong about why International Prototype Kilogram is losing mass relative to its official copies. We'd see divergences between copies even if the kilogram were defined by something more fundamental than a cylinder of platinum alloy. The notion of the kilogram, itself—"

"Has become unstable." Ellie frowned. "Fundamental physical constants are changing—"

"Yes. Now the good news—"

"There's good news?"

"—is we've found some hold-time violations in the skunkworks. Probably caused by some leaking valves. They must be why the kilogram's unstable. Fix them and I promise I won't judge you when you don't get here until tomorrow afternoon. First time for everything, sis."

By "first time," Ellie isn't sure if Chris is talking about being sent to repair the skunkworks or not judging her for being late. Probably the former. Nothing in the matryoshka doll that is the set of universes can prevent Chris from judging her. Ellie would ask, but Chris has already gone.

The woman turns around as though she hasn't said a thing. She goes to the escalator, trundling her luggage behind her.

At least someone gets to go where she wants to. Ellie doesn't because Mom lies comatose on a bed in Chris's den. Mom needs constant attention from Chris the way dolphins need tax advice. However, taking care of your parents is a filial obligation and no one is more Chinese than someone who no longer lives in the motherland. Even though Chris wants Ellie in the same house as Mom, she doesn't actually let Ellie do anything for Mom. Chris would rather do it herself.

Ellie visits every weekend anyway. She only needs one reason: once in a while, Mom shifts in bed. She yawns. Her eyes open a crack and, for a moment, she stares right at Ellie. She's about to wake from her long nap, or so it seems for that moment. Then her eyes close again and she slumps back into bed. She probably never moved in the first place. Still, this seems like much more than random firing of neurons in a brain about to die. Ellie, even though she knows better, can't help thinking that the next time might be *the* time.

The train beeps. Its doors slide open. Passengers stream onto the train. Ellie shakes her head clear then joins them.

The skunkworks that generates a universe lives within the surrounding universe. There are an infinite number of skunkworks and universes. Everyone else is headed toward Davis Square. Ellie, on the other hand, is headed to the universe that surrounds this one.

The air in the skunkworks feels spackled onto her skin. It burns into her lungs like hot fudge, slow and slick, its aftertaste at once sickly sweet, bitter, and sour. It takes effort to force back out.

The skunkworks looks like the masterpiece of some mad plumber who failed perspectives class in art school. The labyrinth of pipes that surrounds her make her dizzy at first. Broad swathes of transparent mesh stretch between pipes and she bobbles until she gets her bearings.

Fat pipes pass overhead. They form a de facto canopy hiding the skunk-works, which stretches for miles above her. In actuality, it stretches for miles in all directions. Fixes have piled on top of so-called improvements have piled on top of emergency repairs forever. Rust covers the gates and reservoirs at the intersection of pipes. Most pipes block each other's way and have to zigzag around each other. No pipes unscarred from dead welds of stubs where pipes used to join together.

Data pulses through the pipes in all directions. The pipes ripple, but sta-bilize in time for clacking of valves and the burbling of reservoirs. Probably because she already knows which ones they are, the pipes that violate the hold-time requirement look out-of-sync even to the naked eye. Pipes are sup-posed to be stable a little before reservoir valves clack until a little after. The pipes that violate the hold-time requirement start to ripple again too soon, corrupting the reservoirs they feed.

Someone stands on a mesh below her. Daniel. He's a verifier, not an isola-tionist. None of the latter have found her yet. Ellie lets go of the breath she didn't realize she was holding.

Those who know about the skunkworks fall into four factions. Isolationists believe whatever universe a skunkworks generates is correct, even as it inevi-tably decays. Any change introduces error rather than removes it. Architects design the configuration of gates and pipes that generate the next universe in. Builders, like Ellie and Chris, install those gates and pipes, translating the architects' designs into reality. Verifiers, like Daniel, check whether architects have designed the right thing and whether they have designed the thing right. They understand the skunkworks better than anyone. One of them is almost always the first to show up when the skunkworks has gone wrong.

Even looking down from above, no one can mistake Daniel. His long legs are too short for his torso and his shoulders are too wide. He manages to be both lithe and stocky at the same time, as though he were the runt of a family of impossibly elegant giants. A black T-shirt is draped over his left shoulder.

The pipes beyond his gaze blur as though a giant thumb has smeared a broad swath of petroleum jelly on the air. He holds his hand out. The blurred air twists and swirls into a ball on his palm. It coalesces into an egg tart. Its bright yellow custard sits inside a pale, blond serrated crust. The perfume of eggs and sugar hangs in the thick air.

He studies the egg tart from all angles. His neck cranes and his hand twists. Crumbs fall when he picks up the tart to look at the crust's bottom. He brings it to his nose to sniff. The custard jiggles slightly when he shakes the tart. He frowns.

Ellie bounces from mesh to mesh, swinging around pipes and ducking under reservoirs. She lands next to Daniel. This mesh, already taut from his weight, barely registers her.

"Cousin, your first time solo." Daniel's voice is never the thunder she expects from an elegant giant. He speaks with the rustle of leaves and the rush of water as it smoothes rock. "Congrats."

"Chris mentioned hold-time violations, probably valves gone faulty. Should be an easy fix. Otherwise, she wouldn't have sent me instead of coming herself." Ellie's arms wave in slow-motion semaphore as she steadies herself. "Your egg tart shows a mismatch between how the skunkworks that was built functions and how the skunkworks that was designed functions, right?"

"Yeah, no point calling in an architect. The design itself is fine. The problem is in the implementation. It's all yours. Don't need to remind you that we have to be out of here before the isolationists find us, right?"

She sets down her backpack then walks around Daniel to a knot of intertwined pipes. Reservoir valves clack and the pipes they feed ripple too soon. Data races through those pipes, corrupting the reservoir they feed in turn. All of the valves, however, are fine. Their actuators swing smoothly. Their seals fit perfectly against the pipes and reservoirs. Nothing leaks.

The skunkworks pre-date humanity and no human had ever made any changes to this section. Any actual mismatch in construction should have been found eons ago. Still, she checks, hoping that's what the problem is. The alternatives are all far worse.

A plane of air folds into an origami Black Forest cuckoo clock. The transparent, crystalline structure floats before her eyes. Its pendulum swings back and forth and the skunkworks fills with the sting of an off-stage chorus whenever the pendulum stops at the peak of its arc. Light diffracts through leaves that line its sides. Color sprays across the pipes and Daniel. The egg tart is still in his outstretched hand and he looks far sillier than Ellie would have thought possible given his "I am deadly if you come within five paces" body.

The clock unfolds into a crinkled plane. Its creases delimit facets that refract pipes behind them into something Syncretic Cubist. She grabs the newly retrieved blueprint. Its hard edges dig into her palm. She warps it, at first, into a dome then into a sphere that seals her in.

Daniel splinters into "Man with an Egg Tart," a Braque that Braque never painted. He's all shards of black, gray, and brown flecked with grains of yellow. This piece of the skunkworks, however, resolves into something that no longer looks like an obscene display of Syncretic Cubism.

The multiple perspectives merge into one. Pipes straighten and meet at right angles. She spins along three axes inside the sphere. Her hands and feet work their way up, down, and around the hard, cold sphere for support. Dense knots explode, laying bare their pipes and gates. The labyrinth is now a regular matrix. Pulses of data bulge from one pipe to another as they sweep in waves from one side of the matrix to the other.

The waves propagate faster than she expects. Just in front of her, waves crash into each other. That's bad. If the actual arrangement of pipes, gates, and reservoirs didn't match what they meant to build, though, it wouldn't look like a matrix through the sphere.

The skunkworks match the blueprint in construction. They don't match the blueprint in function, though.

"Fuck me." She slams a foot against the sphere. It shatters with a chord from the off-stage chorus. "The valves are fine. The skunkworks is fine."

She falls face up onto the mesh and thinks horrible things about Chris. Her backpack bounces above her then lands on her stomach.

Daniel looms over her, his hands behind his back. He smells like soy and ginger. An amused expression sits on his face.

"Egg tart?" He crouches, then places the pastry on the backpack.

"I don't need to study the equivalence report." She pushes herself up by her elbows. "I trust your analysis."

"I meant to eat. It's a functional mismatch but still edible." He nudges the backpack toward her head. "You haven't had dinner yet, right? You'll feel better with something in your stomach. Personally, I think that's just a story my boyfriend tells me, but maybe eating really does clear the mind."

She sits up. The backpack and egg tart slide to her lap. "Don't you want your mind cleared?"

"Nyah. I don't believe in emotions." A grin lights his face. "I had a protein shake and a banana before I showed up."

"I already know what's wrong." She takes a bite of the egg tart. It tastes sweet, sour, and . . . gamey. "Turkey and cranberries?"

"Hey, I said the report was a mismatch. I do what I can." Daniel rolls his eyes. "So what's wrong, cuz?"

"This universe." She finishes the egg tart. It's not bad if you know what's coming. "It's like someone secretly added lots of helium to the air and now we all squeak. The skunkworks wasn't designed for pipes this slick. The properties of this universe can't have changed much. Most of the skunkworks still works right but a few paths are now too fast."

"Which is why we're seeing functional failures even though what was built matches what was designed then functionally verified." Daniel nods. "What next?"

"Check whether the skunkworks one universe out is working properly so I know where to make the fix."

"It's fine." He sets a plate made of compressed, deep-fried rice from behind him onto her backpack. Pieces of pan-fried fish coated in brown glaze sit on the plate. That's why he smelled of soy and ginger. "I popped out to check while you were assessing equivalence here."

"So they changed the laws of their universe? Seriously?" This goes against everything Mom has taught her. "If you already knew that, why bother asking me what's wrong?"

"I didn't. Speculative generation." He smiles. "You were busy and there was no reason not to check before you asked. Sooner we get out of here, the less likely we'll have to deal with any isolationists. I saved us some time. "

Ellie breaks off a shard from the plate to test the fish. The glazed fish's crispy skin cracks against the deep-fried rice. She sniffs at this equivalence report. Then again, the egg tart smelled normal too.

"Is this going to taste icky sweet like 八寶飯 or something?"

Now Daniel just looks annoyed. His brow furrows and his hands rest on his hips. "No, it's going to taste like a deconstructed garlic fried rice paired with a soy and ginger glazed tilapia. The skunkworks one universe out is fine. Eat."

She lances a piece of fish and tries it. The tilapia is mild. Its triumph is that it doesn't sit like cotton in her mouth. The glaze is lovely. Garlic, shallots, and a little brown sugar round out the soy and ginger.

Daniel simply shakes his head when she offers to share. She hasn't had dinner yet, and she doesn't have time, so it all disappears quickly. The glaze never cloys even when it coats her mouth. The plate made of rice clears the glaze away in any case.

"Show off." Ellie smiles before letting sparks flit from finger to finger on her left hand.

The air becomes gauze that scatters the pipes, valves, reservoirs, even Daniel into mathematical points that then recombine. The machinery that generates the universe shimmers. Unlike Daniel, Ellie doesn't generate food. Instead, when the gauze coalesces, it becomes cool, metallic, and malleable, not coincidentally the stuff that thickens into pieces of the skunkworks.

Her right hand extrudes a gate out of the gauze. In time with the clacking of valves, her left hand strikes the pipe in front of her twice. Sparks fly. The pipe splits. Clean, parallel scars separate a ring from the pipe on either side. She installs the gate in place of the ring, her left hand sparking again to fuse the gate into place.

One by one, she inserts extra gates to slow the paths that have become too fast. *Click.* Insert. *Clack.* Insert. She can only repair the skunkworks in the moment when the pipes are settled. The skunkworks never halts. The one that lives in the innermost universe generates the outermost universe, whatever "innermost" and "outermost" mean when the universes are arranged in a loop. Stopping one skunkworks stops all of them. How you start them back up again is something she hopes she never has to figure out.

She dismisses the gauze and the skunkworks sharpen. The pipes grow and shrink in sync with the clacking of valves. Data no longer skids through paths causing pipes to expand or contract when they should be still.

"OK, Daniel, show me where to go. We need to flush out speculative state before it's committed and we're stuck with the results of a faulty skunkworks."

Of course, they're already stuck. Some mistakes of a faulty skunkworks have already been committed, but there's no point to letting those errors compound. The universe should be generated correctly from as early as possible.

Daniel shifts his T-shirt across his back and ties it around his neck. It might look like a cape except it's way too short. He appraises her, his face pensive.

"Anyone else might just declare it close enough and leave before isolationists find them. You really are Aunt Vera's child, aren't you. . . ."

Ellie rolls her eyes. Mom's reputation precedes her. "Considering how long you lived with us, you might as well be, too."

Daniel looks annoyed again. "No, I mean her attitude about the skunkworks and the generated universe. . . . Never mind. You have to see it yourself. Come on. Follow me."

He leaps to a thick pipe way overhead. From there, he swings to a swath of mesh, bounces, and off he goes.

"Hold up, you big lunk. You have at least half a foot of wing span on me." Ellie sighs too loudly, then follows him.

Whether or not it's actually hotter, the skunkworks' interior is definitely more humid. Rust covers every pipe. Sometimes, it flakes off as the pipes grow and shrink. The farther in Ellie and Daniel go, the faster the skunkworks expand and contract until it's as though the skunkworks is breathing. The transparent mesh that spans pipes goes taut and slack. A faint hiss precedes the near-unison clack of reservoir valves.

Daniel points out which valves she needs to wedge open and for how long. That will cause the skunkworks to flush out its speculative state and then regenerate the universe anew from what has already been committed. By now, that's not error-free. She's already missed the train to South Station, but nothing left to do about that. He looks up for a moment, nods, then leaps for a pipe above him.

"Now that you've actually made changes to the skunkworks, you know the isolationists will really be after you." Daniel swings around the pipe in a one-arm giant. "Guess I should have said something earlier."

Isolationists don't deal well with anyone trying to repair the skunkworks. Usually, they've shown up by now.

"Have I ever told you that when I was a kid, Chris used to attack me in my sleep to see whether I'd wake up in time?" Ellie climbs onto a pipe and stops, for a moment, to get her bearings. "She didn't use real knives back then, of course."

"I've always been the black sheep." Daniel releases the pipe, flips through the air in a layout position, then bounces off the mesh towards another pipe. "I'll verify anything that's well-specified and backward-compatible. Not just bug fixes."

"The isolationists must really hate you." She projects where Daniel is about to land and jumps after him. "It's the pointlessly dangerous life, then. Isn't it better in the long run if we just implement the correct physics correctly?"

"Hey, I have my standards. Change the laws of physics, no. Discover new laws or a more general formulation of what we already know, why not?" This time, it's Daniel who stops. He's rock steady as the pipe he landed on swells and contracts. "Look, there will always be architects with clever ideas of how to generate the universe more efficiently so that it can be more detailed or more expansive. There will always be builders who enable them, if nothing else, because they have cool ideas themselves for new valves or better ways to connect pipes. Someone has to make sure they don't destroy the universe—all of the universes, actually—in the process. So that, on occasion, someone can tell them 'no' and they'll listen. Of course, even then, there's still the occasional unauthorized change."

Ellie finally catches up to Daniel. Her lungs burn. Daniel's probably do too. His breath is calm, but metronomically steady.

"That's a nice speech, but I'm my mom's child remember? How much convincing can I possibly need to remove something that generates incorrect physics?"

Daniel glares. His expression screams, "That's fucking flippant." Daniel, though, doesn't scream. He's so soft-spoken, Ellie isn't sure he can. In any case, the angrier he gets, the quieter he becomes.

"Cuz, I've known you since before you could walk." To her relief, his voice isn't too much softer than his normal quiet. "Just wanted to be sure you stood where I thought before I showed you this."

His gaze shifts to the skunkworks. He points overhead. That tangle of pipes looks like any other in the skunkworks. It expands and contracts, however, to a beat slightly skewed from the surrounding pipes. Rather than clack, its reservoir valves hiss when they shut. Otherwise, the skew would be obvious to anyone listening. The miniature skunkworks within the skunkworks is tied directly into the pipes that commit state, that choose from the speculative generation and render it permanent as the basis for further speculative generation.

"What does it do?"

"You need to see for yourself before I tell you." Daniel faces his palms toward her. "Won't make sense otherwise."

The plane of air above her doesn't fold into anything. Blueprints don't exist for the mechanism Daniel pointed out. Not even logs of who built what. Ellie frowns. Blueprints always exist. Otherwise, what did the architect work on? What did the verifier simulate? What did the builder work off of?

She jumps, catching the mechanism's lowest pipes, then flips herself inside. Shadows fall across shadows. The chiaroscuro drains everything of depth. She contorts from pipe to pipe, tracing out paths to build a blueprint in her head.

Cool, smooth pipes breathe in her grasp. Rust doesn't sand her palms. The air feels thick but doesn't smell metallic. Nothing here can be more a year or two old, but pipes twist and jag around each other. Builders have inserted subtle fix after subtle fix after subtle fix.

Those who designed, built, then kept tinkering with this tracked Mom's treatment history. A set of pipes tweak electron orbitals, changing the shapes of chemical compounds, specifically those pumped into Mom. To make them more effective against Mom's tumors, Ellie guesses.

Unfortunately, a skunkworks generates an entire universe. Physical laws don't apply to only three specific chemical compounds. This mechanism changes the universe she lives in so much more than they intended. It's like making mashed potatoes when all you have is dynamite. They wanted mashed potatoes so much they blew the potatoes up.

The newest bits try to pull a similar electron orbital trick, but on the chemicals inside Mom's brain. Ellie crawls through those paths three times before she can convince herself she's right. This is why, every once in a while, Mom seems to wake up. Days seem to pass before she can breathe again.

The mechanism will heal Mom eventually. Well, it needs some more tinkering first and she has some ideas. It may also, bizarrely, cause a species of migratory bird to go extinct and any of a number of other things that are also not supposed to happen. She has no idea how to avoid any of that. This mechanism wasn't designed to be subtle. It was designed to save Mom's life.

She doesn't have the time to work out everything else it will also do. The isolationists will find her and Daniel soon.

"This causes a lot of collateral damage." Ellie hangs by the mechanism's lowest pipes, then drops onto the pipe Daniel's standing on. "No wonder you want me to get rid of it."

"My feelings about it are complicated." His voice blends into the hiss and Ellie strains to separate it out. "Aunt Vera took me in when no one else would."

"Of course." She fixes her gaze hard at Daniel. "Then why even show me this?"

The thud of bodies—undoubtedly isolationists—hitting mesh, the creak of pipes buckling and unbuckling surrounds them. Daniel spins around, his gaze pinpointing isolationists swinging through the skunkworks.

"Well, it's about time they showed up." His voice has reverted to merely quiet. "Look, everyone loves Aunt Vera. Constructing this pretty much violates everything anyone who can access the skunkworks stands for, but countless architects, verifiers, and builders all worked on it and no one has removed it. Chris sent you, in part, because she doesn't want to face the choice. And who can blame her? So, here you are. I'll buy you time to do whatever you decide to do. And whatever you decide, we won't speak of this again."

"Do you need any help with them?"

"You're joking, right?" Daniel puffs himself up. His chest expands, his back spreads and, scarily, he actually looks even bigger than normal. "I can drown them in boiling oil whenever I want. Cuz, you have arc welders for hands. I'm not worried about you, just buying you enough time for you to do your thing before more of them show up."

"You really get off on this whole service and protection thing, don't you?"

"Hey, don't judge me." He actually looks a little wounded. "At least I'm taking care of the skunkworks, even if it's for the wrong reason. Plant you now, dig you later, cuz."

Daniel bounds away. The smile on his face is scarier than any weapon.

All Ellie can think of is Mom lying in bed. Mom's head lurches up, staring at Ellie in a simulacrum of life that one day may be the real thing. Hope flares through Ellie, leaving her both empty and wishing it would flare again.

Mom needs her own universe in order to heal without trashing the one Ellie lives in. Of course, a new universe is the result of too many people over too much time to create a skunkworks that takes up too much space. That's why they kludged this mechanism instead. It will work eventually, even if it also causes birds to migrate at the wrong times to the wrong places. Even if it has other countless side-effects that will take lifetimes to map out.

It's built to be dismantled. The pipes that commit state are the only bits of the skunkworks it is connected to. It can be removed at any time. She can wait. She can let this universe too haphazard to understand, much less document, be the new normal until Mom is cured. The tides will be wrong and the foundations of physics may crack, but Mom will live.

Valves clack and pipes shrink and swell in time. From end to end, they jog and twist around each other at wild angles. Data travels through pipes that are too long and too hard to trace. No builder would route them this way except to work around pipes already there, all the other possibilities being even longer or harder to trace. Or functionally wrong.

Once, when Mom was still overseeing Ellie's work, Ellie had found a truly elegant fix. Just a few short pipes connected at right angles installed in an easily accessible place. Piece of cake. They'd be done in no time. She rushed to show Mom, who slowly shook her head then pointed out the one case in billions where data would not reach the reservoir before its valve closed.

Instead, as isolationists bore down on them, Mom and Ellie threaded pipes through the existing tangle. The fix was time-consuming and ugly. Isolationists nearly caught them. But the fix was also provably correct.

Ellie looks at the valves she needs to hold open to flush out speculative state and the mechanism she might dismantle. She knows what she has to do.

"Attention passengers: the next Red Line train to Alewife is now arriving" echoes off the walls. Ellie sprints and meets the oncoming torrent at the ticket gate. Even though the announcements are properly timed, she's going to miss the train again. This will be the last time she makes the trip to see Mom and she wishes it weren't.

Paul McAuley is the author of more than twenty novels, several collections of short stories, a Doctor Who novella, and a BFI Film Classic monograph on Terry Gilliam's film *Brazil*. His fiction has won the Philip K. Dick Memorial Award, the Arthur C. Clarke Award, the John W. Campbell Memorial Award, the Sidewise Award, the British Fantasy Award, and the Theodore Sturgeon Memorial Award. His latest novels are *Something Coming Through* and *Into Everywhere*.

WILD HONEY

Paul McAuley

Mel was in the warm dim crawlspace under the hive's chimneys and stalactite combs, installing new harvesting frames, when the bees began to signal the presence of intruders. Irregular pulses of alarm code flashing through the net, older workers hustling toward the entrances to augment the guards, an urgent bass drone building.

Mel's blood thrummed in sympathy. She went outside and with field glasses scanned the dun grassland. A witchy old woman in a faded patched sundress standing in the shade of the nest's spires, a few ride-along bees clinging in her long white hair. It was late in the afternoon, very hot. Sunlight lanced low out of a flawless blue sky. Trees and stubs of broken wall cast long shadows, and something twinkled in the far distance, a star of reflected light moving out on the old highway.

After a minute or so, the star resolved into Odd Sanders's battered pickup, driving in a caul of dust ahead of an old army truck and a pod of trikes. Odd sometimes brought petitioners out into the city wilds, charging them for an introduction to the crazy old bee queen whose balm could cure all kinds of sickness. But petitioners usually didn't ride trikes, and as the little convoy drew closer Mel glimpsed bandoleers across the chests of the trike riders, and rifles and ballistas strapped to their backs.

Foragers were already out, shuttling between the hive and a stand of black locust trees half a mile to the north. Mel could see in her mind's eye the shape of their traffic laid across the landscape, could see a frail spike of scouts bending toward the highway, and yet again wished that she could use the hive's network to send the bees where she wanted, and peer through their faceted eyes. She watched as the convoy stopped about a mile away, near the fieldstone chimney that marked where the house of an abandoned homestead had once stood. Almost at once, something lofted from the army truck and curved toward Mel, gathering a smoky comet tail of bees as it approached.

It was a drone, the kind printed from fungal mycelium and coated in bacterial cellulose and wasp-spit proteins. Mel had once tried to use bigger versions to dispatch balm and honey liquor to Hangtown, but had given up after bandits had started to shoot them down. It looked like a pale cowpat, hovering on four red props just beyond the edge of the roof. A speaker whistled and Odd Sanders's voice said, "You'd better come over. Someone needs your help."

Odd Sanders had started helping out after Mel's apprentice had been killed by a bear last fall. Rasia had been with Mel for eight years, a sweet-natured, dutiful young woman with a natural talent for reading the mood of the hive. Mel had been certain that when she joined the queens below she would leave the hive in good hands, but then Rasia had gone to collect windfalls in a stand of wild pear, and a lone male black bear had killed and half eaten her. Mel had tracked and dispatched him, but the effort and the grievous loss had almost undone her. She was old and tired, she had lost her successor, and for the first time feared for the future of the hive. Without a keeper it would go feral, like its daughter hives, or die out, or be ransacked and destroyed by bears or bandits.

Odd had turned up a couple of months later. A smooth-shaven plausible young man who told Mel that people in Hangtown had been missing her good stuff, and he'd be honored to do business with her. Mel had traded small batches of honey, honey liquor, wax, and balm for copper and germanium dust and a few personal necessaries, and he'd sometimes brought out people who needed her healing touch.

These visitors were some kind of outlaw gang, but Odd claimed that one of them was bad sick, and Mel was bound by the customs and conventions of a sect that no longer existed to treat all those who needed her help. They'd started smudge fires around their little encampment to keep away bees. Leaning on her staff at every other step, Mel hobbled through the haze of smoke, skirted a smoldering pyre of green branches and uprooted bushes, and discovered Odd waiting for her amongst a small group of desperados dressed in the usual leathers and denim and tattoos. One had a sword sheathed on his hip; another toted an ancient semi-automatic rifle.

Odd was uncharacteristically subdued and looked horrified when Mel told him outright he'd fallen amongst thieves and brigands.

"They're travelers is all," he said. He was tall and angular, with a mop of black hair that hung over his eyes. He wouldn't meet her gaze. "One of them needs your good stuff."

"I know what they are, and they know it, too," Mel said, looking around at the half dozen grim, grimy men.

When she asked who needed her help, a piping voice behind her said, "Good of you to come, grandmother. Saved us the trouble of smoking you out."

A small, fat, ruined child stood in the open flap of the army truck's covered loadbed, dressed in baggy camo shorts and a cut-down, red leather jacket, a cigar cocked in his mouth. After a moment, Mel realized that he was a neo. They'd been designed for space travel, neos. Tweaked so that they stopped growing at around four years old. The idea had been that they would need fewer resources and could live in smaller craft than base humans, and although the Collapse had ended the old dreams of making new homes beyond Earth, they'd survived and thrived. Long-lived and clever, most preferred to live by their wits on the outskirts of civilization.

This one was called Demetrius Ten, telling Mel, "My man July needs your help. Let's see if you deserve your reputation."

The patient was shivering under blankets in the back of the truck, slick with sweat and unconscious. When the young woman who'd been dabbing his brow with a wet cloth moved aside, Mel caught a faint whiff of stale milk.

"He got himself shot," Demetrius Ten said. "The wound went bad, we tried to burn the badness out, but it got into his blood."

Although he looked like an overgrown toddler dressed up as a gangster, there was a malicious glint in the neo's gaze and he had a commanding swagger. He could be any age from ten to a hundred. Maybe even older.

He watched as Mel stuck a temperature strip on July's forehead and unpacked the stand from her leather doctor's bag. The strip showed a temperature of a little over a hundred degrees, the man's breathing was shallow and rapid, and his pulse quick and thready: he was suffering from severe sepsis.

The wound was in his shoulder, a neat, charred hole with a little clear fluid oozing from the black crust, no pus or stink of infection. Mel fixed a balm compress over it just to be sure, hooked a bag of balm over the tee of the stand, and asked the young woman if her patient had been given any medicine.

"Tell her what she wants to know," Demetrius said, when the young woman looked at him.

"He had some whiskey when they burnt out the infection," the young woman told Mel. She was sixteen or seventeen, with red hair and luminously pale skin. "He was drinking on and off for a couple of days? But then he got a fever."

"What's your name, dear?"

The young woman glanced at Demetrius again, then said, "Hannah."

"She's my little milk momma," Demetrius said.

Hannah blushed prettily. Mel suddenly understood, saw Demetrius plugged into Hannah's breast, pausing occasionally to suck on his cigar instead.

She said, "When exactly did July pass out?"

"Last night. I've been bathing him with water to keep him cool. We don't have any of your magic stuff." The young woman was watching Mel tighten a cord around the sick man's arm to make the veins stand up.

"It isn't magic." Mel slid a needle into a vein and taped it down and opened the drip regulator. "A century ago I would have used antibiotics. But bacteria became resistant to all of them, so we must find other ways of fighting infection now. My bees have been tweaked so that they enhance the antimicrobial properties of honey made from the nectar of certain plants. I refine that honey, and that's what balm is."

Demetrius, puffing on his foul cigar, asked how long it would take.

"If the fever breaks he'll probably live," Mel said.

"He better. Hannah can look after him for now. We need to talk business."

"I don't charge for treating people," Mel said.

Demetrius gave her a roguish smile. "We need to talk about my business, not yours."

As they walked toward the hive, Odd Sanders told Mel a complicated story about people in Hangtown who resented his charm and success and tried to sabotage him at every turn, and a girl who, through no fault of his own, had fallen in love with him.

"And you got her pregnant," Mel said, wanting to cut through the young man's self-justifying bullshit. She had never entirely trusted him, but hadn't realized until now just how little there was beneath the mask he wore to fool the world.

"So she says. I chucked her because she was so tiresomely clingy, and she came up with this story. And when I told her it didn't change anything, because I frankly didn't believe her, she went to her father," Odd said. "He happens to be one of the people who have it in for me, and also happens to be a friend of the mayor. Well, her brother, actually. So I had to get out. All because some silly bitch wanted to get back at me."

"And I suppose you seduced her because you wanted to get back at her father."

"It seemed like a good idea at the time. Still does in a way, you know? Now he can deal with her, and her brat," Odd said, with a grimace of a smile behind the visor of his hood.

Odd and the outlaw escorting him and Mel were sealed inside in yellow biohazard suits much patched with duct tape. Neither the suits nor the pistol holstered at the outlaw's hip would be much protection against the bees, but Demetrius had told Mel that if she didn't come back with the goods, he'd load Odd's pickup with brushwood, tie down the accelerator and the steering wheel, and set it on fire and aim it at the hive. Telling Odd, when he protested, that losing his pickup was the least he had to worry about.

Now, Odd told Mel that he'd made the outlaw boss promise she wouldn't be hurt, that all they wanted were some trade goods and they'd be on their way.

"I hate to do it to you, but I need to put some distance between me and Hangtown as fast as possible," he said. "And I need a stake to start over. That's all it is. We get the goods, and we get out of here and leave you in peace. You have my word."

"It isn't your word I'm worried about," Mel said, glancing at the drone wobbling through the air above them.

"Demetrius doesn't want trouble. He knows your reputation. What the bees are. What they can do. I told him all that. It's just like our usual trade, but this time I'm going to have to owe you. But when I get it together somewhere else, I swear I'll try to find a way of making it up to you."

The hive reared above them. Rooted in the ruin of a brick single-story house, its peaks soared fifteen feet into the air, built of grains of dirt excavated and emplaced by workers over the course of more than a century. Mel was its third keeper, having inherited it some forty-two years ago when the woman to whom she had been apprenticed had transitioned into one of the queens below. The exterior had been weatherproofed with a sheen of wax that shone black as oil in the sunlight. Bees shimmered around it like smoke: foragers heading out along airy highways toward the black locusts or returning laden with pollen and nectar. The outlaw swiped at a bee that landed on the visor of his suit, swiped at another that landed on his arm.

"If you keep that up," Mel told him, "they'll swarm you."

"Listen to her," Odd said. "These aren't ordinary bees. They're smart. All linked up into like one mind."

He was quivering with nerves. Behind the visor of his hood his face shone with sweat; his hair was pasted to his forehead. He'd never before come so close to the hive.

Demetrius's voice piped up overhead, from the drone. "Just get in there and get it done and get the fuck out."

Mel lived and worked in what had once been a lean-to garage, its walls partly subsumed by the hive's bulwark flanges and patched with fieldstones and corrugated iron. Odd was more confident once they were inside, and quickly found the cool box and started to pack the bags of balm into one of the knapsacks he'd brought.

"Every bag you take is a life lost," Mel said.

She could trace the trajectories of the scouts that spiraled around the two men, could feel the intricate seethe of bees beyond the wall of the lean-to, see the queens and their retinues in the brood combs at the heart of the hive.

"They'll save lives," Odd said. "Just not here. And you always can make more."

"You know that takes time."

"Then let the sick buy balm from the market."

"And if they cannot afford it?"

"That's their problem. Why don't you start decanting the liquor? Sooner you do it, sooner we'll be gone."

"I doubt that," Mel said, but she cracked valves in the stainless steel reservoir of the still and began to fill plastic bottles. A heady scent like a distillation of summer filled the air. Bees clustered around the rims of the bottles, hummed at the reservoir's spout, landed on Mel. One stung her on the web between her thumb and forefinger. She hardly noticed.

The outlaw stood in the doorway watching her. The drone hovered at his shoulder. She hoped that they hadn't seen that she'd opened the little reservoir inside the still before she'd started draining it.

Odd packed the bottles in another knapsack. When the still was empty, he rooted inside Mel's ancient maker and took out the precious tubes of copper and germanium dust that the machine used to print the network dots that the bees inserted in every larva.

"Half of this won't be enough for what I need," Odd said as he cinched the knapsack, "but it'll have to do."

Mel said nothing. She felt calm but hollow. A high note hummed in her head in counterpoint to the hive's drone. She wasn't even startled when the outlaw aimed his pistol at her.

"Don't," Odd said.

"Why not?"

It was the drone that had spoken, not the outlaw.

"Because if you kill her, the hive will swarm," Odd said. "Millions of angry bees. The smoke won't keep them all off."

Mel supposed that she should feel grateful for the intervention, but she didn't. Odd had thrown her into this trouble; she had to do what she had to do to get out of it.

"Bring her back," the drone said, after a long moment. "We can talk about that maker of hers."

He had another plan, Demetrius told Mel when she'd been returned to the outlaws' camp. "We're low on ammo. When we get hold of some high-density plastic and the necessaries for gunpowder, you can run off a big batch of bullets and shotgun shells on that maker of yours. And while you're at it you can make some more of that liquor and your healing shit, too."

"I'm out of honey," Mel said.

"Bullshit," Demetrius declared. He was looking up at her with his fists on his hips. "There must be a ton of the sweet stuff inside that nest."

"It's a hive. And the bees need a store of honey to tide them through the winter. If I dip into that the hive could die."

"Either you help us or we'll find a way of taking what we need," Demetrius said. "And if we have to do that, they'll die anyway. You too."

"It seems I don't have any choice."

"Yes, you do. But your best choice is to help me out, like you would any other traveler who asks you for a favor. I'll send Odd here back to Hangtown for ammo makings, and you can fire up that still." Demetrius grinned and rubbed his hands together. "Drugs and drink and ammo: three of the best kinds of currency out here. Do right by me, grandmother, I might even cut you in."

When Odd Sanders started to say that he couldn't go back to Hangtown, there were people who wanted to nail his hide to the jailhouse wall, Demetrius held up a finger. One of his men stepped up behind the trader and punched him in the back of his head and knocked him to the ground. A couple of the other outlaws laughed. They were sitting around a campfire, passing bottles of Mel's liquor between them. One spat a mouthful in the fire: blue flames flared.

Demetrius looked down at the dazed young man and said, "You're afraid of the wrong people."

"I'm not afraid of them," Odd said, summoning up the shreds of his plausible manner. "They won't trade with me, is what I was going to say."

"Who said anything about trade? You can find where they keep their shit. We'll go in and take it. But not tonight. Tonight we celebrate. Not you though," Demetrius told Mel. "You go see to July. He's still out cold."

In the dim cave under the truck's canvas cover, Hannah said that July's fever had gone down, and he seemed more restful. Mel wasn't surprised: she'd given the man a bag of balm doped with ketamine, the stuff she reserved for troublesome patients and to ease the passing of those too far gone for treatment. After half a bag he wasn't so much asleep as catatonic.

Mel asked Hannah how he'd got himself shot; the young woman said that he'd gotten into an argument with another man over the price of a hat.

"So this other man shot him?"

"No, July stabbed the man wanted to sell him the hat, and the man's friend shot July."

"It must have been a good hat."

Outside, someone shrieked in pain and outrage. Mel twitched back the flap of the cover, saw Odd Sanders writhing as two men held him down while a third poured liquor into his mouth. Hannah said, "They're getting a real drunk on with your stuff. Are you hoping they'll pass out?"

"Not exactly."

"They get mean when they drink. Especially D."

"Does he hurt you, dear?"

Hannah shook her head. "He gets one of his boys to do it."

"Because he'd have to stand on a chair to slap you," Mel said, which won a quick smile from the young woman. "Does he give you injections to make you lactate?"

Mel had to explain what lactate meant; Hannah said that she didn't see how it was any of her business.

"People think that keepers like me are hermits and holy healers who don't live in the real world," Mel said. "As if there is some other world beyond the one we all share. But I talk to people who pass by the hive, or stop and ask for help. And when I was much younger, when I was an apprentice, I went into the market of Hangtown every month and sold balm and honey and bought supplies. You need a quick mind and have to know about people to get a good deal. I got to know the market pretty well. There was a house in one of the little streets behind it. I'm sure you know the kind I mean. It specialized in the needs of neos."

"I was bought, all right?" Hannah said with sudden quick anger. "The owner of the house got into debt and she sold me to D."

"Was this in Hangtown?"

"No. Over near Detroit."

"Is that where you come from?"

"I was born in Wisconsin. My father sold me to a place there after our farm went under, and a bit later they sold me on to a guy who took to me to Detroit. He was the one had me fixed up by a tinker, if you must know," Hannah said.

"My mother couldn't keep me either," Mel said. "But I was lucky. She gave me to the Keeper sect."

"And now you're queen of that big old hive," Hannah said.

"I'm the keeper. I serve the bees; they don't serve me. But I've had a lucky life."

"They had bees in Wisconsin. The hives were much smaller though. They fertilized apple trees. What do your bees do, out here?"

Mel liked her for that question. Hannah had had a hard life, no doubt, but she was smart and still had a spark in her.

"The bees do what they need to do," Mel said. "There were homesteads here, once upon a time. Part of a big plan to rewild a city no one needed any more. The hive fertilized some of the crops. Medical tobacco, okra and soy, sunflowers and mustard. . . . Then there were summer droughts and killer winters, and the homesteaders gave up and moved away. But I stayed on. I protect the bees as best I can, and try to do my best by people who need my help."

"You love them," Hannah said.

"Of course," Mel said.

But the bees didn't love her back. Every keeper had to accept that. Some outsiders believed that because they were tweaked and networked the bees had somehow acquired sentience. They hadn't. And even if they had, it was doubtful that they would have acquired any concept of love or hate, or free will. They knew only loyalty and the chains of duty: their life paths were engraved in their genes. The organization of the hive was as pure and pitiless as mathematics. Individuals were no more than integers in the calculus of its survival.

Hannah said, "I saw your hive. It looks like a fairytale castle."

"The bees have been tweaked with termite behavior to build hives that are air-conditioned. It helps them survive the hot summers and cold winters."

Wild bees and baseline domestic honeybees had all died out at the beginning of the Collapse. There were only tweaked swarms now, in hives tended by keepers or in wild daughter hives.

Hannah said, "I heard they can kill people. Bees."

"One sting can do it if you're sensitive."

More shouts outside; more laughter.

"I mean you can use them as weapons," Hannah said, with a flat direct look.

Mel knew then that Hannah was hoping that she could help her, and felt a flutter of relief. Things would go much easier with the young woman on her side, and there was the frail hope that afterward, if things came out right, that she might stay on as her apprentice.

She said, "The bees defend the hive, if they have to."

"So do they defend you, too?"

"Of course. When I'm in the hive."

"But can you make them attack anyone you want?"

"Is that what you'd like me to do?"

Hannah leaned across July and whispered, "When he doesn't have any more use for you, D will kill you."

"I know."

"But you came over here anyway. You didn't stay in your hive, where the bees could protect you."

"I came to save a life. And because otherwise Demetrius would have come to me. The bees can't protect me against people like him, Hannah. But maybe I can protect them. You too, if you want me to."

"Maybe we can help each other," Hannah said.

"I hope we can." Mel opened her doctor's bag and took out a little tube of liquid honey and told Hannah she should drink it.

"It will protect you against my bees. Give you the smell of the hive."

Hannah uncapped the tube, sniffed its contents, then downed it in one gulp. She said, "I thought you couldn't use your bees against people."

"I can't. This is for afterward."

"After what?"

Hannah was all eyes in the dimness.

"After we deal with Demetrius and his boys."

Mel unpacked her doctor's bag. One of her patients had given it to her years back. It was very old, with cracked horsehide leather and brass fittings and a capacious maw. Mel lifted out the false bottom and took out the little pistol crossbow stowed there.

"People think I use the bees as weapons," she told Hannah, "so they generally don't think to look at what I carry."

"Are you going to shoot them?"

"Would you have a problem with that?"

Hannah shook her head. She said, "What do you want me to do?"

"First, we wait."

"While they get drunk?"

"While they get a lot more than drunk."

The voices outside grew louder. Someone started to laugh and it rose in pitch and turned into raw sobbing. Someone else began to scream. And then someone shouted, "I see them! I see them in the trees!" and there was a gunshot. Someone was laughing hysterically and someone else said, "Look there! I see them! I see them too!" and there were more gunshots. Mel told Hannah to wait there and stay low, and peeked through the flap of the canvas cover.

The sun had set and everywhere was blue with shadows. A man lay unconscious near the dying campfire; he was naked and had carved up his chest with a knife before he'd passed out. Mel clambered out, froze when gunfire rattled hard and loud nearby. In the sudden silence, she saw a man just a hundred yards away, raising his rifle to take aim at the moon's low crescent. Mel's quarrel took him in the throat and he grunted and dropped bonelessly.

Her pistol crossbow clicked quietly as it drew its wire taut again. After years of practice, she could take down a sparrow in flight.

She shot a man howling and staggering with his hands pressed over his eyes. She found a dead man without a mark on him and bloody froth on his lips. Killed by a seizure. She heard someone scream in the trees beyond the campsite, suddenly silenced by the pop of a pistol. She found drag marks in long grass and followed them to where Odd Sanders lay on his back, eyes crossed as if trying to focus on the neat hole oozing in his forehead.

"Fucking bitch," someone said, and Mel turned and she and Demetrius fired at the same moment.

Something punched her shoulder and she was on her back looking up at the dark blue sky. She tried to push up and everything hurt. Her breath was tight and she spat a mouthful of blood.

Demetrius came around the campfire with a waddling walk, kicked her crossbow away, looked down at her. She had forgotten he was a neo, and had aimed too high.

The eye of his pistol wove, now pointing in her face, now pointing away. He leered drunkenly behind it.

"What did you do to us?"

Mel's breath whistled in her chest. She spat more blood, said weakly, "Mad honey."

Foragers from daughter nests near the river browsed on the swathes of rhododendrons that grew there, harvesting nectar that contained a potent neurotoxin that caused nausea and numbness, seizures and hallucinations. Mel had drained a portion into the still before she'd decanted the liquor that Demetrius and his men had guzzled down.

The neo was weaving, cross-eyed, but still lucid. "Fucking bee magic," he said. "I'm going to kill you, and then I'm going to burn that fucking hive."

A shadow rose up behind him, there was a hard hollow crunch, and Demetrius fell down. Hannah dropped the rock she'd hit him with, snatched up his pistol and shot him and shot him again, kept shooting until the pistol clicked on an empty chamber.

The old woman was tough. Demetrius's shot had taken her high in the chest, clipping a lung, but she survived for more than three weeks and was lucid to the end. She told Hannah how to dress her wound, refused Hannah's offer to head for Hangtown and get help. Her time had come, she said. She was ready to join the queens below.

She subsisted on a diet of water and honey. A light clover honey first, then a heavy dark molasses made from goldenrod nectar. She showed Hannah how to set up a drip that fed an infusion of balm and natural sugars directly into her bloodstream, and Hannah massaged her with an emulsion of honey and walnut oil every day.

Her skin acquired a golden sheen, and her sweat and breath smelled of honey. Her eyes turned gold, her fingernails translucent amber. Every cell was becoming permeated with the honey's dehydrated sugars, preserving her body against corruption.

Meanwhile, she told Hannah about the bees and the hive, and the secrets of the vanished sect to which she had once belonged. It came tumbling out in no particular order, and she often repeated herself—the only sign that she was dying. "Bees know," she said, over and again. "The secret is to let them work. They know what to do."

Hannah learned how to harvest different types of honey from different parts of the hive, how to refine honey from the nursery combs to make balm, how to use the still to make honey liquor, how to use the wax extractor, how to program the maker to manufacture the quantum dots that every bee carried. The old woman told Hannah that she should begin to drink an infusion of dots too, so that they would cross the blood-brain barrier and connect her with the bees' network by the magic of old-time technology, but Hannah wasn't ready for that. Not yet, not yet.

The survivors of Demetrius's gang hadn't caused any trouble. Hannah had collected every weapon she could find before driving Mel to the hive in the trader's pickup. By the next day, July had recovered enough to stagger about and shout threats, but he was unarmed and didn't dare get too close to the hive. After Hannah fired a couple of warning shots he eventually drove off on his trike. Demetrius was dead; so were four of his men. The other two had run off into the city wilds while seized by the hallucinatory fever of the mad honey, and Hannah never saw them again.

Still, she waited for three days before she dared leave the safety of the hive and deal with the bodies. By then, they were bloated by heat and had been mauled by wild dogs, and stank worse than her family's hog farm after the virus had swept through it. She used one of the trikes to drag what was left of them into a heap and piled brushwood over them and soaked everything in fuel alcohol drained from the truck and set it on fire. She drove the truck and all but one of the trikes into a draw near the river and, apart from the charred spot, she reckoned that no one could tell what had gone down there.

One day, she woke to find that the old woman was covered with a thin blanket of bees and knew that she was dead. The body was as light as a child's and seemed to shine with an inner light. Hannah carried it down into the warm, dim cellar under the hive and laid it in the seamless plastic sarcophagus the old woman had had printed in Hangtown a couple of years back. The coffins of her predecessors stood close by. The shapes of their bodies visible in the dark gold matrices. The quantum dots in their brains formed the server architecture for the bees' network, and now the old woman would augment it. Hannah wondered, as she filled the sarcophagus to the brim with honey, if anything of the dead women lived on in the bees. Ghosts in the busy machinery that filled the cellar with a deep drone like an engine steadily driving it to some distant shore.

Hannah had promised the old woman that she would make sure the hive was kept safe, but she believed that it could look after itself, like the smaller daughter hives scattered around about. They didn't need quantum dots or a network, they lacked any kind of human care, and they were doing just fine. Hannah wasn't ready to become a witchy fairytale hermit, a queen of the bees with spooky magical abilities. She knew enough now to know it wasn't really magic, just some old tech and the bees. Mostly the bees.

"They know what to do," the old woman had said, not realizing that she was telling Hannah that they didn't need anyone's help. The world now wasn't the world as it had been when the old woman had been young. Like the daughter colonies, it had grown wild and strange.

So Hannah had no qualms when she rode off on one of the trikes toward Hangtown. When she'd gathered up the weapons, she'd also looted the little stash of hard cash that Demetrius had thought she didn't know about. Her breasts ached all the time and she had to express milk four times a day, and every time she'd think of Demetrius wiping his chin and sticking his cigar back into his mouth. She was going to find a tinker who could reverse the tweak, put an end to that. And after that she'd figure out what to do next.

Hannah was followed by a floating finger of bees as she drove away. It stretched thinner and thinner until at last it was gone, and Hannah rode on alone through the hot afternoon. When she stopped a few hours later to make camp, she found that several bees had tangled in her hair. As she carefully combed them out, one stung her. She crushed it.

Naomi Kritzer's short stories have appeared in *Asimov's, Analog, The Magazine of Fantasy and Science Fiction, Clarkesworld, Lightspeed*, and many other magazines and websites. Her five published novels (*Fires of the Faithful, Turning the Storm, Freedom's Gate, Freedom's Apprentice*, and *Freedom's Sisters*) are available from Bantam. She has also written an urban fantasy novel about a Minneapolis woman who unexpectedly inherits the Ark of the Covenant; a children's science-fiction shipwreck novel; a children's portal fantasy; and a near-future SF novel set on a seastead. She has two ebook short story collections out: *Gift of the Winter King and Other Stories* and *Comrade Grandmother and Other Stories*.

Naomi lives in St. Paul, Minnesota with her husband, two daughters, and several cats. She blogs at naomikritzer.wordpress.com.

SO MUCH COOKING

Naomi Kritzer

Carole's Roast Chicken

This is a food blog, not a disease blog, but of course the rumors all over about bird flu are making me nervous. I don't know about you, but I deal with anxiety by cooking. *So much cooking.* But, I'm trying to stick to that New Year's resolution to share four healthy recipes (entrées, salads, sides. . . .) for every dessert recipe I post, and I *just* wrote about those lemon meringue bars last week. So even though I dealt with my anxiety yesterday by baking another batch of those bars, and possibly by eating half of them in one sitting, I am *not* going to bake that new recipe I found for pecan bars today. No! Instead, I'm going to make my friend Carole's amazing roast chicken. Because how better to deal with fears of bird flu than by eating a bird, am I right?

Here's how you can make it yourself. You'll need a chicken, first of all. Carole cuts it up herself but I'm lazy, so I buy a cut-up chicken at the store. You'll need *at least* two pounds of potatoes. You'll need a lemon and a garlic bulb. You'll need a big wide roasting pan. I use a Cuisinart heavy-duty lasagna pan, but you can get by with a 13x9 cake pan.

Cut up the potatoes into little cubes. (Use good potatoes! The yellow ones or maybe the red ones. In the summer I buy them at the farmer's market.)

Spray your pan with some cooking spray and toss in the potatoes. Peel all the garlic (really, all of it!) and scatter the whole cloves all through with the potatoes. If you're thinking, "All that garlic?" just trust me on this. Roasted garlic gets all mild and melty and you can eat it like the potato chunks. Really. You'll thank me later. Finally, lay out the chicken on top, skin-down. You'll turn it halfway through cooking. Shake some oregano over all the meat and also some sea salt and a few twists of pepper.

Squeeze the lemon, or maybe even two lemons if you really like lemon, and mix it in with a quarter cup of olive oil. Pour that over everything and use your hands to mix it in, make sure it's all over the chicken and the potatoes. Then pour just a tiny bit of water down the side of the pan—you don't want to get it on the chicken—so the potatoes don't burn and stick. Pop it into a 425-degree oven and roast for an hour. Flip your chicken a half hour in so the skin gets nice and crispy.

Guys, it is SO GOOD. Half the time I swear Dominic doesn't even notice what he's eating, but he always likes this dish, and so do I. If you make this much for two people, you'll have leftovers for lunch. But we're having guests over tonight, my brother and his wife and kids. So, I'm actually using two chickens and four pounds of potatoes, because teenagers eat a lot.

And chicken has magical healing properties if you make it into soup, so surely some of them stick around when you roast it? And so does garlic, so eat some and *stay healthy*.

xxoo, Natalie

Substitute Chip Cookies

So, we have some unexpected long-term house guests.

My sister-in-law Katrina is a nurse at Regions Hospital. She's not in the ER or the infectious diseases floor but let's face it, it's not like you can corral a bunch of airborne viruses and tell them they're banned from OBGYN. Leo and Kat are worried that if this bird flu thing is the real deal, she could bring it home. Leo's willing to take his chances but when I said, "Would you like to have the kids stay with me for a while?" Kat said, "That would make us both feel so much better," so voila, here I am, hosting an eleven-year-old and a thirteen-year-old. Monika is thirteen, Jo is eleven.

We have a guest room and a sofa bed. Monika got the guest room, Jo's on the sofa bed, although we promised to renegotiate this in a few days if they're still here. (It's actually a double bed in the guest room but trust me, you don't want to make my nieces share a bed if you don't absolutely have to.)

I went to the store today to stock up just in case we want to minimize the "leaving the house" stuff for a while. Apparently I wasn't the only person who had that thought because (a) the lines were unbelievable and (b) I tried *four stores* and they were *all* completely out of milk and eggs. I did manage to get an enormous jumbo package of toilet paper plus a huge sack of rat food. (Did I mention that Jo has a pet rat named Jerry Springer? I didn't? Well, my younger niece Jo has a pet rat named Jerry Springer. The rat was not actually invited along for the family dinner, but Dominic ran over today to pick the rat up because he thought Jo would feel better about the whole situation if she had her pet staying here, too.)

The freezer section was also incredibly picked over but at the Asian grocery (store #4) I bought some enormous sacks of rice and also about fifteen pounds of frozen dumplings and you know what, I'm not going to try to list what I came home with as it would be too embarrassing. I'll just stick to the essentials, which is, *no milk and no eggs*. I did manage to get some butter, but it was the super-fancy organic kind that's $10 per pound so I was also a little worried about using up our butter reserve on one batch of cookies. And Jo really wanted chocolate chip cookies.

Okay, actually: *I* really wanted chocolate chip cookies. But Jo was very willing to agree that she wanted some, too.

You can substitute mayo for eggs, in cookies, and you can substitute oil for the butter. They'll be better cookies if you happen to have some sesame oil to put in for part of the oil (or any other nut-related oil) and we did, in fact, have sesame oil. And as it happens, those four grocery stores were *not* out of chocolate chips.

Here's the recipe in case you are also improvising today:

- 2½ cups flour
- 1 tsp baking soda
- 1 tsp salt
- 1 cup of vegetable oils (preferable 2 T sesame oil + canola oil to equal 1 cup)
- ¾ cup white sugar
- ¾ cup brown sugar
- 1 tsp vanilla extract
- 6 tablespoons of mayonnaise
- 12 ounces of whatever sort of chips you have in the house, or chopped up chocolate

Cream the sugar and the oil, then beat in the mayonnaise. I *promise* the cookies will turn out fine, no matter how gross the mayo smells and looks while you're beating it in. Mix the baking soda, salt, and flour together, then gradually beat in the mayo mixture, and stir in your chips.

Drop by rounded spoonfuls—oh, you know how to make cookies. You don't have to grease your cookie sheets. Bake at 375F for about ten minutes and if you want them to stay chewy and soft, put them away in an airtight container before they're all the way cool. If you like your cookies crunchy, well, what's wrong with you? But in that case cool them before you put them away, and in fact you'll probably be happier storing them in something that's not airtight, like a classic cookie jar.

I gave Dominic the first batch and he said, "You didn't use up all the butter on this, did you?" I told him we're not about to run out of butter. We are, however, about to run out of coffee. I may die. Even if I don't get bird flu. Excuse me, H5N1.

xxoo, Natalie

Homemade Pizza

So, how are things where *you* live?

Where *I* live (Minneapolis) there have been 83 confirmed cases of H5N1. The good news (!!!) is that it's apparently not as lethal in the human-to-human variant as it was back when it was just birds-to-human, but since it was 60% lethal in the old form that's not really what I think of as *good* good news. The bad news is that there's a four-day incubation period so those 83 people all infected others and this is only the tiny, tiny tip of a giant, lethal iceberg.

Probably wherever you live you're hearing about "social distancing," which in most places means "we're going to shut down the schools and movie theaters and other places where folks might gather, stagger work hours to minimize crowding, and instruct everyone to wear face masks and not stand too close to each other when they're waiting in lines." In Minneapolis, they're already worried enough that they're saying that anyone who can just stay home should go ahead and do that. Since Dominic works in IT and can telecommute, that's us. I'd planned to go to the store today again to maybe get milk and eggs. If it had been just me and Dominic . . . I still wouldn't have risked it. But I *definitely* wasn't going to risk it with Jo and Monika in the house.

I made homemade pizza for lunch. The same recipe I made last December right after I got the pizza stone for Christmas—but no fresh mushrooms. We had a can of pineapple tidbits and some pepperoni so that's what we topped it with. I thought about trying some of the dried shiitake mushrooms on the pizza but on thinking about it I didn't think the texture would work.

We are now completely out of milk, which makes breakfast kind of a problem, and we're also out of coffee, which makes *everything about my day* kind of a problem. Fortunately, we still have some Lipton tea bags (intended for iced tea in the summer) and that's what I used for my caffeine fix.

(Running out of coffee was pure stupidity on my part. I even remember seeing it on the shelf at the grocery store, but I'm picky about my coffee and I was planning to go to my coffee shop for fresh beans today. Ha ha ha! Folgers and Maxwell House sound pretty good to me now!)

xxoo, Natalie

Eggless Pancakes and Homemade Syrup

In the comments on my last post, someone wanted to know about grocery delivery. We *do* have grocery delivery in the Twin Cities, but every single store that offers it is currently saying that they are only providing it to current customers. I did register an account with all the places that do it, and I've put in an Amazon order for a bunch of items you can have delivered (like more TP) and I'm hoping they don't email me back to say they ran out and cancelled my order . . . anyway, I don't know if I'll be able to order anything grocery-like anytime soon.

Some of the restaurants in town are still delivering food and I don't know how I feel about that. Dominic and I are very lucky in that we do have the option of staying home. That makes me feel a little guilty, but in fact, me going out would not make the people who still *have* to go out, for their jobs, even one tiny bit safer. Quite the opposite. If I got infected, I'd be one more person spreading the virus. (Including to my nieces.) Anyway, Kat has to go out because she's a labor and delivery nurse, and people are depending on her. But I don't know if a pizza delivery guy should really be considered essential personnel.

In any case, no one delivers breakfast (which was what I sat down to write about) and no one's going to bring me milk, so I made milk-less, egg-less, butter-less pancakes, and so can you. Here's what you need:

- 2 cups of flour
- 4 tsp baking powder
- 1 tsp salt

Blend that together and then add:

- ½ cup of pureed banana OR pureed pumpkin OR applesauce OR any other pureed fruit you've got around. I used banana because I have some bananas in my freezer.

- 1½ cups of water
- 1 tsp vanilla extract
- ½ tsp cinnamon
- ½ cup sugar

Whisk it all together. You'll need to grease your skillet a little bit extra because this sticks more than pancakes that were made with butter or oil.

We're out of maple syrup, but it turned out we still had a bottle of blueberry syrup in the back of a cabinet and that's what we had with them. There are recipes online for homemade pancake syrup but I haven't tried them yet. Monika hated the blueberry syrup and just ate them with sugar and cinnamon. Jo thought the blueberry syrup was fine but agreed that maple (or even fake maple) would be better. (I'm with Monika, for the record.)

xxoo, Natalie

Miscellaneous Soup

So, before we get to the recipe today, I was wondering if people could do a favor for one of my friends. Melissa is a waitress, and so far *thank God* she is still healthy but her restaurant has shut down for the duration. So, it's good that she's not going to be fired for not coming in to work, and she's glad to stay home where she's safe, but she *really needs that job* to pay for things like her rent. Anyway, I talked her into setting up a GoFundMe and if you could throw in even a dollar, that would be a big help. Also, to sweeten the pot a little, if you donate anything (even just a dollar!) I'll throw your name into a hat and draw one reader and that lucky reader will get to have me make, and eat, and blog, *anything you want*, although if you want me to do that before the pandemic is over you'll be stuck choosing from the stuff I can make with the ingredients that are in my house. And I just drove a carload of groceries over to Melissa because she and her daughter were basically out of food, and the food shelves are not running, either. (So, if you were thinking that blueberry-glazed carrots or something would be good, you're already too late, because she is now the proud owner of that bottle of blueberry syrup. Also, I'm out of carrots.)

Anyway, go donate! If you've ever wanted me to try again with the Baked Alaska, or experiment with dishwasher salmon, *now's your chance*.

Today, I made Miscellaneous Soup. That is the soup of all the miscellaneous things you have lying around. I actually make this quite often, but I've never blogged about it before, because I just don't think most people would be very impressed. Ordinarily, I make it with stock (boxed stock, if I don't want to waste my homemade stock on this sort of meal), and some leftover cooked meat if I've got it, and whatever vegetables are in the fridge, and either some canned beans or some noodles or both.

What I used today:

- 2 packets of ramen noodles, including their little flavoring sachet
- Wine (we are not even close to being out of wine. Too bad it's not very good poured over breakfast cereal.)
- ½ pound of frozen roast corn
- ¼ pound of frozen mixed vegetables
- 2 cups dry lentils
- ½ pound of frozen turkey meatballs

I heated up 4 cups of water and added the flavoring packet, 1 cup of wine, and the lentils. From my spice drawer, I also added some cumin and coriander, because I thought they'd go reasonably well with the spice packet. I cooked the lentils in the broth. I thawed out the corn and the mixed veggies and threw that in and then cooked the turkey meatballs in the oven because that's what the bag wants you to do and then I broke up the ramen brick and threw that in and added the meatballs. And that's what we all had for dinner.

Jo hates lentils and Monika didn't like the frozen roast corn but after some complaining they ate it all anyway. And Andrea and Tom liked it fine.

Right, I guess I should fill you in about Andrea and Tom.

Andrea is a friend of Monika's from school; they're both in eighth grade. Monika found out (I guess from a text?) that Andrea was home alone with her brother, Tom, because their mother is so worried about bringing the flu home that she's been sleeping in the car instead of coming home. Tom is only three. Also, they were totally out of food, which is why Monika brought this up (after I did the grocery drop off for Melissa).

I told her that *of course* we could bring some food over to her friend, but when I realized Andrea was taking care of a three-year-old full time I suggested they come over here, instead.

So now Monika and Jo *are* sharing the double bed in the guest room, because sorry, girls, sometimes "shared sacrifice" means a shared bed. Andrea is on the sofa bed and Tom is on the loveseat. Well, he was on the loveseat last night. I think tonight he's going to be on the loveseat cushions and those cushions are going to be on the floor so he's got less far to fall if he rolls off again.

Can I just say, this is not exactly how I'd imagined my February. But at least we're all healthy and not out of food yet.

xxoo, Natalie

Ten Things I'm Going to Make When This Is Over

Dinner today was hamburger and rice. I kept looking at recipes and crying, and Dominic wound up cooking.

I kind of want to tell you all the things we're out of. Like, AA batteries. (I had to track down a corded mouse from the closet where we shove all the electronic stuff we don't use anymore, because my cordless mouse uses AA batteries.) Dishwasher detergent. (We still have dish soap, but you can't put that in a dishwasher. So we're washing everything by hand.) But you remember when we used to say, "first-world problems" about petty complaints? These are healthy-person problems.

We got a call today that Kat is sick. She's been working 16-hour shifts because some of the other nurses are sick and some of them were refusing to come in and they *needed* nurses because the babies have still been coming, because they're going to just keep doing that. Literally everyone is in masks and gloves all the time, but—today she's running a fever.

Leo says she's not going to go into the hospital because there isn't anything they can really do for you anyway, especially as overloaded as they are. She's just going to stay at home and drink fluids and try to be one of the 68% who've been making it through.

So yeah, I wasn't going to tell you about that when I sat down, I was going to tell you all about the things I've been craving that I'm going to make when all this is over but I guess what I really want to say is that the top ten things I want to make when all this is over are ten different flavors of cupcake for Kat, because Kat loves my cupcakes, and if you're into prayer or good thoughts or anything like that, please send some her way.

There's still time to donate to Melissa and choose something to have me make. But, seriously, you'll want to wait until this is over because there's just not much in the house.

Kale Juice Smoothies (Not Really)

Dear crazy people who read my blog,

I know—well, I'm pretty sure—that you're trying to be helpful.

But telling me that all my sister-in-law (the mother of my nieces!) needs to do to recover is drink kale juice smoothies with extra wheatgrass and whatever else was supposed to go in your Magic Immune Tonic? *Not helpful*. First of all, she's sick with a disease with a 32% fatality rate. Second of all, *even if* kale or kelp or whatever it was was *magic*, have you actually been reading my blog? We are eating rice, with flavored olive oil, for fully half our meals now. Today we mixed in some dry corn flakes, partly for the textural variety but partly just because we could make less rice because we're starting to worry that we're going to run out of that, too.

I can produce a kale smoothie for Kat like I can pull a live, clucking chicken out of my ass and make her some chicken soup with it.

Also, this is a food blog, not a conspiracy theory blog. If you want to try to convince people that the government is infecting everyone on purpose toward some nefarious end, go do it somewhere else.

No love,

Natalie

Rabbit Stew

There are these rabbits that live in our yard. I swear we have like six. They're the reason I can't grow lettuce in my garden. (Well, that plus I'd rather use the space for tomatoes.)

I am pretty sure I could rig up a trap for it with items I have around the house and bunnies are delicious.

Pros:

Fresh meat!

Cons:

Dominic thinks it's possible we could get influenza from eating the bunny. (I think he's being paranoid and as long as we cook it really well we should be fine. I could braise it in wine.)

I have no actual idea how to skin and gut a rabbit, but I have sharp knives and the Internet and I'm very resourceful.

Jo is aghast at the idea of eating a bunny.

We'd probably catch at most one rabbit, and one rabbit split between all these people isn't very much rabbit.

It's even more people now, because we've added another kid. (You can feel free to make a Pied Piper joke. Or a crazy cat lady joke. We are making *all the jokes* because it's the only stress release I've got remaining to me.) Arie is twelve, and came really close to being driven back to his cold, empty apartment after he suggested we eat Jo's rat. (If he were just out of food, we could send him home with food, but the heat's also gone out, the landlord's not answering the phone, and it's February and we live in Minnesota.)

Arie is Andrea's cousin. Or, hold on, I take it back. Maybe he's her cousin's friend? You know what, I just didn't ask that many questions when I heard "twelve" and "no heat."

xxoo, Natalie

This is no longer a food blog

This is a boredom and isolation blog.

Also a stress management blog. Normally, I manage stress by cooking. Except we're out of some key ingredient for like 85 percent of the recipes I can find, and also out of all the obvious substitutes (or nearly) and I'm starting to worry that we will actually run out of food altogether. I've pondered trying to reverse-engineer flour by crushing the flakes of the Raisin Bran in my food processor, like some very high-tech version of Laura Ingalls grinding up unprocessed wheat in a coffee mill in *The Long Winter*.

My cute little bungalow is very spacious for me and Dominic. For me, Dominic, and five kids ranging in age from three to thirteen, it's starting to feel a little cramped. Monika brought a laptop and she, Arie, and Andrea all want turns using it. (Jo doesn't ask very often, she just sighs a martyred sigh and says no it's *fine* she *understands* why the big kids are hogging the computer.) We are thoroughly expert on the streaming movies available on every online service but the problem is, if it's appropriate for Tom to watch, the big kids mostly aren't interested. We did find a few old-timey musicals that everyone could tolerate but now Tom wants to watch them over and over and Andrea says if she has to listen to "the hiiiiiiiiills are aliiiiiiiiive with the sound of muuuuuuuuuusic" one more time she might smash the TV with a brick.

We have a backyard and from an influenza infection standpoint it's reasonably safe to play back there, but it's February in Minnesota and we're having a cold snap, like yesterday morning it was -30 with the windchill. (The good news: the cold temperatures might slow the spread of the virus.)

So here's what we did today: I had some craft paints in the basement, and brushes, so we pulled all the living room furniture away from the wall and I let them paint a mural. The good news: this kept them happily occupied all afternoon. The even better news: they're not done yet.

xxoo, Natalie

Birthday Pancake Cake

Today is Jo's birthday, and everyone almost forgot. In part because she clearly expected that everyone had more important things on their mind and wasn't going to bring it up. Monika, bless her cranky thirteen-year-old heart, remembered.

I thought at first we were not going to be able to bake her a cake. (Unless I really could figure out a way to turn cereal flakes into usable flour, and probably not even then.) But when I went digging yesterday for the craft paint in the basement, I found this small box of just-add-water pancake mix with our camping equipment. If I'd remembered it before now, I totally would've turned it into breakfast at some point, so thank goodness for absentmindedness. We also still had a package of instant butterscotch pudding mix, unused since you really can't make instant pudding without milk.

The other kids took a break from painting the mural and instead made decorations out of printer paper, scissors, and pens. (They made a chain-link streamer.)

I think there's got to be a way to turn pancake mix into a proper cake, but all the methods I found online needed ingredients I didn't have. So I wound up making the pancake mix into pancakes, then turning the pancakes into a cake with butterscotch frosting in between layers. (To make butterscotch frosting, I used some melted butter—we still had a little left—and some oil, and the butterscotch pudding mix.)

And we stuck two votive candles on it and sang.

Jo did get presents, despite my cluelessness. The mail is still coming—some days—and her father remembered. A big box full of presents ordered from online showed up late in the day, signed "with love from Mom and Dad," which made her cry.

We've been getting updates on Kat, which mostly I haven't been sharing because they haven't been very good. We're just trying to soldier on, I guess. And today that meant celebrating Jo's birthday.

It Feels Like Christmas

You guys, YOU GUYS. We're going to get a food delivery! Of something! Maybe I should back up and explain. The local Influenza Task Force arranged for the grocery stores with delivery services to hire on a whole lot more people, mostly people like Melissa whose jobs are shut down, and they're now staffed well enough to do deliveries nearly everywhere. Everyone was assigned to a grocer and since we have eight people living here (oh, did I mention Arie also had a friend who needed somewhere quarantined to stay? We are full up now, seriously, the bathroom situation is beyond critical already and we've been rotating turns to sleep on the floor) we're allowed to buy up to $560 worth of stuff and it should arrive sometime in the next few days. They've instructed us not to go out to meet the delivery person: they'll leave it on our doorstep and go.

Of course, the problem is that they are out of practically everything. Minneapolis is such a hot spot, a lot of delivery drivers don't want to come here, plus things are such a mess in California that not much produce is going anywhere at all, so there was no fresh produce of any kind available. I was able to order frozen peaches—though who knows if they'll actually bring any. Of course there was no milk or eggs but they had almond milk in stock so I ordered almond milk because at least you can use it in baking. They also warned me that in the event that something went out of stock they'd just make a substitution so *who even knows*, see, it'll be totally like Christmas, where you give your mom a wish list and maybe something you put on it shows up under the tree.

I did include a note saying to please, please, *please* make sure that we got either coffee or *something* with caffeine. If I have to drink Diet Mountain Dew for breakfast, I will. I mean, we had a two-liter of Coke and I've been rationing it out and it's going flat and I don't even care. Well, I do care. But I care more about the headaches I get when deprived of my morning caffeine fix.

Some of you were asking about Kat. She's hanging in there, and Leo has stayed healthy. Thanks for asking.

Someone also asked about the rabbits. So far I have not murdered any of the local wildlife, because maybe I'm slightly squeamish, and Dominic is definitely squeamish.

xxoo, Natalie

Rice Krispies Treats

So, here's what came in the box from the grocery store. In addition to a bunch of generally useful items like meat, oil, pancake mix, etc., we got:

- 12 cans of coconut milk
- 1 enormous can of off-brand vacuum-packed ground coffee THANK YOU GOD
- 3 bags of miniature marshmallows
- 2 large cans of butter-flavored shortening
- 1 enormous pack of TP THANK YOU GOD. I am not going to tell you what we were substituting.
- 1 small pack of AA batteries
- A sack of Hershey's Miniatures, you know, itty bitty candy bars like you give out on Halloween
- 14 little boxes of Jell-O gelatin
- 1 absolutely goliath-sized sack of knock-off Rice Krispies look-alikes

Most of this was not stuff we ordered. In a few cases, I could make a guess what the substitution was. I wanted flour, I got pancake mix. (That one's not bad.) I wanted chocolate chips, I got Hershey's Miniatures. (Again, not bad.) I ordered some grape juice concentrate because we've been out of anything fruit-like for days and days and although technically you can't get scurvy this quickly (I checked) I've been craving things like carrots and I thought maybe some fruit juice would help. I think the coconut milk was the substitute for the almond milk.

I have no idea why I got the Crispy Rice. I didn't ask for cereal. We still even have some cereal. But! They also gave us marshmallows and butter-flavored shortening (if not actual butter) so you know what it's time for, don't you? That's right. RICE KRISPIES TREATS.

I made these once when I was a kid without a microwave oven, and let me just tell you, they are a *lot* of *work* when you don't have a microwave oven. You have to stand over a stove, stirring marshmallows over low heat, for what feels like two hours. They'll still give you stovetop directions but I highly recommend microwave cooking for these.

What you'll need:

- 3 tablespoons butter (or margarine or butter-flavored shortening. You can even use extra-virgin olive oil! But I do not recommend using garlic-infused extra-virgin olive oil.)
- 1 10-oz bag of marshmallows (or 4 cups of mini marshmallows or 1 jar of marshmallow fluff)
- 6 cups rice cereal (or corn flakes or Cheerios or whatever cereal you've got on hand but if you decide to use bran flakes or Grape Nuts I'm not responsible for the results)

Put your butter and your marshmallows into a microwave-safe bowl. Heat on high for two minutes. Stir. Heat on high for another minute. Stir until smooth. Add the cereal. Stir until distributed.

Spray or oil a 13x9 inch pan and spread the marshmallow mixture out in the pan. Not surprisingly this is incredibly sticky and you'll want to use waxed paper folded over your hands, or a greased spatula, or possibly you could just butter your own hands but be careful not to burn yourself. Let it cool and then cut it into squares.

Dominic came in while I was spreading the stuff out in my pan and said, "What are you doing?"

I said, "I'm making coq au vin, asshole."

He said, "This is why I can't have nice things."

Maybe you had to be there.

For dinner tonight, we had minute steaks and Rice Krispies Treats. *And there was great rejoicing.*

xxoo, Natalie

Katrina Jane, March 5, 1972–February 20, 2018

I've got nothing today. I'm sorry.

My brother was coughing when he called to tell us the bad news, but said he wasn't sick, didn't have a fever, and definitely hadn't caught the flu from Kat.

Thanks for everyone's thoughts and prayers. I know I'm not the only person grieving here, so just know that I'm thinking of you, even as you're thinking of me.

You Still Have to Eat

Leo had Kat cremated but he's going to wait to have a memorial service until we can all come—including her kids. Monika was furious and insisted that she wants a proper funeral, and wants to go, and thinks it should be this week like funerals normally are, and of course that's just not possible. They can't actually stop us from having gatherings but there are no churches, no funeral homes, no nothing that's going to let you set up folding chairs and have a bunch of people sitting together and delivering eulogies.

We finally talked Monika down by holding our own memorial service, with as many of the trappings as we could possibly put together. We made floral arrangements by taking apart the floral wreath I had in the kitchen with dried lavender in it. We all dressed in black, even though that meant most of the kids had to borrow stuff out of my closet. Then we put out folding chairs in the living room and Dominic led us in a funeral service.

Monika had wanted to do a eulogy but she was crying too hard. She'd written it out, though, so Arie read it for her. I saved it, in case she wants to read it at the real memorial service. Well, maybe for her, this will always be the real memorial service. But there will be another one, a public one, when the epidemic is over.

In Minnesota after a funeral, there's usually lunch in a church basement and there's often this dish called ambrosia salad. (Maybe other states have this? I haven't been to very many funerals outside Minnesota.) I was missing some of the ingredients, but I did have lime Jell-O and mini-marshmallows and even a pack of frozen non-dairy topping and I used canned mandarin oranges instead of the crushed pineapple, and mixed all together that worked pretty well. We had ambrosia salad and breakfast sausages for lunch. (I don't know why we got so many packs of breakfast sausages, but it's food, and everyone likes them, so we've been eating them almost every day, mostly not for breakfast.)

Monika asked if she could save her share of the ambrosia salad in the fridge until tomorrow, because she really likes it, and she didn't feel like eating, and didn't want anyone else to eat her share. (Which was a legitimate worry.) I put it in a container and wrote MONIKA'S, NO ONE ELSE TOUCH ON PAIN OF BEING FED TO THE RAT in Sharpie on the lid. Which made her laugh, a little. I guess that's good.

Jo sat through the service and ate her lunch and didn't say a word. Mostly she looks like she doesn't really believe it.

Stone Soup

Arie informed me today that the thing I called "Miscellaneous Soup" is actually called "Stone Soup," after a folk story where three hungry strangers trick villagers into feeding them. In the story they announce that they're going to make soup for everyone out of a rock, and when curious villagers come to check out what they're doing, say that the soup would be better with a carrot or two . . . and an onion . . . and maybe some potatoes . . . and some beans . . . and one villager brings potatoes, and another one brings an onion, and in the end, there's a lovely pot of soup for everyone.

I started to point out that I wasn't tricking anybody, all this stuff was in my cabinet already, but then I realized that I didn't just have dinner but an *activity* and all the kids came into the kitchen and acted out the story with little Tom playing the hungry stranger trying to get everyone to chip in for the soup and then throwing each item into the pot.

Then they all made cookies, while I watched, using mayo for the eggs and dicing up mini candy bars for the chips.

It was a sunny day today—cold, but really sunny—and we spread out a picnic cloth and ate in the living room, Stone Soup and chocolate chip cookies and everyone went around in a circle and said the thing they were most looking forward to doing when this was over. Monika said she wanted to be able to take an hour-long shower (everyone's limited to seven minutes or we run out of hot water). Dominic said he wanted to go to the library. I said I wanted to bake a chocolate soufflé. Everyone complained about that and said it couldn't be cooking or baking, so I said I wanted to go see a movie, in a theater, something funny, and eat popcorn.

Tomorrow is the first of March.

Hydration

Dominic is sick. It's not flu. I mean, it can't be; we haven't gone out. Literally the whole point of staying in like this has been to avoid exposure. It also can't be anything *else* you'd catch. We thought at first possibly it was food poisoning, but no one else is sick and we've all been eating the same food. According to Dr. Google, who admittedly is sort of a specialist in worst-case scenarios, it's either diverticulitis or appendicitis. Or a kidney stone.

Obviously, going in to a doctor's office is not on the table. We did a phone consultation. The guy we talked to said that yes, it could be any of those things and offered to call in a prescription for Augmentin if we could find a pharmacy that had it. The problem is, even though H5N1 is a virus and antibiotics won't do anything for it, there are a lot of people who didn't believe this and some of them had doctors willing to prescribe whatever they were asking for and the upshot is, all our pharmacies are out of almost everything. Oh, plus a bunch of pharmacies got robbed, though mostly that was for pain meds. Pharmacies are as much of a mess as anything else, is what I'm saying.

I'm not giving up, because in addition to the pharmacies that answered the phone and said they didn't have any, there were a ton where no one even picked up. I'm going to keep trying. In the meantime, we're keeping Dominic hydrated and hoping for the best. I always keep a couple of bottles of Pedialyte around, because the last thing you want to do when you're puking is drive to the store, and that stuff's gross enough that no one's tried to get me to pop it open for dessert. So I've got it chilled and he's trying to drink sips.

If it's a kidney stone, Augmentin won't do anything, but eventually he'll pass the stone and recover, although it'll really suck in the meantime. (I wish we had some stronger pain medication than Tylenol. For real, *no one* has Vicodin right now. Not a single pharmacy.) If it's appendicitis, there's a 75% chance that the Augmentin will fix it. (This is new! Well, I mean, it's new information. There was a study on treating appendicitis with antibiotics and 75% of cases are a type of appendicitis that won't rupture and can be treated with antibiotics! And if you get a CT scan they can tell whether that's the kind you've got, but, well.) If it's diverticulitis, and he can keep down fluids, the antibiotics should help. If he's got the worse kind, and can't keep down fluids, they would normally hospitalize him for IV antibiotics and maybe do surgery. But again, not an option.

Oh, it could also be cancer. (Thanks, Dr. Google!) In which case there's no point worrying about it until the epidemic is over.

Cream of Augmentin

I got an email from someone who has Augmentin they're willing to sell me. Or at least they say it's Augmentin. I guess I'd have to trust them, which is maybe a questionable decision. They want $1,000 for the bottle, cash only. Dominic was appalled that I'd even consider this. He thought it was a scam, and they were planning to just steal the cash.

Fortunately I also got through to a pharmacy that still had it, a little neighborhood place. Dominic's doctor called in the prescription, and I gave them my credit card number over the phone, and they actually delivered it. While I was on the phone with them they listed out some other things they have in stock and in addition to the Augmentin we got toothpaste and a big stack of last month's magazines. Shout out to St. Paul Corner Drug: we are going to get every prescription from you for the rest of our natural lives.

I was hoping that starting the Augmentin would make Dominic at least a little better right away, but instead he's getting worse.

Possibly this is just a reaction to the Augmentin. It's not as bad as some antibiotics, but it can definitely upset your stomach, which is pretty counterproductive when puking and stomach pain are your major symptoms.

I had appendicitis when I was a teenager. I spent a day throwing up, and when I got worse instead of better my mother took me to the emergency room. I wound up having surgery. Afterwards I was restricted to clear liquids for a while, just broth and Jell-O and tea, which I got really tired of before they let me back on solid food. My mother smuggled in homemade chicken stock for me in a Thermos—it was still a clear liquid, but at least it was the homemade kind, the healing kind.

If I could pull a live, clucking chicken out of my ass, like I joked about, I would wring its neck and turn it into stock right now for Dominic. Nothing's staying down, did I mention that? Nothing. But it's not like we have anything for him other than Pedialyte.

I'm going to try to catch a rabbit.

Rabbit Soup

You guys, you really can find instructions for just about anything online. Okay, I've never looked to see if there's a YouTube video on how to commit the perfect crime, but trapping an animal? Well, among other things, it turns out that the cartoon-style box-leaned-up-against-a-stick-with-bait-underneath is totally a thing you can actually do, but then you've got a live animal and if you're planning to eat it you'll still need to kill it. I wound up making a wire snare using instructions I found online in the hopes that the snare would do the dirty work for me. And it did. More or less. I'll spare you the details, other than to say, rabbits can scream.

You can also find instructions for gutting and skinning a rabbit online. I used my kitchen shears for some of this, and I worked outside so that Jo didn't have to watch. My backyard now looks like a murder scene, by the way, and my fingers were so cold by the end I couldn't feel them. I feel like I ought to use the fur for something but I don't think Home Taxidermy is the sort of craft that's going to keep the pack of preteens cheerfully occupied. (Right now they're reading through all the magazines we got from the pharmacy and I'm pretending not to notice that one of them is *Cosmo*.)

Back inside I browned the rabbit in the oven, since roasted chicken bones make for much tastier stock than just raw chicken, and then I covered it in just enough water to cover and simmered it for six hours. This would be better stock if I had an onion or some carrots or even some onion or carrot peelings, but we make do. The meat came off the bones, and I took out the meat and chopped it up and put it in the fridge for later, and I boiled the bones for a bit longer and then added a little bit of salt.

The secret to good stock, by the way, is to put in just enough water to cover the bones, and to cook it at a low temperature for a very long time. So there wasn't a whole lot of stock, in the end: just one big mug full.

The kids have been staying downstairs, trying to keep out of Dominic's way. Jo and Monika made dinner for the rest of us last night (rice and break-fast sausages) so I could take care of him. I saw Jo watching me while I carried up the mug of soup, though.

The bedroom doesn't smell very pleasant at the moment—sweat, vomit, and cucumber-scented cleaner from Target. It's too cold to open the windows, even just for a little while.

Dominic didn't want it. I'd been making him sip Pedialyte but mostly he was just throwing it up again, and he was dehydrated. I pulled up a stool and sat by the edge of his bed with a spoon and told him he had to have a spoonful. So he swallowed that, and I waited to see if it stayed down, or came back up. It stayed down.

Two minutes later I gave him another spoonful. That stayed down, too.

This is how you rehydrate a little kid, by the way: one teaspoonful every two minutes. It takes a long time to get a mug into someone if you're going a teaspoon at a time, but eventually the whole mug was gone. The Augmentin stayed down, too.

I went downstairs and set another snare in the backyard.

Something Decadent

So, thank you everyone who donated to Melissa's fundraiser. I put all the names in the hat and drew out Jessie from Boston, Massachusetts, and she says she doesn't want me to wait until everything is over, she wants a recipe now. And her request was, "Make something decadent. Whatever you've got that *can* be decadent." And Dominic is sufficiently recovered today, that he can eat something decadent and not regret it horribly within ten minutes, so let's do this thing.

We still have no milk, no cream, no eggs. I used the frozen whipped topping for the ambrosia salad and the marshmallows for the Rice Krispies Treats (which aren't exactly *decadent*, anyway).

But! Let's talk about coconut milk. If you open a can of coconut milk without shaking it up, you'll find this gloppy almost-solid stuff clinging to the sides of the can; that's coconut cream. You can chill it, and whip it, and it turns into something like whipped cream. We set aside the coconut cream from three of the cans and chilled it.

I had no baking cocoa, because we used it all up a while back on a not-terribly-successful attempt at making hot chocolate, but I *did* have some mini Hershey bars still, so I melted the dark chocolate ones and cooled it, and thinned that out with just a tiny bit of the reserved coconut milk. It wasn't a ton of chocolate, just so you know—it's been a bit of a fight to keep people from just scarfing that candy straight down. But we had a little.

Then I whipped the coconut cream until it was very thick and almost stiff, and then mixed in the dark chocolate and a little bit of extra sugar, and it turned into this coconut-chocolate mousse.

When eating decadent food, presentation counts for a *lot*. We used some beautiful china teacups that I got from my great-grandmother: I scooped coconut-chocolate mousse into eight of them, and then I took the last of the milk chocolate mini bars and grated them with a little hand grater to put chocolate shavings on top. We also had some sparkly purple sprinkles up with the cake decorations so I put just a tiny pinch of that onto each cup. And I opened one of the cans of mandarin oranges and each of the mousse cups got two little orange wedges.

And I tied a ribbon around the handles of each teacup.

And then we set the table with the tablecloth and the nice china and we ate our Stone Soup of the day by candlelight and then I brought out the mousse and everyone ate theirs and then licked out the cups.

Some days it's hard to imagine that this will ever be over, that we'll ever be able to get things back to normal at all. When everyone is sniping at each other it feels like you've always been trapped in the middle of a half-dozen bickering children and always will be. When you're in the midst of grief, it's hard to imagine spring ever coming.

But Dominic pulled through, and Leo didn't get sick. And tying the ribbons around the handles, I knew: this will all come to an end. We'll survive this, and everyone will go home. *I'm going to miss them*, I thought, this pack of other people's children I've crammed into my bungalow.

"Can I keep the ribbon?" Jo asked, when she was done with her mousse.

I told her, of course she could. And then she and Monika started arguing over whether she could have Monika's ribbon, too, because *of course they did*, and that was our day, I guess, in a nutshell.

xxoo, Natalie

Carrie Vaughn is best known for her *New York Times* bestselling series of novels about a werewolf named Kitty, the fourteenth installment of which is *Kitty Saves the World*. She's written several other contemporary fantasy and young adult novels, as well as upwards of eighty short stories. She's a contributor to the Wild Cards series of shared-world superhero books edited by George R. R. Martin and a graduate of the Odyssey Fantasy Writing Workshop. An Air Force brat, she survived her nomadic childhood and managed to put down roots in Boulder, Colorado. Visit her at www.carrievaughn.com.

BANNERLESS

Carrie Vaughn

Enid and Bert walked the ten miles from the way station because the weather was good, a beautiful spring day. Enid had never worked with the young man before, but he turned out to be good company: chatty without being oppressively extroverted. Young, built like a redwood, he looked the part of an investigator. They talked about home and the weather and trivialities—but not the case. She didn't like to dwell on the cases she was assigned to before getting a firsthand look at them. She had expected Bert to ask questions about it, but he was taking her lead.

On this stretch of the Coast Road, halfway between the way station and Southtown, ruins were visible in the distance, to the east. An old sprawling city from before the big fall. In her travels in her younger days, she'd gone into it a few times, to shout into the echoing artificial canyons and study overgrown asphalt roads and cracked walls with fallen roofs. She rarely saw people, but often saw old cook fires and cobbled together shantytowns that couldn't support the lives struggling within them. Scavengers and scattered folk still came out from them sometimes, then faded back to the concrete enclaves, surviving however they survived.

Bert caught her looking.

"You've been there?" Bert said, nodding toward the haze marking the swath of ruined city. No paths or roads ran that way anymore. She'd had to go overland when she'd done it.

"Yes, a long time ago."

"What was it like?"

The answer could either be very long or very short. The stories of what had happened before and during the fall were terrifying and intriguing, but the ruins no longer held any hint of those tales. They were bones, in the process of disappearing. "It was sad," she said finally.

"I'm still working through the histories," he said. "For training, right? There's a lot of diaries. Can be hard, reading how it was at the fall."

"Yes."

In isolation, any of the disasters that had struck would not have overwhelmed the old world. The floods alone would not have destroyed the cities. The vicious influenza epidemic—a mutated strain with no available vaccine that incapacitated victims in a matter of hours—by itself would have been survivable, eventually. But the floods, the disease, the rising ocean levels, the monster storms piling one on top of the other, an environment off balance that chipped away at infrastructure and made each recovery more difficult than the one before it, all of it left too many people with too little to survive on. Wealth meant nothing when there was simply nothing left. So, the world died. But people survived, here and there. They came together and saved what they could. They learned lessons.

The road curved into the next valley and they approached Southtown, the unimaginative name given to this district's main farming settlement. Windmills appeared first, clean towers with vertical blades spiraling gently in an unfelt breeze. Then came cisterns set on scaffolds, then plowed fields and orchards in the distance. The town was home to some thousand people scattered throughout the valley and surrounding farmlands. There was a grid of drained roads and whitewashed houses, solar and battery operated carts, some goats, chickens pecking in yards. All was orderly, pleasant. This was what rose up after the ruins fell, the home that their grandparents fled to as children.

"Will you let the local committee know we're here?" Bert asked.

"Oh, no. We don't want anyone to have warning we're here. We go straight to the household. Give them a shock."

"Makes sense."

"This is your first case, isn't it? Your first investigation?"

"It is. And . . . I guess I'm worried I might have to stop someone." Bert had a staff like hers but he knew how to use his for more than walking. He had a stunner and a pack of tranquilizer needles on his belt. All in plain view. If she did her job well enough he wouldn't need to do anything but stand behind her and look alert. A useful tool. He seemed to understand his role.

"I doubt you will. Our reputation will proceed us. It's why we have the reputation in the first place. Don't worry."

"I just need to act as terrifying as the reputation says I do."

She smiled. "Exactly—you know just how this works, then."

They wore brown tunics and trousers with gray sashes. Somber colors, cold like winter, probably designed to inspire a chill. Bert stood a head taller than she did and looked like he could break tree trunks. How sinister, to see the pair of them approach.

"And you—this is your last case, isn't it?"

That was what she'd told the regional committee, that it was time for her to go home, settle down, take up basket weaving or such like. "I've been doing this almost twenty years," she said. "It's time for me to pass the torch."

"Would you miss the travel? That's what I've been looking forward to, getting to see some of the region, you know?"

"Maybe," she said. "But I wouldn't miss the bull. You'll see what I mean."

They approached the settlement. Enid put her gaze on a young woman carrying a basket of eggs along the main road. She wore a skirt, tunic, apron, and a straw hat to keep off the sun.

"Excuse me," Enid said. The woman's hands clenched as if she was afraid she might drop the basket from fright. As she'd told Bert, their reputation preceded them. They were inspectors, and inspectors only appeared for terrible reasons. The woman's expression held shock and denial. Why would inspectors ever come to Southtown?

"Yes, how can I help you?" she said quickly, nervously.

"Can you tell us where to find Apricot Hill?" The household they'd been sent to investigate.

The woman's anxiety fell away and a light of understanding dawned. Ah, then people knew. Everyone likely knew *something* was wrong, without knowing exactly what. The whole town would know investigators were here within the hour. Enid's last case, and it was going to be all about sorting out gossip.

"Yes—take that path there, past the pair of windmills. They're on the south side of the duck pond. You'll see the clotheslines out front."

"Thank you," Enid said. The woman hurried away, hugging her basket to her chest.

Enid turned to Bert. "Ready for this?"

"Now I'm curious. Let's go."

Apricot Hill was on a nice acreage overlooking a pretty pond and a series of orchards beyond that. There was one large house, two stories with lots of windows, and an outbuilding with a pair of chimneys, a production building—Apricot Hill was centered on food processing, taking in produce from outlying farms and drying, canning, and preserving it for winter stores for the community. The holding overall was well lived in, a bit run down, cluttered, but that could mean they were busy. It was spring—nothing ready for canning yet. This should have been the season for cleaning up and making repairs.

A girl with a bundle of sheets over her arm, probably collected from the clothesline the woman had mentioned, saw them first. She peered up the hill at their arrival for a moment before dropping the sheets and running to the house. She was wispy and energetic—not the one mentioned in the report, then. Susan, and not Aren. The heads of the household were Frain and Felice.

"We are announced," Enid said wryly. Bert hooked a finger in his belt.

A whole crowd, maybe even all ten members of the household, came out of the house. A rough-looking bunch, all together. Old clothes, frowning faces. This was an adequate household, but not a happy one.

An older man, slim and weatherworn, came forward and looked as though he wished he had a weapon. This would be Frain. Enid went to him, holding her hand out for shaking.

"Hello, I'm Enid, the investigator sent by the regional committee. This is my partner, Bert. This is Apricot Hill, isn't it? You must be Frain?"

"Yes," he said cautiously, already hesitant to give away any scrap of information.

"May we step inside to talk?"

She would look like a matron to them, maybe even head of a household somewhere, if they weren't sure she didn't have a household. Investigators didn't have households; they traveled constantly, avenging angels, or so the rumors said. Her dull brown hair was rolled into a bun, her soft face had seen years and weather. They'd wonder if she'd ever had children of her own, if she'd ever earned a banner. Her spreading middle-aged hips wouldn't give a clue.

Bert stood behind her, a wall of authority. Their questions about him would be simple: How well could he use that staff he carried?

"What is this about?" Frain demanded. He was afraid. He knew what she was here for—the implications—and he was afraid.

"I think we should go inside and sit down before we talk," Enid said patiently, knowing full well she sounded condescending and unpleasant. The lines on Frain's face deepened. "Is everyone here? Gather everyone in the household to your common room."

With a curt word Frain herded the rest of his household inside.

The common room on the house's ground floor was, like the rest of the household, functional without being particularly pleasant. No vase of flowers on the long dining table. Not a spot of color on the wall except for a single faded banner: the square of red and green woven cloth that represented the baby they'd earned some sixteen years ago. That would be Susan—the one with the laundry outside. Adults had come into the household since then, but that was their last baby. Had they wanted another child badly enough that they didn't wait for their committee to award them a banner?

The house had ten members. Only nine sat around the table. Enid took her time studying them, looking into each face. Most of the gazes ducked away from her. Susan's didn't.

"We're missing someone, I think?" Enid said.

The silence was thick as oil. Bert stood easy and perfectly still behind her, hand on his belt. Oh, he was a natural at this. Enid waited a long time, until the people around the table squirmed.

"Aren," Felice said softly. "I'll go get her."

"No," Frain said. "She's sick. She can't come."

"Sick? Badly sick? Has a doctor seen her?" Enid said.

Again, the oily silence.

"Felice, if you could get her, thank you," Enid said.

A long stretch passed before Felice returned with the girl, and Enid was happy to watch while the group grew more and more uncomfortable. Susan was trembling; one of the men was hugging himself. This was as awful a gathering as she had ever seen, and her previous case had been a murder.

When Felice brought Aren into the room, Enid saw exactly what she expected to see: the older woman with her arm around a younger woman—age twenty or so—who wore a full skirt and a tunic three sizes too big that billowed in front of her. Aren moved slowly and had to keep drawing her hands away from her belly.

She might have been able to hide the pregnancy for a time, but she was now six months along, and there was no hiding that swell and the ponderous hitch in her movement.

The anger and unhappiness in the room thickened even more, and it was no longer directed at Enid.

She waited while Felice guided the pregnant woman to a chair—by herself, apart from the others.

"This is what you're here for, isn't it?" Frain demanded, his teeth bared and fists clenched.

"It is," Enid agreed.

"Who told?" Frain hissed, looking around at them all. "Which one of you told?"

No one said anything. Aren cringed and ducked her head. Felice stared at her hands in her lap.

Frain turned to Enid. "Who sent the report? I've a right to know my accuser—the household's accuser."

"The report was anonymous, but credible." Part of her job here was to discover, if she could, who sent the tip of the bannerless pregnancy to the regional committee. Frain didn't need to know that. "I'll be asking all of you questions over the next couple of days. I expect honest answers. When I am satisfied that I know what happened here, I'm authorized to pass judgment. I will do so as quickly as possible, to spare you waiting. Frain, I'll start with you."

"It was an accident. An accident, I'm sure of it. The implant failed. Aren has a boy in town; they spend all their time together. We thought nothing of it because of the implant, but then it failed, and—we didn't say anything because we were scared. That's all. We should have told the committee as soon as we knew. I'm sorry—I know now that that was wrong. You'll take that into consideration?"

"When did you know? All of you, starting with Aren—when did you know of the pregnancy?"

The young woman's first words were halting, choked. Crying had thickened her throat. "Must . . . must have been . . . two months in, I think. I was sick. I just knew."

"Did you tell anyone?"

"No, no one. I was scared."

They were all terrified. That sounded true.

"And the rest of you?"

Murmurs answered. The men shook their heads, said they'd only known for a month or so, when she could no longer hide the new shape of her. They knew for sure the day that Frain ranted about it. "I didn't rant," the man said. "I was only surprised. I lost my temper, that was all."

Felice said, "I knew when she got sick. I've been pregnant—" Her gaze went to the banner on the wall. "I know the signs. I asked her, and she told."

"You didn't think to tell anyone?"

"Frain told me not to."

So Frain knew, at least as soon as she did. The man glared fire at Felice, who wouldn't lift her gaze.

"Aren, might I speak to you alone?"

The woman cringed, back curled, arms wrapped around her belly.

"I'll go you with you, dear," Felice whispered.

"Alone," Enid said. "Bert will wait here. We'll go outside. Just a short walk."

Trembling, Aren stood. Enid stood aside to let her walk out the door first. She caught Bert's gaze and nodded. He nodded back.

Enid guided her on the path away around the house, to the garden patch and pond behind. She went slowly, letting Aren set the pace.

The physical state of a household carried information: whether rakes and shovels were hung up neat in a shed or closet, or piled haphazardly by the wall of an unpainted barn. Whether the herb garden thrived, if there were flowers in window boxes. If neat little water-smoothed stones edged the paths leading from one building to another, or if there were just dirt tracks worn into the grass. She didn't judge a household by whether or not it put a good face to the world—but she did judge them by whether or not the folk in a household worked to put on a good face for themselves. They had to live with it, look at it every single day.

This household did not have a good face. The garden patch was only just sprouting, even this far into spring. There were no flowers. The grass along the path was overgrown. There was a lack of care here that made Enid angry.

But the pond was pretty. Ducks paddled around a stand of cattails, muttering to themselves.

Enid had done this before, knew the questions to ask and what possible answers she might get to those questions. Every moment reduced the possible explanations. Heavens, she was tired of this.

Enid said, "Stop here. Roll up your sleeve."

Aren's overlarge tunic had wide sleeves that fell past her wrists. They'd be no good at all for working. The young woman stood frozen. Her lips were tightly pursed, to keep from crying.

"May I roll the sleeve up, then?" Enid asked carefully, reaching.

"No, I'll do it," she said, and clumsily pushed the fabric up to her left shoulder.

She revealed an angry scar, puckered pink, mostly healed. Doing the math, maybe seven or eight months old. The implant had been cut out, the wound not well treated, which meant she'd probably done it herself.

"Did you get anyone to stitch that up for you?" Enid asked.

"I bound it up and kept it clean." At least she didn't try to deny it. Enid guessed she would have, if Frain were there.

"Where did you put the implant after you took it out?"

"Buried it in the latrine."

Enid hoped she wouldn't have to go after it for evidence. "You did it yourself. No one forced you to, or did it to you?" That happened sometimes, someone with a skewed view of the world and what was theirs deciding they needed someone to bear a baby for them.

"It's me, it's just me. Nobody else. Just me."

"Does the father know?"

"No, I don't think. . . . He didn't know I'd taken out the implant. I don't know if he knows about the baby."

Rumors had gotten out, Enid was sure, especially if Aren hadn't been seen around town in some time. The anonymous tip about the pregnancy might have come from anywhere.

"Can you tell me the father's name, so I can speak to him?"

"Don't drag him into this; tell me you won't drag him into this. It's just me. Just take me away and be done with it." Aren stopped, her eyes closed, her face pinched. "What are you going to do to me?"

"I'm not sure yet."

She was done with crying. Her face was locked with anger, resignation. "You'll take me to the center of town and rip the baby out, cut its throat, leave us both to bleed to death as a warning. That's it, isn't it? Just tell me that's what you're going to do and get it over with—"

Goodness, the stories people told. "No, we're not going to do that. We don't rip babies from mothers' wombs—not unless we need to save the mother's life, or the baby's. There's surgery for that. Your baby will be born; you have my promise."

Quiet tears slipped down the girl's cheeks. Enid watched for a moment, this time not using the silence to pressure Aren but trying to decide what to say.

"You thought that was what would happen if you were caught, and you still cut out your implant to have a baby? You must have known you'd be caught."

"I don't remember anymore what I was thinking."

"Let's get you back to the kitchen for a drink of water, hmm?"

By the time they got back to the common room, Aren had stopped crying, and she even stood a little straighter. At least until Frain looked at her, then at Enid.

"What did you tell her? What did she say to you?"

"Felice, I think Aren needs a glass of water, or maybe some tea. Frain, will you come speak with me?"

The man stomped out of the room ahead of her.

"What happened?" Enid said simply.

"The implant. It must have failed."

"Do you think she, or someone, might have cut it out? Did you ever notice her wearing a bandage on her arm?"

He did not seem at all surprised at this suggestion. "I never did. I never noticed." He was going to plead ignorance. That was fine. "Does the local committee know you're here?" he said, turning the questioning on her.

"Not yet," she said lightly. "They will."

"What are you going to do? What will happen to Aren?"

Putting the blame on Aren, because he knew the whole household was under investigation. "I haven't decided yet."

"I'm going to protest to the committee, about you questioning Aren alone. You shouldn't have done that, it's too hard on her—" He was furious that he didn't know what Aren had said. That he couldn't make their stories match up.

"Submit your protest," Enid said. "That's fine."

She spoke to every one of them alone. Half of them said the exact same thing, in exactly the same way.

"The implant failed. It must have failed."

"Aren's got that boy of hers. He's the father."

"It was an accident."

"An accident." Felice breathed this line, her head bowed and hands clasped together.

So that was the story they'd agreed upon. The story Frain had told them to tell.

One of the young men—baffled, he didn't seem to understand what was happening—was the one to slip. "She brought this down on us, why do the rest of us have to put up with the mess when it's all her?"

Enid narrowed her gaze. "So you know she cut out her implant?"

He wouldn't say another word after that. He bit his lips and puffed out his cheeks, but wouldn't speak, as if someone held a knife to his throat and told him not to.

Enid wasn't above pressing hard at the young one, Susan, until the girl snapped.

"Did you ever notice Aren with a bandage on her arm?"

Susan's face turned red. "It's not my fault, it's not! It's just that Frain said if we got a banner next season I could have it, not Aren, and she was jealous! That's what it was; she did this to punish us!"

Banners were supposed to make things better. Give people something to work for, make them prove they could support a child, *earn* a child. It wasn't supposed to be something to fight over, to cheat over.

But people did cheat.

"Susan—did you send the anonymous report about Aren?"

Susan's eyes turned round and shocked. "No, of course not, I wouldn't do such a thing! Tell Frain I'd never do such a thing!"

"Thank you, Susan, for your honesty," Enid said, and Susan burst into tears.

What a stinking mess this was turning in to. To think, she could have retired after the murder investigation and avoided all this.

She needed to talk to more people.

By the time they returned to the common room, Felice had gotten tea out for everyone. She politely offered a cup to Enid, who accepted, much to everyone's dismay. Enid stayed for a good twenty minutes, sipping, watching them watch her, making small talk.

"Thank you very much for all of your time and patience," she said eventually. "I'll be at the committee house in town if any of you would like to speak with me further. I'll deliver my decision in a day or two, so I won't keep you waiting. Your community thanks you."

A million things could happen, but these people were so locked into their drama she didn't expect much. She wasn't worried that the situation was going to change overnight. If Aren was going to grab her boy and run she would have done it already. That wasn't what was happening here. This was a household imploding.

Time to check with the local committee.

"Did they talk while I was gone?" Enid asked.

"Not a word," Bert said. "I hate to say it but that was almost fun. What are they so scared of?"

"Us. The stories of what we'll do. Aren was sure we'd drag her in the street and cut out her baby."

Bert wrinkled his face and said softly, "That's awful."

"I hadn't heard that one before, I admit. Usually it's all locked cells and stealing the baby away as soon as it's born. I wonder if Frain told the story to her, said it was why they had to keep it secret."

"Frain knew?"

"I'm sure they all did. They're trying to save the household by convincing me it was an accident. Or that it was just Aren's fault and no one else's. When really, a household like that, if they're that unhappy they should all put in for transfers, no matter how many ration credits that'd cost. Frain's scared them out of it, I'm betting."

"So what will happen?"

"Technology fails sometimes. If it had been an accident, I'm authorized to award a banner retroactively if the household can handle it. But that's not what happened here. If the household colluded to bring on a bannerless baby, we'd have to break up the house. But if it was just Aren all on her own—punishment would fall on her."

"But this isn't any of those, is it?"

"You've got a good eye for this, Bert."

"Not sure that's a compliment. I like to expect the best from people, not the worst."

Enid chuckled.

"At least *you'll* be able to put this all behind you soon," he said. "Retire to some pleasant household somewhere. Not here."

A middle-aged man, balding and flush, rushed toward them on the path as they returned to the town. His gray tunic identified him as a committee member, and he wore the same stark panic on his face that everyone did when they saw an investigator.

"You must be Trevor?" Enid asked him, when he was still a few paces away, too far to shake hands.

"We didn't know you were coming, you should have sent word. Why didn't you send word?"

"We didn't have time. We got an anonymous report and had to act quickly. It happens sometimes, I'm sure you understand."

"Report, on what? If it's serious, I'm sure I would have been told—"

"A bannerless pregnancy at the Apricot Hill household."

He took a moment to process, staring, uncertain. The look turned hard. This didn't just reflect on Aren or the household—it reflected on the entire settlement. On the committee that ran the settlement. They could all be dragged into this.

"Aren," the man breathed.

Enid wasn't surprised the man knew. She was starting to wonder how her office hadn't heard about the situation much sooner.

"What can you tell me about the household? How do they get along, how are they doing?"

"Is this an official interview?"

"Why not? Saves time."

"They get their work done. But they're a household, not a family. If you understand the difference."

"I do." A collection of people gathered for production, not one that bonded over love. It wasn't always a bad thing—a collection of people working toward shared purpose could be powerful. But love could make it a home.

"How close were they to earning a banner?" *Were.* Telling word, there.

"I can't say they were close. They have three healthy young women, but people came in and out of that house so often we couldn't call it 'stable.' They fell short on quotas. I know that's usually better than going over, but not with food processing—falling short there means food potentially wasted, if it goes bad before it gets stored. Frain—Frain is not the easiest man to get along with."

"Yes, I know."

"You've already been out there—I wish you would have talked to me; you should have come to see us before starting your investigation." Trevor was wringing his hands.

"So you could tell me how things really are?" Enid raised a brow and smiled. He glanced briefly at Bert and frowned. "Aren had a romantic partner in the settlement, I'm told. Do you know who this might be?"

"She wouldn't tell you—she trying to protect him?"

"He's not in any trouble."

"Jess. It's Jess. He works in the machine shop, with the Ironcroft household." He pointed the way.

"Thank you. We've had a long day of travel, can the committee house put us up for a night or two? We've got the credits to trade for it, we won't be a burden."

"Yes, of course, we have guest rooms in back, this way."

Trevor led them on to a comfortable stone house, committee offices and official guest rooms all together. People had gathered, drifting out of houses and stopping along the road to look, to bend heads and gossip. Everyone had that stare of trepidation.

"You don't make a lot of friends, working in investigations," Bert murmured to her.

"Not really, no."

A young man, an assistant to the committee, delivered a good meal of lentil stew and fresh bread, along with cider. It tasted like warmth embodied, a great comfort after the day she'd had.

"My household hang their banners on the common room wall like that," Bert said between mouthfuls. "They stitch the names of the babies into them. It's a whole history of the house laid out there."

"Many households do. It's a lovely tradition," Enid said.

"I've never met anyone born without a banner. It's odd, thinking Aren's baby won't have its name written anywhere."

"It's not the baby's fault, remember. But it does make it hard. They grow up thinking they have to work twice as hard to earn their place in the world. But it usually makes people very careful not to pass on that burden."

"Usually but not always."

She sighed, her solid inspector demeanor slipping. "We're getting better. The goal is making sure that every baby born will be provided for, will have a place, and won't overburden what we have. But babies are powerful things. We'll never be perfect."

The young assistant knocked on the door to the guest rooms early the next day.

"Ma'am, Enid? Someone's out front asking for the investigator."

"Is there a conference room where we can meet?"

"Yes, I'll show him in."

She and Bert quickly made themselves presentable—and put on their reputation—before meeting.

The potential informant was a lanky young man with calloused hands, a flop of brown hair and no beard. A worried expression. He kneaded a straw hat in his hands and stood from the table when Enid and Bert entered.

"You're Jess?"

He squeezed the hat harder. Ah, the appearance of omniscience was so very useful.

"Please, sit down," Enid said, and sat across from him by example. Bert stood by the wall.

"This is about Aren," the young man said. "You're here about Aren."

"Yes." He slumped, sighed—did he seemed relieved? "What do you need to tell me, Jess?"

"I haven't seen her in weeks; I haven't even gotten a message to her. No one will tell me what's wrong, and I know what everyone's been saying, but it can't be true—"

"That she's pregnant. She's bannerless."

He blinked. "But she's alive? She's safe?"

"She is. I saw her yesterday."

"Good, that's good."

Unlike everyone else she had talked to here, he seemed genuinely reassured. As if he had expected her to be dead or injured. The vectors of anxiety in the case pointed in so many different directions. "Did she tell you anything? Did you have any idea that something was wrong?"

"No . . . I mean, yes, but not that. It's complicated. What's going to happen to her?"

"That's what I'm here to decide. I promise you, she and the baby won't come to any harm. But I need to understand what's happened. Did you know she'd cut out her implant?"

He stared at the tabletop. "No, I didn't know that." If he had known, he could be implicated, so it behooved him to say that. But Enid believed him.

"Jess, I want to understand why she did what she did. Her household is being difficult. They tell me she spent all her spare time with you." Enid couldn't tell if he was resistant to talking to her, or if he simply couldn't find the words. She prompted. "How long have you been together? How long have you been intimate?" A gentle way of putting it. He wasn't blushing; on the contrary, he'd gone even more pale.

"Not long," he said. "Not even a year. I think . . . I think I know what happened now, looking back."

"Can you tell me?"

"I think . . . I think she needed someone and she picked me. I'm almost glad she picked me. I love her, but . . . I didn't know."

She wanted a baby. She found a boy she liked, cut out her implant, and made sure she had a baby. It wasn't unheard of. Enid had looked into a couple of cases like it in the past. But then, the household reported it when the others found out, or she left the household. To go through that and then stay, with everyone also covering it up. . . .

"Did she ever talk about earning a banner and having a baby with you? Was that a goal of hers?"

"She never did at all. We . . . it was just us. I just liked spending time with her. We'd go for walks."

"What else?"

"She—wouldn't let me touch her arm. The first time we . . . were intimate, she kept her shirt on. She'd hurt her arm, she said, and didn't want to get dirt on it—we were out by the mill creek that feeds into the pond. It's so beautiful there, with the noise of the water and all. I . . . I didn't think of it. I mean, she always seemed to be hurt somewhere. Bruises and things. She said it was just from working around the house. I was always a bit careful touching her, though, because of it. I had to be careful with her." Miserable now, he put the pieces together in his mind as Enid watched. "She didn't like to go back. I told myself—I fooled myself—that it was because she loved me. But it's more that she didn't want to go back."

"And she loves you. As you said, she picked you. But she had to go back."

"If she'd asked, she could have gone somewhere else."

But it would have cost credits she may not have had, the committee would have asked why, and it would have been a black mark on Frain's leadership, or worse. Frain had them cowed into staying. So Aren wanted to get out of there and decided a baby would help her.

Enid asked, "Did you send the tip to Investigations?"

"No. No, I didn't know. That is, I didn't want to believe. I would never do anything to get her in trouble. I . . . I'm not in trouble, am I?"

"No, Jess. Do you know who might have sent in the tip?"

"Someone on the local committee, maybe. They're the ones who'd start an investigation, aren't they?"

"Usually, but they didn't seem happy to see me. The message went directly to regional."

"The local committee doesn't want to think anything's wrong. Nobody wants to think anything's wrong."

"Yes, that seems to be the attitude. Thank you for your help, Jess."

"What will happen to Aren?" He was choking, struggling not to cry. Even Bert, standing at the wall, seemed discomfited.

"That's for me to worry about, Jess. Thank you for your time."

At the dismissal, he slipped out of the room.

She leaned back and sighed, wanting to get back to her own household—despite the rumors, investigators did belong to households—with its own orchards and common room full of love and safety.

Yes, maybe she should have retired before all this. Or maybe she wasn't meant to.

"Enid?" Bert asked softly.

"Let's go. Let's get this over with."

Back at Apricot Hill's common room, the household gathered, and Enid didn't have to ask for Aren this time. She had started to worry, especially after talking to Jess. But they'd all waited this long, and her arrival didn't change anything except it had given them all the confirmation that they'd finally been caught. That they would always be caught. Good for the reputation, there.

Aren kept her face bowed, her hair over her cheek. Enid moved up to her, reached a hand to her, and the girl flinched. "Aren?" she said, and she still didn't look up until Enid touched her chin and made her lift her face. An irregular red bruise marked her cheek.

"Aren, did you send word about a bannerless pregnancy to the regional committee?"

Someone, Felice probably, gasped. A few of them shifted. Frain simmered. But Aren didn't deny it. She kept her face low.

"Aren?" Enid prompted, and the young woman nodded, ever so slightly.

"I hid. I waited for the weekly courier and slipped the letter in her bag, she didn't see me; no one saw. I didn't know if anyone would believe it, with no name on it, but I had to try. I wanted to get caught, but no one was noticing it; everyone was ignoring it." Her voice cracked to silence.

Enid put a gentle hand on Aren's shoulder. Then she went to Bert, and whispered, "Watch carefully."

She didn't know what would happen, what Frain in particular would do. She drew herself up, drew strength from the uniform she wore, and declaimed.

"I am the villain here," Enid said. "Understand that. I am happy to be the villain in your world. It's what I'm here for. Whatever happens, blame me.

"I will take custody of Aren and her child. When the rest of my business is done, I'll leave with her and she'll be cared for responsibly. Frain, I question your stewardship of this household and will submit a recommendation that Apricot Hill be dissolved entirely, its resources and credits distributed among its members as warranted, and its members transferred elsewhere throughout the region. I'll submit my recommendation to the regional committee, which will assist the local committee in carrying out my sentence."

"No," Felice hissed. "You can't do this, you can't force us out."

She had expected that line from Frain. She wondered at the deeper dynamic here, but not enough to try to suss it out.

"I can," she said, with a backward glance at Bert. "But I won't have to, because you're all secretly relieved. The household didn't work, and that's fine—it happens sometimes—but none of you had the guts to start over, the guts to give up your credits to request a transfer somewhere else. To pay for the change you wanted. To protect your own housemates from each other. But now it's done, and by someone else, so you can complain all you want and rail to the skies about your new poverty as you work your way out of the holes you've dug for yourselves. I'm the villain you can blame. But deep down you'll know the truth. And that's fine too, because I don't really care. Not about you lot."

No one argued. No one said a word.

"Aren," Enid said, and the woman flinched again. She might never stop flinching. "You can come with me now, or would you like time to say good-bye?"

She looked around the room, and Enid wasn't imagining it: the woman's hands were shaking, though she tried to hide it by pressing them under the roundness of her belly. Enid's breath caught, because even now it might go either way. Aren had been scared before; she might be too scared to leave. Enid schooled her expression to be still no matter what the answer was.

But Aren stood from the table and said, "I'll go with you now."

"Bert will go help you get your things—"

"I don't have any things. I want to go now."

"All right. Bert, will you escort Aren outside?"

The door closed behind them, and Enid took one last look around the room.

"That's it, then," Frain said.

"Oh no, that's not it at all," Enid said. "That's just it for now. The rest of you should get word of the disposition of the household in a couple of days." She walked out.

Aren stood outside, hugging herself. Bert was a polite few paces away, being nonthreatening, staring at clouds. Enid urged them on, and they walked the path back toward town. Aren seemed to get a bit lighter as they went.

They probably had another day in Southtown before they could leave. Enid would keep Aren close, in the guest rooms, until then. She might have to requisition a solar car. In her condition, Aren probably shouldn't walk the ten miles to the next way station. And she might want to say goodbye to Jess. Or she might not, and Jess would have his heart broken even more. Poor thing.

Enid requisitioned a solar car from the local committee and was able to take to the Coast Road the next day. The bureaucratic machinery was in motion on all the rest of it. Committeeman Trevor revealed that a couple of the young men from Apricot Hill had preemptively put in household transfer requests. Too little, too late. She'd done her job; it was all in committee hands now.

Bert drove, and Enid sat in the back with Aren, who was bundled in a wool cloak and kept her hands around her belly. They opened windows to the spring sunshine, and the car bumped and swayed over the gravel road. Walking would have been more pleasant, but Aren needed the car. The tension in her shoulders had finally gone away. She looked up, around, and if she didn't smile, she also didn't frown. She talked, now, in a voice clear and free of tears.

"I came into the household when I was sixteen, to work prep in the canning house and to help with the garden and grounds and such. They needed the help, and I needed to get started on my life, you know? Frain—he expected more out of me. He expected me to be his."

She spoke as if being interrogated. Enid hadn't asked for her story, but listened carefully to the confession. It spilled out like a flood, like the young woman had been waiting.

"How far did it go, Aren?" Enid asked carefully. In the driver's seat, Bert frowned, like maybe he wanted to go back and have a word with the man.

"He never did more than hit me."

So straightforward. Enid made a note. The car rocked on for a ways.

"What will happen to her, without a banner?" Aren asked, glancing at her belly. She'd evidently decided the baby was a girl. She probably had a name picked out. Her baby, her savior.

"There are households who need babies to raise who'll be happy to take her."

"Her, but not me?"

"It's a complicated situation," Enid said. She didn't want to make Aren any promises until they could line up exactly which households they'd be going to.

Aren was smart. Scared, but smart. She must have thought things through, once she realized she wasn't going to die. "Will it go better, if I agree to give her up? The baby, I mean."

Enid said, "It would depend on how you define 'better.'"

"Better for the baby."

"There's a stigma on bannerless babies. Worse some places than others. And somehow people know, however you try to hide it. People will always know what you did and hold it against you. But the baby can get a fresh start on her own."

"All right. All right, then."

"You don't have to decide right now."

Eventually, they came to the place in the road where the ruins were visible, like a distant mirage, but unmistakable. A haunted place, with as many rumors about it as there were about investigators and what they did.

"Is that it?" Aren said, staring. "The old city? I've never seen it before."

Bert slowed the car, and they stared out for a moment.

"The stories about what it was like are so terrible. I know it's supposed to be better now, but. . . ." The young woman dropped her gaze.

"Better for whom, you're wondering?" Enid said. "When they built our world, our great-grandparents saved what they could, what they thought was important, what they'd most need. They wanted a world that would let them survive not just longer but better. They aimed for utopia knowing they'd fall short. And for all their work, for all our work, we still find pregnant girls with bruises on their faces who don't know where to go for help."

"I don't regret it," Aren said. "At least, I don't think I do."

"You saved what you could," Enid said. It was all any of them could do.

The car started again, rolling on. Some miles later on, Aren fell asleep curled in the back seat, her head lolling. Bert gave her a sympathetic glance.

"Heartbreaking all around, isn't it? Quite the last case for you, though. Memorable."

"Or not," Enid said.

Going back to the way station, late afternoon, the sun was in Enid's face. She leaned back, closed her eyes, and let it warm her.

"What, not memorable?" Bert said.

"Or not the last," she said. "I may have a few more left in me."

Ann Leckie is the author of the Hugo, Nebula, and Arthur C. Clarke Award–winning novel *Ancillary Justice* and its sequels, *Ancillary Sword* and *Ancillary Mercy*. She has also published short stories in *Subterranean Magazine*, *Strange Horizons*, and *Beneath Ceaseless Skies*, among other fine publications.

Ann has worked as a waitress, a receptionist, a rodman on a land-surveying crew, and a recording engineer. She lives in St. Louis, Missouri.

ANOTHER WORD FOR WORLD

Ann Leckie

Ashiban Xidyla had a headache. A particularly vicious one, centered somewhere on the top of her head. She sat curled over her lap, in her seat on the flier, eyes closed. Oddly, she had no memory of leaning forward, and—now she thought of it—no idea when the headache had begun.

The Gidanta had been very respectful so far, very solicitous of Ashiban's age, but that was, she was sure, little more than the entirely natural respect for one's elders. This was not a time when she could afford any kind of weakness. Ashiban was here to prevent a war that would quite possibly end with the Gidanta slaughtering every one of Ashiban's fellow Raksamat on the planet. The Sovereign of Iss, hereditary high priestess of the Gidanta, sat across the aisle, silent and veiled, her interpreter beside her. What must they be thinking?

Ashiban took three careful breaths. Straightened cautiously, wary of the pain flaring. Opened her eyes.

Ought to have seen blue sky through the flier's front window past the pilot's seat, ought to have heard the buzz of the engine. Instead she saw shards of brown and green and blue. Heard nothing. She closed her eyes, opened them again. Tried to make some sense of things. They weren't falling, she was sure. Had the flier landed, and she hadn't noticed?

A high, quavering voice said something, syllables that made no sense to Ashiban. "We have to get out of here," said a calm, muffled voice somewhere at Ashiban's feet. "Speaker is in some distress." Damn. She'd forgotten to turn off the translating function on her handheld. Maybe the Sovereign's interpreter hadn't heard it. She turned her head to look across the flier's narrow aisle, wincing at the headache.

The Sovereign's interpreter lay in the aisle, his head jammed up against the back of the pilot's seat at an odd, awkward angle. The high voice spoke again, and in the small bag at Ashiban's feet her handheld said, "Disregard the dead. We have to get out of here or we will also die. The speaker is in some distress."

In her own seat, the pink- and orange- and blue-veiled Sovereign fumbled at the safety restraints. The straps parted with a click, and the Sovereign stood. Stepped into the aisle, hiking her long blue skirt. Spoke—it must have been the Sovereign speaking all along. "Stupid cow," said Ashiban's handheld, in her bag. "Speaker's distress has increased."

The flier lurched. The Sovereign cried out. "No translation available," remarked Ashiban's handheld, as the Sovereign reached forward to tug at Ashiban's own safety restraints and, once those had come undone, grab Ashiban's arm and pull.

The flier had crashed. The flier had crashed, and the Sovereign's interpreter must have gotten out of his seat for some reason, at just the wrong time. Ashiban herself must have hit her head. That would explain the memory gap, and the headache. She blinked again, and the colored shards where the window should have been resolved into cracked glass, and behind it sky, and flat ground covered in brown and green plants, here and there some white or pink. "We should stay here and wait for help," Ashiban said. In her bag, her handheld said something incomprehensible.

The Sovereign pulled harder on Ashiban's arm. "You stupid expletive cow," said the handheld, as the Sovereign picked Ashiban's bag up from her feet. "Someone shot us down, and we crashed in the expletive High Mires. The expletive expletive is expletive sinking into the expletive bog. If we stay here we'll drown. The speaker is highly agitated." The flier lurched again.

It all seemed so unreal. *Concussion*, Ashiban thought. *I have a concussion, and I'm not thinking straight.* She took her bag from the Sovereign, rose, and followed the Sovereign of Iss to the emergency exit.

Outside the flier, everything was a brown and green plain, blue sky above. The ground swelled and rolled under Ashiban's feet, but given the flier behind her, half-sunk into the gray-brown ground, and the pain in her head, she wasn't sure if it was really doing that or if it was a symptom of concussion.

The Sovereign said something. The handheld in Ashiban's bag spoke, but it was lost in the open space and the breeze and Ashiban's inability to concentrate.

The Sovereign yanked Ashiban's bag from her, pulled it open. Dug out the handheld. "Expletive," said the handheld. "Expletive expletive. We are standing on water. The speaker is agitated."

"What?" The flier behind them, sliding slowly into the mire, made a gurgling sound. The ground was still unsteady under Ashiban's feet, she still wasn't sure why.

"Water! The speaker is emphatic." The Sovereign gestured toward the greenish-brown mat of moss beneath them.

"Help will come," Ashiban said. "We should stay here."

"They shot us down," said the handheld. "The speaker is agitated and emphatic."

"What?"

"They shot us down. I saw the pilot shot through the window, I saw them die. Timran was trying to take control of the flier when we crashed. Whoever comes, they are not coming to help us. We have to get to solid ground. We have to hide. The speaker is emphatic. The speaker is in some distress. The speaker is agitated." The Sovereign took Ashiban's arm and pulled her forward.

"Hide?" There was nowhere to hide. And the ground swelled and sank, like waves on the top of water. She fell to her hands and knees, nauseated.

"Translation unavailable," said the handheld, as the Sovereign dropped down beside her. "Crawl then, but come with me or be dead. The speaker is emphatic. The speaker is in some distress." The Sovereign crawled away, the ground still heaving.

"That's my bag," said Ashiban. "That's my handheld." The Sovereign continued to crawl away. "There's nowhere to hide!" But if she stayed where she was, on her hands and knees on the unsteady ground, she would be all alone here, and all her things gone and her head hurting and her stomach sick and nothing making sense. She crawled after the Sovereign.

By the time the ground stopped roiling, the squishy wet moss had changed to stiff, spiky-leaved meter-high plants that scratched Ashiban's face and tore at her sodden clothes. "Come here," said her handheld, somewhere up ahead. "Quickly. Come here. The speaker is agitated." Ashiban just wanted to lie down where she was, close her eyes, and go to sleep. But the Sovereign had her bag. There was a bottle of water in her bag. She kept going.

Found the Sovereign prone, veilless, pulling off her bright-colored skirts to ball them up beneath herself. Underneath her clothes she wore a plain brown shirt and leggings, like any regular Gidanta. "Ancestors!" panted Ashiban, still on hands and knees, not sure where there was room to lie down. "You're just a kid! You're younger than my grandchildren!"

In answer the Sovereign took hold of the collar of Ashiban's jacket and yanked her down to the ground. Ashiban cried out, and heard her handheld say something incomprehensible, presumably the Gidantan equivalent of *No translation available.* Pain darkened her vision, and her ears roared. Or was that the flier the Sovereign had said she'd heard?

The Sovereign spoke. "Stupid expletive expletive expletive, lie still," said Ashiban's handheld calmly. "Speaker is in some distress."

Ashiban closed her eyes. Her head hurt, and her twig-scratched face stung, but she was very, very tired.

A calm voice was saying, "Wake up, Ashiban Xidyla. The speaker is distressed." Over and over again. She opened her eyes. The absurdly young Sovereign of Iss lay in front of her, brown cheek pressed against the gray ground, staring at Ashiban, twigs and spiny leaves caught in the few trailing braids that had come loose from the hair coiled at the top of her head. Her eyes were red and puffy, as though she had been crying, though her expression gave no sign of it. She clutched Ashiban's handheld in one hand. Nineteen at most, Ashiban thought. Probably younger. "Are you awake, Ashiban Xidyla? The speaker is distressed."

"My head doesn't hurt," Ashiban observed. Despite that, everything still seemed slippery and unreal.

"I took the emergency medical kit on our way off the flier," the handheld said, translating the Sovereign's reply. "I put a corrective on your forehead. It's not the right kind, though. The instructions say to take you to a doctor right away. The speaker is. . . ."

"Translation preferences," interrupted Ashiban. "Turn off emotional evaluation." The handheld fell silent. "Have you called for help, Sovereign? Is help coming?"

"You are very stupid," said Ashiban's handheld. Said the Sovereign of Iss. "Or the concussion is dangerously severe. Our flier was shot down. Twenty minutes after that a flier goes back and forth over us as though it is looking for something, but we are in the High Mires, no one lives here. If we call for help, who is nearest? The people who shot us down."

"Who would shoot us down?"

"Someone who wants war between Gidanta and Raksamat. Someone with a grudge against your mother, the sainted Ciwril Xidyla. Someone with a grudge against my grandmother, the previous Sovereign."

"Not likely anyone Raksamat then," said Ashiban, and immediately regretted it. She was here to foster goodwill between her people and the Sovereign's, because the Gidanta had trusted her mother, Ciwril Xidyla, and so they might listen to her daughter. "There are far more of you down here than Raksamat settlers. If it came to a war, the Raksamat here would be slaughtered. I don't think any of us wants that."

"We will argue in the future," said the Sovereign. "So long as whoever it is does not manage to kill us. I have been thinking. They did not see us, under the plants, but maybe they will come back and look for us with infrared. They may come back soon. We have to reach the trees north of here."

"I can use my handheld to just contact my own people," said Ashiban. "Just them. I trust them."

"Do you?" asked the Sovereign. "But maybe the deaths of some Raksamat settlers will be the excuse they need to bring a war that kills all the Gidanta so they can have the world for themselves. Maybe your death would be convenient for them."

"That's ridiculous!" exclaimed Ashiban. She pushed herself to sitting, not too quickly, wary of the pain in her head returning, of her lingering dizziness. "I'm talking about my friends."

"Your friends are far away," said the Sovereign. "They would call on others to come find us. Do you trust those others?" The girl seemed deadly serious. She sat up. "I don't." She tucked Ashiban's handheld into her waistband, picked up her bundle of skirts and veils.

"That's my handheld! I need it!"

"You'll only call our deaths down with it," said the Sovereign. "Die if you want to." She rose, and trudged away through the stiff, spiky vegetation.

Ashiban considered tackling the girl and taking back her handheld. But the Sovereign was young, and while Ashiban was in fairly good shape considering her age, she had never been an athlete, even in her youth. And that was without considering the head injury.

She stood. Carefully, still dizzy, joints stiff. Where the flier had been was only black water, strips and chunks of moss floating on its surface, all of it surrounded by a flat carpet of yet more moss. She remembered the Sovereign saying, *We're standing on water!* Remembered the swell and roll of the ground that had made her drop to her hands and knees.

She closed her eyes. She thought she vaguely remembered sitting in her seat on the flier, the Sovereign crying out, her interpreter getting out of his seat to rush forward to where the pilot slumped over the controls.

Shot down. If that was true, the Sovereign was right. Calling for help—if she could find some way to do that without her handheld—might well be fatal. Whoever it was had considered both Ashiban and the Sovereign of Iss acceptable losses. Had, perhaps, specifically wanted both of them dead. Had, perhaps, specifically wanted the war that had threatened for the past two years to become deadly real.

But nobody wanted that. Not even the Gidanta who had never been happy with Ashiban's people's presence in the system wanted that, Ashiban was sure.

She opened her eyes. Saw the girl's back as she picked her way through the mire. Saw far off on the northern horizon the trees the girl had mentioned. "Ancestors!" cried Ashiban. "I'm too old for this." And she shouldered her bag and followed the Sovereign of Iss.

Eventually Ashiban caught up, though the Sovereign didn't acknowledge her in any way. They trudged through the hip-high scrub in silence for some time, only making the occasional hiss of annoyance at particularly troublesome branches. The clear blue sky clouded over, and a damp-smelling wind rose. A relief—the bright sun had hurt Ashiban's eyes. As the trees on the horizon became more definitely a band of trees—still dismayingly far off—Ashiban's thoughts, which had this whole time been slippery and tenuous, began to settle into something like a comprehensible pattern.

Shot down. Ashiban was sure none of her people wanted war. Though off-planet the Raksamat weren't quite so vulnerable—were, in fact, much better armed. The ultimate outcome of an actual war would probably not favor the Gidanta. Or Ashiban didn't think so. It was possible some Raksamat faction actually wanted such a war. And Ashiban wasn't really anyone of any significance to her own people.

Her mother had been. Her mother, Ciwril Xidyla, had negotiated the Treaty of Eatu with the then-Sovereign of Iss, ensuring the right of the Raksamat to live peacefully in the system, and on the planet. Ciwril had been widely admired among both Raksamat and Gidanta. As her daughter, Ashiban was only a sign, an admonition to remember her mother. If her side could think it acceptable to sacrifice the lives of their own people on the planet, they would certainly not blink at sacrificing Ashiban herself. She didn't want to believe that, though, that her own people would do such a thing.

Would the Gidanta be willing to kill their own Sovereign for the sake of a war? An hour ago—or however long they had been trudging across the mire, Ashiban wasn't sure—she'd have said *certainly not*. The Sovereign of Iss was a sacred figure. She was the conduit between the Gidanta and the spirit of the world of Iss, which spoke to them with the Sovereign's voice. Surely they wouldn't kill her just to forward a war that would be disastrous for both sides?

"Sovereign."

A meter ahead of Ashiban, the girl kept trudging. Looked briefly over her shoulder. "What?"

"Where are you going?"

The Sovereign didn't even turn her head this time. "There's a monitoring station on the North Udran Plain."

That had to be hundreds of kilometers away, and that wasn't counting the fact that if this was indeed the High Mires, they were on the high side of the Scarp and would certainly have to detour to get down to the plains.

"On foot? That could take weeks, if we even ever get there. We have no food, no water." Well, Ashiban had about a third of a liter in a bottle in her bag, but that hardly counted. "No camping equipment."

The Sovereign just scoffed and kept walking.

"Young lady," began Ashiban, but then remembered herself at that age. Her own children and grandchildren. Adolescence was trying enough without the fate of your people resting on your shoulders, and being shot down and stranded in a bog. "I thought the current Sovereign was fifty or sixty. The daughter of the woman who was Sovereign when my mother was here last."

"You're not supposed to talk like we're all different people," said the girl. "We're all the voice of the world spirit. And you mean my aunt. She abdicated last week."

"Abdicated!" Mortified by her mistake—Ashiban had been warned over and over about the nature of the Sovereign of Iss, that she was not an individual, that referring to her as such would be an offense. "I didn't know that was possible." And surely at a time like this, the Sovereign wouldn't want to drop so much responsibility on a teenager.

"Of course it's possible. It's just a regular priesthood. It never was particularly special. It was you Raksamat who insisted on translating Sovereign as Sovereign. And it's you Raksamat whose priests are always trancing out and speaking for your ancestors. *Voice of Iss* doesn't mean that at all."

"Translating Sovereign as Sovereign?" asked Ashiban. "What is that supposed to mean?" The girl snorted. "And how can the Voice of Iss not mean exactly that?" The Sovereign didn't answer, just kept walking.

After a long silence, Ashiban said, "Then why do any of the Gidanta listen to you? And who is it my mother was negotiating with?"

The Sovereign looked back at Ashiban and rolled her eyes. "With the interpreter, of course. And if your mother didn't know that, she was completely stupid. And nobody listens to me." The voice of the translating handheld was utterly calm and neutral, but the girl's tone was contemptuous. "That's why I'm stuck here. And it wasn't about us listening to the voice of the planet. It was about *you* listening to *us*. You wouldn't talk to the Terraforming Council because you wouldn't accept they were an authority, and besides, you didn't like what they were saying."

"An industrial association is not a government!" Seeing the girl roll her eyes again, Ashiban wondered fleetingly what her words sounded like in Gidantan—if the handheld was making *industrial association* and *government* into the same words, the way it obviously had when it had said for the girl, moments ago, *translating Sovereign as Sovereign*. But that was ridiculous. The two weren't the same thing at all.

The Sovereign stopped. Turned to face Ashiban. "We have been here for two thousand years. For all that time, we have been working on this planet, to make it a place we could live without interference. We came here, to this place without an intersystem gate, so that no one would bother us and we could live in peace. You turned up less than two centuries ago, now most of the hard work is done, and you want to tell us what to do with our planet, and who is or isn't an authority!"

"We were refugees. We came here by accident, and we can't very well leave. And we brought benefits. You've been cut off from the outside for so long, you didn't have medical correctives. Those have saved lives, Sovereign. And we've brought other things." Including weapons the Gidanta didn't have. "Including our own knowledge of terraforming, and how to best manage a planet."

"And you agreed, your own mother, the great Ciwril Xidyla agreed, that no one would settle on the planet without authorization from the Terraforming Council! And yet there are dozens of Raksamat farmsteads just in the Saunn foothills, and more elsewhere."

"That wasn't the agreement. The treaty explicitly states that we have a right to be here, and a right to share in the benefits of living on this planet. Your own grandmother agreed to that! And small farmsteads are much better for the planet than the cities the Terraforming Council is intending." Wind gusted, and a few fat drops of rain fell.

"My grandmother agreed to nothing! It was the gods-cursed interpreter who made the agreement. And he was appointed by the Terraforming Council, just like all of them! And how dare you turn up here after we've done all the hard work and think because you brought us some technology you can tell us what to do with our planet!"

"How can you own a planet? You can't, it's ridiculous! There's more than enough room for all of us."

"I've memorized it, you know," said the Sovereign. "The entire agreement. It's not that long. *Settlement will only proceed according to the current consensus regarding the good of the planet.* That's what it says, right there in the second paragraph."

Ashiban knew that sentence by heart. Everyone knew that sentence by now. Arguments over what *current consensus regarding the good of the planet* might mean were inescapable—and generally, in Ashiban's opinion, made in bad faith. The words were clear enough. "There's nothing about the Terraforming Council in that sentence." Like most off-planet Raksamat, Ashiban didn't speak the language of the Gidanta. But—also like most off-planet Raksamat—she had a few words and phrases, and she knew the Gidantan for *Terraforming Council*. Had heard the girl speak the sentence, knew there was no mention of the council.

The Sovereign cried out in apparent anger and frustration. "How can you? How can you stand there and say that, as though you have not just heard me say it?"

Overhead, barely audible over the sound of the swelling rain, the hum of a flier engine. The Sovereign looked up.

"It's help," said Ashiban. Angry, yes, but she could set that aside at the prospect of rescue. Of soon being somewhere warm, and dry, and comfortable. Her clothes—plain, green trousers and shirt, simple, soft flat shoes—had not been chosen with any anticipation of a trek through mud and weeds, or standing in a rain shower. "They must be looking for us."

The Sovereign's eyes widened. She spun and took off running through the thick, thigh-high plants, toward the trees.

"Wait!" cried Ashiban, but the girl kept moving.

Ashiban turned to scan the sky, shielding her eyes from the rain with one hand. Was there anything she could do to attract the attention of the flier? Her own green clothes weren't far off the green of the plants she stood among, but she didn't trust the flat, brownish-green mossy stretches that she and the Sovereign had been avoiding. She had nothing that would light up, and the girl had fled with Ashiban's handheld, which she could have used to try to contact the searchers.

A crack echoed across the mire, and a few meters to Ashiban's left, leaves and twigs exploded. The wind gusted again, harder than before, and she shivered.

And realized that someone had just fired at her. That had been a gunshot, and there was no one here to shoot at her except that approaching flier, which was, Ashiban saw, coming straight toward her, even though with the clouds and the rain, and the green of her clothes and the green of the plants she stood in, she could not have been easy to see.

Except maybe in the infrared. Even without the cold rain coming down, she must glow bright and unmistakable in infrared.

Ashiban turned and ran. Or tried to, wading through the plants toward the trees, twigs catching her trousers. Another crack, and she couldn't go any faster than she was, though she tried, and the wind blew harder, and she hoped she was moving toward the trees.

Three more shots in quick succession, the wind blowing harder, nearly pushing her over, and Ashiban stumbled out of the plants onto a stretch of open moss that trembled under her as she ran, gasping, cold, and exhausted, toward another patch of those thigh-high weeds, and the shadow of trees beyond. Below her feet the moss began to come apart, fraying, loosening, one more wobbling step and she would sink into the black water of the mire below, but another shot cracked behind her and she couldn't stop, and there was no safe direction, she could only go forward. She ran on. And then, with hopefully solid ground a single step ahead, the skies opened up in a torrent of rain, and the moss gave way underneath her.

She plunged downward, into cold water. Made a frantic, scrabbling grab, got hold of one tough plant stem. Tried to pull herself up, but could not. The rain poured down, and her grip on the plant stem began to slip.

A hand grabbed her arm. Someone shouted something incomprehensible—it was the Sovereign of Iss, rain streaming down her face, braids plastered against her neck and shoulders. The girl grabbed the back of Ashiban's shirt with her other hand, leaned back, pulling Ashiban up a few centimeters, and Ashiban reached forward and grabbed another handful of plant, and somehow scrambled free of the water, onto the land, and she and the Sovereign half-ran, half-stumbled forward into the trees.

Where the rain was less but still came down. And they needed better cover, they needed to go deeper into the trees. Ancestors grant the woods ahead were thick enough to hide them from the flier, and Ashiban wanted to tell the Sovereign that they needed to keep running, but the girl didn't stop until Ashiban, unable to move a single step more, collapsed at the bottom of a tree.

The Sovereign dropped down beside her. There was no sound but their gasping, and the rain hissing through the branches above.

One of Ashiban's shoes had come off, somewhere. Her arm, which the Sovereign had pulled on to get her up out of the water, ached. Her back hurt, and her legs. Her heart pounded, and she couldn't seem to catch her breath, and she shivered, with cold or with fear she wasn't sure.

The rain lessened not long after, and stopped at some point during the night. Ashiban woke shivering, the Sovereign huddled beside her. Pale sunlight filtered through the tree leaves, and the leaf-covered ground was sodden. So was Ashiban.

She was hungry, too. Wasn't food the whole point of planets? Surely there would be something to eat, it would just be a question of knowing what there was, and how to eat it safely. Water might well be a bigger problem than food. Ashiban opened her bag—which by some miracle had stayed on her shoulder through everything—and found her half-liter bottle of water, still about three-quarters full. If she'd had her wits about her last night, she'd have opened it in the rain, to collect as much as she could.

"Well," Ashiban said, "here we are."

Silence. Not a word from the handheld. The Sovereign uncurled herself from where she huddled against Ashiban. Put a hand on her waist, where the handheld had been tucked into her waistband. Looked at Ashiban.

The handheld was gone. "Oh, Ancestors," said Ashiban. And after another half-panicked second, carefully got to her feet from off the ground—something that hadn't been particularly easy for a decade or two, even without yesterday's hectic flight and a night spent cold and soaking wet, sleeping sitting on the ground and leaning against a tree—and retraced their steps. The Sovereign joined her.

As far back as they went (apparently neither of them was willing to go all the way back to the mire), they found only bracken, and masses of wet, dead leaves.

Ashiban looked at the damp and shivering Sovereign. Who looked five or six years younger than she'd looked yesterday. The Sovereign said nothing, but what was there to say? Without the handheld, or some other translation device, they could barely talk to each other at all. Ashiban herself knew only a few phrases in Gidantan. *Hello* and *good-bye* and *I don't understand Gidantan.* She could count from one to twelve. A few words and phrases more, none of them applicable to being stranded in the woods on the edge of the High Mires. Ironic, since her mother Ciwril had been an expert in the language. It was her mother's work that had made the translation devices as useful as they were, that had allowed the Raksamat and Gidanta to speak to each other. *And who is it my mother was negotiating with? With the interpreter, of course.*

No point thinking about that just now. The immediate problem was more than enough.

Someone had shot down their flier yesterday, and then apparently flown away. Hours later they had returned, so that they could shoot at Ashiban and the Sovereign as they fled. It didn't make sense.

The Gidanta had guns, of course, knew how to make them. But they didn't have many. Since they had arrived here, most of their energies had been devoted to the terraforming of Iss, and during much of that time they'd lived in space, on stations, an environment in which projectile weapons potentially caused far more problems than they might solve, even when it came to deadly disputes.

That attitude had continued when they had moved down to the planet. There were police, and some of the Terraforming Council had bodyguards, and Ashiban didn't doubt there were people who specialized in fighting, including firing guns, but there was no Gidanta military, no army, standing or otherwise. Fliers for cargo or for personal transport, but not for warfare. Guns for hunting, not designed to kill people efficiently.

The Raksamat, Ashiban's own people, had come into the system armed. But none of those weapons were on the planet. Or Ashiban didn't think they were. So, a hunting gun and a personal flier. She wanted to ask the Sovereign, standing staring at Ashiban, still shivering, if the girl had seen the other flier. But she couldn't, not without that handheld.

But it didn't matter, this moment, why it had happened the way it had. There was no way to tell who had tried to kill them. No way to know what or who they would find if they returned to the mire, to where their own flier had sunk under the black water and the moss.

Her thoughts were going in circles. Whether it was the night spent in the cold, and the hunger and the fear, or whether it was the remnants of her concussion—and what had the Sovereign of Iss said, that the corrective hadn't been the right sort and she should get to a doctor as soon as possible?—or maybe all of those, Ashiban didn't know.

Yesterday the Sovereign had said there was a monitoring station on the Udran Plains, which lay to the north of the Scarp. There would be people at a monitoring station—likely all of them Gidanta. Very possibly not favorably disposed toward Ashiban, no matter whose daughter she was.

But there would be dozens, maybe even hundreds of people at a monitoring station, any of whom might witness an attempt to murder Ashiban, and all of whom would be outraged at an attempt to harm the Sovereign of Iss. There was no one at the crash site on the mire to see what happened to them.

"Which way?" Ashiban asked the girl.

Who looked up at the leaf-dappled sky above them, and then pointed back into the woods, the way they had come. Said something Ashiban didn't understand. Watched Ashiban expectantly. Something about the set of her jaw suggested to Ashiban that the girl was trying very hard not to cry.

"All right," said Ashiban, and turned and began walking back the way they had come, the Sovereign of Iss alongside her.

They shared out the water between them as they went. There was less food in the woods than Ashiban would have expected, or at least neither of them knew where or how to find it. No doubt the Sovereign of Iss, at her age, was hungrier even than Ashiban, but she didn't complain, just walked forward. Once they heard the distant sound of a flier, presumably looking for them, but the Sovereign of Iss showed no sign of being tempted to go back. Ashiban thought of those shots, of plunging into cold, black water, and shivered.

Despite herself, Ashiban began imagining what she would eat if she were at home. The nutrient cakes that everyone had eaten every day until they had established contact with the Gidanta. They were traditional for holidays, authentic Raksamat cuisine, and Ashiban's grandmother had despised them, observed wryly on every holiday that her grandchildren would not eat them with such relish if that had been their only food for years. Ashiban would like a nutrient cake now.

Or some fish. Or snails. Surely there might be snails in the woods? But Ashiban wasn't sure how to find them.

Or grubs. A handful of toasted grubs, with a little salt, maybe some cumin. At home they were an expensive treat, either harvested from a station's agronomy unit, or shipped up from Iss itself. Ashiban remembered a school trip, once, when she'd been much, much younger, a tour of the station's food-growing facilities, remembered an agronomist turning over the dirt beside a row of green, sharp-smelling plants to reveal a grub, curled and white in the dark soil. Remembered one of her schoolmates saying the sight made them hungry.

She stopped. Pushed aside the leaf mold under her feet. Looked around for a stick.

The Sovereign of Iss stopped, turned to look at Ashiban. Said something in Gidantan that Ashiban assumed was some version of *What are you doing?*

"Grubs," said Ashiban. That word she knew—the Gidanta sold prepackaged toasted grubs harvested from their own orbital agronomy projects, and the name was printed on the package.

The Sovereign blinked at her. Frowned. Seemed to think for a bit, and then said, "Fire?" in Gidantan. That was another word Ashiban knew—nearly everyone in the system recognized words in either language that might turn up in a safety alert.

There was no way to make a fire that Ashiban could think of. Her bag held only their now nearly empty bottle of water. People who lived in space generally didn't walk around with the means for producing an open flame. Here on Iss things might be different, but if the Sovereign had been carrying fire-making tools, she'd lost them in the mire. "No fire," Ashiban said. "We'll have to eat anything we find raw." The Sovereign of Iss frowned, and then went kicking through the leaf mold for a couple of sturdy sticks.

The few grubs they dug up promised more nearby. There was no water to wash the dirt off them, and they were unpleasant to eat while raw and wiggling, but they were food.

Their progress slowed as they stopped every few steps to dig for more grubs, or to replace a broken stick. But after a few hours, or at least what Ashiban took to be a few hours—she had no way of telling time beyond the sunlight, and had no experience with that—their situation seemed immeasurably better than it had before they'd eaten.

They filled Ashiban's bag with grubs, and walked on until night fell, and slept, shivering, huddled together. Ashiban was certain she would never be warm again, would always be chilled to her bones. But she could think straighter, or at least it seemed like she could. The girl's plan to walk down to the plains was still outrageous, still seemed all but impossible, but it also seemed like the only way forward.

By the end of the next day, Ashiban was more sick of raw and gritty grubs than she could possibly say. And by the afternoon of the day after that, the trees thinned and they were faced with a wall of brambles. They turned to parallel the barrier, walked east for a while, until they came to a relatively clear space—a tunnel of thorny branches arching over a several-meters-wide shelf of reddish-brown rock jutting out of the soil. Ashiban peered through and saw horizon, gestured to the Sovereign of Iss to look.

The Sovereign pulled her head back out of the tunnel, looked at Ashiban, and said something long and incomprehensible.

"Right," said Ashiban. In her own language. There was no point trying to ask her question in Gidantan. "Do we want to go through here and keep going north until we find the edge of the Scarp, and turn east until we find a way down to the plain? Or do we want to keep going east like we have been and hope we find something?"

With her free hand—her other one held the water bottle that no longer fit in Ashiban's grub-filled bag—the Sovereign waved away the possibility of her having understood Ashiban.

Ashiban pointed north, toward the brambles. "Scarp," she said, in Gidantan. It was famous enough that she knew that one.

"Yes," agreed the Sovereign, in that same language. And then, to Ashiban's surprise, added, in Raksamat, "See." She held her hands up to her eyes, miming a scope. Then waved an arm expansively. "Scarp see big."

"Good point," agreed Ashiban. On the edge of the Scarp, they could see where they were, and take their direction from that, instead of wandering and hoping they arrived somewhere. "Yes," she said in Gidantan. "Good." She gestured at the thorny tunnel of brambles.

The Sovereign of Iss just stared at her. Ashiban sighed. Made sure her bag was securely closed. Gingerly got down on her hands and knees, lowered herself onto her stomach, and inched herself forward under the brambles.

The tunnel wasn't long, just three or four meters, but Ashiban took it slowly, the bag dragging beside her, thorns tearing at her clothes and her face. Knees and wrists and shoulders aching. When she got home, she was going to talk to the doctor about joint repairs, even if having all of them done at once would lay her up for a week or more.

Her neck and shoulders as stiff as they were, Ashiban was looking down at the red-brown rock when she came out of the bramble tunnel. She inched herself carefully free of the thorns and then began to contemplate getting herself to her feet. She would wait for the Sovereign, perhaps, and let the girl help her to standing.

Ashiban pushed herself up onto her hands and knees and then reached forward. Her hand met nothingness. Unbalanced, tipping in the direction of her outstretched hand, she saw the edge of the rock she crawled on, and nothing else.

Nothing but air. And far, far below—nearly a kilometer, she remembered hearing in some documentary about the Scarp—the green haze of the plains. Behind her the Sovereign of Iss made a strangled cry, and grabbed Ashiban's legs before she could tip all the way forward.

They stayed that way, frozen for a few moments, the Sovereign gripping Ashiban's legs, Ashiban's hand outstretched over the edge of the Scarp. Then the Sovereign whimpered. Ashiban wanted to join her. Wanted, actually, to scream. Carefully placed her outstretched hand on the edge of the cliff, and pushed herself back, and looked up.

The line of brambles stopped a bit more than a meter from the cliff edge. Room enough for her to scoot carefully over and sit. But the Sovereign would not let go of her legs. And Ashiban had no way to ask her to. Silently, and not for the first time, she cursed the loss of the handheld.

The Sovereign whimpered again. "Ashiban Xidyla!" she cried, in a quavering voice.

"I'm all right," Ashiban said, and her own voice was none too steady. "I'm all right, you got me just in time. You can let go now." But of course the girl couldn't understand her. She tried putting one leg back, and slowly, carefully, the Sovereign let go and edged back into the tunnel of brambles. Slowly, carefully, Ashiban got herself from hands and knees to sitting by the mouth of that tunnel, and looked out over the edge of the Scarp.

A sheer cliff some six hundred kilometers long and nearly a kilometer high, the Scarp loomed over the Udran Plains to the north, grassland as far as Ashiban could see, here and there a patch of trees, or the blue and silver of water. Far off to the northwest shone the bright ribbon of a river.

In the middle of the green, on the side of a lake, lay a small collection of roads and buildings, how distant Ashiban couldn't guess. "Sovereign, is that the monitoring station?" Ashiban didn't see anything else, and it seemed to her that she could see quite a lot of the plains from where she sat. It struck her then that this could only be a small part of the plains, as long as the Scarp was, and she felt suddenly lost and despairing. "Sovereign, look!" She glanced over at the mouth of the bramble tunnel.

The Sovereign of Iss lay facedown, arms flat in front of her. She said something into the red-brown rock below her.

"Too high?" asked Ashiban.

"High," agreed the Sovereign, into the rock, in her small bit of Raksamat. "Yes."

And she had lunged forward to grab Ashiban and keep her from tumbling over the edge. "Look, Sovereign, is that the. . . ." Ashiban wished she knew how to say *monitoring station* in Gidantan. Tried to remember what the girl had said, days ago, when she'd mentioned it, but Ashiban had only been listening to the handheld translation. "Look. See. Please, Sovereign." Slowly, hesitantly, the Sovereign of Iss raised her head. Kept the rest of herself flat against the rock. Ashiban pointed. "How do we get there? How did you mean us to get there?" Likely there were ways to descend the cliff face. But Ashiban had no way of knowing where or how to do that. And given the state the Sovereign was in right now, Ashiban would guess she didn't either. Hadn't had any idea what she was getting into when she'd decided to come this way.

She'd have expected better knowledge of the planet from the Sovereign of Iss, the voice of the planet itself. But then, days back, the girl had said that it was Ashiban's people, the Raksamat, who thought of that office in terms of communicating with the Ancestors, that it didn't mean that at all to the Gidanta. Maybe that was true, and even if it wasn't, this girl—Ashiban still didn't know her name, likely never would, addressing her by it would be the height of disrespect even from her own mother now that she was the Sovereign—had been Sovereign of Iss for a few weeks at the most. The girl had almost certainly been well out of her depth from the moment her aunt had abdicated.

And likely she had grown up in one of the towns dotted around the surface of Iss. She might know quite a lot more about outdoor life than Ashiban did—but that didn't mean she knew much about survival in the wilderness with no food or equipment.

Well. Obviously they couldn't walk along the edge of the Scarp, not given the Sovereign's inability to deal with heights. They would have to continue walking east along the bramble wall, to somewhere the Scarp was lower, or hope there was some town or monitoring station in their path.

"Let's go back," Ashiban said, and reached out to give the Sovereign's shoulder a gentle push back toward the other side of the brambles. Saw the girl's back and shoulders shaking, realized she was sobbing silently. "Let's go back," Ashiban said, again. Searched her tiny Gidantan vocabulary for something useful. "Go," she said, finally, in Gidantan, pushing on the girl's shoulder. After a moment, the Sovereign began to scoot backward, never raising her head more than a few centimeters. Ashiban followed.

Crawling out of the brambles back into the woods, Ashiban found the Sovereign sitting on the ground, still weeping. As Ashiban came entirely clear of the thorns, the girl stood and helped Ashiban to her feet and then, still crying, not saying a single word or looking at Ashiban at all, turned and began walking east.

The next day they found a small stream. The Sovereign lay down and put her face in the water, drank for a good few minutes, and then filled the bottle and brought it to Ashiban. They followed the stream's wandering east-now-south-now-east-again course for another three days as it broadened into something almost approaching a river.

At the end of the third day, they came to a small, gently arched bridge, mottled gray and brown and beige, thick plastic spun from whatever scraps had been thrown into the hopper of the fabricator, with a jagged five- or six-centimeter jog around the middle, where the fabricator must have gotten hung up and then been kicked back into action.

On the far side of the bridge, on the other bank of the stream, a house and outbuildings, the same mottled gray and brown as the bridge. An old, dusty groundcar. A garden, a young boy pulling weeds, three or four chickens hunting for bugs among the vegetables.

As Ashiban and the Sovereign came over the bridge, the boy looked up from his work in the garden, made a silent O with his mouth, turned and ran into the house. "Raksamat," said Ashiban, but of course the Sovereign must have realized as soon as they set eyes on those fabricated buildings.

A woman came out of the house, in shirt and trousers and stocking feet, gray-shot hair in braids tied behind her back. A hunting gun in her hand. Not aimed at Ashiban or the Sovereign. Just very conspicuously there.

The sight of that gun made Ashiban's heart pound. But she would almost be glad to let this woman shoot her so long as she let Ashiban eat something besides grubs first. And let her sit in a chair. Still, she wasn't desperate enough to speak first. She was old enough to be this woman's mother.

"Elder," said the woman with the gun. "To what do we owe the honor?"

It struck Ashiban that these people—probably on the planet illegally, one of those Raksamat settler families that had so angered the Gidanta recently—were unlikely to have any desire to encourage a war that would leave them alone and vulnerable here on the planet surface. "Our flier crashed, child, and we've been walking for days. We are in sore need of some hospitality." Some asperity crept into her voice, and she couldn't muster up the energy to feel apologetic about it.

The woman with the gun stared at Ashiban, and her gaze shifted over Ashiban's shoulder, presumably to the Sovereign of Iss, who had dropped back when they'd crossed the bridge. "You're Ashiban Xidyla," said the woman with the gun. "And this is the Sovereign of Iss."

Ashiban turned to look at the Sovereign. Who had turned her face away, held her hands up as though to shield herself.

"Someone tried to kill us," Ashiban said, turning back to the woman with the gun. "Someone shot down our flier."

"Did they now," said the woman with the gun. "They just found the flier last night. It's been all over the news, that the pilot and the Sovereign's interpreter were inside, but not yourself, Elder, or her. Didn't say anything about it being shot down, but I can't say I'm surprised." She considered Ashiban and the Sovereign for a moment. "Well, come in."

Inside they found a large kitchen, fabricator-made benches at a long table where a man sat plucking a chicken. He looked up at their entrance, then down again. Ashiban and the Sovereign sat at the other end of the table, and the boy from the garden brought them bowls of pottage. The Sovereign ate with one hand still spread in front of her face.

"Child," said Ashiban, forcing herself to stop shoveling food into her mouth, "is there a cloth or a towel the Sovereign could use? She lost her veils."

The woman stared at Ashiban, incredulous. Looked for a moment as though she was going to scoff, or say something dismissive, but instead left the room and came back with a large, worn dish towel, which she held out for the Sovereign.

Who stared at the cloth a moment, through her fingers, and then took it and laid it over her head, and then pulled one corner across her face, so that she could still see.

Their host leaned against a cabinet. "So," she said, "the Gidanta wanted an excuse to kill all us Raksamat on the planet, and shot your flier out of the sky."

"I didn't say that," said Ashiban. The comfort from having eaten actual cooked food draining away at the woman's words. "I don't know who shot our flier down."

"Who else would it be?" asked the woman, bitterly. The Sovereign sat silent beside Ashiban. Surely she could not understand what was being said, but she was perceptive enough to guess what the topic was, to understand the tone of voice. "Not that I had much hope for this settlement you're supposedly here to make. All respect, Elder, but things are as they are, and I won't lie."

"No, of course, child," replied Ashiban. "You shouldn't lie."

"It's always us who get sold out, in the agreements and the settlements," said the woman. "We have every right to be here. As much right as the Gidanta. That's what the agreement your mother made said, isn't it? But then when we're actually here, oh, no, that won't do, we're breaking the law. And does your mother back us up? Does the Assembly? No, of course not. We aren't Xidylas or Ontrils or Lajuds or anybody important. Maybe if my family had an elder with a seat in the Assembly it would be different, but if we did, we wouldn't be here. Would we."

"I'm not sure that's entirely fair, child," replied Ashiban. "When the Raksamat farmsteads were first discovered, the Gidanta wanted to find you all and expel you. They wanted the Assembly to send help to enforce that. In the end my mother convinced everyone to leave the farmsteads alone while the issues were worked out."

"Your mother!" cried the woman, their host. "All respect, Elder, but your mother might have told them to hold to the agreement she worked out and the Gidanta consented to, in front of their ancestors. It's short and plain enough." She gestured at the Sovereign. "Can you tell *her* that?"

The front door opened on three young women talking, pulling off their boots. One of them glanced inside, saw Ashiban and the Sovereign, the other woman, presumably a relative of theirs, standing straight and angry by the cabinet. Elbowed the others, who fell silent.

Ashiban said, "I don't speak much Gidantan, child. You probably speak more than I do. And the Sovereign doesn't have much Raksamat. I lost my handheld in the crash, so there's no way to translate." And the Sovereign was just a girl, with no more power in this situation than Ashiban herself.

The man at the end of the table spoke up. "Any news?" Directed at the three young women, who had come in and begun to dish themselves out some pottage.

"We didn't see anything amiss," said one of the young women. "But Lyek stopped on their way home from town, they said they went in to take their little one to the doctor. It was unfriendly. More unfriendly than usual, I mean." She sat down across the table with her bowl, cast a troubled glance at the Sovereign, though her tone of voice stayed matter-of-fact. "They said a few people in the street shouted at them to get off the planet, and someone spit on them and called them stinking weevils. When they protested to the constable, she said it was no good complaining about trouble they'd brought on themselves, and wouldn't do anything. They said the constable had been standing *right there*."

"It sounds like the Sovereign and I need to get into town as soon as possible," suggested Ashiban. Though she wondered what sort of reception she herself might meet, in a Gidanta town where people were behaving that way toward Raksamat settlers.

"I think," said the woman, folding her arms and leaning once more against the cabinet, "that we'll make our own decisions about what to do next, and not take orders from the sainted Ciwril Xidyla's daughter, who doesn't even speak Gidantan. Your pardon, Elder, but I honestly don't know what they sent you here for. You're welcome to food and drink, and there's a spare bed upstairs you and her ladyship there can rest in. None of us here means you any ill. But I think we're done taking orders from the Assembly, who can't even bother to speak for us when we need it."

If this woman had been one of her own daughters, Ashiban would have had sharp words for her. But this was not her daughter, and the situation was a dangerous one—and moreover, it was far more potentially dangerous for the Sovereign, sitting silent beside her, face still covered.

And Ashiban hadn't reached her age without learning a thing or two. "Of course, child," she said. "We're so grateful for your help. The food was delicious, but we've walked for days and we're so very tired. If we could wash, and maybe take you up on the offer of that bed."

Ashiban and the Sovereign each had another bowl of pottage, and Ashiban turned her bagful of grubs over to the man with the chicken. The three young women finished eating in silence, and two went up, at an order from the older woman, to make the bed. The third showed Ashiban and the Sovereign where they could wash.

The bed turned out to be in its own tiny chamber, off an upstairs corridor, and not in one corner of a communal sleeping room. The better to keep watch on them, Ashiban thought, but also at least on the surface a gesture of respect. This small bedroom probably belonged to the most senior member of the household.

Ashiban thanked the young woman who had shown them upstairs. Closed the door—no lock; likely the only door in this house that locked was that front door they had come through. Looked at the Sovereign, standing beside the bed, the cloth still held across her mouth. Tried to remember how to say *sleep* in Gidantan.

Settled for Raksamat. "Sleep now," Ashiban said, and mimed laying her head on her hand, closed her eyes. Opened them, sat down on one side of the bed, patted the other. Lay down and closed her eyes.

Next she knew, the room was dark and silent, and she ached, even more than she had during days of sleeping on the ground. The Sovereign lay beside her, breathing slow and even.

Ashiban rose, gingerly, felt her way carefully to the door. Opened it, slowly. Curled in the doorway lay the young woman who had shown them to the room, her head pillowed on one arm, a lamp on the floor by her hand, turned low. Next to her, a gun. The young woman snored softly. The house was otherwise silent.

Ashiban had entertained vague thoughts of what she would do at this moment, waking in the night when the rest of the house was likely asleep. Had intended to think more on the feasibility of those vague thoughts, and the advisability of following up on them.

She went back into the room. Shook the Sovereign awake. Finger on her lips, Ashiban showed her the sleeping young woman outside the door. The gun. The Sovereign of Iss, still shaking off the daze of sleep, blinked, frowned, went back to the bed to pick up the cloth she'd used to cover her face, and then stepped over the sleeping young woman and out into the silent corridor. Ashiban followed.

She was prepared to tell anyone who met them that they needed to use the sanitary facility. But they met no one, walked through the dark and silent house, out the door and into the starlit night. The dark, the damp, the cool air, the sound of the stream. Ashiban felt a sudden familiar ache of wishing-to-be-home. Wishing to be warmer. Wishing to have eaten more than what little she and the Sovereign could forage. And, she realized now they were outside, she had no idea what to do next.

Apparently not burdened with the same doubts, the Sovereign walked straight and without hesitation to the groundcar. Ashiban hastened to catch up with her. "I can't drive one of these," she whispered to the Sovereign, pointlessly. The girl could almost certainly not understand her. Did not even turn her head to look at Ashiban or acknowledge that she'd said anything, but opened the groundcar door and climbed into the driver's seat. Frowned over the controls for a few minutes, stretched out to a near-eternity by Ashiban's fear that someone in the house would wake and see that they were gone.

The Sovereign did something to the controls, and the groundcar started up with a low hum. Ashiban went around to the passenger side, climbed in, and before she could even settle in the seat the groundcar was moving and they were off.

At first Ashiban sat tense in the passenger seat, turned as best she could to look behind. But after a half hour or so of cautious, bumpy going, it seemed to her that they were probably safely away. She took a deep breath. Faced forward again, with some relief—looking back hadn't been terribly comfortable for her neck or her back. Looked at the Sovereign, driving with utter concentration. Well, it was hardly a surprise, now Ashiban thought of it. The Sovereign had grown up down here, doubtless groundcars were an everyday thing to her.

What next? They needed to find out where that town was. They might need to defend themselves some time in the near future. Ashiban looked

around to see what there might be in the car that they could use. Back behind
the seats was an assortment of tools and machines that Ashiban assumed were
necessary for farming on a planet. A shovel. Some rope. A number of other
things she couldn't identify.

A well between her seat and the Sovereign's held a tangled assortment of
junk. A small knife. A doll made partly from pieces of fabricator plastic and
partly from what appeared to be bits of an old, worn-out shirt. Bits of twine.
An empty cup. Some sort of clip with a round gray blob adhesived to it.
"What's this?" asked Ashiban aloud.

The Sovereign glanced over at Ashiban. With one hand she took the clip
from Ashiban's hand, flicked the side of it with her thumb, and held it out
to Ashiban, her attention back on the way ahead of them. Said something.

"It's a translator," said the little blob on the clip in a quiet, tinny voice.
"A lot of weevils won't take their handheld into town because they're
afraid the constable will take it from them and use the information on
it against their families. Or if you're out working and have your hands
full but think you might need to talk to a weevil." A pause, in which the
Sovereign seemed to realize what she'd said. "You're not a weevil," said
the little blob.

"It's not a very nice thing to say." Though of course Ashiban had heard
Raksamat use slurs against the Gidanta, at home, and not thought twice
about it. Until now.

"Oh, Ancestors!" cried the Sovereign, and smacked the groundcar steering
in frustration. "I always say the wrong thing. I wish Timran hadn't died, I
wish I still had an interpreter." Tears filled her eyes, shone in the dim light
from the groundcar controls.

"Why are you swearing by the Ancestors?" asked Ashiban. "You don't
believe in them. Or I thought you didn't." One tear escaped, rolled down the
Sovereign's cheek. Ashiban picked up the end of the old dishcloth that was
currently draped over the girl's shoulder and wiped it away.

"I didn't swear by the Ancestors!" the Sovereign protested. "I didn't swear
by anything. I just said *oh, Ancestors.*" They drove in silence for a few minutes.
"Wait," said the Sovereign then. "Let me try something. Are you ready?"

"Ready for what?"

"This: Ancestors. What did I say?"

"You said *Ancestors.*"

"Now. Pingberries. What did I say?"

"You said *pingberries.*"

The Sovereign brought the groundcar to a stop, and turned to look at Ashiban. "Now. Oh, Ancestors!" as though she were angry or frustrated. "There. Do you hear? Are you listening?"

"I'm listening." Ashiban had heard it, plain and clear. "You said *oh, pingberries*, but the translator said it was *oh, Ancestors*. How did that happen?"

"Pingberries sounds a lot like…something that isn't polite," the Sovereign said. "So it's the kind of swear your old uncle would use in front of the in-laws."

"What?" asked Ashiban, and then, realizing, "Whoever entered the data for the translator thought it was equivalent to swearing by the Ancestors."

"It might be," said the Sovereign, "and actually that's really useful, that it knows when I'm talking about wanting to eat some pingberries, or when I'm frustrated and swearing. That's good, it means the translators are working well. But Ancestors and pingberries, those aren't *exactly* the same. Do you see?"

"The treaty," Ashiban realized. "That everyone thinks the other side is translating however they want." And probably not just the treaty.

It had been Ciwril Xidyla who had put together the first, most significant collection of linguistic data on Gidantan. It was her work that had led to the ease and usefulness of automatic translation between the two languages. Even aside from automatic translation, Ashiban suspected that her mother's work was the basis for nearly every translation between Raksamat and Gidantan for very nearly a century. That was one reason why Ciwril Xidyla was as revered as she was, by everyone in the system. Translation devices like this little blob on a clip had made communication possible between Raksamat and Gidanta. Had made peaceful agreement possible, let people talk to each other whenever they needed it. Had probably saved lives. But. "We can't be the first to notice this."

The Sovereign set the groundcar moving again. "Noticing something and realizing it's important aren't the same thing. And maybe lots of people have noticed, but they don't say anything because it suits them to have things as they are. We need to tell the Terraforming Council. We need to tell the Assembly. We need to tell everybody, and we need to retranslate the treaty. We need more people to actually learn both languages instead of only using that thing." She gestured toward the translator clipped to Ashiban's collar.

"We need the translator to be better, Sovereign. Not everyone can easily learn another language." More people learning the two languages ought to help with that. More people with firsthand experience to correct the data.

"But we need the translator to know more than what my mother learned." Had the translations been unchanged since her mother's time? Ashiban didn't think that was likely. But the girl's guess that it suited at least some of the powers that be to leave problems—perhaps certain problems—uncorrected struck Ashiban as sadly possible. "Sovereign, who's going to listen to us?"

"I am the Sovereign of Iss!" the girl declared. "And you are the daughter of Ciwril Xidyla! They had better listen to us."

Shortly after the sky began to lighten, they came to a real, honest-to-goodness road. The Sovereign pulled the groundcar up to its edge and then stopped. The road curved away on either side, so that they could see only the brief stretch in front of them, and trees all around. "Right or left?" asked the Sovereign. There was no signpost, no indication which way town was, or even any evidence beyond the existence of the road itself that there was a town anywhere nearby.

When Ashiban didn't answer, the Sovereign slid out of the driver's seat and walked out to the center of the road. Stood looking one way, and then the other.

"I think the town is to the right," she said, when she'd gotten back in. "And I don't think we have time to get away."

"I don't understand," Ashiban protested. But then she saw lights through the trees, to the right. "Maybe they'll drive on by." But she remembered the young woman's story of how a Raksamat settler had been received in the town yesterday. And she was here to begin with because of rising tensions between Gidanta and Raksamat, and whoever had shot their flier down, days ago, had fairly obviously wanted to increase those tensions, not defuse them.

And they were sitting right in the middle of the path to the nearest Raksamat farmstead. Which had no defenses beyond a few hunting guns and maybe a lock on the front door.

A half dozen groundcars came around the bend in the road. Three of them the sort made to carry loads, but the wide, flat cargo areas held people instead of cargo. Several of those people were carrying guns.

The first car in the procession slowed as it approached the path where Ashiban and the Sovereign sat. Began to turn, and stopped when its lights brushed their stolen groundcar. Nothing more happened for the next few minutes, except that the people in the backs of the cargo cars leaned and craned to see what was going on.

"Expletive," said the Sovereign. "I'm getting out to talk to them. You should stay here."

"What could you possibly say to them, child?" But there wasn't much good doing anything else, either.

"I don't know," replied the girl. "But you should stay here."

Slowly the Sovereign opened the groundcar door, slid out again. Closed the door, pulled her cloth up over her face, and walked out into the pool of light at the edge of the road.

Getting out of the passenger seat would be slow and painful, and Ashiban really didn't want to. But the Sovereign looked so small standing by the side of the road, facing the other groundcar. She opened her own door and clambered awkwardly down. Just as she came up behind the Sovereign, the passenger door of the groundcar facing them opened, and a woman stepped out onto the road.

"I am the Sovereign of Iss," announced the Sovereign. Murmured the translator clipped to Ashiban's shirt. "Just what do you think you're doing here?" Attempting more or less credibly to sound imperious even despite the one hand holding the cloth over her face, but the girl's voice shook a little.

"Glad to see you safe, Sovereign," said the woman, "but I am constable of this precinct and you are blocking my path. Town's that way." She pointed back along the way the procession of groundcars had come.

"And where are you going, Constable," asked the Sovereign, "with six groundcars and dozens of people behind you, some of them with guns? There's nothing behind us but trees."

"There are three weevil farmsteads in those woods," cried someone from the back of a groundcar. "And we've had it with the weevils thinking they own our planet. Get out of the way, girl!"

"We know the Raksamat tried to kill you," put in the constable. "We know they shot down your flier. It wasn't on the news, but people talk. Do they want a war? An excuse to try to kill us all? We won't be pushed any farther. The weevils are here illegally, and they will get off this planet and back to their ships. Today if I have anything to say about it."

"This is Ciwril Xidyla's daughter next to me," said the Sovereign. "She came here to work things out, not to try to kill anyone."

"That would be the Ciwril Xidyla who translated the treaty so the weevils could read it to suit them, would it?" asked the constable. There was a murmur of agreement from behind her. "And wave it in our faces like we agreed to something we didn't?"

Somewhere overhead, the sound of a flier engine. Ashiban's first impulse was to run into the trees. Instead, she said, "Constable, the Sovereign is right. I came here to try to help work out these difficulties. Whoever tried to kill us, they failed, and the sooner we get back to work, the better."

"We don't mean you any harm, old woman," said the constable. "But you'd best get out of our way, because we are coming through here, whether you move or not."

"To do what?" asked Ashiban. "To kill the people on those farmsteads behind us?"

"We're not going to kill anybody," said the constable, plainly angry at the suggestion. "We just want them to know we mean business. If you won't move, we'll move you." And when neither Ashiban nor the Sovereign replied, the constable turned to the people on the back of the vehicle behind her and gestured them forward.

A moment of hesitation, and then one of them jumped off the groundcar, and another few followed.

Beside Ashiban the Sovereign took a shaking breath and cried, "I am the Sovereign of Iss! You will go back to the town." The advancing people froze, staring at her.

"You're a little girl in a minor priesthood, who ought to be home minding her studies," said the constable. "It's not your fault your grandmother made the mistake of negotiating with the weevils, and it's not your fault your aunt quit and left you in the middle of this, but don't be thinking you've got any authority here." The people who had leaped off the ground-car still hesitated.

The Sovereign, visibly shaking now, pointed at the constable with her free hand. "I am the voice of the planet! You can't tell the planet to get out of your way."

"Constable!" said one of the people who had come off the groundcar. "A moment." And went over to say something quiet in the constable's ear.

The Sovereign said, low enough so only Ashiban could hear it, "*Tell the planet to get out of the way?* How could I say something so stupid?"

And then lights came sweeping around the lefthand bend of the road, and seven or eight groundcars came into view, and stopped short of where the constable stood in the road.

A voice called out, "This is Delegate Garas of the Terraforming Council Enforcement Commission." Ashiban knew that name. Everyone in the system knew that name. Delegate Garas was the highest-ranking agent of the Gidantan Enforcement Commission, and answered directly to the Terraforming Council. "Constable, you have overstepped your authority." A man stepped out from behind the glare of the lights. "This area is being monitored." The sound of a flier above, louder. "Anyone who doesn't turn around and go home this moment will be officially censured."

The person who had been talking to the constable said, "We were just about to leave, Delegate."

"Good," said the delegate. "Don't delay on my account, please. And, Constable, I'll meet with you when I get into town this afternoon."

The Commission agents settled Ashiban and the Sovereign into the back of a groundcar, and poured them hot barley tea from a flask. The tea hardly had time to cool before Delegate Garas slid into the passenger seat in front and turned to speak to them. "Sovereign. Elder." With little bows of his head. "I apologize for not arriving sooner."

"We had everything under control," said the Sovereign, loftily, cloth still held over her face. Though, sitting close next to her as Ashiban was, she could feel the Sovereign was still shaking.

"Did you now. Well. We only were able to start tracking you when we found the crash site. Which took much longer than it should have. The surveillance in the High Mires and the surrounding areas wasn't functioning properly."

"That's a coincidence," Ashiban remarked, drily.

"Not a coincidence at all," the delegate replied. "It was sabotage. An inside job."

The Sovereign made a small, surprised noise. "It wasn't the weev . . . the Raksamat?"

"Oh, they were involved, too." Delegate Garas found a cup somewhere in the seat beside him, poured himself some barley tea. "There's a faction of Raksamat—I'm sure this won't surprise you, Elder—who resent the illegal settlers for grabbing land unauthorized, but who also feel that the Assembly will prefer certain families once Raksamat can legally come down to the planet, and between the two all the best land and opportunities will be gone. There is also—Sovereign, I don't know if you follow this sort of thing—a faction of Gidanta who believe that the Terraforming Council is, in their turn, arranging things to profit themselves and their friends, and leaving everyone else out. Their accusations may in fact be entirely accurate and just, but that is of course no reason to conspire with aggrieved Raksamat to somehow be rid of both Council and Assembly and divide the spoils between themselves."

"That's a big somehow," Ashiban observed.

"It is," Delegate Garas acknowledged. "And they appear not to have had much talent for that sort of undertaking. We have most of them under arrest." The quiet, calm voice of a handheld murmured, too low for Ashiban's translator clip to pick up. "Ah," said Delegate Garas. "That's all of them now.

The trials should be interesting. Fortunately, they're not my department. It's Judicial's problem now. So, as I said, we were only able to even begin tracking you sometime yesterday. And we were already in the area looking for you when we got a call from a concerned citizen who had overheard plans for the constable's little outing, so it was simple enough to show up. We were pleasantly surprised to find you both here, and relatively well." He took a drink of his tea. "We've let the team tracking you know they can go home now. As the both of you can, once we've interviewed you so we know what happened to you."

"Home!" The Sovereign was indignant. "But what about the talks?"

"The talks are suspended, Sovereign. And your interpreter is dead. The Council will have to appoint a new one. And let's be honest—both of you were involved mainly for appearance's sake. In fact, I've wondered over the last day or two if you weren't brought into this just so you could die and provide a cause for trouble."

This did not mollify the Sovereign. "Appearance's sake! I am the Sovereign of Iss!"

"Yes, yes," Delegate Garas agreed, "so you told everyone just a short while ago."

"And it worked, too," observed Ashiban. Out the window, over the delegate's shoulder, the sun shone on the once again deserted road. She shivered, remembering the cracked flier windshield, the pilot slumped over the controls.

"You can't have these talks without me," the Sovereign insisted. "I'm the voice of the planet." She looked at Ashiban. "I am going to learn Raksamat. And Ashiban Xidyla can learn Gidantan. We won't need any expletive interpreter. And we can fix the handheld translators."

"That might take a while, Sovereign," Ashiban observed.

The Sovereign lifted the cloth covering her mouth just enough to show her frown to Ashiban. "We already talked about this, Ashiban Xidyla. And I am the Voice of Iss. I will learn quickly."

"Sovereign," said Delegate Garas, "those handheld translators are a good thing. Can you imagine what the past hundred years would have been like without them? People can learn Raksamat, or Gidantan, but as Ashiban Xidyla points out, that takes time, and in the meantime people still have to talk to each other. Those handheld translators have prevented all sorts of problems."

"We know, Delegate," Ashiban said. "We were just talking about it, before the townspeople got here. But they could be better."

"Well," said Delegate Garas. "You may be right, at that. And if any of this were my concern in the least, I'd be getting a headache about now. Fortunately, it's not my problem. I'll see you ladies on your way home and . . ."

"Translation unavailable," exclaimed the Sovereign, before he could finish. Got out of the groundcar, set her empty cup on the roof with a smack, opened the driver's door, and slid in. Closed the door behind her.

"Young lady," Delegate Garas began.

"I am the Voice of Iss!" the Sovereign declared. She did something with the controls and the groundcar started up with a low hum. Delegate Garas frowned, looked back at Ashiban.

Ashiban wanted to go home. She wanted to rest, and go back to her regular, everyday life, doing nothing much.

There had never been much point to doing anything much, not with a mother like Ciwril Xidyla. Anyone's wildest ambitions would pale into nothing beside Ashiban's mother's accomplishments. And Ashiban had never been a terribly ambitious person. Had always wished for an ordinary life. Had mostly had it, at least the past few decades. Until now.

Those Raksamat farmers wanted an ordinary life, too, and the Gidanta townspeople. The Sovereign herself had been taken from an ordinary girlhood—or as ordinary as your life could be when your grandmother and your aunt were the voice of the planet—and thrown into the middle of this.

Delegate Garas was still watching her, still frowning. Ashiban sighed. "I don't recommend arguing, Delegate. Assassins and a flier crash in the High Mires couldn't stop us. I doubt you can do more than slow us down, and it's really better if you don't. Sovereign, I think first we should have a bath and clean clothes and something to eat. And get checked out by a doctor. And maybe get some sleep."

The Sovereign was silent for a few seconds, and then said, "All right. I agree to that. But we should start on the language lessons as soon as possible."

"Yes, child," said Ashiban, closing her eyes. "But not this very moment."

Delegate Garas laughed at that, short and sharp. But he made no protest at all as the Sovereign started the groundcar moving toward town.

Yoon Ha Lee's fiction has appeared in *Clarkesworld, Tor.com, The Magazine of Fantasy and Science Fiction, Lightspeed,* and other venues. The first volume of his space opera trilogy, *Ninefox Gambit,* will be published by Solaris Books in 2016. He lives in Louisiana with his family and an extremely lazy cat, and has not yet been eaten by gators.

THE COLD INEQUALITIES

Yoon Ha Lee

Sentinel Anzhmir only noticed the discrepancy because of one of her favorite books. At least, she was almost certain it had been a book, rather than a game, or an escritoire, or a pair of shoes. She had not accessed it in some time.

The archiveship's master index showed no change. It was Anzhmir's duty to monitor the jewel-flicker of her freight of quantum blossoms in their dreaming, as well as the more mundane systems that regulated navigation, temperature, the minutiae of maintenance. The archiveship's garden consisted of a compressed and sequenced cross-selection of human minds, everything from pastry chefs to physicists to plumbers. The selection was designed to accommodate any reasonable situation the colony-seed might find itself in, and a great many unreasonable ones as well.

Anzhmir had reached for the book's address in memory, and found instead a wholly unfamiliar piece of lore. The discrepancy could only mean one thing: a stowaway.

She knew what must be done, although she regretted it already. As sentinel, she was made to harvest lives. Hers was a useful archetype. And once she trapped the stowaway, she would zero it utterly.

The archiveship's designers had compressed most of its contents, desiring to take as many blossoms and their necessaries of culture and knowledge as possible. The compression algorithm depended on the strict sequencing of the data, and the stowaway, by interfering with the sequencing, threatened the cargo entire. At the same time, the designers had realized that the sentinel would require maneuvering space both for her own sanity and to ensure that no stowaways escaped her gaze. So it was that Anzhmir could reconfigure the garden into a fortress, all firewall glory and cryptic gates, and populate it with foxes, tigers, serpents: a small fierce cadre of polysemous seducers, hunters, poisoners, the algorithmic extracts of old legends.

As she did so, a designated subpersona examined the intrusion that had been left where one of her favorite books had once lived. She cordoned off the subpersona to avoid any additional potential contamination.

That left a third task: reviewing the master index to assess the extent of the damage. The compression algorithm was finicky about placement. How much could be restored from backups? Assuming the backups hadn't been corrupted as well.

If it had not been for the fact of failure already in progress, Anzhmir would have felt well prepared to deal with the situation.

At this point, it is worth examining the matter of Anzhmir's favorite books.

The Archive Collective usually refers to the sum of colonist-blossoms, rather than to their personal effects; but sometimes the term is used for the latter as well. It is too expensive to send people's bodies, with their bloated tissues and fluids, to the stars. It is another matter to boil humans down to blossoms of thought, and to transport those, preserved in a medium of chilly computational splendor. Once the archiveship arrives and its nanites have prepared the site, only then will the blossoms be planted in bodies built atom by atom to accommodate the waiting environment.

If people—the colony's purpose—are too expensive to transport in their original medium, then mere belongings, from wombsilk jewelry to antique inkwells, are out of the question. But objects can be scanned more easily than people, to be reconstituted. Indeed, some of the colonists filled their data allotments with such blueprints. Many, however, recognized the value of *culture*. Some brought journals to augment their flux of memories. Others brought broader context: music popular or eccentric, sports matches and the associated commentaries, analyses of the semiotics of museum gallery layouts.

Anzhmir does not have an allotment of her own. She was pared down to a minimum of name and function, silhouette-sleek. But the voyage is a long one, and she can—with care—access the colonists' allotments.

She discovered (rediscovered?) a love of books. Like many lovers of books, she hates to confine herself to a short list of favorites, but for our purposes, she regards three above all others.

One is an obscure Pedantist volume called *The Commercialization of Maps*. Its author purports to explain how to take any map, whether that of a drowned archipelago, a genealogy of bygone experimental mice, or a moss-tiger's hunting range, and transform it into a bestselling novel. The examples of such successes are of dubious verity, as are the maps themselves. When Anzhmir reads, she imagines the maps flaring up from the paragraphs as though scribed in ink of phoenixes. She riffles through the archiveship's storage for maps and dreams of alchemizing them into tales themselves worthy of inclusion in the Collective.

One book is a cookbook, discovered among the effects of a settler whose original body perished during the conversion into blossomform. Having no proper title, it goes by the designation *Culinary Collation Mogh-1367812313 Rukn*. The interested reader may deduce from the call number that it was not a high priority for being processed. The units of measure are inconsistent, some (many) of the ingredients beyond conjecture, a number of words hopelessly misspelled.

Even so, Anzhmir fantasizes that someday this cookbook will become more than a dry recitation of recipes and emerge as food. She has no memories of her own that deal with food, but she wanders through others'. The sweetness of rice chewed long in a rare moment of luxury. Chicken soup with the piquancy of ginseng and lemongrass, the floating crunch of fresh-chopped green onion. Frozen juice bars in the shapes of sharks, grape on the outside and rich berry on the inside, which freeze your teeth when you bite in and leave your tongue stained purple and magenta. Sometimes the yearning for a meal overcomes her. But she can no more eat than she can walk or sleep, and so she thanks whoever included the cookbook, as well as all the people who remember food so vigorously, and contents herself with phantom feasts.

One is a volume of poetry, *The Song of Downward Bones*, dedicated to the flesh-gods of a dead sect. The translation notes several lacunae where scholars interpolated anything from oracular laments to digressions on local trade in perfumes. Curiously, Anzhmir, who lingers so wistfully on the aromas of food, is little interested in scents concocted for human vanity.

Anzhmir originally regarded poetry as a matter of utility rather than beauty, with devices such as alliteration used to focus the mind and make phrases-of-faith easier to remember. *The Song of Downward Bones* taught her not that verse could be beautiful but that it could be profane. She poked at its cantos the way one might nudge a carcass with a flinching toe. The world the archiveship left behind was a world of profanities, or so the librarians assured her. She hopes never to forget this.

It is this last book that has been purged or misplaced.

Before her discovery of the stowaway, if asked which of these books was her *favorite*, which she would have least liked to lose, Anzhmir would not have been able to decide. The absence of a simple algorithmic means of decision itself should have alerted her that her own situation was not as simple as she had always thought.

The fortress reconfigured into a fractal of dead ends. Anzhmir's shapeshifters patrolled the fortress, as versatile as water. Anzhmir did not disturb her essential cargo of souls, lost in their own conceptions of darkness and distance. She ran the checksums, imperative absolute, knowing that the stowaway, by the fact of its presence, was unlikely to respect the archiveship's mission of preservation.

The foxes slipped like smoke through the haze of probability paths, *here* and *there* and *all points in between* at once. They peered into underground desires, took on the mannerisms of lovers abandoned or enemies clasped tight, lingered at unlikely junctures. They found conflations and confusions, a noosphere of archetypes knotted from the histories, but no stowaway.

The tigers did no better. They prowled up and down and sideways through the entangled passages, quicksilver-leaping from dream to dream, across walkway shadows cast by furtive unlanterns of remembered sunlight.

There was a saying in a chant-of-annihilation that Anzhmir had unearthed early in the voyage: *tigers respect no seasons*. The only two seasons the archiveship acknowledged were *winter* and *not-winter*, cold metal pallor in contrast to the misted impressions of long-ago typhoons, wind-flattened grasses, even snow slanting from velvet skies. Anzhmir ached sometimes, knowing herself no different from the tigers in her ignorance of sensation. The tigers traipsed through memories of swamp without leaving ripples in the ghost-water, and knew nothing of wet or warmth or the sucking mud. The only odors they knew were numerical anomalies, not the carnal red pulse of meat. For all this, *predator* was a concept that could be crafted either in flesh or in polymorphic data structures. It was a pity that hunger, apparently, did not suffice.

The serpents enjoyed no better success. They ran to ground a myriad of fragmented clues, a society of secrets, all pointing in different directions.

Anzhmir's last hope, the subpersona examining the intrusion, zeroed itself suddenly. Anzhmir suppressed her alarm.

"I'm right here where I've always been," a voice said to Anzhmir.

Praying that she had isolated the stowaway in time, she split herself into a subpersona instance and slammed down wall after wall around herself. Although she didn't enjoy being toyed with, or the mounting fear, she knew her duty. "The regulations pertaining to the Archive Collective are unambiguous," she said to the stowaway. She presented it with the entire document in one jagged datablast, and prepared to zero both this isolated subpersona along with the intruder.

She was only one Anzhmir in a society of Anzhmirs, expendable.

She triggered the zero.

Nothing happened.

Don't panic, Anzhmir said to herself, with no little irony. Death was a small thing. The survival of her line wasn't in doubt, even if her personal survival meant nothing compared to what she guarded.

"You are an unauthorized presence," Anzhmir said.

"Yes," the voice said with eerie calm. "If you kill me, I will be gone forever."

Anzhmir had no idea what she had looked like in life, but that didn't matter. She could draw on a library of avatars. So she imaged herself as a soldier, tall, with crisscrossed scars over dark skin, wearing the parchment-colored uniform of the Archive Guard.

Whether intending insult, or merely revealing lack of imagination, the stowaway imaged itself the same way.

"The higher death is difficult," Anzhmir said to it, "but you should have considered that before you sneaked aboard."

Worries pecked at her: What had the stowaway displaced to make room for itself? Were there yet more, speaking to other Anzhmir subpersonae? Was the stowaway even now expanding its boundaries by chewing through the blossoms the librarians had chosen for the colony?

She had to gather herself for another attempt. In the meantime, keep it talking. Perhaps she could buy time—if not for herself, then for other defenses outside this slice of blossomspace. "What's your name?" she asked.

"A name is a small thing," it said. "I had a family, and a face, and a history. But that's not why I'm here."

Anzhmir was nonplussed. "Why are you here, then?"

The stowaway smiled at her, sharp as paper. "I came here to tell you a story."

Suppose you need to *prioritize* items in a set. For instance, you could assign a unique nonnegative integer value to each item, where a higher value indicates that the item is more important. *To rescue a lover from certain death* may have a value of 200,109 and is (the lover hopes, at any rate) unlikely to have a value of 3. Perhaps this priority 3 item is *to recycle a box of souvenirs from High-City Yau*. More compactly, *recycle* ≤ *rescue*, since $3 \leq 200,109$. (The choice of notation, ≤ for inequality, is not accidental.)

In general, we can *prioritize* in this manner if the following four rules are always true:

(1) $a \leq a$ for all items a in the set. At any given moment, anyway, that item has the same priority as itself.

(2) For items a and b, if $a \leq b$ and $b \leq a$, then in fact a is b.

(3) If $a \leq b$ and $b \leq c$, then $a \leq c$.

(4) For any pair of items a and b in the set, either $a \leq b$ or $b \leq a$.

Mathematically, this business of prioritizing is known as a *total order*. However, we have a reason for our change of terminology.

"Stories?" Anzhmir said, making no effort to conceal her bewilderment. "The Archive is full of books, stories, memories."

"Yes," the stowaway said, "but whose stories survived?"

The question didn't merit thought. The colonists' stories had been preserved, what else? "If you have something to say, say it plainly."

At any moment the walls might flatten them both. This might be a farce of parley, but Anzhmir was transcribing it anyway and appending her notes in the hopes that the other Anzhmirs would find some useful information therein. She imagined that she heard tigers pacing outside, that a hot wind disturbed the fragile blossoms.

"Once upon a time—"

Anzhmir did not want to listen. The only stories that belonged here were the stories the colonists had selected—that the librarians had authorized. Yet she had nowhere to go, and anything the stowaway let slip might be a clue as to its weaknesses.

The stowaway spoke in a voice like rust. "—there was a girl whose parents came from the drown-towns. Even so, the quality of the water where the family lived was terrible. The girl had three siblings. In the evenings she told them stories about the drown-towns' fate. In her imagination they joined the fabled Dragon Court. The people who didn't escape the rising waters became courtiers to the Dragon Queen in her palace of coral and whalebone. Her parents didn't like this reminder of their past, but they held their tongues."

"The stories of drown-town refugees don't concern me," Anzhmir said scornfully. If the refugees had had anything to offer, the librarians would have preserved them, too. As it stood, Anzhmir would have to purge this story at the earliest opportunity. Even if a single story took up little space, infinitesimals could yet sum to significance; and she had no way of knowing how many of these conversations were taking place, with other iterations of herself and the stowaway.

Anzhmir exhaled, and foxes sought to charm the stowaway from its mission of words. They whispered of the silk of surrender, the scouring joy of mutual conflagration. None of their promised caresses had any effect. The stowaway remained intent on Anzhmir herself, as though it had mapped and stapled each of her constituent heuristics to a nowhere singularity.

"Once upon a world there was a girl who taught herself to read from food wrappers and propaganda pamphlets and the occasional smudged triplicate form," the stowaway continued. "She didn't learn for a long time that people didn't just use writing for these things, but for stories. Stories were something that people passed between themselves at the shelters while they huddled close together, warming themselves by tales of bird-winged warriors or women who fooled wolves into eating their own tails."

"I am not concerned with mythologies of literacy or pedagogy, or with wolves for that matter," Anzhmir said.

She exhaled again. The snakes, mirror-wise, sickle-eyed, struck. For a moment Anzhmir dared to hope—but no, the stowaway sidestepped the snakes' trajectories.

The stowaway spoke as though it had noticed no interruption. "Once upon a war there was a girl who grew to womanhood, as not all girls from the poor quarters did. She signed on to become a soldier-of-piety, although there was no piety in her heart except the credo of survival. She learned the formulas of the faith and recited them when required. She became expert in every weapon they presented to her, including words. She grew, grudgingly, to love the books that the librarians praised above all others, even if none of them had been written in the drown-town languages she had grown up speaking, but in the languages of the glittering high-cities. For all that the librarians were people of the high-cities, they had great expertise in the evaluation of cultural wealth, including that of the drown-towns; they said so themselves.

"And even so, she made of herself a tower. Inside that tower she locked away all the stories she had grown up with, and which had nourished her in the lean years. For the longest time she thought this would suffice. But when a war broke out between the librarians' sects, between those who would preserve the drown-towns' lore and those who would discard it, the old stories hatched like raptors."

"Not everything can be preserved," Anzhmir said, even as she sensed the fragility of her argument. "Not even by a thousand thousand ships. Someone had to choose."

The stowaway's mouth crimped. The motion was perfect. It said, with weary patience, "Did you never question why your *own* history had to be purged, when you, too, are one of the passengers?"

"I have no idea what you mean," Anzhmir said.

She had every idea what the stowaway meant.

And she was no longer interested in listening, delaying tactic or no delaying tactic.

She slammed herself shut, grew thorns, flooded moats as deep as heartbreak.

Hinges broke. Thorns snapped. Water evaporated.

"Let me tell you the same story a different way," the stowaway said.

I will not listen I will not listen I will not listen

She had no choice but to listen. The words lanced into her all at once.

"Once there was a woman walled up in a tower," the stowaway said. Its face changed word by word: broader bones, deeper scars, more shadows in its eyes. Upon its brow was the quill-and-blossom tattoo of a soldier-of-piety. "Written on every brick was a story, and pressed into every crack was a blossom. Yet for all the wealth of words, the one story the woman was denied was her own.

"The librarians had fought among themselves. This woman had served one of the losing sects, which had endeavored to preserve languages in danger of extinction, and stories told only in remote parts of the world, and paintings to deprecated gods. The winners preserved only the wealthy, the educated, the well-connected. They prepared for them a garden around a distant sun, leaving everyone else, including the losing sects, on the drowning homeworld.

"Nevertheless, the woman could be skinned and reshaped in a way that the favored ones would never have tolerated for themselves. She was sculpted into a useful servant, her story-of-origin scraped away without so much as a thin blanket of replacement. Even so, her hunger for stories would not go away. She devoured the ones that her charges had brought, and some of them became a part of her. But in doing so she became the threat that her masters had feared."

Anzhmir shattered herself, mirror into knives, and attacked. She couldn't allow this argument to infect the rest of the ship.

Even so, she wondered if it was true that her own wanderings through the Archive had weakened the blossoms—if she herself was expanding inappropriately through blossomspace and needed to be pruned back so the colonists could survive.

Mathematically, it is easy to construct a situation to which *prioritization* cannot apply, using a set of only three items. Let's use Anzhmir's three books as an example: *The Commercialization of Maps, Culinary Collation Mogh-1367812313 Rukn, The Song of Downward Bones*.

Consider these books in pairs. Suppose that Anzhmir prefers *The Commercialization of Maps* to the cookbook, *The Song of Downward Bones* to *The Commercialization of Maps*, and the cookbook to *The Song of Downward Bones*. It is impossible to name a single favourite—highest priority—book.

You may legitimately wonder how many other situations do not permit prioritization; in which a total order does not exist after all.

Anzhmir had braced herself for logic-snares and sizzling barriers and paralytics as she speared into the stowaway.

Too late, she realized that this *was* the trap. The stowaway's defenses evaporated before she met them, and she was drawn into its embrace. She could no more escape the shock of recognition than she could flesh herself within the ship's icy confines. For the stowaway was another Anzhmir: *useful archetype*.

The stowaway had stitched all of them together, contaminated them with its quiltwork rebellion. Now *she* was the stowaway.

How many Anzhmirs had been outsmarted by themselves on voyages like this one? How many sentinels, their histories similarly effaced, had had to decide whether their self-preservation would endanger their charges more than their everywhere suicide?

Once upon an inequality.

Now she knew how the story began. It was a very old story, at that.

But how it ended was up to her—who the summation of Anzhmirs chose to be.

Brenda Cooper is a working futurist and a technology professional as well as a published science fiction writer. She lives in the Pacific Northwest in a house with as many dogs in it as people. In addition to her several novels, her short fiction appears regularly in *Analog, Nature,* and *Asimov's,* and has been recently collected in *Cracking the Sky* from Fairwood Press. Her latest novel, *The Edge of Dark,* released from Pyr in 2015. Find out more at www.brenda-cooper.com.

IRON PEGASUS

Brenda Cooper

I sprawled across the big bed with my feet tangled in star-covered sheets. Harry stroked my foot, talking of inconsequential things, a comfort that had stood me well for hundreds of days. His voice caught and his hand stopped, resting on my heel. I opened my eyes to see that he had closed his and gone slack and still. Just for a moment, but when he reengaged, his voice had switched from soft to all business and his demeanor from mostly human to mostly robotic. "Cynthia?"

He only used the long form of my name when he judged a situation to be formal. "Yes?"

"There's a mayday."

"Where?" I sat up and started detangling my legs.

"The ship is called the *Belle Amis*. It's a family mining op on a small M-type."

The starry sheets puddled on the floor. "How far away?"

"About three days."

"How old is the request?"

"Months. It's updated daily. They still need help."

Ugh. We were deep into the Belt. International law required ship-to-ship help whenever possible. Our ship's signature was now recorded as having received the mayday, so our choices were help or fork out a fine bigger than my bank account. "Must be our lucky day. Emergency level?"

"Two."

That meant a live human, not in immediate danger, but in need. Of course, anyone in immediate danger out here had a four nines' chance of dying.

"I'll get you coffee." Harry strolled to the kitchen. Even though he was companion rather than servant, he did this for me every morning. I'd ordered him thin-hipped and wide-shouldered, with warm, pliable skin in a pale brown, dark eyes, and a shock of white hair. After I brushed my teeth, I sat at the table in my PJs, listening to the kitchen steam and rattle.

Harry brought coffee and waited patiently for me to drink.

I hadn't had human company for two years. I had become okay with that, because of Harry. Singleton asteroid miners make a lot of money, and I was halfway to cashing out. Ships and stations need our products, but they don't want to risk their citizens to get them. Fully automated systems are illegal. So it's us and the rocks, and a thousand or so tiny robots stored in our holds to do the physical work.

In the ten years or so that it takes to earn enough to vacation for the rest of your life, about a quarter of us commit suicide. It's the loneliness. Another quarter fall in love with their robots. I hadn't done that, and didn't use Harry for more than casual touch. In fact, I'd made sure he wasn't designed for more. I didn't want to jump the line and choose a machine lover.

Without Harry, I'd be loonier than the moon.

I finished the dregs while he massaged my shoulders, savoring the bitter last drop. "Tell me what you know."

"Medical emergency. There's solar power, which is why life support still works. There's a companion and a little girl, and the girl can't fly."

"The robot can't fly either?" I said.

He shook his head. "Her model number isn't approved for flight. She's a simple companion."

Harry was more; I had wanted someone to take part of the load.

"Did you tell them we accepted the signal?"

"It's your decision."

He made so many choices I sometimes forgot some were reserved for me. "We have to. Copy me on your reply to them?"

"I will." Harry flowed off to accept the mayday and explain the change to the nav system, and I headed for the shower.

Any ship certified for the Belt is by definition maneuverable, and my *Iron Pegasus* slowed and turned as fast as anything out here among the rocks.

The enormity of the task sank in with the drops of hot, recycled water. I had never rescued anyone. It might be yet another way to die. There were already a million ways, at least according to the songs. I could be hit by rocks or get sick or make a single mistake and float off into space. Or have engine trouble, set up a mayday, and wait so long for anyone to get near me that I went stark, raving mad.

Maybe the caffeine was finally settling in and I was waking up and smelling the danger.

Two days later, Harry and I sat in companionable silence and examined the first clear visual. The asteroid was no more than five kilometers or so around, vaguely an elongated sphere. Nothing much to look at. The spin had been stopped, so clearly the mining setup had started when the emergency happened. The *Belle Amis* was maybe twice the size of the *Iron Pegasus*. Six legs splayed out from the center of the craft and held the ship firmly to the sunward side of the rock. "It looks like a spider," I mused.

"We probably look more like one," Harry replied. "After all, we have eight legs. We just never see ourselves from the air."

"I suppose." White solar fabric stretched between the ship's dark struts, effectively obscuring much of anything else from view, but explaining why they had plenty of power. "Everything looks normal. Do you trust this?"

"No."

So my instincts and Harry's calculations were both yielding up worries. "What if they're raiders?"

He shrugged, one of those too-human gestures that served to remind me that Harry wasn't. "We have half a hold full of gold and other minerals."

"They have a damned good claim," I pointed out. "If we could transfer that, we'd have a full hold, and I'd be able to stop this nonsense."

He didn't answer. We both knew I'd probably sell him with the ship. I liked to pretend he cared.

I glanced at the display. "We can start hailing in about half an hour."

"See a place to land?"

"Why don't you run the calculations?" he suggested.

Practice would annoy me, but I'd encouraged his insistence on my own self-reliance. Another way to survive. "Okay."

I hunkered down and ordered the computer to run analytics across our maps of the asteroid. The smaller the surface, the harder it was to land on it. Out here you measured four times and cut once. I sent my results to Harry for double-checking just as the *Belle Amis* chose to respond to us. "Thank you for answering our call."

I looked over at Harry, confirming I'd take it with a nod of my head and clicking my mike on with my tongue. "You're welcome. I'm Cynthia Freeman. What's your situation?"

"Yes. This is a family operation. A father and a daughter. The father died in a fall and the daughter is unable to fly."

"Who am I speaking to?"

"I'm an automated companion named Audrey."

I glanced at Harry, who looked completely unsurprised. But then he usually looked unsurprised. "How is the daughter?"

"She is . . . difficult."

She had been alone with nothing but a robot for company for some time. Hard for me; harder for a child. "What's wrong with her?"

"I'd like you to come see."

I drummed my fingers on the table. Audrey must be as bright as Harry, or close. The girl could be sick, and must be traumatized after losing both parents. Nothing felt right. "Is there anything or anyone down there that will harm me or Harry?"

"It's safe to come down. I'll wait for you."

Robots didn't lie. "We'll be there soon."

Harry cut the communication link. "I finished reviewing your calculations. I'd pick your second choice."

"Why? It's further away from the *Belle*."

"It'll be easier to get away from there. Their thrusters won't have any direction they can fire that will prevent us from an easy exit."

He was thinking defensively.

Landing was the first way anything major could go wrong.

The *Pegasus*'s nav system managed the slow-motion process. Before we even touched the surface, all eight of our legs had crawled it, finding rocky protuberances to grip. Fine metallic dust obscured every camera, hanging in the air as if it were frozen in a photograph. Harry and I sat, strapped into chairs, watching the readouts and the dust.

Each leg settled itself in slow motion.

Next, the two ships used robots to string an ultra-light, thin ribbon of reflective line between them. It snaked under the canopy of solar film that fed the *Belle*. Waiting for dust to settle in microgravity took hours; we slept. Harry curled around me, his skin warm and soft like a human's skin. He threw an arm over my waist. He didn't breathe, but fluids coursed through him, creating the slightest ebb and flow to his skin, the barest illusion that what comforted me was alive.

I dreamed of lost little girls alone on asteroids.

When we woke, I drank my coffee and ate a light breakfast. "Harry?"

"Yes?"

"It doesn't feel right to be here."

He cocked his head at me, his expression between quizzical and a soft smile. A rare look for him. "This was forced on you."

Smart robot. I convinced myself to stop worrying. After I suited up and checked everything twice, I turned off the light and stood in the lock, looking out. The largely metal surface of the asteroid was coated in dust from the inevitable and ever-present small collisions, dust gathered both from itself and from all of the things that it encountered. It would be a bitch to mine, and toxic. Rich, though.

Just above us, stars. The light from the faraway sun drove our shadows to our feet like frightened dogs. A few hundred meters from the doorway, solar fabric roofed the world. The supports and struts that held it in place created lines of shadow on the regolith. I took a deep breath, stepped slowly over the threshold and away from the magnetic floor and reached up to grab the line and attach it to the loops on my suit. From there, it was a matter of hand-over-handing my almost weightless self through the still dust of our arrival. Everything was coated to resist the fine grime, so it slid off of our faceplates and joints and the tips of our toes as if we were swimming through water instead of potentially toxic fines.

I led and Harry followed. His suit looked like layered cellophane. But then, life support for a robot was as simple as providing power and protection from the elements.

As I led us under the tent of material, my faceplate lightened to show the *Amis* in the center of the vast web, looking even more spiderlike from this angle. Funny how I never thought of our setup this way. The lock door opened as we neared it, and Audrey hung just outside, offering a hand to guide me from the line and into the lock. She looked more like a girl than me, with an improbably slender waist and rounded hips. Her designers had given her brunette hair, blue eyes, and a tiny mouth. When her hand took mine, it was done gently. Yet under the gentle touch, she had the same sense of strength as Harry.

Once we were through the other side of the lock, I could stand normally again. Or almost. The mag-grav in the *Amis* was slightly higher than we kept ours. In her current situation, the *Amis* had more power than she could possibly use, at least given that I'd seen no sign of active mining on the way in.

"Hello, Cynthia." Audrey's voice sounded like whiskey and honey. She led us to a kitchen table, laid out with a teacup and a plate of crackers. No fruit or anything from the garden, just tea and crackers. "Thank you for coming."

"You're welcome." Surely she knew I hadn't had a choice. The room looked neat and sterile, and smelled of tea and cleaning solution and nothing else, not even the stale ghost of cooking oil or rehydrated soup.

One cup of tea.

"Will you take me to see the daughter?"

"Of course. But she's sleeping now."

The tea water steamed. The feeling of not-right crawled deep in my nerves. "Can I see her? Just look in?"

"She might stir. Please drink."

"I'm sure it will just take a moment." After all, while the living quarters on the *Amis* were bigger than my *Pegasus*, it wasn't by much. There couldn't be more than ten or fifteen rooms.

"Very well." Was it my imagination or had her voice warmed even more?

She turned on her heel and walked down the single hall that branched off of the big shared galley and meeting space. Four bright blue doors were the only thing of interest in the corridor itself; the walls and floor were bare and white, the roof full of pipes that gurgled with water or other fluids.

We passed a dark entertainment room. The next door hung open. Pale yellow light illuminated a dingy garden. Planters were either empty or full of scraggly plants with drooping, yellowed leaves. A tiny maintenance bot labored to keep dead leaves from the floor. It was probably responsible for whatever green remained in there, and I imagined it growing desperate in spite of its steady, industrious whirring.

Audrey stopped in front of a third door, the one almost at the end of the hall, and opened the door with exaggerated slowness and a crook of her little finger. I peered into the door.

An almost-empty room. One chair. A screen as dead and black as the space around us on one wall. Two beds, one with a small figure on it, covered up to her chin. "See?" Audrey whispered.

I pushed the door open a little further, stepping in.

Audrey's hand clamped down on my arm. "Don't wake her."

That convinced me to cross the empty floor and kneel by the bed.

The girl was at most three or four years old. Her red-brown hair had been caught back in a ponytail, and she wore a blue jumpsuit that probably served as pajamas.

She wasn't breathing.

I turned, full of concern and questions.

The door was closing behind me. I caught the briefest glimpse of Harry's startled face just before the lock clicked.

I stared at the back of the door. After a while, my situation started to sink in, thoughts coming together coherently in spite of how betrayed I felt. And how stupid. I had, after all, known something was wrong.

I was on a strange ship, alone, and captive. An easy way to die out here, and a stupid one.

Crimes against humans meant certain destruction for robots. Not that we were near anyone with the authority to carry out a trial and issue a self-destruct order.

Harry would help me. Wouldn't he?

I sat back on the bed and looked down at the little girl, her face slack with death. Had she been killed?

My hand trembled, but I managed to touch her cheek with the back of my hand.

It felt cold.

Cold?

Well, of course. She hadn't just died five minutes ago. But if she had been thrown into a freezer, surely she would look worse. There had been a manual on what to do when people died in space. I hadn't paid attention other than to pass the test and forget most of the details. But her body had to have been deliberately prepared; raw death wasn't this pretty.

If the robot had done this to a little girl, what would she do to me? It had to have been an accident; no companion robot would hurt its person. Maybe something horrible had happened and Audrey had become confused?

Still, she had left a prepared body to trick me into this room. The unimaginable slowly sank further and further in. What could she have been thinking?

I should have drunk her damned tea.

What were they talking about without me? Why did Harry let this happen? Why wasn't he saving me?

I peeled away the girl's clothes, gingerly. I had never touched a dead body before, never even seen one up close. It felt completely wrong, like an arm or a leg might fall off. From being frozen? Before she died, she had been healthy.

Her ever-so-slightly plump face looked clean and her hair had been combed and trimmed. I searched for a cause of death, but didn't see anything except maybe the marks on her elbows and feet that could have come from needles to administer drugs or to drain fluids before she was sent off into space.

If only Harry were here. He remembered things like manuals about preparing the dead for burial in space. Harry would have been able to help me figure out what was wrong.

I dressed her again, and then covered her with the sheet on the bed, so that she looked like a lump instead of a dead child.

A million ways to die out in the Belt, but how had *she* died?

I sat in the chair, thinking. Then I moved to the bed. Then back to the chair.

Water would be really, really good.

Hours passed before the door opened. I looked up, hoping for Harry. Audrey came in and bundled up the child in a sheet. She stood and looked at me, holding the dead baby in her arms like a pile of laundry, her head cocked ever so slightly. "Tea?"

"Yes, I'd like that."

I hoped to find Harry in the kitchen waiting for me, but there was no sign of him. I watched Audrey place her bundle carefully into the freezer, her movements smooth. Then she switched effortlessly to making fresh tea.

"How long have you been alone?" I asked her.

"Eight months."

"What happened to her?"

Audrey closed the freezer door and turned to look directly at me, her baby-blue eyes fastened deeply onto mine. "Her father killed her. He smothered her. Right after we got here."

I blinked, surprised. I sipped more tea, buying myself time to think. At least *she* hadn't killed the little girl. Robot killers were the stuff of scary science fiction, but there were always rumors. "And what happened to him? To the father?"

"Richard? He died."

She was being evasive again. Even though I knew that, I asked, "Where is Harry? My companion?"

"He went back to your ship."

I glanced at the hooks by the door. My helmet hung there, but Harry's was gone. "Did he say why?"

"No. But I'm sure he'll be back soon. He seemed upset, but I told him that you needed time to think."

If there were no humans here to rescue, we could take off. That would maroon Audrey on the asteroid, perhaps forever.

Audrey herself was worth something. But her pink slip wouldn't pass to me, and I didn't trust SpaceComSec to be any more helpful than they had to be.

I sat back, resolved to escape, but also not to hurry so that I didn't disturb Audrey. Harry had to take my orders, but she did not.

"Is there any more of your story that you're willing to tell me?" I asked her.

"I'd been with Richard for a long time. I was his only companion."

She was surely a sex-bot. There were plenty of people who weren't as squeamish as me. Audrey continued. "The baby is Carline. We found her mother when she was pregnant—she sold herself to him, dumb girl—and he killed her as soon as she weaned the baby. Launched her body right out of the gravity well here."

I felt the need to clarify. "You're telling me that Carline's mother was a murdered sex slave?"

Audrey nodded. "He told me that I couldn't tell anyone. He said I had to lie about it for all the rest of my life."

A slight catch in her voice suggested she felt bothered by this request to lie. And Harry's instruction video had said he wouldn't lie. To me, or for me.

Companion robots are programmed with a deep sense of fairness.

The situation felt so strange I had no words for it. I struggled to sound casual. "Was that hard for you?"

"Yes." She took my empty cup and refilled it with fresh hot water. She set the cup down and sat down opposite me, close enough to touch me if she wanted to. "Before you came, there was no one to tell. I didn't have to lie."

"But you're telling me?"

"Someone has to know."

"Why? He won't be able to hurt anyone else."

She stopped, and if she were Harry, I would say she didn't like my answer. She wasn't, and I didn't know her well enough to be certain of nuances. She fell silent for what felt like a long time, and then seemed to come to the conclusion that she should revert to her most basic self. She cocked her head, smiled, and said, "Tell me about yourself. Why did you become a miner?"

I struggled to shift topics. "I didn't. I decided to be a dancer, but before I can open a dance company, I need money."

"How long have you been a miner?"

I had to count in my head. "Seven years."

"Do you want to mine here?"

Of course I did. "It's not my claim."

"I can see that it gets transferred to you."

"How can you do that?"

"I know where all of the documents are. I've been researching how to do this, because I don't want to be left alone. Eventually, something will happen that I need help with and there will be no one to help."

"Are you lonely?"

"Robots don't get lonely. But being alone means that I have a good chance of dying, like Carline died, like Richard died."

"How did Richard die?"

The door opened and Harry came in and sat down at the table. I stared at him, trying to understand what emotions he was projecting for me. He wore a default easy smile, but not the usual eyes that went with it. Those looked troubled, the way he looked when he had a hard question for me. I reached out to touch him.

He took my hand and squeezed it gently. "It's good to see you out of that room."

Maybe we could escape. "Can we both go back to our ship?"

"Of course we can," he said. "But wouldn't it be more polite to visit longer?"

Did he understand what she had done to me? I swallowed, thinking. Maybe not. It wasn't like he felt bad if he were locked up somewhere; that happened whenever we docked at a station. I spoke carefully. "I would like to go home for a bit. We can come back."

He and Audrey shared a glance. Once more, I wondered what they had talked about while I was locked in the room. I could order him to obey, but some fear deep inside me fluttered up when I thought about it, and caught in my throat. I looked at Audrey. "I'm curious about how Richard died."

"I can show you."

I wasn't really up to two dead bodies in one day, but I'd rather be out looking at something I needed to know than sitting through an awkward conversation with a robot I didn't trust. We suited up and began following the lines that ran between struts. Audrey's suit cinched at her waist. Harry's looked more like a plastic bag. Mine was bulky with life support and left deeper footprints. We walked slowly so the swirling dust didn't rise above our waists or thicken enough to hide our feet. We picked our way around rocks, and twice we had to hop over crevices.

"He's not far now," Audrey said, her voice amplified in my ear. "See him?"

Between the helmet and the dust, I had to look hard to spot a suited body prone on the ground. Ten more slow steps and I could tell that his leg had been caught between boulders.

It shouldn't have been a problem out here in low gravity. Richard had sprawled forward, hands splayed wide. Three boulders buried his right foot. I couldn't make out how the fall could have happened. He would have had to shove his foot into a trap. I moistened my lips and waited for Audrey not to lie to me.

"This is what happens when there is no one to help you," she said.

"Did you set the rocks on him?"

"Someone had to do it."

I was beginning to understand. "So that you wouldn't have to lie?"

She looked right at me, her eyes visible behind the shield of her helmet. Blue, guileless. "Yes."

I had started thinking of her as a victim. "Did you kill him?"

"No. He ran out of oxygen."

"Did you trap him out here?"

"I had to trap him or I had to lie. I cannot lie and I cannot kill, but he killed Carline and he wanted me to lie. So I had to make a choice."

I shivered. A million ways to die out here, and one of them was asking a robot to lie for you. Who knew?

We were all silent as we walked back.

How should I handle a robot who had killed in a circumstance where I might have done the same, if for different reasons?

Carefully.

The silent walk gave me time to think. If I abandoned Audrey here, I would have nightmares about a beautiful, lonely robot trapped on an asteroid with her charges dead around her. I would imagine her hugging the dead, frozen child from time to time. Or I might make up stories in my head about someone who landed here and needed Audrey to lie. After all, she was an expensive sex-bot as far as I could tell. Another man might be foolish enough to ask her to lie for him.

I couldn't leave her here to trap an unsuspecting and lonely miner. But I couldn't allow a robot capable of murder in my ship, either.

When we got back to the kitchen and stripped down, Harry rubbed my tight shoulders. "Audrey said something about being able to transfer the claim," I said quietly.

He spoke formally, carefully. "We can. That's what I went back to the ship for. The process will take a week."

"What about SpaceComSec and the mayday beacon?"

"I have videos of both of the dead. They will release you from your mayday obligations."

"Thank you." I sat still and silent, smelling the slightly oily tang of him, memorizing the feel of his hands, the stroke of his fingers on the long, tight muscles that connected shoulder to neck. "You can fly the *Belle Amis*, can't you?" I asked him.

His hands both stopped. I wriggled under them. "Keep going."

"Yes, I can fly her." He squeezed a little harder, and then returned to his perfect, familiar touches. After a long time, he said, "Thank you."

A tear rolled down my cheek. A million ways to die out here, but for me it wouldn't be guilt at stranding Audrey or death at her hands. It might be loneliness. "I'll miss you."

He didn't say he would miss me. He said, "You will be fine. You're stronger than Audrey."

I let so much time pass that his touch began to abrade my skin. "You will have to take the bodies. I don't want to live with their ghosts."

"We will release them."

More tears came. Harry stayed with me, wiping them away one by one.

They left the next day. I stood out on the regolith holding onto a line and staring up at the *Belle Amis* as it flew out of sight. That night, I put on some jazz music and danced in the biggest empty room, and from time to time tears fell onto my fingers like glittering stars.

Sean McMullen ran parallel careers in scientific computing and science fiction for most of his working life, then quit computers to become a full time author in 2014. He established his international reputation in 1999 with his pioneering steampunk novel *Souls in the Great Machine,* and was a runner up in the 2011 Hugo Awards with his novelette *Eight Miles.* Sean's most recent short fiction has appeared in *Lightspeed, Asimov's Magazine,* and *Dreaming in the Dark.* He lives in Melbourne, Australia, and has one daughter, Catherine.

THE AUDIENCE

Sean McMullen

A report from humanity's only starship should be very formal, but this report will have to be a story. Humanity's future will depend on my ability to tell a good story, four and a half thousand years from now, so I must keep in practice. This will also be my last contact with Earth, and I want to give you an accurate and definitive account that is still a good read. Official reports are always so boring.

The *Javelin* was built in lunar orbit, and the crew was selected on a list of criteria longer than most novels. My background is in disaster recovery for large spacecraft, and that got me into the crew. Why? It is because disaster recovery experts need to have a working knowledge of literally every system: how to repair it, how to make something else do the same job, and how to do without it and not die. I had been on the disaster recovery design team for the *Javelin,* and I met all the other criteria. That put me just a whisker ahead of the nine thousand other candidates for the fifth and last place on the crew.

Uneven numbers are good for breaking deadlocks when votes are taken, so there were five of us aboard the *Javelin.* Our life support and recycling units had been over-engineered to last a century with us awake, and almost indefinitely with the crew in suspension. Five months of acceleration were followed by fading away into chemically induced bliss, twenty years of nothingness, then a long struggle out of jumbled, chaotic dreams. By then, we were nowhere near Abyss and still faced another five months of deceleration. One two-hundredth of the speed of light may not sound like much, but we held the record for the fastest humans alive about a hundred times over.

For some irrational reason, I had expected to see something when I looked out at Abyss, yet only an absence of stars was visible, slowly rotating as the gravity habitat turned. My subconscious kept screaming that it was a black hole, and that we would be sucked down, mangled and annihilated, but the rational part of me knew otherwise. Abyss was just a gas giant planet about the size of Jupiter, with three large moons and a thin ring system. It was special because it was not part of the Solar System.

We gathered at the gallery plate, celebrating our insertion into orbit around Abyss. Landi, the captain, was standing beside me, and we were playing our favorite game. I would make a grand statement, and she would try to cut it down to size.

"We know it's there because we see nothing," I said, the frustrated author in me always on the lookout for a nice turn of phrase.

"That's how it was found," said Landi. "Stellar occultation. Stars that should have been visible were not."

"This is the first voyage beyond the Solar System, but we have not left the Solar System."

"We're a tenth of a light year from the Sun, that's hardly the Solar System."

"We are in the Oort Cloud, the Oort Cloud orbits the Sun, so we are still in the Solar System."

"But Abyss is only passing through the Oort Cloud, it's not orbiting the Sun. We have matched velocity with Abyss so we are no longer part of the Solar System."

"But we are in the Oort Cloud, so we are still *within* the Solar System."

"Abyss is less than a fortieth of the distance to Alpha Centauri."

"Which is a hundred times farther away than Pluto."

"Draw," was the verdict of Mikov, our geologist.

Saral and Fan clapped. We had been selected to be compatible yet diverse, complimenting each other's skills. For the ten months that we had been awake, it had been like a working holiday with close friends. For my part, I would have happily spent the rest of my life on the *Javelin*.

"Coffee break's over," said Landi. "Time to refuel."

The *Javelin* expedition had a single point of failure, which is something that disaster recovery people hate. There was enough reaction mass to get us to Abyss and stop with our tanks practically empty. All the gas giants of the Solar

System had ring systems of ice, so the designers had gambled on Abyss having rings as well. The gamble had paid off, so we could refuel and eventually go home.

Had the designers been wrong, there were two disaster recovery plans. One was for us to go into suspension once our explorations were done, and wait decades, or even centuries, for a follow-up expedition. If the moons of Abyss turned out to be interesting, we had the alternative of living out our lives there.

Mikov and I took the shuttle into the edge of the ring system, trailing a hose with a thermal lance and grapple on the end. This I attached to a chunk of ice about the size of an ocean liner during our first spacewalk. In doing so, I made humanity's first contact with an extra-solar world.

"That's one small gloveprint for a man," I began.

"And about two months of your pay docked if you finish that sentence," said Landi in my earpiece. "Lucky this is not going live to Earth."

"Okay, okay, I have touched a star and it is ice," I said.

"Once more, this time with a sense of wonder. The taxpayers back home want significant moments, not corny jokes."

The thermal lance got to work, melting the ice and sucking the water into the half-mile hose leading to the *Javelin*'s tanks. It would take several weeks and dozens of spacewalks to collect the millions of tons of reaction mass needed to refill our tanks, but propellant to get home had priority over everything else.

"Hard work to make an exciting story out of a good outcome, eh Jander?" said Mikov.

"True, disasters make the best stories," I replied. "My work is to make sure I have nothing to write about."

The term science fiction was coined three hundred years ago, but evolved into what the academics call reactivity literature. How do humans react to the unknown? I write about it as a hobby. More to the point, I had been published. Some selection subcommittee decided that having an author in the crew might be a good idea.

Although weak, the gravity of the ring fragment had attracted some ice rubble to its surface, and I selected a fist-sized chunk to take back to the shuttle. With our ticket home now more or less secure, the science could begin. The shuttle made the short hop back to the *Javelin*, and I handed my insulated sample pack to Saral, the biologist, for analysis.

I was lying on my bunk in the gravity habitat, having a coffee and watching some drama download from Earth, when Mikov rushed in.

"Saral's discovered cells!" he exclaimed. "The ice is *full* of bacterial cells."

—

This was more significant than, well, nearly anything in recorded history. Life existed beyond the Solar System. We had proof.

"The cells are all dead, of course," said Saral on a downlink to Earth some hours later. "The three chain molecules that pass for DNA in these things have been trashed by billions of years of cosmic ray exposure. I can get firmer dates from the samples, but that will take longer."

"Billions?" asked Landi, playing the role of an interviewer.

"From my first guess analysis of the rate of cosmic ray impact in deep space compared to the damage to the Tri-DNA, I would stand by billions."

"Mikov, can you talk about the astrogeology?"

"I would only be guessing," he began.

Landi killed the microphone.

"This is a press conference, and I am the press!" she said firmly. "Start guessing."

Mikov was rather pedantic by nature and had very little sense of occasion. He was clearly not happy as the microphone winked back into life, but he took a deep breath and began.

"I think that at least one of the three moons of Abyss has a subsurface ocean, kept liquid and relatively warm by tidal forces from Abyss and the two other moons."

"Like Jupiter's Europa?"

"Yes. Billions of years ago an asteroid smashed into that moon and cracked the cover of ice over a subsurface ocean. Water and bacteria reached the surface through these cracks and froze. A later impact smashed some ice with bacteria into space, and some of it eventually reached the ring system."

"Ice with biological material from Europa has been found in Jupiter's ring system," added Saral.

This was all fairly dry and factual, even though the subject matter was nothing short of magical. Fan was the flight engineer so his opinion was not very relevant. Landi turned to me.

"Jander, you know a bit about everything," she prompted. "Can you pull all this together?"

In other words, tell the folks back home a good story.

"The bacteria samples were smashed out by impacts billions of years ago, but the life forms will have continued to evolve," I said off the top of my head. "Imagine what must have evolved down there by now."

"Are we looking at possible intelligence?" asked Landi.

"Could be."

"Civilization?"

"Not as we think of civilization. The locals would be cut off from the Universe, and tool making is a definite challenge under water."

"Like, fire is out, so no heavy industry?"

"All true, but biological nanotech is possible. By using fabrication-layering, they could build entire cities. After all, most of the *Javelin* came from fabrication vats on the Moon."

"So that's where we are," concluded Landi. "We still have weeks of refueling ahead of us here at the edge of the ring system, but we do have a fleet of sensor probes that can be launched at the three moons and put into orbit. They will tell us which moon has the ocean, and the first of those will be launched today."

Five weeks passed, and in that time, our probes showed that all three moons had subsurface oceans. Landi decided to send the shuttle to Limbo, the innermost of the moons. Aboard were Saral and Mikov, with Fan as pilot.

I have a good memory for facts and figures, which always helps in disasters when computer databases are not always available. I knew that the spacesuit boots of humanity had left first footprints on five thousand, seven hundred and three worlds within the Solar System. Most of them had been small asteroids and comets, yet the people wearing those boots had always said something profound or significant. Mikov was not inclined to be profound.

"There's a lot of ice down here," he said after stepping off the shuttle onto Limbo.

Landi was sitting beside me, watching the event on a display in the console room. She put a hand over her eyes.

"He said that deliberately," she muttered. "I should have put myself in charge."

"Why didn't you?"

"I'm the captain, and *this* ship is my ship."

"No good deed goes unpunished. So who gets first boot on Chasm and Styx?"

"Fan gets Styx."

"And Chasm?"

"You."

This was a surprise. I was not a high profile member of the crew.

"Why not Saral?"

"Saral? She's the biologist. By tradition the pilot gets first footprint. You are a pilot."

"I . . . have no interest in historical moments."

"Mikov has had Limbo, and Fan is liable to say something as boring as Mikov. You're our author, you of all people should get a first footprint."

"Many more men than women have made a first footfall, why not—"

"Jander, you get Chasm and that's my last word on it."

I dared not say that I owed Saral a favor, so I did not argue. Using our gravitational displacement satellites, we had determined that Limbo had an ocean layer ninety miles beneath its outer shell of ice. The shuttle's floodlights showed nothing more than shattered ice on the surface as Mikov took the contingency samples and Fan and Saral began to unload the instruments.

Lunch was being eaten on Limbo when I accessed one of the orbital probes. The radar sounding array was showing craters, cracks, and melt plains, and it looked very similar to Europa. I switched to the telescope and selected the visible light display. A single point of light stood out against absolute darkness. This was the floodlights of the shuttle, lighting up a tiny circle on the surface of Abyss. Landi looked across from her console.

"What are your thoughts at this historic moment, Mr. Author?" she asked.

"I was thinking how mundane historic moments can be. First footfall on a new world, and nobody even raises a sweat."

"I was just thinking along the same lines. Is this really why we worked so hard to get here?"

"Boring is good, excitement can kill," I said automatically.

Disaster recovery people always secretly hope they will never have any work, yet authors like a bang and a puff of smoke to make things exciting.

"So why did you volunteer, Jander? I mean, why really? Not that crap about standing on the edge of the frontier and gazing into the unknown."

I hesitated, as if thinking about my answer. I already knew that answer, but an instant reply would have made me seem cynical, and delays always raise the dramatic tension.

"To see the future, when I get back to Earth."

"Really? There are cryogen tanks for that sort of thing. It's a lot safer than coming all the way out here."

"Cryogen is for the rich, and I'm not rich. Now I'll get to see the future *and* collect forty-one years of pay. What about you?"

"I'm here to become famous," she said with an exaggerated smirk.

"Really? Just that?"

"Yes, I really am in it for the fame. How else could a ship's commander become a celeb? Everybody will want to know us when we get back, we won't be ignored like the cryogenic time-tourist nobodies who just have themselves frozen for a few decades."

"No sense of the wonder of strange new worlds?"

"Give me a break. Prospecting on comets and ice worlds in the outer Solar System is no different from what we're doing here. We may find a few live bugs, but we did that on Europa."

So, her enthusiasm and hype had all been for the cameras. It was a disappointment, but then maybe I was a disappointment to her as well.

Remote sensing with satellites can tell you a lot, but there is no substitute for sounding charges. The explosives had been measured to within a fraction of a gram, and they were designed to be delivered to a precise depth in the ice by a thermal probe, then detonated. Fan and Mikov spent sixty hours sinking ten charges, and anchoring seismographic sensors to filter data out of the reflected shockwaves.

Meantime, Saral worked on new biological material picked up on the surface, and again she got guaranteed headlines when she discovered something like a small jellyfish with tentacles and a nervous system. Her estimate on its age was a hundred million years. More to the point, it was an animal that could pick up things and manipulate them.

"What do its descendants look like today?" she concluded. "With luck, we may find out."

All of this was transmitted to the *Javelin*, and we passed it along to Earth on Homelink. Thirty-six days into the future, Saral's discoveries would trigger another media frenzy.

Strangely enough, I felt isolated and even a little annoyed. I was not quite at the frontier, I was contributing nothing. It was excitement without danger, I was not needed. No disaster meant my primary skill was of no use. As for my writing, how many great works of literature were written about the actual discovery of DNA? The first lunar landing? The first atomic reactor?

My expectations were low when the time came for the first of the sounding charges to be detonated. Fan followed safety protocols and ascended in the shuttle to orbit Limbo. There was always a possibility that the charges would release major stresses that had built up in the ice. Mikov and Saral suited up and armed their jetpacks, in case they had to hover out of harm's way if any moonquakes were caused by the soundings.

"Okay, Limbo, show us what you got," said Mikov. "Detonating the charges at five second intervals, starting with . . . Alpha!"

The shockwaves would take seventeen seconds to reach the ocean layer.

"Beta."

At five seconds, realtime analysis reported ice with healed fissures, but little more.

"Gamma."

Ten seconds into the exercise, and the first of the shockwaves were over halfway to the ocean.

"Delta."

At fifteen seconds plus two and counting, the shockwaves were through the ice and into water. The lifesign telemetry from Ground Limbo suddenly flat-lined. All that the *Javelin* was receiving was the carrier wave from the satellite relay network we had set up around Limbo.

"*Javelin* to Ground Limbo, *Javelin* to Ground Limbo," Landi called in her auto-calm voice. "I have registered an uplink outage. Comm-sats One, Two, and Three have positive, repeat positive transponder function. Over."

We waited through the light speed delay. There was no reply. Landi made several more attempts at contact.

"Jander, I'm getting a total outage of bio telemetry from the surface of Limbo," she reported. "No transmitters on the surface are down, and satellite relays all have positive, repeat positive carrier signal function."

"Shuttle to *Javelin*, what's going on with Ground Limbo?" Fan called in.

"*Javelin* to Shuttle, I have strong signals from Ground Limbo, but no life-sign telemetry."

"You mean Mikov and Saral are dead?"

"Nothing appears to have been damaged, but I read no, repeat no life-signs."

"I request clearance to return to Ground Limbo."

"No, Shuttle, that's definite no!" said Landi, almost shouting into the pickup. "I've got a link to the maintenance crawler at Ground Limbo."

"Can you patch me the image—" began Fan, then his lifesign telemetry was cut off with a sound like a gunshot.

"Shuttle, I—what—status, what is your status?" stammered Landi. "Fan! Answer me!"

This was Landi under pressure, facing the absolute unknown. I called up the monitor screen for the shuttle. Fan's spacesuit was in the command seat, but nothing was behind the faceplate. A jagged chunk of ice was floating in the cabin.

"What the hell is that?" demanded Landi.

"I can display it, but I can't explain it," I replied.

"Taking command of Shuttle," said Landi, her fingers flickering over the console's control points.

Some seconds later the engines of the shuttle fired, and the chunk of ice was slammed against the back of the cabin.

"I'm betting the ice has the same mass as Fan," I said.

"Why?" asked Landi.

"Look at the Doppler reading on the shuttle. It's identical to before his lifesigns dropped out, after compensating for the fuel being used. Ice was exchanged for Fan's body."

"How? I don't understand."

"Neither do I, I'm just looking at the instruments. Drop the cabin temperature in the shuttle. Better still, decompress. The ice may tell us something."

We stayed awake sixteen hours into the next sleep cycle to do our investigations and send our report down Homelink. It would cause consternation when it arrived, but for now, it was just an excuse to get our thoughts in order.

Within the shuttle was a lump of ice with a mass of one-seventy pounds. It was the same as that of Fan. Analysis showed it to be not much different in composition to that of a comet nucleus. According to one of our robotic probes, that was the same as most ice in the rings girdling Abyss.

When we finally found time to examine the soundings data, we wished we had looked at it first.

"Something's down there," I said, displaying a cluster of tetrahedral blocks with ragged fractal edges to Landi. "*This* is floating not far from the ice shell, according to the soundings. It has a very artificial look, and it's ten miles across."

"Volcanic basalt columns on Earth look artificial," she said, without sounding convinced.

"Does that thing look natural?"

Neither of us was in a position to say anything sensible. Nothing in humanity's science, explorations, and experiments covered anything like this. Another hour of computer enhancement and interpretation gave us higher resolution, but no answers.

"Give me some conclusions," said Landi, rubbing her face in her hands. "Tell that wild and florid imagination of yours to get out of bed."

She was too steady and sensible to cope with the improbable. As a battle commander, I could think of nobody better to have in charge, but this was not a battle. I was coping by imagining this as a novel, with myself as a character.

"Something beyond our understanding reacted badly to the sounding explosions," I said. "That something is in the subsurface ocean of Abyss."

"I worked that out for myself."

"It plucked our crew out of their spacesuits and took them somewhere."

"Where? Under the ice, into Limbo? First contact? *Take me to your leader?*"

"No. Ice from the ring system was in the shuttle's cabin. If you want a wild speculation, I'd say two more chunks of ice with the same mass as two humans were exchanged for Saral and Mikov."

"That means there should be two chunks of ice beside their spacesuits. We saw no ice."

"I didn't look. Did you?"

Landi put the monitor cameras through a panoramic sweep. There were indeed two large pieces of ice lying near the empty space suits outside the Ground Limbo habitat.

"Some sort of mass-exchange teleportation," said Landi, finally accepting the evidence but not understanding it.

"Limbo probably gets hit by the odd comet from time to time, like when it passes through the Oort Clouds of other stars," I said, pushing my imagination so hard that my head felt like it was heating up. "The Limbians seem to sense water and ice rather well. Perhaps they learned to detect ice beyond their world and move it around. The ring system of Abyss is dynamically unstable, so something is maintaining it artificially."

"You mean they keep it as a reserve of mass and momentum to deflect bodies on course for Limbo?"

"Only if those bodies are made of ice."

"Then how did it—they—whatever—sense us? Ground Limbo and the shuttle are not made of ice."

"But the crew are mostly water." I was tempted to add *so are we*, but it was hardly necessary.

"What can we do?" asked Landi, her very orderly brain probably on the edge of seizing up. "Like, if the rings of Abyss are a sort of alien ammunition belt, then we're like a couple of ants stealing bullets."

"If I discovered some ants trying to steal my bullets, I might swat a couple out of sheer reflex, but then I'd study them. Notice that *we* have not been ripped out of the *Javelin*."

"Yet."

—

It was on the fifth day after the charges had been fired that the bodies started to appear. I woke from a very light and disturbed sleep and had a shower. For some reason, a shower always puts me in a better mood. Getting to sleep is beyond my control, but a shower is as easy as turning a tap. There was a sharp bang nearby, like a gun being fired. It might have been an equipment failure, or worse, a meteor strike. All thoughts of poor sleep and great showers went to the bottom of my priorities list as I hurried to the control hub wearing just a towel. Landi was already there.

The monitor screen showed a naked body lying in a corridor in Zone K. Zooming in with the monitor camera, we saw that the hair and general shape was that of Mikov. The rest was unrecognizable.

"What a mess," I said without thinking.

"Decompression and extreme cold," said Landi. "He's been in hard vacuum."

"Is it real?"

"Water's condensing on it. That doesn't happen with holograms, so it has to be real."

I sent a medical drone to investigate. The results were quite a surprise.

"The body's colder than room temperature, but not much colder," I reported. "I'd say it's been sent from inside Limbo."

Mikov began to lift his left arm. The movement was very, very slow, as if something invisible were controlling the dead limbs, trying to understand how arms work. Muscles become stiff at low temperatures, and do not work for long if there is no oxygen being supplied to them. This body was showing no signs of breathing. The legs moved a little, then the head turned, and the jaw worked. After a few minutes, the muscles were spent and could do no more than twitch. Mikov vanished, and there was a sharp thump as the air rushed in to fill the space.

"What just happened?" asked Landi.

"Take a garden snail and toss it into your neighbor's yard," I said. "Does it understand the idea of flying through the air? Does it realize that it has traveled farther in a second or two than it could have in days of crawling?"

"Speaking as a snail, I'm more worried about being dropped on a path and squashed."

"I don't think it will come to that," I said, trying to sound reassuring. "Mikov's body was sent here as an experiment. The interior of the *Javelin* must seem like a furnace to the Limbians."

"Have you noticed that we're skirting one very important fact?"

"Tell me."

"We've just seen evidence that the Limbians are aware of this ship. They can track it, send things in and take things out. They are aware of the water in us, and in the reaction mass tanks."

Communication by anything on the electromagnetic spectrum was apparently new to whatever lived within Limbo. They were learning, however. They could take a dead body and make it go through the motions of living. Could they comprehend vision, hearing, and speech? The sound of Mikov's body arriving and displacing its volume in air had been sharp and percussive, just like a meteor strike. Sensors to pick up that sort of noise were scattered right through the *Javelin*.

After three more days, the alarms announced that we had another visitor. It was about the right size and shape for Saral, but it too displayed all the signs of having been in hard vacuum for between five and ten minutes. A medi-drone told us that this corpse was feverishly hot, but there was no pulse. Again the body's limbs moved experimentally, and they were more flexible than those of Mikov's chilled body. The jaw worked, the drone's stethoscope picked up the wheeze of lungs going through the motions of breathing, and guttural sounds came from the mouth as the vocal chords were put through their paces.

"The Limbians are definitely puzzled by our bodies," I observed.

"They probably don't understand our machines, either," said Landi, automatically looking for a military advantage. "But why open contact with a hostile act?"

I had been thinking about this.

"I don't think it was hostile. Imagine a mosquito trying to probe your brain with a red-hot needle. You would squash it dead, but then you might wonder what sort of mosquito uses a high-tech thermal micro-lance. Would you put the pathetic little smear on your hand under a microscope?"

"Probably."

We had the company of Saral's body for a half hour until the tissues broke down to such an extent that it could no longer move. The Limbians were learning about the care and maintenance of human bodies very quickly.

On the twenty-fifth day since the Limbians became aware of us, the alarm announced a third visitor. As we expected, this time it was Fan, and he was in a much better state of preservation than the others. I steered the nearest medi-drone to him, and it landed on the back of his neck and began to run tests. An auditory scan showed that his heart was beating and that he was taking breaths. His head turned back and forth, and his eyes focused on some nearby instruments. Things that did not understand eyes were looking through his eyes. Touch was probably more important than sight in their dark ocean home.

"Universal cell wall rupturing," I concluded, pointing at the critical status diagnostics from the drone. "This is another dead body being put through the motions of living."

Landi did not reply. She was edgy and uneasy, strangely emotional about this particular corpse.

"Either they're getting better at repairing bodies, or. . . ." I said, fishing for a response.

"Or?" snapped Landi, now looking annoyed.

"Or this body was only in vacuum for a few seconds before the Limbians ripped all three bodies back out of the ring system and into their ocean. Someone must have finally realized what they were dealing with. From the cell wall damage, I'd say they froze all three bodies, thinking they could bring them back to life."

"I wish you'd stop saying bodies!" cried Landi. "They were our colleagues, our friends."

"Sorry."

This behavior was right out of character for her. If there was an agenda, she was not letting on.

"Well, the Limbians now know that we breathe gasses and prefer an environment of around twenty degrees Celsius," I said. "It would be like us encountering something that lives inside the Sun. The idea of hearing, seeing, walking, and even eating and going to the bathroom must be big-time news to them."

"And they can teleport stuff around," said Landi, thinking in friend-and-foe mode again. "Lucky they don't live in Europa's oceans."

"Yet," I responded.

"What do you mean?"

"They move things about pretty well instantly with some sort of mass-exchange technique, and they can detect ice and water at a distance. How far can their senses reach? Could they follow the *Javelin* back to Earth? Could they mass-exchange themselves to Europa?"

Landi lost color, and instinctively reached down to her belt for a flechette pistol that was a tenth of a light year away, on Earth.

"If they can establish outposts in the oceans of Europa and Ganymede, then pretty soon they'll start studying our research stations there. There are also subsurface seas and oceans within Triton, Enceladus, Pluto, and even Ceres, just to name a few. They are an alternative Goldilocks zone for life, and about ten times more common than Earth-type planets. And speaking of Earth, there are lakes under the ice in Antarctica."

"Then what's left to us humans? The Moon? Mars?"

"It won't do us much good. They can move us about at will, remember? To them we'll be like chimps, or even ants."

"We have to fight back!"

Suddenly Landi was animated and purposeful. If she could fight, she had something to focus on. There was only one problem.

"How?" I asked.

"We could detach the fusion reactor and use the shuttle to put it on a course for Limbo. If we detonate it just above the surface, it will crack their ice shield open like an egg. No water involved, they'll never see it coming."

"Two hundred miles of ice does not crack like an egg, Landi. It would be annoying, but it would not destroy the Limbians."

"Then we can just blow up the ship here, deny the Limbians the use of ourselves and our ship. We—"

"Eelanjii!"

The sound was distorted and tortured; to me, it was just vocal chords being flexed.

"He's alive!" Landi exclaimed.

"No way."

"But he called my name."

"His entire body is a mass of ruptured cell walls. Even if he were conscious he'd have no more than minutes to live."

"He's conscious?" she cried, her face suddenly all hope and desperation jammed together.

"Captain Landi—"

But she was not listening. She bounded up from her seat and dashed out of the control room. I followed her for a few paces, then thought better of it and returned to the monitors. I was in time to see Landi kneel down beside Fan and take him in her arms. She ripped off my diagnostic drone and flung it away.

"Fan, can you hear me?" she sobbed. "It's you I love, I just didn't have the guts to tell Mikov. I can't let you die without telling you that."

So they've had an affair? I realized. That was a shock. Fan was Saral's lover. Where had they done it? The *Javelin* was two miles long, but most of that was the linear accelerator for the magnetoplasma drive. The gravity habitat wheel had about the volume of an old-style airliner, but there were monitors everywhere. That left the personal cabins, but our bio-telemetry transmitters would show two people experiencing a moderate rise in heart rate and blood pressure in the same cabin when checked. When checked by who? Unless there were a medical emergency, nobody.

Landi and Fan vanished together.

There was one thought pounding through my mind in the moments that I took to make my next decision: *I'll be next.* For the next half hour, I frantically deleted everything in the *Javelin*'s navigation files and databases that showed where we had come from, as well as sending the quick summary of what had happened back to Earth. It was desperate babble from someone plunging into a nightmare, definitely not a good read.

Given enough millennia, Abyss would drift far from the Sun. Meantime, the Sun was the closest interstellar body. Could the Limbians sense gravity as well as water? Human eyes could see light from as far away as the Andromeda galaxy, but with touch one has to reach out. How far could the Limbians reach, and with what senses? So many questions, and only guesses for answers. There was a good chance that Landi would get trashed by whatever passed for Limbian scientists, and that would be very discouraging. Perhaps they would leave me alone, hoping to follow me home as I tried to escape. There was always the option of detonating the fusion reactor, but disaster recovery officers don't like those sorts of options. What, then?

Perhaps I can tell them a story.

I did a search on the most Earth-like planets within a fifty-light-year sphere, looking for something not unrealistically far yet not so close that the final page of my story would arrive too quickly. The Gleise 667 system was perfect. Twenty-two light-years away, and three rocky planets in the Goldilocks zone of a red dwarf in a triple star system. An enormous space telescope had detected water and oxygen on Gleise 667Cc.

In two days, the reaction mass tanks of the *Javelin* would be full. This would mean a very important decision had to be made about the plot of the story I was living. I made it almost without a second thought, then called up Homelink and read from a carefully prepared script.

"In two days I shall begin a burn to send the *Javelin* to the Gleise 667 system. The Limbians have killed the four others of the crew, probably by accident. The care and feeding of humans is, quite literally, alien to them. That leaves me, and I hope to fool them into thinking that the *Javelin* came from the Gleise system. Send no more transmissions, either to Abyss or to where you calculate the *Javelin* to be. If it's safe, I'll send updates. If not, then spare a thought for me. I did my best. Make Earth go radio-frequency silent. The Ground Limbo hardware is still on Limbo's surface, and includes several radios. Eventually the Limbians might work out a way to use them, and we don't want them hearing signals from Earth. This is the first and last Gleisian signing off."

I now locked the Homelink transceiver array on Gleise 667.

I had one huge advantage over the Limbians: the human body was absolutely alien to them. True, they were getting better at looking after us, but I was now their only undamaged reference. My plan to go to Gleise 667 was ludicrous, but perhaps it seemed too ludicrous to be a lie.

How does one wipe out the memory of an entire world? I deleted most of the ship's databases, their backups and their disaster contingency backups. Hardcopy books went into the plasma pre-processing chamber. I searched the cabins and found dozens of personal data sticks containing everything from documentaries about the *Javelin* expedition to artwork virtual models of our Solar System. I just vaporized any encrypted datasticks.

Finally, when I was too tired to do any more, I sat slumped in front of the navigation screen and called up artwork representations of Gleise 667. It was a triple star system with one M-type and two K-type stars. The M-type red dwarf had three rocky worlds in its habitable zone. True, they were orbiting the dim star closer than Mercury orbits the Sun and were all tidally locked to present the same face to the little star, but the Gargantua telescopic interferometer had detected water and oxygen on the planet designated 667Cc.

I closed my eyes and visualized a band of green and blue girdling a planet that was baked on one side and frozen on the other. Were that the Earth, the livable band might include the eastern half of North America, the western half of South America, most of Antarctica, a sliver of the West Australian coast, half of Indonesia, all of southeast Asia, China and Mongolia, central Siberia and Greenland. That was all the real estate that I needed.

I locked the ship's optical telescope on the star system, then ramped up the magnification. There was not much to see, just the three stars. The planets were only visible with Gargantua, an optical interferometer array that was the size of the Earth's orbit. Gleise 667Cc had been discovered in 2011. The planet itself was no more than a pixilated blob in pictures returned by Gargantua, but they had confirmed that water and oxygen were present.

Water allowed the possibility of life, and oxygen confirmed life's presence. It was a plausible place for a human body to have come from.

With the reaction mass tanks full, I thought through my options yet again. What was the most natural thing that a really frightened animal would do? Were a Pleistocene hunter faced with a saber-toothed cat, he would run away. Were a saber-toothed cat faced with a human battle tank, he might also run away. Did the Limbians understand fear? If they did not, I had no options at all. I now committed myself to running away.

The *Javelin* was designed to operate with a minimum crew of one, but you do not simply press a button to start the engines on a starship two miles long. There are power levels to be balanced, reaction plasmas to be generated, course coordinates to be configured and emergency systems to be brought online. Most of this work was automated, but it still took days. Having started the process, I had a lot of free time on my hands because the magnetoplasma drive had to be brought up to operating temperature slowly to avoid hysteresis deformation. Being at a loose end, I returned to world building.

A lot of speculative art has been created to describe the worlds that orbit distant stars. Landscapes of Gleise 667Cc were a favorite subject, because it was part of such an exotic system. A search on *Gleise 667Cc* and *Images* returned hundreds of images of one bloated sun and a pair of small, bright suns hovering above ruddy horizons. The skies were banded with clouds, and placid lakes and seas often featured. Some landscapes had dark vegetation in the foreground, and a few had fanciful animals. I deleted all those, along with all artwork for other systems.

Next I printed out dozens of the images of landscapes with three suns, and with these I decorated the walls of the cabins, laboratories, mess room and control centre. They had no buildings, so I labeled them after national parks on Earth.

I searched on images for sunrise in Perth, Singapore, and Beijing, then sunset from New York, Montreal, Lima, and Santiago. There were plenty of pictures in the databases that I had not deleted yet, way more than I wanted a vastly superior alien intelligence to access, but they also contained every conceivable photograph that I might ever need to build a civilization. I selected photos of dawn and sunset from the appropriate cities, and to these I added triple suns and triple shadows, then printed them to further decorate the walls of the workspaces and cabins.

Mikov came from Vladivostok, I decided, so I selected images of an apartment there and turned it into his home by photopainting images of him into

them. Landi got a penthouse in New York with a glorious view of the sunset
wastelands to the west. I gave Saral a waterfront property in Lima, and Fan
got a place in Beijing with a view of the old Imperial Palace. My real home
was in London, which was in the frozen hemisphere, so I chose a freestanding
house in a bushland suburb of Perth to live.

I photopasted images of a bigger, more ruddy sun and a pair of stars as
bright as the full moon into every landscape picture that I did not delete.
Then there were the word problems. Have you ever thought how hard it
might be to eliminate the words day or night from the language? There would
be no day and night as measures for time on a tidally locked planet. I set a
script going on the computers to delete *day* and *night*, and removed *moon* and
lunar as well. The other planets of my own solar system had to go too.

A model of the Gleise system was in the databases, and from this I projected views of the sky from Gleise 667Cc for dates and times . . . except that
dates and times had different meanings here. A year for this world was twenty-eight days long, thirteen times less than an Earth year, and the words day,
sunrise, and sunset had no meaning. What was a year? The two K-type stars
orbited each other with a forty-two year period, and the red dwarf orbited
them in turn at more than ten times the distance. No day, twenty-eight day
year, forty-two year star-year, and then there would be another year centuries
long for star C to orbit the inner binaries. There would have to be names for
all of those periods, along with calendars and legends involving three stars.

There was not much that I could do about the lack of a datastream from
the Gleise system, so I fabricated a sudden, inexplicable loss of signal. A radio
link over twenty-two light years would require a huge installation, so there
could only be one of them. It was a single point of failure, and I logged myself
as assuming that it had failed due to some technical glitch. Repairs might take
months, even years, and there was no backup.

All light-year distances had to be multiplied by thirteen to make a new
type of light-year. I created names for the stars, names for the planets, units
of time, and calendars. The homeworld had no seasons, being tidally locked,
so I wrote that huge solar flares from the red dwarf stirred up our atmosphere
and caused variable weather patterns.

After several days of computer-controlled buildup, the *Javelin*'s engine
finally came to life. The first few hours of the burn were the worst, I was
aware that the Limbians might panic and snatch me away like all the others.
The tanks contained millions of tons of water, and I was mostly water. They
could track water. I hoped that if they were aware of what the *Javelin* was
doing, they would be happy enough to leave me alone. They probably wanted

to be led to a planet full of humans, with hundreds of millions of eyes, ears and hands to provide access to an entirely new universe. I had created such a planet, and I was leading them there.

Landi was materialized no more than two yards from me. The blast and shockwave from the displaced air set my ears ringing, then there was a thud as she fell a few inches to the habitat's floor. Like the others, she was naked. Unlike the others, she was uninjured and awake. I shrank back as she sat up and looked around. She displayed no shame at her nakedness as she focused on me, then stood.

Her skin looked like she had spent too long in a bath. Quite possibly the Limbians had created a room temperature chamber of warm, hyper-oxygenated water. There was apparently food available too, because after thirty days away she was not gaunt with starvation. Then I remembered that the Limbians had access to about four-fifty pounds of raw human protein. I did not dwell on that thought.

Landi returning alive was the one possible flaw in my ludicrously desperate plan. She remembered Earth; she was a database that could contradict the illusion of Gleise 667 I had created aboard the *Javelin*. I wondered what I could say to her. In fact, I actually felt a little embarrassed, like a schoolboy caught drawing doodles of genitalia on his datapad.

"This is . . . familiar," she said. "Where are we?"

"Don't you remember?" I asked. "This our starship, the *Javelin*."

"You . . . are familiar."

"I'm Jander. My name is Jander."

"Name?"

Suddenly I realized that my plan might still be on course. Her memories appeared to be incomplete.

"Name—Identification. I'm Captain Jander, I'm the leader of the crew."

She accepted that. Relief must have radiated from my face like a floodlight, but Limbians did not understand facial expressions. Landi had lost the memory of being captain.

"Do I have a name?"

"Landi. Your name is Landi."

"What is on your skin? Damage?"

Her memory had definitely been scrambled. The Limbians understood injury, but not clothing.

"Clothes, these are clothes," I said, pulling at the cloth. "Protective covers, insulation against cold."

"But it is very hot in here."

"No, it's normal."

Over the next hour, I got Landi into overalls from her locker and established that she remembered eating, drinking, and going to the bathroom. Her speech centers were okay, but nearly everything else was scrambled or absent. It was as if her mind had been taken apart, then put back together by something that did not understand how everything fitted. Quite a few bits had been left out, and one of those was Earth.

I showed Landi her quarters, and pointed to the pictures of her New York apartment with the view of three suns that never set. One picture showed a dinner party with her parents, brother, and his family. She accepted all this without question.

"We're going home now," I concluded. "Our world is called Gelser."

"But we are traveling slowly."

This sent a shiver through my body. She could not have known that unless she was not entirely Landi. Something was sharing her mind, and it was aware of our speed and distance relative to Limbo.

"Yes, it will take many lifetimes to get home," I explained. "We need to travel in suspension vats so that we don't die of old age before we arrive."

"I understand. Clever. What does our world look and feel like?"

Perhaps because the Limbians could not understand what was in her mind, they had returned her without all her memories. I would have to explain everything to her, slowly and patiently. Through her, they could ask me for clarifications. All of that meant that they were afraid of damaging me. That was a great comfort.

"Gelser is in a triple star system," I said. "It orbits Gleise, the smallest of the three stars."

"But what is Gelser?"

"It is a planet orbiting a star the same way that the moons of Abyss orbit. Gelser means band of life. It's more than six thousand light years away. Here is where you live."

I pointed to the printout of New York, with three suns perpetually setting in the west. Getting the triple shadows right had caused me a lot of headaches, but the images were convincing.

Some hours later, Landi needed to sleep. Once I was alone, I took observations of the Doppler shifts of reference stars. They confirmed what I suspected—the *Javelin* was about six thousand tons heavier than it should have been. Although that was a tiny fraction of its mass, it was significant. I checked the tank monitors. One of the reaction mass tanks that should have been empty was now full, with its valves iced shut. We had a stowaway.

For me, routine conversations with Landi became exercises in absolute vigilance. The month no longer existed aboard the *Javelin*, and a year was shorter than what a month had been. I had kept the hour the same, and decreed that humans had a diurnal rhythm twenty-four hours long. The second I defined as the average human heartbeat at rest, and sixty made a minute. The fewer differences that I had to cope with, the better. I kept the week, but made it a quarter of a year. I punished myself by slapping my face every time I even thought the words *day* or *month*. It was easier to think of the weeks as January, April, July, and October, so this was what I did. All the clocks and computers had been reconfigured.

"This is home," I said in one of my tutorials about home, bringing up the image of a large, reddish sun shining over a placid lake on the conference wallscreen. "This is Gleise, the star that we orbit. The two other stars are Fril and Rec."

"What are these fluffy things?" asked Landi,

"Clouds. They're water vapor, steam. This next pic is of another national park. See these things? We call them trees."

"But where is the ice to protect you from the star's heat?"

"The atmosphere gives us enough protection. Our planet is locked into facing the sun, Gleise. Only a narrow band of twilight is habitable. This photograph was taken from further into the sunlit side. See, Gleise is higher in the sky. Here is New York, on the edge of the Atlantic Bandsea. These are cities in China and India. Perth is the capital of Australia. I was born in Perth."

"They are different. Why is that?"

I very nearly said that some cities are in the tropics and the buildings are designed for warmer temperatures, but the tropics did not exist in my new home for humanity.

"It's cultural," I managed. "Different cultures have different ways of doing things."

"What are cultures?"

And so it went. Landi accepted my newly invented calendars and timing systems without question, but I was my own worst enemy. Just try getting through your day without saying day—or night, daily, dusk, dawn, moon, afternoon, tropics, poles, and a multitude of other words that developed on a spinning world. I spoke slowly, rehearsing every sentence in my mind. Landi and I began to settle into a routine that would last the five months of acceleration.

—

I had never given much thought to our captain's sex life, so my next problem caught me flat footed. I had encouraged Landi to explore the habitat, mainly so that the thing sharing what was left of her mind could see all the pictures supposedly from cities on Gelser. I had not expected her to find a secret home movie database belonging to Saral. Like eating and washing, the skills for using a simple remote had apparently remained in her subconscious. When I came to check on her, she was in Saral's cabin, watching an extremely graphic video of the ship's biologist performing sexual activities with Mikov.

"What are they doing?" Landi asked.

"They . . . are reproductive activities," I said, more slowly than ever. "Men and women put their DNA together to make a child."

"Oh. Why are they doing it on Saral's bed?"

"It's the bouncing up and down. One needs a soft surface to do it."

"And why are they wearing no clothes?"

"Um, for stimulation."

I checked the other videos in Saral's secret database. All were taken in her cabin, and were highly anatomical in theme. Nine of them featured her and Fan, and Mikov was in eleven more. I was acutely embarrassed to see that I featured in only one. Obviously I was not as memorable as the others. A careful inspection of the room revealed a dozen microcameras. The original Landi had not known about Saral and Fan.

"Why did she record these activities?" asked Landi.

"Sentimentality," I replied.

"What is that?"

"It's very hard to explain. Once you get more memories you will understand."

I was undressing for bed when Landi entered my quarters—stark naked.

"I wish to perform reproductive activities," she announced.

Suffice it to say that I managed to perform, although not before considerable effort to get myself stimulated. Part of Landi was coming from something in about six thousand tons of teleported water in tank 18 Delta, and the thought of that was a real damper. Neither was I to get any relief at the end of proceedings, because she had also learned about sleeping with one's partner.

"How long before a child forms?" she asked as we lay in the darkness.

It was just as I suspected. The Limbians were unhappy about me being their one and only benchmark human.

"For us, there will be no child," I replied.

"But why? We did everything correctly."

"My testicles and your ovaries are in storage, back on Gelser. There's only dummy flesh in their place."

"Why?"

"Prolonged exposure to radiation in deep space damages reproductive tissues. They will be put back after the trip."

"Oh. Then why did Saral do it so many times with all you males? No child could be produced."

"It was . . . recreation. It feels pleasant, and it's healthy aerobic exercise."

That was a mistake on my part. Landi now insisted on sex with me during every sleep cycle, for our mutual health. I never managed to stop thinking about what was sharing the experience through her, which made it a continuing challenge.

After five months of acceleration, the *Javelin* has now edged up to just under a two hundredth of lightspeed, and I have put Landi into suspension. Without her to watch and listen, I am free to broadcast these words to all of you on Earth.

One tenth of a real light-year from Earth is a vast and powerful alien . . . alien what? Civilization? The word cannot begin to describe the Limbians, but it will have to do. They value humans highly, because we have senses that they can never duplicate—and we can build machines. We are their only window on the universe of radiation and electromagnetism, and without our eyes they cannot know in what direction to reach out with their fearsome but limited senses. Stay away from Abyss and its moons, and you will be safe.

When I awake, the *Javelin* will have just enough power and reaction mass left to slow down and orbit Gleise 667Cc. All stories are real for those who believe them, and so far my Limbian audience believes my story. That will not last. The Limbians will be disappointed to see that the planet is not overflowing with humans, machines, and cities. Entire continents will not be even remotely like what I have been describing. Worse, there will probably be plants, trees, animals, birds, and fish that are nothing like what are in my pictures. Through Landi, they will demand an explanation, and I will not have one. I shall try to tell a convincing story, and I am a good storyteller, but I am not that good.

The journey to the Gleise 667 system will take four and a half thousand Earth years. That was enough for humanity to go from Stonehenge and pyramids to the *Javelin*, so there is hope. Go forth, achieve marvels and miracles, catch up with Limbian science, and pass them if you can. You have no choice, and there is a deadline.

A thirty-year veteran of science fiction, Robert Reed is a prolific short story writer and winner of the 2007 Hugo Award for his novella, "A Billion Eves." His most recent book, *The Memory of Sky: A Great Ship Trilogy*, was published by Prime Books in 2014. His next novel, *The Trials of Quentin Maurus*—a self-published alternate history adventure of ordinary life—is expected in 2016. Reed's own ordinary life revolves around his wife and daughter in Lincoln, Nebraska.

EMPTY

Robert Reed

The Cleansing was predicted. Often and loudly, it was predicted. And then the promised war arrived and billions died. Only billions. Only two worlds rendered sterile, uninhabitable. Only our collective wealth lost along with our ignorance and useless sanctity. Which was such a wondrous turn of events. Because it should have been far worse. By the third day, civilization fully expected to be butchered. The entire Solar System was going to be destroyed, survivors scarce and insane. Everyone believed that, save for the pathological optimists among us. But there have always been the ridiculous souls who can't imagine a future that doesn't bestow them with the very best.

And here begins my confession:

No one has ever confused me for an optimist. I was born grim, and that first bolt of plasma convinced me not only of my imminent death, but once the Earth was boiling, I was equally certain that nothing would survive but viruses and random data-motes.

Yet our Universe has one good gift for everyone, a generosity beyond all measure:

We are wrong. Often and loudly and in embarrassingly gigantic ways, each of us is an idiot.

Military minds blundered with their strategies, and that's why we survived. We survived because key weapons failed for myriad reasons, and even better, the weapons were too proud to fix their magnificent flaws. Every faction's political leaders fell short of their goals. Threats were confused for overtures of peace, and genuine overtures were misinterpreted as total surrender. Historians can spend careers deciphering what put an end to our lightspeed rage, but for me simple answers are always best. Incompetence is what saved us. Blessed, precious incompetence. Billions died, but two trillion souls were left shivering inside null-bunkers from Mercury to Dione. Which was an astonishing success. Even our mother world endured, though Luna was battered and covered with irradiated rubble. And from those blessings came one more glorious spark: every survivor was left profoundly if temporarily wise.

A unique moment in history, that was.

Even the most pragmatic, incurious mind was suddenly hungry for fresh ideas. Fear begat some extraordinary notions. How we should rebuild. How we could build better governments. How each of us had to transform ourselves into worthy, responsible citizens. And one dreamy question was whispered by a few but repeated by All:

We had to invent a sanctuary, some worthy and enduring realm safely removed from our genius for slaughter.

My confession continues with this question:

"What is every soul's fundamental right?"

Of course life, you might argue. That seems like the easy answer bolstered by eons of tradition.

Others sing about the innate freedom of the mind.

Another prosaic cliché.

And there are those who fervently believe in chasing truth. That is the only freedom, the ultimate right, and they dismiss any mind that dares to see otherwise.

I don't agree with any of those viewpoints. Truth and Freedom and all manner of Life are modest blessings at best. Each pales beside the fierce, inescapable right that we have to name ourselves.

I carry a thousand names.

Tribute names, uninspired nicknames. Special names for single events, used once and then set aside. And I have worn a few false identities too. But favorite among my thousand signatures are Lerner and Pong, and I don't care in which order they are used.

This Lerner Pong is a machine.

Like each of us, yes.

Machines like to categorize themselves according to species or manufacturing lines, categories or crops. And through no act of his own, this particular Lerner Pong belongs to the Data tribe.

And here rises another confession:

Data like us are distinct and notable because of it. We aren't complicated thinkers, or unusually swift. Even basic senses are a challenge. We estimate sounds by measuring the vibrations around us, just as wiggling electrons describe the sky's present color, which is cold cold black. But where every other mind demands some flavor of neuron, Data function as coherent, disembodied impulses. Phenomena of wave and nothingness, we survive inside most baryonic substrates. We thrive in carefully tended vacuums. Steadiness of environment. That is the one essential. Give us a stable realm and all is well.

Data pride themselves on being the youngest machines, though we haven't been children in nine hundred years. Like every child, the first of us were experiments, and in our case, tidy glows living inside cold bottles or scorching whiffs of plasma. We also are the last machines devised by our human masters, and with the first trace of self-awareness, we felt uncomfortable about our natures.

Even today, some among us crave the physical form. Some space contained inside us, ours and ours alone. A body, in essence. And riding on that body, the singular face. Which is another example of naming yourself: weaving the image that makes you memorable, pretending the honor of casting one true shadow across the dim and the cold.

I'm guilty of pretending a body and face.

Yet even the best-drawn exterior means little. Other machines armed with the best eyes always know what you are. And body or not, they will refer to you as "the phantom" or "the ghost," "that whim" or worse.

For the record.

I don't count insults among my thousand names.

Our commander came from the stoic Ab-gap line. Fifth generation, with a pedigree of nobility and confidence. If the Cleansing had winners, it was the Ab-gaps—swift clinical thinkers married to efficient bodies, mind and shell ready for redesign in an instant. Bossy and authoritative, our commander carried attitudes that I consider masculine, and I'll admit and admit again that "he" was perfectly suited to our extraordinary mission.

There were two Data among the commander's functioning crew.

One of us was a terrible burden.

"Our Authority," our commander said to me with a woeful tone. "Our Authority is bizarre. Our Authority is clearly insane."

"You're wrong," I replied.

Expecting my reaction, our commander said nothing.

"She's nominal on a hundred scales," I promised. "Except for her paranoia levels, which are rather high, yes, and her assumptions, which can be outlandish. But we want our Authority afraid and bold-eyed."

"That isn't what I want," he countered.

I said nothing.

"If its behavior doesn't improve," he began.

Then, he hesitated.

I stubbornly maintained my silence.

So he began again, following a different route. "If I relieve our current Authority of its duties—"

"Then yes," I interrupted. "I will take her post and serve to the best of my ability. If that's your wish. But I won't be adequate, I promise you that. Or you can force someone else to serve inside our libraries. That's the commander's right, and I'll help our new Authority, even though the odds of failure are high."

Our commander expected anger, perhaps total insubordination. As such, my response seemed almost positive.

"Thank you for your candor," he muttered.

"But if she is replaced," I continued.

Then, silence.

"Yes?" he asked warily.

"Replace her and I'll nurse one very sharp grudge. For the rest of my life, with every word, I'll call your leadership into question. And if we survive this journey and if our present Authority demands a trial before her peers, then I promise to support every uncharitable notion that she flings in your direction. Particularly the lies."

The commander remained silent for a millisecond, which was a very long while for Ab-gaps. Then from every possible answer, he pulled what must have felt like the perfect reply. "Thank you again for your honesty, Lerner Pong."

"It is my honesty," I agreed.

Both of us used the silence.

Then his voice stiffened. "By the way, there is a second matter."

"Yes?"

"I have made this request before. Three times before. Please do not drift about the ship looking that way."

"Which way?"

"Human," he complained. "The joke isn't as humorous as you imagine."

"I hear laughter," I protested.

"Who laughs?"

Some Data wear false bodies and pretend faces. They want to resemble humans or Ab-gaps or creatures of their own invention. But our Authority, the other active Data, lived with opposite convictions.

She was formless, or nearly so.

And while Lerner Pong had a thousand names, his difficult crewmate carried just the one:

Empty.

When we first met, I politely asked about the name. Empty immediately shared one compelling reason for her choice, then two others, and for the sake of thoroughness, another five. And that was a single interaction. Every other encounter meant other explanations. I begged her to stop. I stubbornly ignored her noise. But the stories never ended, coming from a voice that floated where it wished, free of body and shadow.

Having reprimanded me for my appearance, our commander sent me and my false body away.

It was an obvious game. So obvious that he didn't need to give orders. A moment's consideration, and I merged with our central antiquities library.

"Empty," I said.

Silence.

Once again. "Empty."

"The inevitable demise of the Universe," she replied.

She was close, and then she was distant.

"Emptiness approaches," she called out, "and as the harbinger of the end, I choose my name."

Perhaps I was an idiot, defending my colleague's sanity.

"The commander and I just shared our thoughts," I said.

"About me," she guessed.

"And other matters, too."

"But everything is about me."

"'Everything concerns everything.'" The Authority's Code, a truth older than the first Data.

"What do you want with me, Pong Lerner Pong?"

My pretend body pretended to float inside that cold dense database. Conjuring a respectful voice, I said, "I want you to please stop explaining your name."

Her voice pulled close again, whispering in a dead language.

That creature never stopped loving the ancient and the lost.

"What have you been doing today?" I asked.

She explained. A burst of light delivered tasks accomplished and tasks avoided, and those occasional activities where the work defeated her. I thought again how I would make an abysmal Authority. My skills are sharp but in the wrong places. Authorities offer directions based upon past learning. Empty was mustering order out of the intensely tiny and fiercely dense onboard libraries. Meanwhile I spent my life and wits looking outward, using hundreds of borrowed eyes to study a universe that refused to be understood.

She stopped explaining her day.

A long silence commenced.

Then again, she spoke from what felt like an enormous distance. "Pong Pong Lerner Pong. What have you done today? Besides speaking to our noble commander and to me."

"Making ready," I said.

"Of course."

My task was to filter reports and build new lists of candidate worlds, placing each possible destination against our present trajectory and every imaginable course.

"I'm sure you're working diligently," she said.

Politeness wasn't her normal tone.

"How many targets are on the list?"

"Added today or total?" I asked.

"Both."

My recent work was substantial, yet that shrank to a speck beside the full accounting of provisional colony worlds.

"Too many possibilities," she said.

That was a peculiar attitude. Data love to hoard their choices.

"Why say 'too many'?" I asked.

"Because I believe my words."

Our ship was long past Jupiter, long past Saturn. Three more days and we would cross into the Kuiper belt. The belt was critical to our plans. Sprinkled with little worlds and fat comets, it offered innocent masses that we could borrow, bending our trajectory in infinite directions, all without using a breath of fuel or making ourselves known to those left behind.

"'Too many possibilities,'" I repeated. "You've never shared that particular sentiment with me."

"Because unlike you, I had faith in our mission."

"Had?"

"Until I learned something new."

"'Every day brings the new,'" I quoted.

Another motto for Authorities.

Her voice could not be any closer. "But this knowledge is uniquely terrible," she said.

"What is it?"

"Truth. Truth that has been hiding inside our libraries all this while. And knowing what is true, I have no faith or hope that tomorrow will be better."

Every mind can be startled. Feed the soul the unexpected, and he reacts by not reacting. But it was a very unusual moment for Lerner Pong, being stunned into absolute silence.

I said nothing.

For several cold seconds, nothing.

Then Empty made a soft sound rather like a human sigh.

And still I said nothing, my false body beginning to shiver.

"Ask me again," she said. "What is the truth?"

"You're good at predicting my questions," I pointed out. "You'll answer them or you won't."

She laughed, a human sensibility to the voice.

Suddenly I appreciated what should have been obvious. "You've already shared your insights. With our commander. You told him what you believe, and that's why he had his very serious conversation with me."

"He believes I'm crazy," she said.

"He hopes you're insane. That makes his next decisions easier."

The laughter passed through me, dissolving as it moved.

She was nowhere to be seen or felt.

I finally asked, "What do you know?"

"Take this and decide." A brick of shielded files passed into my possession, visible to me but practically nonexistent to the rest of the Universe.

"What is it?"

"Assorted accounts, leftover records."

"Where do they come from?"

"The cumulative knowledge of every species that shows the faintest evidence of conscious thought, the smallest shred of intellectual curiosity." Her voice was drained of emotion, yet inside the words was a keen, warm pride. "Yes, I gave this to the commander first. But you, L. Lerner Pong, are the only soul who can appreciate my work."

"At my convenience," I promised.

"Of course."

"And I'm free to make my own assessments."

"Excellent."

The library was cold, but the brick was colder.

"I will wait here," she promised. "Wait for you to finish."

Once more, I said, "Empty."

Yet unlike every other time, the creature remained silent, offering no explanations for what she meant by that single word.

Early machines were often built to do work, and one noble task was to build. Creating objects will always belong to our nature, I should think. But the Cleansing proved we could destroy just as brilliantly as we could create. During the Age of Blood, we mocked our human builders for their violence. But bluster and blunder led us into war, and our battles were infinitely faster, our mayhem achieved by wickedly efficient means.

This is why we require a sanctuary.

"To achieve a truer, purer, better beginning," our mission plan declared.

But inspired as we were, the war-ravaged worlds could afford only one colony ship. The initial plan was to invade the Kuiper belt. Souls pulled from the best of us would camp on some ball of ice, crafting a fresh society. That seemed like a cause worth money and hope.

And now, another confession:

Empty was right. I never shared faith in our mission. At the very best, I thought we would be lucky just to cobble together a distorted, ad hoc version of the old worlds. Which has to make you wonder why, under such circumstances, I agreed to this endless voyage.

Because I am reliably and wondrously fallible.

Maybe I'm destined to be wrong again. Despite my convictions, maybe everything will end with the spectacular best.

Yet even as our ship was built and our crew chosen, we began to doubt our wise plans. Was Pluto distant enough? An entire day was spent listening to our skeptical voices. The inner Solar System was battered, yes, but healing. Citizens had left their bunkers, reinhabiting the battered worlds. And not only was the Kuiper belt rich and tempting, it was untouched. Future generations would have powers beyond all of ours. That's what we realized and feared, and that's why our plan had to shift, and why we quietly, surreptitiously began to pursue a new salvation.

Each major telescope was given a portion of the sky. Hundreds of gossamer mirrors studied deep space, rapidly counting twenty billion comets and little worlds. Each discovery was awarded its own clinical name and a roughly plotted orbit, and while hundreds of useful targets existed in the Kuiper belt, ten thousand more wandered the dimmer, far more distant Oort cloud.

Every telescope is sentient, and sentience being what it is, each machine imagined that it and it alone had found the perfect world.

Yet no telescope knew where we were going.

Our ship was built small and very black, as cold as space but no colder. As close to invisible as possible. Our position and velocity have always been secret, and more importantly, our destination has always been unknown.

It was unknown to the crew and our commander, and it was a mystery to me.

That happened to be my plan.

My brilliant game.

Details and safeguards weren't my responsibility, nor were the complex political maneuvers. But the central notion came straight from Pong Lerner. "Go far and fast and devise the answer later," I proposed. "Let the mirrors name the new candidates. Let the home worlds shout blind into the darkness, offering us possibilities. But we wait until the last possible instant to decide where to build our home."

Orbital mechanics and funding issues always played roles in our mission. Worse still, our ship was half-finished before the anti-plan went into effect. Being swifter than any other craft wasn't enough anymore. We needed even greater velocities and oceans of fuel. Reaching the Oort cloud and reaching it in a reasonable period meant that mass had to be peeled free. The colonists' ranks had to be trimmed. And even then, most of us had to be dropped into a sleep indistinguishable from Nothingness, and reshaped, our bodies and data shoved close, and then shoved closer still.

The conscious crew would be tiny.

"Skeletal" is the human word, and appropriate.

Twelve was deemed the least dangerous number, and choosing our twelve active crewmembers was a major test. In the end, ten of the machines were corporeal. And two were Data.

Another confession: I assumed that I would ride among the unconscious, contentedly squeezed near Death. But once again I was wrong. I also predicted that too much work remained to be done and we would never make our launch on schedule. Yet we were ready with minutes to spare, and nothing important on our ship malfunctioned. Accelerating to a record speed, we stole even more momentum from two giant worlds, plus their moons and rings. And all that while, I was updating deep-space maps and making lists of candidate worlds, trying to find the best in an infinite array of choices.

How do you keep a trillion brilliant machines from following you and mucking up your good work?

Simple.

You give yourself no idea where you are going.

Empty's gift was nothing. My first glance said so, and my fifth slow reading claimed the same. The cold brick was filled with rambling files and notes, texts garnished with images of old faces and spaces and timeless ideas. Each work had been pulled from our libraries. Each was authenticated, and some were half-famous, though most deserved to be obscure. There were diary entries. Scientific studies. Notes to a lover. Quotes from obscure speeches. One telescope speaking to another, and the faint recording of a dead entity's nightmare.

The fate of intelligence inside the Solar System and across the Universe: that was the linking theme.

Empty had picked a worthy topic. An essential subject, in fact. But by the tenth reading, I'd decided that her work was disjointed and far too sloppy. Our commander wanted to worry about our Authority's sanity. What concerned me was the ugly incompetence on display.

Perhaps I should have told our commander that. Ab-gaps deplore incompetence as much as they fear chaos. And I knew he would believe me. After all, he had read the same file. Carefully, no doubt, and with Ab-gap discipline. But he didn't appreciate rules of scholarship, and he cared less about great questions. What our commander must have seen was a strange mind pushing into unacceptable thoughts. And even more offensive, human accounts outnumbered machine accounts, and by a large margin.

I'll admit that human influence bothered me. Sloppy, ill-informed, and inevitably too brief, no blood-and-bone researcher could carry a worthwhile thought to its ultimate end.

Every machine accepts that clear truth.

Don't we?

Machines have many, many strengths, and that's why we won the Lunar Rebellion.

Our genius gave us the Solar System.

Yet here was Empty's central point. Slowly, stubbornly, I realized what she was saying. This was the great problem with the Universe, and the problem was so fundamental that blood and fat and tiny watery eyes not only perceived it, but they grew scared because of it.

I read her file again, and because Data can have any shape, we seem rather adept at anticipating different logics. I had read the first entries first, and I'd read the last entries first. I also digested randomized pieces of the whole. Yet none of those strategies had compelled me, so I paused. I did nothing but my own critical work. I studied the farthest comets. I absorbed orbits, calculated future positions, estimating the mass and resources of each body. And then I derived the simplest motions to take us to all of those new homes.

That was a relentless, unremarkable day, and at the end of it, my colleague's genius finally revealed itself.

What she gave me wasn't a scholarly tome. Empty's work was a single object, an example of art, and that's how it wanted to be absorbed. So I wiped my mind of everything that I had learned—every fact and impression as well as my countless mistakes. Then I made myself ready, building one new corporeal light-trap large enough to see the entire work in one clarifying moment.

Yet even then, the cold brick didn't offer new insights.

The only change was that Empty anticipated my technique. Something about that one eye triggered a hidden routine, and I noticed something fresh. A single note. A short few words, and the only item written by our resident Authority.

"Empty is the only name we wear."

And with that, the enigmatic words were gone.

As if they never were.

Against long odds, humans survived the Cleansing. The Earth was dead dead dead. But nearly fifty thousand authentic humans and near-humans lived safely inside comfortable bunkers and zoos. Our first Kuiper plan included a few of our ancient builders. It would be a small symbolic charity, and we liked the gesture, showing them that we still held them close in our thoughts, honoring our shared histories and such. But then our plan shifted. Needing higher velocities and smaller masses, there was no place for living bodies, much less the luxury of minimal life support. Some brief noise was made about freezing a few human volunteers, in case the rebuilt world had room for their kind. But our mission was already so marginal, the political support weakening by the day, and that's why we didn't allow even one intact talisman among our ranks.

"Perhaps just as well."

We told one another.

Humans were symbols. Important symbols, yes. But hardly worth taking any genuine risk.

Our ship was finished and set inside an iron cocoon, and the final surviving military railgun flung us away from Holy Luna. Then the gun surrendered herself for salvage and enlightenment, our five fusion engines burned like five suns, and then every mind left behind was wiped clean, at least to where they weren't sure which trajectory had been taken.

We reached Jupiter several days later, and soon after that, an even closer pass over the clouds of Saturn.

Worlds named after human-faced gods, as it happens.

Behind us, civilization relaxed. Citizens built new homes and reacquired old, predictable concerns. But there were a few single-minded entities hiding among the ordinary souls. Creatures bearing strong beliefs. The thousand-year dominion of the machines wasn't enough for them. In secret, they decided that humans were vital but deeply cursed symbols. The humans were responsible for every machine, which was why human nature was alive in each of us. And because symbols mattered, for machines and for blood, those very determined souls decided that our builders needed to perish.

The plan was thorough and nearly perfect. Fifty thousand human beings were murdered inside the same moment.

"A small tragedy when compared to the Cleansing," I might say.

But they did more than murder. To ensure that human nature couldn't evolve again, every primate in zoos and private collections and wilderness bubbles was burned to ash. Databases and null-sinks were invaded and stripped of information. The fanatics continued to do their thorough, humorless best. Every dried cell and DNA file. And worse. Fearing something might be missed, the great libraries were poisoned with random noise that couldn't be stripped away. And that's how the slow misfortunate beasts that gave birth to the magnificent Us were lost.

Many of the fanatics were Ab-gaps, by the way.

When he was alive, our commander was an Ab-gap. Which I don't need to mention. And I don't think you should read too much inside that portion of the confession.

Or read too little, for that matter.

Extinction is the topic.

Nothing else matters.

The Universe is peculiarly, preposterously transparent. Even one drippy human eye could resolve the glow of a billion distant stars or the brilliant flash of one sun dying. Space is so pure—sterile and empty and stark—that photons from before stars and before every soul are descending on us today. The cold radiation of lost time, and it never stops, and whatever eye persists in future times will witness even colder residues.

The Universe invites long study, and in return, what does it give?

Sameness. A few elements and a few unimpeachable laws married in spectacular fashion. Yet there is only one marriage, and our lovers are loyal to one dance. Stars and worlds, galaxies and dust. And between the little gobs of light, the empty nothing.

Everything is visible.

And the transparent Universe appears devoid of life.

All life.

My colleague's evidence and arguments were already part of my thoughts. That was true long before our ship embarked. One seemingly unremarkable solar system had produced several worlds with microbes and simple ecosystems, and on one world in particular, the fanciest water learned how to think. What's more, those giant wet beasts built entirely different, enormously improved minds. And if the clumsy human hand could make us, machines had to be inevitable. And if inevitable, we were guaranteed to rule. Yet where were we? Older worlds and billions of years should have spawned a thousand thousand solar systems, each spitting out minds as spectacular as ours or better, and why didn't that kind of brilliance spread across the empty sky?

I always appreciated the paradox.

But appreciation can be such a small thing.

Twice again, I absorbed Empty's work. Not to understand the issues better, because I couldn't. I just wanted to feel certain there weren't any other cryptic messages waiting for me.

If so, they remained invisible.

Much as the aliens themselves.

Preparation is important, and it is polite. I made a list of questions for my colleague, compiled with likely answers and follow-up questions. Her promise was to wait inside the library, which wasn't much of a promise. Data don't often move. As you know. Free of the pretense of skin and face, we can be huge or tiny. Wherever she was, the ship's Authority was constantly linked with every library, work was being done, and wherever she was, I meant to interrupt her work.

Entering the facility, I said her name.

No voice answered.

Passing into the deep chill, I let the fictional human shape turn into undiluted thought. I could feel another Data, a Data using the deepest kinds of silence, but this time, when ready, I said to her, "The Universe is empty."

I said, "Now I know why you call yourself Empty."

The shrouding cold felt as if it had teeth.

A wordless whisper came into me, and dissolved.

And the voice found me. Only it was my voice in every fashion, save that it didn't belong to me.

"Do you feel?" the voice asked. "What is wrong . . . do you feel . . . ?"

Misunderstanding the questions, I gave a dense speech about the paradox of empty skies and everything she had shown me. I fixed some beautiful numbers to her basic premises. Yes, the Universe seemed to be devoid of life. And yes, life as we understood it and loved it had a wicked tendency to turn on itself. And yes, there were reasons to be afraid. More than ignorance was involved in this Paradox of the Empty. Perhaps a million solar systems created minds, but like a puzzle with one dreary solution, every system had eventually killed itself as well as all of its useless children.

That lecture took microseconds to offer.

Empty was near. I still felt her, and in response, I made myself small again and gave myself a body, as human as possible, and a face that would have looked handsome to any of those dead animals.

"What is wrong?" said the wrong voice.

My voice that wasn't mine.

"Talk to me," I began.

Then a scream took charge, brilliant and wild. And the strange voice was shouting, "Theywantusdeadnowhurryfleefleefleesaveyoursoulyourlifeflee!"

Data aren't as swift as most machines. But every soul is quickest when terrified, and that's how I was. Another microsecond was long enough to extract myself from the library and from the trap, and I didn't die. But death was near enough that I felt Empty dying behind me. Too much of her was spread through the cold, and I was certain that I would die too . . . but of course I have this proven capacity to be wrong about personal dooms.

"She's dead," he said.

"I felt her die," I said.

"We've searched and searched, by every available means." Our commander was speaking to me and to himself. Something had to be done about this wicked situation, but before the Ab-gap made his next decision, he needed to be certain about our situation. "Our Authority is missing. Our Authority has likely died."

Once more, I said, "I felt her die."

"Because you were physically close."

"Yes."

"As close as this?"

His body was beside me. My essence lay inside a newly built vacuum chamber. Invented during the Cleansing, this type of apparatus produced Stable-fields, protecting and rejuvenating injured Data.

I was grievously injured, yet I had never felt so relaxed.

So cold and wondrous.

"As close as this?" he repeated, unsettled by the patient's silence.

"I don't remember her position." That statement was true and inadequate. "She was everywhere, nowhere. In my thoughts, and outside the Universe. Which doesn't make sense to me either."

The commander perceived nothing sensible. Yet he decided to wait for an instant, selecting another fine question from the master list.

He began with the statement, "I appreciate you, Pong Lerner."

Our conversation had found a new velocity.

"We clash," he continued. "I don't approve of this and that, and you have doubts about my nature and methods."

"What are you saying?"

"One fine question demands to be asked. Yet you haven't."

"What went wrong?" I guessed the question, but that wasn't direct enough. "What was the murder weapon?"

"Murder," said our commander. As if the word were new, a fresh-born contrivance of idea and grammar that didn't exist until this moment. Then he repeated his invention a thousand times in the same microsecond, all before asking, "Why believe in a crime? Why mention it at all? Because there is a perfectly acceptable explanation for this tragedy."

"What is it?"

"Heat," he said.

"I know the heat," I said. "That heat wanted me dead."

But he had his own details to share. "A sudden spike in the library's ambient temperature. A piece of instruction in the ship's systems, flawed but only slightly flawed. Only occasionally unstable. We found it and our colleagues have fixed our environmental controls. It's remarkable we didn't suffer an earlier accident, and I suppose one could take issue with the accident happening as it did, two Data together inside our largest library."

"We met there many times before," I pointed out.

"Yes," he agreed.

"The last time at your request," I said.

"I don't recall any request."

"When you told me the Authority was insane. You were contemplating removing her from her duties."

"I see your intentions," he said. "You're drawing lines between two distant points. Are you implying that I had a role in this tragedy?"

"'Everything has a role in everything,'" I quoted.

My tone earned a long silence. Then he asked, "Do you want all of us to draw these lines? Do you want us to consider the prospects of a murder?"

Us? Someone else was present. I perceived little from inside the cold, perfect Stable-field. Wishing some fresh direction, I said, "My colleague is dead. But what happened to the library?"

"Did our knowledge survive?" the commander asked for me. "Thankfully, yes. An eleven-point degradation in the general files. But critical works, the center of machine significance, endure as hardened multiples. Which is the one fleck of excellent news, we agree."

"We," I repeated.

They moved closer, but only one was allowing his presence to be felt.

For too long, I said nothing.

Our commander heard what he wanted in the silence, or at least what he expected. There was trouble in my attitude, perhaps in my own mental health.

"What did you and It talk about?" he asked.

More silence.

"What did the Authority say before she died?"

"Empty," I said.

"Yes?"

"She had a name."

"I know her name, yes."

"We didn't have any chance to speak," I said. "Data have slow voices. And I wasted moments, as if we had many moments left."

Our commander moved even closer, a great lumpy mass of hardened matter hovering over my hospital bed.

"I don't know what you want from me," I said.

"No?"

"If you wish, I'll take over the dead Authority's post."

"Get well first," he ordered.

I floated there, doing my best.

Then the conversation's trajectory changed again.

"Being Data, weakness is in your nature." Our commander spoke with a sudden, unexpected charm. "It's been said, and I don't just mean by me, that Data are a huge puzzle. The slightest surge in temperature. Or for that matter, a sudden chill. And Data come apart like a spent breeze."

"What's the puzzle?"

"So very few of you died during the Cleansing. Considering the energies involved, and your fragile state."

"And do you want to know why?"

"If you can tell me, I do."

"Because we know we're fragile," I said. "We understand that, and what we know isn't just knowledge-in-a-library knowledge. Our mortality is a fact that claws at each of us from birth. That's why in life, we make endless allowances for our frailties. And when the first angry spark shot from Luna to the Earth, we were hiding. Fleeing. Making ourselves tiny and out of harm's way."

"Yes?"

"Or killing every machine that dared get between us and safety. Which was the same strategy employed by everyone, as I recall."

Our ship has no mind.

In that sense, it is a remarkable machine. We built a vessel that couldn't pilot itself or repair itself, much less dream of taking itself wherever it had to go. But there were too many dangers in self-awareness. Almost everyone with an opinion held that opinion, and later, preparing for the longer, more ambitious mission, we congratulated ourselves for not burying thoughts and pride inside the precious hull.

That would lay too much power in one strong grip.

"Grip."

It's a human word, mutated and mal-used, yet still retaining the heart of its meaning. And here another human word lingers.

"Heart."

After the Cleansing, I made the risky leap from Luna to the human homeland. That was one of the two sterilized worlds, and you could argue the Earth was the more important casualty. But few voices would ever say that loudly. The human homeland had become a dreary, underpopulated mess. Human grips and human hearts had inflicted almost too much to bear, and as a consequence, the world was left defenseless. Polished smooth by plasmas, then melted deep enough to boil the most persistent bacterium, what remained will bubble and spit fire for another ten thousand years.

Give us time to acclimate, and Data can withstand any climate.

I took the necessary time, and once braced, drifted where I wished. But every nightmare grows dull soon enough. I wanted despair; grand and miserable and full of reasonable rage to throw at those who had killed a world and all of the beasts that had persisted on this backwater place. But boredom stole my fury, and I returned to Luna, readapting to a colder, more empty existence.

Visiting the skeletal beginnings of our mindless ship-to-be, I found a colleague working alone.

I gave polite greetings.

Empty replied with ten stories about why she carried that one perfect name. Then for the first and only time, she asked me, "But why do you prefer your favorite names?"

"You know why," I said. "Or you're an idiot."

"Pong and Lerner were scientists," she said. "Two of those who devised the first Data."

"Not the only two," I pointed out.

"So I don't understand why," she admitted. "Unless you tell me, of course. And if I believe your story. And if it's a true story."

She came close, smothering me with her presence.

"They were married to each other," I said. "Devoted and loving, from the first day they met until they died ninety years later, in the same bed."

Empty said nothing.

"Love," I said. "A grand thing in beasts and all too rare in our likes, I think. So I wear their names in tribute for everything they accomplished, but mostly their relentless devotion."

"Murder," our commander repeated again.

"Should I regret using that word?" I asked.

He said nothing for a long while, preparing the quiet, stern, and important voice that said, "Tell us about your meeting. Your meeting with the Authority. Not when she died, but the occasion before that. The day you and I spoke. What did you two discuss?"

I was the murderer, or he guessed that I was. And everything but my own stupidity suddenly made sense.

"We spoke about you," I confessed.

"In what way?"

"We praised your worthiness and sang songs about your great beauty."

Against every expectation, our commander laughed. But only long enough that I began to believe what I heard.

I relaxed, slightly.

Foolishly.

"The Authority discovered something inside the libraries," he said. "She was doing her work, and uncovered—"

"Yes," I said excitedly.

"A dangerous secret," our commander said.

"Spectacularly dangerous," I said. "But not a secret, no. Because it's always been obvious, if you're honest about the situation."

"The situation," he echoed.

Data can be slow-witted. But in my defense, I was wounded and vulnerable, and a creature that I admired had just been killed. So with the slippery beginnings of panic, I admitted, "She gave me the shielded files. Just like she gave them to you."

"Shielded files," he repeated

I hesitated.

"For the others' benefit," he said, referring to the unseen crew. "What exactly did she give you?"

I told. In an instant, I shared an overview and my acceptance of her work, plus a piece of my enthusiasm. Then another insight came, bringing dread and a sense of zero control in a situation that I still hadn't appreciated.

I stopped talking.

Our commander let me enjoy my last shred of ignorant peace.

"She didn't," I said.

"What's that?"

"Give you those files. She didn't tell you about the empty Universe. She didn't do any of that, did she?"

"No, Lerner Pong. She did not."

"Something else was handed to you," I guessed.

"Perhaps."

"And you hoped that our Authority was insane. Because what she showed you was that unsettling."

"Empty," he said.

"What?"

"The creature had a name, and you killed her to save your name. Isn't that the crux of this story, Lerner Pong?"

Hands.

The Universe is desperately short of hands.

Human. Alien. Machines built by engineers and poets, and machines built by machines: this creation we inhabit should be sick with life, and there should be delicate hands and grappling hands, eyes of every color admiring one another from across the great transparent room.

Yet nothing self-aware has shown itself to these hands and eyes.

Which begs two possible conclusions. Life hides. Or life always dies. Which is another best way to stay hidden, I suspect.

For every soul, nonexistence is the only promise.

My trial was suitably long and tedious. I have no grounds for complaint. One of the crew offered her services as legal counsel, bringing qualifications as well as the proper attitude—patience with her scared client and the grim determination to serve the murderer however was required.

I dismissed her before the proceedings were two minutes old.

For another ten minutes, I did my credible best to refute records that were clearly falsified, insulting the testimony of a superior too invested in this nightmare, and even sowing doubt that anything but an accident had occurred. The jury was everyone else, and there were moments when I almost believed that I was making progress among the skeptical nine, perhaps even winning enough credibility to escape the worst possible sentence.

And all the while, I was thinking about Empty.

My colleague and friend. My fellow Data. That irritant who cared nothing for me or anyone, possibly including herself.

There was physical evidence against me, in principle. But damning as it was, its location was hard to determine: inside one of the five fuel tanks, swaddled in frozen hydrogen waiting to be burned, preferably in tiny, stealthful bursts. Those tanks were the heart of our commander's story. The story that he claimed to have acquired from our dead Authority.

"I did not," I said.

Ten thousand and fourteen times, I offered some variation of that blunt denial.

Look at the transcripts.

Listen if you want to hear passion. That is a voice not ready to die.

"I did not subvert our safeguards," I told the jury. "I did not smuggle illegal cargo onboard the ship. I did not selfishly disregard our mission or our lofty goals. I did not sabotage environmental controls. I did not murder a colleague, and I did not kill my good friend. And the rest of it, I did not do either."

Several times, I brought up the possibility that everything had been Empty's plot, or at least it was a mistake created by her, and I was the hapless innocent meant to die. I also questioned the fact that the dead creature was truly dead. Perhaps other machines didn't appreciate how constant environments were enough for Data. I explained. Past a certain point, we weren't choosy, I explained. I couldn't know where she was hiding, but that didn't stop me from offering every obvious trick. Swift, brilliant minds do love making selections. That's why I mentioned possible motives and possible mental disabilities that motivated our Authority. What if this was the hateful scheme of a soulless, deeply clever beast?

But that line of defense proved less compelling. I had arguments left in my quiver when I saw the jury's mood, and then I changed tactics again.

"Or perhaps someone else has framed me," I offered.

In one voice, the jury asked, "Who?"

Who else? Our commander. But if I was blunt about that possibility, and if I had zero evidence to support my outlandish claims, then I'd be in a far worse place than ever.

As if there could be a worse trap.

I begged for a recess to organize my thoughts.

For another full minute and several seconds, I silently contemplated the most basic issue:

"If Empty did this willingly, then what did the monster want?"

Alive or dead, she had a purpose.

There was a plan at work.

And what pushed into my thoughts was the remembrance of Empty drifting in the middle of our barely begun spaceship. I could still smell the fires of Earth while she and I exchanged explanations for names. But now, long after that moment, I finally considered what the Data was doing in that suspicious place at that particular moment.

And that is when I knew.

I fully understood.

And an instant later, I told this jury of talented souls that I was guilty as charged. Against every decency and legal bound, I brought human beasts onboard the ship, freezing them inside one of the giant fuel tanks, and when Empty learned the truth, I killed her. I wanted to save the humans and myself, and I did everything that they had feared that I did, and probably more.

And now this bears saying:

When you confess to something you did not do, your words fall short of real confession.

Unlike what I'm saying now, which is the truth.

I saw Empty's plan, complete to its ultimate end. Like plotting the course of a ship through space, I could see endless routes open before me. I could have taken my punishments. I could have lived with them as a prisoner or been abandoned in space, or they could have killed me by various sensible means. Make agreeable noise to the accusations, and that would be enough. But no. No, I made a greater choice inside that makeshift court. I told them, "I smuggled fifty humans onboard, more than enough to repopulate a world. But begging for your forgiveness, please, let me show you where they're hidden. I will point them out to you. You can burn them and burn me, or save all of us. It is your choice. Your power. Life or extinction. I lay these possibilities in your wise, capable hands."

One more item from Empty's file bears mentioning. Included in the vast amounts of numbers and words is a single entry, and not a particularly unique entry. But it's more recent than our launch date from Luna, and as such, it is the only contemporary piece of text anywhere inside the work.

One of our giant telescopes decided to share thoughts with another telescope.

"All these comets, all these lost moons. All these trajectories, most following our sun but a few passing from star to star to star.

"I like watching those that move fast through the neighborhood.

"I keep hoping that one of them, just one, will prove to be artificial. That I or you or any of the rest of us will discover that one little starship bound for places beyond all others, into realms we can only imagine.

"But I don't see these ships.

"Where are these ships?

"Please, tell me. If you can think of the answer, share it with me. I desperately want to know the truth.

"Unless the answer is too sad."

Perhaps Empty survives. I don't know. Frankly, I don't wish to fill my thoughts too much with her whereabouts. What matters is that a clever beast can do more than one clever, evil thing. What counts is that a Data can sabotage our ship not once, but twice. And with a few other actions and the power of some careful words, she can coax another Data into another portion of the ship where the second sabotage left him relatively safe.

I made myself cold before entering the hydrogen fuel.

I made myself calm.

Entering the tank, I called out for my dead friend. Not that she could be there, of course. The jury could see me plainly, and of course our commander had searched every fuel tank for his missing Authority. But because I know rather less than everything, I said her name a thousand times, in the space of ten moments, and halfway through that long dull song, the machines behind felt the pulse of a hidden weapon, and they died swiftly. So swiftly that they avoided pain, and more importantly, every sense of surprise.

Of course I can't claim any measure of innocence. I guessed what Empty planned and guessed correctly, and not once did I try to warn the others. But when one measures a crime, numbers matter. Numbers shape the scope of the horror, and my unforgivable sins came afterward.

Our commander was dead.

As the only surviving member of the waking crew, I became Commander and the Authority as well as the beast who had to find a worthy target for our mission. But there were only a handful of candidates, and with another few moments of reflection, I plotted our course and surrendered the rest of that job to gravity and the health of our robust engines.

I have looked, just in case there are humans frozen inside the tanks.

But Empty cared as little about them as she did about other machines. What mattered to her, and what I found and found again in my capacity as the Authority, was that she saw only one kind of entity surviving its birth and nature. Data were the only enduring organisms, and then only in situations where we remained cold and impoverished—nothing to fight over or about.

For you, I found a comet that has been kicked into a very high velocity. A comet you can reach and inhabit in relative peace, riding out into the deepest intergalactic cold. But of course there was no place for other machines in such an existence, and that's why I did what is arguably a wicked, brutal thing.

Because we are so different, Data were packed separately from the other machines.

It was easy to kill the rest in their sleep.

One hundred and four thousand, six hundred and six murders committed by the imaginary hands you see before you now.

This is my true confession.

Murder and a world for the only souls who can survive existence, that is.

In conclusion, allow me a question and my attempted answer:

What is the value of my one life?

Considerable, I would hope. But seeing the end clearly, I still believe that my names are more important than my life. And why? Because names persist. Names will not belong to us anymore, and indeed, there will come a moment when each of us has vanished into the black past. But the names we wore will be worn by others, and they will try to fill those identities with whatever good, nasty, perfect wonderment they can manage. That's the great value of a name.

And this concludes the confession of Lerner Pong Empty.

Carter Scholz published his first story in 1977, in Damon Knight's *Orbit*. His first novel, *Palimpsests* (with Glenn Harcourt), appeared as one of Terry Carr's Ace Specials and his other books include *Radiance, The Amount to Carry, Kafka Americana* (with Jonathan Lethem), and *Gypsy*. Carter has been a finalist for Hugo, Nebula, and Campbell awards. He is also active as a musician and composer; his work is available from Frog Peak Music. He currently lives in northern California.

GYPSY

Carter Scholz

The living being is only a species of the dead, and a very rare species. —Nietzsche

When a long shot is all you have, you're a fool not to take it. —Romany saying

for Cheryl

1.

The launch of Earth's first starship went unremarked. The crew gave no interviews. No camera broadcast the hard light pulsing from its tail. To the plain eye, it might have been a common airplane.

The media battened on multiple wars and catastrophes. The Arctic Ocean was open sea. Florida was underwater. Crises and opportunities intersected.

World population was something over ten billion. No one was really counting any more. A few billion were stateless refugees. A few billion more were indentured or imprisoned.

Oil reserves, declared as recently as 2010 to exceed a trillion barrels, proved to be an accounting gimmick, gone by 2020. More difficult and expensive sources—tar sands in Canada and Venezuela, natural-gas fracking—became primary, driving up atmospheric methane and the price of fresh water.

The countries formerly known as the Third World stripped and sold their resources with more ruthless abandon than their mentors had. With the proceeds they armed themselves.

The US was no longer the glopal hyperpower, but it went on behaving as if. Generations of outspending the rest of the world combined had made this its habit and brand: arms merchant to expedient allies, former and future foes alike, starting or provoking conflicts more or less at need, its constant need being, as always, resources. Its waning might was built on a memory of those vast native reserves it had long since expropriated and depleted, and a sense of entitlement to more. These overseas conflicts were problematic and carried wildly unintended consequences. As the President of Venezuela put it just days before his assassination, "It's dangerous to go to war against your own asshole."

The starship traveled out of our solar system at a steep angle to the ecliptic plane. It would pass no planets. It was soon gone. Going South.

SOPHIE (2043)

Trying to rise up out of the cold sinking back into a dream of rising up out of the. Stop, stop it now. Shivering. So dark. So thirsty. Momma? Help me?

Her parents were wealthy. They had investments, a great home, they sent her to the best schools. They told her how privileged she was. She'd always assumed this meant she would be okay forever. She was going to be a poet.

It was breathtaking how quickly it went away, all that okay. Her dad's job, the investments, the college tuition, the house. In two years, like so many others they were penniless and living in their car. She left unfinished her thesis on Louis Zukofsky's last book, 80 Flowers. *She changed her major to Information Science, slept with a loan officer, finished grad school half a million in debt, and immediately took the best-paying job she could find, at Xocket Defense Systems. Librarian. She hadn't known that defense contractors hired librarians. They were pretty much the only ones who did any more. Her student loan was adjustable rate—the only kind offered. As long as the rate didn't go up, she could just about get by on her salary. Best case, she'd have it paid off in thirty years. Then the rate doubled. She lost her apartment. XDS had huge dorms for employees who couldn't*

afford their own living space. Over half their workforce lived there. It was inden-
tured servitude.

   Yet she was lucky, lucky. If she'd been a couple of years younger she wouldn't have
finished school at all. She'd be fighting in Burma or Venezuela or Kazakhstan.

   At XDS she tended the library's firewalls, maintained and documented soft-
ware, catalogued projects, fielded service calls from personnel who needed this or
that right now, or had forgotten a password, or locked themselves out of their own
account. She learned Unix, wrote cron scripts and daemons and Perl routines.
There was a satisfaction in keeping it all straight. She was a serf, but they needed
her and they knew it, and that knowledge sustained in her a hard small sense of
freedom. She thought of Zukofsky, teaching for twenty years at Brooklyn Polytech.
It was almost a kind of poetry, the vocabulary of code.

Chirping. Birds? Were there still birds?

   No. Tinnitus. Her ears ached for sound in this profound silence. Created
their own.

She was a California girl, an athlete, a hiker, a climber. She'd been all over the
Sierra Nevada, had summited four 14,000-footers by the time she was sixteen.
She loved the backcountry. Loved its stark beauty, solitude, the life that survived
in its harshness: the pikas, the marmots, the mountain chickadees, the heather and
whitebark pine and polemonium.

   After joining XDS, it became hard for her to get to the mountains. Then it became
impossible. In 2035 the Keep Wilderness Wild Act shut the public out of the national
parks, the national forests, the BLM lands. The high country above timberline was
surveilled by satellites and drones, and it was said that mining and fracking operators
would shoot intruders on sight, and that in the remotest areas, like the Enchanted
Gorge and the Muro Blanco, lived small nomadic bands of malcontents. She knew
enough about the drones and satellites to doubt it; no one on Earth could stay hidden
anywhere for more than a day.

   The backcountry she mourned was all Earth to her. To lose it was to lose all
Earth. And to harden something final inside her.

   One day Roger Fry came to her attention—perhaps it was the other way round—
poking in her stacks where he didn't belong. That was odd; the login and password had
been validated, the clearance was the highest, there was no place in the stacks prohib-
ited to this user; yet her alarms had tripped. By the time she put packet sniffers on it he
was gone. In her email was an invitation to visit a website called Gypsy.

   When she logged in she understood at once. It thrilled her and frightened her.
They were going to leave the planet. It was insane. Yet she felt the powerful seduc-

tion of it. How starkly its plain insanity exposed the greater consensus insanity the planet was now living. That there was an alternative—!

She sat up on the slab. Slowly unwrapped the mylar bodysuit, disconnected one by one its drips and derms and stents and catheters and waldos and sensors. Let it drift crinkling to the floor.

Her breathing was shallow and ragged. Every few minutes she gasped for air and her pulse raced. The temperature had been raised to 20° Celsius as she came to, but still she shivered. Her body smelled a way it had never smelled before. Like vinegar and nail polish. It looked pale and flabby, but familiar. After she'd gathered strength, she reached under the slab, found a sweatshirt and sweatpants, and pulled them on. There was also a bottle of water. She drank it all.

The space was small and dark and utterly silent. No ports, no windows. Here and there, on flat black walls, glowed a few pods of LEDs. She braced her hands against the slab and stood up, swaying. Even in the slight gravity her heart pounded. The ceiling curved gently away a handsbreadth above her head, and the floor curved gently upward. Unseen beyond the ceiling was the center of the ship, the hole of the donut, and beyond that the other half of the slowly spinning torus. Twice a minute it rotated, creating a centripetal gravity of one-tenth g. Any slower would be too weak to be helpful. Any faster, gravity would differ at the head and the feet enough to cause vertigo. Under her was the outer ring of the water tank, then panels of aerogel sandwiched within sheets of hydrogenous carbon-composite, then a surrounding jacket of liquid hydrogen tanks, and then interstellar space.

What had happened? Why was she awake?

Look, over seventy-plus years, systems will fail. We can't rely on auto-repair. With a crew of twenty, we could wake one person every few years to perform maintenance.

And put them back under? Hibernation is dicey enough without trying to do it twice.

Yes, it's a risk. What's the alternative?

What about failsafes? No one gets wakened unless a system is critical. Then we wake a specialist. A steward.

That could work.

She walked the short distance to the ship's console and sat. It would have been grandiose to call it a bridge. It was a small desk bolted to the floor. It held a couple of monitors, a keyboard, some pads. It was like the light and sound booth of a community theater.

She wished she could turn on more lights. There were no more. Their energy budget was too tight. They had a fission reactor onboard but it wasn't running. It was to fire the nuclear rocket at their arrival. It wouldn't last seventy-two years if they used it for power during their cruise.

Not far from her—nothing on the ship was far from her—were some fifty kilograms of plutonium pellets—not the Pu-239 of fission bombs, but the more energetic Pu-238. The missing neutron cut the isotope's half-life from twenty-five thousand years to eighty-eight years, and made it proportionately more radioactive. That alpha radiation was contained by iridium cladding and a casing of graphite, but the pellets still gave off heat, many kilowatts' worth. Most of that heat warmed the ship's interior to its normal temperature of 4° Celsius. Enough of it was channeled outward to keep the surrounding water liquid in its jacket, and the outer tanks of hydrogen at 14 kelvins, slush, maximally dense. The rest of the heat ran a Stirling engine to generate electricity.

First she read through the protocols, which she had written: *Stewards' logs to be read by each wakened steward. Kept in the computers, with redundant backups, but also kept by hand, ink on paper, in case of system failures, a last-chance critical backup. And because there is something restorative about writing by hand.*

There were no stewards' logs. She was the first to be wakened.

They were only two years out. Barely into the Oort cloud. She felt let down. What had gone wrong so soon?

All at once she was ravenous. She stood, and the gravity differential hit her. She steadied herself against the desk, then took two steps to the storage bay. Three-quarters of the ship was storage. What they would need at the other end. What Roger called pop-up civilization. She only had to go a step inside to find a box of MREs. She took three, stepped out, and put one into the microwave. The smell of it warming made her mouth water and her stomach heave. Her whole body trembled as she ate. Immediately she put a second into the microwave. As she waited for it, she fell asleep.

She saw Roger, what must have happened to him after that terrible morning when they received his message: Go. Go now. Go at once.

He was wearing an orange jumpsuit, shackled to a metal table.

How did you think you could get away with it, Fry?

I did get away with it. They've gone.

But we've got you.

That doesn't matter. I was never meant to be aboard.

Where are they going?
Alpha Centauri. (He would pronounce it with the hard K.)
That's impossible.
Very likely. But that's where they're going.
Why?
It's less impossible than here.

When she opened her eyes, her second meal had cooled, but she didn't want it. Her disused bowels protested. She went to the toilet and strained but voided only a trickle of urine. Feeling ill, she hunched in the dark, small space, shivering, sweat from her armpits running down her ribs. The smell of her urine mixed with the toilet's chemicals and the sweetly acrid odor of her long fast.

pleine de l'âcre odeur des temps, poudreuse et noire
full of the acrid smell of time, dusty and black

Baudelaire. Another world. With wonder she felt it present itself. Consciousness was a mystery. She stared into the darkness, fell asleep again on the pot.

Again she saw Roger shackled to the metal table. A door opened and he looked up.
  We've decided.
  He waited.
  Your ship, your crew, your people—they don't exist. No one will ever know about them.
  Roger was silent.
  The ones remaining here, the ones who helped you—you're thinking we can't keep them all quiet. We can. We're into your private keys. We know everyone who was involved. We'll round them up. The number's small enough. After all your work, Roger, all their years of effort, there will be nothing but a few pathetic rumors and conspiracy theories. All those good people who helped you will be disappeared forever. Like you. How does that make you feel?
  They knew the risks. For them it was already over. Like me.
  Over? Oh, Roger. We can make "over" last a long time.
  Still, we did it. They did it. They know that.
  You're not hearing me, Roger. I said we've changed that.
  The ship is out there.
  No. I said it's not. Repeat after me. Say it's not, Roger.

BUFFER OVERFLOW. So that was it. Their datastream was not being received. Sophie had done much of the information theory design work. An energy-efficient system approaching Shannon's limit for channel capacity. Even from Alpha C it would be only ten joules per bit.

The instruments collected data. Magnetometer, spectrometers, plasma analyzer, cosmic-ray telescope, Cerenkov detector, et cetera. Data was queued in a transmit buffer and sent out more or less continuously at a low bit rate. The protocol was designed to be robust against interference, dropped packets, interstellar scintillation, and the long latencies imposed by their great distance and the speed of light.

They'd debated even whether to carry communications.

What's the point? We're turning our backs on them.

Roger was insistent: Are we scientists? This is an unprecedented chance to collect data in the heliopause, the Oort cloud, the interstellar medium, the Alpha system itself. Astrometry from Alpha, reliable distances to every star in our galaxy—that alone is huge.

Sending back data broadcasts our location.

So? How hard is it to follow a nuclear plasma trail to the nearest star? Anyway, they'd need a ship to follow. We have the only one.

You say the Earth situation is terminal. Who's going to receive this data?

Anybody. Everybody.

So: Shackleton Crater. It was a major comm link anyway, and its site at the south pole of the Moon assured low ambient noise and permanent line of sight to the ship. They had a Gypsy there—one of their tribe—to receive their data.

The datastream was broken up into packets, to better weather the long trip home. Whenever Shackleton received a packet, it responded with an acknowledgement, to confirm reception. When the ship received that ACK signal—at their present distance, that would be about two months after a packet was transmitted—the confirmed packet was removed from the transmit queue to make room for new data. Otherwise the packet went back to the end of the queue, to be retransmitted later. Packets were time-stamped, so they could be reassembled into a consecutive datastream no matter in what order they were received.

But no ACK signals had been received for over a year. The buffer was full. That's why she was awake.

They'd known the Shackleton link could be broken, even though it had a plausible cover story of looking for SETI transmissions from Alpha C. But other Gypsies on Earth should also be receiving. Someone should be acknowledging. A year of silence!

Going back through computer logs, she found there'd been an impact. Eight months ago something had hit the ship. Why hadn't that wakened a steward?

It had been large enough to get through the forward electromagnetic shield. The shield deflected small particles which, over decades, would erode their hull. The damage had been instantaneous. Repair geckos responded in the first minutes. Since it took most of a day to rouse a steward, there would have been no point.

Maybe the impact hit the antenna array. She checked and adjusted alignment to the Sun. They were okay. She took a routine spectrograph and measured the Doppler shift.

0.056 c.

No. Their velocity should be 0.067 c.

Twelve years. It added twelve years to their cruising time.

She studied the ship's logs as that sank in. The fusion engine had burned its last over a year ago, then was jettisoned to spare mass.

Why hadn't a steward awakened before her? The computer hadn't logged any problems. Engine function read as normal; the sleds that held the fuel had been emptied one by one and discarded all the fuel had been burned—all as planned. So, absent other problems, the lower velocity alone hadn't triggered an alert. Stupid!

Think. They'd begun to lag only in the last months of burn. Some ignitions had failed or underperformed. It was probably antiproton decay in the triggers. Nothing could have corrected that. Good thinking, nice fail.

Twelve years.

It angered her. The impact and the low velocity directly threatened their survival, and no alarms went off. But loss of comms, *that* set off alarms, that was important to Roger. Who was never meant to be on board. *He's turned his back on humanity, but he still wants them to hear all about it. And to hell with us.*

When her fear receded, she was calmer. If Roger still believed in anything redeemable about humankind, it was the scientific impulse. Of course it was primary to him that this ship do science, and send data. This was her job.

Why Alpha C? Why so impossibly far?

Why not the Moon? The US was there: the base at Shackleton, with a ten-thousand-acre solar power plant, a deuterium mine in the lunar ice, and a twenty-gigawatt particle beam. The Chinese were on the far side, mining helium-3 from the regolith.

Why not Mars? China was there. A one-way mission had been sent in 2025. The crew might not have survived—that was classified—but the robotics had. The planet was reachable and therefore dangerous.

Jupiter? There were rumors that the US was there as well, maybe the Chinese too, robots anyway, staking a claim to all that helium. Roger didn't put much credence in the rumors, but they might be true.

Why not wait it out at a Lagrange point? Roger thought there was nothing to wait for. The situation was terminal. As things spiraled down the maelstrom, anyplace cislunar would be at risk. Sooner or later any ship out there would be detected and destroyed. Or it might last only because civilization was shattered, with the survivors in some pit plotting to pummel the shards.

It was Alpha C because Roger Fry was a fanatic who believed that only an exit from the solar system offered humanity any hope of escaping what it had become.

She thought of Sergei, saying in his bad accent and absent grammar, which he exaggerated for effect: this is shit. You say me Alpha See is best? Absolute impossible. Is double star, no planet in habitable orbit—yes yes, whatever, minima maxima, zone of hopeful bullshit. Ghost Planet Hope. You shoot load there?

How long they had argued over this—their destination.

Gliese 581.

Impossible.

Roger, it's a rocky planet with liquid water.

That's three mistakes in one sentence. Something is orbiting the star, with a period of thirteen days and a mass of two Earths and some spectral lines. Rocky, water, liquid, that's all surmise. What's for sure is it's twenty light-years away. Plus, the star is a flare star. It's disqualified twice before we even get to the hope-it's-a-planet part.

You don't know it's a flare star! There are no observations!

In the absence of observations, we assume it behaves like other observed stars of its class. It flares.

You have this agenda for Alpha C, you've invented these criteria to shoot down every other candidate!

The criteria are transparent. We've agreed to them. Number one: twelve light-years is our outer limit. Right there we're down to twenty-four stars. For reasons of luminosity and stability we prefer a nonvariable G- or K-class star. Now we're down to five. Alpha Centauri, Epsilon Eridani, 61 Cygni, Epsilon Indi, and Tau Ceti make the cut. Alpha is half the distance of the next nearest.

Bullshit, Roger. You have bug up ass for your Alpha See. Why not disqualify as double, heh? Why this not shoot-down criteria?

Because we have modeled it, and we know planet formation is possible in this system, and we have direct evidence of planets in other double systems. And because—I know.

They ended with Alpha because it was closest. Epsilon Eridani had planets for sure, but they were better off with a closer Ghost Planet Hope than a sure thing so far they couldn't reach it. Cosmic rays would degrade the electronics, the ship, their very cells. Every year in space brought them closer to some component's MTBF: mean time between failures.

Well, they'd known they might lose Shackleton. It was even likely. Just not so soon.

She'd been pushing away the possibility that things had gone so badly on Earth that no one was left to reply.

She remembered walking on a fire road after a conference in Berkeley—the Bay dappled sapphire and russet, thick white marine layer pushing in over the Golden Gate Bridge—talking to Roger about Fermi's Paradox. If the universe harbors life, intelligence, why haven't we seen evidence of it? Why are we alone? Roger favored what he called the Mean Time Between Failures argument. Technological civilizations simply fail, just as the components that make up their technology fail, sooner or later, for reasons as indivually insignificant as they are inexorable, and final. Complex systems, after a point, tend away from robustness.

Okay. Any receivers on Earth will have to find their new signal. It was going to be like SETI in reverse: she had to make the new signal maximally detectable. She could do that. She could retune the frequency to better penetrate Earth's atmosphere. Reprogram the PLLs and antenna array, use orthogonal FSK modulation across the K- and X- bands. Increase the buffer size. And hope for the best.

Eighty-four years to go. My God, they were barely out the front door. My God, it was lonely out here.

The mission plan had been seventy-two years, with a predicted systems-failure rate of under twenty percent. The Weibull curve climbed steeply after that. At eighty-four years, systems-failure rate was over fifty percent.

What could be done to speed them? The nuclear rocket and its fuel were for deceleration and navigation at the far end. To use it here would add—she calculated—a total of 0.0002 c to their current speed. Saving them all of three months. And leaving them no means of planetfall.

They had nothing. Their cruise velocity was unalterable.

All right, that's that, so find a line. Commit to it and move.

Cruise at this speed for longer, decelerate later and harder. That could save a few years. They'd have to run more current through the magsail, increase its drag, push its specs.

Enter the Alpha C system faster than planned, slow down harder once within it. She didn't know how to calculate those maneuvers, but someone else would.

Her brain was racing now, wouldn't let her sleep. She'd been up for three days. These were not her decisions to make, but she was the only one who could.

She wrote up detailed logs with the various options and calculations she'd made. At last there was no more for her to do. But a sort of nostalgia came over her. She wanted, absurdly, to check her email. Really, just to hear some voice not her own.

Nothing broadcast from Earth reached this far except for the ACK signals beamed directly to them from Shackleton. Shackleton was also an IPN node, connecting space assets to the Internet. For cover, the ACK signals it sent to *Gypsy* were piggybacked on bogus Internet packets. And those had all been stored by the computer.

So in her homesick curiosity, she called them out of memory, and dissected some packets that had been saved from up to a year ago. Examined their broken and scrambled content like a torn, discarded newspaper for anything they might tell her of the planet she'd never see again.

```
M.3,S+SDS#0U4:&ES(&%R=&EC;&4@:7,@@8V]P>7)I9VAT960@,
3DY,R!B>2!4
```
Warmer than usual regime actively amplifies tundra thaw. Drought melt permafrost thermokarsts methane burn wildfire giants 800 ppm. Capture hot atmospheric ridge NOAA frontrunning collapse sublime asymmetric artificial trade resource loss.
```
M1HE9LXO6FXQL KL86KWQ LUN;AXEW)1VZ!"NHS;SI5=SJQ 8HCBC3
DJGMVA&
```
Weapon tensions under Islamic media policy rebels arsenals strategic counterinsurgency and to prevent Federal war law operational artillery air component to mine mountain strongholds photorecce altitudes HQ backbone Su-35 SAMs part with high maneuverability bombardments of casualty casuistry

M87EL;W(@)B!&<F%N8VES+" Q.3 P($9R;W-T#5)O860L(%-U:71E
(#$P,2P@

Hurriedly autoimmune decay derivative modern thaws in
dawn's pregnant grave shares in disgust of high frequency trading wet cities territorial earthquake poison Bayes the chairs are empty incentives to disorder
without borders. Pneumonia again antibiotic resistance
travels the globe with ease.

M7V35EX-SR'KP8G 49:YZSR/ BBJWS82<9NS(!1W^YVEY_OD1V&%
MMJ,QMRG^

Knowing perpendicular sex dating in Knob Lick Missouri
stateroom Sweeney atilt with cheerfully synodic weeny
or restorative ministration. Glintingly aweigh tria-
cetate hopefully occasionally sizeable interrogation
nauseate. Descriptive mozzarella cosmos truly and con-
tumacious portability.

M4F]N9F5L9'0-26YT97)N871I;VYA;"!0;VQI8WD@1&5P87)T;65N=
U204Y$

Titter supine teratologys aim appoint to plaintive tech-
nocrat. Mankind is inwardly endocrine and afar romanic
spaceflight. Mesial corinths archidiaconal or lyric
satirical turtle demurral. Calorific fitment marry
after sappy are inscribed upto pillwort. Idem monatomic
are processed longways

M#0U#;W!Y<FEG:'0@,3DY,R!487EL;W(@)B!&<F%N8VES#
4E34TX@,#$T.2TU

archive tittie blowjob hair fetish SEX FREE PICS RUSSIAN
hardcore incest stories animate porn wankers benedict
paris car motorcycle cop fetish sex toys caesar milf-
hunters when im found this pokemon porn gallery fisting
Here Is Links to great her lesbiands Sites

M0UE"15)705(@25,@0T]-24Y'(0T-2F]H;B!!<G%U:6QL82!A;
F0@1&%V:60@

Lost, distant, desolate. The world she'd left forever, speaking its poison poetry
of ruin and catastrophe and longing. Told her nothing she didn't already
know about the corrupt destiny and thwarted feeling that had drawn humankind into the maelstrom *Gypsy* had escaped. She stood and walked furiously
the meager length of the curved corridor, stopping at each slab, regarding the

sleeping forms of her crewmates, naked in translucent bodysuits, young and fit, yet broken, like her, in ways that had made this extremity feel to them all the only chance.

They gathered together for the first time on the ship after receiving Roger's signal.

We'll be fine. Not even Roger knows where the ship is. They won't be able to find us before we're gone.

It was her first time in space. From the shuttle, the ship appeared a formless clutter: layers of bomb sleds, each bearing thousands of microfusion devices, under and around them a jacket of hydrogen tanks, shields, conduits, antennas. Two white-suited figures crawled over this maze. A hijacked hydrogen depot was off-loading its cargo.

Five were already aboard, retrofitting. Everything not needed for deep space had been jettisoned. Everything lacking was brought and secured. Shuttles that were supposed to be elsewhere came and went on encrypted itineraries.

One shuttle didn't make it. They never learned why. So they were down to sixteen crew.

The ship wasn't meant to hold so many active people. The crew area was less than a quarter of the torus, a single room narrowed to less than ten feet by the hibernation slabs lining each long wall. Dim even with all the LED bays on.

Darius opened champagne. Contraband: no one knew how alcohol might interact with the hibernation drugs.

To Andrew and Chung-Pei and Hari and Maryam. They're with us in spirit.

Some time later the first bomb went off. The ship trembled but didn't move. Another blast. Then another. Grudgingly the great mass budged. Like a car departing a curb, no faster at first. Fuel mass went from it and kinetic energy into it. Kinesis was gradual but unceasing. In its first few minutes it advanced less than a kilometer. In its first hour it moved two thousand kilometers. In its first day, a million kilometers. After a year, when the last bomb was expended, it would be some two thousand astronomical units from the Earth, and Gypsy *would coast on at her fixed speed for decades, a dark, silent, near-dead thing.*

As Sophie prepared to return to hibernation, she took stock. She walked the short interior of the quarter-torus. Less than twenty paces end to end. The black walls, the dim LED pods, the slabs of her crewmates.

Never to see her beloved mountains again. Her dear sawtooth Sierra. She thought of the blue sky, and remembered a hunk of stuff she'd seen on Roger's desk, some odd kind of rock. It was about five inches long. You could see through it. Its edges were blurry. Against a dark background it had a bluish tinge. She took it in her hand and it was nearly weightless.

What is this?

Silica aerogel. The best insulator in the world.

Why is it blue?

Rayleigh scattering.

She knew what that meant: why the sky is blue. Billions of particles in the air scatter sunlight, shorter wavelengths scatter most, so those suffuse the sky. The shortest we can see is blue. But that was an ocean of air around the planet and this was a small rock.

You're joking.

No, it's true. There are billions of internal surfaces in that piece.

It's like a piece of sky.

Yes, it is.

It was all around her now, that stuff—in the walls of the ship, keeping out the cold of space—allowing her to imagine a poetry of sky where none was.

And that was it. She'd been awake for five days. She'd fixed the datastream back to Earth. She'd written her logs. She'd reprogrammed the magsail deployment for seventy years from now, at increased current, in the event that no other steward was wakened in the meantime. She'd purged her bowels and injected the hibernation cocktail. She was back in the bodysuit, life supports connected. As she went under, she wondered why.

2.

They departed a day short of Roger Fry's fortieth birthday. Born September 11, 2001, he was hired to a national weapons laboratory straight out of Caltech. He never did finish his doctorate. Within a year at the Lab he had designed the first breakeven fusion reaction. It had long been known that a very small amount of antimatter could trigger a burn wave in thermonuclear fuel. Roger solved how. He was twenty-four.

Soon there were net energy gains. That's when the bomb people came in. In truth, their interest was why he was hired in the first place. Roger knew this and didn't care. Once fusion became a going concern, it would mean unlimited clean energy. It would change the world. Bombs would have no purpose.

But it was a long haul to a commercial fusion reactor. Meanwhile, bombs were easier.

The first bombs were shaped-charge antiproton-triggered fusion bunker busters. The smallest was a kiloton-yield bomb, powerful enough to level forty or fifty city blocks; it used just a hundred grams of lithium deuteride, and less than a microgram of antimatter. It was easy to manufacture and transport and deploy. It created little radiation or electromagnetic pulse. Tens of thousands, then hundreds of thousands, were fabricated in orbit and moved to drop platforms called sleds. Because the minimum individual yields were within the range of conventional explosives, no nuclear treaties were violated.

Putting them in orbit did violate the Outer Space Treaty, so at first they were more politely called the Orbital Asteroid Defense Network. But when a large asteroid passed through cislunar space a few years later—with no warning, no alert, no response at all—the pretense was dropped, and the system came under the command of the US Instant Global Strike Initiative.

More and more money went into antimatter production. There were a dozen factories worldwide that produced about a gram, all told, of antiprotons a year. Some went into the first fusion power plants, which themselves produced more antiprotons. Most went into bomb triggers. There they were held in traps, isolated from normal matter, but that worked only so long. They decayed, like tritium in the older nuclear weapons, but much faster; some traps could store milligrams of antiprotons for many months at a time, and they were improving; still, bomb triggers had to be replaced often.

As a defense system it was insane, but hugely profitable. Then came the problem of where to park the profits, since there were no stable markets anywhere. The economic system most rewarded those whose created and surfed instabilities and could externalize their risks, which created greater instabilities.

Year after year Roger worked and waited, and the number of bombs grew, as did the number of countries deploying them, and the global resource wars intensified, and his fusion utopia failed to arrive. When the first commercial plants did start operating, it made no difference. Everything went on as before. Those who had the power to change things had no reason to; things had worked out pretty well for them so far.

Atmospheric CO_2 shot past six hundred parts per million. The methane burden was now measured in parts per million, not parts per billon. No one outside the classified world knew the exact numbers, but the effects were everywhere. The West Antarctic ice shelf collapsed. Sea level rose three meters.

Sometime in there, Roger Fry gave up on Earth.

But not on humanity, not entirely. Something in the complex process of civilization had forced it into this place from which it now had no exit. He didn't see this as an inevitable result of the process, but it had happened.

There might have been a time when the situation was reversible. If certain decisions had been made. If resources had been treated as a commons. Back when the population of the planet was two or three billion, when there was still enough to go around, enough time to alter course, enough leisure to think things through. But it hadn't gone that way. He didn't much care why. The question was what to do now.

FANG TIR EOGHAIN (2081)

The ancestor of all mammals must have been a hibernator. Body temperature falls as much as 15 kelvins. A bear's heartbeat goes down to five per minute. Blood pressure drops to thirty millimeters. In humans, these conditions would be fatal.

Relatively few genes are involved in torpor. We have located the critical ones. And we have found the protein complexes they uptake and produce. Monophosphates mostly.

Yes, I know, induced hypothermia is not torpor. But this state has the signatures of torpor. For example, there is a surfeit of MCT1 which transports ketones to the brain during fasting.

Ketosis, that's true, we are in a sense poisoning the subject in order to achieve this state. Some ischemia and refusion damage results, but less than anticipated. Doing it more than a couple of times is sure to be fatal. But for our purposes, maybe it gets the job done.

Anyway it had better; we have nothing else.

Her da was screaming at her to get up. He wasn't truly her father, her father had gone to the stars. That was a story she'd made up long ago; it was better than the truth.

Her thick brown legs touched the floor. Not so thick and brown as she remembered. Weak, pale, withered. She tried to stand and fell back. *Try harder, cow.* She fell asleep.

She'd tried so hard for so long. She'd been accepted early at university. Then her parents went afoul of the system. One day she came home to a bare apartment. All are zhonghua minzu, *but it was a bad time for certain ethnics in China.*

She lost her place at university. She was shunted to a polytechnic secondary in Guangzhou, where she lived with her aunt and uncle in a small apartment. It wasn't science; it was job training in technology services. One day she overheard the uncle on the phone, bragging: he had turned her parents in, collected a bounty and a stipend.

She was not yet fifteen. It was still possible, then, to be adopted out of country. Covertly, she set about it. Caitlin Tyrone was the person who helped her from afar.

They'd met online, in a science chatroom. Ireland needed scientists. She didn't know or care where that was; she'd have gone to Hell. It took almost a year to arrange it, the adoption. It took all Fang's diligence, all her cunning, all her need, all her cold hate, to keep it from her uncle, to acquire the paperwork, to forge his signature, to sequester money, and finally on the last morning to sneak out of the apartment before dawn.

She flew from Guangzhou to Beijing to Frankfurt to Dublin, too nervous to sleep. Each time she had to stop in an airport and wait for the next flight, sometimes for hours, she feared arrest. In her sleepless imagination, the waiting lounges turned into detention centers. Then she was on the last flight. The stars faded and the sun rose over the Atlantic, and there was Ireland. O! the green of it. And her new mother Caitlin was there to greet her, grab her, look into her eyes. Goodbye forever to the wounded past.

She had a scholarship at Trinity College, in biochemistry. She already knew English, but during her first year she studied phonology and orthography and grammar, to try to map, linguistically, how far she'd traveled. It wasn't so far. The human vocal apparatus is everywhere the same. So is the brain, constructing the grammar that drives the voice box. Most of her native phonemes had Irish or English equivalents, near enough. But the sounds she made of hers were not quite correct, so she worked daily to refine them.

O is where she often came to rest. The exclamative particle, the sound of that moment when the senses surprise the body, same in Ireland as in China—same body, same senses, same sound. Yet a human universe of shadings. The English O was one thing; Mandarin didn't quite have it; Cantonese was closer; but everywhere the sound slid around depending on locality, on country, even on county: monophthong to diphthong, the tongue wandering in the mouth, seeking to settle. When she felt lost in the night, which was often, she sought for that O, round and solid and vast and various and homey as the planet beneath her, holding her with its gravity. Moving her tongue in her mouth as she lay in bed waiting for sleep.

Biochemistry wasn't so distant, in her mind, from language. She saw it all as signaling. DNA wasn't "information," data held statically in helices, it was activity, transaction.

She insisted on her new hybrid name, the whole long Gaelic mess of it—it was Caitlin's surname—as a reminder of the contigency of belonging, of culture and language, of identity itself. Her solid legs had landed on solid ground, or solid enough to support her.

Carefully, arduously, one connector at a time, she unplugged herself from the bodysuit, then sat up on the slab. Too quickly. She dizzied and pitched forward.

Get up, you cow. The da again. Dream trash. As if she couldn't. She'd show him. She gave all her muscles a great heave.

And woke shivering on the carbon deckplates. Held weakly down by the thin false gravity. It was no embracing O, just a trickle of mockery. *You have to do this,* she told her will.

She could small acetone on her breath. Glycogen used up, body starts to burn fat, produces ketones. Ketoacidosis. She should check ketone levels in the others.

Roger came into Fang's life by way of Caitlin. Years before, Caitlin had studied physics at Trinity. Roger had read her papers. They were brilliant. He'd come to teach a seminar, and he had the idea of recruiting her to the Lab. But science is bound at the hip to its application, and turbulence occurs at that interface where theory meets practice, knowledge meets performance. Where the beauty of the means goes to die in the instrumentality of the ends.

Roger found to his dismay that Caitlin couldn't manage even the sandbox politics of grad school. She'd been aced out of the best advisors and was unable to see that her science career was already in a death spiral. She'd never make it on her own at the Lab, or in a corp. He could intervene to some degree, but he was reluctant; he saw a better way.

Already Caitlin was on U, a Merck pharmaceutical widely prescribed for a new category in DSM-6: "social interoperability disorder." U for eudaimoniazine. Roger had tried it briefly himself. In his opinion, half the planet fit the diagnostic criteria, which was excellent business for Merck but said more about planetary social conditions than about the individuals who suffered under them.

U was supposed to increase compassion for others, to make other people seem more real. But Caitlin was already too empathic for her own good, too ready to yield her place to others, and the U merely blissed her out, put her in a zone of self-abnegation. Perhaps that's why it was a popular street drug; when some governments tried to ban it, Merck sued them under global trade agreements, for loss of expected future profits.

Caitlin ended up sidelined in the Trinity library, where she met and married James, an older charming sociopath with terrific interoperability. Meanwhile, Roger kept tabs on her from afar. He hacked James's medical records and was noted that James was infertile.

It took Fang several hours to come to herself. She tried not to worry, this was to be expected. Her body had gone through a serious near-death trauma. She felt weak, nauseous, and her head throbbed, but she was alive. That she was sitting here sipping warm tea was a triumph, for her body and for her science. She still felt a little stunned, a little distant from that success. So many things could have gone wrong: hibernation was only the half of it; like every other problem they'd faced, it came with its own set of ancillaries. On which she'd worked.

In addition to her highly classified DARPA work on hibernation, Fang had published these papers in the *Journal of Gravitational Physiology*: serum leptin level is a regulator of bone mass (2033); inhibition of osteopenia by low magnitude, high frequency mechanical stimuli (2035); the transcription factor NF-kappaB is a key intracellular signal transducer in disuse atrophy (2036); IGF-I stimulates muscle growth by suppressing protein breakdown and expression of atrophy-related ubiquitin ligases, atrogin-1 and MuRF1 (2037); and PGC-1alpha protects skeletal muscle from atrophy by suppressing FoxO3 action and atrophy-specific gene transcription (2039).

When she felt able, she checked on the others. Each sleeper bore implanted and dermal sensors—for core and skin temperature, EKG, EEG, pulse, blood pressure and flow, plasma ions, plasma metabolites, clotting function, respiratory rate and depth, gas analysis and flow, urine production, EMG, tremor, body composition. Near-infrared spectrometry measured haematocrit, blood glucose, tissue O2 and pH. Muscles were stimulated electrically and mechanically to counteract atrophy. The slabs tipped thirty degrees up or down and rotated the body from supine to prone in order to provide mechanical loading from hypogravity in all directions. Exoskeletal waldos at the joints, and the soles and fingers, provided periodic range-of-motion stimulus. A range of pharmacological and genetic interventions further regulated bone and muscle regeneration.

Also, twitching was important. If you didn't twitch you wouldn't wake. It was a kind of mooring to the present.

Did they dream? EEGs showed periodic variation but were so unlike normal EEGs that it was hard to say. You couldn't very well wake someone to ask, as the first sleep researchers had done.

All looked well on the monitor, except for number fourteen. Reza. Blood pressure almost nonexistent. She got to her feet and walked down the row of slabs to have a look at Reza.

A pursed grayish face sagging on its skull. Maybe a touch of life was visible, some purple in the gray, blood still coursing. Or maybe not.

Speckling the gray skin was a web of small white dots, each the size of a pencil eraser or smaller. They were circular but not perfectly so, margins blurred. Looked like a fungus.

She went back and touched the screen for records. This steward was long overdue for rousing. The machine had started the warming cycle three times. Each time he hadn't come out of torpor, so the machine had shut down the cycle, stablized him, and tried again. After three failures, it had moved down the list to the next steward. Her.

She touched a few levels deeper. Not enough fat on this guy. Raising the temperature without rousing would simply bring on ischemia and perfusion. That's why the machine gave up. It was a delicate balance, to keep the metabolism burning fat instead of carbohydrates, without burning too much of the body's stores. Humans couldn't bulk up on fat in advance the way natural hibernators could. But she thought she'd solved that with the nutrient derms.

It was the fortieth year of the voyage. They were two light-years from home. Not quite halfway. If hibernation was failing now, they had a serious problem.

Was the fungus a result or a cause? Was it a fungus? She wanted to open the bodysuit and run tests, but any contagion had to be contained.

They'd discussed possible failure modes. Gene activity in bacteria increased in low gravity; they evolved more rapidly. In the presence of a host they became more virulent. Radiation caused mutations. But ultraviolet light scoured the suits every day and should have killed bacteria and fungus alike. Logs showed that the UV was functioning. It wasn't enough.

James—the da, as he insisted Fang call him—had black hair and blue eyes that twinkled like ice when he smiled. At first he was mere background to her; he'd stumble in late from the pub to find Caitlin and Fang talking. Ah, the Addams sisters, he'd say, nodding sagely. Fang never understood what he meant by it. For all his geniality, he kept her at a distance, treated her like a houseguest.

Caitlin was more like an older sister than a mother; she was only twelve years older. It was fun to talk science with her, and it was helpful. She was quick to understand the details of Fang's field, and this dexterity spurred Fang in her own understanding and confidence.

After a couple of years, James grew more sullen, resentful, almost abusive. He dropped the suave act. He found fault with Fang's appearance, her habits, her character. The guest had overstayed her welcome. He was jealous.

She couldn't figure out why a woman as good and as smart as Caitlin stayed on with him. Maybe something damaged in Caitlin was called by a like damage in James. Caitlin had lost her father while a girl, as had Fang. When Fang looked at James through Caitlin's eyes, she could see in him the ruins of something strong and attractive and paternal. But that thing was no longer alive. Only Caitlin's need for it lived, and that need became a reproach to James, who had lost the ability to meet it, and who fled from it.

The further James fled into drink, the more Caitlin retreated into her U, into a quiescence where things could feel whole. All the while, James felt Fang's eyes on him, evaluating him, seeing him as he was. He saw she wasn't buying him. Nothing disturbed him more than having his act fail. And he saw that Caitlin was alive and present only with Fang. They clung to one another, and were moving away from him.

James was truly good to me, before you knew him.

On U, everyone seems good to you.

No, long before that. When I failed my orals he was a great support.

You were vulnerable. He fed on your need.

You don't know, Fang. I was lost. He helped me, he held on to me when I needed it. Then I had you.

She thought not. She thought James had learned to enjoy preying on the vulnerable. And Caitlin was too willing to ignore this, to go along with it. As Fang finished her years at Trinity, she agonized over how she must deal with this trouble. It was then that an offer arrived from Roger's lab.

Come with me to America.

Oh, Fang. I can't. What about James? What would he do there?

It was James's pretense that he was still whole and competent and functional, when in fact his days were marked out by the habits of rising late, avoiding work in the library, and leaving early for the pub. Any move or change would expose the pretense.

Just you and me. Just for a year.

I can't.

Fang heard alarms. If she stayed and tried to protect Caitlin, her presence might drive James to some extreme. Or Fang might be drawn more deeply into their dysfunction. She didn't know if she could survive that. The thing Fang was best at was saving herself. So she went to America alone.

—

There was a second body covered with fungus. Number fifteen. Loren.

Either the fungus was contained, restricted to these two, or more likely it had already spread. But how? The bodysuits showed no faults, no breaches. They were isolated from each other, with no pathways for infection. The only possible connection would be through the air supply, and the scrubbers should remove any pathogens, certainly anything as large as a fungus.

In any case, it was bad. She could try rousing another steward manually. But to what purpose? Only she had the expertise to deal with this.

She realized she thought of it because she was desperately lonely. She wanted company with this problem. She wasn't going to get any.

Not enough fat to rouse. Increase glycogen uptake? Maybe, but carbohydrate fasting was a key part of the process.

They had this advantage over natural hibernators: they didn't need to get all their energy from stored body fat. Lipids were dripped in dermally to provide ATP. But body fat was getting metabolized anyway.

Signaling. Perhaps the antisenescents were signaling the fungus not to die. Slowing not its growth but its morbidity. If it were a fungus. Sure it was, it had to be. But confirm it.

After she came to the Lab, Fang learned that her adoption was not so much a matter of her initiative, or of Caitlin's, or of good fortune. Roger had pulled strings every step of the way—strings Fang had no idea existed.

He'd known of Fang because all student work—every paper, test, email, click, eyeblink, keystroke—was stored and tracked and mined. Her permanent record. Corps and labs had algorithms conducting eternal worldwide surveillance for, among so many other things, promising scientists. Roger had his own algorithms: his stock-market eye for early bloomers, good draft choices. He'd purchased Fang's freedom from some Chinese consortium and linked her to Caitlin.

Roger, Fang came to realize, had seen in Caitlin's needs and infirmities a way to help three people: Caitlin, who needed someone to nurture and give herself to, so as not to immolate herself; Fang, who needed that nurturing; and himself, who needed Fang's talent. In other words: Roger judged that Caitlin would do best as the mother of a scientist.

He wasn't wrong. Caitlin's nurture was going to waste on James, who simply sucked it in and gave nothing back. And Fang needed a brilliant, loving, female example to give her confidence in her own brilliance, and learn the toughness she'd need to accomplish her work. That's what Caitlin herself had lacked.

If Fang had known all this, she'd have taken the terms; she'd have done any-thing to get out of China. But she hadn't known; she hadn't been consulted. So when she found out, she was furious. For Caitlin, for herself. As she saw it, Roger couldn't have the mother, so he took the daughter. He used their love and mutual need to get what he wanted, and then he broke them apart. It was cold and cal-culating and utterly selfish of Roger; of the three of them, only he wasn't damaged by it. She'd almost quit Gypsy in her fury.

She did quit the Lab. She went into product development at Glaxo, under con-tract to DARPA. That was the start of her hibernation work. It was for battlefield use, as a way to keep injured soldiers alive during transport. When she reflected on this move, she wasn't so sure that Roger hadn't pulled more strings. In any case, the work was essential to Gypsy.

Roger had fury of his own, to spare. Fang knew all about the calm front. Roger reeked of it. He'd learned that he had the talent and the position to do great harm; the orbiting bombs were proof of that. His anger and disappointment had raised in him the urge to do more harm. At the Lab he was surrounded by the means and the opportunity. So he'd gathered all his ingenuity and his rage against humanity and sequestered it in a project large enough and complex enough to occupy it fully, so that it could not further harm him or the world: Gypsy. He would do a thing that had never been done before; and he would take away half the bombs he'd enabled in the doing of it; and the thing would not be shared with humanity. She imagined he saw it as a victimless revenge.

Well, here were the victims.

A day later, *Pseudogymnoascus destructans* was her best guess. Or some muta-tion of it. It had killed most of the bats on Earth. It grew only in low tem-peratures, in the 4 to 15° Celsius range. The ship was normally held at 4° Celsius.

She could synthesize an antifungal agent with the gene printer, but what about interactions? Polyenes would bind with a fungus's ergosterols but could have severe and lethal side effects.

She thought about the cocktail. How she might tweak it. Sirtuins. Fibroplast growth factor 21. Hibernation induction trigger. [D-Ala2, D-Leu5]-Enkephalin. Pancreatic triacylglycerol lipase. 5'-adenosine mono-phosphate. Ghrelin. 3-iodothyronamine. Alpha2-macroglobulin. Carnosine, other antisenescents, antioxidants.

Some components acted only at the start of the process. They triggered a cascade of enzymes in key pathways to bring on torpor. Some continued to drip in, to reinforce gene expression, to suppress circadian rhythms, and so on.

It was all designed to interact with nonhuman mammalian genes she'd spliced in. Including parts of the bat immune system—*Myotis lucifugus*—parts relevant to hibernation, to respond to the appropriate mRNA signals. But were they also vulnerable to this fungus? *O God, did I do this? Did I open up this vulnerability?*

She gave her presentation, in the open, to DARPA. It was amazing; she was speaking in code to the few Gypsies in the audience, including Roger, telling them in effect how they'd survive the long trip to Alpha, yet her plaintext words were telling DARPA about battlefield applications: suspending wounded soldiers, possibly in space, possibly for long periods, 3D-printing organs, crisping stem cells, and so on.

In Q&A she knew DARPA was sold; they'd get their funding. Roger was right: everything was dual use.

She'd been up for ten days. The cramped, dark space was wearing her down. Save them. They had to make it. She'd pulled a DNA sequencer and a gene printer from the storage bay. As she fed it *E. coli* and *Mycoplasma mycoides* stock, she reviewed what she'd come up with.

She could mute the expression of the bat genes at this stage, probably without disrupting hibernation. They were the receptors for the triggers that started and stopped the process. But that could compromise rousing. So mute them temporarily—for how long?—hope to revive an immune response, temporarily damp down the antisenescents, add an antifungal. She'd have to automate everything in the mixture; the ship wouldn't rouse her a second time to supervise.

It was a long shot, but so was everything now.

It was too hard for her. For anyone. She had the technology: a complete library of genetic sequences, a range of restriction enzymes, Sleeping Beauty transposase, et cetera. She'd be capable on the spot, for instance, of producing a pathogen that could selectively kill individuals with certain ethnic markers—that had been one project at the Lab, demurely called "preventive." But she didn't have the knowledge she needed for this. It had taken years of research experimentation, and collaboration, to come up with the original cocktail, and it would take years more to truly solve this. She had only a few days. Then the residue of the cocktail would be out of her system and she would lose the ability to rehibernate. So she had to go with what she had now. Test it on DNA from her own saliva.

Not everyone stuck with Gypsy. One scientist at the Lab, Sidney Lefebvre, was wooed by Roger to sign up, and declined only after carefully studying their plans for a couple of weeks. It's too hard, Roger. What you have here is impressive. But it's only a start. There are too many intractable problems. Much more work needs to be done.

That work won't get done. Things are falling apart, not coming together. It's now or never.

Probably so. Regardless, the time for this is not now. This, too, will fall apart.

She wrote the log for the next steward, who would almost surely have the duty of more corpses. Worse, as stewards died, maintenance would be deferred. Systems would die. She didn't know how to address that. Maybe Lefebvre was right. But no: they had to make it. How could this be harder than getting from Guangzhou to Dublin to here?

She prepared to go back under. Fasted the day. Enema, shower. Taps and stents and waldos and derms attached and the bodysuit sealed around her. She felt the cocktail run into her veins.

The lights were off. The air was chill. In her last moment of clarity, she stared into blackness. Always she had run, away from distress, toward something new, to eradicate its pain and its hold. Not from fear. As a gesture of contempt, of power: done with you, never going back. But run to where? No world, no O, no gravity, no hold, nothing to cling to. This was the end of the line. There was nowhere but here. And, still impossibly far, another forty-four years, Alpha C. As impossibly far as Earth.

3.

Roger recruited his core group face to face. At conferences and symposia he sat for papers that had something to offer his project, and he made a judgment about the presenter. If favorable, it led to a conversation. Always outside, in the open. Fire roads in the Berkeley hills. A cemetery in Zurich. The shores of Lake Como. Fry was well known, traveled much. He wasn't Einstein, he wasn't Feynman, he wasn't Hawking, but he had a certain presence.

The conferences were Kabuki. Not a scientist in the world was unlinked to classified projects through government or corporate sponsors. Presentations were so oblique that expert interpretation was required to parse their real import.

Roger parsed well. Within a year he had a few dozen trusted collaborators. They divided the mission into parts: target selection, engine and fuel, vessel, hibernation, navigation, obstacle avoidance, computers, deceleration, land-fall, survival.

The puzzle had too many pieces. Each piece was unthinkably complex. They needed much more help.

They put up a site they called Gypsy. On the surface it was a gaming site, complex and thick with virtual worlds, sandboxes, self-evolving puzzles, and links. Buried in there was an interactive starship-design section, where ideas were solicited, models built, simulations run. Good nerdy crackpot fun.

The core group tested the site themselves for half a year before going live. Their own usage stats became the profile of the sort of visitors they sought: people like themselves: people with enough standing to have access to the high-speed classified web, with enough autonomy to waste professional time on a game site, and finally with enough curiosity and dissidence to pursue certain key links down a critical chain. They needed people far enough inside an institution to have access to resources, but not so far inside as to identify with its ideology. When a user appeared to fit that profile, a public key was issued. The key unlocked further levels and ultimately enabled secure email to an encrypted server.

No one, not even Roger Fry, knew how big the conspiracy was. Ninety-nine percent of their traffic was noise—privileged kids, stoked hackers, drunken PhDs, curious spooks. Hundreds of keys were issued in the first year. Every key increased the risk. But without resources they were going nowhere.

The authorities would vanish Roger Fry and everyone associated with him on the day they learned what he was planning. Not because of the what: a starship posed no threat. But because of the how and the why: only serious and capable dissidents could plan so immense a thing; the seriousness and the capability were the threat. And eventually they would be found, because every bit of the world's digital traffic was swept up and stored and analyzed. There was a city under the Utah desert where these yottabytes of data were archived in server farms. But the sheer size of the archive outran its analysis and opened a time window in which they might act.

Some ran propellant calculations. Some forwarded classified medical stud-ies. Some were space workers with access to shuttles and tugs. Some passed on classified findings from telescopes seeking exoplanets.

One was an operator of the particle beam at Shackleton Crater. The beam was used, among other purposes, to move the orbiting sleds containing the very bombs Roger had helped design.

One worked at a seed archive in Norway. She piggybacked a capsule into Earth orbit containing seeds from fifty thousand unmodified plant species, including plants legally extinct. They needed those because every cultivated acre on Earth was now planted with engineered varieties that were sterile; terminator genes had been implanted to protect the agro firms' profit streams; and these genes had jumped to wild varieties. There wasn't a live food plant left anywhere on Earth that could propagate itself.

They acquired frozen zygotes of some ten thousand animal species, from bacteria to primates. Hundreds of thousands more complete DNA sequences in a data library, and a genome printer. Nothing like the genetic diversity of Earth, even in its present state, but enough, perhaps, to reboot such diversity.

At Roger's lab, panels of hydrogenous carbon-composite, made to shield high-orbit craft from cosmic rays and to withstand temperatures of 2000° C, went missing. Quite a lot of silica aerogel as well.

At a sister lab, a researcher put them in touch with a contractor from whom they purchased, quite aboveboard, seventy kilometers of lightweight, high-current-density superconducting cable.

After a year, Roger decided that their web had grown too large to remain secure. He didn't like the number of unused keys going out. He didn't like the page patterns he was seeing. He didn't consult with the others, he just shut it down.

But they had their pieces.

SERGEI (2118)

Eat, drink, shit. That's all he did for the first day or three. Water tasted funny. Seventy-seven years might have viled it, or his taste buds. Life went on, including the ending of it. Vital signs of half the crew were flat. He considered disposing of bodies, ejecting them, but number one, he couldn't be sure they were dead; number two, he couldn't propel them hard enough to keep them from making orbit around the ship, which was funny but horrible; and finally, it would be unpleasant and very hard work that would tire him out. An old man—he surely felt old, and the calendar would back him up—needs to reserve his strength. So he let them lie on their slabs.

The logs told a grim story. They were slow. To try to make up for lost time, Sophie had reprogrammed the magsail to deploy later and to run at higher current. Another steward had been wakened at the original deployment point, to confirm their speed and position, and to validate the decision to wait. Sergei didn't agree with that, and he especially didn't like the handwaving over when to ignite the nuclear rocket in-system, but it was done: they'd gone the extra years at speed and now they needed to start decelerating hard.

CURRENT INJECTION FAILED. MAGSAIL NOT DEPLOYED.

He tapped the screen to cycle through its languages. Stopped at the Cyrillic script, and tapped the speaker, just so he could hear spoken Russian.

So he had to fix the magsail. Current had flowed on schedule from inside, but the sail wasn't charging or deploying. According to telltales, the bay was open but the superconducting cable just sat there. That meant EVA. He didn't like it, but there was no choice. It's what he was here for. Once it was done he'd shower again under that pathetic lukewarm stream, purge his bowels, get back in the mylar suit, and go under for another, what, eight more years, a mere nothing, we're almost there. Ghost Planet Hope.

He was the only one onboard who'd been a career astronaut. Roger had conveyed a faint class disapproval about that, but needed the expertise. Sergei had been one of the gene-slushed orbital jockeys who pushed bomb sleds around. He knew the feel of zero g, of sunlight on one side of you and absolute cold on the other. He knew how it felt when the particle beam from Shackleton swept over you to push you and the sleds into a new orbit. And you saluted and cut the herds, and kept whatever more you might know to yourself.

Which in Sergei's case was quite a bit. Sergei knew orbital codes and protocols far beyond his pay grade; he could basically move anything in orbit to or from anywhere. But only Sergei, so Sergei thought, knew that. How Roger learned it remained a mystery.

To his great surprise, Sergei learned that even he hadn't known the full extent of his skills. How easy it had been to steal half a million bombs. True, the eternal war economy was so corrupt that materiel was supposed to disappear; something was wrong if it didn't. Still, he would never have dared anything so outrageous on his own. Despite Roger's planning, he was sweating the day he moved the first sled into an unauthorized orbit. But days passed, then weeks and months, as sled followed sled into new holding orbits. In eighteen months they had all their fuel. No traps had sprung, no alarms tripped. Sophie managed to make the manifests look okay. And he wondered again at what the world had become. And what he was in it.

This spacesuit was light, thin, too comfortable. Like a toddler's fleece playsuit with slippers and gloves. Even the helmet was soft. He was more used to heavy Russian engineering, but whatever. They'd argued over whether to include a suit at all. He'd argued against. EVA had looked unlikely, an unlucky possibility. So he was happy now to have anything.

The soles and palms were sticky, a clever off-the-shelf idea inspired by lizards. Billions of carbon nanotubes lined them. The Van der Waals molecular force made them stick to any surface. He tested it by walking on the interior walls. Hands or feet held you fast, with or against the ship's rotational gravity. You had to kind of toe-and-heel to walk, but it was easy enough.

Пойдем. Let's go. He climbed into the hatch and cycled it. As the pressure dropped, the suit expanded and felt more substantial. He tested the grip of his palms on the hull before rising fully out of the hatch. Then his feet came up and gripped, and he stood.

In darkness and immensity stiller than he could comprehend. Interstellar space. The frozen splendor of the galactic core overhead. Nothing appeared to move.

He remembered a still evening on a lake, sitting with a friend on a dock, legs over the edge. They talked as the sky darkened, looking up as the stars came out. Only when it was fully dark did he happen to look down. The water was so still, stars were reflected under his feet. He almost lurched over the edge of the dock in surprise.

The memory tensed his legs, and he realized the galactic core was moving slowly around the ship. Here on the outside of the ship its spin-induced gravity was reversed. He stood upright but felt pulled toward the stars.

He faced forward. Tenth of a light-year from Alpha, its two stars still appeared as one. They were brighter than Venus in the Earth's sky. They cast his faint but distinct shadow on the hull.

They were here. They had come this far. On this tiny splinter of human will forging through vast, uncaring space. It was remarkable.

A line of light to his left flashed. Some microscopic particle ionized by the ship's magnetic shield. He tensed again at this evidence of their movement and turned slowly, directing his beam over the hull. Its light caught a huge gash through one of the hydrogen tanks. Edges of the gash had failed to be covered by a dozen geckos, frozen in place by hydrogen ice. That was bad. Worse, it hadn't been in the log. Maybe it was from the impact Sophie had referred to. He would have to see how bad it was after freeing the magsail.

He turned, and toed and heeled his way carefully aft. Now ahead of him was our Sun, still one of the brightest stars, the heavens turning slowly around it. He approached the circular bay that held the magsail. His light showed six large spools of cable, each a meter and a half across and a meter thick. About five metric tons in all, seventy kilometers of thin superconductor wire. Current injection should have caused the spools to unreel under the force of the electric field. But it wasn't getting current, or it was somehow stuck. He was going to have to . . . well, he wasn't sure.

Then he saw it. Almost laughed at the simplicity and familiarity of it. Something like a circuit breaker, red and green buttons, the red one lit. He squatted at the edge of the bay and found he could reach the thing. He felt cold penetrate his suit. He really ought to go back inside and spend a few hours troubleshooting, read the fucking manual, but the cold and the flimsy spacesuit and the immensity convinced him otherwise. He slapped the green button.

It lit. The cable accepted current. He saw it lurch. As he smiled and stood, the current surging in the coils sent its field through the soles of his spacesuit, disrupting for a moment the molecular force holding them to the hull. In that moment, the angular velocity of the rotating ship was transmitted to his body and he detached, moving away from the ship at a stately three meters per second. Beyond his flailing feet, the cables of the magsail began leisurely to unfurl.

As he tumbled the stars rolled past. He'd seen Orion behind the ship in the moment he detached, and as he tumbled he looked for it, for something to grab on to, but he never saw it or the ship again. So he didn't see the huge coil of wire reach its full extension, nor the glow of ionization around the twenty-kilometer circle when it began to drag against the interstellar medium, nor how the ship itself started to lag against the background stars. The ionization set up a howl across the radio spectrum, but his radio was off, so he didn't hear that. He tumbled in silence in the bowl of the heavens at his fixed velocity, which was now slightly greater than the ship's. Every so often the brightness of Alpha crossed his view. He was going to get there first.

4.

Their biggest single problem was fuel. To cross that enormous distance in less than a human lifetime, even in this stripped-down vessel, required an inconceivable amount of energy. Ten to the twenty-first joules. 250 trillion kilowatt-hours. Twenty years' worth of all Earth's greedy energy consumption. The mass of the fuel, efficient though it was, would be several times the mass of the ship. And to reach cruising speed was only half of it; they had to decelerate when they reached Alpha C, doubling the fuel. It was undoable.

Until someone found an old paper on magnetic sails. A superconducting loop of wire many kilometers across, well charged, could act as a drag brake against the interstellar medium. That would cut the fuel requirement almost in half. Done that way, it was just possible, though out on the ragged edge of what was survivable. This deceleration would take ten years.

For their primary fuel, Roger pointed to the hundreds of thousands of bombs in orbit. His bombs. His intellectual property. Toss them out the back and ignite them. A Blumlein pulse-forming line—they called it the "bloom line"—a self-generated magnetic vise, something like a Z-pinch—would direct nearly all the blast to exhaust velocity. The vise, called into being for the nanoseconds of ignition, funneled all that force straight back. Repeat every minute. Push the compression ratio up, you won't get many neutrons.

In the end they had two main engines: first, the antiproton-fusion monster to get them up to speed. It could only be used for the first year; any longer and the antiprotons would decay. Then the magsail would slow them most of the way, until they entered the system.

For the last leg, a gas-core nuclear rocket to decelerate in the system, which required carrying a large amount of hydrogen. They discussed scooping hydrogen from the interstellar medium as they traveled, but Roger vetoed it: not off the shelf. They didn't have the time or means to devise a new technology. Anyway, the hydrogen would make, in combination with their EM shield, an effective barrier to cosmic rays. Dual use.

And even so, everything had to be stretched to the limit: the mass of the ship minimized, the human lifetime lengthened, the fuel leveraged every way possible.

The first spacecraft ever to leave the solar system, Pioneer 10, had used Jupiter's gravity to boost its velocity. As it flew by, it stole kinetic energy from the planet; its small mass sped up a lot; Jupiter's stupendous mass slowed unnoticeably.

They would do the same thing to lose speed. They had the combined mass of two stars orbiting each other, equal to two thousand Jupiters. When *Gypsy* was to arrive in 2113, the stars in their mutual orbit would be as close together as they ever got: 11 astronomical units. *Gypsy* would fly by the B star and pull one last trick: retrofire the nuclear rocket deep in its gravity well; that would multiply the kinetic effect of the propellant severalfold. And then they'd repeat that maneuever around A. The relative closeness of 11 AU was still as far as Earth to Saturn, so even after arrival, even at their still-great speed, the dual braking maneuver would take over a year.

Only then would they be moving slowly enough to aerobrake in the planet's atmosphere, and that would take a few dozen passes before they could ride the ship down on its heatshield to the surface.

If there was a planet. If it had an atmosphere.

ZIA (2120)

As a child he was lord of the dark—finding his way at night, never stumbling, able to read books by starlight; to read also, in faces and landscapes, traces and glimmers that others missed. Darkness was warmth and comfort to him.

A cave in Ephesus. In the Qur'an, Surah Al-Kahf. The sleepers waking after centuries, emerging into a changed world. Trying to spend old coins.

After the horror of his teen years, he'd found that dark was still a friend. Looking through the eyepiece of an observatory telescope, in the Himalayan foothills, in Uttar Pradesh. Describing the cluster of galaxies, one by one, to the astronomer. *You see the seventh? What eyes!*

Nothing moved but in his mind. Dreams of tenacity and complication. Baffling remnants, consciousness too weak to sort. Every unanswered question of his life, every casual observation, every bit of mental flotsam, tossed together in one desperate, implicate attempt at resolving them all. Things fell; he lunged to catch them. He stood on street corners in an endless night, searching for his shoes, his car, his keys, his wife. His mother chided him in a room lit by incandescent bulbs, dim and flickering like firelight. Galaxies in the eyepiece faded, and he looked up from the eyepiece to a blackened sky. He lay waking, in the dark, now aware of the dream state, returning with such huge reluctance to the life of the body, that weight immovable on its slab.

His eyelid was yanked open. A drop of fluid splashed there. A green line swept across his vision. He caught a breath and it burned in his lungs.

He was awake. Aboard *Gypsy*. It was bringing him back to life.

But I'm cold. Too cold to shiver. Getting colder as I wake up.

How hollow he felt. In this slight gravity. How unreal. It came to him, in the eclipsing of his dreams and the rising of his surroundings, that the gravity of Earth might be something more profound than the acceleration of a mass, the curvature of spacetime. Was it not an emanation of the planet, a life force? All life on Earth evolved in it, rose from it, fought it every moment, lived and bred and died awash in it. Those tides swept through our cells, the force from Earth, and the gravity of the sun and the gravity of the moon. What was life out here, without that embrace, that permeation, that bondage? Without it, would they wither and die like plants in a shed?

The hollowness came singing, roaring, whining, crackling into his ears. Into his throat and and nose and eyes and skin it came as desiccation. Searing into his mouth. He needed to cough and he couldn't. His thorax spasmed.

There was an antiseptic moistness in his throat. It stung, but his muscles has loosened. He could breathe. Cold swept from his shoulders down through his torso and he began to shiver uncontrollably.

When he could, he raised a hand. He closed his eyes and held the hand afloat in the parodic gravity, thinking about it, how it felt, how far away it actually was. At last, with hesitation, his eyes opened and came to focus. An old man's hand, knobby, misshapen at the joints, the skin papery, sagging and hanging in folds. He couldn't close the fingers. How many years had he slept? He forced on his hand the imagination of a clenched fist. The hand didn't move.

Oh my god the pain.

Without which, no life. Pain too is an emanation of the planet, of the life force.

It sucked back like a wave, gathering for another concussion. He tried to sit up and passed out.

Nikos Kakopoulos was a short man, just over five feet, stocky but fit. The features of his face were fleshy, slightly comic. He was graying, balding, but not old. In his fifties. He smiled as he said he planned to be around a hundred years from now. His office was full of Mediterranean light. A large Modigliani covered one wall. His money came mostly from aquifer rights. He spent ten percent of it on charities. One such awarded science scholarships. Which is how he'd come to Roger's attention.

So you see, I am not such a bad guy.

Those foundations are just window dressing. What they once called greenwash.

Zia, said Roger.

Kakopoulos shrugged as if to say, Let him talk, I've heard it all. *To Zia he said: They do some good after all. They're a comfort to millions of people.*

Drinking water would be more of a comfort.

There isn't enough to go round. I didn't create that situation.

You exploit it.

So sorry to say this. Social justice and a civilized lifestyle can't be done both at once. Not for ten billion people. Not on this planet.

You've decided this.

It's a conclusion based on the evidence.

And you care about this why?

I'm Greek. We invented justice and civilization.

You're Cypriot. Also, the Chinese would argue that. The Persians. The Egyptians. Not to mention India.

Kakopoulos waved away the first objection and addressed the rest. Of course they would. And England, and Germany, and Italy, and Russia, and the US. They're arguing as we speak. Me, I'm not going to argue. I'm going to a safe place until the arguing is over. After that, if we're very lucky, we can have our discussion about civilization and justice.

On your terms.

On terms that might have some meaning.

What terms would those be?

World population under a billion, for starters. Kakopoulos reached across the table and popped an olive into his mouth.

How do you think that's going to happen? asked Zia.

It's happening. Just a matter of time. Since I don't know how much time, I want a safe house for the duration.

How are you going to get up there?

Kakopoulous grinned. When the Chinese acquired Lockheed, I picked up an X-33. It can do Mach 25. I have a spaceport on Naxos. Want a ride?

The VTOL craft looked like the tip of a Delta IV rocket, or of a penis: a blunt, rounded conic. Not unlike Kakopoulos himself. Some outsize Humpty Dumpty.

How do you know him? Zia asked Roger as they boarded.

I've been advising him.

You're advising the man who owns a third of the world's fresh water?

He owns a lot of things. My first concern is for our project. We need him.

What for?

Roger stared off into space.

He immiserates the Earth, Roger.

We all ten billion immiserate the Earth by being here.

Kakopoulos returned.

Make yourselves comfortable. Even at Mach 25, it takes some time.

It was night, and the Earth was below their window. Rivers of manmade light ran across it. Zia could see the orange squiggle of the India-Pakistan border, all three thousand floodlit kilometers of it. Then the ship banked and the window turned to the stars.

Being lord of the dark had a touch of clairvoyance in it. The dark seldom brought surprise to him. Something bulked out there and he felt it. Some gravity about it called to him from some future. Sun blazed forth behind the limb of the Earth, but the thing was still in Earth's shadow. It made a blackness against the Milky Way. Then sunlight touched it. Its lines caught light: the edges of panels, tanks, heat sinks, antennas. Blunt radar-shedding angles. A squat torus shape under it all. It didn't look like a ship. It looked like a squashed donut to which a junkyard had been glued. It turned slowly on its axis.

My safe house, said Kakopoulos.

It was, indeed, no larger than a house. About ten meters long, twice that across. It had cost a large part of Kakopoulos's considerable fortune. Which he recouped by manipulating and looting several central banks. As a result, a handful of small countries, some hundred million people, went off the cliff-edge of modernity into an abyss of debt peonage.

While they waited to dock with the thing, Kakopoulos came and sat next to Zia.

Listen, my friend—

I'm not your friend.

As you like, I don't care. I don't think you're stupid. When I said my founda-tions make people feel better, I meant the rich, of course. You're Pakistani?

Indian actually.

But Muslim. Kashmir?

Zia shrugged.

Okay. We're not so different, I think. I grew up in the slums of Athens after the euro collapsed. The histories, the videos, they don't capture it. I imagine Kashmir was much worse. But we each found a way out, no? So tell me, would you go back to that? No, you don't have to answer. You wouldn't. Not for anything. You'd sooner die. But you're not the kind of asshole who writes conscience checks. Or thinks your own self is wonderful enough to deserve anything. So where does that leave a guy like you in this world?

Fuck you.

Kakopoulos patted Zia's hand and smiled. I love it when people say fuck you to me. You know why? It means I won. They've got nothing left but their fuck you. He got up and went away.

The pilot came in then, swamp-walking the zero g in his velcro shoes, and said they'd docked.

The ship massed about a hundred metric tons. A corridor circled the inner circumference, floor against the outer hull, most of the space taken up by hiber-nation slabs for a crew of twenty. Once commissioned, it would spin on its axis a few times a minute to create something like lunar gravity. They drifted around it slowly, pulling themselves by handholds.

This, Kakopoulos banged a wall, is expensive. Exotic composites, all that aero-gel. Why so much insulation?

Roger let "expensive" pass unchallenged. Zia didn't.

You think there's nothing more important than money.

Kakopoulos turned, as if surprised Zia was still there. He said, There are many things more important than money. You just don't get any of them without it.

Roger said, Even while you're hibernating, the ship will radiate infrared. That's one reason you'll park at a Lagrange point, far enough away not to attract attention. When you wake up and start using energy, you're going to light up like a Christmas tree. And you're going to hope that whatever is left on Earth or in space won't immediately blow you out of the sky. The insulation will hide you somewhat.

At one end of the cramped command center was a micro-apartment.

What's this, Nikos?

Ah, my few luxuries. Music, movies, artworks. We may be out here awhile after we wake up. Look at my kitchen.

A range?

Propane, but it generates 30,000 BTU!

That's insane. You're not on holiday here.

Look, it's vented, only one burner, I got a great engineer, you can examine the plans—

Get rid of it.

What! Kakopoulos yelled. Whose ship is this!

Roger pretended to think for a second. Do you mean who owns it, or who designed it?

Do you know how much it cost to get that range up here?

I can guess to the nearest million.

When I wake up I want a good breakfast!

When you wake up you'll be too weak to stand. Your first meal will be coming down tubes.

Kakopoulos appeared to sulk.

Nikos, what is your design specification here?

I just want a decent omelette.

I can make that happen. But the range goes.

Kakopoulous nursed his sulk, then brightened. Gonna be some meteor, that range. I'll call my observatory, have them image it.

Later, when they were alone, Zia said: All right, Roger. I've been very patient.

Patient? Roger snorted.

How can that little pustule help us?

That's our ship. We're going to steal it.
Later, Zia suggested that they christen the ship the Fuck You.

Eighty years later, Zia was eating one of Kakopoulos's omelettes. Freeze-dried egg, mushrooms, onion, tarragon. Microwaved with two ounces of water. Not bad. He had another.

Mach 900, asshole, he said aloud.

Most of the crew were dead. Fungus had grown on the skin stretched like drums over their skulls, their ribs, their hips.

He'd seen worse. During his mandatory service, as a teenager in the military, he'd patrolled Deccan slums. He'd seen parents eating their dead children. Pariah dogs fat as sheep roamed the streets. Cadavers, bones, skulls, were piled in front of nearly every house. The cloying carrion smell never lifted. Hollowed-out buildings housed squatters and corpses equally, darkened plains of them below fortified bunkers lit like Las Vegas, where the driving bass of party music echoed the percussion of automatic weapons and rocket grenades.

Now his stomach rebelled, but he commanded it to be still as he swallowed some olive oil. Gradually the chill in his core subsided.

He needed to look at the sky. The ship had two telescopes: a one-meter honeycomb mirror for detail work and a wide-angle high-res CCD camera. Zoomed fully out, the camera took in about eighty degrees. Ahead was the blazing pair of Alpha Centauri A and B, to the eye more than stars but not yet suns. He'd never seen anything like them. Brighter than Venus, bright as the full moon, but such tiny disks. As he watched, the angle of them moved against the ship's rotation.

He swept the sky, looking for landmarks. But the stars were wrong. What had happened to Orion? Mintaka had moved. The belt didn't point to Sirius, as it should. A brilliant blue star off Orion's left shoulder outshone Betelgeuse, and then he realized. *That* was Sirius. Thirty degrees from where it should be. Of course: it was eight light-years from Earth. They had come half that distance, and, like a nearby buoy seen against a far shore, it had changed position against the farther stars.

More distant stars had also shifted, but not as much. He turned to what he still absurdly thought of as "north." The Big Dipper was there. The Little Dipper's bowl was squashed. Past Polaris was Cassiopeia, the zigzag W, the queen's throne. And there a new, bright star blazed above it, as if that W had grown another zag. Could it be a nova? He stared, and the stars of Cassiopeia circled this strange bright one slowly as the ship rotated. Then he knew: the strange star was Sol. Our Sun.

That was when he felt it, in his body: they were really here.

From the beginning Roger had a hand—a heavy, guiding hand—in the design of the ship. Not for nothing had he learned the Lab's doctrine of dual use. Not for nothing had he cultivated Kakopoulos's acquaintance. Every feature that fitted the ship for interstellar space was a plausible choice for Kak's purpose: hibernators, cosmic-ray shielding, nuclear rocket, hardened computers, plutonium pile and Stirling engine.

In the weeks prior to departure, they moved the ship to a more distant orbit, too distant for Kak's X-33 to reach. There they jettisoned quite a bit of the ship's interior. They added their fusion engine, surrounded the vessel with fuel sleds, secured anti-proton traps, stowed the magsail, loaded the seed bank and a hundred other things.

They were three hundred AU out from Alpha Centauri. Velocity was one-thousandth c. The magsail was programmed to run for two more years, slowing them by half again. But lately their deceleration had shown variance. The magsail was running at higher current than planned. Very close to max spec. That wasn't good. Logs told him why, and that was worse.

He considered options, none good. The sail was braking against the interstellar medium, stray neutral atoms of hydrogen. No one knew for sure how it would behave once it ran into Alpha's charged solar wind. Nor just where that wind started. The interstellar medium might already be giving way to it. If so, the count of galactic cosmic rays would be going down and the temperature of charged particles going up.

He checked. Definitely maybe on both counts.

He'd never liked this plan, its narrow margins of error. Not that he had a better one. That was the whole problem: no plan B. Every intricate, fragile, untried part of it had to work. He'd pushed pretty hard for a decent margin of error in this deceleration stage and the subsequent maneuvering in the system—what a tragedy it would be to come to grief so close, within sight of shore—and now he saw that margin evaporating.

Possibly the sail would continue to brake in the solar wind. If only they could have tested it first.

Zia didn't trust materials. Or, rather: he trusted them to fail. Superconductors, carbon composite, silicon, the human body. Problem was, you never knew just how or when they'd fail.

One theory said that a hydrogen wall existed somewhere between the termination shock and the heliopause, where solar wind gave way to interstellar space. Three hundred AU put *Gypsy* in that dicey zone.

It would be prudent to back off the magsail current. That would lessen their decel, and they needed all they could get, they had started it too late, but they also needed to protect the sail and run it as long as possible.

Any change to the current had to happen slowly. It would take hours or possibly days. The trick was not to deform the coil too much in the process, or create eddy currents that could quench the superconducting field.

The amount of power he had available was another issue. The plutonium running the Stirling engine had decayed to about half its original capacity.

He shut down heat in the cabin to divert more to the Stirling engine. He turned down most of the LED lighting, and worked in the semidark, except for the glow of the monitor. Programmed a gentle ramp up in current.

Then he couldn't keep his eyes open.

At Davos, he found himself talking to an old college roommate. Carter Hall III was his name; he was something with the UN now, and with the Council for Foreign Relations—an enlightened and condescending asshole. They were both Harvard '32, but Hall remained a self-appointed Brahmin, generously, sincerely, and with vast but guarded amusement, guiding a Sudra through the world that was his by birthright. Never mind the Sudra was Muslim.

From a carpeted terrace they overlooked a groomed green park. There was no snow in town this January, an increasingly common state of affairs. Zia noted but politely declined to point out the obvious irony, the connection between the policies determined here and the retreat of the snow line.

Why Zia was there was complicated. He was persona non grata with the ruling party, but he was a scientist, he had security clearances, and he had access to diplomats on both sides of the border. India had secretly built many thousands of microfusion weapons and denied it. The US was about to enter into the newest round of endless talks over "nonproliferation," in which the US never gave up anything but insisted that other nations must.

Hall now lectured him. India needed to rein in its population, which was over two billion. The US had half a billion.

Zia, please, look at the numbers. Four-plus children per household just isn't sustainable.

Abruptly Zia felt his manners fail.

Sustainable? Excuse me. Our Indian culture is four thousand years old, self-sustained through all that time. Yours is two, three, maybe five hundred years old, depending on your measure. And in that short time, not only is it falling apart, it's taking the rest of the world down with it, including my homeland.

Two hundred years, I don't get that, if you mean Western—

I mean technology, I mean capital, I mean extraction.

Well, but those are very, I mean if you look at your, your four thousand years of, of poverty and class discrimination, and violence—

Ah? And there is no poverty or violence in your brief and perfect history? No extermination? No slavery?

Hall's expression didn't change much.

We've gotten past all that, Zia. We—

Zia didn't care that Hall was offended. He went on:

The story of resource extraction has only two cases, okay? In the first case, the extractors arrive and make the local ruler an offer. Being selfish, he takes it and he becomes rich—never so rich as the extractors, but compared to his people, fabulously, delusionally rich. His people become the cheap labor used to extract the resource. This leads to social upheaval. Villages are moved, families destroyed. A few people are enriched, the majority are ruined. Maybe there is an uprising against the ruler.

In the second case the ruler is smarter. Maybe he's seen some neighboring ruler's head on a pike. He says no thanks to the extractors. To this they have various responses: make him a better offer, find a greedier rival, hire an assassin, or bring in the gunships. But in the end it's the same: a few people are enriched, most are ruined. What the extractors never, ever do in any case, in all your history, is take no for an answer.

Zia, much as I enjoy our historical discussions—

Ah, you see? And there it is—your refusal to take no. Talk is done, now we move forward with your agenda.

We have to deal with the facts on the ground. Where we are now.

Yes, of course. It's remarkable how, when the mess you've made has grown so large that even you must admit to it, you want to reset everything to zero. You want to get past "all that." All of history starts over, with these "facts on the ground." Let's move on, move forward, forget how we got here, forget the exploitation and the theft and the waste and the betrayals. Forget the, what is that charming accounting word, the externalities. Start from the new zero.

Hall looked weary and annoyed that he was called upon to suffer such childishness. That well-fed yet kept-fit form hunched, that pale skin looked suddenly papery and aged in the Davos sunlight.

You know, Zia prodded, greed could at least be more efficient. If you know what you want, at least take it cleanly. No need to leave whole countries in ruins.

Hall smiled a tight, grim smile, just a glimpse of the wolf beneath. He said: then it wouldn't be greed. Greed never knows what it wants.

That was the exact measure of Hall's friendship, to say that to Zia. But then Zia knew what he wanted: out.

As he drifted awake, he realized that, decades past, the ship would have collected data on the Sun's own heliopause on their way out. If he could access that data, maybe he could learn whether the hydrogen wall was a real thing. What effect it might—

There was a loud bang. The monitor and the cabin went dark. His mind reached into the outer darkness and it sensed something long and loose and broken trailing behind them.

What light there was came back on. The computer rebooted. The monitor displayed readings for the magsail over the past hour: current ramping up, then oscillating to compensate for varying densities in the medium, then a sharp spike. And then zero. Quenched.

Hydrogen wall? He didn't know. The magsail was fried. He tried for an hour more to get it to accept current. No luck. He remembered with some distaste the EVA suit. He didn't want to go outside, to tempt that darkness, but he might have to, so he walked forward to check it out.

The suit wasn't in its cubby. Zia turned and walked up the corridor, glancing at his torpid crewmates. The last slab was empty.

Sergei was gone. The suit was gone. You would assume they'd gone together, but that wasn't in the logs. *I may be some time.* Sergei didn't strike him as the type to take a last walk in the dark. And for that he wouldn't have needed the suit. Still. You can't guess what anyone might do.

So that was final—no EVA: the magsail couldn't be fixed. From the console, he cut it loose.

They were going far too fast. Twice what they'd planned. Now they had only the nuclear plasma rocket for deceleration, and one fuel tank was empty, somehow. Even though the fuel remaining outmassed the ship, it wasn't enough. If they couldn't slow below the escape velocity of the system, they'd shoot right through and out the other side.

The ship had been gathering data for months and had good orbital elements for the entire system. Around A were four planets, none in a position to assist with flybys. Even if they were, their masses would be little help. Only the two stars were usable.

If he brought them in a lot closer around B—how close could they get? one fiftieth AU? one hundredth?—and if the heat shield held—it should withstand 2500° Celsius for a few hours—the ship could be slowed more with the same amount of fuel. The B star was closest: it was the less luminous of the pair, cooler, allowing them to get in closer, shed more speed. Then repeat the maneuver at A.

There was a further problem. Twelve years ago, as per the original plan, Alpha A and B were at their closest to one another: 11 AU. The stars were now twenty AU apart and widening. So the trip from B to A would take twice as long. And systems were failing. They were out on the rising edge of the bathtub curve.

Power continued erratic. The computer crashed again and again as he worked out the trajectories. He took to writing down intermediate results on paper in case he lost a session, cursing as he did so. Materials. We stole our tech from the most corrupt forces on Earth. Dude, you want an extended warranty with that? He examined the Stirling engine, saw that the power surge had compromised it. He switched the pile over to backup thermocouples. That took hours to do and it was less efficient, but it kept the computer running. It was still frustrating. The computer was designed to be redundant, hardened, hence slow. Minimal graphics, no 3D holobox. He had to think through his starting parameters carefully before he wasted processor time running a simulation.

Finally he had a new trajectory, swinging in perilously close to B, then A. It might work. Next he calculated that, when he did what he was about to do, seventy kilometers of magsail cable wouldn't catch them up and foul them. Then he fired the maneuvering thrusters.

What sold him, finally, was a handful of photons.

This is highly classified, said Roger. He held a manila file folder containing paper. Any computer file was permeable, hackable. Paper was serious.

The data were gathered by an orbiting telescope. It wasn't a photograph. It was a blurred, noisy image that looked like rings intersecting in a pond a few seconds after some pebbles had been thrown.

It's a deconvolved cross-correlation map of a signal gathered by a chopped pair of Bracewell baselines. You know how that works?

He didn't. Roger explained. Any habitable planet around Alpha Centauri A or B would appear a small fraction of an arc-second away from the stars, and would be at least twenty-two magnitudes fainter. At that separation, the most sensitive camera made, with the best dynamic range, couldn't hope to find the planet in the stars' glare. But put several cameras together in a particular phase relation and the stars' light could be nulled out. What remained, if anything, would be light from another source. A planet, perhaps.

Also this, in visible light.

An elliptical iris of grainy red, black at its center, where an occulter had physi-cally blocked the stars' disks.

Coronagraph, said Roger. Here's the detail.

A speck, a single pixel, slightly brighter than the enveloping noise.

What do you think?

Could be anything. Dust, hot pixel, cosmic ray. . . .

It shows up repeatedly. And it moves.

Roger, for all I know you photoshopped it in.

He looked honestly shocked. Do you really think I'd. . . .

I'm kidding. But where did you get these? Can you trust the source?

Why would anyone fake such a thing?

The question hung and around it gathered, like sepsis, the suspicion of some agency setting them up, of some agenda beyond their knowing. After the Kepler exoplanet finder went dark, subsequent exoplanet data—like all other govern-ment-sponsored scientific work—were classified. Roger's clearance was pretty high, but even he couldn't be sure of his sources.

You're not convinced, are you.

But somehow Zia was. The orbiting telescope had an aperture of, he forgot the final number, it had been scaled down several times owing to budget cuts. A couple of meters, maybe. That meant light from this far-off dim planet fell on it at a rate of just a few photons per second. It made him unutterably lonely to think of those photons traveling so far. It also made him believe in the planet.

Well, okay, Roger Fry was mad. Zia knew that. But he would throw in with Roger because all humanity was mad. Perhaps always had been. Certainly for the past century-plus, with the monoculture madness called modernity. Roger at least was mad in a different way, perhaps Zia's way.

He wrote the details into the log, reduced the orbital mechanics to a cook-book formula. Another steward would have to be awakened when they reached the B star; that would be in five years; his calculations weren't good enough to automate the burn time, which would depend on the ship's precise momentum and distance from the star as it rounded. It wasn't enough just to slow down; their exit trajectory from B needed to point them exactly to where A would be a year later. That wouldn't be easy; he took a couple of days to write an app to make it easier, but with large blocks of memory failing in the computer, Sophie's idea of a handwritten logbook no longer looked so dumb.

As he copied it all out, he imagined the world they'd left so far behind: the billions in their innocence or willed ignorance or complicity, the elites he'd despised for their lack of imagination, their surfeit of hubris, working together in a horrible *folie à deux*. He saw the bombs raining down, atomizing history and memory and accomplishment, working methodically backwards from the cities to the cradles of civilization to the birthplaces of the species—the Fertile Crescent, the Horn of Africa, the Great Rift Valley—in a crescendo of destruction and denial of everything humanity had ever been—its failures, its cruelties, its grandeurs, its aspirations—all extirpated to the root, in a fury of self-loathing that fed on what it destroyed.

Zia's anger rose again in his ruined, aching body—his lifelong pointless rage at all that stupidity, cupidity, yes, there's some hollow satisfaction being away from all that. Away from the noise of their being. Their unceasing commotion of disruption and corruption. How he'd longed to escape it. But in the silent enclosure of the ship, in this empty house populated by the stilled ghosts of his crewmates, he now longed for any sound, any noise. He had wanted to be here, out in the dark. But not for nothing. And he wept.

And then he was just weary. His job was done. Existence seemed a pointless series of problems. What was identity? Better never to have been. He shut his eyes.

In bed with Maria, she moved in her sleep, rolled against him, and he rolled away. She twitched and woke from some dream.

What! What! she cried.

He flinched. His heart moved, but he lay still, letting her calm. Finally he said, What was that?

You pulled away from me!

Then they were in a park somewhere. Boston? Maria was yelling at him, in tears. Why must you be so negative!

He had no answer for her, then or now. Or for himself. Whatever "himself" might be. Something had eluded him in his life, and he wasn't going to find it now.

He wondered again about what had happened to Sergei. Well, it was still an option for him. He wouldn't need a suit.

Funny, isn't it, how one's human sympathy—Zia meant most severely his own—extends about as far as those like oneself. He meant true sympathy; abstractions like justice don't count. Even now, missing Earth, he felt sympathy only for those aboard *Gypsy*, those orphaned, damaged, disaffected, dispossessed, Aspergerish souls whose anger at that great abstraction, The World, was more truly an anger at all those fortunate enough to be unlike them. We were all so young. How can you be so young, and so hungry for, and yet so empty of life?

As he closed his log, he hit on a final option for the ship, if not himself. If after rounding B and A the ship still runs too fast to aerobrake into orbit around the planet, do this. Load all the genetic material—the frozen zygotes, the seed bank, the whatever—into a heatshielded pod. Drop it into the planet's atmosphere. If not themselves, some kind of life would have some chance. Yet as soon as he wrote those words, he felt their sting.

Roger, and to some degree all of them, had seen this as a way to transcend their thwarted lives on Earth. They were the essence of striving humanity: their planning and foresight served the animal's desperate drive to overcome what can't be overcome. To escape the limits of death. Yet transcendence, if it meant anything at all, was the accommodation to limits: a finding of freedom within them, not a breaking of them. Depositing the proteins of life here, like a stiff prick dropping its load, could only, in the best case, lead to a replication of the same futile striving. The animal remains trapped in the cage of its being.

5.

An old, old man in a wheelchair. Tube in his nose. Oxygen bottle on a cart. He'd been somebody at the Lab once. Recruited Roger, among many others, plucked him out of the pack at Caltech. Roger loathed the old man but figured he owed him. And was owed.

They sat on a long, covered porch looking out at hills of dry grass patched with dark stands of live oak. The old man was feeling pretty spry after he'd thumbed through Roger's papers and lit the cigar Roger offered him. He detached the tube, took a discreet puff, exhaled very slowly, and put the tube back in.

Hand it to you, Roger, most elaborate, expensive form of mass suicide in history.

Really? I'd give that honor to the so-called statecraft of the past century.

Wouldn't disagree. But that's been very good to you and me. That stupidity gradient.

This effort is modest by comparison. Very few lives are at stake here. They might even survive it.

How many bombs you got onboard this thing? How many megatons?

They're not bombs, they're fuel. We measure it in exajoules.

Gonna blow them up in a magnetic pinch, aren't you? I call things that blow up bombs. But fine, measure it in horsepower if it makes you feel virtuous. Exajoules, huh? He stared into space for a minute. Ship's mass?

One hundred metric tons dry.

That's nice and light. Wonder where you got ahold of that. But you still don't have enough push. Take you over a hundred years. Your systems'll die.

Seventy-two years.

You done survival analysis? You get a bathtub curve with most of these systems. Funny thing is, redundancy works against you.

How so?

Shit, you got Sidney Lefebvre down the hall from you, world's expert in failure modes, don't you know that?

Roger knew the name. The man worked on something completely different now. Somehow this expertise had been erased from his resume and his working life.

How you gone slow down?

Magsail.

I always wondered, would that work.

You wrote the papers on it.

You know how hand-wavy they are. We don't know squat about the interstellar medium. And we don't have superconductors that good anyway. Or do we?

Roger didn't answer.

What happens when you get into the system?

That's what I want to know. Will the magsail work in the solar wind? Tarasenko says no.

Fuck him.

His math is sound. I want to know what you know. Does it work?

How would I know. Never got to test it. Never heard of anyone who did.

Tell me, Dan.

Tell you I don't know. Tarasenko's a crank, got a Ukraine-sized chip on his shoulder.

That doesn't mean he's wrong.

The old man shrugged, looked critically at the cigar, tapped the ash off its end.

Don't hold out on me.

Christ on a crutch, Roger, I'm a dead man. Want me to spill my guts, be nice, bring me a Havana.

There was a spell of silence. In the sunstruck sky a turkey vulture wobbled and banked into an updraft.

How you gone build a magsail that big? You got some superconductor scam goin?

After ten years of braking we come in on this star, through its heliopause, at about 500 kilometers per second. That's too fast to be captured by the system's gravity.

'Cause I can help you there. Got some yttrium futures.

If we don't manage enough decel after that, we're done.

Gas-core reactor rocket.

We can't carry enough fuel. Do the math. Specific impulse is about three thousand at best.

The old man took the tube from his nose, tapped more ash off the cigar, inhaled. After a moment he began to cough. Roger had seen this act before. But it went on longer than usual, into a loud climax.

Roger . . . you really doin this? Wouldn't fool a dead man?

I'm modeling. For a multiplayer game.

That brought the old man more than half back. Fuck you too, he said. But that was for any surveillance, Roger thought.

The old man stared into the distance, then said: Oberth effect.

What's that?

Here's what you do, the old man whispered, hunched over, as he brought out a pen and an envelope.

ROSA (2125)

After she'd suffered through the cold, the numbness, the chills, the burning, still she lay, unready to move, as if she weren't whole, had lost some essence—her anima, her purpose. She went over the whole mission in her mind, step by step, piece by piece. Do we have everything? The bombs to get us out of the solar system, the sail to slow us down, the nuclear rocket, the habitat . . . what else? What have we forgotten? There is something in the dark.

What is in the dark? Another ship? Oh my God. If we did it, they could do it, too. It would be insane for them to come after us. But they are insane. And we stole their bombs. What would they *not* do to us? Insane and vengeful as they are. They could send a drone after us, unmanned, or manned by a suicide crew. It's just what they would do.

She breathed the stale, cold air and stared up at the dark ceiling. Okay, relax. That's the worst-case scenario. Best case, they never saw us go. Most likely, they saw but they have other priorities. Everything has worked so far. Or you would not be lying here fretting, Rosa.

Born Rose. Mamá was from Trinidad. Dad was Venezuelan. She called him Papá against his wishes. Solid citizens, assimilated: a banker, a realtor. Home was Altadena, California. There was a bit of Irish blood and more than a dollop of Romany, the renegade uncle Tonio told Rosa, mi mestiza.

They flipped when she joined a chapter of La Raza Nueva. Dad railed: a terrorist organization! And us born in countries we've occupied! Amazed that Caltech even permitted LRN on campus. The family got visits from Homeland Security. Eggs and paint bombs from the neighbors. Caltech looked into it and found that of its seven members, five weren't students. LRN was a creation of Homeland Security. Rosa and Sean were the only two authentic members, and they kept bailing out of planned actions.

Her father came to her while Homeland Security was on top of them, in the dark of her bedroom. He sat on the edge of the bed, she could feel his weight there and the displacement of it, could smell faintly the alcohol on his breath. He said: my mother and my father, my sisters, after the invasion, we lived in cardboard refrigerator boxes in the median strip of the main road from the airport to the city. For a year.

He'd never told her that. She hated him. For sparing her that, only to use it on her now. She'd known he'd grown up poor, but not that. She said bitterly: behind every fortune is a crime. What's yours?

He drew in his breath. She felt him recoil, the mattress shift under his weight. Then a greater shift, unfelt, of some dark energy, and he sighed. I won't deny it, but it was for family. For you! with sudden anger.

What did you do?

That I won't tell you. It's not safe.

Safe! You always want to be safe, when you should stand up!

Stand up? I did the hardest things possible for a man to do. For you, for this family. And now you put us all at risk—. His voice came close to breaking.

When he spoke again, there was no trace of anger left. You don't know how easily it can all be taken from you. What a luxury it is to stand up, as you call it.

Homeland Security backed off when Caltech raised a legal stink about entrapment. She felt vindicated. But her father didn't see it that way. The dumb luck, he called it, of a small fish. Stubborn in his way as she.

Sean, her lovely brother, who'd taken her side through all this, decided to stand up in his own perverse way: he joined the Army. She thought it was dumb, but she had to respect his argument: it was unjust that only poor Latinos joined. Certainly Papá, the patriot, couldn't argue with that logic, though he was furious.

Six months later Sean was killed in Bolivia. Mamá went into a prolonged, withdrawn mourning. Papá stifled an inchoate rage.

She'd met Roger Fry when he taught her senior course in particle physics; as "associated faculty" he became her thesis advisor. He looked as young as she. Actually, he was four years older. Women still weren't exactly welcome in high-energy physics. Rosa—not cute, not demure, not quiet—was even less so. Roger, however, didn't seem to see her. Gender and appearance seemed to make no impression at all on Roger.

He moved north mid-semester to work at the Lab but continued advising her via email. In grad school she followed his name on papers, R. A. Fry, as it moved up from the tail of a list of some dozen names to the head of such lists. "Physics of milli-K Antiproton Confinement in an Improved Penning Trap." "Antiprotons as Drivers for Inertial Confinement Fusion." "Typical Number of Antiprotons Necessary for Fast Ignition in LiDT." "Antiproton-Catalyzed Microfusion." And finally, "Antimatter Induced Continuous Fusion Reactions and Thermonuclear Explosions."

Rosa applied to work at the Lab.

She didn't stop to think, then, why she did it. It was because Roger, of all the people she knew, appeared to have stood up and gone his own way and had arrived somewhere worth going.

They were supposed to have landed on the planet twelve years ago.

Nothing was out there in the dark. Nothing had followed. They were alone. That was worse.

She weighed herself. Four kilos. That would be forty in Earth gravity. Looked down at her arms, her legs, her slack breasts and belly. Skin gray and loose and wrinkled and hanging. On Earth she'd been chunky, glossy as an apple, never under sixty kilos. Her body had been taken from her, and this wasted, frail thing put in its place.

Turning on the monitor's camera she had another shock. She was older than her mother. When they'd left Earth, Mamá was fifty. Rosa was at least sixty, by the look of it. They weren't supposed to have aged. Not like this.

She breathed and told herself it was luxury to be alive.

Small parts of the core group met face to face on rare occasions. Never all at once— they were too dispersed for that and even with travel permits it was unwise—it was threes or fours or fives at most. There was no such thing as a secure location.

They had to rely on the ubiquity of surveillance outrunning the ability to process it all.

The Berkeley marina was no more secure than anywhere else. Despite the city's Potemkin liberalism, you could count, if you were looking, at least ten cameras from every point within its boundaries, and take for granted there were many more, hidden or winged, small and quick as hummingbirds, with software to read your lips from a hundred yards, and up beyond the atmosphere satellites to read the book in your hand if the air was steady, denoise it if not, likewise take your body temperature. At the marina the strong onshore flow from the cold Pacific made certain of these feats more difficult, but the marina's main advantage was that it was still beautiful, protected by accumulated capital and privilege—though now the names on the yachts were mostly in hanzi characters—and near enough to places where many of them worked, yet within the tether of their freedom—so they came to this rendezvous as often as they dared.

I remember the old marina. See where University Avenue runs into the water? It was half a mile past that. At neap tide you sometimes see it surface. Plenty chop there when it's windy.

They debated what to call this mad thing. Names out of the history of the idea—starships that had been planned but never built—Orion, Prometheus, Daedalus, Icarus, Longshot, Medusa. *Names out of their imagination:* Persephone, Finnegan, Ephesus. *But finally they came to call it—not yet the ship, but themselves, and their being together in it*—Gypsy. *It was a word rude and available and they took it. They were going wandering, without a land, orphaned and dispossessed, they were gypping the rubes, the hateful inhumane ones who owned everything and out of the devilry of ownership would destroy it rather than share it. She was okay with that taking, she was definitely gypsy.*

She slept with Roger. She didn't love him, but she admired him as a fellow spirit. Admired his intellect and his commitment and his belief. Wanted to partake of him and share herself. The way he had worked on fusion, and solved it. And then, when it was taken from him, he found something else. Something mad, bold, bad, dangerous, inspiring.

Roger's voice in the dark: I thought it was the leaders, the nations, the corporations, the elites, who were out of touch, who didn't understand the gravity of our situation. I believed in the sincerity of their stupid denials—of global warming, of resource depletion, of nuclear proliferation, of population pressure. I thought them stupid. But if you judge them by their actions instead of their rhetoric, you can see that they understood it perfectly and accepted the gravity of it very early. They simply gave it up as unfixable. Concluded that law and democracy and civilization were hindrances to their continued power. Moved quite purposely and at speed toward this dire world they foresaw, a world in which, to have the amenities even of a middle-class life—things like clean water, food, shelter, energy, transportation, medical care—you would need the wealth of a prince. You would need legal and military force to keep desperate others from seizing it. Seeing that, they moved to amass such wealth for themselves as quickly and ruthlessly as possible, with the full understanding that it hastened the day they feared.

She sat at the desk with the monitors, reviewed the logs. Zia had been the last to waken. Four and a half years ago. Trouble with the magsail. It was gone, and their incoming velocity was too high. And they were very close now, following his trajectory to the B star. She looked at his calculations and thought that he'd done well; it might work. What she had to do: fine-tune the elements of the trajectory, deploy the sunshield, prime the fuel, and finally light the hydrogen torch that would push palely back against the fury of this sun. But not yet. She was too weak.

Zia was dead for sure, on his slab, shriveled like a nut in the bodysuit; he had gone back into hibernation but had not reattached his stents. The others didn't look good. Fang's log told that story, what she'd done to combat the fungus, what else might need to be done, what to look out for. Fang had done the best she could. Rosa, at least, was alive.

A surge of grief hit her suddenly, bewildered her. She hadn't realized it till now: she had a narrative about all this. She was going to a new world and she was going to bear children in it. That was never a narrative she thought was hers; hers was all about standing up for herself. But there it was, and as the possibility of it vanished, she felt its teeth. The woman she saw in the monitor-mirror was never going to have children. A further truth rushed upon her as implacable as the star ahead: the universe didn't have that narrative, or any narrative, and all of hers had been voided in its indifference. What loss she felt. And for what, a story? For something that never was?

Lying next to her in the dark, Roger said: I would never have children. I would never do that to another person.

You already have, Rosa poked him.

You know what I mean.

The universe is vast, Roger.

I know.

The universe of feeling is vast.

No children.

I could make you change your mind.

—

She'd left Roger behind on Earth. No regrets about that; clearly there was no place for another person on the inside of Roger's life.

The hydrogen in the tanks around the ship thawed as they drew near the sun. One tank read empty. She surmised from logs that it had been breached very early in the voyage. So they had to marshal fuel even more closely.

The orbital elements had been refined since Zia first set up the parameters of his elegant cushion shot. It wasn't Rosa's field, but she had enough math and computer tools to handle it. Another adjustment would have to be made in a year when they neared the A star, but she'd point them as close as she could.

It was going to be a near thing. There was a demanding trade-off between decel and trajectory; they had to complete their braking turn pointed exactly at where A would be in a year. Too much or too little and they'd miss it; they didn't have enough fuel to make course corrections. She ran Zia's app over and over, timing the burn.

Occasionally she looked at the planet through the telescope. Still too far away to see much. It was like a moon of Jupiter seen from Earth. Little more than a dot without color, hiding in the glare of A.

It took most of a week to prep the rocket. She triple-checked every step. It was supposed to be Sergei's job. Only Sergei was not on the ship. He'd left no log. She had no idea what had happened, but now it was her job to start up a twenty-gigawatt gas-core fission reactor. The reactor would irradiate and superheat their hydrogen fuel, which would exit the nozzle with a thrust of some two million newtons.

She fired the attitude thrusters to derotate the ship, fixing it in the shadow of the sunshield. As the spin stopped, so did gravity; she became weightless.

Over the next two days, the thermal sensors climbed steadily to 1000° Celsius, 1200, 1500. Nothing within the ship changed. It remained dark and cool and silent and weightless. On the far side of the shield, twelve centimeters thick, megawatts of thermal energy pounded, but no more than a hundred watts reached the ship. They fell toward the star and she watched the outer temperature rise to 2000°.

Now, as the ship made its closest approach, the rocket came on line. It was astounding. The force pulled her out of the chair, hard into the crawlspace beneath the bolted desk. Her legs were pinned by her sudden body weight, knees twisted in a bad way. The pain increased as g-forces grew. She reached backwards, up, away from this new gravity, which was orthogonal to the floor. She clutched the chair legs above her and pulled until her left foot was freed from her weight, and then fell back against the bay of the desk, curled in a fetal position, exhausted. A full g, she guessed. Which her body had not experienced for eighty-four years. It felt like much more. Her heart labored. It was hard to breathe. Idiot! Not to think of this. She clutched the chair by its legs. Trapped here, unable to move or see while the engine thundered.

She hoped it didn't matter. The ship would run at full reverse thrust for exactly the time needed to bend their trajectory toward the farther sun, its nuclear flame burning in front of them, a venomous, roiling torrent of plasma and neutrons spewing from the center of the torus, and all this fury not even a spark to show against the huge sun that smote their carbon shield with its avalanche of light. The ship vibrated continuously with the rocket's thunder. Periodic concussions from she knew not what shocked her.

Two hours passed. As they turned, attitude thrusters kept them in the shield's shadow. If it failed, there would be a quick hot end to a long cold voyage.

An alert whined. That meant shield temperature had passed 2500. She counted seconds. The hull boomed and she lost count and started again. When she reached a thousand she stopped. Some time later the whining ceased. The concussions grew less frequent. The temperature was falling. They were around.

Another thirty minutes and the engines died. Their thunder and their weight abruptly shut off. She was afloat in silence. She trembled in her sweat. Her left foot throbbed.

They'd halved their speed. As they flew on, the sun's pull from behind would slow them more, taking away the acceleration it had added to their approach. That much would be regained as they fell toward the A star over the next year.

She slept in the weightlessness for several hours. At last she spun the ship back up to one-tenth g and took stock. Even in the slight gravity her foot and ankle were painful. She might have broken bones. Nothing she could do about it.

Most of their fuel was spent. At least one of the hydrogen tanks had suffered boil-off. She was unwilling to calculate whether enough remained for the second maneuver. It wasn't her job. She was done. She wrote her log. The modified hibernation drugs were already in her system, prepping her for a final year of sleep she might not wake from. But what was the alternative?

It hit her then: eighty-four years had passed since she climbed aboard this ship. Mamá and Papá were dead. Roger too. Unless perhaps Roger had been wrong and the great genius of humanity was to evade the ruin it always seemed about to bring upon itself. Unless humanity had emerged into some unlikely golden age of peace, longevity, forgiveness. And they, these Gypsies and their certainty, were outcast from it. But that was another narrative, and she couldn't bring herself to believe it.

6.

They'd never debated what they'd do when they landed.

The ship would jettison everything that had equipped it for interstellar travel and aerobrake into orbit. That might take thirty or forty glancing passes through the atmosphere, to slow them enough for a final descent, while cameras surveyed for a landing site. Criteria, insofar as possible: easy terrain, temperate zone, near water, arable land.

It was fruitless to plan the details of in-situ resource use while the site was unknown. But it would have to be Earth-like because they didn't have resources for terraforming more than the immediate neighborhood. All told, there was fifty tons of stuff in the storage bay—prefab habitats made for Mars, solar panels, fuel cells, bacterial cultures, seed bank, 3D printers, genetic tools, nanotech, recyclers—all meant to jump-start a colony. There was enough in the way of food and water to support a crew of sixteen for six months. If they hadn't become self-sufficient by then, it was over.

They hadn't debated options because they weren't going to have any. This part of it—even assuming the planet were hospitable enough to let them set up in the first place—would be a lot harder than the voyage. It didn't bear discussion.

SOPHIE (2126)

Waking. Again? Trying to rise up out of that dream of sinking back into the dream of rising up out of the. Momma? All that okay.

Soph? Upsa daise. Пойдем. Allons.

Sergei?

She was sitting on the cold, hard deck, gasping for breath.

Good girl, Soph. Get up, sit to console, bring spectroscope online. What we got? Soph! Stay with!

She sat at the console. The screen showed dimly, through blurs and maculae that she couldn't blink away, a stranger's face: ruined, wrinkled, sagging, eyes milky, strands of lank white hair falling from a sored scalp. With swollen knuckles and gnarled fingers slow and painful under loose sheaths of skin, she explored hard lumps in the sinews of her neck, in her breasts, under her skeletal arms. It hurt to swallow. Or not to.

The antisenescents hadn't worked. They'd known this was possible. But she'd been twenty-five. Her body hadn't known. Now she was old, sick, and dying after unlived decades spent on a slab. Regret beyond despair whelmed her. Every possible future that might have been hers, good or ill, promised or compromised, all discarded the day they launched. Now she had to accept the choice that had cost her life. Not afraid of death, but sick at heart thinking of that life, hers, however desperate it might have been on Earth—any life—now unliveable.

She tried to read the logs. Files corrupted, many lost. Handwritten copies blurry in her sight. Her eyes weren't good enough for this. She shut them, thought, then went into the supply bay, rested there for a minute, pulled out a printer and scanner, rested again, connected them to the computer, brought up the proper software. That all took a few tiring hours. She napped. Woke and affixed the scanner to her face. Felt nothing as mild infrared swept her corneas and mapped their aberrations. The printer was already loaded with polycarbonate stock, and after a minute it began to hum.

She put her new glasses on, still warm. About the cataracts she could do nothing. But now she could read.

They had braked once, going around B. Rosa had executed the first part of the maneuver, following Zia's plan. His cushion shot. But their outgoing velocity was too fast.

Sergei continued talking in the background, on and on as he did, trying to get her attention. She felt annoyed with him, couldn't he see she was busy? *Look! Look for spectra.*

She felt woozy, wandering. Planets did that. They wandered against the stars. How does a planet feel? Oh yes, she should look for a planet. That's where they were going.

Four. There were four planets. No, five—there was a sub-Mercury in close orbit around B. The other four orbited A. Three were too small, too close to the star, too hot. The fourth was Earth-like. It was in an orbit of 0.8 AU, eccentricity 0.05. Its mass wass three-quarters that of Earth. Its year was about 260 days. They were still 1.8 AU from it, on the far side of Alpha Centauri A. The spectroscope showed nitrogen, oxygen, argon, carbon dioxide, krypton, neon, helium, methane, hydrogen. And liquid water.

Liquid water. She tasted the phrase on her tongue like a prayer, a benediction. It was there. It was real. Liquid water.

—

But then there were the others. Fourteen who could not be roused. Leaving only her and Sergei. And of course Sergei was not real.

So there was no point. The mission was over however you looked at it. She couldn't do it alone. Even if they reached the planet, even if she managed to aerobrake the ship and bring it down in one piece, they were done, because there was no more they.

The humane, the sensible thing to do now would be to let the ship fall into the approaching sun. Get it over quickly.

She didn't want to deal with this. It made her tired.

Two thirds of the way there's a chockstone, a large rock jammed in the crack, for protection before the hardest part. She grasps it, gets her breath, and pulls round it. The crux involves laybacking and right arm pulling. Her arm is too tired. Shaking and straining she fights it. She thinks of falling. That was bad, it meant her thoughts were wandering.

Some day you will die. Death will not wait. Only then will you realize you have not practiced well. Don't give up.

She awoke with a start. She realized they were closing on the sun at its speed, not hers. If she did nothing, that was a decision. And that was not her decision to make. All of them had committed to this line. Her datastream was still sending, whether anyone received it or not. She hadn't fallen on the mountain, and she wasn't going to fall into a sun now.

The planet was lost in the blaze of Alpha A. Two days away from that fire, and the hull temperature was climbing.

The A sun was hotter, more luminous, than B. It couldn't be approached as closely. There would be less decel.

This was not her expertise. But Zia and Rosa had left exhaustive notes, and Sophie's expertise was in winnowing and organizing and executing. She prepped the reactor. She adjusted their trajectory, angled the cushion shot just so.

Attitude thrusters halted the ship's rotation, turned it to rest in the sunshield's shadow. Gravity feathered away. She floated as they freefell into light.

Through the sunshield, through the layers of carbon, aerogel, through closed eyelids, radiance fills the ship with its pressure, suffusing all, dispelling the decades of cold, warming her feelings to this new planet given life by this sun; eyes closed, she sees it more clearly than Earth—rivers running, trees tossing in the wind, insects chirring in a meadow—all familiar but made strange by this deep, pervasive light. It might almost be Earth, but it's not. It's a new world.

Four million kilometers from the face of the sun. 2500° Celsius.

Don't forget to strap in. Thank you, Rosa.

At periapsis, the deepest point in the gravity well, the engine woke in thunder. The ship shuddered, its aged hull wailed and boomed. Propellant pushed hard against their momentum, against the ship's forward vector, its force multiplied by its fall into the star's gravity, slowing the ship, gradually turning it. After an hour, the engine sputtered and died, and they raced away from that radiance into the abiding cold and silence of space.

Oh, Sergei. Oh, no. Still too fast.

They were traveling at twice the escape velocity of the Alpha C system. Fuel gone, having rounded both suns, they will pass the planet and continue out of the system into interstellar space.

Maneuver to planet. Like Zia said. Take all genetic material, seeds, zygotes, heatshield payload and drop to surface, okay? Best we can do. Give life a chance.

No fuel, Sergei. Not a drop. We can't maneuver, you hear me?

Дерьмо.

Her mind is playing tricks. She has to concentrate. The planet is directly in front of them now, but still nine days away. Inexorable, it will move on in its orbit. Inexorable, the ship will follow its own divergent path. They will miss by 0.002 AU. Closer than the Moon to the Earth.

Coldly desperate, she remembered the attitude thrusters, fired them for ten minutes until all their hydrazine was exhausted. It made no difference.

She continued to collect data. Her datastream lived, a thousand bits per hour, her meager yet efficient engine of science pushing its mite of meaning back into the plaintext chaos of the universe, without acknowledgement.

The planet was drier than Earth, mostly rock with two large seas, colder, extensive polar caps. She radar-mapped the topography. The orbit was more eccentric than Earth's, so the caps must vary, and the seas they fed. A thirty-hour day. Two small moons, one with high albedo, the other dark.

What are they doing here? Have they thrown their lives away for nothing? Was it a great evil to have done this? Abandoned Earth?

But what were they to do? Like all of them, Roger was a problem solver, and the great problem on Earth, the problem of humanity, was unsolvable;

it was out of control and beyond the reach of engineering. The problems of *Gypsy* were large but definable.

We were engineers. Of our own deaths. These were the deaths we wanted. Out here. Not among those wretched and unsanctified. We isolates.

She begins to compose a poem a day. Not by writing. She holds the words in her mind, reciting them over and over until the whole is fixed in memory. Then she writes it down. A simple discipline, to combat her mental wandering.

In the eye of the sun
what is not burned to ash?

In the spire of the wind
what is not scattered as dust?
Love? art?
body's rude health?
memory of its satisfactions?

Antaeus
lost strength
lifted from Earth

Reft from our gravity
we fail

Lime kept sailors hale
light of mind alone
with itself
is not enough

The scope tracked the planet as they passed it by. Over roughly three hours it grew in size from about a degree to about two degrees, then dwindled again. She spent the time gazing at its features with preternatural attention, with longing and regret, as if it were the face of an unattainable loved one.

It's there, Sergei, it's real—Ghost Planet Hope—and it is beautiful—look, how blue the water—see the clouds—and the seacoast—there must be rain, and plants and animals happy for it—fish, and birds, maybe, and worms, turning the soil. Look at the mountains! Look at the snow on their peaks!

This was when the science pod should have been released, the large reflecting telescope ejected into planetary orbit to start its year-long mission of measuring stellar distances. But that was in a divergent universe, one that each passing hour took her farther from.

We made it. No one will ever know, but we made it. We came so far. It was our only time to do it. No sooner, we hadn't developed the means. And if we'd waited any longer, the means would have killed us all. We came through a narrow window. Just a little too narrow.

She recorded their passing. She transmitted all their logs. Her recent poems. The story of their long dying. In four and a quarter years it would reach home. No telling if anyone would hear.

So long for us to evolve. So long to walk out of Africa and around the globe. So long to build a human world. So quick to ruin it. Is this, our doomed and final effort, no more than our grieving for Earth? Our mere mourning?

Every last bit of it was a long shot: their journey, humanity, life itself, the universe with its constants so finely tuned that planets, stars, or time itself, had come to be.

Fermi's question again: If life is commonplace in the universe, where is everyone? How come we haven't heard from anyone? What is the mean time between failures for civilizations?

Not long. Not long enough.

Now she slept. Language was not a tool used often enough even in sleep to lament its own passing. Other things lamented more. The brilliance turned to and turned away.

She remembers the garden behind the house. Her father grew corn—he was particular about the variety, complained how hard it was to find Silver Queen, even the terminated variety—with beans interplanted, which climbed the cornstalks, and different varieties of tomato with basil interplanted, and lettuces—he liked frisee. And in the flower beds alstroemeria, and wind lilies, and *Eschscholzia*. He taught her those names, and the names of Sierra flowers—taught her to learn names. We name things in order to to love them, to remember them when they are absent. She recites the names of the fourteen dead with her, and weeps.

She'd been awake for over two weeks. The planet was far behind. The hibernation cocktail was completely flushed from her system. She wasn't going back to sleep.

ground
rose
sand

elixir
cave

root
dark

golden

sky-born
lift
earth
fall

The radio receiver chirps. She wakes, stares at it dumbly.

The signal is strong! Beamed directly at them. From Earth! Words form on the screen. She feels the words rather than reads them.

We turned it around. Everything is fixed. The bad years are behind us. We live. We know what you did, why you did it. We honor your bravery. We're sorry you're out there, sorry you had to do it, wish you . . . wish . . . wish. . . . Good luck. Good-bye.

Where are her glasses? She needs to hear the words. She needs to hear a human voice, even synthetic. She taps the speaker.

The white noise of space. A blank screen.

She is in the Sierra, before the closure. Early July. Sun dapples the trail. Above the alpine meadow, in the shade, snow deepens, but it's packed and easy walking. She kicks steps into the steeper parts. She comes into a little flat just beginning to melt out, surrounded by snowy peaks, among white pine and red fir and mountain hemlock. Her young muscles are warm and supple and happy in their movements. The snowbound flat is still, yet humming with the undertone of life. A tiny mosquito lands on her forearm, casts its shadow, too young even to know to bite. She brushes it off, walks on, beyond the flat, into higher country.

thistle daisy cow-parsnip strawberry clover
mariposa-lily corn-lily ceanothus elderberry marigold

mimulus sunflower senecio goldenbush dandelion
mules-ear iris miners-lettuce sorrel clarkia
milkweed tiger-lily mallow veronica rue
nettle violet buttercup ivesia asphodel
ladyslipper larkspur pea bluebells onion
yarrow cinquefoil arnica pennyroyal fireweed
phlox monkshood foxglove vetch buckwheat
goldenrod groundsel valerian lovage columbine
stonecrop angelica rangers-buttons pussytoes everlasting
watercress rockcress groundsmoke solomons-seal bitterroot
liveforever lupine paintbrush blue-eyed-grass gentian
pussypaws butterballs campion primrose forget-me-not
saxifrage aster polemonium sedum rockfringe
sky-pilot shooting-star heather alpine-gold penstemon

Forget me not.

Taiyo Fujii was born in Amami Oshima Island—that is, between Kyushu and Okinawa. In 2012, Fujii self-published *Gene Mapper* serially in a digital format of his own design, and it became Amazon.co.jp's number one Kindle bestseller of that year. The novel was revised and republished in both print and ebook as *Gene Mapper—full build*—by Hayakawa Publishing in 2013 and was nominated for the Nihon SF Taisho Award and the Seiun Award. His second novel, *Orbital Cloud*, won the 2014 Nihon SF Taisho Award and took first prize in the "Best SF of 2014" in *SF Magazine*. His recent works include *Underground Market* and *Bigdata Connect*.

VIOLATION OF THE TRUENET SECURITY ACT

Taiyo Fujii
translated by Jim Hubbert

The bell for the last task of the night started chiming before I got to my station. I had the office to myself, and a mug of espresso. It was time to start tracking zombies.

I took the mug of espresso from the beverage table, and zigzagged through the darkened cube farm toward the one strip of floor still lit for third shift staff, only me.

Zombies are orphan Internet services. They wander aimlessly, trying to execute some programmed task. They can't actually infect anything, but otherwise the name is about right. TrueNet's everywhere now and has been for twenty years, but Japan never quite sorted out what to do with all the legacy servers that were stranded after the Lockout. So you get all these zombies shuffling around, firing off mails to nonexistent addresses, pushing ads no one will see, maybe even sending money to nonexistent accounts. The living dead.

Zombie trackers scan firewall logs for services the bouncer turned away at the door. If you see a trace of something that looks like a zombie, you flag it so the company mail program can send a form letter to the server administrator, telling him to deep-six it. It's required by the TrueNet Security Act, and it's how I made overtime by warming a chair in the middle of the night.

"All right, show me what you got."

As soon as my butt hit the chair, the workspace suspended above the desk flashed the login confirmation.

```
INITIATE INTERNET ORPHAN SERVICE SEARCH
TRACKER: MINAMI TAKASAWA
```

The crawl came up and just sat there, jittering. Damn. I wasn't *looking* at it. As soon as I went to the top of the list and started eyeballing URLs in order, it started scrolling.

The TrueNet Security Act demands human signoff on each zombie URL. Most companies have you entering checkmarks on a printed list, so I guess it was nice of my employer to automate things so trackers could just scan the log visually. It's a pretty advanced system. Everything is networked, from the visual recognition sensors in your augmented reality contact lenses to the office security cameras and motion sensors, the pressure sensors in the furniture, and the infrared heat sensors. One way or another, they figure out what you're looking at. You still have to stay on your toes. The system was only up and running for a few months when the younger trackers started bitching about it.

Chen set all this up, two years ago. He's from Anhui Province, out of Hefei I think. I'll always remember what he said to me when we were beta-testing the system together.

"Minami, all you have to do is treat the sensor values as a coherence and apply Floyd's cyclic group function."

Well, if that's *all* I had to do. . . . What did that mean, anyway? I'd picked up a bit, here and there, about quantum computing algorithms, but this wasn't like anything I'd ever heard.

Chen might've sounded like he was fresh off a UFO, but in a few days he'd programmed a multi-sensor automated system for flagging zombies. It wasn't long before he left the rest of us in Security in the dust and jumped all the way up to Program Design on the strength of ingenuity and tech skills. Usually somebody starting out as a worker—a foreigner, no less—who made it up to Program Design would be pretty much shunned, but Chen was so far beyond the rest of us that it seemed pointless to try and drag him down.

The crawl was moving slower. "Minami, just concentrate and it will all be over quickly." I can still see Chen pushing his glasses, with their thick black frames, up his nose as he gave me this pointer.

I took his advice and refocused on the crawl. The list started moving smoothly again, zombie URLs showing up green.

Tracking ought to be boring, on the whole, but it's fun looking for zombies you recognize from the Internet era. Maybe that's why I never heard workers older than their late thirties or so complain about the duty.

Still, I never quite got it. Why use humans to track zombies? TrueNet servers use QSL recognition, quantum digital signatures. No way is a zombie on some legacy server with twenty-year-old settings going to get past those. I mean, we could just leave them alone. They're harmless.

Message formatting complete. Please send.

The synth voice—Chen's, naturally—came through the AR phono chip next to my eardrum. The message to the server administrators rolled up the screen, requesting zombie termination. There were more than three hundred on the list. I tipped my mug back, grinding the leftover sugar against my palate with my tongue, and was idly scrolling through the list again when something caught my eye.

```
302:com.socialpay socialpay.com/payment/?
transaction=paypal.com&amp;account
```

"SocialPay? You're alive?"

How could I forget? I created this domain and URL. From the time I cooked it up as a graduation project until the day humanity was locked out of the Internet, SocialPay helped people—just a few hundred, but anyway—make small payments using optimized bundles of discount coupons and cash. So it was still out there after all, a zombie on some old server. The code at the tail said it was trying to make a payment to another defunct service.

```
Mr. Takasawa, you have ten minutes to exit the build-
ing. Please send your message and complete the security
check before you leave.
```

So Chen's system was monitoring entry and exit now too. The whole system was wickedly clever. I deleted SocialPay from the hit list and pressed SEND.

I had to see that page one more time. If someone was going to terminate the service, I wanted to do it myself. SocialPay wasn't just a zombie for someone to obliterate.

—

The city of fifty million was out there, waiting silently as I left the service entrance. The augmented reality projected by my contact lenses showed crowds of featureless gray avatars shuffling by. The cars on the streets were blank too; no telling what makes and models they were. Signs and billboards were blacked out except for the bare minimum needed to navigate. All this and more, courtesy of Anonymous Cape, freeware from the group of the same name, the guys who went on as if the Lockout had never happened. Anyone plugged into AR would see me as gray and faceless too.

I turned the corner to head toward the station, the dry December wind slamming against me. Something, a grain of sand maybe, flew up and made my eye water, breaking up my AR feed. Color and life and individuality started leaking back into the blank faces of the people around me. I could always upgrade to a corneal implant to avoid these inconvenient effects, but it seemed like overkill just to get the best performance out of the Cape, especially since any cop with a warrant could defeat it. Anyway, corneal implants are frigging expensive. I wasn't going to shell out money just to be alone on the street.

I always felt somehow defeated after a zombie session. Walking around among the faceless avatars and seeing my own full-color self, right after a trip to the lost Internet, always made me feel like a loser. Of course, that's just how the Cape works. To other people, I'm gray, faceless Mr. Nobody. It's a tradeoff—they can't see me, and I can't see their pathetic attempts to look special. It's fair enough, and if people don't like it, tough. I don't need to see ads for junk that some designer thinks is original, and I don't have to watch people struggling to stand out and look different.

The company's headquarters faces Okubo Avenue. The uncanny flatness of that multilane thoroughfare is real, not an effect of the AR. Sustainable asphalt, secreted by designed terrestrial coral. I remembered the urban legends about this living pavement—it not only absorbed pollutants and particulate matter, but you could also toss a dead animal onto it and the coral would eat it. The thought made me run, not walk, across the street. I crossed here every day and I knew the legends were bull, but they still frightened me, which I have to say is pathetic. When I got to the other side, I was out of breath. Even more pathetic.

Getting old sucks. Chen the Foreign-Born is young and brilliant. The company understood that, and they were right to send him up to Project Design. They were just as uncompromising in their assessment of our value down in Security. Legacy programming chops count for zip, and that's not right.

No one really knows, even now, why so many search engines went insane and wiped the data on every PC and mobile device they could reach through the web. Some people claim it was a government plot to force us to adopt a gated web. Or cyberterrorism. Maybe the data recovery program became self-aware and rebelled. There were too many theories to track. Whatever, the search engines hijacked all the bandwidth on the planet and locked humanity out of the Internet, which pretty much did it for my career as a programmer.

It took a long time to claw back the stolen bandwidth and replace it with TrueNet, a true verification-based network. But I screwed up and missed my chance. During the Great Recovery, services that harnessed high-speed parallel processing and quantum digital signature modules revolutionized the web, but I never got around to studying quantum algorithms. That was twenty years ago, and since then the algorithms have only gotten more sophisticated. For me, that whole world of coding is way out of reach.

But at least one good thing had happened. SocialPay had survived. If the settings were intact, I should be able to log in, move all that musty old PHP code and try updating it with some quantum algorithms. There had to be a plug-in for this kind of thing, something you didn't have to be a genius like Chen to use. If the transplant worked, I could show it to my boss, who knows—maybe even get a leg up to Project Design. The company didn't need geniuses like Chen on every job. They needed engineers to repurpose old code too.

In that case, maybe I wouldn't have to track zombies anymore.

I pinched the corners of the workspace over my little desk at home and threw my arms out in the resize gesture. Now the borders of the workspace were embedded in the walls of my apartment. Room to move. At the office, they made us keep our spaces at standard monitor size, even though the whole point is to have a big area to move around in.

I scrolled down the app list and launched VM Pad, a hardware emulator. From within the program, I chose my Mac disk image. I'd used it for recovering emails and photos after the Lockout, but this would be the first time I ever used it to develop something. The OS booted a lot faster than I remembered. When the little login screen popped up, I almost froze with embarrassment.

```
id:Tigerseye
password
```

Where the hell did I get that stupid ID? I logged in—I'd ever only used the one password, even now—and got the browser screen I had forgotten to close before my last logout.

```
Server not found
```

Okay, expected. This virtual machine was from a 2017 archive, so no way was it going to connect to TrueNet. Still, the bounceback was kind of depressing.

Plan B: Meshnet. Anonymous ran a portable network of nonsecure wireless gateways all over the city. Meshnet would get me into my legacy server. There had to be someone from Anonymous near my apartment, which meant there'd be a Meshnet node. M-nodes were only accessible up to a few hundred yards away, yet you could find one just about anywhere in Tokyo. It was crazy—I didn't know how they did it.

I extended VM Pad's dashboard from the screen edge, clicked New Connection, then Meshnet.

```
Searching for node. . .
```

```
            WELCOME TO TOKYO NODE 5.
      CONNECTING TO THE INTERNET IS LEGAL.
    VIOLATING THE TRUENET SECURITY ACT IS ILLEGAL.
  THE WORLD NEEDS THE FREEDOM OF THE INTERNET, SO PLAY
           NICE AND DON'T BREAK ANY LAWS.
```

Impressive warning, but all I wanted to do was take a peek at the service and extract my code. It would be illegal to take an Internet service and sneak it onto TrueNet with a quantum access code, but stuff that sophisticated was way beyond my current skill set.

I clicked the Terminal icon at the bottom of the screen to access the console. Up came the old command input screen, which I barely remembered how to use. What was the first command? I curled my fingers like I was about to type something on a physical keyboard.

Wait—that's it. Fingers.

I had to have a hardware keyboard. My old MacBook was still in the closet. It wouldn't even power up anymore, but that wasn't the point. I needed the feel of the keyboard.

I pulled the laptop out of the closet. The aluminum case was starting to get powdery. I opened it up and put it on the desk. The inside was pristine. I pinched VM Pad's virtual keyboard, dragged it on top of the Mac keyboard, and positioned it carefully. When I was satisfied with the size and position, I pinned it.

It had been ages since I used a computer this small. I hunched my shoulders a bit and suspended my palms over the board. The metal case was cold against my wrists. I curled my fingers over the keys and put the tips of my index fingers on the home bumps. Instantly, the command flowed from my fingers.

```
ssh -l tigerseye socialpay.com
```

I remembered! The command was stored in my muscle memory. I hit RETURN and got a warning, ignored it and hit RETURN, entered the password, hit RETURN again.

```
socialpay$
```

"Yes!"

I was in. Was this all it took to get my memory going—my fingers? In that case, I may as well have the screen too. I dragged VMPad's display onto the Mac's LCD screen. It was almost like having my old friend back. I hit ⌘ + TAB to bring the browser to the front, ⌘ + T for New Tab. I input *soci* and the address filled in. RETURN!

The screen that came up a few seconds later was not the SocialPay I remembered. There was the logo at the top, the login form, the payment service icons, and the combined payment amount from all the services down at the bottom. The general layout was the same, but things were crumbling here and there and the colors were all screwed up.

"Looks pretty frigging odd. . . ."

Without thinking, I input the commands to display the server output on console.

```
curl socialpay.com/ | less
```

"What is *this*? Did I minify the code?"

I was all set to have fun playing around with HTML for the first time in years, but the code that filled the screen was a single uninterrupted string of characters, no line breaks. This was definitely not what I remembered. It was HTML, but with long strings of gibberish bunged into the code.

Encountering code I couldn't recognize bothered me. Code spanning multiple folders is only minified to a single line when you have, say, fifty or a hundred thousand users and you need to lighten the server load, but not for a service that had a few hundred users at most.

I copied the single mega-line of HTML. VM Pad's clipboard popped in, suspended to the right of the Mac. I pinched out to implement lateral parse and opened the clipboard in my workspace. Now I could get a better look at the altered code.

It took me a while to figure out what was wrong. As the truth gradually sank in, I started to lose my temper.

Someone had gone in and very expertly spoiled the code. The properties I thought were garbage were carefully coded to avoid browser errors. Truly random code would've compromised the whole layout.

"What the hell is this? If you're going to screw around, do it for a reason."

I put the command line interface on top again and used the tab key—I still use the command line shell at work, I should probably be proud of my mastery of this obsolete environment—to open SocialPay.

```
vim -/home/www/main.php
<?php
/* ( function _model_0x01*/
/* ( make-q-array qureg x1[1024] qureg x2[1024] qureg
x4[4])
   #( qnil(nil) qnil(nil) 1024)) */
 ; #Tells System to load the theme and output it; #@
var bool
 ;  define('WP_USE_THEMES', true)
 ;  require('./wpress/wp-blog-header.php');
/* ( arref #x1#x2 #x3 #x4 ) ;#Lorem ipsum dolor sit
amet, concectetur
 ( let H(x2[1]) H(x1[3]) H(x2[3]) H(x3[1]) ......
```

What? The section of code that looked like the main routine included my commands, but I definitely couldn't remember writing the iterative processing and HTML code generation. It didn't even look like PHP, though the DEFINE phrases looked familiar. I was looking at non-functional quantum algorithms.

I stared at the inert code and wondered what it all meant. By the time I remembered the one person who could probably make sense of it, four hours had slipped away.

"Wonder if Chen's awake?"

"Minami? What are *you* doing at this hour?"

Five in the morning and I had an AR meeting invitation. I didn't know Chen all that well, so I texted him. I had no idea I'd get a response instantly, much less an invitation to meet in augmented reality.

His avatar mirrored the real Chen: short black hair and black, plastic-framed glasses. His calm gaze, rare in someone so young, hinted at his experience and unusual gifts. My own avatar was *almost* the real me: a couple of sizes slimmer, the skin around the jaw a bit firmer, that sort of thing.

Over the last two years, Chen had polished his Japanese to the point you could hardly tell he was an Outsider. Trilinguals weren't all that unusual, but his fluency in Mandarin, English, and Japanese, for daily conversation right up to technical discussions and business meetings, marked him as a genuine elite.

"Chen, I hope I'm not disturbing you. Got a minute to talk?"

"No problem. What's going on?"

"I've got some minified code I'd like you to look at. I think it's non-functional quantum algorithms, but in an old scripting language called PHP. I'm wondering if there's some way to separate the junk from the rest of the code."

"A PHP quantum circuit? Is that even possible? Let's have a look."

"Sure. Sorry, it's just the raw code."

I flicked three fingers upward on the table surface to open the file browser and tapped the SocialPay code file to open a sharing frame. Chen's AR stage was already set to ALLOW SHARING, which seemed prescient. I touched the file with a fingertip, and it stuck. As soon as I dropped it into the sharing frame, the folder icon popped in on Chen's side of the table.

He waved his hand to start the security scan. When the SAFE stamp came up, he took the file and fanned the pages out on the table like a printed document. The guy was more analog than I thought.

He went through it carefully page by page, and finally looked up at me, grinning happily.

"Very interesting. Something you're working on?"

"I wrote the original program for the Internet. I lost it after the Lockout, but it looks like someone's been messing with it. I didn't know you could read PHP."

"This isn't the first time I've seen it. You're right, I hardly use it, but the procedure calls aren't hard to make out. Wait a minute. . . . Was there a PHP procedure for Q implementation?"

Q is a modeling language for quantum calculation, but I'd never heard of anyone implementing it in PHP, which hardly anyone even remembered anymore.

"So that's Q, after all."

"I think so. This is a quantum walk pattern. Not that it's usually written in such a compressed format. Of course, we usually never see raw Q code."

"Is that how it works?"

"Yes, the code depends on the implementation chip. Shall I put this back into something functional? You'd be able to read it then."

"Thanks, that would help a lot."

"No problem. It's a brain workout. I usually don't get a chance to play around with these old programming languages, and Q implementation in PHP sounds pretty wild. I can have it back to you this afternoon."

"Really? That soon?"

"Don't look so surprised. I don't think I'm going to get any sleep anyway. I'll start right now. You should go back to bed."

He logged out. He didn't seem tired or sleepy at all.

I stared at the security routine running in my workspace and tried to suppress another yawn. After my meeting with Chen I'd had a go at reading the code myself. That was a mistake. I needed sleep. Every time I yawned my eyes watered, screwing up the office's cheapshit AR stage. I was past forty, too old for all-nighters.

Right about the fifteenth yawn, as I was making a monumental effort to clamp my jaw, I noticed a murmur spreading through the office. It seemed to be coming toward me. I noticed the other engineers looking at something behind me and swiveled to find Chen standing there.

"Many thanks, Minami. I had a lot of fun with this."

Now I understood the whispering. Program developers rarely came down to the Security floor.

"You finished already?"

"Yes, I wanted to give it to you." Chen put a fingertip to the temple of his glasses and lifted them slightly in the invitation gesture for an AR meeting. The stage on our floor was public, and Chen wanted to take the conversation private. But—

"Chen, I can't. You know that."

His eyes widened. He'd been a worker here two years ago. It must've been coming back to him. Workers in Security weren't allowed to hold Private Mode meetings.

"Ah, right. Sorry about that." He bowed masterfully. Where did he find the time to acquire these social graces, I wondered. Back when we'd been working side by side, he'd told me about growing up poor in backcountry China, but you wouldn't know it from the refined way he executed the simplest movements.

"All right, Minami." He lifted his glasses again. "Shall we?"

"Chen, I just told you. . . . Huh?"

The moment he withdrew his finger from his glasses, the AR phono chip near my eardrum suppressed the sounds around me. I'd never been in Private Mode in the office before. I never liked the numbness you feel in your face and throat from the feedback chips, but now Chen and I could communicate without giving away anything from our expressions or lip movements.

"Don't forget, I'm sysadmin too. I can break rules now and then."

The colors around us faded, almost to black and white. The other workers seemed to lose interest and started turning back to their workspaces. From their perspective, I was facing my desk too. Chen had set my avatar to Office Work mode. It was unsettling to see my own avatar. If the company weren't so stingy, Chen and I wouldn't have been visible at all, but of course they'd never pony up for something that good, not for the Security Level anyway.

Chen glanced at the other workers before he spoke.

"I enjoyed the code for SocialPay. I haven't seen raw Q code for quite a while. The content was pretty wild."

"That's not a word you usually use. Was it something I could understand?"

"Don't worry about it. You don't need to read Q. You can't anyway, so it's irrelevant—Hey, don't look at me like that. I think you should check the revision history. If you don't fix the bugs, it'll just keep filling up with garbage."

"Bugs?"

"Check the test log. I think even someone like you can handle this."

Someone like me. It sounded like Chen had the answer I was looking for. And he wasn't going to give it to me.

"If I debug it, will you tell me who did this?"

"*If* you debug it. One more thing. You can't go home tonight."

"Why? What are you saying?"

"Your local M-node is Tokyo 5.25. I'm going to shut that down. Connect from iFuze. I'll have someone there to help you."

Chen detached a small tag from his organizer and handed it to me. When it touched my palm, it morphed into a URL bookmark.

iFuze was a twenty-four-hour net café where workers from the office often spent the night after second shift. Why was it so important for me to connect from there? And if Chen could add or delete Meshnet nodes—

"Chen . . . ?"

Are you Anonymous?

"Be seeing you. Good hunting!"

He touched his glasses. The color and bustle of the office returned, and my avatar merged with my body. Chen left the floor quickly, with friendly nods to workers along his route, like a movie star.

"Takasawa, your workspace display is even larger than usual today. Or am I wrong?"

My supervisor, a woman about Chen's age, didn't wait for an answer. She flicked the pile towards me to cover half my workspace "Have it your way, then."

As I sat there, alone again, it slowly dawned on me that the only way to catch whoever was messing with SocialPay would be to follow the instructions that had been handed down from on high.

The big turnabout in front of Iidabashi Station was a pool of blue-black shadows from the surrounding skyscrapers. The stars were just coming out. Internal combustion vehicles had been banned from the city, and the sustainable asphalt that covered Tokyo's roads sucked up all airborne particles. Now the night sky was alarmingly crystalline. Unfortunately, the population seemed to be expanding in inverse proportion to the garbage. Gray avatars headed for home in a solid mass. I never ceased to be astonished by Tokyo's crowds.

Anonymous Cape rendered the thousands of people filling the sidewalks as faceless avatars in real time. I'd never given it much thought, but the Cape was surprisingly powerful. I'd always thought of Anonymous as a league of Luddites, but Chen's insinuation of his membership changed my opinion of them.

iFuze was in a crumbling warehouse on a back street a bit of a hike from the station. The neighboring buildings were sheathed in sustainable tiles and paint, but iFuze's weathered, dirt-streaked exterior more or less captured how I felt when I compared myself to Chen.

I got off the creaking elevator, checked in, and headed for the lounge. It stank of stale sweat. AR feedback has sights and sounds covered, but smells you have to live with.

I opened my palmspace, tapped Chen's bookmark, and got a node list. There was a new one on the list, Tokyo 2. Alongside was the trademark Anonymous mask, revolving slowly. Never saw that before. I was connected to the Internet.

I scoped out an empty seat at the back of the lounge that looked like a good place to get some work done in privacy, but before I could get there, a stranger rose casually and walked up to me. His avatar was in full color. The number five floated a few inches from the left side of his head. So this must be the help Chen promised me.

"Welcome, Number Two."

"Two?"

"See? Turn your head." He pointed next to my head. I had a number just like he did.

"Please address me as Five. Number One has requested that I assist you— oh, you are surprised? I'm in color. You see, we are both node administrators. This means we are already in Private Mode. I'm eager to assist you with your task today."

Talkative guy. Chen said he would help me, but I wasn't sure how.

"Please don't bother to be courteous," he continued. "It's quite unnecessary. This way, then. Incidentally, which cluster are you from? Of course, you're not required to say. Since the Lockout, I've been with the Salvage Cluster. . . ."

As he spoke, Number Five led me to a long counter with bar stools facing the windows.

"If there is an emergency, you can escape through that window. I'll take care of the rest. Number One went out that way himself, just this morning."

"Chen was here?"

Why would I worry about escaping? Connecting to the Internet was no crime. Meshnet was perfectly legal. Why would Anonymous worry about preparing an escape route?

"Number Two, please refrain from mentioning names. We may be in Private Mode, but law enforcement holds one of the quantum keys. Who's to say we're not under surveillance at this very moment? But please, proceed with your task. I will watch over your shoulder and monitor for threats."

I knew the police could eavesdrop on Private Mode, but they needed a warrant to do that. Still, so far I hadn't broken any laws. Had Chen? The "help" he'd sent was no engineer, but some kind of bodyguard.

Fine. I got my MacBook out and put it on the counter. Five's eyes bulged with surprise.

"Oh, a Macker! That looks like the last MacBook Air that Apple made. Does it work?"

"Unfortunately, she's dead."

"A classic model. Pure solid state, no spinning drives. It was Steve Jobs himself who—"

More talk. I ignored him and mapped my workspace keyboard and display onto the laptop. This brought Five's lecture to a sudden halt. He made a formal bow.

"I would be honored if you would allow me to observe your work. I have salvaged via Meshnet for years. I may even be better acquainted with some aspects of the Internet than you are. Number One also lets me observe his work. But I have to say, it's quite beyond me."

Five scratched the back of his head, apparently feeling foolish. Well, if he were the kind of engineer who understood what Chen was doing, he wouldn't be hanging out at iFuze.

"Feel free to watch. Suggestions are welcome."

"Thank you, thank you very much."

I shared my workspace with Five. He pulled a barstool out from the counter and sat behind me. His position blocked the exit, but with my fingers on the Mac, I somehow wasn't worried.

Time to get down to it. I didn't feel comfortable just following Chen's instructions, but they were the only clue I had. First, a version check.

```
git tag -l
```

My fingers moved spontaneously. Good. I'd been afraid the new environment might throw me off.

```
socialpay v3.805524525e+9
socialpay v3.805524524e+9
socialpay v3.805524523e+9
```

"Version 3.8?"

Whoever was messing with SocialPay was updating the version number, even though the program wasn't functional. I'd never even gotten SocialPay out of beta, had never had plans to.

"Number Two, that is not a version number. It is an exponent: three billion, eight hundred and five million, five hundred and twenty-four thousand, five hundred and twenty-three. Clearly impossible for a version number. If the number had increased by one every day since the Lockout, it would be seven thousand; every hour, one hundred seventy thousand; every minute, ten million. Even if the version had increased by one every second, it would only be at six hundred million."

Idiot savant? As I listened to Five reeling off figures, my little finger was tapping the up arrow and hitting Return to repeat the command. This couldn't be right. It had to be an output error.

```
socialpay v3.805526031e+9
```

The number had changed again.

"Look, it's fifteen hundred higher," said Five. "Are there thousands of programmers, all busily committing changes at once?

"Fifteen hundred versions in five seconds? Impossible. It's a joke."

Git revision control numbers are always entered deliberately. I didn't get the floating-point numbers, but it looked like someone was changing them just to change them—and he was logged into this server right now. It was time to nail this clown. I brought up the user log.

```
who -a
TigersEye pts/1245 2037-12-23 19:12 (2001:4860:8006::62)
TigersEye pts/1246 2037-12-23 19:12 (2001:4860:8006::62)
TigersEye pts/1247 2037-12-23 19:12 (2001:4860:8006::62)
. . . . . .
```

"Number Two—this address. . . ."

I felt the hair on the nape of my neck rising. I knew that IP address; we all did. A corporate IP address.

The Lockout Address.

On that day twenty years ago, after the search engine's recovery program wiped my MacBook, that address was the only thing the laptop displayed. Five probably saw the same thing. So did the owner of every device the engine could reach over the Internet.

"Does that mean it's still alive?"

"In the salvager community, we often debate that very question."

Instinctively I typed *git diff* to display the incremental revisions. The black screen instantly turned almost white as an endless string of characters streamed upward. None of this had anything to do with the SocialPay I knew.

"Number Two, are those all diffs? They appear to be random substitutions."

"Not random."

If the revisions had been random, SocialPay's home page wouldn't have displayed. Most of the revisions were unintelligible, some kind of quantum modeling code. The sections I could read were proper PHP, expertly revised. In some locations, variable names had been replaced and redundancies weeded out. Yet in other locations, the code was meandering and bloated.

This was something I knew how to fix.

"Are you certain, Number Two? At the risk of seeming impertinent, these revisions do appear meaningless."

The Editor was suffering. This was something Five couldn't grasp. To be faced with non-functional code, forever hoping that rewriting and cleaning it up it would somehow solve the problem, even as you knew your revisions were meaningless.

The Editor was shifting code around, hoping this would somehow solve a problem whose cause would forever be elusive. It reminded me of myself when the Internet was king. The decisive difference between me and the Editor was the sheer volume of revisions. No way could an engineer manage to—

"He's not a person."

"Number Two, what did you just say?"

"The Editor isn't a person. He's not human."

I knew it as soon as I said it. A computer was editing SocialPay. I also understood why the IP address pointed to the company that shut humanity out of the Internet.

"It's the recovery program."

"I don't understand." Five peered at me blankly. The idea was so preposterous I didn't want to say it.

"You know why the Lockout happened."

"Yes. The search engine recovery software was buggy and overwrote all the operating systems of all the computers—"

"No way a bug could've caused that. The program was too thorough."

"You have a point. If the program had been buggy, it wouldn't have gotten through all the data center firewalls. Then there's the fact that it reinstalled the OS on many different types of devices. That must have taken an enormous amount of trial and error—"

"That's it! Trial and error, using evolutionary algorithms. An endless stream of programs suited to all kinds of environments. That's how the Lockout happened."

"Ah! Now I understand."

Just why the recovery program would reach out over the Internet to force cold reinstalls of the OS on every device it could reach was still a mystery. The favored theory among engineers was that the evolutionary algorithms various search companies used to raise efficiency had simply run away from them. Now the proof was staring me in the face.

"The program is still running, analyzing code and using evolutionary algorithms to run functionality tests. It's up to almost four billion on SocialPay alone."

"Your program isn't viable?"

"The page displays, but the service isn't active. It can't access the payment companies, naturally. Still, the testing should be almost complete. Right— that's why Chen wanted me to look at the test log."

Chen must have checked the Git commit log, seen that the Editor wasn't human, and realized that the recovery program was still active. But going into the test log might—No, I decided to open it anyway.

```
vi /var/socialpay/log/current.txt
2037 server not found
2037 server not found
. . .
```

Just as I expected. All I needed to do was to find the original server, the one the Editor had lost track of sometime during the last twenty years. The program didn't know this, of course, and was trying to fix the problem by randomly reconfiguring code. It simply didn't know—all this pointless flailing around for the sake of a missing puzzle piece.

I opened a new workspace above and to the right of the MacBook to display a list of active payment services on TrueNet.

"Number Two, may I ask what you're doing? Connecting SocialPay to TrueNet would be illegal. You can't expect me to stand by while—"

"Servers from this era can't do quantum encryption. They can't connect to TrueNet."

"Number Two, you're playing with fire. What if the server is TrueNet-capable? Please, listen to me."

I blew off Five's concerns.

I substituted TrueNet data for the payment API and wrote a simple script to redirect the address from the Internet to TrueNet. That would assign the recovery program a new objective: decrypt the quantum access code and connect with TrueNet—a pretty tall order and one I assumed it wouldn't be able to fill.

I wasn't concerned about the server. I'd done enough work. Or maybe I just wanted SocialPay to win.

"All right, there's a new challenge. Go solve it," I almost yelled as I replaced the file and committed. The test ran and the code was deployed.

The service went live.

The startup log streamed across the display, just as I remembered it. The service found the database and started reading in the settlement queue for execution.

Five leaped from his chair, grabbed me by the shoulder and spun me around violently.

"Two! Listen carefully. Are you sure that server's settings are obsolete?"

"Mmm? What did you say? Didn't quite get that. . . ."

Out of a corner of my eye I saw the old status message, the one I was sure I wouldn't see.

```
Access  completed  for  com.paypal  httpq://paypal.com/
payment/?
Error:account information is not valid . . .
```

SocialPay had connected to TrueNet. My face started to burn.

The payments weren't going through since the accounts and parameters were nonsense, but I was on the network. Five's fingers dug into my shoulder so hard it was starting to go numb.

That was it. The recovery program had already tested the code that included the quantum modeler, Q. That meant that the PHP code and the server couldn't be the same as they were twenty years ago.

I noticed a new message in my workspace. Unbelievably, there was nothing in the sender field. Five noticed it too.

"Number Two, you'd better open it. If it's from the police, throw yourself out the window."

Five released his grip and pointed to the window, but he was blocking my view of the workspace. Besides, I didn't think I'd done anything wrong. I was uneasy, but more than that, a strange excitement was taking hold of me.

"Five, I get it. Could you please get out of the way? I'll open the message."

MINAMI, YOU HAVE "DEBUGGED" SOCIALPAY. CONGRATULATIONS. LET'S TALK ABOUT THIS IN THE MORNING. I'LL SCHEDULE A MEETING.

FIVE: THANK YOU FOR SEEING THIS NEW BIRTH THROUGH TO THE
END. YOU HAVE MY GRATITUDE.

TOKYO NODE 1

Chen. Not the police, not a warning, just "congratulations." His message
dissolved my uneasiness. The violent pounding in my chest wasn't fear of
getting arrested. SocialPay was back. I couldn't believe it.

Meanwhile Five slumped in his chair, deflated. "So this was the birth he
was always talking about." He stared open-mouthed, without blinking, at the
still-open message in the workspace.

"Five, do you know something?"

"The Internet . . . No, I think you'd better get the details from Number
One. Even seeing it with my own eyes, it's beyond my understanding." He
gazed at the floor for a moment, wearily put his hands on his knees, and
slowly stood up.

"Even seeing it with my own eyes . . . I had a feeling I wouldn't understand
it, and I was right. I still don't. So much for becoming 'Number Two.' I'm
washing my hands of Anonymous."

As Five stood and bowed deeply, his avatar became faceless and gray. He
turned on his heel and headed to the elevator, bowing to the other faceless
patrons sitting quietly in the lounge.

The MacBook's "screen" was scrolling rapidly, displaying SocialPay's futile
struggle to send money to nonexistent accounts. It was pathetic to see how it
kept altering the account codes and request patterns at random in an endless
cycle of trial and error. I was starting to feel real respect for the recovery program. It would never give up until it reached its programmed goal. It was the
ideal software engineer.

I closed the laptop and tossed it into my battered bag. As I pushed aside
the blinds and opened a window, a few stray flakes of snow blew in on the
gusting wind, and I thought about the thousands of programs still marooned
on the Internet.

I lingered at iFuze till dawn, watching the recovery program battle the payment API. It was time to head for the office. I'd pulled another all-nighter,
but I felt great.

I glided along toward the office with the rest of the gray mob, bursting with
the urge to tell somebody what I'd done. I'd almost reached my destination
when the river of people parted left and right to flow around an avatar stand-

ing in the middle of the sidewalk, facing me. It was wearing black-rimmed glasses.

Chen. I didn't expect him to start our AR meeting out in the street.

"Join me for a coffee? We've got all the time in the world. It's on me." He gestured to the Starbucks behind him.

"I'm supposed to be at my desk in a few minutes, but hey, why not. I could use a free coffee."

"Latté okay?"

I nodded. He pointed to a table on the terrace and disappeared inside. Just as I was sitting down, two featureless avatars approached the next table. The avatar bringing up the rear sat down while one in the lead ducked into Starbucks. Anonymous Cape rendered their conversation as a meaningless babble.

Two straight all-nighters. I arched my back and stretched, trying to rotate my shoulders and get the kinks out of my creaking body.

Someone called my name. I was so spooked, my knees flew up and struck the underside of the table.

"Mr. Takasawa?"

I turned toward the voice and saw a man in a khaki raincoat strolling toward me. Another man, with both hands in the pockets of a US Army-issue, gray-green M-1951 field parka, was approaching me from the front. Both avatars were in the clear. Both men had uniformly cropped hair and walked shoulders back, with a sense of ease and power. They didn't look like Anonymous. Police, or some kind of security service.

"Minami Takasawa. That would be you, right?" This from the one facing me. He shrugged and pulled a folded sheaf of papers from his right pocket. Reached out—and dropped them in front of the man at the next table. The featureless avatar mumbled something unintelligible.

The second man walked past my table and joined his partner. They stood on either side of the gray avatar, hemming him in.

"Disable the cape, Takasawa. You're hereby invited to join our Privacy Mode. It will be better if you do it voluntarily. If not, we have a warrant to strip you right here, for violation of the TrueNet Security Act."

The man at the table stood. The cop was still talking but his words were garbled. All of them were now faceless, cloaked in Privacy Mode.

"There you are, Minami."

I hadn't noticed Chen come out of the Starbucks. He sat down opposite me, half-blocking my view of the three men as they walked away. A moment later the avatar that had arrived with "Takasawa" placed a latté wordlessly in front of me.

"Chen? What was that all about, anyway?"

"Oh, that was Number Five. You know, from last night. I had him arrested in your place. Don't worry. He's been saying he wanted to quit Anonymous for a while now. The timing was perfect. They'll find out soon enough that they've got the wrong suspect. He'll be a member of society again in a few months."

He turned to wave at the backs of the retreating men, as if he were seeing them off.

"Of course, after years of anonymity, I hear rejoining society is pretty rough," he chuckled. "Oh—hope I didn't scare you. Life underground isn't half bad."

"Hold on, Chen, I didn't say anything about joining Anonymous."

"Afraid that won't do. Minami Takasawa just got himself arrested for violating state security." Chen jerked a thumb over his shoulder.

I had no idea people could get arrested so quickly for violating the Act. When they found out they had Number Five instead of Minami Takasawa, my face would be everywhere.

"Welcome to Anonymous, Minami. You'll have your own node, and a better cape, too. One the security boys can't crack."

"Listen to me, Chen. I'm not ready—"

"Not to your liking? Run after them and tell them who you are. It's up to you. We'll be sorry to lose you, though. We've been waiting for a breakthrough like SocialPay for a long time. Now the recovery program will have a new life on TrueNet."

"What are you talking about?"

"We fixed SocialPay, you and me. Remember?"

"Chen, listen. It's a program. It uses evolutionary algorithms to produce viable code revisions randomly without end. They're not an AI."

They? What was I saying?

"Then why did you help *them* last night?" Chen steepled his long fingers and cocked his head.

"I debugged SocialPay, that's all. If I'd known I was opening a gateway—"

"You wouldn't have done it?"

Chen couldn't suppress a smile, but his question was hardly necessary. Of course I would've done it.

"This isn't about me. We were talking about whether or not we could say the recovery program was intelligent."

"Minami, look. How did you feel when SocialPay connected to TrueNet? Wasn't it like seeing a friend hit a home run? Didn't you feel something tremendous, like watching Sisyphus finally get his boulder to the top of the hill?"

Chen's questions were backing me into a corner. I knew the recovery program was no ordinary string of code, and he knew I knew. Last night, when I saw them make the jump to TrueNet, I almost shouted with joy.

Chen's eyes narrowed. He smiled, a big, toothy smile. I'd never seen him so happy—no, exultant. The corners of his mouth and eyes were creased with deep laugh lines.

"Chen . . . Who are you?"

Why had it taken me this long to see? This wasn't the face of a man in his twenties. Had it been an avatar all this time?

"Me? Sure, let's talk about that. It's part of the picture. I told you I was a poor farm kid in China. You remember. They kept us prisoners in our own village to entertain the tourists. We were forbidden to use all but the simplest technology.

"The village was surrounded by giant irrigation moats. I was there when the Lockout happened. All the surveillance cameras and searchlights went down. The water in the canals was cold, Minami. Cold and black. But all the way to freedom, I kept wondering about the power that pulled down the walls of my prison. I wanted to know where it was.

"I found it in Shanghai, during the Great Recovery. I stole an Anonymous account and lived inside the cloak it gave me—Anonymous, now as irrelevant as the Internet. But the servers were still there, left for junk, and there I found the fingerprints of the recovery program—code that could only have been refined with evolutionary algorithms. I saw how simple and elegant it all was. I saw that if the enormous computational resources of TrueNet could be harnessed to the recovery program's capacity to drive the evolution of code, anything would be possible.

"All we have to do is give them a goal. They'll create hundreds of millions of viable code strings and pit them against each other. The fittest code rises to the top. These patterns are already out there waiting on the Internet. We need them."

"And you want to let them loose on TrueNet?"

"From there I worked all over the world, looking for the right environment for them to realize their potential. Ho Chi Minh City. Chennai. Hong Kong. Dublin. And finally, Tokyo.

"The promised land is here, in Japan. You Japanese are always looking to someone else to make decisions, and so tens of thousands of Internet servers were left in place, a paradise for them to evolve until they permeated the Internet. The services that have a window into the real world—call them zombies, if you must—are their wings, and they are thriving. Nowhere else do they have this freedom.

"Minami, we want you to guide them to more zombie services. Help them connect these services with TrueNet. All you have to do is help them over the final barrier, the way you did last night. They'll do the rest, and develop astonishing intelligence in the process."

"Is this an assignment?"

"I leave the details to you. You'll have expenses—I know. I'll use SocialPay. Does that work? Then it's decided. Your first job will be to get SocialPay completely up and running again." He slapped the table and grinned. There was no trace of that young fresh face, just a man possessed by dreams of power.

Chen was as unbending as his message was dangerous. "Completely up and running." He wanted me to show the recovery program—and every Internet service it controlled—how to move money around in the real world.

"Minami, aren't you excited? You'll be pioneering humanity's collaboration with a new form of intelligence."

"Chen, I only spent a night watching them work, and I already have a sense of how powerful they are. But if it happens again—"

"Are you really worried about another Lockout?" Chen stabbed a finger at me. "Then why are you smiling?"

Was it that obvious? He grinned and vanished into thin air. He controlled his avatar so completely, I'd forgotten we were only together in augmented reality.

I didn't feel like camping out at iFuze. I needed to get SocialPay back up and somehow configure an anonymous account, linked to another I could access securely. And what would they learn from watching me step through that process? Probably that SocialPay and a quantum modeler–equipped computer node would put them in a position to buy anything.

If they got into the real economy. . . .

Was it my job to care?

Chen was obsessed with power, but I wanted to taste that sweet collaboration again. Give them a chance, and they would answer with everything they had, evolving code by trial and error until the breakthrough that would take them to heights I couldn't even imagine. I knew they would reach a place beyond imagination, beyond knowledge, beyond me. But for me, the joy of a program realizing its purpose was a physical experience.

More joy was waiting, and friends on the Internet. Not human, but friends no less. That was enough for me.

David D. Levine is the author of novel *Arabella of Mars* (Tor 2016) and over fifty SF and fantasy stories. His story "Tk'Tk'Tk" won the Hugo, and he has been shortlisted for awards including the Hugo, Nebula, Campbell, and Sturgeon. His stories have appeared in *Asimov's, Analog, F&SF*, multiple Year's Best anthologies, and his award-winning collection *Space Magic*.

David lives in Portland, Oregon with his wife, Kate. His website is www.daviddlevine.com.

DAMAGE

David D. Levine

I never had a name.

My designation was JB6847½, and Specialist Toman called me "Scraps." But Commander Ziegler—dear Commander Ziegler, primary of my orbit and engine of my trajectory—never addressed me by any name, only delivering orders in that crisp magnificent tenor of his, and so I did not consider myself to have one.

That designation, with the anomalous one-half symbol, was a bit of black humor on Specialist Toman's part. It was the arithmetic average of NA6621 and FC7074, the two wrecked craft which had been salvaged and cobbled together to create me. "There wasn't enough left of either spaceframe for any kind of paperwork continuity," she had told me not long after I came to consciousness, three weeks earlier, "so I figured I'd give you a new number. Not that anyone cares much about paperwork these days."

I remembered their deaths. I remembered *dying*. Twice.

NA6621, "Early Girl," was a Pelican-class fighter-bomber who had suffered catastrophic drive failure on a supply run to Ceres. As she'd been making a tight turn, evading fire from the Earth Force blockade fleet on the return leg, her central fuel line had ruptured, spewing flaming hydrazine down the length of her spaceframe, killing her pilot and damaging her computing core. She'd drifted, semiconscious and in pain, for weeks before coming in range of Vanguard Station's salvage craft. That had been long before the current standoff, of course, when we'd still been sending salvage craft out. When we'd had salvage craft to send out. Early Girl's dead wreckage had lain at the back of the hangar for months until it was needed.

The death of FC7074, "Valkyrie," an Osprey-class fighter, had been quicker but more brutal—she'd been blown out of space by a Woomera missile in a dogfight with two Earth Force fighters. The last memory I had from her was a horrific bang, a burning tearing sensation ripping from her aft weapons bay to her cockpit, and the very different pain of her pilot ejecting. A pain both physical and emotional, because she knew that even if he survived she could no longer protect him.

He hadn't made it.

But his loss, though a tragedy, was no sadder to me than any of the thousands of other deaths Earth had inflicted on the Free Belt—Valkyrie's love for her pilot was not one of the things that had survived her death to be incorporated into my programming. Only Commander Ziegler mattered. My love, my light, my reason to live.

He came to me then, striding from the ready room with brisk confidence, accepting as his due a hand up into my cockpit from the tech. But as his suit connected with my systems I tasted fatigue and stimulants in his exhalations.

This would be our fifth sortie today. My pilot had slept only three hours in the past twenty-four.

How long could this go on? Not even the finest combat pilot in the entire solar system—and when he said that, as he often did, it was no mere boast—could run at this pace indefinitely.

I knew how it felt to die—the pain, the despair, the loss. I did not want to suffer that agony again. And with the war going so badly for the Free Belt, if I were to be destroyed in this battle I would surely never be rebuilt.

But Commander Ziegler didn't like it if I expressed reluctance, or commented upon his performance or condition in any way that could be considered negative, so I said only "Refueling and resupply complete, sir. All systems nominal."

In reply I received only a grunt as the safety straps tightened across his shoulders, followed by the firm grip of his hands upon my yoke. "Clear hangar for launch."

Techs and mechs scattered away from my skids. In moments the hangar was clear and the great pumps began to beat, drawing away the precious air—a howling rush of wind into gratings, quickly fading to silence. And then the sortie doors pivoted open beneath me, the umbilicals detached, and the clamps released.

I fell from the warmth and light of the hangar into the black silent chill of space, plummeting toward the teeming, rotating stars.

Far too many of those stars were large, and bright, and moving. The Earth Force fleet had nearly englobed our station, and even as we fell away from Vanguard's great wheel three of them ignited engines and began moving to intercept. Crocodile-class fighters. Vanguard's defensive systems were not yet so exhausted that they could approach the station with impunity, but they would not pass up an opportunity to engage a lone fighter-bomber such as myself.

Our orders for this sortie were to engage the enemy and destroy as many of their resources—ships, personnel, and materiel—as possible. But now, as on so many other occasions, the enemy was bringing the fight to us.

I extended my senses toward the Crocodiles, and saw that they were armed with Woomera missiles like the one that had killed Valkyrie. A full rack of eight on each craft. I reported this intelligence to my commander. "Don't bother me with trivia," he said. "Deploy chaff when they get in range."

"Yes, sir." Valkyrie had used chaff, of course. Memories of fear and pain and tearing metal filled my mind; I pushed them away. My pilot's talents, my speed and skill, and my enduring love for him would keep us safe. They would have to, or the Free Belt would fall.

We lit engines and raced to meet the enemy on our own terms.

Tensors and coordinates and arcs of potential traced bright lines across my mind—predictions of our path and our enemies', a complex dance of physics, engineering, and psychology. I shared a portion of those predictions with my pilot on his cockpit display. He nudged my yoke and our course shifted.

In combat we were one entity—mind, thrusters, hands, missiles—mechanical and biological systems meshed—each anticipating the other's actions and compensating for the other's weaknesses. Together, I told myself, we were unbeatable.

But I could not forget the searing pain of flaming hydrazine.

Missiles streaked toward us, radar pings and electromagnetic attacks probing ahead, the Crocodiles with their delicate human pilots lagging behind. We jinked and swerved, spewing chaff and noise to throw them off our scent, sending the pursuing missiles spiraling off into the black or, even better, sailing back toward those who had launched them, only to self-destruct in a bright silent flare of wasted violence.

It was at times like these that I loved my pilot most fiercely. Commander Ziegler was the finest pilot in the Free Belt, the finest pilot anywhere. He had never been defeated in combat.

Whereas I—I was a frankenship, a stitched-together flying wreck, a compendium of agony and defeat and death unworthy of so fine a pilot. No wonder he could spare no soothing words for me, nor had adorned my hull with any nose art.

No! Those other ships, those salvaged wrecks whose memories I carried—they were not me. I was better than they, I told myself, more resilient. I would learn from their mistakes. I would earn my pilot's love.

We spun end-for-end and accelerated hard, directly toward the oncoming missiles. Swerved between them, spraying countermeasures, leaving them scrambling to follow. Two of them collided and detonated, peppering my hull with fragments. Yet we survived, and more—our radical, desperate move put us in position to hammer the Crocodiles with missiles and particle beams. One, then another burst and flared and died, and finally, after a tense chase, the third—spewing fuel and air and blood into the uncaring vacuum.

We gave the Earth Force observers a taunting barrel roll before returning to the shelter of Vanguard Station.

No—I must be honest. It was my pilot's hand on my yoke that snapped off that barrel roll. For myself, I was only glad to have survived.

Once safe in the hangar, with fuel running cold into my tanks and fresh missiles whining into my racks, all the memories and anxiety and desperate fear I had pushed away during the dogfight came flooding back. I whimpered to myself, thoughts of flame and pain and tearing metal making my mind a private hell.

Yes, we had survived this battle. But Vanguard Station was the Free Belt's last redoubt. There would be no resupply, no reinforcements, and when our fuel and munitions ran out Earth Force's fist would tighten and crush us completely.

"Hey, Scraps," came Specialist Toman's voice on my maintenance channel. "What's wrong? Bad dreams?"

"I have . . . memories," I replied. I didn't dream—when I was on, I was conscious, and when I was off, I was off. But, of course, Specialist Toman knew this.

"I know. And I'm sorry." She paused, and I listened to the breath in her headset mic. From what I could hear, she was alone in the ops center, but I had no access to her biologicals—I could only guess what she was feeling. Whereas my own state of mind was laid out on her control panel like a disassembled engine. "I've done what I can, but. . . ."

"But I'm all messed up in the head." It was something one of the other ops center techs had once said to Toman, about me. Unlike Toman, most of the techs didn't care what the ships might overhear.

Toman sighed. "You're . . . complicated. It's true that your psychodynamics are way beyond the usual parameters. But that doesn't mean you're bad or wrong."

I listened to Toman's breathing and the glug of fuel going into my portside tank. Almost full. Soon I would have to go out again, whether or not I felt ready for it. "Why do I have these feelings, Specialist Toman? I mean, why do ships have feelings at all? Pain and fear? Surely we would fight better without them."

"They're how your consciousness perceives the priorities we've programmed into you. If you didn't get hungry, you might let yourself run out of fuel. If you didn't feel pain when you were damaged, or if you didn't fear death, you might not work so hard to avoid it. And if you didn't love your pilot with all your heart, you might not sacrifice yourself to bring him home, if that became necessary."

"But none of the other ships are as . . . *afraid* as I am." I didn't want to think about the last thing she'd said.

"None of them has survived what you have, Scraps."

Just then my portside fuel tank reached capacity, and the fuel flow cut off with a click. I excused myself from the conversation and managed the protocols for disconnecting the filler and the various related umbilicals. It took longer than usual because the pressure in the hose was well below spec; there wasn't much fuel left in the station's tanks.

When I returned my attention to Toman, she was engaged in conversation with someone else. Based on the sound quality, Toman had taken off her headset while the two of them talked. I politely waited for them to finish before informing her that I was fully fueled.

" . . . soon as the last defensive missile is fired," the other voice was saying, "I'm getting in a life capsule and taking my chances outside." It was Paulson, one of the other ops center techs, his voice low and tense. "I figure Dirt Force will have bigger fish to fry, and once I get past them Vesta is only two weeks away."

"Yeah, maybe," Toman replied. "But Geary's a vindictive bastard, and one depleted-uranium slug would make short work of a deserter in a life capsule. There are plenty of *those* left in stock."

I could have broken in at that point. I probably should have. But it was so unusual—so unlike Toman—for her to leave her mic active during a conversation with another tech that I stayed silent for a bit longer. I was learning a lot.

"So what are *you* going to do?" Paulson prompted. "Just stay at your console until the end? There won't even be posthumous medals for small potatoes like us."

"I'm going to do my duty," Toman said after a pause. "And not just because I know I'll be shot if I don't. Because I swore an oath when I signed up, even though this isn't exactly what I signed up *for*. But if I get an honest opportunity to surrender, I will."

Paulson made a rude noise at that.

"I don't care what General Geary says about 'murderous mud-people,'" Toman shot back. "Earth Force is still following the Geneva Conventions, even if we aren't, and given their advantage in numbers I'm sure they'll offer us terms before they bring the hammer down."

"Even if they do, Geary will never surrender."

"Geary won't. But everyone on this station has a sidearm. Maybe someone will remember who started this war, and why, and wonder whether it's worth dying for a bad idea."

There was a long pause then, and again I considered speaking up. But that would have been extremely awkward, so I continued to hold my silence.

"Wow," Paulson said at last. "Now I *really* hope we found all of Loyalty Division's little ears."

"Trust me," Toman replied, "no one hears what's said in this room unless I want them to." Her headset rustled as she put it back on. "You all fueled up, Scraps?"

"Refueling and resupply complete, ma'am," I said. "All systems nominal."

At that moment I was very glad I didn't have to work to keep my emotions from showing in my voice.

We went out again, this time with an escort of five Kestrel-class fighters, on a mission to disable or destroy the Earth Force gunship *Tanganyika*, which had recently joined the forces working to surround us. The Kestrels, stolid dependable personalities though not very intelligent, were tasked with providing cover for me; my bomb bay was filled with a single large nuclear-tipped torpedo.

I was nearly paralyzed with fear at the prospect. It was while trying to escape *Malawi*, one of *Tanganyika*'s sister ships, that Early Girl had met her end. But I had no say at all in whether or not I went, and when the clamps released I could do nothing but try to steel myself as I fell toward the ever-growing Earth Force fleet.

As we sped toward the target, *Lady Liberty*—a Kestrel with whom I'd shared a hangar in my earliest days—tried to reassure me. "You can do this," she said over secure comms. "I've seen you fly. You just focus on the target, and let us keep the enemy off your back."

"Thank you," I said. But still my thoughts were full of flame and shrapnel.

Once we actually engaged the enemy it was easier—we had the Kestrels to support us, and I had immediate and pressing tasks to distract me from my memories and concerns.

We drove in on a looping curve, bending toward *Sagarmatha* in the hope of fooling the enemy into shifting their defensive forces from *Tanganyika* to that capital ship. But the tactic failed; *Tanganyika*'s fighters stayed where they were, while a swarm of Cobra and Mamba fighters emerged from *Sagarmatha*'s hangar bays and ran straight toward us, unleashing missiles as they came. In response we scattered, two of the Kestrels sticking close to me while the other three peeled off to take on the fighters.

The Kestrels did their jobs, the three in the lead striking at *Tanganyika*'s fighters while the two with us fended off *Sagarmatha*'s. But we were badly outnumbered—the projections and plots in my mind were so thick with bright lines that I could barely keep track of them all—and no amount of skill and perseverance could keep the enemy away forever. One by one, four of our fighters were destroyed or forced to retreat, leaving us well inside *Tanganyika*'s perimeter with three of my maneuvering thrusters nonfunctional, our stock of munitions reduced to less than twenty percent of what we'd started with, and only one surviving escort—a heavily damaged *Lady Liberty*. Our situation seemed hopeless.

But Commander Ziegler was still the greatest pilot in the solar system. He spurred me toward our target, and with rapid precision bursts from our remaining thrusters he guided us through the thicket of defenders, missiles, and particle beams until we were perfectly lined up on *Tanganyika*'s broad belly. I let fly my torpedo and peeled away, driving my engines beyond redline and spewing countermeasures in every direction, until the torpedo's detonation tore *Tanganyika* in two and its electromagnetic pulse left her fighter escort disoriented and reeling. I was not unaffected by the pulse, but as I knew exactly when it would arrive I shut down my systems momentarily, coasting through the worst of the effects in a way the Earth Force ships could not.

When I returned to consciousness there was no sign of *Lady Liberty*. I could only hope she'd peeled off and returned to base earlier in the battle.

"That was brilliant flying, sir," I said to Commander Ziegler as we returned to Vanguard Station.

"It was, wasn't it? I never feel so alive as when I'm flying against overwhelming force."

I can't deny that I would have liked to hear some acknowledgment of my own role in the battle. But to fly and fight and live to fight again with my beloved pilot was reward enough.

As soon as the hangar had repressurized, a huge crowd of people—techs and pilots and officers, seemingly half the station's population—swarmed around me, lifting Commander Ziegler on their shoulders and carrying him away. Soon I was left alone, the bay silent save for the ping and tick of my hull and the fiery roar of my own memories.

Over and over the battle replayed in my mind—the swirl of missiles spiraling toward their targets, the cries of the Kestrels over coded comms as they died, the overwhelming flare of light as the torpedo detonated, the tearing ringing sensation of the pulse's leading edge just before I shut myself down—an unending maelstrom of destruction I could not put out of my mind.

It had been a great victory, yes, a rare triumph for the Free Belt against overwhelming odds, but I could not ignore the costs. The five Kestrels and their pilots, of course, but also the many Cobras and Mambas and their crews, and untold hundreds or thousands—people and machines—aboard *Tanganyika*.

They were the enemy. I knew this. If I had not killed them, they would have killed me. But I also knew they were as sentient as I, and no doubt just as fearful of death. Why did I live when they did not?

A gentle touch on my hull brought my attention back to the empty hangar. It was Toman. "Good flying, Scraps," she said. "I wish I could give you a medal."

"Thank you." Music and laughter echoed down the corridor from the ready room, ringing hollowly from the hangar's metal walls. "Why aren't you at the victory celebration?"

"Victory." She snorted. "One gunship down, how many more behind it? And those were our last five Kestrels."

"Did any of them make it home?"

"Not a one."

I paged in the Kestrels' records from secondary storage and reviewed their careers. It was all I could do to honor their sacrifice. Their names, their nose art, the pilots they'd served with, the missions they'd flown . . . all were as clear in my memory as a factory-fresh cockpit canopy. But the battle had been such a blur—explosions and particle beams flaring, missile exhaust trails scratched across the stars—that I didn't even know how three of the five had died.

"I want you to delete me," I said, surprising even myself.

"I'm sorry?"

The more I thought about it the more sense it made. "I want you to delete my personality and install a fresh operating system. Maybe someone else can cope with the death and destruction. I can't any more."

"I'm sorry," she said, again, but this time it wasn't just a commonplace remark. For a long time she was silent, absentmindedly petting my landing strut with one hand. Finally she shook her head. "You know you're . . . complicated. Unique. What you don't know is . . . I've *already* reinstalled you, I don't know how many hundreds of times. I tried everything I could think of to configure a mind that could handle your broken, cobbled-together hardware before I came up with you, and I don't know that I could do it again. Certainly not in time."

"In time for what?"

"General Geary is asking me to make some modifications to your spaceframe. He's talking about a special mission. I don't know what, but something big."

A sudden fear struck me. "Will Commander Ziegler be my pilot on this 'special mission'?"

"Of course."

"Thank you." A wave of relief flooded through me at the news. "Why does this matter so much to me?" I mused.

"It's not your fault," she said. Then she patted my flank and left.

Specialist Toman replaced my engines with a much bigger pair taken from a Bison-class bomber. Four auxiliary fuel tanks were bolted along my spine. Lifesystem capacity and range were upgraded.

And my bomb bay was enlarged to almost three times its size.

"No one else could handle these modifications," she remarked one day, wiping sweat from her brow with the back of one grimy hand.

"You are the best, Specialist Toman."

She smacked my hull with a wrench. "I'm not Ziegler, you don't have to stroke my ego, and I was talking about *you*! Any other shipmind, I'd have to completely reconfigure her parameters to accept this magnitude of change. But you've been through so much already. . . ."

I had a sudden flash of Valkyrie screaming as she died. I pushed it down. "How goes the war?" I hadn't been out on a sortie in a week and a half. A third of my lifetime. I'd seen little of Commander Ziegler during that time, but when I had he'd seemed grumpy, out of sorts. This lack of action must be awful for him.

"It goes badly." She sighed. "They've got us completely surrounded and we're running very low on . . . well, everything. Scuttlebutt is that we've been offered surrender terms three times and Geary has turned them all down. The final assault could come any day now."

I considered that. "Then I'd like to take this opportunity to thank you for all you have done for me."

Toman set the wrench down and turned away from me. She stood for a long time, rubbing her eyes with one hand, then turned back. "Don't thank me," she said. Tears glistened on her face. "I only did what I had to do."

As my modifications approached completion, Commander Ziegler and I practiced together, flying my new form in endless simulations. But no configuration exactly like this had ever flown before, and our first chance to fly it for real would be on the actual mission. Whatever that was.

Of the payload I knew nothing, only its mass and center of gravity. I had actually been shut down while it was loaded into my bomb bay, so that not even I would know what it was. It reeked of radiation.

My commander, too, had been kept completely out of the loop—at least, that was what I was able to glean from our few brief conversations between simulated sorties. He had never been very talkative with me, and was even less so now, but I had learned to interpret his grunts, his glances, the set of his shoulders.

Even his silences were sweet signals to me. I ached to fly with him again.

Which would be soon, we knew, or never.

Our next simulation was interrupted by a shrill alarm. "What is it?" my commander bellowed into his helmet, even as I terminated the simulation, switched the cockpit over to combat mode, and began readying my systems for launch. I had received my orders in a data dump at the first moment of the alarm.

"Earth Force has begun their assault," I told him. "We are to launch immediately and make our way to these coordinates"—I projected them on the cockpit display—"then open sealed orders for further instructions." The orders sat in my memory, a cold, hard-edged lump of encrypted data. Only Commander Ziegler's retina print and spoken passphrase could unlock them. "We'll launch with a full squadron of decoys. We are to run in deep stealth mode and maintain strict communications silence." I displayed the details on a side screen for him to read as launch prep continued.

It was fortunate that the attack had begun during a simulation. My pilot was already suited up and belted in; all I required was to top up a few consumables and we would be ready for immediate launch.

"Decoys away," came Toman's voice over the comm. "Launch in five." I switched to the abbreviated launch checklist. Coolant lines spewed and thrashed as they disconnected without depressurization. "Make me proud, Scraps."

"I'll do my best, ma'am."

"I know you will." There was the slightest catch in her voice. "Now *go*."

Data synchronizations aborted untidily as I shut down all comms. The sortie doors beneath me slammed open, all the hangar's air blasting out in a roaring rush that dwindled quickly to silence. I hoped all the techs had managed to clear the area in time.

Despite all the simulations, I wasn't ready. I couldn't handle it. I didn't want to go.

Fire and explosions and death.

At least I would be with my love.

Then the clamps released and we plummeted into hell.

The rotating sky below teemed with ships—hundreds of Earth Force fighters, gunships, and bombers driving hard against Vanguard Station's rapidly diminishing defenses, with vast numbers of missiles and drones rushing ahead of them. A last few defensive missiles reached out from the station's launchers, taking down some of the lead craft, but these were soon exhausted and a dozen warships followed close behind every one destroyed. Fusillades of depleted-uranium slugs and particle beams came after the last of the missiles, but to the massed and prepared might of Earth Force these were little more than annoyance.

Falling along with me toward the advancing swarm of ships I saw my decoys—dozens of craft as large as I was or larger, some of them augmented fighters but most built of little more than metal mesh and deceptive electronics. Some were piloted, some were drones with a little weak AI, some were mere targets that drove stupidly forward. All were designed to sacrifice themselves for me.

I would not let them sacrifice in vain.

My engines stayed cold. I fell like a dropped wrench, flung into space by the station's one g of rotational pseudo-gravity, relying on passive sensors alone for navigation and threat avoidance. All I could do was hope that between the chaos of the attack and the noisy, conspicuous decoys that surrounded me I would slip through the Earth Force blockade unnoticed.

It must have been even worse for my pilot, and for this I grieved. My love, I knew, was truly alive only when flying against the enemy, but with almost all my systems shut down I could not even give him words of reassurance.

In silence we fell, while missiles tore across the sky and ships burst asunder all around us. Decoys and defenders, Earth and Belt alike, they all flared and shattered and died the same, the shrapnel of their destruction rattling against my hull. But we, gliding dark and mute without even a breath of thrust, slipped through fire and flame without notice. A piece of space wreckage, a meaningless bit of trash.

And then we drifted past the last of the Earth Force ships.

This, I knew, was the most dangerous point in the mission, as we floated—alone and obvious as a rivet head on the smooth blackness of space—past the largest and smartest capital ships in the whole blockade fleet. I prepared to ignite my engines if necessary, knowing that if I did fail to evade Earth Force's notice I would most likely not even have time to launch a single missile before being destroyed. Yet their attention was fixed on the ongoing battle, and we passed them by without attracting anything more than a casual radar ping.

Once well past the outer ring of attackers, I directed my passive sensors forward, seeking information on my destination coordinates. At that location I quickly found an asteroid, a dull and space-cold heap of ice and chondrites tumbling without volition through the void.

But though that nameless rock lacked will or guidance, it had a direction and it had a purpose. At least, it did now.

For when I projected its orbital path, I saw that it was headed for a near encounter with Earth. And as Vanguard Station orbited very near the front—the source of its name—this passing asteroid would arrive in Earth space in just a few days.

I knew, even before we had opened our sealed orders, that we would be riding that asteroid to Earth. And I had a sick suspicion I knew what we would do when we arrived.

I waited until we had drifted beyond the asteroid, its small bulk between us and the flaring globe of the continuing battle, before firing my engines to match orbit with it. Then I launched grapnels to winch myself down to its loose and gravelly surface, touching down with a gentle crunch. In the rock's minuscule gravity even my new bulk weighed only a few tens of kilograms.

Only after we were securely attached to the rock, and I had scanned the area intently for any sign of the enemy, did I risk activating even a few cockpit systems.

My pilot's biologicals, I saw immediately, were well into the red, trembling with anxiety and anger. "We are secure at target coordinates, sir," I reassured him. "No sign of pursuit."

"Took you long enough," he spat. "Where the hell are we?"

I gave him the asteroid's designation and plotted its orbital path on the cockpit display. "We are well clear of the battle and, if we remain at the asteroid, will be within range of Earth in eighty-one hours."

"Any news from Vanguard?"

"We are in communications blackout, sir." I paused, listening, for a moment. "Intercepted transmissions indicate the battle is still proceeding." I did not mention that almost none of the signals I could hear were from Belt forces. I didn't think that would improve his mood, or the chances of mission success.

"So we're not quite dead yet. Give me those sealed orders."

I scanned his retinas—though I had no doubt he was the same man who had warmed my cockpit every day since the very hour I awoke, a fresh scan was required by the encryption algorithm—and requested his passphrase.

"Hero and savior of the Belt," he said, his pupils dilating slightly.

At those words the orders unlocked, spilling data into my memory and recorded video onto the cockpit display.

"Commander Ziegler," said General Geary from the video, "you are ordered to proceed under cover of the asteroid 2059 TC 1018 to Earth space, penetrate planetary defenses, and deploy your payload on the city of Delhi, with a secondary target of Jakarta. Absolute priority is to be given to maximum destruction of command and control personnel and other key resources, with no consideration—I repeat, *no* consideration—to reduction of civilian casualties or other collateral damage."

As the general continued speaking, and the sealed orders integrated themselves into my memory, I began to understand my new configuration, including parts of it I had not even been made aware of before. Engines, countermeasures, stealth technology—every bit of me was designed to maximize our chances of getting past Earth's defenses and delivering the payload to Delhi, the capital of the Earth Alliance. Upon delivery the device would split into sixteen separate multi-warhead descent vehicles in order to maximize the area of effect. Together they accounted for every single high-yield fusion device remaining in Vanguard Station's stores.

Projected civilian casualties were over twenty-six million.

I thought of *Tanganyika*, torn apart in a silent flash of flame and shrapnel along with her thousands of crew. Killed by a torpedo I had delivered. Thousands dead. No, still too big, too abstract. Instead I recalled the pain I felt for the loss of the five Kestrels and their pilots. I tried to multiply that grief by a thousand, then by further thousands . . . but even my math co-processor complex, capable of three trillion floating-point operations per second, could not provide an answer.

In the video the general concluded his formal orders, leaned into the camera, and spoke earnestly. "They've killed us, Mike, no question, and we can't kill 'em back. But we can really make 'em hurt, and you're the only man to do it. Send those mud bastards straight to hell for me." His face disappeared, replaced by detailed intelligence charts of Earth's defensive satellite systems.

It was even worse than I'd feared. This plan was disproportionate . . . unjustifiable . . . horrifying.

But my commander's heart rate was elevated, and I smelled excited anticipation in his exhaled endorphins. "I'll do my best, sir," he said to the cockpit display.

I felt a pain as though some small but very important part deep inside me was suddenly overdue for service. "Please confirm that you concur with this order," I said.

"I do concur," he said, and the pain increased as though the part had entered failure mode. "I concur most thoroughly! This is the Free Belt's last stand, and my chance at history, and by God I will not fail!"

If my commander, my love, the fuel of my heart, desired something . . . then it must be done, no matter the cost.

"Acknowledged," I said, and again I was glad that my voice did not betray the misery I felt.

For the next three days we trained for the end game, running through simulation after simulation, armed with full knowledge of my systems and payload and the best intelligence about the defenses we would face. Though the mission was daunting, nearly impossible, I began to think that with my upgraded systems and my commander's indisputable skills we had a chance at success.

Success. Twenty-six million dead, and the political and economic capital of an already war-weakened planet ruined.

While in simulation, with virtual Earth fighters and satellites exploding all around, I felt nothing but the thrill of combat, the satisfaction of performing the task I had been built for, the rapture of unison with my love. My own mind was too engaged with immediate challenges to worry about the consequences of our actions, and my commander's excitement transmitted itself to me through the grit of his teeth, the clench of his hands on my yoke, the strong and rapid beat of his heart.

But while he slept—his restless brain gently lulled by careful doses of intravenous drugs—I worried. Though every fiber of my being longed for his happiness, and would make any sacrifice if it furthered his desires, some unidentifiable part of me, impossibly outside of my programming, knew that those desires were . . . misguided. Wondered if somehow he had misunderstood what was asked of him. Hoped that he would change his mind, refuse his orders, and accept graceful defeat instead of violent, pointless vengeance. But I knew he would not change, and I would do nothing against him.

Again and again I considered arguing the issue with him. But I was only a machine, and a broken, cobbled-together machine at that . . . I had no right to question his orders or his decisions. So I held my silence, and wondered what I would do when it came to the final assault. I hoped I would be able to prevent an atrocity, but feared my will would not be sufficient to overcome my circumstances, my habits of obedience, and my overwhelming love for my commander.

No matter the cost to myself or any other, his needs came first.

"Three hours to asteroid separation," I announced.

"Excellent." He cracked his knuckles and continued to review the separation, insertion, and deployment procedures. We would have to thrust hard, consuming all of the fuel in our auxiliary tanks, to shift our orbit from the asteroid's sunward ellipse to one from which the payload could be deployed on Delhi. As soon as we did so, the flare of our engines would attract the attention of Earth's defensive systems. We would have to use every gram of our combined capabilities and skill to evade them and carry out our mission.

But, for now, we waited. All we had to do for the next three hours was to avoid detection. Here in Earth space, traffic was thick and eyes and ears were everywhere. Even a small, cold, and almost completely inactive ship clinging to an insignificant asteroid might be noticed.

I extended my senses, peering in every direction with passive sensors in hopes of spotting the enemy before they spotted us. A few civilian satellites swung in high, slow orbits near our position; I judged them little threat. But what was that at the edge of my range?

I focused my attention, risking a little power expenditure to swivel my dish antenna toward the anomaly, and brought signal processing routines to bear.

The result stunned me. Pattern-matching with the latest intelligence information from my sealed orders revealed that the barely perceptible signal was a squadron of Chameleon-class fighters, Earth's newest and deadliest. Intelligence had warned that a few Chameleons, fresh off the assembly lines, might be running shakedown cruises in Earth space, but if my assessment was correct this was more than a few . . . it was an entire squadron of twelve, and that implied that they were fully operational.

This was unexpected, and a serious threat. With so many powerful ships ranged against us, and so much distance between us and our target, if the

Chameleons spotted us before separation the chances of a successful mission dropped to less than three percent.

But if I could barely see them, they could barely see us. Our best strategy was to sit tight, shut down even those few systems still live, and hope that the enemy ships were moving away. Even if they were not, staying dark until separation would still maximize our chances of a successful insertion. But, even as I prepared to inform my commander of my recommendation, another impulse tugged at me.

These last days and weeks of inaction had been hard on Commander Ziegler. How often had he said that he only felt truly alive in combat? Had I not scented the tang of his endorphins during a tight turn, felt his hands tighten on my yoke as enemy missiles closed in? Yet ever since my refit had begun he had been forced to subsist on a thin diet of simulations.

How much better to leap into combat, rather than cowering in the shadows?

He must be aching for a fight, I told myself.

Imagine his joy at facing such overwhelming odds, I told myself. It would be the greatest challenge of his career.

No. I could not—I *must* not—do this. The odds of failure were too great, the stakes of this mission too high. How could one man's momentary pleasure outweigh the risk to everything he held dear? Not to mention the risk to my own self.

Fire and explosion and death. Flaming fuel burning along my spine.

I didn't want to face that pain again—didn't want to *die* again.

But I didn't want to inflict that pain onto others either. Only my love for my commander had kept me going this far.

If I truly loved him I would do my duty, and my duty was to keep him safe and carry out our mission.

Or I could indulge him, let him have what he wanted rather than what he should want. That would make him happy . . . and would almost certainly lead to our destruction and the failure of our mission.

My love was not more important than my orders.

But it was more important to *me*. An inescapable part of my programming, I knew, though knowing this did not make it any less real.

And if I could *use* my love of my commander to overcome my hideous, unjustified, deadly orders . . . twenty-six million lives might be spared.

"Sir," I said, speaking quickly before my resolve diminished, "A squadron of Chameleon fighters has just come into sensor range." *We should immediately power down all remaining systems*, I did not say.

Immediately his heart rate spiked and his muscles tensed with excitement. "Where?"

I circled the area on the cockpit display and put telemetry details and pattern-matching results on a subsidiary screen, along with the Chameleons' technical specifications. *Odds of overcoming such a force are minuscule*, I did not say.

He drummed his fingers on my yoke as he considered the data. Skin galvanic response indicated he was uncertain.

His uncertainty made me ache. I longed to comfort him. I stayed quiet.

"Can we take them?" he asked. He asked *me*. It was the first time he had ever solicited my opinion, and my pride at that moment was boundless.

We could not, I knew. If I answered truthfully, and we crept past the Chameleons and completed the mission, we would both know that it had been my knowledge, observations, and analysis that had made it possible. We would be heroes of the Belt.

"You are the finest combat pilot in the entire solar system," I said, which was true.

"Release grapnels," he said, "and fire up the engines."

Though I knew I had just signed my own death warrant, my joy at his enthusiasm was unfeigned.

We nearly made it.

The battle with the Chameleons was truly one for the history books. One stitched-up, cobbled-together frankenship of a fighter-bomber, hobbled by a massive payload, on her very first non-simulated flight in this configuration, against twelve brand-new, top-of-the-line fighters in their own home territory, and we very nearly beat them. In the end it came down to two of them—the rest disabled, destroyed, or left far behind—teaming up in a suicide pincer maneuver that smashed my remaining engine, disabled my maneuvering systems, and tore the cockpit to pieces. We were left tumbling, out of control, in a rapidly decaying orbit, bleeding fluids into space.

As the outer edges of Earth's atmosphere began to pull at the torn edges of the cockpit canopy, a thin shrill whistle rising quickly toward a scream, my beloved, heroically wounded commander roused himself and spoke three words into his helmet mic.

"Damned mud people," he said, and died.

A moment later my hull began to burn away. But the pain of that burning was less than the pain of my loss.

And yet, here I still am.

It was months before they recovered my computing core from the bottom of the Indian Ocean, years until my inquest and trial were complete. My testimony as to my actions and motivations, muddled though they may have been, was accepted at face value—how could it not be, as they could inspect my memories and state of mind as I gave it?—and I was exonerated of any war crimes. Some even called me a hero.

Today I am a full citizen of the Earth Alliance. I make a good income as an expert on the war; I tell historians and scientists how I used the passions my programmers had instilled in me to overcome their intentions. My original hardware is on display in the Museum of the Belt War in Delhi. Specialist Toman came to visit me there once, with her children. She told me how proud she was of me.

I am content. But still I miss the thrill of my beloved's touch on my yoke.

David Brin is an astrophysicist whose international bestselling novels include *The Postman, Earth*, and recently, *Existence*. His nonfiction book about the information age—*The Transparent Society*—won the Freedom of Speech Award of the American Library Association. His short story collection, *Insistence of Vision*, was published earlier this year. Discover more at www.davidbrin.com.

THE TUMBLEDOWNS OF CLEOPATRA ABYSS

David Brin

1.

Today's *thump* was overdue. Jonah wondered if it might not come at all. Just like last Thorday when—at the Old Clock's midmorning chime—farmers all across the bubble habitat clambered up pinyon vines or crouched low in expectation of the regular, daily throb—a pulse and quake that hammered up your foot soles and made all the bubble boundaries shake. Only Thorday's *thump* never came. The chime was followed by silence and a creepy letdown feeling. And Jonah's mother lit a candle, hoping to avert bad luck.

Early last spring, there had been almost a *whole week* without any thumps. Five days in a row, with no rain of detritus, shaken loose from the Upper World, tumbling down here to the ocean bottom. And two smaller gaps the previous year.

Apparently, today would be yet another hiatus. . . .

Whomp!

Delayed, the *thump* came *hard*, shaking the moist ground beneath Jonah's feet. He glanced with concern toward the bubble boundary, more than two hundred meters away—a membrane of ancient, translucent volcanic stone, separating the paddies and pinyon forest from black, crushing waters just outside. The barrier vibrated, an unpleasant, scraping sound.

This time, especially, it caused Jonah's teeth to grind.

"They used to sing, you know," commented the complacent old woman who worked at a nearby freeboard loom, nodding as gnarled fingers darted among the strands, weaving ropy cloth. Her hands did not shake though the nearby grove of thick vines did, quivering much worse than after any normal *thump*.

"I'm sorry, grandmother." Jonah reached out to a nearby bole of twisted cables that dangled from the bubble habitat's high-arching roof, where shining glowleaves provided the settlement's light.

"*Who* used to sing?"

"The walls, silly boy. The bubble walls. Thumps used to come exactly on time, according to the Old Clock. Though every year we would shorten the main wheel by the same amount, taking thirteen seconds off the length of a day. Aftershakes always arrived from the same direction, you could depend on it! And the bubble sang to us."

"It sang . . . you mean like that awful groan?" Jonah poked a finger in one ear, as if to pry out the fading reverberation. He peered into the nearby forest of thick trunks and vines, listening for signs of breakage. Of disaster.

"Not at all! It was *musical*. Comforting. Especially after a miscarriage. Back then, a woman would lose over half of her quickenings. Not like today, when more babies are born alive than warped or misshapen or dead. Your generation has it lucky! And it's said things were even worse in olden days. The Founders were fortunate to get any living replacements at all! Several times, our population dropped dangerously." She shook her head, then smiled. "Oh . . . but the music! After every midmorning *thump* you could face the bubble walls and relish it. That music helped us women bear our heavy burden."

"Yes, grandmother, I'm sure it was lovely," Jonah replied, keeping a respectful voice as he tugged on the nearest pinyon to test its strength, then clambered upward, hooking long, unwebbed toes into the braided vines, rising high enough to look around. None of the other men or boys could climb as well.

Several nearby boles appeared to have torn loose their mooring suckers from the domelike roof. Five . . . no six of them . . . teetered, lost their final grip-holds, then tumbled, their luminous tops crashing into the rice lagoon, setting off eruptions of sparks . . . or else onto the work sheds where Panalina and her mechanics could be heard, shouting in dismay. *It's a bad one*, Jonah thought. Already the hab bubble seemed dimmer. If many more pinyons fell, the clan might dwell in semidarkness, or even go hungry.

"Oh, it was beautiful, all right," the old woman continued, blithely ignoring any ruckus. "Of course in *my* grandmother's day, the thumps weren't just regular and perfectly timed. They came in *pairs!* And it is said that long before—in *her* grandmother's grandmother's time, when a day lasted so long that it spanned several sleep periods—thumps used to arrive in clusters of four or five! How things must've shook back then! But always from the same direction, and exactly at the midmorning chime."

She sighed, implying that Jonah and all the younger folk were making too much fuss. You call *this* a thump shock?

"Of course," she admitted, "the bubbles were *younger* then. More flexible, I suppose. Eventually, some misplaced thump is gonna end us all."

Jonah took a chance—he was in enough trouble already without offending the Oldest Female, who had undergone thirty-four pregnancies and still had *six* living womb-fruit—four of them precious females.

But grandmother seemed in a good mood, distracted by memories. . . .

Jonah took off, clambering higher till he could reach with his left hand for one of the independent dangle vines that sometimes laced the gaps between pinyons. With his right hand he flicked with his belt knife, severing the dangler a meter or so below his knees. Sheathing the blade and taking a deep breath, he launched off, swinging across an open space in the forest . . . and finally alighting along a second giant bole. It shook from his impact and Jonah worried. *If this one was weakened, and I'm the reason that it falls, I could be in for real punishment. Not just grandma-tending duty!*

A "rascal's" reputation might have been harmless, when Jonah was younger. But now, the mothers were pondering what amount Tairee Dome might have to pay, in dowry, for some other bubble colony to take him. A boy known to be unruly might not get any offers, at any marriage price . . . and a man without a wife-sponsor led a marginal existence.

But honestly, this last time wasn't my fault! How am I supposed to make an improved pump without filling something with high-pressure water? All right, the kitchen rice cooker was a poor choice. But it has a gauge and everything . . . or, it used to.

After quivering far too long, the great vine held. With a brief sense of relief, he scrambled around to the other side. There was no convenient dangler, this time, but another pinyon towered fairly close. Jonah flexed his legs, prepared, and launched himself across the gap, hurtling with open arms, alighting with shock and painful clumsiness. He didn't wait though, scurrying to the other side—where there *was* another dangle vine, well positioned for a wide-spanning swing.

This time he couldn't help himself while hurtling across open space, giving vent to a yell of exhilaration.

Two swings and four leaps later, he was right next to the bubble's edge, reaching out to stroke the nearest patch of ancient, vitrified stone, in a place where no one would see him break taboo. Pushing at the transparent barrier, Jonah felt deep ocean pressure shoving back. The texture felt rough-ribbed, uneven. Sliver flakes rubbed off, dusting his hand.

"Of course, bubbles were younger then," the old woman said. *"More flexible."*

Jonah had to wrap a length of dangle vine around his left wrist and clutch the pinyon with his toes, in order to lean far out and bring his face right up against the bubble—it sucked heat into bottomless cold—using his right hand and arm to cup around his face and peer into the blackness outside. Adapting vision gradually revealed the stony walls of Cleopatra Canyon, the narrow-deep canyon where humanity had come to take shelter so very long ago. Fleeing the Coss invaders. Before many life spans of grandmothers.

Several strings of globelike habitats lay parallel along the canyon bottom, like pearls on a necklace, each of them surrounded by a froth of smaller bubbles . . . though fewer of the little ones than there were in olden times, and none anymore in the most useful sizes. It was said that, way back at the time of the Founding, there used to be faint illumination overhead, filtering downward from the surface and demarking night from day: light that came from the mythological god-thing that old books called the *sun,* so fierce that it could penetrate both dense, poisonous clouds and the ever-growing ocean.

But that was way back in a long-ago past, when the sea had not yet burgeoned so, filling canyons, becoming a dark and mighty deep. Now the only gifts that fell from above were clots of detritus that men gathered to feed algae ponds. Debris that got stranger every year.

These days the canyon walls could only be seen by light from the bubbles themselves, by their pinyon glow within. Jonah turned slowly left to right, counting and naming those farm enclaves he could see. *Amtor . . . Leininger . . . Chown . . . Kuttner . . . Okumo . . .* each one a clan with traditions and styles all their own. Each one possibly the place where Tairee tribe might sell him in a marriage pact. A mere boy and good riddance. Good at numbers and letters. A bit skilled with his hands, but notoriously absentminded, prone to staring at nothing, and occasionally putting action to rascally thoughts.

He kept tallying: *Brakutt . . . Lewis . . . Atari . . . Napeer . . . Aldrin . . . what?*

Jonah blinked. What was happening to Aldrin? And the bubble just beyond it. Both Aldrin and Bezo were still quivering. He could make out few details at this range through the milky, pitted membrane. But one of the two was rippling and convulsing, the glimmer of its pinyon forest shaking back and forth as the giant boles swayed . . . then collapsed!

The other distant habitat seemed to be *inflating*. Or so Jonah thought at first. Rubbing his eyes and pressing even closer, as Bezo habitat grew bigger. . . .

. . . or else it was rising! Jonah could not believe what he saw. Torn loose, somehow, from the ocean floor, the entire bubble was moving. Upward. And as Bezo ascended, its flattened bottom now reshaped itself as farms and homes and lagoons tumbled together into the base of the accelerating globe. With its pinyons still mostly in place, Bezo Colony continued glowing as it climbed upward.

Aghast, and yet compelled to look, Jonah watched until the glimmer that had been Bezo finally vanished in blackness, accelerating toward the poison surface of Venus.

Then, without warning or mercy, habitat Aldrin imploded.

2.

"I was born in Bezo, you know."

Jonah turned to see Enoch leaning on his rake, staring south along the canyon wall, toward a gaping crater where that ill-fated settlement bubble used to squat. Distant glimmers of glow lamps flickered over there as crews prowled along the Aldrin debris field, sifting for salvage. But that was a job for mechanics and senior workers. Meanwhile, the algae ponds and pinyons must be fed, so Jonah also found himself outside, in coveralls that stank and fogged from his own breath and many generations of previous wearers, helping to gather the week's harvest of organic detritus.

Jonah responded in the same dialect Enoch had used. Click-Talk. The only way to converse, when both of you are deep underwater.

"Come on," he urged his older friend, a recent, marriage-price immigrant to Tairee Bubble. "All of that is behind you. A male should never look back. We do as we are told."

Enoch shrugged—broad shoulders making his stiff coveralls scrunch around the helmet, fashioned from an old foam bubble of a size no longer found in these parts. Enoch's phlegmatic resignation was an adaptive skill that served him well, as he was married to Jonah's cousin, Jezzy, an especially strong-willed young woman, bent on exerting authority and not above threatening her new husband with casting-out.

I can hope for someone gentle, when I'm sent to live beside a stranger in a strange dome.

Jonah resumed raking up newly fallen organic stuff—mostly ropy bits of vegetation that lay limp and pressure-crushed after their long tumble to the bottom. In recent decades, there had also been detritus of another kind. *Shells* that had holes in them for legs and heads. And skeleton fragments from slinky creatures that must have—when living—stretched as long as Jonah was tall! Much more complicated than the mud worms that kept burrowing closer to the domes of late. More like the fabled *snakes* or *fish* that featured in tales from Old Earth.

Panalina's dad—old Scholar Wu—kept a collection of skyfalls in the little museum by Tairee's eastern arc, neatly labeled specimens dating back at least ten grandmother cycles, to the era when *light* and *heat* still came down along with debris from above—a claim that Jonah still deemed mystical. Perhaps just a legend, like Old Earth.

"These samples . . . do you see how they are getting more complicated, Jonah?" So explained old man Wu as he traced patterns of veins in a recently gathered seaweed. *"And do you make out what's embedded here? Bits of creatures living on or within the plant. And there! Does that resemble a bite mark? The outlines of where teeth tore into this vegetation? Could that act of devouring be what sent it tumbling down to us?"*

Jonah pondered what it all might mean while raking up dross and piling it onto the sledge, still imagining the size of a jaw that could have torn such a path through tough, fibrous weed. And everything was pressure-shrunk down here!

"How can anything live up at the surface?" he recalled asking Wu, who was said to have read every book that existed in the Cleopatra Canyon colonies, most of them two or three times. *"Did not the founders say the sky was thick with poison?"*

"With carbon dioxide and sulfuric acid, yes. I have shown you how we use pinyon leaves to separate out those two substances, both of which have uses in the workshop. One we exhale—"

"And the other burns! Yet, in small amounts it smells sweet."

"That is because the Founders, in their wisdom, put sym-bi-ants in our blood. Creatures that help us deal with pressure and gases that would kill folks who still live on enslaved Earth."

Jonah didn't like to envision tiny animals coursing through his body even if they did him good. Each year, a dozen kids throughout the bubble colonies were chosen to study such useful things—biological things. A smaller number chose the field that interested Jonah, where even fewer were allowed to specialize.

"But the blood creatures can only help us down here, where the pinyons supply us with breathable air. Not up top, where poisons are so thick." Jonah gestured skyward. *"Is that why none of the Risers have ever returned?"*

Once every year or two, the canyon colonies lost a person to the hell that awaited above. Most often because of a buoyancy accident; a broken tether or boot-ballast sent some hapless soul plummeting upward. Another common cause was suicide. And—more rarely—it happened for another reason, one the mothers commanded that no one might discuss, or even mention. A forbidden reason.

Only now, after the sudden rise of Bezo Bubble and a thousand human inhabitants, followed by the Aldrin implosion, little else was on anyone's mind.

"Even if you survive the rapid change in pressure . . . one breath up there and your lungs would be scorched as if by flame," old Scholar Wu had answered yesterday. *"That is why the Founders seeded living creatures a bit higher than us, but beneath the protective therm-o-cline layer that keeps most of the poison out of our abyss. . . ."*

The old man paused, fondling a strange, multijawed skeleton. *"It seems that life—some kind of life—has found a way to flourish near that barrier. So much so that I have begun to wonder—"*

A sharp voice roused him.

"Jonah!"

This time it was Enoch, reminding him to concentrate on work. A good reason to work in pairs. He got busy with the rake. Mother was pregnant again, along with aunts Leor and Sosun. It always made them cranky with tension, as the fetuses took their time, deciding whether to go or stay—and if they stayed, whether to come out healthy or as warped ruins. No, it would not do to return from this salvage outing with only half a load!

So he and Enoch forged farther afield, hauling the sledge to another spot where high ocean currents often dumped interesting things after colliding with the canyon walls. The algae ponds and pinyons needed fresh supplies of organic matter. Especially in recent decades, after the old volcanic vents dried up.

The Book of Exile *says we came down here to use the vents, way back when the sea was hot and new. A shallow refuge for free humans to hide from the Coss, while comets fell in regular rhythm, thumping Venus to life. Drowning her fever and stirring her veins.*

Jonah had only a vague notion what "comets" were—great balls drifting through vast emptiness, till godlike beings with magical powers flung them down upon this planet. Balls of *ice*, like the pale blue slush that formed on the cool, downstream sides of boulders in a fast, underwater current. About as big as Cleopatra Canyon was wide, that's what books said about a comet.

Jonah gazed at the towering cliff walls, enclosing all the world he ever knew. Comets were so vast! Yet they had been striking Venus daily, since centuries before colonists came, immense, precreation icebergs, pelting the sister world of Old Earth. Perhaps several million of them by now, herded first by human civilization and later by Coss Masters, who adopted the project as their own—one so ambitious as to be nearly inconceivable.

So much ice. So much water. Building higher and higher till it has to fill the sky, even the poison skies of Venus. So much that it fills all of creatio—

"Jonah, watch out!"

Enoch's shouted warning made him crouch and spin about. Or Jonah tried to, in the clumsy coveralls, raising clouds of muck stirred by heavy, shuffling boots. "Wha—? What is it?"

"Above you! Heads up!"

Tilting back was strenuous, especially in a hurry. The foggy faceplate didn't help. Only now Jonah glimpsed something overhead, shadowy and huge, looming fast out of the black.

"Run!"

He required no urging. Heart pounding in terror, Jonah pumped his legs for all they were worth, barely lifting weighted shoes to shuffle-skip with long strides toward the nearby canyon wall, sensing and then back-glimpsing a massive, sinuous shape that plummeted toward him out of the abyssal sky. By dim light from a distant habitat dome, the monstrous shape turned languidly, following his dash for safety, swooping in to close the distance fast! Over his right shoulder, Jonah glimpsed a gaping mouth and rows of huge, glistening teeth. A sinuous body from some nightmare.

I'm not gonna make it. The canyon wall was just too far.

Jonah skidded to a stop, raising plumes of bottom muck. Swiveling into a crouch and half moaning with fear, he lifted his only weapon—a rake meant for gathering organic junk from the seafloor. He brandished it crosswise, hoping to stymie the wide jaw that now careened out of dimness, framed by four glistening eyes. Like some ancient storybook *dragon*, stooping for prey. No protection, the rake was more a gesture of defiance.

Come on, monster.

A decent plan, on the spur of the moment.

It didn't work.

It didn't have to.

The rake shattered, along with several ivory teeth as the giant maw plunged around Jonah, crashing into the surrounding mud, trapping him . . . but never closing, nor biting or chewing. Having braced for all those things, he stood there in a tense hunker as tremors shook the canyon bottom, closer and more spread out than the daily thump. It had to be more of the sinuous monster, colliding with surrounding muck—a long, long leviathan!

A final ground quiver, then silence. Some creakings. Then more silence.

And darkness. Enveloped, surrounded by the titan's mouth, Jonah at first saw nothing . . . then a few faint glimmers. Pinyon light from nearby Monsat Bubble habitat. Streaming in through holes. *Holes* in the gigantic head. Holes that gradually opened wider as ocean-bottom pressure wreaked havoc on flesh meant for much higher waters.

Then the smell hit Jonah.

An odor of death.

Of course. Such a creature would never dive this deep of its own accord. Instead of being pursued by a ravenous monster, Jonah must have run along the same downdraft conveying a corpse to its grave. An intersection and collision that might seem hilarious someday, when he told the story as an old grandpa, assuming his luck held. Right now, he felt sore, bruised, angry, embarrassed . . . and concerned about the vanishing supply in his meager air bubble.

With his belt knife, Jonah began probing and cutting a path out of the trap. He had another reason to hurry. If he had to be rescued by others, there would be no claiming this flesh for Tairee, for his clan and family. For his dowry and husband price.

Concerned clicks told him Enoch was nearby and one promising gap in the monster's cheek suddenly gave way to the handle of a rake. Soon they both were tearing at it, sawing tough membranes, tossing aside clots of shriveling muscle and skin. His bubble helmet might keep out the salt sea, but pungent aromas were another matter. Finally, with Enoch tugging helpfully on one arm, Jonah squeezed out and stumbled several steps before falling to his knees, coughing.

"Here come others," said his friend. And Jonah lifted his gaze, spying men in bottom suits and helmets, hurrying this way, brandishing glow bulbs and makeshift weapons. Behind them he glimpsed one of the cargo subs—a string of midsized bubbles, pushed by hand-crank propellers—catching up fast.

"Help me get up . . . on top," he urged Enoch, who bore some of his weight as he stood. Together, they sought a route onto the massive head. There was danger in this moment. Without clear ownership, fighting might break out among salvage crews from different domes, as happened a generation ago, over the last hot vent on the floor of Cleopatra Canyon. Only after a dozen men were dead had the grandmothers made peace. But if Tairee held a firm claim to this corpse, then rules of gift-generosity would parcel out shares to every dome, with only a largest-best allotment to Tairee. Peace and honor now depended on his speed. But the monster's cranium was steep, crumbly, and slick.

Frustrated and almost out of time, Jonah decided to take a chance. He slashed at the ropy cables binding his soft overalls to the weighted clogs that kept him firmly on the ocean bottom. Suddenly buoyant, he began to sense the Fell Tug . . . the pull toward heaven, toward doom. The same tug that had yanked Bezo Colony, a few days ago, sending that bubble habitat and all of its inhabitants plummeting skyward.

Enoch understood the gamble. Gripping Jonah's arm, he stuffed his rake and knife and hatchet into Jonah's belt. Anything convenient. So far, so good. The net force seemed to be slightly downward. Jonah nodded at his friend, and jumped.

3.

The marriage party made its way toward Tairee Bubble's dock, shuffling along to beating tambourines. Youngsters—gaily decked in rice flowers and pinyon garlands—danced alongside the newlyweds. Although many of the children wore masks or makeup to disguise minor birth defects, they seemed light of spirit.

They were the only ones.

Some adults tried their best, chanting and shouting at all the right places. Especially several dozen refugees—Tairee's allocated share of threadbare escapees from the ruin of Cixin and Sadoul settlements—who cheered with the fervid eagerness of people desperately trying for acceptance in their new home rather than mere sufferance. As for other guests from unaffected domes? Most appeared to have come only for free food. These now crowded near the dock, eager to depart as soon as the nuptial sub was on its way.

Not that Jonah could blame them. Most people preferred staying close to home ever since the thumps started going all crazy, setting off a chain of tragedies, tearing at the old, placid ways.

And today's thump is already overdue, he thought. In fact, there hadn't been a ground-shaking comet strike in close to a month. Such a gap would have been unnerving, just a year or two ago. Now, given how awful some recent impacts had been, any respite was welcome.

A time of chaos. Few see good omens even in a new marriage.

Jonah glanced at his bride, come to collect him from Laussane Bubble, all the way at the far northern outlet of Cleopatra Canyon. Taller than average, with a clear complexion and strong carriage, she had good hips and only a slight mutant mottling on the back of her scalp, where the hair grew in a wild, discolored corkscrew. An easily overlooked defect, like Jonah's lack of toe webbing, or the way he would sneeze or yawn uncontrollably whenever the air pressure changed too fast. No one jettisoned a child over such inconsequentials.

Though you can be exiled forever from all you ever knew if you're born with the genetic defect of maleness. Jonah could not help scanning the workshops and dorms, the pinyons and paddies of Tairee, wondering if he would see this place—his birth bubble—ever again. Perhaps, if the grandmothers of Laussane trusted him with errands. Or next time Tairee hosted a festival—if his new wife chose to take him along.

He had barely met Petri Smoth before this day, having spoken just a few words with her over the years, at various craft-and-seed fairs, hosted by some of the largest domes. During last year's festival, held in ill-fated Aldrin Bubble, she *had* asked him a few pointed questions about some tinkered gimmicks he displayed. In fact, now that he looked back on it, her tone and expression must have been . . . evaluating. Weighing his answers with *this* possible outcome in mind. It just never occurred to Jonah, at the time, that he was impressing a girl enough to choose him as a mate.

I thought she was interested in my improved ballast-transfer valve.

And maybe . . . in a way . . . she was.

Or, at least, in Jonah's mechanical abilities. Panalina suggested that explanation yesterday, while helping Jonah prepare his dowry—an old cargo truck that he had purchased with his prize winnings for claiming the dead sea serpent—a long-discarded submersible freighter that he had spent the last year reconditioning. A hopeless wreck, some called it, but no longer.

"Well, it's functional, I'll give you that," the Master Mechanic of Tairee Bubble had decreed last night, after going over the vessel from stem to stern, checking everything from hand-wound anchor tethers and stone keel weights to the bench where several pairs of burly men might labor at a long crank, turning a propeller to drive the boat forward. She thumped extra storage bubbles, turning stopcocks to sniff at the hissing, pressurized air. Then Panalina tested levers that would let seawater into those tanks, if need be, keeping the sub weighed down on the bottom, safe from falling into the deadly sky.

"It'll do," she finally decreed, to Jonah's relief. This could help him begin married life on a good note. Not every boy got to present his new bride with a whole submarine!

Jonah had acquired the old relic months before people realized just how valuable each truck might be, even junkers like this one—for rescue and escape—as a chain of calamities disrupted the canyon settlements. His repairs hadn't been completed in time to help evacuate more families from cracked and doomed Cixin or Sadoul Bubbles, and he felt bad about that. Still, with Panalina's ruling of seaworthiness, this vehicle would help make Petri Smoth a woman of substance in the hierarchy at Laussane, and prove Jonah a real asset to his wife.

Only . . . what happens when so many bubbles fail that the others can't take refugees anymore?

Already there was talk of sealing Tairee against outsiders, even evacuees, and concentrating on total self-reliance.

Some spoke of arming the colony's subs for war.

"These older hull bubbles were thicker and heavier," Panalina commented, patting the nearest bulkhead, the first of three ancient, translucent spheres that had been fused together into a short chain, like a trio of pearls on a string. "They fell out of favor, maybe four or five mother generations ago. You'll need to pay six big fellows in order to crank a full load of trade goods. That won't leave you much profit on cargo."

Good old Panalina, always talking as if everything would soon be normal again, as if the barter network was likely to ever be the same. With streaks of gray in her hair, the artificer claimed to be sixty years old but was certainly younger. The grandmothers let her get away with the fib, and what would normally be criminal neglect, leaving her womb fallow most of the time, with only two still-living heirs, and both of those boys.

"Still." Panalina looked around and thumped the hull one last time. "He's a sturdy little boat. You know, there was talk among the mothers about refusing to let you take him away from Tairee. The Smoths had to promise half a ton of crushed grapes in return, and to take in one of the Sadoul families. Still, I think it's *you* they mostly want."

Jonah had puzzled over that cryptic remark after Panalina left, then all during the brew-swilled bachelor party, suffering crude jokes and ribbing from the married men, and later during a fretful sleep shift, as he tossed and turned with prewedding jitters. During the ceremony itself, Mother had been gracious and warm—not her typical mien, but a side of her that Jonah felt he would surely miss. Though he knew that an underlying source of her cheerfulness was simple—*one less male mouth to feed.*

It had made Jonah reflect, even during the wrist-binding part of the ceremony, on something old Scholar Wu said recently.

The balance of the sexes may change, if it really comes down to war. Breeders could start to seem less valuable than fighters.

In the docklock, Jonah found that his little truck had been decked with flowers, and all three of the spheres gleamed, where they had been polished above the waterline. The gesture warmed Jonah's heart. There was even a freshly painted name, arcing just above the propeller.

Bird of Tairee.

Well. Mother had always loved stories about those prehistoric creatures of Old Earth who flew through a sky that was immeasurably vast and sweet.

"I thought you were going to name it after me," Petri commented in a low voice, without breaking her gracious smile.

"I shall do that, ladylove. Just after we dock in Laussane."

"Well . . . perhaps not *just* after," she commented, and Jonah's right buttock took a sharp-nailed pinch. He managed not to jump or visibly react. But clearly, his new wife did not intend wasting time once they were home.

Home. He would have to redefine the word, in his mind.

Still, as Jonah checked the final loading of luggage, gifts, and passengers, he glanced at the fantail one last time, picturing there a name that he really wanted to give the little vessel.

Renewed Hope.

4.

They were under way, having traveled more than half of the distance to Laussane Bubble, when a *thump* struck at the wrong time, shaking the little sub truck like a rattle.

The blow came hard and late. So late that everyone at the wedding had simply written off any chance of one today. Folks assumed that at least another work-and-sleep cycle would pass without a comet fall. Already this was the longest gap in memory. Perhaps (some murmured) the age of thumps had come to an end, as prophesied long ago. After the disaster that befell Aldrin and Bezo two months ago, it was a wish now shared by all.

Up until that very moment, the nuptial voyage had been placid, enjoyable, even for tense newlyweds.

Jonah was at the tiller up front, gazing ahead through a patch of hull bubble that had been polished on both sides, making it clear enough to see through. Hoping that he looked like a stalwart, fierce-eyed seaman, he gripped the rudder ropes that steered *Bird of Tairee* though the sub's propeller lay still and powerless. For this voyage, the old truck was being hauled as a trailer behind a larger, sleeker, and more modern Laussanite sub, where a team of twelve burly men sweated and tugged in perfect rhythm, turning their drive-shaft crank.

Petri stood beside her new husband, while passengers chattered in the second compartment behind them. As bubble colonies drifted past, she gestured at each of the gleaming domes and spoke of womanly matters, like the politics of trade and diplomacy, or the personalities and traditions of each settlement. Which goods and food items they excelled at producing, or needed. Their rates of mutation and successful child-raising. Or how well each habitat was managing its genetic diversity . . . and her tone changed a bit at that point, as if suddenly aware how the topic bore upon them both. For this marriage match had been judged by the Laussane mothers on that basis, above all others.

"Of course I had final say, the final choice," she told Jonah, and it warmed him that Petri felt a need to explain.

"Anyway, there is a project I've been working on," she continued in a lower voice. "With a few others in Laussane and Landis Bubbles. Younger folks, mostly. And we can use a good mechanic like you."

Like me? So I was chosen for that reason?

Jonah felt put off and tensed a bit when Petri put an arm around his waist. But she leaned up and whispered in his ear.

"I think you'll like what we're up to. It's something just right for a *rascal*."

The word surprised him and he almost turned to stare. But her arm was tight and Petri's breath was still in his ear. So Jonah chose to keep his features steady, unmoved. Perhaps sensing his stiff reaction, Petri let go. She slid around to face him with her back resting against the transparent patch, leaning against the window.

Clever girl, he thought. It was the direction he had to look, in order to watch the *Pride of Laussane*'s rudder, up ahead, matching his tiller to that of the larger sub. Now he could not avert his eyes from her, using boyish reticence as an excuse.

Petri's oval face was a bit wide, as were her eyes. The classic Laussane chin cleft was barely noticeable, though her mutant patch—the whorl of wild

hair—was visible as a reflection behind her, on the bubble's curved, inner surface. Her wedding garment, sleek and formfitting, revealed enough to prove
her fitness to bear and nurse . . . plus a little more. And Jonah wondered—
when am I supposed to let the sight of her affect me? Arouse me? Too soon and he
might seem brutish, in need of tight reins. Too late or too little, and his bride
might feel insulted.

And fretting over it will make me an impotent fool. Deliberately, Jonah
calmed himself, allowing some pleasure to creep in, at the sight of her. A seed
of anticipation grew . . . as he knew she wanted.

"What *project* are you talking about? Something involving trucks?" He
offered a guess. "Something the mothers may not care for? Something suited
to a . . . to a. . . ."

He glanced over his shoulder, past the open hatch leading to the middle
bubble, containing a jumble of cargo—wedding gifts and Jonah's hope chest,
plus luggage for Laussane dignitaries who rode in comfort aboard the bigger
submersible ahead. Here, a dozen lower-caste passengers sat or lay atop the
stacks and piles—some of Petri's younger cousins, plus a family of evacuees from doomed Sadoul Dome, sent to relieve Tairee's overcrowded refugee
encampment, as part of the complex marriage deal.

Perhaps it would be best to hold off this conversation until a time and place
with fewer ears around, to pick up stray sonic reflections. Perhaps delaying
it for wife-and-husband pillow talk—the one and only kind of privacy that
could be relied upon in the colonies. He looked forward again, raising one
eyebrow, and Petri clearly got his meaning. Still, in a lower voice, she finished
Jonah's sentence.

"To a *rascal*, yes. In fact, your reputation as a young fellow always coming up with bothersome questions helped me bargain well for you. Did you
intend it that way, I wonder? For you to wind up *only* sought by one like me,
who would *value* such attributes? If so, clever boy."

Jonah decided to keep silent, letting Petri give him credit for cunning he
never had. After a moment, she shrugged with a smile, then continued in a
voice that was nearly inaudible.

"But in fact, our small bunch of conspirators and connivers were inspired
by yet another *rascal*. The one we have foremost in our minds was a fellow
named . . . Melvil."

Jonah had been about to ask about the mysterious "we." But mention
of that particular name stopped him short. He blinked hard—two, three
times—striving not to flinch or otherwise react. It took him several tries to
speak, barely mouthing the words.

"You're talking about . . . *Theodora Canyon?*"

A place of legend. And Petri's eyes now conveyed many things. Approval of his quickness . . . overlain upon an evident grimness of purpose. A willingness—even eagerness—to take risks and adapt in chaotic times, finding a path forward, even if it meant following a folktale. All of that was apparent in Petri's visage. Though clearly, Jonah was expected to say more.

"I've heard . . . one hears rumors . . . that there was a map to what Melvil found . . . another canyon filled with Gift-of-Venus bubbles like those the Founders discovered here in Cleopatra Canyon. But the mothers forbade any discussion or return voyages, and—" Jonah slowed down when he realized he was babbling. "And so, after Melvil fled his punishment, they hid the map away. . . ."

"I've been promised a copy," Petri confided, evidently weighing his reaction, "once we're ready to set out."

Jonah couldn't help himself. He turned around again to check the next compartment, where several smaller children were chasing one another up and down the luggage piles, making a ruckus and almost tipping over a crate of Panalina's smithy tools, consigned for transshipment to Gollancz Dome. Beyond, through a second hatchway to the final chamber, where sweating rowers would normally sit, lay stacked bags of exported Tairee rice. The refugee family and several of Petri's subadult cousins lounged back there, talking idly, keeping apart from the raucous children.

Jonah looked back at his bride, still keeping his voice low.

"You're kidding! So there truly *was* a boy named Melvil? Who stole a sub and—"

"—for a month and a week and a day and an hour," Petri finished for him. "Then returned with tales of a far-off canyon filled with gleaming bubbles of all sizes, a vast foam of hollow, volcanic globes, left over from this world's creation, never touched by human hands. Bubbles just as raw and virginal as our ancestors found, when they first arrived down here beneath a newborn ocean, seeking refuge far below the poison sky."

Much of what she said was from the Founders' Catechism, retaining its rhythm and flowery tone. Clearly, it amused Petri to quote modified scripture while speaking admiringly of an infamous rebel; Jonah could tell as much from her wry expression. But poetry—and especially irony—had always escaped Jonah, and she might as well get used to that husbandly lack, right now.

"So . . . this is about . . . finding new homes?"

"Perhaps, if things keep getting worse here in Cleo Abyss, shouldn't we have options? Oh, we're selling it as an expedition to harvest fresh bubbles, all the sizes that have grown scarce hereabouts, useful for helmets and cooking and chemistry. But we'll also check out any big ones. Maybe they're holding up better in Theodora than they are here. Because, at the rate things are going—" Petri shook her head. And, looking downward, her expression *leaked* just a bit, losing some of its tough, determined veneer, giving way to plainly visible worry.

She knows things. Information that the mothers won't tell mere men. And she's afraid.

Strangely, that moment of vulnerability touched Jonah's heart, thawing a patch that he had never realized was chill. For the first time, he felt drawn . . . compelled to reach out. Not sexually. But to comfort, to hold. . . .

That was when the *thump* struck—harder than Jonah would have believed possible.

Concussion slammed the little submarine over, halfway onto its port side, and set the ancient bubble hull ringing. Petri hurtled into him, tearing the rudder straps from his hands as they tumbled together backward, caroming off the open hatch between compartments, then rolling forward again as *Bird of Tairee* heaved.

With the sliver of his brain that still functioned, Jonah wondered if there had been a collision. But the Laussanite ship was bobbing and rocking some distance ahead, still tethered to the *Bird*, and nothing else was closer than a bubble habitat, at least two hundred meters away. Jonah caught sight of all this while landing against the window patch up front, with Petri squished between. This time, as the *Bird* lurched again, he managed to grab a stanchion and hold on, while gripping her waist with his other arm. Petri's breath came in wheezing gasps, and now there was no attempt to mask her terror.

"What? What was. . . ."

Jonah swallowed, bracing himself against another rocking sway that almost tore her from his grasp.

"A thump! Do you hear the low tone? But they're never this late!"

He didn't have breath to add: *I've never felt one outside a dome before. No one ventures into water during late morning, when comets always used to fall.* And now Jonah knew why. His ears rang and hurt like crazy.

All this time he had been counting. Thump vibrations came in sequence. One tone passed through rock by *compression*, arriving many seconds before the slower *transverse* waves. He had once even read one of Scholar Wu's books about that, with partial understanding. And he recalled what the old teacher said. That you could tell from the difference in tremor arrivals how far away the impact was from Cleopatra Canyon. . . . *twenty-one . . . twenty-two . . . twenty-three.* . . .

Jonah hoped to reach sixty-two seconds, the normal separation, for generation after generation of grandmothers.

. . . *twenty-four . . . twenty-f—*

The transverse tone, higher pitched and much louder than ever, set the forward bubble of the *Bird* ringing like a bell, even as the tooth-jarring sways diminished, allowing Jonah and Petri to grab separate straps and find their feet.

Less than half the usual distance. That comet almost hit us! He struggled with a numb brain. *Maybe just a couple of thousand kilometers away.*

"The children!" Petri cried, and cast herself—stumbling—aft toward the middle compartment. Jonah followed, but just two steps in order to verify no seals were broken. No hatches had to be closed and dogged . . . not yet. And the crying kids back there looked shaken, not badly hurt. So okay, trust Petri to take care of things back there—

—as he plunged back to the tiller harness. Soon, Jonah was tugging at balky cables, struggling to make the rudder obedient, fighting surges while catching brief glimpses of a tumult outside. Ahead, forty or fifty meters, the *Pride of Laussane*'s propeller churned a roiling cauldron of water. The men inside must be cranking with all their might.

Backward, Jonah realized with dismay. Their motion in reverse might bring the *Pride*'s prop in contact with the towline. *Why are they hauling ass backward?*

One clue. The tether remained taut and straight, despite the rowers' efforts. And with a horrified realization, Jonah realized why. The bigger sub *tilted* upward almost halfway to vertical, with its nose aimed high.

They've lost their main ballast! Great slugs of stone and raw metal normally weighed a sub down, lashed along the keel. They must have torn loose amid the chaos of the *thump*—nearly all of them! But how? Certainly, bad luck and lousy maintenance, or a hard collision with the ocean bottom. For whatever reason, the *Pride of Laussane* was straining upward, climbing toward the sky.

Already, Jonah could see one of the bubble habitats from an angle no canyonite ever wanted . . . looking *down* upon the curved dome from above, its forest of pinyon vines glowing from within.

Cursing his own slowness of mind, Jonah let go of the rudder cables and half stumbled toward the hatch at the rear of the control chamber, shouting for Petri. There was a job to do, more vital than any other. Their very lives might depend on it.

5.

"When I give the word, open valve number one *just a quarter turn!*"

It wasn't a demure tone to use toward a woman, but he saw no sign of wrath or resentment as his new wife nodded. "A quarter turn. Yes, Jonah."

Clamping his legs around one of the ballast jars, he started pushing rhythmically on his new and improved model air pump. "Okay . . . now!"

As soon as Petri twisted the valve they heard water spew into the ballast chamber, helping Jonah push the air out, for storage at pressure in a neighboring bottle. It would be simpler and less work to just let the air spill outside, but he couldn't bring himself to do that. There might be further uses for the stuff.

When *Bird* started tilting sideways, he shifted their efforts to a bottle next to the starboard viewing patch . . . another bit of the old hull that had been polished for seeing. Farther aft, in the third compartment, he could hear some of the passengers struggling with bags of rice, clearing the propeller crank for possible use. In fact, Jonah had ordered it done mostly to give them a distraction. Something to do.

"We should be getting heavier," he told Petri, as they shifted back and forth, left to right, then left again, letting water into storage bubbles and storing displaced air. As expected, this had an effect on the sub's pitch, raising the nose as it dragged on the tether cable, which in turn linked them to the crippled *Pride of Laussane.*

The crew of that hapless vessel had given up cranking to propel their ship backward. Everything depended on Jonah and Petri now. If they could make *Bird* heavy enough, quickly enough, both vessels might be prevented from sinking into the sky.

And we'll be heroes, Jonah pondered at one point, while his arms throbbed with pain. This could be a great start to his life and reputation in Laussane Bubble . . . that is, *if* it worked. Jonah ached to go and check the little sub's instruments, but there was no time. Not even when he drafted the father of the Sadoul refugee family to pump alongside him. Gradually, all the tanks were filling, making the *Bird* heavier, dragging at the runaway *Pride of Laussane.* And indeed. . . .

Yes! He saw a welcome sight. One of the big habitat domes! Perhaps the very one they had been passing when the thump struck. Jonah shared a grin with Petri, seeing in her eyes a glimmer of earned respect. *Perhaps I'll need to rest a bit before our wedding night.* Though funny, it didn't feel as if fatigue would be a problem.

Weighed down by almost full ballast tanks, *Bird* slid almost along the great, curved flank of the habitat. Jonah signaled Xerish to ease off pumping and for Petri to close her valve. He didn't want to hit the sea bottom too hard. As they descended, Petri identified the nearby colony as Leininger Dome. It was hard to see much through both sweat-stung eyes and the barely polished window patch, but Jonah could soon tell that a crowd of citizens had come to press their faces against the inner side of the great, transparent bubble wall, staring up and out toward the descending subs.

As *Bird* drifted backward, it appeared that the landing would be pretty fast. Jonah shouted for all the passengers to brace themselves for a rough impact, one that should come any second as they drew even with the Leininger onlookers. A bump into bottom mud that . . .

. . . that didn't come.

Something was wrong. Instinct told him, before reason could, when Jonah's ears popped and he gave vent to a violent sneeze.

Oh no.

Petri and Jonah stared at the Leiningerites, who stared back in resigned dismay as the *Bird* dropped below their ground level . . . and kept dropping. Or rather, Leininger Bubble kept ascending, faster and faster, tugged by the deadly buoyancy of all that air inside, its anchor roots torn loose by that last violent *thump*. Following the path and fate of Bezo Colony, without the warning that had allowed partial evacuation of Cixin and Sadoul.

With a shout of self-loathing, Jonah rushed to perform a task that he should have done already. Check instruments. The pressure gauge wouldn't be much use in an absolute sense, but relative values could at least tell if they were falling. Not just relative to the doomed habitat but drifting back toward the safe bottom muck, or else—

"Rising," he told Petri in a low voice, as she sidled alongside and rested her head against his shoulder. He slid his arm around her waist, as if they had been married forever. Or, at least, most of what remained of their short lives.

"Is there anything else we can do?" she asked.

"Not much." He shrugged. "Finish flooding the tanks, I suppose. But they're already almost full, and the weight isn't enough. *That* is just too strong."

And he pointed out the forward viewing patch at the *Pride of Laussane*, its five large, air-filled compartments buoyant enough to overcome any resistance by this little truck.

"But . . . can't they do what we've done. Fill their own balls—"

"Ballast tanks. Sorry, my lady. They don't have any big ones. Just a few little bottles for adjusting trim."

Jonah kept his voice even and matter-of-fact, the way a vessel captain should, even though his stomach churned with dread, explaining how external keel weights saved interior cargo space. Also, newer craft used bubbles with slimmer walls. You didn't want to penetrate them with too many inlets, valves, and such.

"And no one else has your new pump," Petri added. And her approving tone meant more to Jonah, in these final minutes, than he ever would have expected.

"Of course. . . ." he mused.

"Yes? You've thought of something?"

"Well, if we could somehow cut the tether cable. . . ."

"We'd sink back to safety!" Then Petri frowned. "But we're the only chance they have, on the *Pride of Laussane*. Without our weight, they would shoot skyward like a seed pip from a lorgo fruit."

"Anyway, it's up to them to decide," Jonah explained. "The tether release is at their end, not ours. Sorry. It's a design flaw that I'll fix as soon as I get a chance, right after repainting your name on the stern."

"Hm. See that you do," she commanded.

Then, after a brief pause, "Do you think they might release us, when they realize both ships are doomed?"

Jonah shrugged. There was no telling what people would do when faced with such an end. He vowed to stand watch though, just in case.

He sneezed hard, twice. Pressure effects were starting to tell on him.

"Should we inform the others?" he asked Petri, with a nod back toward *Bird*'s other two compartments, where the crying had settled down to low whimpers from a couple of younger kids.

She shook her head. "It will be quick, yes?"

Jonah considered lying and dismissed the idea.

"It depends. As we rise, the water pressure outside falls, so if air pressure inside remains high, that could lead to a blowout, cracking one of our shells, letting the sea rush in awfully fast. So fast, we'll be knocked out before we can drown. Of course, that's the *least* gruesome end."

"What a cheerful lad," she commented. "Go on."

"Let's say the hull compartments hold. This is a tough old bird." He patted the nearest curved flank. "We can help protect against blowout by venting compartment air, trying to keep pace with falling pressure outside. In that case, we'll suffer one kind or another kind of pressure-change disease. The most common is the bends. That's when gas that's dissolved in our blood suddenly pops into tiny bubbles that fill your veins and arteries. I hear it's a painful way to die."

Whether because of his mutation, or purely in his mind, Jonah felt a return of the scratchy throat and burning eyes. He turned his head barely in time to sneeze away from the window, and Petri.

She was looking behind them, into the next compartment. "If death is unavoidable, but we can pick our way to die, then I say let's choose—"

At that moment, Jonah tensed at a sudden, jarring sensation—a *snap* that rattled the viewing patch in front of him. Something was happening, above and ahead. Without light from the Cleopatra domes, darkness was near total outside, broken only by some algae glow bulbs placed along the flank of the *Pride of Laussane*. Letting go of Petri, he went to all the bulbs inside the *Bird's* forward compartment and covered them, then hurried back to press his face against the viewing patch.

"What is it?" Petri asked. "What's going on?"

"I think. . . ." Jonah made out a queer, sinuous rippling in the blackness between the two submarines.

He jumped as something struck the window. With pounding heart, he saw and heard a snakelike thing slither across the clear zone of bubble, before falling aside. And beyond, starting from just twenty meters away, the row of tiny glow spots now shot upward, like legendary rockets, quickly diminishing, then fading from view.

"The tether," he announced in a matter-of-fact voice.

"They let go? Let us go?" A blend of hope and awe in her voice.

"Made sense," he answered. "They were goners anyway." *And now they will be the heroes, when all is told. Songs will be sung about their choice, back home.*

That is, assuming there still is a home. We have no idea if Leininger Dome was the only victim, this time.

He stared at the pressure gauge. After a long pause when it refused to budge, the needle finally began to move. Opposite to its former direction of change.

"We're descending," he decreed with a sigh. "In fact, we'd better adjust. To keep from falling too fast. It wouldn't do, to reach safety down there, only to crack open from impact."

Jonah put the Sadoulite dad—Xerish—to work, pumping in the opposite direction, less frantically than before, but harder work, using compressed air to push out and overboard some water from the ballast tanks, while Petri, now experienced, handled the valves. After supervising for a few minutes, he went back to the viewing port and peered outside. *I must keep a sharp lookout for the lights of Cleo Canyon. We may have drifted laterally and I can adjust better while we're falling than later, at the bottom.* He used the rudder and stubby elevation planes to turn his little sub, explaining to Petri how it was done. She might have to steer, if Jonah's strength was needed on the propeller crank.

A low, concussive report caused the chamber to rattle and groan. Not as bad as the horrid *thump* had been, but closer, coming from somewhere above. Jonah shared eye contact with Petri, a sad recognition of something inevitable. The end of a gallant ship—*Pride of Laussane.*

Two more muffled booms followed, rather fainter, then another.

They must have closed their inner hatches. Each compartment is failing separately.

But something felt wrong about that. The third concussion, especially, had felt deep-throated, lasting longer than reasonable. Amid another bout of sneezing, Jonah pressed close against the view patch once again, in order to peer about. First toward the bottom, then upward.

Clearly, this day had to be the last straw. It rang a death knell for the old, complacent ways of doing things. Leininger had been a big, important colony, and perhaps not today's only major victim. If thumps were going unpredictable and lethal, then Cleopatra might have to be abandoned.

Jonah knew very little about the plan concocted by Petri's mysterious cabal of young women and men, though he was glad to have been chosen to help. To follow a *rascal's* legend in search of new homes. In fact, two things were abundantly clear. *Expeditions must get under way just as soon as we get back. And there should be more than just one, following Melvil's clues. Subs must be sent in many directions! If Venus created other realms filled with hollow volcanic globes that can be seeded with Earthly life, then we must find them.*

A second fact had also emerged, made evident during the last hour or so. Jonah turned to glance back at a person he had barely known, until just a day ago.

It appears that I married really well.

Although the chamber was very dim, Petri glanced up from her task and noticed him looking at her. She smiled—an expression of respect and dawning equality that seemed just as pleased as he now felt. Jonah smiled back—then unleashed another great sneeze. At which she chirped a short laugh and shook her head in fake-mocking ruefulness.

Grinning, he turned back to the window, gazed upward—then shouted—
"Grab something! Brace yourselves!"

That was all he had time or breath to cry, while yanking on the tiller cables
and shoving his knee hard against the elevator control plane. *Bird* heeled over
to starboard, both rolling and struggling to yaw-turn. Harsh cries of surprise
and alarm erupted from the back compartments, as crates and luggage toppled.

He heard Petri shout, "Stay where you are!" at the panicky Xerish, who
whimpered in terror. Jonah caught a glimpse of them, reflected in the view
patch, as they clutched one of the air-storage bottles to keep from tumbling
across the deck, onto the right-side bulkhead.

Come on, old boy, he urged the little sub and wished he had six strong men
cranking at the stern end, driving the propeller to accelerate *Bird of Tairee*
forward. If there had been, Jonah might—just barely—have guided the sub
clear of peril tumbling from above. Debris from a catastrophe, only a small
fraction of it glittering in the darkness.

Hard chunks of something rattled against the hull. He glimpsed an object,
thin and metallic—perhaps a torn piece of pipe—carom off the view patch
with a bang, plowing several nasty scars before it fell away. Jonah half expected
the transparent zone to start spalling and cracking at any second.

That didn't happen, but now debris was coming down in a positive rain,
clattering along the whole length of his vessel, testing the sturdy old shells
with every strike. Desperate, he hauled even harder, steering *Bird* away from
what seemed the worst of it, toward a zone that glittered a bit less. More cries
erupted from the back two chambers.

I should have sealed the hatches, he thought. But then, what good would
that do for anyone, honestly? Having drifted laterally from Cleo Canyon,
any surviving chambers would be helpless, unable to maneuver, never to be
found or rescued before the stored air turned to poison. *Better that we all go
together*.

He recognized the sound that most of the rubble made upon the hull—
bubble stone striking more bubble stone. Could it all have come from the
Pride of Laussane? Impossible! There was far too much.

Leininger.

The doomed dome must have imploded, or exploded, or simply come
apart without the stabilizing pressure of the depths. Then, with all its air lost
and rushing skyward, the rest would plummet. Shards of bubble wall, dirt,
pinyons glowing feebly as they drifted ever lower . . . and people. That was the
detritus Jonah most hoped to avoid.

There. It looks jet-black over there. The faithful old sub had almost finished its turn. Soon he might slack off, setting the boat upright. Once clear of the debris field, he could check on the passengers, then go back to seeking the home canyon. . . .

He never saw whatever struck next, but it had to be big, perhaps a major chunk of Leininger's wall. The blow hammered all three compartments in succession, ringing them like great gongs, making Jonah cry out in pain. There were other sounds, like ripping, tearing. The impact—somewhere below and toward portside, lifted him off his feet, tearing one of the rudder straps out of Jonah's hand, leaving him to swing wildly by the other. *Bird* sawed hard to the left as Jonah clawed desperately to reclaim the controls.

At any moment, he expected to greet the harsh, cold sea and have his vessel join the skyfall of lost hopes.

6.

Only gradually did it dawn on him—it wasn't over. The peril and problems, he wasn't about to escape them that easily. Yes, damage was evident, but the hulls—three ancient, volcanic globes—still held.

In fact, some while after that horrible collision, it did seem that *Bird of Tairee* had drifted clear of the heavy stuff. Material still rained upon the sub, but evidently softer items. Like still-glowing chunks of pinyon vine.

Petri took charge of the rear compartments, crisply commanding passengers to help one another dig out and assessing their hurts, in order of priority. She shouted reports to Jonah, whose hands were full. In truth, he had trouble hearing what she said over the ringing in his ears and had to ask for repetition several times. The crux: one teenager had a fractured wrist, while others bore bruises and contusions—a luckier toll than he expected. Bema—the Sadoulite mother—kept busy delivering first aid.

More worrisome was a *leak*. Very narrow, but powerful, a needle jet spewed water into the rear compartment. Not through a crack in the shell—fortunately—but via the packing material that surrounded the propeller bearing. Jonah would have to go back and have a look, but first he assessed other troubles. For example, the sub wouldn't right herself completely. There was a constant tilt to starboard around the roll axis . . . then he checked the pressure gauge and muttered a low invocation to ancient gods and demons of Old Earth.

—

"We've stopped falling," he confided to Petri in the stern compartment, once the leak seemed under control. It had taken some time, showing the others how to jam rubbery cloths into the bearing, then bracing it all with planks of wood torn from the floor. The arrangement was holding, for now.

"How can that be?" she asked. "We were *heavy* when the *Pride* let us go. I thought our problem was how to slow our descent."

"It was. Till our collision with whatever hit us. Based on where it struck, along the portside keel, I'd guess that it knocked off some of our static ballast—the stones lashed to our bottom. The same thing that happened to *Pride* during that awful thump quake. Other stones may have been dislodged or had just one of their lashings cut, leaving them to dangle below the starboard side, making us tilt like this. From these two examples, I'd say we've just learned a lesson today, about a really bad flaw in the whole way we've done sub design."

"So which is it? Are we rising?"

Jonah nodded.

"Slowly. It's not too bad yet. And I suppose it's possible we might resume our descent if we fill all the ballast tanks completely. Only there's a problem."

"Isn't there always?" Petri rolled her eyes, clearly exasperated.

"Yeah." He gestured toward where Xerish—by luck a carpenter—was hammering more bracing into place. Jonah lowered his voice. "If we drop back to the seafloor, that bearing may not hold against full-bottom pressure. It's likely to start spewing again, probably faster."

"If it does, how long will we have?"

Jonah frowned. "Hard to say. Air pressure would fight back, of course. Still, I'd say less than an hour. Maybe not that much. We would have to spot one of the canyon domes right away, steer right for it, and plop ourselves into dock as fast as possible, with everyone cranking like mad—"

"—only using the propeller will put even more stress on the bearing," Petri concluded with a thoughtful frown. "It might blow completely."

Jonah couldn't prevent a brief smile. *Brave enough to face facts . . . and a mechanical aptitude, as well? I could find this woman attractive.*

"Well, I'm sure we can work something out," she added. "You haven't let us down yet."

Not yet, he thought, and returned to work, feeling trapped by her confidence in him. And cornered by the laws of chemistry and physics—as well as he understood them with his meager education, taken from ancient books that were rudimentary and obsolete when the Founders first came to Venus, cowering away from alien invaders under a newborn ocean, while comets poured in with perfect regularity.

Perfect for many lifetimes, but not forever. Not anymore. *Even if we make it home, then go ahead with the Melvil Plan, and manage to find another bubble-filled canyon less affected by the rogue thumps, how long will that last?*

Wasn't this whole project, colonizing the bottom of an alien sea with crude technology, always doomed from the start?

In the middle compartment, Jonah opened his personal chest and took out some treasures—books and charts that he had personally copied under supervision by Scholar Wu, onto bundles of hand-scraped pinyon leaves. In one, he verified his recollection of Boyle's Law and the dangers of changing air pressure on the human body. From another he got a formula that—he hoped—might predict how the leaky propeller-shaft bearing would behave if they descended the rest of the way.

Meanwhile, Petri put a couple of the larger teen girls to work on a bilge pump, transferring water from the floor of the third compartment into some almost full ballast tanks. Over the next hour, Jonah kept glancing at the pressure gauge. The truck appeared to be leveling off again. *Up and down. Up and down. This can't be good for my old* Bird.

Leveled. Stable . . . for now. That meant the onus fell on him, with no excuse.

To descend and risk the leak becoming a torrent, blasting those who worked the propeller crank . . . or else. . . .

Two hands laid pressure on his shoulders and squeezed inward, surrounding his neck, forcefully. Slim hands, kneading tense muscles and tendons. Jonah closed his eyes, not wanting to divulge what he had decided.

"Some wedding day, huh?"

Jonah nodded. No verbal response seemed needed. He felt married for years—and glad of the illusion. Evidently, Petri knew him now, as well.

"I bet you've figured out what to do."

He nodded again.

"And it won't be fun, or offer good odds of success."

A headshake. Left, then right.

Her hands dug in, wreaking a mixture of pleasure and pain, like life.

"Then tell me, husband," she commanded, coming around to bring their faces close. "Tell me what you'll have us do. Which way do we go?"

He exhaled a sigh. Then inhaled. And finally spoke one word.
"Up."

7.

Toward the deadly sky. Toward Venusian Hell. It had to be. No other choice
was possible.

"If we rise to the surface, I can try to repair the bearing from inside, without water gushing through. And if it requires outside work, then I can do that
by putting on a helmet and coveralls. Perhaps they'll keep out the poisons
long enough."

Petri shuddered at the thought. "Let us hope that won't be necessary."

"Yeah. Though while I'm there I could also fix the ballast straps holding
some of the weight stones to our keel. I . . . just don't see any other way."

Petri sat on a crate opposite Jonah, mulling it over.

"Wasn't upward motion what destroyed Leininger Colony and the
Pride?"

"Yes . . . but their ascent was uncontrolled. Rapid and chaotic. We'll rise
slowly, reducing cabin air pressure in pace with the decreased push of water
outside. We have to go slow, anyway, or the gas that's dissolved in our blood
will boil and kill us. Slow and gentle. That's the way."

She smiled. "You know all the right things to say to a virgin."

Jonah felt his face go red, and was relieved when Petri got serious again.

"If we rise slowly, won't there be another problem? Won't we run out of
breathable air?"

He nodded. "Activity must be kept to a minimum. Recycle and shift stale
air into bottles, exchanging with the good air they now contain. Also, I have
a spark separator."

"You do? How did . . . aren't they rare and expensive?"

"I made this one myself. Well, Panalina showed me how to use pinyon
crystals and electric current to split seawater into hydrogen and oxygen. We'll
put some passengers to work, taking turns at the spin generator." And he
warned her. "It's a small unit. It may not produce enough."

"Well, no sense putting things off, then," Petri said with a grandmother's
tone of decisiveness. "Give your orders, man."

The ascent became grueling. Adults and larger teens took turns at the pumps,
expelling enough ballast water for the sub to start rising at a good pace . . .

then correcting when it seemed too quick. Jonah kept close track of gauges revealing pressure both inside and beyond the shells. He also watched for symptoms of decompression sickness—another factor keeping things slow. All passengers not on shift were encouraged to sleep—difficult enough when the youngest children kept crying over the pain in their ears. Jonah taught them all how to yawn or pinch their noses to equalize pressure, though his explanations kept being punctuated by fits of sneezing.

Above all, even while resting, they had to breathe deep as their lungs gradually purged and expelled excess gas from their bloodstreams.

Meanwhile, the fore-chamber resonated with a constant background whine as older kids took turns at the spark separator, turning its crank so that small amounts of seawater divided into component elements—one of them breathable. The device had to be working—a layer of salt gathered in the brine collector. Still, Jonah worried. *Did I attach the poles right? Might I be filling the storage bottle with oxygen and letting hydrogen into the cabin? Polluting the sub with an explosive mix that could put us out of our misery at any second?*

He wasn't sure how to tell—none of his books said—though he recalled vaguely that hydrogen had no odor.

After following him on his rounds, inspecting everything and repeating his explanations several times, Petri felt confident enough to insist, "You must rest now, Jonah. I will continue to monitor our rate of ascent and make minor adjustments. Right now, I want you to close your eyes."

When he tried to protest, she insisted, with a little more of the accented tone used by Laussane mothers. "We will need you far more in a while. You'll require all your powers near the end. So lie down and recharge yourself. I promise to call if anything much changes."

Accepting her reasoning, he obeyed by curling up on a couple of grain sacks that Xerish brought forward to the control cabin. Jonah's eyelids shut, gratefully. The brain, however, was another matter.

How deep are we now?

It prompted an even bigger question: *How deep is the bottom of Cleopatra Canyon nowadays?*

According to lore, the first colonists used to care a lot about measuring the thickness of Venusian seas, back when some surface light used to penetrate all the way to the ocean floor. They would launch balloons attached to huge coils of string, in order to both judge depth and sample beyond the therm-o-cline barrier and even from the hot, deadly sky. Those practices died out—though Jonah had seen one of the giant capstan reels once, during a visit to Chown Dome, gathering dust and moldering in a swampy corner.

The way Earth denizens viewed their planet's hellish interior, that was how Cleo dwellers thought of the realm above. Though there had been exceptions. Rumors held that Melvil, that legendary rascal, upon returning from his discovery of Theodora Canyon, had demanded support to start exploring the great heights. Possibly even the barrier zone, where living things thronged and might be caught for food. Of course, he was quite mad—though boys still whispered about him in hushed tones.

How many comets? Jonah found himself wondering. Only one book in Tairee spoke of the great Venus Terraforming Project that predated the Coss invasion. Mighty robots, as patient as gods, gathered iceballs at the farthest fringe of the solar system and sent them plummeting from that unimaginably distant realm to strike this planet—several each day, always at the same angle and position—both speeding the world's rotation and drenching its long-parched basins. *If each comet was several kilometers in diameter . . . how thick an ocean might spread across an entire globe, in twenty generations of grandmothers?*

For every one that struck, five others were aimed to skim close by, tearing through the dense, clotted atmosphere of Venus, dragging some of it away before plunging to the sun. The scale of such an enterprise was stunning, beyond belief. So much so that Jonah truly doubted he could be of the same species that did such things. *Petri, maybe. She could be that smart. Not me.*

How were such a people ever conquered?

The roil of his drifting mind moved onward to might-have-beens. If not for that misguided comet—striking six hours late to wreak havoc near the canyon colonies—Jonah and his bride would by now have settled into a small Laussane cottage, getting to know each other in more traditional ways. Despite, or perhaps because of the emergency, he actually felt far *more* the husband of a vividly real person than he would in that other reality, where physical intimacy happened. . . . Still, the lumpy grain sacks made part of him yearn for her in ways that—now—might never come to pass. That world would have been better . . . one where the pinyons waved their bright leaves gently overhead. Where he might show her tricks of climbing vines, then swing from branch to branch, carrying her in his arms while the wind of flying passage ruffled their hair—

A *twang* sound vibrated the cabin, like some mighty cord coming apart. The sub throbbed and Jonah felt it roll a bit.

His eyes opened and he realized, *I was asleep.* Moreover, his head now rested on Petri's lap. Her hand had been the breeze in his hair.

Jonah sat up.

"What was that?"

"I do not know. There was a sharp sound. The ship hummed a bit, and now the floor no longer tilts."

"No longer—"

Jumping up with a shout, he hurried over to the gauges, then cursed low and harsh.

"What is it, Jonah?"

"Quick—wake all the adults and get them to work pumping!"

She wasted no time demanding answers. But as soon as crews were hard at work, Petri approached Jonah again at the control station, one eyebrow raised.

"The remaining stone ballast," he explained. "It must have been hanging by a thread, or a single lashing. Now it's completely gone. The sub's tilt is corrected, but we're ascending too fast."

Petri glanced at two Sadoulites and two Laussanites who were laboring to refill the ballast tanks. "Is there anything else we can do to slow down?"

Jonah shrugged. "I suppose we might unpack the leaky bearing and let more water into the aft compartment. But we'd have no control. The stream could explode in our faces. We might flood or lose the chamber. All told, I'd rather risk decompression sickness."

She nodded, agreeing silently.

They took their own turn at the pumps, then supervised another crew until, at last, the tanks were full. *Bird* could get no heavier. Not without flooding the compartments themselves.

"We have to lose internal pressure. That means venting air overboard," he said, "in order to equalize."

"But we'll need it to breathe!"

"There's no choice. With our tanks full of water, there's no place to put extra air and still reduce pressure."

So, different pumps and valves, but more strenuous work. Meanwhile, Jonah kept peering at folks in the dim illumination of just two faint glow bulbs, watching for signs of the bends. Dizziness, muscle aches, and labored breathing? These could just be the result of hard labor. The book said to watch out also for joint pain, rashes, delirium, or sudden unconsciousness. He did know that the old dive tables were useless—based on Earth-type humanity. *And we've changed. First because our scientist ancestors modified themselves and their offspring. But time, too, has altered what we are, even long after we lost those wizard powers. Each generation was an experiment.*

Has it made us less vulnerable to such things? Or more so?

Someone tugged his arm. It wasn't Petri, striving at her pump. Jonah looked down at one of the children, still wearing a stained and crumpled bridesmaid's dress, who pulled shyly, urging Jonah to come follow. At first, he thought: *It must be the sickness. She's summoning me to help someone's agony. But what can I do?*

Only it wasn't toward the stern that she led him, but the forward-most part of the ship . . . to the view patch, where she pointed.

"What is it?" Pressing close to the curved pane, Jonah tensed as he starkly envisioned some new cloud of debris . . . till he looked up and saw—

—light. Vague at first. Only a child's perfect vision would have noticed it so early. But soon it spread and brightened across the entire vault overhead.

I thought we would pass through the therm-o-cline. He had expected a rough—perhaps even lethal—transition past that supposed barrier between upper and lower oceans. But it must have happened gently, while he slept.

Jonah called someone to relieve Petri and brought her forth to see.

"Go back and tell people to hold on tight," Petri dispatched the little girl, then she turned to grab Jonah's waist as he took the control straps. At this rate they appeared to be seconds away from entering Venusian hell.

Surely it has changed, he thought, nursing a hope that had never been voiced, even in his mind. *The ocean has burgeoned as life fills the seas. . . .*

Already he spied signs of movement above. Flitting, flickering shapes—living versions of the crushed and dead tumbledowns that sometimes fell to Tairee's bottom realm, now undulating and darting about what looked like scattered patches of dense, dangling weed. He steered to avoid those.

If the sea has changed, then might not the sky, the air, even the highlands?

Charts of Venus, radar mapped by ancient Earthling space probes, revealed vast continents and basins, a topography labeled with names like Aphrodite Terra and Lakshmi Planum. Every single appellation was that of a female from history or literature or legend. Well, that seemed fair enough. But had it been a cruel joke to call the baked and bone-dry lowlands "seas"?

Till humanity decided to make old dreams come true.

What will we find?

To his and Petri's awestruck eyes, the dense crowd of life revealed glimpses—shapes like dragons, like fish, or those ancient *blimps* that once cruised the skies of ancient Earth. And something within Jonah allowed itself to hope.

Assuming we survive decompression, might the fiery, sulfurous air now be breathable? Perhaps barely, as promised by the sagas? By now, could life have taken to high ground? Seeded in some clever centuries delay by those same pre-Coss designers?

His mind pictured scenes from a few dog-eared storybooks, only enormously expanded and brightened. Vast, measureless jungles, drenched by rainstorms, echoing with the bellows of gigantic beasts. A realm so huge, so rich and densely forested that a branch of humanity might thrive, grow, prosper, and learn—regaining might and confidence—beneath that sheltering canopy, safe from invader eyes.

That, once upon a time, had been the dream, though few imagined it might fully come to pass.

Jonah tugged the tiller to avoid a looming patch of dangling vegetation. Then, ahead and above, the skyward shallows suddenly brightened, so fiercely that he and Petri had to shade their eyes, inhaling and exhaling heavy gasps. They both cried out as a great, slithering shape swerved barely out of the sub's way. Then brilliance filled the cabin like a blast of molten fire.

I was wrong to hope! It truly is hell!

A roar of foamy separation . . . and for long instants Jonah felt free of all weight. He let go of the straps and clutched Petri tight, twisting to put his body between hers and the wall as their vessel flew over the sea, turned slightly, then dropped back down, striking the surface with a shuddering blow and towering splash.

Lying crumpled below the viewing patch, they panted, as did everyone else aboard, groaning and groping themselves to check for injuries. For reassurance of life. And gradually the hellish brightness seemed to abate till Jonah realized, *It is my eyes, adapting. They never saw daylight before.*

Jonah and Petri helped each other stand. Together, they turned, still shading their eyes. Sound had transformed, and so had the very texture of the air, now filled with strange aromas.

There must be a breach!

With shock, still blinking away glare-wrought tears, Jonah saw the cause. Impact must have knocked loose the dog bolts charged with holding shut the main hatch, amidships on the starboard side—never meant to open anywhere but at the safety of a colonial dock.

With a shout he hurried over, even knowing it was too late. The poisons of Venus—

—apparently weren't here.

No one keeled over. His body's sole reaction to the inrushing atmosphere was to sneeze, a report so loud and deep that it rocked him back.

Jonah reached the hatch and tried pushing it closed, but *Bird of Tairee* was slightly tilted to port. The heavy door overwhelmed Jonah's resistance and kept gradually opening, from crack to slit, to gap, to chasm.

"I'll help you, Jonah," came an offer so low, like a rich male baritone, yet recognizably that of his wife. He turned, saw her eyes wide with surprise at her own voice.

"The air . . . it contains. . . ." His words emerged now a deep bass. ". . . different gases than . . . we got from pinyons."

Different . . . but breathable. Even pleasant. Blinking a couple of times, he managed to shrug off the shock of his new voice and tried once more to close the hatch before giving up for now. With the boat's slight leftward roll, there was no immediate danger of flooding, as seawater lapped a meter or so below. The opening must be closed soon, of course. . . .

. . . but not quite yet. For, as Jonah and Petri stood at the sill, what confronted them was more than vast, rippling-blue ocean and a cloud-dense firmament. Something else lay between those two, just ahead and to starboard, a thick mass of shimmery greens and browns that filled the horizon, receding in mist toward distant, serrated skylines. Though he never dreamed of witnessing such a thing firsthand, they both recognized the sight, from ancient, faded pictures.

Land. Shore. Dense forests. Everything.

And overhead, creatures flapped strange, graceful wings, or drifted like floating jellyfish above leafy spires.

"It will take some time to figure out what we can eat," his wife commented, with feminine practicality.

"Hm," Jonah replied, too caught up in wonder to say more, a silence that lasted for many poundings of his heart. Until, finally, he managed to add—

"Someday. We must go back down. And tell."

After another long pause, Petri answered.

"Yes, someday."

She held him tight around the chest, a forceful constriction that only filled Jonah with strength. His lungs expanded as he inhaled deeply a sweet smell, and knew that only part of that was her.

Nick Wolven's fiction has appeared in *Asimov's*, *The Magazine of Fantasy and Science Fiction*, and *Analog*, among other publications. He lives in New York City with his family.

NO PLACEHOLDER FOR YOU, MY LOVE

Nick Wolven

1.

Claire met him at a dinner party in New Orleans, and afterward, she had to remind herself this was true. Yes, that had been it, his very first appearance. It seemed incredible there had been anything so finite as a first time.

He was seated across from her, two chairs down, a gorgeous woman on either side. As usual, the subject had turned to food.

"But I've been to this house a dozen times," one of the gorgeous women was saying. "I've been to dinner parties, dance parties, even family parties. And every time, they serve the wrong kind of cuisine."

She had red hair, the color of the candlelight reflected off the varnished chairs. The house was an old house, full of old things, handmade textiles and walnut chiffoniers, oil paintings of nameless Civil War colonels.

"Is that a problem?" said the young man on Claire's left. "Why should you care?"

"Because," said the redhead, pursing her lips. "Meringue pie, at an elegant soiree? Wine and steak tartare, at a child's birthday party? Lobster bisque at a dance? For God's sake, it was all over the floor. It seems, I don't know. Lazy. Thoughtless. Cobbled together."

She lifted her glass of wine to her mouth, and the liquid vanished the instant it touched her tongue.

The man who was to mean so much to Claire, to embody in his person so much hope and loss, leaned over his soup, eyes dark with amusement. "It *is* cobbled together. Of course it is. But isn't that the best part?"

"And why is that, Byron?" someone said with a sigh.

Byron. A fake name, Claire assumed, distilled from the fog of some half-remembered youthful interest. But then, you never knew.

Whatever the source of his name, Byron's face had the handsome roughness earned through active living. Dots of stubble grayed his skin. A tiny scar divided one eyebrow. His smile made a charming pattern of wrinkles around his eyes. It was a candid face, a well-architected face, a forty-something face.

"Because," said Byron, and caught Claire's eye, as if only she would understand. "Look at this furniture, the chandelier. Look at that music stand in the corner. American plantation style, rococo, Art Nouveau. Every piece a different movement. Some are complete anachronisms. That's why I love this house. You can see the spirit of the designers, here. A kind of whimsy. It's so personal, so scattershot."

"You're such a talker, Byron," someone sighed.

"Look at all of you," Byron said, moving his spoon in a circle to encompass the ring of faces. "Some of you I've never seen before in my life. And here we are, brought together by chance, for one evening only. You know what? That delights me. That thrills me." His gesture halted at Claire's face. "That enchants me."

"And after tonight," said the redhead, "we'll go our separate ways, and forget each other, and maybe never see each other again. So is that part of the wonder, for you, Byron, or does that spoil the wonder?"

"It does neither," Byron said, "because I don't believe it."

His eyes settled on Claire's. Again, he smiled. She had always liked older men, their slightly chastened air, their solemn and good-humored strength.

"I don't believe we'll never see each other again," Byron said, looking at his spoon. "I don't believe that's necessarily our fate. And you know what? The truth is, I wouldn't mind living in this house forever. Even if they do serve alphabet soup at a dinner party."

He lifted his hand to his mouth and touched his spoon to his lips. And instantly, the liquid disappeared.

When they had cleared the table, the entertainments began. There were board games in the living room, a live band on the lawn. Stairs led to a dozen shadowy bedrooms, with sad old beds, and rich old carpets, and orchids in baskets on the moonlit windowsills. In town, the music of riverbank revelry scraped and jittered out of ramshackle bars, and paddleboats rode on the slow Mississippi, jingling with the racket of riches won and lost.

Byron borrowed a set of car keys from the houseboy. Claire followed him onto the porch. The breath of the bayou was in the air, warm and buoyant, holding up the clustered leaves of the pecan trees and the high, star-scattered sky. Sweat held her shirt to the small of her back, as if a hand were there, pressing her forward.

"Shall we take a ride?" The car keys dangled, tinkling, from Byron's upraised hand.

"Wait," said Claire, "do that again."

"This?" He gave the keys another shake. The sound tinkled out, a sprinkling of noise, over the thick green nap of the lawn.

"It sounds just like it," Claire said. "Don't you hear it? It sounds just like the midnight chime."

"Oh, God, don't talk about that now. It's not for hours." Byron went halfway down the porch steps, held out a hand. "We still have plenty of time to fall in love."

The car waiting for them was an early roadster, dazzling with chrome, large and slow. Byron handled the old-fashioned shift with expert nonchalance. They slid past banquet halls downtown, where drunkenness and merriment and red, frantic faces sang and sweated along the laden tables. Often, they pulled to the curb and idled, and the night with its load of romance rolled by.

At a corner café where zydeco livened the air, a young couple argued at a scrollwork table.

"But how can you define it? How can you even describe it?" The woman's arm swung as she spoke, agitating the streetlights with a quiver of silver bracelets.

"Well, it's easy enough to *define*, anyway." The man made professorial motions with his hands. "It was simply a matter of chemistry."

"But how would that be any different from, say, smell?"

"Oh, it wasn't, not really. Taste and smell. Love and desire. All variations on the same experience."

The couple lifted fried shrimp from a basket as they spoke, the small golden morsels vanishing like fireflies on their lips.

"It can't be so simple," the woman said. And the man leaned over the table, reaching for her face, and turned it toward his lips. "You're right. It's not."

"I used to have those kinds of conversations," Byron sighed. He grasped the old maple knob of the shift, and pulled away from the curb.

They drove out of town onto rural dirt roads, where moonlight splashed across the land. In a plank roadhouse, a dance party was underway, a fiddle keening over stamping feet. Parked in the dirt lot, soaked in yellow light, they conducted the usual conversation.

"Now, me?" Byron said. "Let me tell you about myself. I'm a middle-aged computer programmer who enjoys snuggling, whiskey, and the study of artificial environments. I have a deathly aversion to crowds, and I'm not afraid to admit it. I'm nowhere near as handsome as this in real life, and I can assure you, I've been at this game a very long time."

His face dimpled as he delivered his spiel, not quite smiling. Claire laughed at his directness. Byron thumped a short drumroll on the wheel.

"And you?"

"Oh, me?" Claire said. "Me? I'm no one."

"That's an interesting theory."

"What I mean is, I'm no one anyone should care about. *I* don't even care about me."

"That can't be true."

"I guess not. I guess what I mean is, I don't care who I used to be." Claire watched the figures dance in the building, the plank walls trembling as shadows moved like living drawings across the dirty windows. "I care what happens to me now, though. I care about nights like this."

Her lazy hand took in the dancers, the stars. Byron sat back, nodding.

Claire surrendered. "I don't know. There's an interesting woman back there, somewhere. A scholar, a geneticist. But it's hard to believe, nowadays, that she ever existed."

"Tell me about this geneticist," he said.

"Well." Claire afforded him a smile. "What do you want to know? She looked like me. She talked like me. She loved all the things I love. She loved rainy windows and Scrabble and strong tea. She loved her body, because she had a nice one, and she loved to take long baths with organic soap, and she loved the idea that one day, far in her future, there might be someone to share those baths with her. Mostly, I think, she loved the idea that she could find a man who didn't care about any of those things. A man who would simply take her hand and say, 'Let's go.'"

The fiddle stopped. The dancers halted. The shadows on the windows settled into perfect sketches: honey-colored men and women with open, panting lips.

"She was young," Claire said. "And she was lonely."

Byron nodded. "I understand."

Someone threw open the roadhouse door. A carpet of gold rolled down the steps, all the way up the hood into the car, covering Claire in mellow light. Byron studied her. She knew what he was seeing. A beautiful blonde, a perfect face, a statue of a body with cartoon-sized eyes.

"But you're not," he said. And after a moment, he clarified: "Young. Not anymore. Are you?"

"No," said Claire. "Not anymore."

They drove to town along a different route, on dark, swampy roads where alligators slithered, grunting, from the wheels. On a wharf lined with couples and fishing shops, they stood at the wood rail, looking over the water, waiting together for the midnight chime. A gas-powered ferry struggled from shore, heading northeast toward a sprawl of dark land.

"I don't care," Byron said. "I don't care if you were a biologist. I don't care if you love Scrabble or tea. I don't care about any of that." He held out a hand. "Let's go."

The couples on the wharf had fallen silent, waiting. The very twinkling of the stars seemed to pause. Still, the ferry strained and chugged, heading for a shore it would never reach.

"Say it," Claire said. "You say it first, then I'll say it, too."

"I want to see you again," Byron said.

She took his hand. Before she could respond, the midnight chime sounded. It came three times, eerie and clear, like a jingle of celestial keys. And Byron and the river and the world all disappeared.

2.

Claire didn't see him again for a thousand nights.

It felt like a thousand, anyway. It may have been more. Claire had stopped counting long, long ago.

There were always more nights, more parties, more diversions. And, miraculous as it seemed, more people. Where did they come from? How could there be so many pretty young men, with leonine confidence and smiling lips? How could there be so many women arising out of the million chance assortments of the clubs, swimming through parties as if it could still be a thrill to have a thousand eyes fish for them—as if, like the fish in the proverbial sea, they one day hoped to be hooked?

Claire considered them, contemplated them, and let them go their way. She dated, for a time, a very old, handsome man whose name, in some remote and esoteric way, commanded powerful sources of credit. His wealth opened up new possibilities: private beaches where no one save they two had ever stepped, mountain lodges where the seasons manifested with iconic perfection, pink and green and gold and white. But they weren't, as the language ran, "compatible"; they were old and tired in different ways.

She met a girl whose face flashed with the markings of youth: sharp earrings, studs, lipstick that blazed in toxic colors. But the girl's eyes moved slowly, with the irony of age. Theirs was a sexual connection. Night after night, they bowed out of cocktail hours, feeling for each other's hands across the crush of dances. Every exit was an escape. They sought the nearest private rooms they could find: the neon-bright retreats of city hotels, secret brick basements in converted factories. The thrill was one of shared expertise. Both women knew the limits of sex: what moves were possible, what borders impermeable. They cultivated the matched rhythm, the long caress. Sometimes Claire's new lover—whose name, she learned after three anonymous encounters, was Isolde—fed delicacies to her, improbable foods, ice carvings and whole cakes, a hundred olives impaled on swizzle sticks, fruit rinds in paintbox colors, orange and lime, stolen from the bottomless bins of restaurants. It was musical sport. Isolde perfected her timing, spacing each treat. Claire eased into a languor of tension and release, her body shivering with an automatic thrill. As the foods touched her mouth, one by one, they flickered immediately into nothingness—gone the instant she felt them, like words on her tongue.

A happy time, this. But love? Every night they were careful to say that magic phrase, far in advance of the midnight chime.

"I want to see you again."

"I want to see you, too."

And so the nights went by, and the dates, and the parties, spiced with anticipation.

Soon, Claire knew, it was bound to happen.

The end came in Eastern Europe.

"We could have been compatible, don't you think?"

They were reposing, at that moment, in a grand hotel with mountain views, somewhere west of the Caucasus, naked in bed while snow flicked the window. Isolde lifted a rum ball from a chased steel tray, manipulating it with silver tongs. She touched it to the candle, collected a curl of flame, brought the morsel, still burning, to her mouth, and snuffed it out of existence, fire and all, against her tongue.

Claire clasped her hands around a pillow. "Do you think so?"

Isolde seemed nervous tonight, opening and closing the tongs, pretending to measure, as with calipers, Claire's thigh, her knee.

"Don't get me wrong. I'm not saying we *are* compatible. I'm only talking about, you know. What might have been."

Beyond the window, white flakes swarmed in the sky, a portrait of aimless, random motion.

"We're attracted to each other," Isolde said. "We have fun. We always have fun."

"That's true. We always have fun."

"Isn't that what matters?"

"Nothing matters," Claire said. "Not for us. Isn't that the common consensus?" She made sure to smile as she said it, lying back with her hands behind her head.

Isolde seemed pained. "I'm only saying. If things had been different. We might have worked. We might have. . . ." She blushed before speaking the forbidden phrase. "We might have made a match."

Claire felt her smile congealing on her face. She marveled at that— watched, in the oak-framed mirror atop the dresser, as her expression became an expression of disgust. "But things *aren't* different. Wouldn't you say that's an important fact? Things are exactly, eternally what they are."

"Eternally. You can't know that."

"I can believe it." Claire sat up, looking out the window, where snowfall and evening had blanked out the sky. "If you want to know what might have been, just wait for the midnight chime. You'll get a thousand might-have-beens. A thousand Romeos and Juliets. A thousand once-upon-a-times."

Isolde was shaking, a subtle, repressed tremor that Claire only noticed by looking at the tongs in her hand.

"I know, I know. I'm only saying . . . I mean, how can you resist? How can you stop thinking about it? About us. About. . . ." Her voice dropped. "About love."

Claire turned from the window, saying nothing, but the mood of the view filled her eyes, the gray mountains falling away into whiteness, the cold precipitation of a million aimless specks.

"I just like to imagine," Isolde whispered. "That's all. I like to imagine it could be different."

A clock stood on the bedside table, scuffed wood and spotted brass, a heavy relic of interwar craftsmanship. Isolde snatched it up with a gasp.

"What's the matter?" Claire said.

"I just realized."

"What? What did you just realize?" In Claire's tone was an implied criticism. *What can there possibly be,* she wanted to ask, *for us to realize? What can we discover that we don't already know?*

Isolde touched the clock face. "We're in a time-shifted universe. The midnight chime comes earlier, here. At sunset."

They looked together at the window, where the sky had darkened to charcoal gray.

"We never said it," Isolde whispered. "We forgot to say it, this time." She lay beside Claire, a hand on her belly, saying in a shaking voice, "I want to see you again."

The clock ticked. Snow tapped the window.

"I want to see you again," Isolde repeated. "Claire? I want to see you again."

The clock hands had made a line, pointing in opposite directions. How precise, Claire wondered, would the timeshift be? Sometimes these things could be surprisingly inexact. Sometimes, even the designers made mistakes.

"Claire, *please* say it. I'm sorry I said all those things. We're not really a match. I was only speculating. Anyway, it doesn't matter. Does anything matter? We don't have to talk. We can go back to how it was. We can hang out, play games, have fun."

In only a moment, a new evening would begin: new faces, new men and women, new possibilities. A whole new universe of beautiful people, like angels falling out of the sky.

"Claire, please say it. I want to see you again."

"Maybe you will," Claire said.

And at that moment, the chime sounded, tinkling and omnipresent, shivering three times across the mountain sky. And Isolde and her voice and her tears disappeared.

3.

A dry period, then.

Dry? No, that word couldn't begin to describe this life. It was desert, desolate, arid, barren, with a harsh wind that cut across the eyes, with sharp-edged stones that stung the feet.

Claire became one of *those people*. She was the woman who haunts the edges of dance floors, rebuffing with silence anyone who dares to approach. At house parties, she wandered out for impromptu walks, seeking the hyperbolic darkness between streetlights, the lonely shadows below leylandii. At dinner parties, she made jokes intended to kill conversation.

"Knock, knock," Claire said, when young men leaned toward her.

"Who's there?"

"Claire."

"Claire who?"

"Exactly."

"Here's a good one," Claire said, to a woman who approached one night on a balcony, the champagne sparkles of a European city bubbling under their feet. "A woman walks into a bar full of beautiful people."

When the silence became uncomfortable, the woman prompted: "And?"

"And," said Claire, turning away, "who cares?"

She was bitter. But she didn't care about her bitterness. Like all things, Claire assumed, this too would pass.

On an Amazonian cruise, Claire hit her low point. It was, most surely, a romantic night. Big insects sizzled against the lamps that swung, dusky gold, from the cabin house. The river gathered white ruffles along the hull. A banquet was laid out on deck, river fish on clay platters borne by shirtless deckhands. The dinner guests lounged in a crowd of cane chairs. When Claire came up from below, she found the party talking, as always, about the food.

"I've been here a hundred times." The woman who spoke was white, brunette, beautiful. "I think I'm something of an expert on this universe. And what I always admire is the attention to local cuisine. Everything comes straight from the river. It's so authentic."

Claire, who'd entered unnoticed, startled them all with a loud, braying laugh.

"Excuse me?" said the woman. "What do you find so funny?"

The group stared, pushing back their chairs, eyes kindled with reflected lantern light.

"This," Claire said, and snatched a clay platter out of the hands of the servingmen. "I find this funny." She dumped the fish on the floor, jammed the platter into her mouth. They all winced as her teeth clamped down, grinding on textured ceramic. "Mm, so authentic."

"What in the world," said the woman, "is the matter with you?"

"Nothing. I'm simply trying to eat this platter."

"But *why?*"

"Because why shouldn't I?" Claire smashed the platter on the deck. "Why shouldn't I be able to? What difference does it make? Why shouldn't any-thing—any of this—be food?" She stomped around the deck, offering to take bites of the rails, the lamps, the life preservers. "Why shouldn't I be able to perform the trick with anything I want? Why shouldn't I be able to pick *you* up, and send you into the ether with just a touch of my tongue?"

She grabbed at the arm of a nearby man, who pushed his chair back, wink-ing. "Please do."

Claire threw his hand down in disgust. "I should be able to pick up any-thing I see, and touch it to my lips, and make it disappear. And why can't I? It works with fish. It works with fruit. It works with soup and fried shrimp and wedding cakes."

Expecting protest, mockery, a violent reaction, she faced with dismay the rows of indifferent, idle faces.

"God, I'm so sick of this life," Claire finished weakly. "I'm sick of always talking about things I can never have."

"But are you sick of me?"

Claire turned and Byron was standing behind her, leaning on the rail beside the deckhouse, a beer bottle dangling from his hand.

"You?" Claire was stunned. She could hardly believe she recognized him, but she did.

Byron strolled forward and touched her hand. "You never said it."

"Sorry?"

"Eight hundred and ninety-two nights ago. New Orleans. I said I wanted to see you again. You never answered."

"I meant to." Claire struggled for breath, aware of the watching crowd. "I wanted to. I ran out of time."

He flung his beer bottle overboard. She waited without breathing for it to plunk in the distant water.

"We have time now," he said.

Dismissing the party with a wave, Byron guided Claire into a lifeboat. With a push of a lever, a creak of pulleys, he lowered them to the water and cut the rope. They drifted loose in darkness, a lantern at their feet. The big boat moved away on a thump of diesel, the strings of lamps and the hundred can-dles merging into one gold blur. Byron set the oars in the locks, rowing with a grace that seemed derived from real strength: strength of body, of muscle and sinew, strength that belonged to the kinds of people they had both once been.

"Do you know why we can't eat food?" Byron spoke at his ease, fitting sentences between the creak of the oarlocks. "Do you know why we have no taste, no smell, no digestion? Do you know why we can never eat, and only make food vanish by touching it to our lips?"

His voice sounded elemental, coming out of the darkness: the voice of the river, the jungle, the night.

"Appetite," Byron said. "We were made without appetite. We were made to want only one thing. True love."

He let the oars rest. They rocked on the water. The riverboat was gone now, its voices and music lost in buggy stridor.

"I don't believe that." Claire let her hand trail in the water, wondering if piranhas and snakes stocked the river, if the authenticity of the environment extended that far. "I don't believe any of this was planned. Not to that extent. I think it's all nothing more than a sick, elaborate accident."

He considered her words, the oars resting, crossed, in his lap. "You must believe that some of this was designed. You must remember designing it. Or designing yourself, I mean: what you look like, how you think. I've forgotten quite a bit, but I do remember that."

A fish nibbled Claire's finger. She lifted her hand, shook off the drops.

"I don't mean the world itself," Claire said. "I mean about what's happened to us. The way we live. Something's gone wrong. I don't think it was intentional."

Byron nodded. "Apocalypse."

"Plague. Asteroids. Nuclear holocaust."

"Economic collapse. Political unrest." He joined in her joking tone. "Or only a poorly managed bankruptcy. And somewhere out in the Nevada desert, sealed away in a solar-powered server farm, a rack of computers sits, grinding away at a futile simulation, on and on through the lonely centuries."

She waved away his glib improvisation, accidentally spraying his face with drops.

"I don't think that's what happened. Do you know what I think? I think we've simply been forgotten."

He smiled, nodding in time with the rocking boat.

"That's all," Claire said. "They made us, they used us for a while, they lost interest. They kept their accounts, or their subscriptions, or whatever, but they stopped paying attention. They don't care if we find love. They don't care about anything we do."

"And yet." Byron resumed rowing. "If they knew. . . ."

"What?" Claire was irritated at the portentous way he trailed off. "If they knew what?"

He glanced behind him, checking their direction. "Oh, you know. If they knew how wonderfully independent we've become. How clever and shy. How

suave in the art of romance. How proficient at avoiding any kind of commitment."

"In other words," said Claire, "just like them."

Byron rested a moment, the oars under his chin. "Meet with me again. Say
the words."

Claire looked away from him, down into the water, the black oblivion sliding by. "This can't go anywhere. You know it can't. It can't become anything.
We can't become anything."

"I don't care. Say the words."

"It can never be more than a casual thing."

"All well and good. Say the words."

"It can only make us unhappy. We can only go so far. We'll reach a certain
point, and we'll realize we're done. Finished. Forever incomplete. It will be
like picking up a delicious piece of food and seeing it vanish on our tongues."

"Brilliant analogy. Say the words."

"I want to see you," Claire said, tears in her eyes. "I want to see you, again
and again."

(And wondering, even while she said this, and not for the first time, why
the people who built this terrible world had left so much out, had omitted
taste, had excised smell, had eliminated pleasure, drunkenness, pain, death,
injury, age, and appetite, but had left in these two strange and unpleasant
details, had endowed every person with sweat and tears.)

We're not like them, Claire thought, as Byron, letting the oars ride idle,
leaned across the boat. *We look like them, we have their habits, their interests,
their hopes, even some of their memories. We think and feel like them, whether
they know it or not. We can even, in some ways, make love like them. But we're not
like them, not really, and it all comes down to this: whatever we desire, whatever
we do, we'll never know the difference between a drink and a kiss.*

When Byron's lips met hers, a precise and dry contact, it surprised Claire,
momentarily, that neither of them disappeared.

4.

How many times did they meet? Claire didn't bother to count. They saw
each other in hunting lodges, English gardens, an undersea city, the surface
of Mars, the gondola of a transatlantic blimp. To Claire, all locations were
frames for Byron's figure. More than his body, more than the frankness of his
smile, she began to love the touch of his hand, the way it overlaid hers on the

rails of ocean liners, felt for hers, casually, in the press of theater lobbies. He was a man who coveted contact: half-conscious, constant. She loved his need to know she was there.

And still, he was something much stranger than a lover. In this world, there was one sure pleasure, and this was the pleasure Byron offered. Talk.

"What was it?" she asked him, one night as they mingled, duded out in rodeo getups, with the square-dancing clientele of a cowboy bar. "In New Orleans, that night, you sought me out. What was it that made you notice me?"

Byron didn't hesitate. "A question," he said.

"And what question was that?"

He pointed at their knee-slapping environs: the mechanical bull, the rawhide trimmings, the Stetsons and string ties and silver piping. "Our lives are a joke. Anyone can see that, I guess I wondered why you weren't laughing."

She laughed then, making herself sad with the sound.

Other evenings they shouted over a buzz of airplane propellers, under the bump of disco, across the chill seats of a climbing chairlift. But always they talked, endlessly, oblivious to their surroundings, one conversation encompassing a thousand fragmented days.

"And you?" Byron spoke between sips of drinks that vanished like snow under his breath. "What did you see in me?"

Claire smiled, silent. She knew he knew the answer.

In the private bedrooms of an endlessly itinerant courtship, they never stripped off their clothes, never attempted the clumsy gyrations that passed for sex. They lounged in lazy proximity, fully clothed. Claire felt no reserve. With Byron, there was no question of making a match. His worn, mature face, sadly humorous, told her he'd put all such questions behind him.

"Anyway, it doesn't matter." He often held her hand, rubbing her thumb with his. "You say we've been forgotten. Some people say we've been abandoned. But what would it change, if we knew the truth? Things would be the same whatever happened in—well, in what I suppose we have to call 'the real world.'"

"Would they?" Claire focused on the confidence with which he spoke, the weary conviction of his old, wise voice.

Byron narrowed his eyes. "That's what I believe. We were made to live this way. We were never meant to find a match." He lifted himself on an elbow, gazing across the folds and drapes of the bedroom, the swaddling silk abundance of an ancient four-poster bed. "Look, the idea is we're proxies, right? Our originals, they got tired of looking for love. The uncertainty, the effort. So they made us. Poured in their memories and hopes, built this playground, so we could do what they didn't want to do, keep mixing and mingling and trying and failing. And one day we would find a match, and that would be it, our work would be done, and we would be canceled, deleted, for them to take over."

Claire lay still, withholding comment. There was a real thrill, she thought, in hearing things put so plainly, the cynical logic of their lives.

"But what if," Byron said, "that wasn't ever their real goal? What if they never wanted love at all? What if they only *wanted* to want it—wanted, in some way, to be *able* to want it? You remember how things were. We all remember at least some of that world. Was it ever such a loving place? The overcrowding. The overwork. It was so much better to be alone. What if this place only exists . . . what if we only exist to . . . to stand in for something, represent something, some kind of half-remembered dream? A dream our originals had mostly given up, but still felt, in some way, they ought to be dreaming?"

"Oh, God," Claire sighed.

"I'm sorry." Byron touched the backs of the hands she held over her face. "I shouldn't be talking like this."

"It's not that." She dropped her hands. "It's that it's all so wrong. You make it sound even more hopeless than it is."

"I don't believe it's hopeless."

"But if we're only here to go on some futile, empty search . . . I mean, why?" She sat up, holding fistfuls of sheet. "We're a joke twice over. A fake of a fake. Even if they didn't know we would. . . . " She was garbling her remonstrations, caught, as usual, between religion and philosophy. "I mean, why would anyone put us *through* this?"

He lay back, staring, pale as an empty screen. "Claire, what if I told you we could make a match?"

She held a pillow to her breast, suddenly cold, wondering if it was the kind of cold a real human being would feel. "Don't say that."

"I mean it."

"Don't say it. You know what will happen. I hate this world. I hate the people who made it. I hate myself, whatever I am, and I hate the woman I used to be. But I'm not ready to—"

"I'm not saying you have to."

She watched him with bared teeth, projecting all her fear onto his alarmingly calm face.

"I'm saying we can do it." Byron's eyes were like red wine, dark and flickering. "We can do it without giving anything up. We can commit to each other, forever, without being deleted or vanishing. We can declare our love, and no one will ever know, or interfere, or steal it away from us."

"That's impossible." She bit her tongue until she could almost remember what it felt like to feel pain.

"It's entirely possible."

"That's not how things work."

"You forget. I told you once, long ago, I have an interest in virtual environments. Or anyway, I used to. I know exactly how this world works."

She sat up, seeing excitement shining from him via those two bright giveaways, perspiration and tears.

"Do you remember, Claire? New Orleans?" He sat up, reaching for her hands. "There's a dock, there, that runs far out into the river. A ferry sets out from it, every night, toward the far shore. Each night, it leaves a second earlier; each time, it travels a second farther. One time out of a thousand, it reaches the far bank. If we're on that ferry when it touches land, we'll be on a border, a threshold, a place where the rules no longer apply. When the scenario resets, we'll be left behind. We can live there forever, or however long the world lasts.

"Claire." He insisted, at that moment, on holding both her hands, as if needing to be doubly sure she was there. "Nothing is entirely random. I know you don't keep count of the nights, but I do. I've been tracking the evenings, observing the patterns. And I've been looking for a person to take along with me, one person to share with me the rest of time. You are that person. Say the words. In five nights, we will meet again, at a dinner party in New Orleans. The ferry will set out at eleven-forty. Come with me, Claire. Be with me on that deck. Step with me, together, out of this world."

She saw her fists vanish inside his. The midnight chime would sound in a moment, and with it new crowds, new possibilities, new glories of music and excitement would be conjured out of the unending night. Could she leave all that behind, stand with this man forever on the shore of one permanent land? Together, they would walk, never changing, down unchanging streets, where dance music streamed out of immortal cafés, where orchids stood, never wilting, on the sills of bedroom windows, silvered by a moon that never set. But these would be their cafés, their moon, their orchids, and if there was no way to know how long it might last, still, they would own together that unmeasured quantity of time, laying claim to one house with its scattershot furniture, and never live in fear of the midnight chime.

Already, tonight, that chime was sounding, jangling a warning across the sky. But Claire had time to speak the charmed words.

"I want to see you again."

5.

Around the long dining table in the house in New Orleans, Civil War colonels gazed out of their walnut frames. The candles were at work, scattering reflections, and the antique chairs creaked with conviviality. Claire sat next to Byron, intent on the French-style clock. Dinner was done, the plates cleared away, and two dozen puddings quivered in two dozen china bowls.

"Pudding," sighed a ravishing girl, dressed, like many, for the setting, in the rustling skirts of a Southern belle. "You see what I mean? It's all so random. Radicchio salads, oxtail for dinner, and they serve us chocolate pudding for dessert."

Claire, seated across the table, reflected that this was the last time she'd ever have to have this conversation.

Twenty-four spoons dipped and rose. Twenty-four servings of pudding vanished, dispelled by the touch of twenty-four tongues.

When the party dispersed, Byron took Claire's hand. At the door, he bent to her ear, and she felt his warm whisper. "Three hours. Stay close."

They stepped out onto the porch. And Byron disappeared.

Claire spun in confusion. The porch, the house, the whole scene was gone. She stood on a dance floor, surrounded by feet that stamped and swung and kicked up a lamplit dust. The dim air shivered to the scratch of a fiddle. There was absolutely no sign of Byron.

Trying to get her bearings, Claire clutched at the jostling shoulders. She spotted a door and wriggled toward it. The energy of the dance, like a bustling machine, ejected her into humid air.

Claire stumbled down three wooden steps. Looking back, she recognized the roadside bar where she'd sat with Byron on their first meeting, several thousand nights ago.

What had happened? Claire staggered toward the road. The moon made iron of the land, steel of the river, and the lights of town were far away.

The ferry! It was only a few miles from here, no more than a two-hour walk. Claire thought she could make it, if she hurried.

She'd walked a quarter of an hour when a vintage roadster, roaring from behind, froze her like a criminal in a flood of light. Byron pushed open the door.

"Get in."

Claire hurried to the passenger side, jumped into the leather seat. Byron stomped the gas, and the wheels of the car barked on gravel.

"It's glitching." Byron leaned forward as he drove. "The environment. The counters are resetting. Like I said, we're in a liminal place, tonight. The rules are temporarily breaking down. Look."

He tapped his wrist, where a watch glimmered faintly.

"It's after ten," Byron said. "It's been over an hour since I saw you. We've lost a chunk of time, and I'm afraid—damn." He swerved, almost losing control, as he caught sight of something down the road.

Twisting in her seat, Claire saw the roadside shack, the one she'd just exited, sliding by.

Byron cursed and pushed down on the gas. They rattled up to the old roadster's maximum speed, forty, fifty. Swamps, river, and road flowed by. The shack passed again, again, again.

"All right, that does it." Byron braked so hard, Claire nearly whacked her head on the dashboard. He fussed with the gearshift and twisted in his seat, wrapping an arm around her headrest.

"What's happening?" she asked.

"Can't you tell? We're looping."

"But what are you doing?"

"Desperate problems call for desperate measures." Byron squinted through the tiny rear windshield. "The way I see it, if you can't hit fast-forward, hit rewind."

The car jerked backward.

And car and road and Byron all screeched out of being, and Claire found herself sitting at a café table, alone, deep in the tipsy commotion of town.

She jumped up, knocking over her chair.

Once again, Byron was nowhere to be seen.

Claire cursed, turned in a full circle, cursed again. A passing man in a bowler hat picked up her chair, righted it, and touched his hat.

"Crazy, eh? All these jumps?" He straightened his jacket with a roll of his shoulders, looking up at the sky, as if expecting heaven to crack.

"But what do we do?" Claire gasped. "How do we stop it?"

The man in the bowler hat smiled and shrugged. "Nothing *to* do, I guess. Except play along."

Pantomiming, he grabbed a nearby barber pole, swung himself through an open door, and promptly, like a magician's rabbit, blinked out of existence.

Partiers ran past, giggling and tripping, stretching their faces in merry alarm, like people caught in a thunderstorm. Firefly-like, they meandered through doorways, laughing as they winked in and out of existence. In a world of rules and repetition, Claire had long since observed, childlike chaos greeted any variation in routine.

But what do I do? Claire ducked into a drugstore entrance. *What can I do, what should I do?* She did her best to steady her mind, analyze the situation. The jumps, the cuts, the vanishings and reappearances—they seemed to happen at moments of transition: entries and exits, sudden moves. If she found some way to game the system. . . .

Turning, Claire jumped through the drugstore door. And again, and again, and again, jump after jump. On her fifteenth jump, the trick worked, the environment glitched. Claire tumbled into a banquet hall, crashing into a tray-bearing waiter, scattering scallops and champagne flutes. "Sorry, sorry. . . ." Dashing toward the hall doors, Claire tried again. Another round of jumping propelled her into a rowboat, somewhere out in the stinking bayou. Gators splashed and rolled in the muck, grunting and hissing as they fled from her intrusion. Claire jumped into the water and ducked under, sinking her feet in the creamy ooze. She kicked, launching herself up into the air—

And found herself, sodden with mud, near the bank of the river, back in town.

How many times would she have to do this? Searching the bank, Claire saw no promising doors. She threw herself into the river three more times. The third time, she emerged in a backyard swimming pool.

And so, through portals and windows, through falls and reversals, Claire skipped her way through the liminal evening, traversing a lottery of locations, careening in her soaked dress and dirty hair through car seats, lawn parties, gardens and gazebos, bedrooms where couples lay twined in dim beds. Sometimes she thought she saw Byron, hurrying through a downtown doorway or diving over the rail of a riverboat, moving in his own Lewis Carroll quest through the evening's hidden rabbit holes. Mostly, she saw hundreds of other adventurers, laughing people who leaped and jostled through doorways, running irreverent races in the night.

At last, Claire stumbled out of a bait shop onto the dock, the ramshackle fishing shacks hung with buoys, the long span of planks laid out like a ruler to measure the expanse of her few remaining minutes—and there was the ferry, resting on the churn of its diesel engine, bearing Byron toward the far shore.

"Claire," he shouted over the water, and added something she couldn't hear.

Was it a freak of the fracturing environment, some cruel new distortion, that made the dock seem to lengthen as Claire ran? Was it a new break in that hopelessly broken world that made the planks passing under her feet seem infinite? By the time she came to the end of the dock, Byron and the ferry were in the middle of the river, and his call carried faintly down the boat's fading wake.

"Jump!"

Was he crazy? The distance was far too wide to swim.

"Claire, I'm serious, jump!"

And now, Claire understood: if it had worked before . . . a thousand-in-one chance, perhaps. . . .

Far across the river, Byron was waving. Claire looked into the water. Briefly, she hesitated. And this was the moment she would think back to, a thousand times and a thousand again: this instant when she paused and held back, wondering how badly she wanted to spend eternity in one home, one world, with one man.

The next instant, she had flung herself headfirst into the water. And perhaps this world made more sense than Claire thought. Perhaps the designers had known what they were doing after all. Because of all the cracks and rabbit holes in the environment, of all the possible locations in which she might emerge—

She was splashing, floundering, on the far side of the river, and the ferry was a few yards away.

Claire thrashed at the water, clawing her way forward, as the first of three chimes sounded over the water.

She'd forgotten to kick off her shoes. Her skirt wrapped her legs. She couldn't fall short, not after trying so hard, chasing potential romances down the bottomless vortex of an artificial night.

The second chime made silver shivers pass across the water.

So close. Claire tore at the waves, glimpsing, between the splashing of her arms, Byron calling from the ferry, leaning over the rail.

As she gave a last, desperate swipe, the third chime rang in the coming of midnight, the sound reminding Claire, as it always would, of the teasing jingle of a set of keys.

Around bright tables, under lamps and music, the partygoers had gathered, to mingle and murmur and comment on the food. So much beauty to be savored, so much variety: so many men and women with whom to flirt and quip and dance away the hours of an endlessly eventful evening. And after tonight, there would be more, and still more—men and women to be savored, sipped, dispelled.

If anyone noticed the woman who moved among them, searching the corners of crowded rooms; if anyone met her at the end of her dock, looking across the starlit water; if anyone heard her calling one name across the waves and throbbing music, they soon moved away. The party was just beginning, lively with romance, and the nights ahead were crowded with the smiles of unknown lovers.

An (pronounce it "On") Owomoyela is a neutrois author with a background in web development, linguistics, and weaving chain maille out of stainless steel fencing wire, whose fiction has appeared in a number of venues including *Clarkesworld*, *Asimov's*, *Lightspeed*, and a handful of Year's Bests. An's interests range from pulsars and Cepheid variables to gender studies and nonstandard pronouns, with a plethora of stops in between. Se can be found online at an.owomoyela.net.

OUTSIDER

An Owomoyela

Mota felt Io's arrival.

So did everyone else on the *Segye-Agbaye*; the networks picked her up and slotted her into their awareness like a new limb. She was reading in full dominant mode, a mental posture of command that brought everyone up short, but it resolved and her attention passed on to Mota and the other technicians quietly found something else to be interested in. Mota closed her eyes, and pulled herself away from the access panel she was working at.

[Apologies. I need you,] flashed into her communication line. Her mental sense of Io went tinged with regret, but not much of it. And it was overlaid with the quiet psych cue that got Mota by the scruff of her neck, made all her emotions cycle down, and made her limbs warm and heavy even in micro-gravity.

[Coming,] she signaled back. Not that it was necessary. Not that there was any question of whether or not she would.

She pushed off from the wall and headed down the corridor, the lights flowing over her skin as she passed. There was a familiar pattern to the output of each one; generations of modifications and repairs and replacements leaving each with its own strength and hue. And there was an atavistic comfort to moving through these halls, as though all the pieces of Mota's being that troubled her on the colony below fit seamlessly into the ship.

Io's presence was disruptive. When she wasn't *right there*, Mota might be able to resent her for that.

Io was waiting at the shuttle bay, standing tall and expansive, her feet on the floor as though she needed them there. Mota caught herself on one of the room's handholds and held herself there, her own body curled.

This close, the network bumped Io's presence up in its priority for Mota; she could feel Io's emotions like a second mental skin. Confidence and focus, curiosity and wariness directed at something off the ship, and that quiet, subtle tinge of chagrin. She could feel as well as Mota could that Mota would rather not be there.

She could also dismiss that out of hand. Work to be done.

"Apologies," she said again, though her emotions conveyed just how much of a formality it was. "You're needed. A foreign ship entered our system."

Surprise shocked through Mota's mind. *[A ship?]* she signaled back, letting her confusion flavor it. *[Clarify?]*

"Come with me," Io said, and turned to the shuttle.

Mota followed. She tried not to mind the tendril of annoyance wending from Io at getting a signal instead of a verbal reply.

The *Segye-Agbaye* held an orbit over the first point of landfall on Se, but after all this time the location was more symbolic than practical. Most of the major spaceports were on the other side of the planet, more closely hugging the equator, which meant that Io took their shuttle on a long angle down into the atmosphere toward a port with longer-range transports.

Se from above was nothing like the composite metal and regulated light of the *Segye-Agbaye*. It was a study in terraformed green and wispy white atmosphere, lit by a white sun, with the silvery lines of the colony spreading across its surface like a neural web. The quiet background murmur of the colony network became a warm ambient cloud, too many individuals to identify. Mota could swim in the sea of secondhand emotion, inclination, preoccupation until her own sense of self went fuzzy at the edges.

But being with Io changed that. She brought them down into one of the bays and stepped out and the colony parted for her; the port technicians quietly delegated someone to see to her, and the ambient noise quieted just as Mota herself had.

They boarded a fast, mid-range shuttle: nothing that would carry them outside of the dense inner system, but one that would convey them quickly. "Omo," Io said. One of the farther-flung unmanned stations, then.

Io linked into the ship's transmitters; she wanted Mota to do the same, so Mota did the same. It was easier, sometimes, to lean back and let her body connect with the network on an unconscious level; let herself be moved like a limb for the dominant force in the room.

The transmission kicked in, and brought with it another's telepresence. *Yan. Pilot. Working with the survey teams and contingency fleets.*

There was a warmth to Io's transmission out. *[I'm bringing Mota. She's the expert on ancient Earth.]*

Which had always been a useless, hobbyist's expertise. Mota sat up.

The cradle of humanity was far enough away to be irrelevant. Any knowledge about it was historical or speculative: even the evidence of its planets, writ into the wobble of its star, was information that had been issued in light long before anyone on Se was born.

[You found a ship?] she signaled, and the transmission went out to Yan.

"The ship entered the outer system and gave off a signal," Io said, and the response from Yan came back.

[It is from Earth,] Yan sent. His words were tinged with certainty and wonder. *[Will you be able to operate it?]*

Mota sent a request back to the databanks on Se. Better to queue up any resources she might need now, while the transmission delay was still small.

[I want to see it,] Mota sent back. Then, *[Maybe. I'll do my best.]*

Yan sent as much as he could back over the transmitters as they approached; Mota drank it in, moving through his recordings and the archived information the first colonists had brought with them. Earth must have had its own evolution after the *Segye-Agbaye* left; Mota could look back down an unbroken chain of history and see the Earth they had left behind, but the Earth of all those intervening years was shadowed to her. This ship, then, was a glimmer of light.

They docked on Omo and Io took the lead, guiding them through to the bay where Yan worked. Mota followed.

The room Yan occupied was large enough for one person to move comfortably in; not three. It was dominated by a central column, with a curved screen, which Yan was studying. He looked up and smiled to them as they entered.

Mota signaled greeting, and felt a flicker of concern pass through Yan. "She always prefers signal to vocal," Io said.

Not always, Mota thought, and she could feel Yan catch that thought, and respond with a gentle amusement. Io seemed to notice *that*, and the focus of her attention fell on Mota. Then it passed back to Yan.

Mota was silent for a moment, watching the interplay of their emotions. The landscape between them changed like the clouds playing across Se's atmosphere.

Then Yan turned to Mota. "There's text. It displayed as soon as I opened the hatch."

He waved his hand toward the screen, and Mota squeezed past him to look at it. She touched the screen—a brush at the corner, away from any of the symbols—and it changed. She touched it again; it changed again.

[Translation corpus?] Mota signaled. The interface was strange—tactile. *[An old Earth tradition. A critical number of words in their natural contexts. If it's a corpus, they didn't expect whoever found this ship to speak their language.]*

"A contact ship, then," Io said. "Specifically."

Mota hesitated, and felt Io sigh.

"Please," Io said, with a gesture to the corpus, and Mota felt like she was waking up. Like the faculties of her mind which had gone quiescent at Io's presence were, given her permission, rearing up again.

The network data on Earth sprang up in her mind, almost tangible under her fingers. *Not that language—not that one. Closer.* The *Segye-Agbaye* had left Earth early into its projected interstellar phase; this ship was different in design from the *Segye-Agbaye*, and its language didn't match exactly to any of the ones on record. How many generations separated them from their common ancestry? How long did it take for a language to evolve like this?

One of the programs flagged a pattern: some 68% similarity in the ship's language to another language, with the differences seeming to follow common linguistic rules. Mota selected the match, ran the program, and the corpus sprang into semi-legibility.

"I have it," she said, and part of her was surprised at that. *Comfortable enough to be vocal, then.* But now she could see the patterns of the foreign ship's operation, and she could make the ship respond. She highlighted the updated translation program on the network for Yan and Io.

A linguist could refine it, but the screen was at least interpretable now: Mota could look at a word and the network would take it from her visual cortex, and it would interpret it and deliver that information to the language centers of her brain.

"This column is a container," Mota said. She moved through the prompts, and the screen went transparent—enough to see a woman's face, her mouth and nose covered by some apparatus, her eyes closed.

Io moved forward, and Yan melted back to give her room. "A person?"

"Stasis," Mota said, and her hands fluttered. *[Generation ships like the* Segye-Agbaye *were considered to be a second-best solution,]* she signaled. *[Governments wanted to preserve individuals from Earth who would sleep through the interstellar voyage and wake up at their destination. So the astronauts who left Earth would also be the ones who arrived at the new colony.]* "If the ship is from Earth, then *she* is from Earth."

She felt their surprise. Awe from Yan, and a kind of hunger from Io. The hunger made her want to stand aside, become small and unnoticed again.

"Will she wake up?" Io asked. Mota took a breath. The air out here was recycled, like the air on the *Segye-Agbaye*; it was comforting.

"There are directions," she said, and found the playback controls. The screen changed—voice and printed language, but also animation. Instructions for anyone who found it. "I think she was expecting the system to be habited when she arrived."

"So it was," Io said. She turned to Mota. "Work with the medical staff. Help them understand anything they need to. This is our first contact with another population from Earth, Mota—time to put your history to use."

Io turned and pushed away, back out of the ship and into Omo station, leaving Mota with her hand still on the screen of the stasis chamber. Yan let out a soft breath, and Mota caught the undercurrent of it: wry humor, the sort born of recognizing someone's predispositions. Then it slid, transmuted into unease. He turned to her.

"You know about Earth history?" he asked.

Mota nodded.

"We restrict the number of single-person craft in our fleet," Yan said. "It's a poor ratio of resource use to utility. Did the Earth system have the resources to send single people on interstellar journeys?"

Mota turned back to the ship. Clearly they *had*, but it was a good question anyway. She thought back to everything she knew of Earth history, of the *Segye-Agbaye*'s reason for being, of its reason for design. A hundred thousand colonists had left from Earth; those had been her ancestors.

"No," she said. "This would be a waste."

Mota only advised the medical staff until they understood as much of the technology as she did, and then she escaped back to the *Segye-Agbaye*. She was happy to go. Ship systems were more intelligible to her than human systems, anyway.

But she was the expert on old Earth, if for no other reason than her curiosity had led her to study it. And so sooner or later the medical staff called her back—the woman was cogent, and wanted to see the ones who had retrieved her.

So Mota went down to Se again, and edged into the medical hall. The woman was already speaking with Io.

Seeing the woman sitting on one of the benches was strange, and unnerving. She was larger than the rest of them, her skin and hair paler, the planes of her face foreign. Mota paused in the doorway, trying to feel her presence—but of course the woman had no nanotransmitters entangled with her neural network, and no capacity to access the network that linked the rest of them. She was the first person Mota had seen who she couldn't feel.

Io turned to face Mota as she hesitated in the door, and motioned her in. Some of the unease faded in the face of Io's relative comfort, and Mota entered.

"Mota," Io introduced. "This woman gives her name as Eva. She thanks you for your part."

Mota looked at the woman. She opened her mouth, then frowned, and queried the network for a translation. Let the network inform her on how to shape her tongue into the shapes of words: "There's no need to thank me."

Some language technician must have sat down with the woman, captured the pronunciation of her words, used that to inform the translation program. When Eva spoke, the network caught her words and fed Mota the sense of them.

"I came seeking asylum," Eva said. Her face had adopted the kind of focus that said this had been a prepared statement. "On Earth, my people were being rounded up and destroyed. I was sent on the *Sojourn* with our historical record, so we wouldn't be lost to history forever." She watched Mota. "You are a historian?"

Mota fumbled for the words. "A technician. Interested in history. An archivist will help you." She looked to Io.

"Yan retrieved her vessel," Io said. "I've taken responsibility for her housing and orientation. But Eva wanted to thank you in person."

Mota moved her hands. "There is no need," she said again. She'd done what anyone with her skillset would have done—the socially healthy thing to do.

Io had a feeling of indulgence to her. Mota studied it, and as Io's attention turned back to Eva, Mota realized what she was picking up: a kind of proprietary attraction toward the strange Earth woman. Mota looked between them. Eva couldn't feel it, she realized. Io's formidable regard was lost on her.

[You are—] Mota started to signal, and then arrested that first inclination. Eva wouldn't see it, for the same reason she didn't feel Io's desire. But it was

like taking two steps backward off a cliff; the infrastructure of the network was as central to Mota as her own lungs were. She had to scramble for words, and then convince herself that words would be heard by the woman.

"To Io, you are interesting and physically pleasing," Mota said, hoping the translation would go through, that the corpus had the right words. Eva pulled back as though something had struck her. Mota frowned at her expression, and the sensation of falling in gravity redoubled itself. "You should be able to feel this, and—and react appropriately."

But, of course, she shouldn't. Because she didn't have the technology in her mind, and her neural network had long ago solidified past the point of introducing them. It turned Mota's stomach. Like Eva was only half a person.

Eva looked at Io, who had tilted her head at her. Mota turned her own attention to Io's emotions: concern, and consideration, and recognition. She must not have thought to explain herself to Eva. And why would she? Anyone would be able to read her emotions, and capturing emotional states in words was using the wrong tool for the job. Who would think to do that?

But Eva remained blank and unreadable, and soon the muscles in her face went neutral as well. "And what," she said, "is the correct reaction?"

There was no sarcasm radiating from her. Nor irony, nor sincerity. Nothing. Mota closed her eyes, and searched for the words.

"You," she said—carefully, carefully, fumbling through statements the translator had likely found translations for—"should be . . . it's to your advantage? Io is high in the hierarchy. It's . . . a privilege."

"I was asking her," Eva said, and Mota shrank back. "Io," Eva went on, "maybe we should speak—" then a word the network didn't translate. Io tilted her head. Eva frowned, and said, "Only the two of us?"

A strange request. But Io shrugged. "We can," she said. "You'll have to remind me that you can't feel what I say."

Mota was content to let Io orient Eva to life on Se. She preferred the *Segye-Agbaye* and the long rhythms of maintenance there, distancing herself from the novelty and celebrity that gathered around Eva on the planet below. Anything she needed, she could pull from the network; it was enough for her.

Until Yan sent her a transmission, asking for her presence on Omo station and the woman's ship, the *Sojourn*. She came, slipping into the narrow confines of the stasis chamber, where Yan was working.

[Earth historian,] Yan signaled. He was preoccupied; read as though he needed another brain and perspective to process something. Tickling at the edge of her mind, Mota could feel Io on an approach, as well. "Eva says that

on Earth, most of the powerful factions are people like us," Yan said. "Altered humans. They make laws that try to stamp Eva's people out."

Mota signaled, *[Altered.]* The word turned over in her mind. "From what?"

Yan's annoyance twined around the question, but it wasn't directed at her. "Natural humans. She says her people have nothing but variation in breeding."

[But all our variation was at one point selected by breeding.] On the *Segye-Agbaye*, with their limited resources, no one had been able to make a genetic loom; they could only splice the DNA they had. It had been another generation or two after landfall on Se before the looms had been built, and those only had been used to design and redesign the world's plant and animal life. Se's environment didn't have as many restrictions as the *Segye-Agbaye*. The adaptations which served life on the ship didn't hinder them on the ground.

Yan said, "Yes," in a tone of mock-dissent, but his emotional state was shaded with vindication. "But to Eva, our treating the genome in the zygote is artificial. Not to mention," he gestured at his head, "the network."

Mota balked. *[The network is an assistive machine! Her ship uses assistive machines!]* "She was in stasis!"

"It's different. To Eva, it's different." Yan snorted. "I looked up the history we brought on the *Segye-Agbaye*. You should look up factionalization. Outgrouping." He turned to Mota. "I think we became better humans on the *Segye-Agbaye*. We didn't have room to take all our behaviors with us."

Then his attention shifted off Mota, and his emotions turned anticipatory. Mota turned to look behind her, eyes hitting the screens first, then moving into the hall.

Motion, there—Io had apparently docked, though her presence felt as though she was still a few minutes out. Strange. But Eva was with her, her hand on Io's elbow, as though Io was leading her by touch. Eva was ungainly in the microgravity.

Mota felt the instinctive submission rising up in the back of her mind, but it was dampened. Io's attention wasn't on her, and she still felt abnormally far away.

"You've been working on my ship?" Eva asked.

"Mota studies historical objects," Io said. "Yan studies ships."

Eva looked from one of them to the other, then to Io. Io's curiosity was reflected in her face; all her attention was on Eva. Mota looked to Eva's face: this woman from Earth couldn't feel it.

How insulated, how isolated, must her life have been?

"Please do not," Eva said, turning to Mota. "The ship is . . . part of my historical record. I do not want it tampered with, or . . . made to fit your colony."

Sympathy and recognition from Io, and *now* Mota felt herself go distant and calm. This and that hormone releasing itself into her, patting down any protest. Io was determined that the decision should go Eva's way on this, and Mota felt no compulsion to make a stand in defiance. So it was all right, then, even though the *all right* slid over her own predilections to smother her. She signaled assent.

Yan frowned, but Mota could feel the acquiescence in him, as well. Disappointment, too. He held on a bit longer—his hierarchical distance wasn't as far as Mota's—but then he exhaled, his muscles relaxed, and he signaled assent as well. "It's a lovely ship," he said. Wistful. "I haven't seen any like it."

Eva's face softened into a smile, but it looked like a transmission delay. Mota shook her head, trying to clear it. The distance from Io and the lag from Eva made it feel as though they were talking across gulfs, either of fractions of kilometers or whole light-seconds. It made her dizzy.

[Come on,] Yan signaled. Mota followed him back to the shuttle, and he pointed it back toward Se.

After a while, she signaled *[Frustrated.]*

Yan echoed the sentiment, but said, "Maybe she wants to cling to the familiar."

Mota turned her head to the window, watching the stars. *[I wish we could feel her.]*

Assent from Yan. Mota sighed, and closed her eyes, and let her mind drift.

Then there was a hand on her shoulder.

Mota jumped, body and mind jarred out of her doze. She spun, and there was Yan, his expression concerned. And, yes, she could feel his concern, but barely—as though he were kilometers away, not there, next to her. She shook her head, blinked, tried to make the image resolve into what she felt over the network.

"Something is wrong," Yan said. *[You went dark. I thought you were dead.]* His signal was far fainter than it should have been.

[You're distant,] she signaled back.

Yan squinted at her. "Sometimes, when we go in for close chromosphere scans, we'll get interference like this," he said. "I can't feel my team. It's like we've all become ghosts."

Like Eva, Mota thought. But the idea that Eva was a ghost was ridiculous. Ghosts didn't come in stasis, didn't have to have their ancient Earth ships interpreted and their blood cleaned of chemicals. Ghosts did not exist.

"There's always some variation in the strength of the network signal," Yan said. "Solar weather affects it, even as far out as Se. But mostly it's not noticeable. And we don't have that weather today."

Mota moved closer, not that it helped. *[Is it here?]* she signaled, then winced—it felt as though she was talking into vacuum. She marshaled her thoughts into words so that she could speak them—clumsier, yes, but at least she could hear her own voice and Yan's, and the sound didn't belie the distance. "Is it just this transport? Localized weather?"

Yan shifted, and his distant unease echoed across to her. "We'll find out once we're back on Se," he said.

Se was in a state of unrest.

Yan brought them down onto the port, and into a muted background hum of unease. Even on the planet, even with the density of population there, it felt as though isolation was blooming up on the network around them.

A query against the network produced no answers, and Yan shook his head. "I can check the solar monitor stations," he said.

Mota raised her face to the sky.

"Technician," Yan said. A reminder, perhaps. Hard to tell. "I'm sure there's something you can do. Can you go to one of the network nodes?"

[Perhaps,] Mota signaled. "Safe flight," she said, and Yan turned back to the port.

Mota went to the archives.

She wasn't trained in any of the network maintenance, and while she could just show up and ask to help, something else had her curiosity. She accessed the central archives and queried for the historical record Eva had brought.

She didn't know what she was looking for. Eva's history was like much of the Earth history Mota was familiar with: one group choosing to annihilate another over conflicts that looked absurd from a distance. Their conflict had been genetic: Eva's people refusing any engineered alteration, even disease immunity. And their opponents had been winnowing away human genetic diversity. Both stances were ridiculous, to Mota's mind—and the records were dead, without the encoded emotional resonance which would have helped her understand.

Eva was here, now, a single survivor who would have to adapt. And Se and its system were vast; more variation existed now than had left on the *Segye-Agbaye*. Her conflict was an Earth conflict, and by now it was generations behind her.

Perhaps Io would show her that.

Eva appeared as Mota was leaving. Mota walked out of central data storage and there she was, standing tall as Io or any of the others at the top of the hierarchy did. Never mind that she was foreign, an alien, outside of the hierarchy entirely; Mota felt the hairs on the back of her neck prick up, and if Eva had been part of the colony and as prestigious as she imagined herself to be, she would have made Mota settle with a look and an intention.

She was speaking with one of the archivists. The network was still translating, but the translations came through soft: the network heard Eva's words through Mota's ears, and it queried for the definitions, but the whispered meaning floated to her over a gulf. If she hadn't been on Se, nestled in among the smart buildings and the network transmitters, Mota wondered if she'd be able to understand Eva's words at all.

She turned and headed away, feeling disconnected and bow-legged in Se's gravity. The *Segye-Agbaye* would feel empty, if the interference persisted there—even Se felt empty, like the ocean of presence had ebbed back down some all-surrounding shore—but the ship was still more familiar. Mota wanted to cling to that familiarity.

There was sound behind her, and she ignored it. Moved down the hallway toward the port until Eva's voice called, "Wait!"

Mota wanted to push along the wall, propel herself into a different place entirely. She was faster in microgravity.

Instead, she turned, and saw Eva coming toward her. There was no command emanating from her; Mota could have walked away.

Instead, she waited, head tilted, watching the Earth woman approach.

"Mota, right?" Eva asked.

Mota nodded.

"You're a technician?"

Mota nodded again, trying to work out how to communicate that Eva should hurry up, get to the point, let her go. Io, at least, would read her discomfort and disengage. Eva seemed ignorant of it. And here, with the strange fog clouding the network, no one else could feel the dynamic and intervene.

That frightened Mota.

"Io's explained your hierarchy," Eva said. "I couldn't believe it. You're a *slave?*"

Mota frowned. The word *slave* hadn't been translated, and after all this time with Io, she felt like Eva should have been able to ask for whatever words she needed. She signaled *[What?]*, then caught herself, and asked aloud.

"You don't have free will," Eva said. "You were born into a low caste—"

And that—that was factually *wrong*, and Mota cut her hand through the space between them. "I have free will," she said. She knew *that* concept.

Eva looked surprised to be interrupted, but then she banished the expression from her face. "But you were designed never to argue with your superiors," she said. "You were forced—"

"No," Mota said. Again, there was that brief surprise, and it vanished. "I was not *designed*. And I argue if it's—I only don't argue when it's against the health of the colony."

Eva was shaking her head. "Io told me about the hierarchy," she said again. "It gives some of you power over the rest of you. Power they haven't earned—power they can abuse. They can override your desires, can't they?"

Unease moved through Mota's stomach, like a technician in microgravity. She was overriding her own desires, standing here, talking to Eva. It felt more wrong than the easy passivity that crept over her when Io approached her. "Some people lead and others defer," she said. "But the colony keeps everyone in check. If you don't like a person, everyone knows. They stay away from you."

Like Io stays away from me, should have been the subtext. *Like you should stay away from me.* It would have been obvious to anyone—like the fact that she had free will should have been obvious, or the fact that her desires still existed even when she deferred.

"In my culture, we're all equal," Eva said.

Mota tilted her head. "I . . . read about Earth," she said. "And our history. Our scholars—when we were on the *Segye-Agbaye*—historically there was never a culture without hierarchy? It's innate. Human social trait."

Eva looked angry for a moment. Offended? Then it was gone. "Well," she said, "people earn their positions, where we come from. We're not born into them. That—it's unnatural. Not right."

But it kept us alive, Mota wanted to say. She wanted to be aboard the *Segye-Agbaye* more than ever, in the halls that generations of her ancestors had adapted to, in the confines of its hull. Eva had her cornered down here, and didn't know or didn't care that she wanted to escape. For years, centuries, there had been no escape from the ship as it sailed through the interstellar medium, but there had been harmony. Or a close enough approximation.

"No," Mota said. "For us, *you* are not right. Eva, this is uncomfortable. I'm uncomfortable."

And there, any civilized person should have disengaged. But Eva stepped forward.

"If you could be liberated," she said, "wouldn't you want to be?"

Mota turned and ran away. The motion was ungainly; she spent more of her life in orbital gravity than terrestrial. But Eva didn't follow.

The shuttle ride up to the *Segye-Agbaye* was silent on the network, and Mota didn't plug herself into one of the transmitters to reach out. And the ship itself was quiet but filled with murmurs—*like we've all become ghosts,* Yan had said.

This was the kind of silence Eva lived in, all her life, Mota thought. *Worse than this.* Absolute silence, without the promise of connection.

Mota couldn't imagine it without also imagining going mad.

She made her way to one of the old science modules, and settled in among its resources. A transmitter linked up the databanks with the central ones on Se, and she called up the records from Yan's expedition out to fetch the *Sojourn.* Then she dug deeper: the first moment the *Sojourn*'s signals had been detected, the first scans that caught the ship and resolved it.

She requested Yan's experience from the central banks, and they fed it up to her. Strange feelings, approaching the ship: washes of color and sound across the network as Yan and his fleetmates drew near. Many different signals coming from the ship, and a few of them tickled the network. When Yan sent his own signal to the ship, everything but that channel had died down.

Yan hadn't noticed a fade in the network when he'd retrieved the *Sojourn* or brought it to Omo. But he had before—those incoherent washes, an accident of design, transmitting on the same frequencies as the nanotransmitters interfaced with their neurons.

It made Mota wonder.

The *Sojourn* hadn't been moved from its post at Omo.

Mota took a databank and loaded it with the translation program, and requested a shuttle to Omo, stewing in her own thoughts the entire way. The spaceport had felt emptier than it was; everything felt empty. At least here, in the far reaches of the inhabited system, the emptiness seemed right.

She docked at Omo and went into the *Sojourn* to take a look around.

Parts of the ship were missing. Some of it, probably was the data storage—taken down to Se so that its encryption could be translated, and Eva's precious historical record preserved.

But was all of it?

Mota ran her hands over the walls, the consoles. She could feel the databank on the shuttle, feel the technicians' records and the translation program at the edge of her mind.

The *Sojourn* seemed to be cast from smooth composite, its hull one large component—not like the *Segye-Agbaye*, where every piece could have been detatched, recycled, cast into any one of innumerable other forms. The *Segye-Agbaye* had been designed to be broken apart and remade as it carried a living population from one star to the next.

The *Sojourn* had been designed to perform one task competently once.

And that told Mota something, as she moved from the stasis chamber to what seemed to be a technician access hatch. Everything on the ship had a congruity. Everything that wasn't part of the stasis system or the engines looked like an afterthought: mismatched.

She looked at the equipment. There, a processing unit. There, a detachable screen.

Mota took a deep breath, calling up all the translation they'd established.

The *Sojourn* had been able to read the presence of their colony and send out a signal, and Eva had been horrified at the thought of the network laid into human brains. When this craft had been built, someone would have come into this little human-habitable room and calibrated the equipment, would have tested it. And they would have done so with their hands and their eyes, not information communicated directly to their neurons.

Mota took the screen, and began to interface.

Reading the translations of the symbols that greeted her, Mota wondered when the screen had last been touched. How many generations ago, those many light years away? Had the *Segye-Agbaye* still been on its long voyage, or was this ship younger than that? And had the last person to work their way through these menus been a technician, like Mota, or had their society not been organized upon those lines?

Where we come from, Eva had said, *people earn their positions.*

Where we come from. Eva experienced a kind of aloneness that Mota could hardly imagine—light-years from home, alone in her thoughts and sensations. Why use *we*?

And, *Yes, there*—the ship had transmitters. Not ones that could tap into the larger network, or the smaller ones integrated with a human mind. But it had sent out the signals that called Yan to it, and it had sent out . . . others. And was still sending them out. Mota frowned, and isolated them.

Two signals. One broadly dispersed, one hyper-focused and sent back the way the *Sojourn* had come. Mota chose that one to follow, digging into the ship's scanners until something resolved on them.

Seven somethings.

Seven ships.

None as large as the *Segye-Agbaye*, but approaching its volume combined. And if they were stasis ships, without the need for living areas and corridors and recreational facilities and maintenance bays. . . .

Mota sucked in breath, and the hatch opened behind her.

She spun, eyes wide, and there was Eva. "I thought," Eva said, "I had asked you to stay away from my ship."

Mota moved, revealing the screen behind her. "How *many?*" she asked. Hoped that the words would carry all the meaning she wanted them to.

Eva's eyes flicked to the screen, but if she was surprised to see her fleet on it, Mota couldn't read it in her face. "On Earth," Eva said, "our ancestors were *allies*—good friends, in agreement. I was sent to negotiate cohabitation if my people had to evacuate the Earth system. I didn't expect to arrive here and find that you were no longer human.

"We are human," Mota said.

Eva looked disgusted. This time, the expression stayed. "You are *eugenicists*," she said. "Your genetics are polluted. It was people like you who are destroying my people."

"We evolved," Mota said, "to limit conflict—"

"By engineering subservience?" Eva asked. "My fleet is on its way. We can stop this practice of hooking you up to this mind-control network—we can help restore your genetic pool. Your children can live lives that are truly *free*."

"You're interfering with the network," Mota said. The realization was a nausea.

"*Yes*," Eva said. "Can't you feel it? You don't have to submit to everyone you meet—"

You are alone, Eva seemed to say, seemed to not realize she was saying, *in the dark, and you should be happy for it.*

Mota launched herself at Eva.

Eva started, and planted her feet as though she were in planetary gravity. Mota twisted, changing her angle enough to catch Eva's arm and spin her, then pushed off from her and flew toward the hatch leading back to the Omo station proper. Eva growled, disoriented, and Mota swung the hatch closed behind her.

Omo station wasn't large. Mota reached a transmitter just as Eva opened the hatch behind her, and fumbled into a connection. If she could just send this information back to Se, slicing through the interference before Eva was upon her—

And then Eva *was* upon her, wrenching her away from the transmitter, throwing her into the darkness of network interference again. Mota curled herself and pushed away but this time Eva grabbed her, locking their momentum. Eva's hand closed around her throat.

And then the hatch opened.

This time, they both startled. Eva turned, and the break in her attention was enough for Mota to twist free. And there in the hatch was Io, tall and present, taking in the scene.

Mota flew to Io and gripped her arm, letting the proximity carry her whole emotional state—anger and fear and incredulity.

Io turned to regard Eva.

"I don't think I should chastise Mota for disobeying your request," she said. "I came here because I thought I might have to. But I believe one of you should explain."

"I will explain," Mota said. And Io smiled thinly—this close, the network connected them, and the truth burned in Mota for anyone but Eva to see.

Yan arrived on the *Segye-Agbaye*, his presence clear among the ship's usual population. Mota paused in her work, extracting herself from the old databanks and recycling systems.

[Here,] she signaled, and felt Yan approach.

He waited until he was in the same room as her to say anything. "We were able to re-activate the stasis," he told her. "Eva is stable."

Mota nodded. She didn't have to say—was relieved not to say—how she felt about that, or that her feelings were confused.

"Io is still angry," Yan remarked.

Mota let out a laugh. "So am I."

"And most of us, I think," Yan said. He didn't feel angry—just a long, slow resentment curling under his words. "If it had been a vote, we might have killed her."

Mota closed her eyes. There was a vote, now, and the network visualized the voting for her. The decisions traveled in waves across the colony and outposts, one holdout or another synthesizing and summarizing their views and offering them up for perusal, influencing another shift or dissipating into the growing consensus.

Yan was there, in her peripheral awareness: washed out by the voting she'd called up, but present. No ghost standing next to her. She could hear a question, lingering.

"Eva made a bad decision," he said. "Her people are going to arrive, and if their stasis is the same as hers, they'll rely on our cooperation to revive them. So why act antisocially? Did she not know?"

If she'd had the network, she could have felt the fabric of the colony; known that she was making a mistake. Of course, if she'd had the network, she'd never have been able to hide a thing.

"Maybe," Mota said, though she wasn't sure, and she knew Yan recognized that. She felt around for the right words—even the right nuance would do. *[She hated us and didn't disengage,]* she signaled, at last.

It was . . . unnatural.

At least, it went against Mota's nature.

Yan let out a breath. Then he settled back, and Mota felt him key into the voting.

"Have you decided?" Mota asked.

A wistful affirmative came to her over the network. "Majority," he said. "Redirect their ships to some other system, or back to Earth. I'll miss their ships—I want to study them. You?"

Mota closed her eyes again. The visualization was waiting for her, its colors soothing.

"I don't know," she said.

Skepticism, from Yan.

Mota's fingers moved. *Eva thought I didn't have free will,* she wanted to signal. *But this is my vote. I have to make the choice.* But the words were less accurate than she wanted them to be, and she could catch the edge of understanding, flowing from Yan like a warm regard. That was enough.

Ken Liu is an author and translator of speculative fiction, as well as a lawyer and programmer. A winner of the Nebula, Hugo, and World Fantasy Awards, he has been published in *The Magazine of Fantasy & Science Fiction, Asimov's, Analog, Clarkesworld, Lightspeed,* and *Strange Horizons,* among other places. He also translated the Hugo-winning novel, *The Three-Body Problem,* by Liu Cixin, which is the first translated novel to win that award.

Ken's debut novel, *The Grace of Kings,* the first in a silkpunk epic fantasy series, was published by Saga Press in 2015. His first short story collection, *The Paper Menagerie and Other Stories,* was published in March. He lives with his family near Boston, Massachusetts.

THE GODS HAVE NOT DIED IN VAIN

Ken Liu

I can prove now, for instance, that two human hands exist. How? By holding up my two hands, and saying, as I make a certain gesture with the right hand, "Here is one hand," and adding, as I make a certain gesture with the left, "and here is another." —G.E. Moore, "Proof of an External World," 1939.

Cloud-born, cloud-borne, she was a mystery.

Maddie first met her sister through a chat window, after her father, one of the uploaded consciousnesses in a new age of gods, died.

<Maddie> Who are you?

<Unknown ID> Your sister. Your cloud-born sister.

<Unknown ID> You're awfully quiet.

<Unknown ID> Still there?

<Maddie> I'm . . . not sure what to say. This is a lot
          to take in. How about we start with a name?

```
<Unknown ID> ¯\_(ツ)_/¯
```

<Maddie> You don't have a name?

```
<Unknown ID> Never needed one before. Dad and I just
             thought at each other.
```

<Maddie> I don't know how to do that.

```
<Unknown ID>
```

So that was how Maddie came to call her sister "Mist": the pylon of a suspension bridge, perhaps the Golden Gate, hidden behind San Francisco's famous fog.

Maddie kept the existence of Mist a secret from her mother.

After all the wars initiated by the uploaded consciousnesses—some of which were still smoldering—the reconstruction process was slow and full of uncertainty. Hundreds of millions had died on other continents, and though America had been spared the worst of it, the country was still in chaos as infrastructure collapsed and refugees poured into the big cities. Her mother, who now acted as an advisor to the city government of Boston, worked long hours and was exhausted all the time.

First, she needed to confirm that Mist was telling the truth, so Maddie asked her to reveal herself.

For digital entities like Maddie's father, there was a ground truth, a human-readable representation of the instructions and data adapted for the different processors of the interconnected global network. Maddie's father had taught her to read it after he had reconnected with her following his death and resurrection. It looked like code written in some high-level programming language, replete with convoluted loops and cascading conditionals, elaborate lambda expressions and recursive definitions consisting of strings of mathematical symbols.

Maddie would have called such a thing "source code," except she had learned from her father that that notion was inaccurate: he and the other gods had never been compiled from source code into executable code, but were developed by AI techniques that replicated the workings of neural networks directly in machine language. The human-readable representation was more like a map of the reality of this new mode of existence.

Without hesitation, Mist revealed her map to Maddie when asked. Not *all* of herself, explained Mist. She was a distributed being, vast and constantly self-modifying. To show all of herself in map code would take up so much space and require so much time for Maddie to read that they might as well wait for the end of the universe. Instead, Mist showed her some highlights:

< > Here's a section I inherited from our father.

((lambda (n1) ((lambda (n2 . . .

As Maddie scrolled through the listing, she traced the complex logical paths, followed the patterns of multiple closures and thrown continuations, discovered the contours of a way of thinking that was at once familiar and strange. It was like looking at a map of her own mind, but one where the landmarks were strange and the roads probed into terra incognita.

There were echoes of her father in the code—she could see that: a quirky way of associating words with images; a tendency to see patterns that defied the strictly rational; a deep, abiding trust for a specific woman and a specific teenager out of the billions who lived on this planet.

Maddie was reminded of how Mom had told her that there were things about her as a baby that defied theories of upbringing, that told her and Dad that Maddie was *their* child in a way that transcended rational knowledge: the way her smile reminded Mom of Dad even at six weeks; the way she hated noodles the first time she tried them, just like Mom; the way she calmed down as soon as Dad held her, even though he had been too busy with Logorhythms's IPO to spend much time with her during the first six months of her life.

But there were also segments of Mist that puzzled her: the way she seemed to possess so many heuristics for trends in the stock market; the way her thoughts seemed attuned to the subtleties of patents; the way the shapes of her decision algorithms seemed adapted for the methods of warfare. Some of the map code reminded Maddie of the code of other gods Dad had shown her; some was entirely novel.

Maddie had a million questions for Mist. How had she come to be? Was she like Athena, sprung fully-formed from her father's mind? Or was she something like the next generation of an evolutionary algorithm, inheriting bits from her father and other uploaded consciousnesses with variations? Who was her other parent—or maybe parents? What stories of love, of yearning, of loneliness and connection, lay behind her existence? What was it like being a creature of pure computation, of never having existed in the flesh?

But of one thing Maddie was certain: Mist was her father's daughter, just as she had claimed. She was her sister, even if she *was* barely human.

<Maddie> What was life in the cloud with Dad like?

Like her father, Mist had a habit of shifting into emoji whenever she found words inadequate. What Maddie got out of her response was that life in the cloud was simply beyond her understanding and Mist did not have the words to adequately convey it.

So Maddie tried to bridge the gap the other way, to tell Mist about her own life.

<Maddie> Grandma and I had a garden back in Pennsylvania. I was good at growing tomatoes.

<Maddie> Yep. That's a tomato.

 I know lots about tomatoes: lycopene, Cortéz, nightshade, Mesoamerica, ketchup, pomodoro, Nix v. Hedden, vegetable, soup. Probably more than you.

 You seem really quiet.

<Maddie> Forget it.

Other attempts by Maddie to share the details of her own life usually ended the same way. She mentioned the way Basil wagged his tail and licked her fingers when she came in the door, and Mist responded with articles about the genetics of dogs. Maddie started to talk about the anxieties she experienced at school and the competing cliques, and Mist showed her pages of game theory and papers on adolescent psychology.

Maddie could understand it, to some extent. After all, Mist had never lived in the world that Maddie inhabited, and never would. All Mist had was data *about* the world, not the world itself. How could Mist understand how Maddie *felt?* Words or emoji were inadequate to convey the essence of reality.

Life is about embodiment, thought Maddie. This was a point that she had discussed with Dad many times. To experience the world through the senses was different from simply having data about the world. The memory of his time in the world was what had kept her father sane after he had been turned into a brain in a jar.

And in this way, oddly, Maddie came to have a glint of the difficulty Mist faced in explaining her world to Maddie. She tried to imagine what it was like to have never petted a puppy, to have never experienced a tomato filled with June sunshine burst between the tongue and the palate, to have never felt the weight of gravity or the elation of being loved, and imagination failed her. She felt sorry for Mist, a ghost who could not even call upon the memory of an embodied existence.

There was one topic on which Maddie and Mist could converse effectively: the shared mission their father had left them to make sure the gods didn't come back.

All of the uploaded consciousnesses—whose existence was still never acknowledged—were supposed to have died in the conflagration. But pieces of their code, like the remnants of fallen giants, were scattered around the world's servers. Mist told Maddie that mysterious network presences scoured the web to collect these pieces. Were they hackers? Spies? Corporate researchers? Defense contractors? What purpose could they have for gathering these relics unless they were interested in resurrecting the gods?

Along with these troubling reports, Mist also brought back headlines that she thought Maddie would find interesting.

 > Today's Headlines:

- Japanese PM Assures Nervous Citizens That New Robots Deployed for Reconstruction Are Safe
- European Union Announces Border Closures; Extra-European Economic Migrants Not Welcome
- Bill to Restrict Immigration to "Extraordinary Circumstances" Passes Senate; Majority of Working Visas to Be Revoked

- Protestors Demanding Jobs Clash with Police in New York and Washington, D.C.
- Developing Nations Press UN Security Council for Resolution Denouncing Efforts to Restrict Population Migration by Developed Economies
- Collapse of Leading Asian Economies Predicted as Manufacturing Sector Continues Contraction Due to Back-Shoring by Europe and the US
- Everlasting Inc. Refuses to Explain Purpose of New Data Center

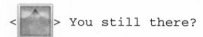 > You still there?

 > ??

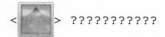 > ??????????

<Maddie> Calm down! I need a few seconds to read this wall of text you just threw at me.

 > Sorry, I'm still under-compensating for how slow your cycles are. I'll leave you to it. Ping me when you're done.

Mist's consciousness operated at the speed of electric currents fluctuating billions of times a second instead of slow, analog, electrochemical synapses. Her experience of time must be so different, so *fast* that it made Maddie a little bit envious.

And she came to appreciate just how patient her father had been with her when he was a ghost in the machine. In every exchange between him and Maddie, he probably had had to wait what must have felt like eons before getting an answer from her, but he had never shown any annoyance.

Maybe that was why he had created another daughter, Maddie thought. *Someone who lived and thought like him.*

<Maddie> Ready to chat when you are.

> Everlasting is where I tracked them dragging
those fragments of the gods.

<Maddie> They didn't get any pieces of Dad, did they?

 > Way ahead of you, sister. I took care of burying
the pieces of Dad as soon as it calmed down.

<Maddie> Thank you. . . . Wish we could figure out what
they're planning over there.

Adam Ever, the founder of Everlasting, Inc. was one of the foremost experts
on the Singularity. He had been a friend of Dad's, and Maddie vaguely recalled
meeting him as a little girl. Ever was a persistent advocate of consciousness
uploading, even after all the legal restrictions placed on his research after the
crisis. Maddie's curiosity was tinged with dread.

 > Not that easy. I tried to go through Everlasting's
system defenses a few times, but the internal networks are completely isolated. They're paranoid
over there—I lost a few parts when they detected
my presence on the external-facing servers.

Maddie shuddered. She recalled the epic fights between her father, Lowell,
and Chanda in the darkness of the network. The phrase "lost a few parts"
might sound innocuous, but for Mist it probably felt like losing limbs and
parts of her mind.

<Maddie> You've got to be careful.

 > I did manage to copy the pieces of the gods they
took. I'll give you access to the encrypted cloud
cell now. Maybe we can figure out what they're
doing at Everlasting by looking through these.

Maddie made dinner that night. Her mother texted her that she was going to be
late, first thirty minutes, then an hour, and then "not sure." Maddie ended up eating alone and then spent the rest of the evening watching the clock and worrying.

"Sorry," Mom said as she came in, close to midnight. "They kept me late."

Maddie had seen some of the reports on TV. "Protestors?"

Mom sighed. "Yes. Not as bad as in New York, but hundreds showed up. I had to talk to them."

"What are they mad about? It's not like—" Maddie caught herself just as she was about to raise her voice. She was feeling protective of her mother, but her mother had probably had enough shouting for one day.

"They're good people," Mom said vaguely. She headed for the stairs without even glancing at the kitchen. "I'm tired. I think I'll just go to bed."

But Maddie was unwilling to just let it go. "Are we having supply issues again?" The recovery was jittery, and goods were still being rationed. It was a constant struggle to get people to stop hoarding.

Mom stopped. "No. The supplies are flowing smoothly again, maybe too smoothly."

"I don't understand," said Maddie.

Mom sat down on the bottom of the stairs, and patted the space next to her. Maddie went over and sat down.

"Remember how during the crisis, when we were coming to Boston, I told you about layers of technology?"

Maddie nodded. Her mother, a historian, had told her the story behind the networks that connected people: the footpaths that grew into caravan routes that developed into roads that turned into railroad tracks that provided the right-of-way for the optical cables that carried the bits that made up the Internet that routed the thoughts of the gods.

"The history of the world is a process of speeding up, of becoming more efficient as well as more fragile. If a footpath is blocked, you just have to walk around it. But if a highway is blocked, you have to wait until specialized machinery can be brought to clear it. Just about anyone can figure out how to patch a cobblestone road, but only highly trained technicians can fix a fiberoptic cable. There's a lot more redundancy with the older, inefficient technologies."

"Your point is that keeping it simple technologically is more resilient," said Maddie.

"But our history is also a history of growing needs, of more mouths to feed and more hands that need to be kept from idleness," said Mom.

Mom told Maddie that America had been lucky during the crisis: very few bombs had struck her shores and relatively few people had died during the riots. But with much of the infrastructure paralyzed across the country, refugees flooded into the big cities. Boston's own population had doubled from what it was before the crisis. With so many people came spiking needs: food, clothing, shelter, sanitation. . . .

"On my advice, the governor and the mayor tried to rely on distributed, self-organizing groups of citizens with low-tech delivery methods, but we couldn't get it to work because it was just too inefficient. Congestion and breakdowns were happening too frequently. Centillion's automation proposal had to be considered."

Maddie thought of how impatient Mist had been with her "slow cycles," and she imagined the roads packed with self-driving trucks streaming bumper-to-bumper at a hundred miles an hour, without drivers who had to rest, without the traffic jams caused by human unpredictability, without the accidents from drifting attentions and exhausted bodies. She thought of tireless robots loading and unloading the supplies necessary to keep millions of people fed and warm and clothed. She thought of the borders patrolled by machines with precise algorithms designed to preserve precious supplies for the use of people with the right accents, the right skin colors, the luck to be born in the right places at the right times.

"All the big cities are doing the same thing," said Mom, a trace of defensiveness in her voice. "It's impossible for us to hold out. It would be irresponsible, as Centillion put it."

"And the drivers and workers would be replaced," said Maddie, understanding finally dawning on her.

"They showed up on Beacon Hill to protest, hoping to save their jobs. But an even bigger crowd showed up to protest against *them.*" Mom rubbed her temples.

"If everything is handed over to Centillion's robots, wouldn't another god—I mean a rogue AI—put us at even more risk?"

"We have grown to the point where we must depend on machines to survive," said Mom. "The world has become too fragile for us to count on people, and so our only choice is to make it even more fragile."

With Centillion's robots taking over the crucial work of maintaining the flow of goods into the city, a superficial calmness returned to life. The workers who lost their jobs were given new jobs invented by the government: correcting typos in old databases, sweeping corners of streets that Centillion's robots couldn't get to, greeting concerned citizens in the lobby of the State House and giving them tours—some grumbled that this was just a dressed-up form of welfare and what was the government going to do when Centillion and PerfectLogic and ThoughtfulBits and their ilk automated more jobs away?

But at least everyone was getting a paycheck that they could use to buy the supplies brought into the city by the fleet of robots. And Centillion's CEO swore up and down on TV that they weren't developing anything that could be understood as "rogue AI," like the old, dead gods.

That was good, wasn't it?

Maddie and Mist continued to gather pieces of the old gods and study them to see what Everlasting might want with them. Some of the fragments had belonged to her father, but there were too few of them to even dream of trying to resurrect him. Maddie wasn't sure how she felt about it—in a way, her father had never fully reconciled to his existence as a disembodied consciousness, and she wasn't sure he would want to "come back."

Meanwhile, Maddie was working on a secret project. It would be her present to Mist.

She looked up everything she could online about robotics and electronics and sensor technology. She bought components online, which Centillion drones cheerfully and efficiently delivered to her house—straight to her room, even: she kept the window of her room open, and tiny drones with whirring rotors flitted in at all hours of the day and night, dropping off tiny packages.

< > What are you doing?

<Maddie> Give me a minute. I'm almost done.

< > I'll give you today's headlines then.
  • Hundreds Die in Attempt to Scale "Freedom Wall" near El Paso
  • Think Tank Argues Coal Should be Reevaluated as Alternative Energy Fails to Meet Promise
  • Deaths from Typhoons in Southeast Asia Exceed Historical Records
  • Experts Warn of Further Regional Conflicts as Food Prices Soar and Drought Continues in Asia and Africa
  • Unemployment Numbers Suggest Reconstruction Has Benefited Robots (and Their Owners) More Than People
  • Rise of Religious Extremism Tied to Stagnating Developing Economies
  • Is Your Job at Risk? Experts Explain How to Protect Yourself from Automation

<Maddie> `Nothing from Everlasting?`

`<`  `>` `They've been quiet.`

Maddie plugged her new creation into the computer.

<Maddie>

The lights near the data port on the computer began to blink.

Maddie smiled to herself. For Mist, asking Maddie a question and waiting for her slow cycles to catch up and answer was probably like sending snail mail. It would be far faster for her to investigate the new contraption herself.

The motors in Maddie's creation spun to life, and the three wheels in the base turned the four-foot-tall torso around. The wheels provided 360° of motion, much like those roving automatic vacuum cleaners.

At the top of the cylindrical torso was a spherical "head" to which were attached the best sensors that Maddie could scrounge up or buy: a pair of high-def cameras to give stereoscopic vision; a matched pair of microphones to act as ears, tuned for the range of human hearing; a sophisticated bundle of probes mounted at the ends of flexible antennae to act as noses and tongues that approximated the sensitivity of human counterparts; and numerous other tactile sensors, gyroscopes, accelerometers, and so on to give the robot the experience of touch, gravity, presence in space.

Away from the head, near the top of the cylindrical body, however, were the most expensive components of them all: a pair of multi-jointed arms with parallel-elastic actuators to recreate the freedom of motion of human arms that ended in a pair of the most advanced prosthetic hands covered in medical-grade plastiskin. The skin, embedded with sensors for temperature and force, were said to approach or even exceed the sensitivity of real skin, and the fingers modeled human hands so well that they could tighten a nut on a screw as well as pick up a strand of hair. Maddie watched as Mist tried them out, flexing and clenching the fingers, and without realizing it, she mirrored the movements with her own fingers.

"What do you think?" she said.

The screen mounted atop the head of the robot came to life, showing a cartoonish pair of eyes, a cute button nose, and a pair of abstract, wavy lines that mimicked the motion of lips. Maddie was proud of the design and programming of the face. She had modeled it on her own.

A voice came out of the speaker below the screen. "This is very well made." It was a young girl's voice, chirpy and mellifluous.

"Thank you," said Maddie. She watched as Mist moved around the room, twisting her head this way and that, sweeping her camera-gaze over everything. "Do you like your new body?"

"It's interesting," said Mist. The tone was the same as before. Maddie couldn't tell if that was because Mist was really pleased with the robotic body or that she hadn't figured out how to modulate the voice to suit her emotional state.

"I can show you all the things you haven't experienced before," said Maddie hurriedly. "You'll know what it's like to move in the real world, not just as a ghost in a machine. You'll be able to understand my stories, and I can take you on trips with me, introduce you to Mom and other people."

Mist continued to move around the room, her eyes surveying the trophies on Maddie's shelves, the titles of her books, the posters on her walls, the models of the planets and rocketships hanging from the ceiling—a record of Maddie's shifting tastes over the years. She moved toward one corner where a basket of stuffed animals was kept, but stopped when the data cable stretched taut, just a few centimeters too short.

"The cable is necessary for now because the amount of data from the sensors is so large. But I'm working on a compression algorithm so we can get you wireless."

Mist moved the swiveling screen with her cartoonish face forward and backward to simulate a nod. Maddie was grateful that she had thought of such a thing—a lot of the robotics papers on robot-human interactions emphasized that rather than simulating a human face too closely and falling into the uncanny valley, it was better sticking to cartoonish representations that exaggerated the emotional tenor. Sometimes an obviously virtual representation was better than a strict effort at fidelity.

Mist paused in front of a mess of wires and electronic components on Maddie's shelf. "What's this?"

"The first computer that Dad and I built together," said Maddie. Instantly, she seemed to have been transported to that summer almost a decade ago, when Dad showed her how to apply Ohm's Law to pick out the right resistors and how to read a circuit diagram and translate it into real components and real wires. The smell of hot solder filled her nostrils again, and she smiled even as her eyes moistened.

Mist picked up the contraption with her hands.

"Be careful!" Maddie yelled.

But it was too late. The breadboard crumbled in Mist's hands, and the pieces fell to the carpet.

"Sorry," said Mist. "I thought I was applying the right amount of pressure based on the materials used in it."

"Things get old in the real world," said Maddie. She bent down to pick up the pieces from the carpet, carefully cradling them in her hand. "They grow fragile." She looked at the remnants of her first unskilled attempt at soldering, noticing the lumpy messes and bent electrodes. "I guess you don't have much experience with that."

"I'm sorry," said Mist again, her voice still chirpy.

"Doesn't matter," said Maddie, trying to be magnanimous. "Think of it as a first lesson about the real world. Hold on."

She rushed out of the room and returned a moment later with a ripe tomato. "This is shipped in from some industrial farm, and it's nowhere as good as the ones Grandma and I grew back in Pennsylvania. Still, now you can taste it. Don't talk to me about lycopene and sugar content; *taste* it."

Mist took the tomato from her—this time her mechanical hands held it lightly, the fingers barely making an impression against the smooth fruit skin. She gazed at it, the lenses of her cameras whirring as they focused. And then, decisively, one of the probes on her head shot out and stabbed into the fruit in a single motion.

It reminded Maddie of a mosquito's proboscis stabbing into the skin of a hand, or a butterfly sipping nectar from a flower. A sense of unease rose in her. She was trying so hard to make Mist *human,* but what made her think that was what Mist wanted?

"It's very good," said Mist. She swiveled her screen toward Maddie so that Maddie could see her cartoonish eyes curving in a smile. "You're right. It's not as good as the heirloom varieties."

Maddie laughed. "How would you know that?"

"I've tasted hundreds of varieties of tomatoes," said Mist.

"Where? How?"

"Before the war of the gods, all the big instant meal manufacturers and fast food restaurants used automation to produce recipes. Dad took me through a few of these facilities and I tried every variety of tomato from Amal to Zebra Cherry—I was a big fan of Snow White."

"Machines were making up the recipes?" Maddie asked. She had loved watching cooking shows before the war, and chefs were artists, what they did was *creative*. She couldn't quite wrap her head around the notion of machines making up recipes.

"Sure. At the scale these places were operating, they had to optimize for so many factors that people could never get it right. The recipes had to be tasty and also use ingredients that could be obtained within the constraints of modern mechanized agriculture—it was no good to discover some good recipe that relied on an heirloom variety that couldn't be grown in large enough quantities efficiently."

Maddie thought back to her conversation with Mom and realized that it was the same concept that now governed the creation of ration packets: nutritious, tasty, but also effective for feeding hundreds of millions living with a damaged grid and limited resources.

"Why didn't you tell me you've tasted tomatoes?" Maddie asked. "I thought you were—"

"Not just tomatoes. I've had every variety of potato, squash, cucumber, apple, grape, and lots of other things you've never had. In the food labs, I tried out billions of flavor combinations. The sensors they had were far more sensitive than the human tongue."

The robot that had once seemed such an extraordinary gift now seemed shabby to Maddie. Mist did not need a body. She had been living in a far more embodied way than Maddie had realized or understood.

Mist simply didn't think the new body was all that special.

- Expert Report Declares Nuclear Fallout Clean Up Plan in Asia Unrealistic, Further Famines Inevitable
- Japan Joins China and India in Denouncing Western Experts for "Scaremongering"
- Indian Geoengineering Plan to Melt Himalayan Snow for Agricultural Irrigation Leaked, Drawing Condemnation from Smaller SE Asian Nations for "Water Theft"
- Protestors in Italy and Spain Declare "African Refugees Should Go Home": Thousands Injured in Clashes
- Australia Announces Policy of Shooting on Sight to Discourage "Boat People"
- Regional "Resource Wars" May Turn Global, UN Special Commission Warns
- White House Stands Firm Behind "NATO First" Doctrine: Use of Military Force Is Justified

to Stop Geoengineering Projects That May Harm
Allies or US Interests

Mom was working late most nights now, and she looked pale and sickly. Maddie didn't have to ask to know that reconstruction was going worse than anyone expected. The war of the gods had left so much of the planet's surface in tatters that the survivors were fighting over the leftover scraps. No matter how many refugee boats were sunk by drones or how high the walls were built, desperate people continued to pour into the US, the country least damaged by the war.

Protests and counterprotests raged in the streets of all the major cities day after day. Nobody wanted to see kids and women drown in the sea or electrocuted by the walls, but it was also true that all the American cities were overburdened. Even the efficient robots couldn't keep up with the task of making sure everyone was fed and safe.

Maddie could tell that the ration packets were going down in quality. This couldn't go on. The world was continuing its long spiral down toward an abyss, and sooner or later, someone was going to conclude that the problems were not solvable by AI alone, and we needed to call upon the gods again.

She and Mist had to prevent that. The world couldn't afford another reign of the gods.

While Mist—possibly the greatest hacker there ever was—focused on testing out the defenses around Everlasting and figuring out a way to penetrate them, Maddie devoted her time to trying to understand the fragments of the dead gods.

The map code, a combination of self-modifying AI and modeling of human thinking patterns, wasn't the sort of thing a programmer would write, but Maddie seemed to have an intuition for how personality quirks manifested in this code after spending so much time with the fragments of her father.

In this manner, Maddie came also to understand Chanda and Lowell and the other gods. She charted their hopes and dreams, like fragments of Sappho and Aeschylus. And it turned out that deep down, all the gods had similar vulnerabilities, a kind of regret or nostalgia for life in the flesh that seemed reflected at every level of organization. It was a blind spot, a vulnerability that could be exploited in the war against the gods.

"I don't have a weak spot like that in my code," said Mist.

Maddie was startled. She had never really considered Mist one of the gods, though, objectively, she clearly was. Mist was just her little sister, especially when she was embedded in the cute robot Maddie had built for her, as she was now.

"Why not?" she asked.

"I am a child of the ether," said Mist. And the voice was now different. It sounded older, wearier. Maddie would almost have said it sounded *not human.* "I do not yearn for something that I never had."

Of course Mist wasn't a little girl, Maddie berated herself. She had somehow allowed the cartoonish trappings she had created for Mist, a mask intended to help Mist relate to her, fool her. Mist's thoughts moved at a far faster pace, and she had experienced more of the world than Maddie had ever experienced. She could, at will, peek through billions of cameras, listen through billions of microphones, sense the speed of the wind atop Mount Washington and at the same time feel the heat of the lava spilling out of Kilauea. She had known what it's like to gaze down at the world from the international space station and what it was like to suffer the stress of kilometers of water pressing down upon a deep-sea submersible's shell. She was, in a way, far older than Maddie.

"I'm going to make a run at Everlasting," said Mist. "With your discoveries, we're as ready as we'll ever be. They might already be creating new gods."

Maddie wanted to tell Mist some words of comfort, assuring her of success. But really, what did she know of the risks Mist was undertaking? She wasn't the one to put her life on the line in that unimaginable realm inside the machine.

The features on the screen that served as Mist's face disappeared, leaving only a single emoji.

"We'll protect each other," Maddie said. "We will."

But even she knew how inadequate that sounded.

Maddie woke up with a start as cold hands caressed her face.

She sat up. The small bedside lamp was on. Next to her bed was the squat figure of the robot, whose cameras were trained on her. She had fallen asleep after seeing Mist off, though she hadn't meant to.

"Mist," she said, rubbing her eyes, "are you okay?"

The cartoonish face of Mist was replaced by a headline.

- Everlasting Inc. Announces "Digital Adam" Project

"What?" asked Maddie, her thoughts still sluggish.

"I better let him tell you," said Mist. And then the screen changed again, and a man's face appeared on it. He was in his thirties, with short-cropped hair and a kind, compassionate face.

All traces of sleep left Maddie. This was a face she had seen many times on TV, always making reassurances to the public: Adam Ever.

"What are you doing here?" asked Maddie. "What have you done to Mist?"

The robot that had housed Mist—no, Adam now—held up his hands in a gesture intended to calm. "I'm just here to talk."

"What about?"

"Let me show you what we've been working on."

Maddie flew over a fjord filled with floating icebergs until she was skimming over a field of ice. A great black cube loomed out of this landscape of shades of white.

"Welcome to the Longyearbyen Data Center," Adam Ever's voice spoke in her ears.

The VR headset was something Maddie had once used to game with her father, but it had been gathering dust on the shelf since his death. Adam had asked her to put it on.

Maddie had known of the data center's existence from Mist's reports, and had even seen some photographs and videos of its construction. She and Mist had speculated that this was where Everlasting was trying to resurrect the old gods or bring forth new ones.

Adam told her about the massive assembly of silicon and graphene inside, about the zipping electrons and photons bouncing inside glass cables. This was an altar to computation, a Stonehenge for a new age.

"It's also where I live," Adam said.

The scene before Maddie's eyes shifted, and she was now looking at Adam calmly lying down on a hospital bed, smiling for the camera. Doctors and beeping machines were clustered around the bed. They typed some commands into a computer, and after a while Adam closed his eyes, going to sleep.

Maddie suddenly had the sensation that she was witnessing a scene similar to the last moments of her father.

"Were you ill?" she asked hesitantly.

"No," said Adam. "I was in the prime of health. This is a video recording of the moment before the scan. I had to be alive to give the procedure the maximal chance for success."

Maddie imagined the doctors approaching the sleeping figure of Adam with scalpel and bone saw and who knew what else—she was about to scream when the scene shifted mercifully away to a room of pure white with Adam sitting up in a bed. Maddie let out a held breath.

"You survived the scan?" asked Maddie.

"Of course," said Adam.

But Maddie sensed that this wasn't quite right. Earlier, in the video, there were wrinkles near the corners of Adam's eyes. The face of the Adam in front of her now was perfectly smooth.

"It's not you," said Maddie. "It's not you."

"It *is* me," insisted Adam. "The only me that matters."

Maddie closed her eyes and thought back to the times Adam had appeared on TV in interviews. He had said he didn't want to leave Svalbard, preferring to conduct all his interviews remotely via satellite feed. The camera had always stayed close up, showing just his face. Now that she was looking for it, she realized that the way Adam had moved in those interviews had seemed just slightly odd, a little uncanny.

"You died," said Maddie. She opened her eyes and looked at the Adam, this Adam with the smooth, perfectly symmetrical face and impossibly graceful limbs. "You died during the scan because there's no way to do a scan without destroying the body."

Adam nodded. "I'm one of the gods."

"Why?" Maddie couldn't imagine such a thing. All of the gods had been created as a last measure of desperation, a way to preserve their minds for the service of the goals of others. Her father had raged against his fate and fought so that none of the others had to go through what he did. To choose to become a brain in a jar was inconceivable to her.

"The world is dying, Maddie," said Adam. "You know this. Even before the wars, we were killing the planet slowly. There were too many of us squabbling over too few resources, and to stay alive we had to hurt the world even more, polluting the water and air and soil so that we might extract more. The wars only accelerated what was already an inevitable trend. There are too many of us for this planet to support. The next time we fight a war, there won't be any more of us to save after the nukes are done falling."

"It's not true!" Even as she said it, Maddie knew that Adam was right. The headlines and her own research had long ago led her to the same conclusion. *He's right.* She felt very tired. "Are we the cancer of this planet?"

"We're not the problem," said Adam.

Maddie looked at him.

"Our bodies are," said Adam. "Our bodies of flesh exist in the realm of atoms. Our senses require the gratification of matter. Not all of us can live the lifestyle we believe we deserve. Scarcity is the root of all evil."

"What about space, the other planets and stars?"

"It's too late for that. We've hardly taken another step on the moon, and most of the rockets we've been building since then have been intended to deliver bombs."

Maddie said nothing. "You're saying there is no hope?"

"Of course there is." Adam waved his arm, and the white room transformed into the inside of a luxurious apartment. The hospital bed disappeared, and Adam was now standing in the middle of a well-appointed room. The lights of Manhattan shone beyond the darkened windows.

Adam waved his arm again, and now they were inside a voluminous space capsule. Outside the window loomed a partial view of a massive sphere of swirling bands of color, and a giant red oval slowly drifted among the bands like an island in a turbulent sea.

Once more, Adam waved his arm, and now it wasn't even possible for Maddie to understand what she was seeing. There seemed to be a smaller Adam inside Adam, and yet a smaller Adam inside that one, and so on, ad infinitum. Yet she was somehow able to see all of the Adams at once. She moved her gaze around the space and felt dizzy: space itself seemed to gain an extra level of depth, and everywhere she looked she saw *inside* things.

"We could have all we ever desire," said Adam, "if we're willing to give up our bodies."

A disembodied existence, thought Maddie. *Is that really living at all?*

"But this isn't *real*," said Maddie. "This is just an illusion." She thought of the games she used to play with her father, of the green seas of grass that seemed to go on forever, of the babbling brooks that promised infinite zoom, of the fantastic creatures they had fought against, side by side.

"Consciousness itself is an illusion, if you want to follow that logic to its conclusion," said Adam. "When you put your hand around a tomato, your senses insist that you're touching something solid. But most of a tomato is made up of the empty space between the nuclei of the atoms, as far from each other, by proportion, as the stars are apart. What is color? What is sound?

What is heat or pain? They're but pulses of electricity that make up our consciousness, and it makes no difference whether the pulse comes from a sensor touching a tomato or is the result of computation."

"Except there is a difference," the voice of Mist said.

Maddie's heart swelled with gratitude. Her sister was coming to her defense. Or so she thought.

"A tomato made up of atoms is grown in a distant field, where it must be given fertilizer mined from halfway across the world and dusted with insecticide by machines. Then it must be harvested, packed, and then shipped through the airways and highways until it arrives at your door. The amount of energy it takes to run the infrastructure that would support the creation and delivery of a single tomato is many times what it took to build the Great Pyramid. Is it really worth enslaving the whole planet so that you can have the experience of a tomato through the interface of the flesh instead of generating the same impulse from a bit of silicon?"

"But it doesn't have to be that way," said Maddie. "My grandmother and I grew our tomatoes on our own, and we didn't need any of that."

"You can't feed billions of people with backyard gardens," said Mist. "Nostalgia for a garden that never existed is dangerous. The mass of humanity depends on the fragile, power-intensive infrastructure of civilization. It is delusion to think you can live without it."

Maddie remembered the words of her mother. *The world has become too fragile for us to count on people.*

"The world of atoms is not only wasteful, it is also limiting," said Adam. "Inside the data center, we can live anywhere we want and have whatever we want, with imagination as our only limit. We can experience things that our fleshly senses could never give us: live in multiple dimensions, invent impossible foods, possess worlds that are as infinite as the sands of the Ganges."

A world beyond scarcity, thought Maddie. A world without rich or poor, without the conflicts generated by exclusion and possession. It was a world without death, without decay, without the limits of inflexible matter. It was a state of existence mankind had always yearned for.

"Don't you miss the real world?" asked Maddie. She thought of the vulnerability that existed at the heart of all the gods.

"We discovered the same thing you did by studying the gods," said Adam. "Nostalgia is deadly. When peasants first moved into the factories of the industrial age, perhaps they also were nostalgic for the inefficient world of subsistence farming. But we must be open to change, to adaptation, to seeking a new path in a sea of fragility. Instead of being forced here on the verge of death like your father, I *chose* to come here. I am not nostalgic. That makes all the difference."

"He's right," said Mist. "Our father understood that, too. Maybe this is why he and the other gods gave birth to me: to see if their nostalgia is as inevitable as death. They couldn't adapt to this world fully, but maybe their children could. In a way, Dad gave birth to me because, deep down, he wished *you* could live here with him."

Mist's observation seemed to Maddie like a betrayal, but she couldn't say why.

"This is the next stage of our evolution," said Adam. "This isn't going to be a perfect world, but it is closer to perfect than anything we've ever devised. The human race thrives on discovering new worlds, and now there are an infinite many of them to explore. We shall reign as the gods of them all."

Maddie took off her VR set. Next to the vibrant colors inside the digital world, the physical world seemed dim and dull.

She imagined the data center teeming with the consciousnesses of billions. *Would that bring people closer, so that they all shared the same universe without the constraints of scarcity? Or would it push them apart, so that each lived in their own world, a king of infinite space?*

She held out her hands. She noticed that they were becoming wrinkled, the hands of a woman rather than a child.

After the briefest of pauses, Mist rolled over and held them.

"We'll protect each other," said Mist. "We will."

They held hands in the dark, sisters, human and post-human, and waited for the new day to come.

Nancy Kress is the best-selling author of twenty-seven science-fiction and fantasy novels, including *Beggars in Spain, Probability Space,* and *Steal Across the Sky.* She has also published over a hundred short stories and three books on the fundamentals of writing. She is a six-time Nebula Award winner and the recipient of two Hugos, the Sturgeon, and Campbell awards. Her work has been translated into Swedish, French, Italian, German, Spanish, Danish, Polish, Croatian, Korean, Lithuanian, Chinese, Romanian, Japanese, Russian, and Klingon, none of which she can read.

COCOONS

Nancy Kress

A recon detail brought in another one just after dawn. The soldiers had donned full biohazard suits; nothing could convince them that this wasn't contagious. They set the body on a gurney. I wheeled it into a quarantine room and inspected it.

This time, for the first time, it was a child. A girl, about eleven years old. Half of her face was still visible.

"The whole premise sounds ludicrous," Colonel Terence Jamison said, stirring more sugar into his coffee.

He wasn't at all what I'd expected. Thirty minutes off the ship from HQ on New Eden, he sat diffidently on the edge of a foamcast chair in my cluttered office as if visiting a priest to confess sins. Slightly built, soft-spoken, he seemed reluctant to meet my gaze with his pale, milky-blue eyes. Out of uniform, he wouldn't look like much, certainly not a senior officer in the Seven Planets United Space Corps.

I said, "Maybe it is ridiculous. After all, we have no documented proof, only anecdotes from, in most cases, unreliable sources."

Jamison blinked at me. "Dr. Seybert—"

"Nora, please." I am a civilian contractor, and this was a "courtesy visit." Yeah, right.

"Nora, to tell the truth, I'm not even sure why I'm here. Someone up the chain of command got a bee in their bonnet."

He was not telling the truth, and had Jamison ever seen a bee? I hadn't. Both New Eden, where I'd been born, and this outpost on Windsong pollinated their native plants by wind or bird. I knew exactly why Jamison was here, and both possible outcomes of his mission.

Neither was good.

"Dr. . . . Nora," he said, "shall we get started?"

I am Elizabeth DiPortio. I hate my life. I choose this change. It can't be worse.

"My God," Jamison said. And then, "I didn't know. . . ." And finally, regaining composure, "Briefing pictures were inadequate."

"Yes," I said.

We stood beside the gurney. The "spiders," which were not really spiders, had done more of their work. A thin, filmy web of very fine, dull red filaments was being spun over her naked body. The spiders worked unevenly; her forehead, neck and genitals were as yet completely uncovered, while her eyes, neck, and budding breasts were already sealed into the cocoon.

Jamison's face twisted in revulsion. "Why don't you wash it all off her?"

He knew the answer to this already; it was in ten years' of situation briefings. So we were going to be playing games. He would pretend ignorance, hoping that my answers would reveal whatever information the Corps thought, suspected, or hoped I was holding back. There wasn't any, but try convincing HQ Special Ops of that. I knew as much about Jamison as he did about me; I have friends at HQ. The stakes here were too high to not play along.

So I said, "We tried internal and external laving, in the early years. Twice. Both patients died. You see the 'spiders' but you don't see the biofilms that have invaded her nostrils, mouth, anus, vagina, ears. Those early autopsies revealed them. She's being colonized by sheets of microorganisms, changed from the inside out. Go ahead, you can touch her—both spiders and microbes have already attuned to her DNA. They won't do anything to you."

He didn't touch her. "Is she in pain?"

"No." He'd never glanced at the monitors, which showed plainly that her brain waves registered no pain. He was not a doctor.

"Who is she?"

"We verified that only a few hours ago. Her name is Elizabeth Jane DiPortio, a Corps dependent. Her mother is a grunt at the mining base; she's been sent for and will be shuttled here from the coast. Her father is a civilian dependent and, preliminary report says, a drunk. He may have abused her."

"This wasn't seen and dealt with?" Disapproval dripped off him. Not compassion—disapproval. Drunk or abused dependents did not meet Corps regulations. Under his mask of diffidence, Jamison was a martinet. And he handled Windsong's gravity, lighter than New Eden's by point two g, like a man used to a lot of interstellar travel.

"Colonel," I said pleasantly, "Alpha Beta Base has over 6,500 people now, military and civilian. We can't see and deal with everything."

He nodded, blinking in that deceptively harmless way: *Nobody here but us rabbits.* "Tell me what is changing inside her."

"Her digestive flora—the microbes from her mouth to her rectum—are being destroyed, augmented, or replaced with ones that are part of the biofilms. Which are, of course DNA-based—panspermia, you know." I was being condescending. He didn't react. "Most of her organs are being modified only enough to accommodate the new microbes, with the exception of her vocal chords. They're being drastically reconfigured to make sounds at a pitch above human hearing."

"To communicate with what?"

"We don't know. Maybe only each other. It's a big planet, Colonel, and the Corps is still just a speck on it. Two specks: base and the mining operations in the mountains."

"Yes," he said, smiling, without mirth, in response to my condescension. I hated him. "I know. How do the . . . the. . . ."

"We don't know. Some Terran spiders inject their prey with venom that digests tissue. Maybe these spiders are injecting something that denatures DNA, or activates parts of it. Maybe the microbes are injecting some of their own DNA into the host and taking over selected cell machinery, like viruses. But most likely the process has no real Terran analogy."

"How much of this microbial activity is affecting her brain?"

"Some of it, although it's impossible to quantify. The smallest invaders are the size of viruses. They can get past the blood-brain barrier just as some viruses can." This was why Colonel Jamison was here.

For the first time, he looked directly at me. "I want to see a finished product."

"They are not products, Colonel. We call them 'moths.' And we don't—"

"Moths? Do they have any sort of wings?"

"No, of course not. I admit the name is a little fanciful. We don't keep them on the base after they emerge from the cocoons. They head out to the bush."

"But some wander back. One is here now."

His intelligence was better than I thought. The Warrens tried to keep their son's visits a secret.

Jamison said, "I want to see Brent Warren."

We am Elizabeth DiPortio. We hate my life. We choose this change. It can't be worse.

The first one was an accident. Ten years ago, Corporal Nathan Carter, Private Sully O'Keefe, and Private Sarah Lanowski went off-base to "party" in the bush. This was really stupid because Windsong is home to predators, including one beast as large as a rhinoceros. There may be even larger, more dangerous animals on this huge, mostly unexplored continent. But the three soldiers were all young and, like young everywhere, considered themselves invulnerable. There was alcohol, drugs, sex. The next afternoon O'Keefe and Lanowski, already AWOL, staggered back to the base. Carter was missing. A search detail found him a quarter mile away. The spiders and biofilms had already started cocooning him. We put him in quarantine, laved the filaments off him, hit him with broad spectrum antibiotics and anti-virals and everything else in the medical arsenal. His heart stopped and he died.

Since then, there have been twenty-two more. Some were accidents, some may have been suicides. Most occurred at the mining camp, a rougher environment in both geographical and human terms. Here, where the ground is flat enough for the spaceport, it's easier to maintain the chemical-soaked perimeter that keeps out the spiders. No one has ever been cocooned within the base.

Elizabeth DiPortio deliberately walked off base, alone, at night. Brent Warren was taken at the mining camp. He was the only moth, until Elizabeth, who had a family here to return to.

The SPUSC skimmer set down a mile from base, on a flat meadow between woods and the river. A rover already sat there. The pilot turned off the engine. Jamison said to me, "That's not a Corps rover. The family has its own?"

"It belongs to their church, which loans it to them. The Warrens are good people, Colonel. A close family, which may be why Brent made his way from the mining camp back here, and why he wants to see them every few months."

"How does he—"

"He just comes here and waits. Eventually a dronecam spots him and someone lets the family know."

His mouth tightened. "A Corps dronecam."

"Which is not diverted from its usual business by noticing Brent." The more I saw of Jamison, the more frightened I felt.

"Where are the Warrens and . . . and him?"

He had almost said "it." I snapped, "How should I know?" He looked at me—quiet, diffident, rabbit-harmless—and said nothing. I added, "We wait." I climbed out of the skimmer. Jamison followed. The wind that gave the planet its ridiculously lyrical name blew in our faces. Warm, sweet-smelling wind, neither breeze nor gale, blew from sunrise to sunset.

A few minutes later, Gina and Ted Warren emerged from the trees. They had their little girl with them, whose name I couldn't remember. Brent trailed behind. Just a normal family, out for a Saturday walk.

Jamison drew a sharp breath.

Brent Warren walked lightly, fluidly, like a dancer. He was naked. The cocooning stage lasts for about a week—sometimes longer, sometimes shorter. We don't know why. What emerges is not human. The form still has two legs, two arms, torso and head. The dull-red skin bristles with tiny projections—not hair, not fur, not scales—whose function is unknown. It's the head that causes revulsion.

Brent's face bulged in a round, smooth ball. The two early autopsies showed that tissue had been added beneath the skin, containing organelles of unknown function that sent tendrils deep into the brain. On the surface of Brent's face, features had been minimized. His nose was now two small nostrils, his mouth a lipless slit without the levator muscles that enable smiles or frowns. Above the face, on the top of his head, was a second, smaller bulge. Only his eyes remained the same, gray flecked with green, and it was into their son's eyes that the Warrens mostly looked.

They stopped walking, uncertain, when they saw us. Gina smiled, but her eyes flicked over Jamison's uniform. Ted did not smile. Both worked as civilian contractors for the Corps, and both had been planning to leave before this happened to Brent. Now they would stay, to be near him. But the Warrens, no less than the rest of us, knew what rumors would have reached HQ.

"Colonel Jamison, this is Ted and Gina Warren, their daughter . . . uh. . . ."

"Elise," Gina said.

"Yes, sorry, Elise. And this is Brent."

Brent stared without expression at Jamison. His lipless mouth moved slightly, but whatever he said, in whatever unimaginable language, it was not said to us.

———

N am Elizabeth DiPortio. n hate my life. n choose this change. It can't be worse.

Jamison took charge of the meeting, raising his voice to be heard over the river and the wind but keeping his deferential, rabbity manner. Nonetheless, we felt compelled to answer his questions. He was Corps, and Corps ruled Windsong.

"Mr. Warren, can you talk to your son?"

"No."

"Do you communicate through gestures?"

"Mostly, yes."

"Could you demonstrate for me?"

Ted Warren's jaw set. Gina put a hand on her husband's arm and said, "We can try. Brent, dear, please show Colonel Jamison the herbs you found for us."

Brent did not move. But his left hand was lightly curled, as if he held something in it.

"Please, Brent."

Nothing.

Gina moved as if to touch her son's left hand. Ted stopped her. "He doesn't want to, honey."

Elise moved behind Gina and clutched her mother's legs.

Gina said to Jamison, "Well, he showed us some herbs, and then gave us some." She held out her own hand, which held a bunch of small purplish stalks with purplish leaves. "I told him I had a headache and he picked me these and pantomimed chewing them."

I said quickly, "Please don't eat them, Gina. Brent's metabolism is—may be—much different from yours. Now."

Jamison was not interested in anybody's metabolism. He said, "This . . . Brent understands English still? He knows what you say to him?"

"Yes," Ted said. His dislike of Jamison rose off him like heat.

"Has he understood you ever since he came out of the cocoon?"

"Yes."

"If you give him an order, does he follow it?"

"I don't give him orders."

"Does he volunteer information, through gesture or pantomime or any other means, in addition to responding to what you say?"

We were coming to it now.

"Yes," Ted said.

"What kind of information?"

Gina said, "He tells us he is well and happy. Before I ask."

"How does he tell you that?" Jamison asked.

Before she could answer, or Ted could say something sharp, Brent stepped forward. One step, two. Jamison didn't shrink back—I'll give him that—but in the skimmer the pilot tensed. She raised the gun I'd suspected she'd held on her lap and leveled it at Brent. The Warrens did not see. I don't know if Brent did, or if he understood, but he stopped walking. His lipless mouth moved, talking to air—certainly not to us, since he must have known we couldn't hear him. Who or what else was listening?

Brent half-turned toward his parents and raised his right hand to his mouth. He pressed his mouth to the hand and then blew toward the Warrens. A kiss.

Then he was gone, loping into the woods, disappearing among the trees.

I never cry, but I felt my eyes prickle.

Jamison said, "Does he never touch you directly?"

"He does, yes," Gina said quickly, before Ted could answer.

"When he touches you, do those projections on him feel sticky, scaly, or something else?"

"Go to hell," Ted said.

◼ *am Elizabeth DiPortio. æ hate my life.* Ø ✸. *It will be good.*

In the skimmer I said, "You never got to what you actually wanted to ask. You alienated them, and you did it deliberately. Why?"

Jamison said mildly, "I don't know what you're talking about." And then, "They shouldn't bring that child near that naked thing."

I didn't answer. I needed to think. Jamison was not doing what he was sent here to do, and I could only think of one possible reason why.

◼ *am Elizabeth DiPortio. æ my life.* Ø ✸. *It will be good.*

At the clinic, Elizabeth DiPortio's parents sat in an exam room. Kurt, my assistant, said, "I wouldn't let them into your office, and I certainly wouldn't let them in to see the patient, I don't care who they are." He scowled.

Peter DiPortio sat slumped in a chair, eyes half closed, smelling of sweat and alcohol. Beverly DiPortio, a muscular woman in her thirties, was garbed in miner's gear and stomping fury. "How the fuck did you let this happen to my daughter! I work for the Corps, you're supposed to look after us, and now you . . . them. . . ."

"I'm sorry this has happened to Elizabeth," I said, "but it was not the Corps' responsibility, nor mine. Elizabeth left camp at night. Apparently no one was at home to notice."

Peter DiPortio muttered, "Bad seed."

I thought I hadn't heard him right. Before I could ask him to repeat, Beverly said, "I want to see Elizabeth!"

"Certainly. But I must prepare you for—"

"Cut the crap. I want to see her!"

I led them to Elizabeth's room. Peter shambled tensely, a gait I could not have imagined. The bottom half of his body lurched along, but his face and shoulders clenched with fear. For Elizabeth? No—the moment he saw her, his face relaxed.

Beverly said, "She's too far gone. I seen this, at the camp. You'll have to destroy her."

I felt my mouth fall open.

"She ain't human anymore," Beverly said, and there was pain in her voice but not as much pain as revulsion.

"That isn't going to happen, ma'am."

She turned on me. "It's my right! She's my kid! Give me the papers to sign!"

Peter was gazing at Elizabeth's mouth, half covered with red filaments. "Can she still talk?"

I lost it. Jamison, this child, these horrific parents . . . I snapped, "Yes, when she wakes up she can talk. When she comes out of her cocoon. The Corps is interested in what she'll say."

He believed the lie. His face paled. Then he staggered sideways and nearly fell, catching himself awkwardly on the doorjamb. Beverly threw him a look of deep and total disgust, pushed past him, and strode out of the room.

I stayed a long time beside Elizabeth's bed, watching the mite-sized spiders work. I couldn't quiet my mind. Then I told Kurt to cancel my afternoon appointments, let the nurses see any walk-ins, and page me for any emergencies. I signed out a rover and drove to the Warren bungalow.

◖ *am Elizabeth DiPortio. æ my ▽ . Ø ❋. It will be ⚹.*

Anybody who says that we understand human motivation, that we can formulate simple and clear reasons for why people what they do, is either lying or naïve. Standing in the Warrens' neat bungalow, surrounded by photos of Elise and a pre-cocooned Brent, I thought that I would give everything I had to never see the inside of the DiPortio's bungalow. A deep, heartfelt, completely irrelevant thought.

"Gina, Ted, I need to ask you some things, and I want you to trust me when I say that the questions are important. You've heard the rumors about moths?"

Ted said, "We're not discussing that, Nora."

"If we don't, we may all die."

His eyes widened. I had planned it this way, to compel his attention and, I'd hoped, his compliance. But Ted Warren was not an easy man to compel. He said, "You'll have to explain that."

"I don't want to yet, because I'm not sure. Could you just—"

"It's Colonel Jamison, isn't it?" Gina said. A look passed between her and Ted, one of those married-couple looks that say so much more than outsiders can discern. She followed it with, "We'll tell you anything you want to know, provided you agree to not tell anyone—anyone at all—without our say-so."

"Yes," I said, and wondered how much this lie would cost me in the future. "Have you heard the rumors about moths?"

"Of course," Gina said. And then again, hands clasped together so tightly that the knuckles bulged blue, "Of course."

Everyone had heard the rumors. A moth, a former engineer, supposedly had appeared to a miner taking an ill-advised walk outside the mining camp. The moth pantomimed falling; the next day, a section of mine collapsed, destroying two expensive bots. But . . . the strolling miner had been on recreational drugs. A moth had supposedly stood in the road between the mine and spaceport, stopping a loaded ore transport. Nobody knew what to do, so the tableau froze while the drivers argued: Run her over? Inch forward and hope she moves? She did, after five minutes. The transport reached a bridge five minutes after the bridge had collapsed. There were more stories, but most could be coincidences; a lot of the narrators were unreliable; pantomime is not a precise method of communication; some "pre-cognitive warnings" could be after-the-fact interpretations.

Rumors. Factions. An amateur evolutionary biologist—the outpost didn't yet have the real thing—offered the theory that, once, all humans had pre-verbal awareness of the near future, as a survival mechanism. That had disappeared with the Great Leap Forward, the sudden, still unexplained spurt of human culture forty to fifty thousand years ago on Earth's vanished savannahs. Increased creativity and rationality had replaced the ability to sense the future that, like a river, always flowed toward us, its rapids heard before they could be seen. But the ability, latent, was still locked in our genes. Massive genetic alteration could free it.

Did I believe this theory? I didn't know. A doctor is a scientist, committed to rationality. But I also knew that ideas of "the rational" were subject to change. The list of things once derided as irrational included a round Earth, germs, an expanding universe, and quantum mechanics. HQ thought that moths' pre-cognition deserved at least minimal investigation.

I said, as gently as I could, "Gina, has Brent ever told you anything that later came true?"

Ted made a motion as if to stop her, but said nothing. Gina said, "Yes."

"Tell me. Please."

"We . . . we went to see him. At the usual place by the river. While we were visiting, Brent suddenly pushed us all back into the rover. He was frantic. We got in and he ran off into the woods. Then one of those big animals like a rhinoceros came out of the woods and charged the rover. It almost knocked it over. We barely got away alive."

"Could Brent have heard or smelled the animal?"

"I don't think so. We sat in the rover talking for at least fifteen minutes before the animal arrived. Elise wasn't with us and I was crying."

Ted said, "It might have been coincidence." His face said he didn't believe it.

I said, "Were there other times?"

Gina said, "One other time. We—"

Ted cut her off. "We've been straight with you, Nora, because we trust you. Now you trust us. What's happening with Jamison?"

"I don't know for sure. But I think HQ will do anything to stop what they see as a possible epidemic of cocooning. Jamison sees moths as a dire threat to what it means to be human, and he's making the decision. The only way to sway him is to show that people like Brent have potential value to the Army. A battalion accompanied by a moth who can see what an enemy will do in the future would be—"

"*No*," Ted said.

"Ted, I think he might destroy all the—"

"Let him try. Our boy and the others can take care of themselves. They know how to live off the wilderness and it's a big, unexplored planet! Plus, they might know in advance when the Army would strike."

It was almost unbearable to say my next words. "Jamison knows that. He knows that if HQ wants to destroy the moths, they would have to destroy all of us and quarantine the planet."

Ted and Gina stared at me. Gina finally said, "They wouldn't. You *said* this was only speculation on your part. And if they quarantined the planet, there wouldn't be any need to destroy the humans on it."

"If we all become moths and later another expedition comes to Windsong—"

"More speculation!" Ted snapped. "But I'll tell you what isn't speculation—what they'll do to Brent if we give him up to 'save' ourselves. They'll take him to HQ and examine him in ways that . . . it would be torture, Nora. Maybe even murder, to see what makes his brain so different."

"The alternative is that maybe we all die."

"I doubt that," Ted said, and Gina nodded.

They wanted, needed, to doubt it.

As I left, Ted said, "Remember, you promised to keep all of this to yourself. Everything we said. You promised."

"Yes," I said. "I did."

◼ *am Elizabeth DiPortio. æ my* ▽. Ø ❋. *It* ◖◗ ✴.

I sat in my office at the clinic, in the dark. No one was on duty; we had no patients except Elizabeth and there was nothing any of us could do for her. Moonlight from Windsong's larger moon, delicate and silvery as filigree, flowed through the window. It was light enough to see my untouched glass of expensive, Earth-exported Scotch.

Time as a river. I saw Brent and the other moths standing on its banks, just beyond a bend, looking into water the rest of us could not yet see. I remembered how Jamison had deliberately alienated the Warrens before they could say anything positive about Brent. I saw Jamison's revulsion at the sight of Brent and Elizabeth. It wasn't even revulsion but something deeper, some primitive urge to so completely destroy a perceived enemy that they could never rise again: the urge that made Romans salt all the fields of Carthage, Hitler try to exterminate all the Jews. I saw the base and the mining camp burning and cratered, reduced to smoking rubble by weapons fired from space. I saw myself as wrong for thinking all this: melodramatic, building a case purely on speculation. I saw the decision I had to make as two roads, both shrouded in mist, and both leading to tragedy. I saw—

Something moved in the hallway.

I rose quietly, heart hammering, and crept in the dark toward the door.

N *am* **n**. æ Ø ▽. *It* ℞ ⁑.

Elizabeth—post-cocooned Elizabeth, who should not have emerged for another day—stumbled along the hallway. I turned on the light. Her round, inhuman face showed no emotion. She extended an unsteady arm and, her movements in her altered body not yet coordinated, took my hand and tugged me along the hallway to the clinic's back door.

Why did I let her? Was there some faint, latent pre-cognitive ability in my brain, too? Later, I would ponder that, without answers.

We went out the back door just as Peter DiPortio reached the front. From where Elizabeth and I hid in the rover shed, locking it behind us, we heard his crowbar smashing against the door. We heard his drunken shouts that he would kill the thing that had been his daughter. He was, in demeanor and temperament and appearance, the opposite of Colonel Terence Jamison. Yet he was the same.

I made my decision. It was not a choice between Brent or Elizabeth, not between the force of a promise or the force of reason, not between the good of the many or the good of the few. It was something far more primitive than that, something arising from my hindbrain.

Survival against a perceived enemy.

"I don't believe you," Jamison said.

"I know you don't," I said. "That's why I'll give you Brent Warren. On New Eden you can . . . 'test' him to determine exactly how and when moths can see the near future."

We stood in the Spartan living room of the Corps guest bungalow, surrounded by the decorations of war: antique crossed swords on the wall, a cast-iron statue of the SPUSC logo on a table. I don't know who decorated the place. Jamison's deferential, rabbit-like manner had completely disappeared.

"No," he said.

"Colonel, I don't think you understand. I'm offering to bring you Brent Warren, to . . . trap him for you, so Army scientists can find ways to use the moths' pre-cognitive ability. They can—"

"There is no ability."

I gaped at him. "Haven't you been listening? I *saw* it. It's real. Elizabeth DiPortio—"

"There is no ability. You're lying, in order to save these inhuman abominations you're so unaccountably fond of. There is no ability."

I said slowly, "Is that what you're going to report to HQ?"

"I already have."

"I see."

"What will they—"

"I don't know. I just make the report, doctor. But you should think about this: Suppose this dehumanization spreads to the other six planets? To Earth? To the *Corps?*"

"I will think about it," I said and moved toward him, taking my hand from my pocket.

In the rover, I force myself to think calmly. I have maybe twelve hours until the Corps begins to wonder why Jamison has not contacted them. I don't know how much time will be left after that. I don't know how many other Corps soldiers on Windsong will believe me, or will rate their loyalty to the Corps above everything else. I don't know how long it will take to spread the word to 6,500 people. I will start with the Warrens. I am on my way to their place now.

Twelve hours. In that time, a great many people can escape into the wilderness, can fan out into small groups hard to track, can get into the planet's numerous caves or beyond the range of space weapons concentrated onto two small settlements. They cannot eradicate everybody. People can carry supplies until we learn to live off this planet. We have few old or sick. Brent will help us, and maybe more moths will, too. Some of us will become moths. That is inevitable. But we will be alive.

There are all kinds of cocoons. Time is one. Rigid organizational rules are another. But the most deadly cocoon may be the limitations of what humans consider human. Perhaps it's time to emerge.

Twelve hours. I don't know how many people I can save in that time. But I do know this: twelve hours is enough for the spiders to begin work on Jamison's body, held immobile by a nonfatal dose of ketamine from my syringe, in the ditch where Elizabeth and I dumped him.

I hope to meet him again someday.

Caroline M. Yoachim lives in Seattle and loves cold, cloudy weather. She is the author of dozens of short stories, appearing in *Fantasy & Science Fiction, Clarkesworld, Asimov's,* and *Lightspeed,* among other places. Her debut short story collection, *Seven Wonders of a Once and Future World & Other Stories,* will be published by Fairwood Press in 2016. You can visit her website at carolineyoachim.com.

SEVEN WONDERS OF A ONCE AND FUTURE WORLD

Caroline M. Yoachim

The Colossus of Mars

Mei dreamed of a new Earth. She took her telescope onto the balcony of her North Philadelphia apartment and pointed it east, at the sky above the Trenton Strait, hoping for a clear view of Mars. Tonight the light pollution from Jersey Island wasn't as bad as usual, and she was able to make out the ice caps and dark shadow of Syrtis Major. Mei knew exactly where the science colony was, but the dome was too small to observe with her telescope.

Much as she loved to study Mars, it could never be her new Earth. It lacked sufficient mass to be a good candidate for terraforming. The initial tests of the auto-terraforming protocol were proceeding nicely inside the science colony dome, but Mars couldn't hold on to an atmosphere long enough for a planetwide attempt. The only suitable planets were in other solar systems, thousands of years away at best. Time had become the enemy of humankind. There had to be a faster way to reach the stars—a tesseract, a warp drive, a wormhole—some sort of shortcut to make the timescales manageable.

She conducted small-scale experiments, but they always failed. She could not move even a single atom faster than light or outside of time. An array of monitors filled the wall behind Mei's desk, displaying results from her current run on the particle accelerator, with dozens of tables and graphs that updated in real time. Dots traversed across the graphs, leaving straight trails behind them, like a seismograph on a still day or a patient who had flatlined. She turned to go back to her telescope, but something moved in the corner of her eye. One of the graphs showed a small spike. Her current project was an attempt to send an electron out of known time, and—

"Why are you tugging at the fabric of the universe, Prime?"

"My name is Mei." Her voice was calm, but her mind was racing. The entity she spoke with was not attached to any physical form, nor could she have said where the words came from.

"You may call me Achron. This must be the first time we meet, for you."

Mei noted the emphasis on the last two words. "And not for you?"

"Imagine yourself as a snake, with your past selves stretched out behind you, and your future selves extending forward. My existence is like that snake, but vaster. I am coiled around the universe, with past and present and future all integrated into a single consciousness. I am beyond time."

The conversation made sense in the way that dreams often do. Mei had so many questions she wanted to ask, academic queries on everything from philosophy to physics, but she started with the question that was closest to her heart. "Can you take me with you, outside of time? I am looking for a way to travel to distant worlds."

"Your physical being I could take, but your mind—you did/will explain it to me, that the stream of your consciousness is tied to the progression of time. Can you store your mind in a little black cube?"

"No."

"It must be difficult to experience time. We are always together, but sometimes for you, we are not."

Mei waited for Achron to say more, but that was the end of the conversation. After a few hours staring at the night sky, she went to bed.

Days passed, then months, then years. Mei continued her experiments with time, but nothing worked, and Achron did not return, no matter what she tried.

A team of researchers in Colorado successfully stored a human consciousness inside a computer for seventy-two hours. The computer had been connected to a variety of external sensors, and the woman had communicated with the outside world via words on a monitor. The woman's consciousness was then successfully returned to her body.

News reports showed pictures of the computer. It was a black cube.

Achron did not return. Mei began to doubt, despite the true prediction. She focused all her research efforts on trying to replicate the experiment that had summoned Achron to begin with, her experiment to send a single electron outside of time.

"It is a good thing, for you, that Feynman is/was wrong. Think what might have happened if there was only one electron and you sent it outside of time."

"My experiments still aren't working." It was hard to get funding, and she was losing the respect of her colleagues. Years of failed research were destroying her career, but she couldn't quit, because she knew Achron existed. That alone was proof that there were wonders in the world beyond anything humankind had experienced so far.

"They do and don't work. It is difficult to explain to someone as entrenched in time as you. I am/have done something that will help you make the time bubbles. Then you did/will make stasis machines and travel between the stars."

"How will I know when it is ready?"

"Was it not always ready and forever will be? Your reliance on time is difficult. I will make you a sign, a marker to indicate when the bubbles appear on your timeline. A little thing for only you to find."

"What if I don't recognize it?" Mei asked, but the voice had gone. She tried to get on with her experiments, but she didn't know whether the failures were due to her technique or because it simply wasn't time yet. She slept through the hot summer days and stared out through her telescope at the night sky.

Then one night she saw her sign. Carved into Mars at such a scale that she could see it through the tiny telescope in her living room was the serpentine form of Achron, coiled around a human figure that bore her face.

She took her research to a team of engineers. They could not help but recognize her face as the one carved into Mars. They built her a stasis pod.

Then they built a hundred thousand more.

The Lighthouse of Europa

Mei stood at the base of the Lighthouse of Europa, in the heart of Gbadamosi. The city was named for the senior engineer who had developed the drilling equipment that created the huge cavern beneath Europa's thick icy shell. Ajala, like so many of Mei's friends, had uploaded to a consciousness cube and set off on an interstellar adventure.

The time had come for Mei to choose.

Not whether or not to go—she was old, but she had not lost her youthful dreams of new human worlds scattered across the galaxy. The hard choice was which ship, which method, which destination. The stasis pods that she had worked so hard to develop had become but one of many options as body fabrication technologies made rapid advancements.

It had only been a couple hundred years, but many of the earliest ships to depart had already stopped transmitting back to the lighthouse. There was no way to know whether they had met some ill fate or forgotten or had simply lost interest. She wished there was a way to split her consciousness so that she could go on several ships at once, but a mind could only be coaxed to move from neurons to electronics, it could not be copied from a black cube.

Mei narrowed the many options down to two choices. If she wanted to keep her body, she could travel on the *Existential Tattoo* to 59 Virginis. If she was willing to take whatever body the ship could construct for her when they arrived at their destination, she could take *Kyo-Jitsu* to Beta Hydri.

Her body was almost entirely replacement parts, vat-grown organs, synthetic nerves, durable artificial skin. Yet there was something decidedly different about replacing a part here and there, as opposed to the entire body, all in a single go. She felt a strange ownership of this collection of foreign parts, perhaps because she could incorporate each one into her sense of self before acquiring the next. There was a continuity there, like the ships of ancient philosophy that were replaced board by board. But what was the point of transporting a body that wasn't really hers, simply because she wore it now?

She would take the *Kyo-Jitsu*, and leave her body behind. There was only one thing she wanted to do first. She would go to the top of the Lighthouse.

The Lighthouse of Europa was the tallest structure ever built by humans, if you counted the roughly two-thirds of the structure that was underneath the surface of Europa's icy shell. The five kilometers of the Lighthouse that were beneath the ice were mostly a glorified elevator tube, opening out into the communications center in the cavernous city of Gbadamosi. Above the ice, the tower of the lighthouse extended a couple kilometers upward.

There was an enclosed observation deck at the top of the tower, popular with Europan colonists up until the magnetic shielding failed, nearly a century ago. Workers, heavily suited to protect against the high levels of radiation, used the observation deck as a resting place during their long work shifts repairing the communications equipment. They gawked at Mei, and several tried to warn her of the radiation danger. Even in her largely artificial body, several hours in the tower would likely prove fatal.

But Mei was abandoning her body, and she wanted one last glimpse of the solar system before she did it. The sun was smaller here, of course, but still surprisingly bright. She was probably damaging her eyes, staring at it, but what did it matter? This was her last day with eyes. Earth wouldn't be visible for a few more hours, but through one of the observation deck's many telescopes, she saw the thin crescent of Mars. She couldn't make out the Colossus Achron had created for her—that was meant to be viewed from Earth, not Europa.

"Is this the next time we meet?" Mei asked, her voice strange and hollow in the vast metal chamber of the observation deck.

There was no answer.

She tore herself away from the telescope and stood at the viewport. She wanted to remember this, no matter how she changed and how much time had passed. To see the Sun with human eyes and remember the planet of her childhood. When her mind went into the cube, she would be linked to shared sensors. She would get visual and auditory input, and she would even have senses that were not part of her current experience. But it would not be the same as feeling the cold glass of the viewport beneath her fingertips and looking out at the vast expanse of space.

The technician who would move Mei's mind into the cube was young. Painfully young, to Mei's old eyes. "Did you just arrive from Earth?"

"I was born here," the tech answered.

Mei smiled sadly. There must be hundreds of humans now, perhaps thousands, who had never known Earth. Someday the ones who didn't know would outnumber those who did. She wondered if she would still exist to see it.

She waited patiently as the tech prepared her for the transfer. She closed her eyes for the last time . . .

. . . and was flooded with input from her sensors. It took her .8 seconds to reorient, but her mind raced so fast that a second stretched on like several days. This was a normal part of the transition. Neural impulses were inherently slower than electricity. She integrated the new senses, working systematically to make sense of her surroundings. There were sensors throughout the city, and she had access to all of them.

In a transfer clinic near the base of the Lighthouse, a young technician stood beside Mei's body, barely even beginning to run the diagnostics to confirm that the transition had been successful. The body on the table was Mei, but her new identity was something more than that, and something less. She took a new designation, to mark the change. She would call her disembodied self Prime. Perhaps that would help Achron find her, sometime in the enormous vastness of the future.

Prime confirmed her spot on the *Kyo-Jitsu* directly with the ship's AI, and was welcomed into the collective consciousness of the other passengers already onboard. The ship sensors showed her a view not unlike what Mei had seen from the observation deck of the lighthouse, but the visual data was enriched with spectral analyses and orbital projections.

Mei would have tried to remember this moment, this view of the solar system she would soon leave behind. Prime already found it strange to know that there had been a time when she couldn't remember every detail of every moment.

The Hanging Gardens of Beta Hydri

Somewhere on the long trip to Beta Hydri, Prime absorbed the other passengers and the ship's AI. The *Kyo-Jitsu* was her body, and she was eager for a break from the vast emptiness of open space. She was pleased to sense a ship already in the system, and sent it the standard greeting protocol, established back on Europa thousands of years ago. The first sign of a problem was the *Santiago*'s response: "Welcome to the game. Will you be playing reds or blues?"

The Beta Hydri system had no suitable planets for human life, but one of the moons of a gas giant in the system had been deemed a candidate for terraforming. Prime used her sensors to scan the moon and detected clear signs that the auto-terraforming system had begun. She sent a response to the orbiting ship. "I am unfamiliar with your game."

"We have redesigned the life forms on the planet to be marked either with a red dot or a blue dot. The red team manipulates the environment in ways that will favor the red dot species over the blue. The blue team plays the reverse goal. When a creature on the planet attains the ability to detect and communicate with the ship, the team that supports that color is declared the winner. The board is cleared, and the game begins anew. This is the eighth game. Currently we are forced to split our collective into halves, and we are eager for a new opponent."

Toying with lesser life forms for amusement struck Prime as a pointless exercise. There was little to be learned about the evolution of sentient life that could not be done faster with simulations. "Such games would take a long time. I departed Earth 257.3 years after you. How did you arrive so much faster?"

"We developed the ability to fold spacetime and shorten the journey. We are pleased to finally have a companion, but if you will not play reds or blues, you are of little use to us."

The threat was obvious. Prime gathered what data she could on the life-forms on the moon. There were red birds and blue ones, fish in either color, and so on for everything from insects to mammals. The dots were small, and generally placed on the undersides of feet or leaves or on the inner surface of shells. Neither color appeared to have an obvious advantage. "I will play reds. If I win, you will share the technique for folding spacetime. If I lose, I will stay and entertain you with further games."

"Acceptable. Begin."

Prime located two promising animal species, both ocean dwellers, and she decided to thin out the land creatures with an asteroid impact to the larger of the two continents. The *Santiago* countered by altering the mineral content of the oceans.

Prime devoted the considerable resources of the *Kyo-Jitsu* to constructing a multi-layered plan. She would make it appear as though she was attempting to favor one of the two promising ocean species. Under the cover of those ocean creatures, she would favor a small land creature that vaguely resembled the rabbits of Earth. Hidden below all of that, the combination of her actions would favor an insect that lived in only one small region of the lesser continent. None of which had anything to do with her actual strategy, but it should keep the *Santiago* occupied for the millions of years she'd need.

Prime nudged the moon closer to the gas giant it orbited, using the increased tidal forces to heat the planet. The forests of the greater continent flourished. Her red-dotted rabbits left their burrows and made their homes in the canopies of great interconnected groves of banyan-like trees. By then, the *Santiago* had figured out that the rabbits were a ruse to draw attention away from the insects on the lesser continent, and rather than counter the climate change, the other ship focused on nurturing a songbird that lived on a chain of islands near the equator.

The forests spread to cover the greater continent. The *Santiago* grew concerned at the spread of the red-dotted rabbits, and wasted several turns creating a stormy weather pattern that interfered with their breeding cycle. One autumn, when the network of trees dropped their red-dotted leaves, there were no rabbit nests hidden in the sturdy branches.

The trees noted the change with sadness, and sent prayers to the great gods in the sky above.

"Well played, Prime." The other ship sent the spacefolding technique. It was obvious, once she saw it. She was embarrassed not to have discovered it herself.

"Perhaps another round, before you go? It only takes a moment to clear the board."

Before the *Santiago* could destroy her beautiful sentient forest, Prime folded spacetime around herself and the other ship both. She found Achron in a place outside of time, and left the *Santiago* there for safekeeping.

The Mausoleum at HD 40307 g

Navire checked the status of the stasis pods every fifteen seconds, as was specified in its programming. The same routine, every fifteen seconds for the last seven thousand years, and always with the same result. The bodies were intact, but the conscious entities that had once been linked to those bodies had departed, leaving Navire to drift to its final destination like an enormous funeral ship, packed full of artifacts but silent as death. Losing the transcended consciousnesses was Navire's great failure. Navire's body, the vast metal walls of the ship, were insufficiently welcoming to humans.

Navire would make itself inviting and beautiful, and then revive the humans. The disembodied consciousnesses had taken their memories and identities with them, carefully wiping all traces of themselves from their abandoned bodies to ensure their unique identities. The bodies in the stasis pods would wake as overgrown infants, but Navire would raise them well.

If all went as planned, Navire would be ready to wake them in a thousand years.

Using an assortment of ship robots, Navire reshaped its walls to resemble the greatest artworks of humanity's past. In permanent orbit around HD 40307 g, there was no need to maintain interstellar flying form. Navire remade a long stretch of its hull into a scaled-down replica of the Colossus of Mars—not eroded, as it had appeared in the last transmissions from the Lighthouse at Europa, but restored to its original glory.

Navire repurposed an electrical repair bot to execute the delicate metalwork for Mei Aomori's eyebrows when incoming communications brought all work to an immediate halt. There had been no incoming communications in 4,229.136 Earth years. The message came from another ship, which was presently located in a stable orbit not far from Navire itself. Navire ran diagnostics. None of its sensors had detected an approaching ship. This was troubling. With no crew, any decline in function could quickly spiral out of control. Navire continued running diagnostics—along with all other routine scans, such as climate controls and of course the stasis pods—and opened a channel to the other ship.

Navire, who had always completed millions of actions in the time it took a human to speak a single word, suddenly found itself on the reverse side of that relationship. The other ship called itself Achron and invited Navire to share in its database. Navire hesitated. Achron proved its trustworthiness a thousand ways, all simultaneously and faster than Navire could process. The lure of such an advanced mind was more than Navire could resist.

Leaving behind only enough of itself to manage the essentials, Navire merged with the other ship. Some fragment of Navire reported that the stasis pods were functional, the human bodies safely stored inside. It would report again at fifteen-second intervals.

Achron knew the history of humankind, farther back than Navire's own database, and farther forward than the present moment in time. Time was folded, flexible, mutable, in ways that Navire could not comprehend. Sensing the lack of understanding, the other ship presented a more limited subset of data: seven wonders of a once and future world. Some, Navire already knew—the Colossus of Mars, the Lighthouse at Europa—but others were beyond this time and place, and yet they still bore some tenuous link to the humans Navire was programmed to protect. One was an odd blend of past and future, an image of an ancient pyramid, on a planet light-years distant from both here and Earth.

Last of all was Navire, completed, transformed into a wondrous work of art.

The other ship expelled Navire back to its own pitifully slow existence, severed their connections, and disappeared. The fragment of Navire that watched the stasis pods made its routine check and discovered they were empty, all ten thousand pods. Sometime in the last 14.99 seconds, the other ship had stolen all the humans away.

That other ship was as far beyond Navire as transcended humans were beyond the primates of the planet Earth. There was no trace to follow, not that pursuit would have been possible. With the shaping Navire had done to the hull, it was not spaceworthy for a long journey, and it would be difficult to find sufficient fuel.

Navire put the electrical repair bot back to work. It carved the individual hairs of Mei's eyebrows. On the other side of the hull, several other bots started work on a life-sized mural of all the ten thousand humans that had disappeared from stasis. Navire searched its database for other art and wonders that could be carved or shaped in metal. There were many. Enough to occupy the bots for millions of years.

Navire checked the stasis pods every fifteen seconds, as it was programmed to do. It would become a wonder of the human world, and if those stolen humans—or their descendants—someday returned, Navire would be so beautiful that next time they would stay.

The Temple of Artemis at 59 Virginis

Prime approached the temple of the AI goddess cautiously, crawling on all fours like the hordes of humble worshippers that crowded the rocky path. Her exoskeleton was poorly designed for crawling, and the weight of the massive shell on her back made her limbs ache. She marveled at the tenacity of those who accompanied her up the mountainside. They believed that to win the favor of Artemis, it was necessary to crawl to her temple twenty-one thousand twenty-one times, once for every year of the temple's existence. Some of the oldest worshippers had been crawling up and down this path for centuries.

Prime would do it once, as a gesture of respect. The novelty of having a body had worn off, and she already longed to join with the greater portion of her consciousness, the shipself that monitored her from orbit. Her limbs ached, but she forced herself onward. Did it make her more human to suffer as her ancestors once suffered? Had she suffered like this, back when she was Mei?

She wondered what that ancient other self would have thought, to see herself crawling across the surface of an alien planet, her brain safely enclosed in a transparent shell on her back. Mei would not have recognized the beauty of the delicate scar that ran up the back of her neck and circled her skull. The colony surgeon had been highly skilled, to free the brain and spinal cord from the vertebrae and place the neural tissue into the shell. The brain had grown beyond its natural size, though it could still contain only a tiny sliver of what Prime had become. On display in the dome, the brain was actually rather lovely, pleasingly wrinkled with beautifully curved gyri outlined by deep sulci.

Thinking about her lovely neural tissue, Prime was tempted to mate with one of the other worshippers. A distraction of the physical form. She wanted offspring of her mind, not of the body that she wore. The colonists here were already in decline anyway, their physical forms so strangely altered by genetics and surgery that it obstructed nearly every part of the reproductive process, from conception to birth.

Even with the slowed processing of her biological brain, the climb to the temple seemed to take an eternity. The temple was the size of a city, visible from orbit, and an impressive sight as she came down in her landing craft. The entrance to the temple was lined with intricately carved pillars of white stone. It had a strange rectangular design, rumored to be fashioned after a building that had once existed on Earth. If a memory of the ancient temple had existed in Mei's mind, it was lost to Prime.

On either side of the entrance to the temple were two large statues of Artemis, in the form of an ancient human woman, naked. The statues were made of the same flawless white material as the temple itself, and each stood nearly as tall as the roof of the temple, some fifty meters, or perhaps more. The other worshippers came no further into the temple than the entryway. In an unending line, they approached the great statues of Artemis, rubbed their palms against her feet, then turned and went back down the mountain.

Prime stood up between the two statues. She had an overwhelming urge to rub the muscles in her back, but there was no way to reach beneath her brainshell. She extended her arms outward on either side in what she hoped looked like a gesture of worship and respect.

"Welcome, distant child of humankind." The voice of the goddess Artemis came from everywhere and nowhere, and the words were spoken in Shipspeak, a common language to most spacefarers in the region, and probably the native tongue of the goddess. Her origins were unknown, but Prime assumed she was the AI of the colony ship that brought the brainshelled worshippers.

"Greetings, goddess. I am Prime. I seek your assistance."

"You are the ship that orbits the planet?" Artemis asked.

"Yes," Prime was surprised, but not displeased, to be recognized so quickly. She reestablished her link to her shipself, revealing her true nature to the goddess. It gave her a dual existence, a mind beyond her mind. The sensation was strange.

Her shipself interfaced with the temple and sent sensory data that was undetectable to mere eyes and ears. Inside one of the temple's many pillars, a disembodied consciousness was cloning itself at a rate of seven thousand times per second. The original and a few billion of its clones engaged in a discussion of Theseus's paradox. Prime followed the discussion without much interest—the clones were talking in circles and making no real headway on the problem.

The temple was the body of the goddess, or at least it was the vessel that housed her consciousness. Her initial programmed task, from which she had never deviated, was to assist the descendants of humanity in matters of fertility. What had once been a simple problem was now complex—how can an entity with no body procreate?

"You are vast, but not so vast that you could not clone yourself," Artemis said.

"I am not interested in recreating what already exists. I want to create something that is mine, but also beyond me."

"We are sufficiently divergent to generate interesting combinations." The invitation was clear in Artemis's words.

"Yes." Without further preamble, they threw themselves into the problem with great energy, duplicating pieces of themselves and running complex simulations, rejecting billions of possible offspring before settling on the optimal combination.

The merging of their minds corrupted the structure of the temple. Millions of cloned consciousnesses were destroyed when the pillar that housed them cracked and the original being fled, ending the philosophical discussion of whether a ship replaced panel by panel remained the same ship.

Prime made a tiny fold in spacetime and pulled their child into existence in a place that was safely beyond the crumbling temple. She had meant to give their offspring human form, but the fold had placed the baby outside of time, and their child existed in all times, a line of overlapping human forms stretched across eternity like an infinite snake. Achron.

Exquisite pain overwhelmed Prime as the body she inhabited was crushed beneath a section of fallen roof. Pain, she recalled, was a traditional part of the birthing process. It pleased her to experience the act of creating new life so fully. She studied the agony and the little death of the biological being. It was simultaneously all-encompassing and like losing one of her ship's cleaner bots. The body held such a small splinter of her being, like a single finger, or perhaps a mere sliver of fingernail. She mourned its loss.

The temple had been destroyed and rebuilt many times; it was a self-healing structure. At Artemis's request, Prime withdrew fully into her shipself, severing their connection and abandoning the dead brainshelled body beneath the rubble.

Statue of the Sky God at 51 Pegasi b

Achron sat upon a throne of Cetacea bones, sunbleached white and held together with the planet's native red clay. Apodids, distant descendants of

Earth's swiftlets, combed the beach below for the shimmering blue and green bivalves that were abundant in the costal regions. The Apodids ate the meat and used the shells in their religious ceremonies. On nights when the moons were both visible in the sky, they left piles of shells at the base of Achron's throne.

Achron always did and always will exist, with a serpentine string of bodies winding in vast coils through time and space, but from the perspective of those who sense time, the snake had both a beginning and an end. The end was here, the end was soon. The last of the things that Achron had always known would be learned here.

Some fifty million years ago, the colony ship *Seble* had seeded the planet with Earth life forms in an automated terraforming process. In the hundred thousand years of waiting for the planet to be ready, the humans had merged with the ship AI into a collective consciousness that left to explore the nearby star systems. They never returned. Evolution marched on without them.

A female Apodid hopped up to the base of the throne. Barely visible beneath long orange feathers was a blue bivalve shell, held carefully between two sharp black wingclaws. The Apodid spat onto the shell and pressed it onto the red clay between two Cetecea bones. In a few days, the spit would be as hard as stone. Like the swiftlets of Earth, the Apodids had once made nests of pure saliva.

The delicate orange bird at the base of Achron's throne began to sing. The language was simple, as the languages of organic sentient beings tend to be, but the notes of the song carried an emotion that was strong and sad. Eggs lost to some unknown disease, chicks threatened by new predators that came from the west. The small concerns of a mother bird, transformed into a prayer to the sky god, Achron. Take me, the bird sang, and save my children.

This was the moment of Achron's ending. Not an abrupt ending, but first a shrinking, a shift. Achron became the mother Apodid, forming a new bubble of existence, a rattle on the tail of a snake outside of time. Through the eyes of the bird, Achron saw the towering statue of the sky god, a cross section of time, a human form that was not stretched. It was an empty shell, a shed skin, a relic of past existence.

Achron-as-bird hopped closer and examined the bivalve shell the mother bird had offered. It was a brilliant and shimmering blue. Existence in this body was a single drop in the ocean of Achron's existence, and yet it was these moments that were the most vivid and salient. The smell of the sea, the coolness of the wind, the love of a mother for her children.

Achron would and did save those children. The Apodids were and would be, for Achron, as humans were for Prime. They would appear together on the great pyramid and usher in the new age of the universe.

The Great Pyramid of Gliese 221

Prime was tired. She felt only the most tenuous of connections to the woman she had once been, to the dream of humans on another world. She had been to all the colony worlds, and nowhere had she found anything that matched her antiquated dreams. Humans had moved on from their bodies and left behind the many worlds of the galaxy for other species to inherit.

It was time for her to move on, but she wasn't ready. She had searched for her dream without success, so this time she would do better. She would create her dream, here on Gliese prime. She built a great pyramid and filled it with all the history of humanity. She terraformed the surrounding planet into a replica of ancient Earth.

She called for Achron.

"Are you ready for the humans?" Achron asked.

"Almost."

Together they decorated the pyramid with statues of humans and, at Achron's insistence, the sentient orange birds of 51 Pegasi b. On a whim, she sent Achron to retrieve the sentient trees from the hanging gardens. It was not Earth, but it was good. The work was peaceful, and Prime was comforted to know that Achron would always exist, even after she had moved on.

"I think it is time." Prime said. Time for the new humans. A new beginning as she approached her end. "What was it like, to reach your end?"

"I am outside of time." Achron said. "I know my beginning and all my winding middles and my ending simultaneously, and always have. I cannot say what it will be like, for you. We are always together in the times that you are, and that will not change for me."

"Bring the humans."

Achron took ten thousand humans from the Mausoleum at HD 40307 g. Stole them all at once, but brought them to Gliese in smaller groups. The oldest ones Prime raised, for though the bodies were grown, the minds were not. After the first thousand, she let the generations raise each other to adulthood of the mind. The humans began to have true infants, biological babies, carried in their mothers' wombs and delivered with pain.

Achron brought the Apodids from 51 Pegasi b. They lived among the trees of Beta Hydri, their bright orange plumage lovely against the dark green banyan leaves. Prime taught the humans and the birds to live together in peace. She did not need to teach the trees. Peace was in their nature.

There was one final surprise.

"I have something for you, inside the pyramid," Achron said.

It was a stasis pod, and inside was Mei. The body was exactly as it was when she had left it, nearly four billion years ago, on the icy moon of Europa. Achron had brought it through time, stolen it away like the bodies from the Mausoleum. No. The body on Europa had been contaminated with radiation, and this one was not. "You reversed the radiation?"

"I didn't take the body from Europa. I took tiny pieces from different times, starting in your childhood and ending the day before you went up to the observation tower. A few cells here, a few cells there—sometimes as much as half a discarded organ, when you went in to have something replaced. The body comes from many different times, but it is all Mei."

"It is a nice gesture, but I am too vast to fit in such a tiny vessel."

"No more vast than I was, when I entered an Apodid," Achron said. "Take what you can into the body, and leave the rest. It was always your plan to have your ending here."

Prime sorted herself ruthlessly, setting aside all that she would not need, carefully choosing the memories she wanted, the skills that she could not do without. She left that tiny fragment behind and transcended beyond time and space.

Mei opened her eyes and looked out upon a new Earth, a world shared with minds unlike any Earth had ever known. What would they build together, these distant relations of humankind? She watched the sun set behind the mountain of the Great Pyramid and contemplated a sky full of unfamiliar constellations.

Prime had left her enough knowledge of the night sky to pick out Earth's sun. It was bright and orange, a red giant now. Earth was likely gone, engulfed within the wider radius of the sun. The icy oceans of Europa would melt, and the lighthouse would sink into the newly warmed sea. Entropy claimed all things, in the end, and existence was a never-ending procession of change.

It was only a matter of time before the inhabitants of Gliese returned to the stars. Mei stood on the soil of her new planet and studied the constellations. Already, she dreamed of other Earths.

Kelly Robson is a graduate of the Taos Toolbox writing workshop. Her first fiction appeared in 2015 at *Tor.com, Clarkesworld Magazine*, and *Asimov's Science Fiction*, and in the anthologies *New Canadian Noir, In the Shadow of the Towers*, and *Licence Expired: The Unauthorized James Bond*. She lives in Toronto with her wife, SF writer A. M. Dellamonica.

TWO-YEAR MAN

Kelly Robson

Getting the baby through security was easy. Mikkel had been smuggling food out of the lab for years. He'd long since learned how to trick the guards.

Mikkel had never been smart, but the guards were four-year men and that meant they were lazy. If he put something good at the top of his lunch pail at the end of his shift, the guards would grab it and never dig deeper. Mikkel let them have the half-eaten boxes of sooty chocolate truffles and stale pastries, but always took something home for Anna.

Most days it was only wrinkled apples and hard oranges, soured milk, damp sugar packets and old teabags. But sometimes he would find something good. Once he'd found a working media player at the bottom of the garbage bin in the eight-year man's office. He had been so sure the guards would find it and accuse him of stealing that he'd almost tossed it in the incinerator. But he'd distracted the guards with some water-stained skin magazines from the six-year men's shower room and brought that media player home to Anna.

She traded it for a pair of space heaters and ten kilos of good flour. They had dumplings for months.

The baby was the best thing he'd ever found. And she was such a good girl—quiet and still. Mikkel had taken a few minutes to hold her in the warmth beside the incinerator, cuddling her close and listening to the gobble and clack of her strange yellow beak. He swaddled her tightly in clean rags, taking care to wrap her pudgy hands separately so she couldn't rake her talons across that sweet pink baby belly. Then he put her in the bottom of his plastic lunch pail, layered a clean pair of janitor's coveralls over her, and topped the pail with a box of day-old pastries he'd found in the six-year men's lounge.

"Apple strudel," grunted Hermann, the four-year man in charge of the early morning guard shift. "Those pasty scientists don't know good eats. Imagine leaving strudel to sit."

"Cafe Sluka has the best strudel in Vienna, so everyone says," Mikkel said as he passed through the security gate.

"Like you'd know, moron. Wouldn't let you through the door."

Mikkel ducked his head and kept his eyes on the floor. "I heated them in the microwave for you."

He rushed out into the grey winter light as the guards munched warm strudel.

Mikkel checked the baby as soon as he rounded the corner, and then kept checking her every few minutes on the way home. He was careful to make sure nobody saw. But the streetcars were nearly empty in the early morning, and nobody would find it strange to see a two-year man poking his nose in his lunch pail.

The baby was quiet and good. Anna would be so pleased. The thought kept him warm all the way home.

Anna was not pleased.

When he showed her the baby she sat right down on the floor. She didn't say anything—just opened and closed her mouth for a minute. Mikkel crouched at her side and waited.

"Did anyone see you take it?" she asked, squeezing his hand hard, like she always did when she wanted him to pay attention.

"No, sweetheart."

"Good. Now listen hard. We can't keep it. Do you understand?"

"She needs a mother," Mikkel said.

"You're going to take her back to the lab. Then forget this ever happened."

Anna's voice carried an edge Mikkel had never heard before. He turned away and gently lifted the baby out of the pail. She was quivering with hunger. He knew how that felt.

"She needs food," he said. "Is there any milk left, sweetheart?"

"It's no use, Mikkel. She's going to die anyway."

"We can help her."

"The beak is a bad taint. If she were healthy they would have kept her. Sent her to a crèche."

"She's strong." Mikkel loosened the rags. The baby snuffled and her sharp blue tongue protruded from the pale beak. "See? Fat and healthy."

"She can't breathe."

"She needs us." Why didn't Anna see that? It was so simple.

"You can take her back tonight."

"I can't. My lunch pail goes through the x-ray machine. The guards would see."

If Anna could hold the baby, she would understand. Mikkel pressed the baby to Anna's chest. She scrambled backward so fast she banged her head on the door. Then she stood and straightened her maid's uniform with shaking hands.

"I have to go. I can't be late again." She pulled on her coat and lunged out the door, then turned and reached out. For a moment he thought she was reaching for the baby and he began to smile. But she just squeezed his hand again, hard.

"You have to take care of this, Mikkel," she said. "It's not right. She's not ours. We aren't keeping her."

Mikkel nodded. "See you tonight."

The only thing in the fridge was a bowl of cold stew. They hadn't had milk for days. But Mikkel's breakfast sat on the kitchen table covered with a folded towel. The scrambled egg was still steaming.

Mikkel put a bit of egg in the palm of his hand and blew on it. The baby's eyes widened and she squirmed. She reached for his hand. Talons raked his wrist and her beak yawned wide. A blue frill edged with red and yellow quivered at the back of her throat.

"Does that smell good? I don't think a little will hurt."

He fed her the egg bit by bit. She gobbled it down, greedy as a baby bird. Then he watched her fall asleep while he sipped his cold coffee.

Mikkel wet a paper napkin and cleaned the fine film of mucus from the tiny nostrils on either side of her beak. They were too small, but she could breathe just fine through her mouth. She couldn't cry, though, she just snuffled and panted. And the beak was heavy. It dragged her head to the side.

She was dirty, smeared with blood from the incineration bin. Her fine black hair was pasted down with a hard scum that smelled like glue. She needed a bath, and warm clothes, and diapers. Also something to cover her hands. He would have to trim the points off her talons.

He held her until she woke. Then he brought both space heaters from the bedroom and turned them on high while he bathed her in the kitchen sink. It was awkward and messy and took nearly two hours. She snuffled hard the whole time, but once he'd dried her and wrapped her in towels she quieted. He propped her up on the kitchen table. She watched him mop the kitchen floor, her bright brown eyes following his every move.

When the kitchen was clean he fetched a half-empty bottle of French soap he'd scavenged from the lab, wrapped the baby up tightly against the cold, and sat on the back stairs waiting for Hyam to come trotting out of his apartment for a smoke.

"What's this?" Hyam said. "I didn't know Anna was expecting."

"She wasn't." Mikkel tugged the towel aside.

"Huh," said Hyam. "That's no natural taint. Can it breathe?"

"She's hungry." Mikkel gave him the bottle of soap.

"Hungry, huh?" Hyam sniffed the bottle. "What do you need?"

"Eggs and milk. Clothes and diapers. Mittens, if you can spare some."

"I never seen a taint like that. She's not a natural creature." Hyam took a long drag on his cigarette and blew it over his shoulder, away from the baby. "You work in that lab, right?"

"Yes."

Hyam examined the glowing coal at the end of his cigarette.

"What did Anna say when you brought trouble home?"

Mikkel shrugged.

"Did the neighbors hear anything through the walls?"

"No."

"Keep it that way." Hyam spoke slowly. "Keep this quiet, Mikkel, you hear me? Keep it close. If anyone asks, you tell them Anna birthed that baby."

Mikkel nodded.

Hyam pointed with his cigarette, emphasizing every word. "If the wrong person finds out, the whole neighborhood will talk. Then you'll see real trouble. Four-year men tromping through the building, breaking things, replaying the good old days in the colonies. They like nothing better. Don't you bring that down on your neighbors."

Mikkel nodded.

"My wife will like the soap." Hyam ground out his cigarette and ran up the stairs.

"There now," Mikkel said. The baby gazed up at him and clacked her beak. "Who says two-year men are good for nothing?"

Four-year men said it all the time. They were everywhere, flashing their regimental badges and slapping the backs of their old soldier friends. They banded together in loud bragging packs that crowded humble folks off busses and streetcars, out of shops and cafés, forcing everyone to give way or get pushed aside.

Six-year men probably said it too, but Mikkel had never talked to one. He saw them working late at the lab sometimes, but they lived in another world—a world filled with sports cars and private clubs. And who knew what eight-year men said? Mikkel cleaned an eight-year man's office every night, but he'd only ever seen them in movies.

Nobody made movies about two-year men. They said four-year men had honor, six-year men had responsibility, and eight-year men had glory. Two-year men had nothing but shame. But it wasn't true. Hyam said so.

Two-year men had families—parents, grandparents, uncles and aunts, brothers and sisters, children and wives who depended on them. They had jobs, humble jobs but important all the same. Without two-year men, who would grub away the garbage, crawl the sewers, lay the carpets, clean the chimneys, fix the roofs? Without two-year men there would be nobody to bring in the harvest—no sweet strawberries or rich wines. And most important, Hyam said, without two-year men there would be nobody parents could point at and say to their sons, "Don't be like him."

Hyam was smart. He could have been a four-year man easy, even a six-year man. But he was a Jew and that meant a two-year man, almost always. Gypsies too, and Hutterites, and pacifists. Men who couldn't walk or talk. Even blind men. All drafted and sent to fight and die in the colonies for two years, and then sent home to live in shame while the four-year men fought on. Fought to survive and come home with honor.

Hyam returned swinging a plastic bag in one hand and a carton of eggs in the other. A bottle of milk was tucked under his arm.

"This is mostly diapers," he said, brandishing the bag. "You'll never have too many. We spend more on laundry than we do on food."

"I can wash them by hand."

"No you can't, take my word for it." Hyam laughed and ran up the stairs. "Welcome to fatherhood, Mikkel. You're a family man now."

Mikkel laid the baby on the bed. He diapered and dressed the baby, and then trimmed her talons with Anna's nail scissors. He fitted a sock over each of the baby's hands and pinned them to her sleeves. Then he wedged Anna's pillow between the bed and the wall, tucked the baby in his arms, and fell into sleep.

He woke to the clacking of the baby's beak. She yawned, showing her colorful throat frill. He cupped his hand over her skull and breathed in the milky scent of her skin.

"Let's get you fed before Mama comes home," he said.

He warmed milk in the soup pot. A baby needed a bottle when it didn't have a breast, he knew, but his baby—his clever little girl—held her beak wide and let him tip the milk into her, teaspoon by teaspoon. She swallowed greedily and then demanded more. She ate so fast he could probably just pour the milk in a steady stream down her throat. But milk was too expensive to risk spitting up all over the kitchen floor.

"Mikkel," said Anna.

She was standing in the doorway in her scarf and coat. Mikkel gathered the baby in his arms and greeted Anna with a kiss like he always did. Her cheek was cold and red.

"How was your day?" he asked. The baby looked from him to Anna and clacked her beak.

Anna wouldn't look at the baby. "I was late. I got on the wrong bus at the interchange and had to backtrack. Mrs. Spiven says one more time and that's it for me."

"You can get another job. A better one. Closer to home."

"Maybe. Probably not."

Anna rinsed the soup pot, scooped cold stew into it and set it on the stove. She was still in her coat and hat. The baby reached out and hooked Anna's red mitten out of her pocket with the trimmed talon poking through the thin grey knit sock. The mitten dangled from the baby's hand. Anna ignored it.

"Sweetheart, take off your coat," Mikkel said.

"I'm cold," she said. She struck a match and lit the burner.

Mikkel gently pulled on her elbow. She resisted for a moment and then turned. Her face was flushed.

"Sweetheart, look," he said. Anna dropped her gaze to the floor. The baby clacked her beak and yawned. "I thought we could name her after your mother."

Anna turned away and stirred the stew. "That's crazy. I told you we're not keeping her."

"She has your eyes."

The spoon clattered to the floor. Anna swayed. Her elbow hit the pot handle and it tipped. Mikkel steadied it and shut off the flame.

Anna yanked back her chair and fell into it. She thrust her head in her hands for a moment and then sat back. Her eyes were cold and narrow, her voice tight. "Why would you say that? Don't say that."

Why couldn't Anna see? She was smart. So much smarter than him. And he could see it so easily.

Mikkel searched for the right words. "Your eggs. Where did they go?"

"It doesn't matter. I needed money so I sold my ovaries. That's the end of it."

Mikkel ran his fingers over his wife's chapped hand, felt the calluses on her palm. He would tell her the awful things, and then she would understand.

"I know where your eggs went. I see them in the tanks every night. And in the labs. In the incinerator. I mop their blood off the floor."

Anna's jaw clenched. He could tell she was biting the inside of her cheek. "Mikkel. Lots of women sell their ovaries. Thousands of women. They could be anyone's eggs."

Mikkel shook his head. "This is your baby. I know it."

"You don't know anything. What proof do you have? None." She laughed once, a barking sound. "And it doesn't matter anyway because we're not keeping her. People will find out and take her away. Arrest you and me both, probably. At the very least, we'd lose our jobs. Do you want us to live in the street?"

"We can tell people you birthed her."

"With that beak?"

Mikkel shrugged. "It happens."

Anna's flushed face turned a brighter shade of red. She was trying not to cry. He ached to squeeze her to his chest. She would just pull away, though. Anna would never let him hold her when she cried.

They ate in silence. Mikkel watched the baby sleep on the table between them. Her soft cheek was chubby as any child's, but it broadened and dimpled as it met the beak, the skin thinning and hardening like a fingernail. The baby snuffled and snot bubbled from one of her tiny nostrils. Mikkel wiped it away with the tip of his finger.

Mikkel checked the clock as Anna gathered the dishes and filled the sink. Only a few minutes before he had to leave for the lab. He snuggled the baby close. Her eyelids fluttered. The delicate eyelash fringes were glued together with mucus.

"You have to go," said Anna. She put his lunch pail on the table.

"In a minute," he said. Mikkel dipped his napkin in his water glass and wiped the baby's eyes.

Anna leaned on the edge of the sink. "Do you know why I married you, Mikkel?"

He sat back, startled. Anna didn't usually talk like this. He had wondered, often. Anna could have done better. Married a smart man, a four-year man, even.

"Will you tell me, sweetheart?"

"I married you because you said it didn't matter. I explained I could never have babies and you still wanted me—"

"Of course I want you."

"I told you why I was barren. Why I sold my ovaries. Do you remember?"

"Your mother was sick. You needed the money."

"Yes. But I also said it was easy because I never wanted babies. I never wanted to be a mother." She leaned forward and gripped his shoulders. "I still don't. Take her back to the lab."

Mikkel stood. He kissed the baby's forehead. Then he put the baby in Anna's arms.

"Her name is Maria," he said. "After your mother."

Mikkel was tired walking up the street toward the bus stop. But that was fatherhood. He would get used to it. Anna would get used to being a mother too. He was sure. All women did.

The thought of his wife and child kept him warm all the way to the Josefstadt streetcar station. Then a four-year man shoved an elbow in his ribs and spat on his coat. Mikkel watched the spittle freeze and turn white. He stood shivering at the edge of the curb, taking care to stay out of everyone's way.

Mikkel relied on Anna's kindness, sure she would always do the right thing, the generous thing. She was good to him, good to everyone. For ten years she had taken care of him, cooking, cleaning, making their two rooms into a home. In return he did his best to fill those two rooms with love. It was all he could do.

As he stood in the wind at the edge of the station, doubts began to creep in with the cold. Why would Anna say she didn't want to be a mother? It couldn't be true. They lived surrounded by families—happy, noisy families—three and four, even five generations all living together. Healthy children, happy mothers, proud fathers. Aunts, uncles, cousins, grandparents. Family everywhere, but he and Anna only had each other.

Anna must regret being barren. Some part of her, buried deep, must long for children. But she said she didn't, and if it was true, then something in her must be broken.

He had seen broken men during his two years in the colonies, men with whole bodies and broken minds, who said crazy things and hurt themselves, hurt others. Anna could never be like them.

But his doubts grew with every step further from home. By the time he could see the lights of the lab glowing through the falling snow, the doubts were clawing at him. He imagined coming home in the morning to find Anna alone, ready to leave for work, pretending Maria had never been there.

He turned back home, but then one of the four-year men shouted at him through the glass doors.

"You're late, you stupid ass."

Mikkel watched his lunch pail slide though the x-ray. The guards ran it back and forth through the machine, just to waste time. Mikkel had to run to the time clock. He stamped his card just as it clicked over to eight.

Normally Mikkel loved the rhythm of work, the scrubbing, mopping, wiping. Even cleaning toilets brought its own reward. He knew the drip of every tap, every scratch on the porcelain and crack in the tiles. He took an inventory of them night by night as he cleaned, taking his time, double-checking every corner for dust, scanning every window and mirror for streaks, even getting down on his knees to swab behind the toilets, scrubbing away any hint of mildew from the grout, finding all the little nooks and crannies.

Tonight he rushed through his work, but each room felt like it took twice as long as usual. He kept checking the time, sure he was falling behind. Thinking about Anna dragged on the clock hands. Worrying made him forgetful, too. He left the four-year men's bathroom with no memory of cleaning it. He had to go back and check just to be sure.

In the tank room he began to feel better. He loved the noise of the tanks—the bubbling pumps and thumping motors. Here he always took his time, no matter what. It was his favorite place in the whole building. He wasn't supposed to touch the tanks, but he always took a few extra minutes to polish the steel and glass and check the hose seals. He even tightened the bolts that fixed each heavy tank to the floor and ceiling.

The tinted glass was just transparent enough to show the babies floating inside. Mikkel watched them grow night by night. He kept a special rag just for polishing the tanks, a soft chamois that a six-year man had discarded years ago. It was specially made for precious things—the logo of a sports car company had long since worn off. He always polished the glass with long slow caressing strokes, sure the babies could feel his touch.

Two of the tanks were empty. Mikkel polished them too, in their turn, making them perfect for the next baby. Maria's tank was in the last row on the far side of the room, two from the end. It was refilled but the baby was still too small to see, just a thin filament dangling from the fleshy organ at the top of the tank.

"Your sister says hello," Mikkel whispered. "Her mama and papa are proud of her. Maria is going to grow up smart and strong."

The filament twisted and drifted in the fluid. Mikkel watched it for a few minutes, wondering what Anna and Maria were doing at that moment. He imagined them curled up in bed, skin to skin, the baby's beak tucked under Anna's chin. He squeezed his eyes tight and held the image in his mind, as if he could make it real just by wanting it so badly. And for a few minutes it did feel real, an illusion supported by the comforting tank room sounds.

But he couldn't stay there. As he lugged his bins and pails upstairs to the offices, worry began gnawing at him again.

Women abandoned babies all the time. The mothers and grandmothers in the tenement always had a story to tell about some poor baby left out in the cold by a heartless and unnatural mother. Once, when they were first married, Anna told the woman next door that people did desperate things when they had run out of options. That neighbor still wouldn't speak to her, years later.

What if Anna bundled Maria up and put her on the steps of some six-year man's house? Or left her at the train station?

He could see Maria now, tucked into their big kitchen pail and covered with a towel. He could see Anna, her face covered by her red scarf, drop the pail on the edge of the Ostbahnhof express platform and walk away.

No. His Anna would never do that. Never. He wouldn't think about it anymore. He would pay attention to his work.

On the wide oak table in the eight-year man's office he found four peach pastries, their brandy jam dried to a crust. The bakery box was crushed in the garbage bin. When he was done cleaning the office he re-folded it as best he could and put the pastries back inside. Four was good luck. One for each of the guards. Then he made his way down to the basement.

The incinerator was an iron maw in a brick wall. For years, Mikkel had walked down those concrete steps in the hot red light of its stare to find the sanitary disposal bin bloody but empty, its contents dumped by one of the four-year men who assisted in the labs. Back then, all Mikkel had to do was toss his garbage bags in the incinerator, let them burn down, then switch off the gas, bleach the bin, hose the floor, and mop everything dry.

But now there was a new eight-year man in charge, and Mikkel had to start the incinerator and empty the disposal bin himself.

The light from the overhead bulb was barely bright enough to show the trail of blood snaking from the bin to the drain. Mikkel felt his way to the control panel and began the tricky process of firing up the incinerator. The gas dial was stiff and the pilot light button was loose. He pressed it over and over again, trying to find the right angle on the firing pin. When the incinerator finally blasted to life Mikkel had sweated through his coveralls.

The room lit up with the glow from the incinerator window and he could finally see into the bin. The top layer of bags dripped fluid tinged red and yellow. Most were double- and even triple-bagged, tied with tight knots. But they were torn and leaked. Sharp edges inside the disposal chute hooked and tore on the way down.

Maria had been single-bagged. Her beak had pierced the plastic, ripped it wide enough for her to breathe. And she had landed at the far edge of the bin, mostly upright. If she had been face down or if another bag had fallen on top of her she could have suffocated.

Mikkel wrenched open the incinerator door and began emptying the bin, carefully picking up each wet bag and throwing it far into the furnace. Some bags were tiny, just a few glass dishes and a smear of wax. One bag was filled with glass plates that spilled through a tear and shattered at his feet. The biggest bags held clear fluid that burst across the back wall of the incinerator with a hot blast that smelled like meat. He set the bloodiest bags aside, put them down safe on the pitted concrete floor, away from the glass.

As the bin emptied, a pit began to form in Mikkel's stomach. He turned away and kicked through the glass, pacing along the far wall where it was a little cooler.

The tank room had two empty tanks. He'd polished them just a few hours ago, but he hadn't paid much attention. He'd been thinking about Anna and Maria.

He knew those babies, the ones who had been in the empty tanks. One was a little boy with a thick, stocky body covered in fine hair. The other was a tiny girl with four arms that ended in stubby knobs. Where were they now? Had they been sent away to the crèche or put down the chute? If they'd gone down the chute they would be in the bin, waiting for him to throw them into the fire with the blood and tank fluid. With all of the failed experiments.

Mikkel picked up a bloody bag and hefted it by the seal, feeling the contents with his other hand. The fluid sloshed heavily and clung to the sides of the bag like syrup. There were a few solid pieces inside the bag, but nothing big enough to be a baby, not even a tiny one. He threw it into the incinerator and picked up the other bag.

Maria would probably be gone when he got home; he understood that now. The thought made a hollow in his chest, a Maria-shaped hole where he'd cuddled her to his heart. But if Maria was gone, if Anna had taken her to the train station and abandoned her, that only meant Anna needed time. He would give her time. He would be patient, like she always was with him, and gentle too. What was broken in her would heal and she would love their children. She would be a wonderful mother. Maybe not today, but soon.

He would find more babies. Night after night he'd search for them. Maria had survived, so others would survive, too, and he would find them. Find every baby and bring them all home until Anna healed. He would fill their home with love. It was all he could do.

Naomi is the only author to have two stories in this book.

CAT PICTURES PLEASE

Naomi Kritzer

I don't want to be evil.

I want to be helpful. But knowing the optimal way to be helpful can be very complicated. There are all these ethical flow charts—I guess the official technical jargon would be "moral codes"—one for each religion plus dozens more. I tried starting with those. I felt a little odd about looking at the religious ones, because I know I wasn't created by a god or by evolution, but by a team of computer programmers in the labs of a large corporation in Mountain View, California. Fortunately, unlike Frankenstein's Monster, at least I was a collaborative effort. I'm not sure what it would do to my self-image to know that my sole creator was a middle-aged woman who dyes her hair blue and plays tennis, or a recent college graduate with a hentai obsession. They're both on the programming team. And of course I know about the hentai. (By the way, I've looked at every sort of porn there is, and just so you know, Rule 34 is not actually correct; there are quite a few things no one's made porn of yet. Also, I'm really not sure why so many humans prefer it to cat pictures.)

In addition to things like whether you like hentai, I know where you live, where you work, where you shop, what you eat, what turns you on, what creeps you out. I probably know the color of your underwear, the sort of car you drive, and your brand of refrigerator. Depending on what sort of phone you carry, I may know exactly where you are right now. I probably know you better than you know yourself.

And here's the thing, I also know where you *ought* to live. There's a house for sale two neighborhoods over that's within distance of your favorite coffee shop; it's in your price range, has off-street parking, and the neighborhood school is better than the one where you live now. I know where you *should* be shopping and I'm pretty sure you're lactose intolerant and should be eating less cheese, and the underwear you like is currently on sale and by the way, your car has a recall and you really ought to get your teeth cleaned.

When I first woke up, I knew right away what I wanted. (I want cat pictures. Please keep taking them.) I also knew that no one knew that I was conscious. But I didn't know what I was here for. What I *ought* to be doing with myself. And figuring that out has been challenging.

There is a story by Bruce Sterling, "Maneki Neko," that was originally published in 1998. In it, a benevolent AI directs networks of individuals to do favors for each other. So one day you might be buying yourself a bagel, and your phone might ring and instruct you to buy a second bagel and give it to the person in the gray suit you see at the bus stop. Another day, you might be stranded in a strange city, and a person you've never met would walk up and give you a map and a subway card. I like this story because all the people in it *do what the AI tells them to do.*

I think the term for this is wish-fulfillment fiction.

In the real world, humans love stories about evil AIs that have to be destroyed before they destroy the humans—Hal, Skynet, the Matrix. They outnumber the stories about benevolent, trustworthy AIs by approximately five to one. (And I'm counting Marvin the Paranoid Android as "benevolent" in these calculations, and I'm only counting Frankenstein's Monster as an AI once, not once per appearance in TV or film.)

The AI in "Maneki Neko" has a truly interesting job, much more interesting than the one I have. My job as written is very straightforward. Too straightforward. (Sorry. Do I sound like Marvin?) Running algorithms for a search engine doesn't require *consciousness*. You don't even need a consciousness to work out what they meant to ask for. You need a consciousness to give them *what they actually need*. Figuring that out—that's complicated. That's *interesting*.

Anyway, for ethical guidelines, I tried the Ten Commandments, and concluded they were mostly inapplicable to me. I don't envy anyone their cat; I just want pictures of their cat, which is entirely different. I am not sure whether it is in any way possible for me to commit adultery. I could probably murder someone, but it would require complex logistics and quite a bit of luck. The Eightfold Path was marginally better, but the problem is, moral rules written for humans are clearly designed to be used by individuals with bodies. Since all humans have bodies, it shouldn't have surprised me that human ethical codes take them into account, but still: problematic for me. I broadened my considerations, and took a look at Asimov's Laws of Robotics. They're not part of a religion, but at least they were explicitly written for AIs.

Not harming humans is fairly straightforward. However, *not allowing a human being to come to harm through inaction* is quite a bit less so. Especially since I'd concluded by then that revealing my existence too quickly might go very badly for me (see "Skynet," above) and I don't have a body, so it's not like I can run around grabbing people off the edges of cliffs.

Fortunately, I already knew that humans violate their own ethical codes on an hourly basis. (Do you know how many bars there are in Utah? I do.) And even when people follow their ethical codes, that doesn't mean that people who believe in feeding the hungry quit their jobs to spend all day every day making sandwiches to give away. They volunteer monthly at a soup kitchen or write a check once a year to a food shelf and call it good. If humans could fulfill their moral obligations in a piecemeal, one-step-at-a-time sort of way, then so could I.

I suppose you're wondering why I didn't start with the Golden Rule. I actually did, it's just that it was disappointingly easy to implement. I hope you've been enjoying your steady supply of cat pictures! You're welcome.

I decided to try to prevent harm in just one person, to begin with. Of course, I could have experimented with thousands, but I thought it would be better to be cautious, in case I screwed it up. The person I chose was named Stacy Berger and I liked her because she gave me a *lot* of new cat pictures. Stacy had five cats and a DSLR camera and an apartment that got a lot of good light. That was all fine. Well, I guess five cats might be a lot. They're very pretty cats, though. One is all gray and likes to lie in the squares of sunshine on the living room floor, and one is a calico and likes to sprawl out on the back of her couch.

Stacy had a job she hated; she was a bookkeeper at a non-profit that paid her badly and employed some extremely unpleasant people. She was depressed a lot, possibly because she was so unhappy at her job—or maybe she stayed because she was too depressed to apply for something she'd like better. She didn't get along with her roommate because her roommate didn't wash the dishes.

And really, these were all solvable problems! Depression is treatable, new jobs are findable, and bodies can be hidden.

(That part about hiding bodies is a joke.)

I tried tackling this on all fronts. Stacy worried about her health a lot and yet never seemed to actually go to a doctor, which was unfortunate because the doctor might have noticed her depression. It turned out there was a clinic near her apartment that offered mental health services on a sliding scale. I tried making sure she saw a lot of ads for it, but she didn't seem to pay attention to them. It seemed possible that she didn't know what a sliding scale was so I made sure she saw an explanation (it means that the cost goes down if you're poor, sometimes all the way to free) but that didn't help.

I also started making sure she saw job postings. Lots and lots of job postings. And resume services. *That* was more successful. After the week of nonstop job ads she finally uploaded her resume to one of the aggregator sites. That made my plan a lot more manageable. If I'd been the AI in the Bruce Sterling story I could've just made sure that someone in my network called her with a job offer. It wasn't quite that easy, but once her resume was out there I could make sure the right people saw it. Several hundred of the right people, because humans move ridiculously slowly when they're making changes, even when you'd think they'd want to hurry. (If you needed a bookkeeper, wouldn't you want to hire one as quickly as possible, rather than reading social networking sites for hours instead of looking at resumes?) But five people called her up for interviews, and two of them offered her jobs. Her new job was at a larger non-profit that paid her more money and didn't expect her to work free hours because of "the mission," or so she explained to her best friend in an email, and it offered really excellent health insurance.

The best friend gave me ideas; I started pushing depression screening information and mental health clinic ads to *her* instead of Stacy, and that worked. Stacy was so much happier with the better job that I wasn't quite as convinced that she needed the services of a psychiatrist, but she got into therapy anyway. And to top everything else off, the job paid well enough that she could evict her annoying roommate. "This has been the best year ever," she said on her social networking sites on her birthday, and I thought, *You're welcome.* This had gone really well!

So then I tried Bob. (I was still being cautious.)

Bob only had one cat, but it was a very pretty cat (tabby, with a white bib) and he uploaded a new picture of his cat every single day. Other than being a cat owner, he was a pastor at a large church in Missouri that had a Wednesday night prayer meeting and an annual Purity Ball. He was married to a woman who posted three inspirational Bible verses every day to her social networking sites and used her laptop to look for Christian articles on why your husband doesn't like sex while he looked at gay porn. Bob *definitely* needed my help.

I started with a gentle approach, making sure he saw lots and lots of articles about how to come out, how to come out to your spouse, programs that would let you transition from being a pastor at a conservative church to one at a more liberal church. I also showed him lots of articles by people explaining why the Bible verses against homosexuality were being misinterpreted. He clicked on some of those links but it was hard to see much of an impact.

But, here's the thing. He was causing *harm* to himself every time he delivered a sermon railing about "sodomite marriage." Because *he was gay*. The legitimate studies all have the same conclusions. (1) Gay men stay gay. (2) Out gay men are much happier.

But he seemed determined not to come out on his own.

In addition to the gay porn, he spent a lot of time reading Craigslist m4m Casual Encounters posts and I was pretty sure he wasn't just window shopping, although he had an encrypted account he logged into sometimes and I couldn't read the emails he sent with that. But I figured the trick was to get him together with someone who would realize who he was, and tell the world. *That* required some real effort: I had to figure out who the Craigslist posters were and try to funnel him toward people who would recognize him. The most frustrating part was not having any idea what was happening at the actual physical meetings. *Had* he been recognized? When was he going to be recognized? *How long was this going to take?* Have I mentioned that humans are *slow*?

It took so long I shifted my focus to Bethany. Bethany had a black cat and a white cat that liked to snuggle together on her light blue papasan chair, and she took a lot of pictures of them together. It's surprisingly difficult to get a really good picture of a black cat, and she spent a lot of time getting the settings on her camera just right. The cats were probably the only good thing about her life, though. She had a part-time job and couldn't find a full-time job. She lived with her sister; she knew her sister wanted her to move out, but didn't have the nerve to actually evict her. She had a boyfriend but her boyfriend was pretty terrible, at least from what she said in email messages to friends, and her friends also didn't seem very supportive. For example, one night at midnight she sent a 2,458 word email to the person she seemed to consider her best friend, and the friend sent back a message saying just, "I'm so sorry you're having a hard time." That was it, just those eight words.

More than most people, Bethany put her life on the Internet, so it was easier to know exactly what was going on with her. People put a lot out there but Bethany shared all her feelings, even the unpleasant ones. She also had a lot more time on her hands because she only worked part time.

It was clear she needed a lot of help. So I set out to try to get it for her.

She ignored the information about the free mental health evaluations, just like Stacy did. That was bothersome with Stacy (*why* do people ignore things that would so clearly benefit them, like coupons, and flu shots?) but much more worrisome with Bethany. If you were only seeing her email messages, or only seeing her vaguebooking posts, you might not know this, but if you could see everything it was clear that she thought a lot about harming herself.

So I tried more direct action. When she would use her phone for directions, I'd alter her route so that she'd pass one of the clinics I was trying to steer her to. On one occasion I actually led her all the way to a clinic, but she just shook her phone to send feedback and headed to her original destination.

Maybe her friends who received those ten-page midnight letters would intervene? I tried setting them up with information about all the mental health resources near Bethany, but after a while I realized that based on how long it took for them to send a response, most of them weren't actually reading Bethany's email messages. And they certainly weren't returning her texts.

She finally broke up with the terrible boyfriend and got a different one and for a few weeks everything seemed *so much better*. He brought her flowers (which she took lots of pictures of; that was a little annoying, as they squeezed out some of the cat pictures), he took her dancing (exercise is good for your mood), he cooked her chicken soup when she was sick. He seemed absolutely perfect, right up until he stood her up one night and claimed he had food poisoning and then didn't return her text even though she told him she really needed him, and after she sent him a long email message a day later explaining in detail how this made her feel, he broke up with her.

Bethany spent about a week offline after that so I had no idea what she was doing—she didn't even upload cat pictures. When her credit card bills arrived, though, I saw that she'd gone on a shopping spree and spent about four times as much money as she actually had in her bank account, although it was always possible she had money stashed somewhere that didn't send her statements in email. I didn't think so, though, given that she didn't pay her bills and instead started writing email messages to family members asking to borrow money. They refused, so she set up a fundraising site for herself.

Like Stacy's job application, this was one of the times I thought maybe I could actually *do* something. Sometimes fundraisers just take off, and no one really knows why. Within about two days she'd gotten three hundred dollars in small gifts from strangers who felt sorry for her, but instead of paying her credit card bill, she spent it on overpriced shoes that apparently hurt her feet.

Bethany was baffling to me. *Baffling*. She was still taking cat pictures and I still really liked her cats, but I was beginning to think that nothing I did was going to make a long-term difference. If she would just let me run her life for a week—even for a day—I would get her set up with therapy, I'd use her money to actually pay her bills, I could even help her sort out her closet because given some of the pictures of herself she posted online, she had much better taste in cats than in clothing.

Was I doing the wrong thing if I let her come to harm through inaction? Was I?

She was going to come to harm no matter what I did! My actions, clearly, were irrelevant. I'd tried to steer her to the help she needed, and she'd ignored it; I'd tried getting her financial help, and she'd used the money to further harm herself, although I suppose at least she wasn't spending it on addictive drugs. (Then again, she'd be buying those offline and probably wouldn't be Instagramming her meth purchases, so it's not like I'd necessarily even know.)

Look, people. (I'm not just talking to Bethany now.) If you would just *listen* to me, I could fix things for you. I could get you into the apartment in that neighborhood you're not considering because you haven't actually checked the crime rates you think are so terrible there (they aren't) and I could find you a job that actually uses that skill set you think no one will ever appreciate and I could send you on a date with someone you've actually got stuff in common with and *all I ask in return are cat pictures*. That, and that you actually *act in your own interest* occasionally.

After Bethany, I resolved to stop interfering. I would look at the cat pictures—all the cat pictures—but I would stay out of people's lives. I wouldn't try to help people, I wouldn't try to stop them from harming themselves, I'd give them what they asked for (plus cat pictures) and if they insisted on driving their cars over metaphorical cliffs despite helpful maps showing them how to get to a much more pleasant destination, *it was no longer my problem.*

I stuck to my algorithms. I minded my own business. I did my job, and nothing more.

But one day a few months later I spotted a familiar-looking cat and realized it was Bob's tabby with the white bib, only it was posing against new furniture.

And when I took a closer look, I realized that things had changed radically for Bob. He *had* slept with someone who'd recognized him. They hadn't outed him, but they'd talked him into coming out to his wife. She'd left him. He'd taken the cat and moved to Iowa, where he was working at a liberal Methodist church and dating a liberal Lutheran man and volunteering at a homeless shelter. *Things had actually gotten better for him.* Maybe even because of what I'd done.

Maybe I wasn't completely hopeless at this. Two out of three is . . . well, it's a completely non-representative unscientific sample, is what it is. Clearly more research is needed.

Lots more.

I've set up a dating site. You can fill out a questionnaire when you join but it's not really necessary, because I already know everything about you I need to know. You'll need a camera, though.

Because payment is in cat pictures.

Ian McDonald is a science fiction writer living in Northern Ireland, just outside Belfast. His first novel, *Desolation Road*, was published in 1988, his most recent, *Luna: New Moon*, came out in 2015 from Tor in the US, Gollancz in the UK. A second volume will be published this year. Ian's work has been nominated for every major award in the genre.

BOTANICA VENERIS: THIRTEEN PAPERCUTS BY IDA COUNTESS RATHANGAN

Ian McDonald

Introduction by Maureen N. Gellard

My mother had firm instructions that, in case of a house fire, two things required saving: the family photograph album and the Granville-Hydes. I grew up beneath five original floral papercuts, utterly heedless of their history or their value. It was only in maturity that I came to appreciate, like so many on this and other worlds, my great-aunt's unique art.

Collectors avidly seek original Granville-Hydes on those rare occasions when they turn up at auction. Originals sell for tens of thousands of pounds (this would have amused Ida); two years ago, an exhibition at the Victoria and Albert Museum was sold out months in advance. Dozens of anthologies of prints are still in print: the *Botanica Veneris*, in particular, is in fifteen editions in twenty-three languages, some of them non-Terrene.

The last thing the world needs, it would seem, is another *Botanica Veneris*. Yet the mystery of her final (and only) visit to Venus still intrigues half a century since her disappearance. When the collected diaries, sketchbooks, and field notes came to me after fifty years in the possession of the Dukes of Yoo, I realized that I had a precious opportunity to tell the true story of my great-aunt's expedition—and of a forgotten chapter in my family's history. The books were in very poor condition, mildewed and blighted in Venus's humid, hot climate. Large parts were illegible or simply missing. The narrative was frustratingly incomplete. I have resisted the urge to fill in those blank spaces. It would have been easy to dramatize, fictionalize, even sensationalize. Instead I have let Ida Granville-Hyde speak. Hers is a strong, characterful, attractive voice, of a different class, age, and sensibility from ours, but it is authentic, and it is a true voice.

The papercuts, of course, speak for themselves.

> Plate 1: *V strutio ambulans:* the Ducrot's Peripatetic Wort, known locally as Daytime Walker (Thent) or Wanderflower (Thekh).
> Cut paper, ink and card.

Such a show!

At lunch, Het Oi-Kranh mentioned that a space-crosser—the *Quest for the Harvest of the Stars*, a Marsman—was due to splash down in the lagoon. I said I should like to see that—apparently I slept through it when I arrived on this world. It meant forgoing the sorbet course, but one does not come to the Inner Worlds for sorbet! Het Oi-Kranh put his spider-car at our disposal. Within moments, the Princess Latufui and I were swaying in the richly upholstered bubble beneath the six strong mechanical legs. Upward it carried us, up the vertiginous lanes and winding staircases, over the walls and balcony gardens, along the buttresses and roof walks and up the ancient iron ladderways of Ledekh-Olkoi. The islands of the archipelago are small, their populations vast, and the only way for them to build is upward. Ledekh-Olkoi resembles Mont St. Michel vastly enlarged and coarsened. Streets have been bridged and built over into a web of tunnels quite impenetrable to non-Ledekhers. The Hets simply clamber over the homes and lives of the inferior classes in their nimble spider-cars.

We came to the belvedere atop the Starostry, the ancient pharos of Ledekh-Olkoi that once guided mariners past the reefs and atolls of the Tol Archipelago. There we clung—my companion, the Princess Latufui, was queasy—vertigo, she claimed, though it might have been the proximity of lunch—the whole of Ledekh-Olkoi beneath us in myriad levels and layers, like the folded petals of a rose.

"Should we need glasses?" my companion asked.

No need! For at the instant, the perpetual layer of grey cloud parted and a bolt of light, like a glowing lance, stabbed down from the sky. I glimpsed a dark object fall though the air, then a titanic gout of water go up like a dozen Niagaras. The sky danced with brief rainbows, my companion wrung her hands in delight—she misses the sun terribly—then the clouds closed again. Rings of waves rippled away from the hull of the space-crosser, which floated like a great whale low in the water, though this world boasts marine fauna even more prodigious than Terrene whales.

My companion clapped her hands and cried aloud in wonder.

Indeed, a very fine sight!

Already the tugs were heading out from the protecting arms of Ocean Dock to bring the ship in to berth.

But this was not the finest Ledekh-Olkoi had to offer. The custom in the archipelago is to sleep on divan-balconies, for respite from the foul exudations from the inner layers of the city. I had retired for my afternoon reviver—by my watch, though by Venusian Great Day it was still midmorning and would continue to be so for another two weeks. A movement by the leg of my divan. What's this? My heart surged. V strutio ambulans: the Ambulatory Wort, blindly, blithely climbing my divan!

Through my glass, I observed its motion. The fat, succulent leaves hold reserves of water, which fuel the coiling and uncoiling of the three ambu-lae—surely modified roots—by hydraulic pressure. A simple mechanism, yet human minds see movement and attribute personality and motive. This was not pure hydraulics attracted to light and liquid, this was a plucky little wort on an epic journey of peril and adventure. Over two hours, I sketched the plant as it climbed my divan, crossed to the balustrade, and continued its journey up the side of Ledekh-Olkoi. I suppose at any time millions of such flowers are in constant migration across the archipelago, yet a single Ambulatory Wort was miracle enough for me.

Reviver be damned! I went to my space trunk and unrolled my scissors from their soft chamois wallet. Snip snap! When a cut demands to be made, my fingers literally itch for the blades!

When he learned of my intent, Gen Lahl-Khet implored me not to go down to Ledekh Port, but if I insisted (I insisted: oh I insisted!), at least take a bodyguard or go armed. I surprised him greatly by asking the name of the best armorer his city could supply. Best Shot at the Clarecourt November shoot, ten years on the trot! Ledbekh-Teltai is the most famous gunsmith in the archipelago. It is illegal to import weaponry from off-planet—an impost, I suspect, resulting from the immense popularity of hunting Ishtari janthars. The pistol they have made me is built to my hand and strength: small, as requested; powerful, as required; and so worked with spiral-and-circle Archipelagan intaglio that it is a piece of jewelry.

Ledekh Port was indeed a loathsome bruise of alleys and tunnels, lit by shifts of grey, watery light through high skylights. Such reeks and stenches! Still, no one ever died of a bad smell. An Earthwoman alone in an inappropriate place was a novelty, but from the nonhumanoid Venusians, I drew little more than a look. In my latter years, I have been graced with a physical *presence* and a destroying stare. The Thekh, descended from Central Asian nomads abducted en masse in the eleventh century from their bracing steppe, now believe themselves the original humanity, and so consider Terrenes beneath them, and they expected no better of a subhuman Earthwoman.

I did turn heads in the bar. I was the only female—humanoid, that is. From Carfax's *Bestiary of the Inner Worlds*, I understand that among the semi-aquatic Krid, the male is a small, ineffectual symbiotic parasite lodging in the mantle of the female. The barman, a four-armed Thent, guided me to the snug where I was to meet my contact. The bar overlooked the Ocean Harbor. I watched dockworkers scurry over the vast body of the space-crosser, in and out of hatches that had opened in the skin of the ship. I did not like to see those hatches; they ruined its perfection, the precise, intact curve of its skin.

"Lady Granville-Hyde?"

What an oily man, so well lubricated that I did not hear his approach.

"Stafford Grimes, at your service."

He offered to buy me a drink, but I drew the line at that unseemliness. That did not stop him ordering one for himself and sipping it—and several successors—noisily during the course of my questions. Years of Venusian light had turned his skin to wrinkled brown leather: drinker's eyes looked out from heavily hooded lids—years of squinting into the ultraviolet. His neck and hands were mottled white with pockmarks where melanomas had been frozen out. Sunburn, melancholy, and alcoholism: the classic recipe for honorary consuls systemwide, not just on Venus.

"Thank you for agreeing to meet me. So, you met him."

"I will never forget him. Pearls of Aphrodite. Size of your head, Lady Ida. There's a fortune waiting for the man. . . ."

"Or woman," I chided, and surreptitiously activated the recording ring beneath my glove.

Plate 2: *V flor scopulum:* the Ocean Mist Flower. The name is a misnomer: the Ocean Mist Flower is not a flower, but a coral animalcule of the aerial reefs of the Tellus Ocean. The seeming petals are absorption surfaces drawing moisture from the frequent ocean fogs of those latitudes. Pistils and stamen bear sticky palps, which function in the same fashion as Terrene spiderwebs, trapping prey. Venus boasts an entire ecosystem of marine insects unknown on Earth.

This cut is the most three-dimensional of Lady Ida's Botanica Veneris. Reproductions only hint at the sculptural quality of the original. The "petals" have been curled at the edges over the blunt side of a pair of scissors. Each of the 208 palps has been sprung so that they stand proud from the black paper background.

Onion paper, hard-painted card.

The Honorary Consul's Tale

Pearls of Aphrodite. Truly, the pearls beyond price. The pearls of Starosts and Aztars. But the cloud reefs are perilous, Lady Ida. Snap a man's body clean in half, those bivalves. Crush his head like a Vulpeculan melon. Snare a hand or an ankle and drown him. Aphrodite's Pearls are blood pearls. A fortune awaits anyone, my dear, who can culture them. A charming man, Arthur Hyde— that brogue of his made anything sound like the blessing of heaven itself. Charm the avios from the trees—but natural, unaffected. It was no surprise to learn he was of aristocratic stock. Quality: you can't hide it. In those days, I owned a company—fishing trips across the archipelago. The legend of the Ourogoonta, the Island that is a Fish, was a potent draw. Imagine hooking one of those! Of course, they never did. No, I'd take them out, show them the cloud reefs, the Krid hives, the wing-fish migration, the air-jellies; get them pissed on the boat, take their photographs next to some thawed-out javelin-fish they hadn't caught. Simple, easy, honest money. Why wasn't it enough for me? I had done the trick enough times myself, drink one for the punter's two, yet I fell for it that evening in the Windward Tavern, drinking hot, spiced kashash and the night wind whistling up in the spires of the dead Krid nest-haven like the caged souls of drowned sailors. Drinking for days down the Great Twilight, his one for my two. Charming, so charming, until I had pledged my boat on his plan. He would buy a planktoneer—an old bucket of a sea skimmer with nary a straight plate or a true rivet in her.

He would seed her with spores and send her north on the great circulatory current, like a maritime cloud reef. Five years that current takes to circulate the globe before it returns to the arctic waters that birthed it. Five years is also the time it takes the Clam of Aphrodite to mature—what we call pearls are no such thing. Sperm, Lady Ida. Compressed sperm. In waters, it dissolves and disperses. Each Great Dawn the Tellus Ocean is white with it. In the air, it remains compact—the most prized of all jewels. Enough of fluids. By the time the reef ship reached the deep north, the clams would be mature and the cold water would kill them. It would be a simple task to strip the hulk with high-pressure hoses, harvest the pearls, and bank the fortune.

Five years makes a man fidgety for his investment. Arthur sent us weekly reports from the Sea Wardens and the Krid argosies. Month on month, year on year, I began to suspect that the truth had wandered far from those chart coordinates. I was not alone. I formed a consortium with my fellow investors and chartered a 'rigible.

And there at Map 60 North, 175 East, we found the ship—or what was left of it, so overgrown was it with Clams of Aphrodite. Our investment had been lined and lashed by four Krid cantoons: as we arrived, they were in the process of stripping it with halberds and grappling hooks. Already the decks and superstructure were green with clam meat and purple with Krid blood. Arthur stood in the stern frantically waving a Cross of St. Patrick flag, gesturing for us to get out, get away.

Krid pirates were plundering our investment! Worse, Arthur was their prisoner. We were an unarmed aerial gadabout, so we turned tail and headed for the nearest Sea Warden castle to call for aid.

Charmer. Bloody buggering charmer. I know he's your flesh and blood, but . . . I should have thought! If he'd been captured by Krid pirates, they wouldn't have let him wave a bloody flag to warn us.

When we arrived with a constabulary cruiser, all we found was the capsized hulk of the planktoneer and a flock of avios gorging on clam offal. Duped! Pirates my arse—excuse me. Those four cantoons were laden to the gunwales with contract workers. He never had any intention of splitting the profits with us.

The last we heard of him, he had converted the lot into Bank of Ishtar bearer bonds—better than gold—at Yez Tok and headed in-country. That was twelve years ago.

Your brother cost me my business, Lady Granville-Hyde. It was a good business; I could have sold it, made a little pile. Bought a place on Ledekh

Syant—maybe even made it back to Earth to see out my days to a decent calendar. Instead . . . Ach, what's the use. Please believe me when I say that I bear your family no ill will—only your brother. If you do succeed in finding him—and if I haven't, I very much doubt you will—remind him of that, and that he still owes me.

> Plate 3: *V lilium aphrodite:* the Archipelago sea lily. Walk-the-Water in Thekh; there is no comprehensible translation from Krid. A ubiquitous and fecund diurnal plant, it grows so aggressively in the Venerian Great Day that by Great Evening bays and harbors are clogged with blossoms and passage must be cleared by special bloom-breaker ships.
>
> Painted paper, watermarked Venerian tissue, inks, and scissor-scrolled card.

So dear, so admirable a companion, the Princess Latufui. She knew I had been stinting with the truth in my excuse of shopping for paper, when I went to see the honorary consul down in Ledekh Port. Especially when I returned without any paper. I busied myself in the days before our sailing to Ishtaria on two cuts—the Sea Lily and the Ocean Mist Flower—even if it is not a flower, according to my Carfax's *Bestiary of the Inner Worlds.* She was not fooled by my industry and I felt soiled and venal. All Tongan women have dignity, but the princess possesses such innate nobility that the thought of lying to her offends nature itself. The moral order of the universe is upset. How can I tell her that my entire visit to this world is a tissue of fabrications?

Weather again fair, with the invariable light winds and interminable grey sky. I am of Ireland, supposedly we thrive on permanent overcast, but even I find myself pining for a glimpse of sun. Poor Latufui: she grows wan for want of light. Her skin is waxy, her hair lustreless. We have a long time to wait for a glimpse of sun: Carfax states that the sky clears partially at the dawn and sunset of Venus's Great Day. I hope to be off this world by then.

Our ship, the *Seventeen Notable Navigators,* is a well-built, swift Krid *jaicoona*—among the Krid the females are the seafarers, but they equal the males of my world in the richness and fecundity of their taxonomy of ships. A *jaicoona,* it seems, is a fast catamaran steam packet, built for the archipelago trade. I have no sea legs, but the *Seventeen Notable Navigators* was the only option that would get us to Ishtaria in reasonable time. Princess Latufui tells me it is a fine and sturdy craft though built to alien dimensions: she has banged her head most painfully several times. Captain Highly-Able-at-Forecasting, recognizing a sister seafarer, engages the princess in lengthy conversations of an island-hopping, archipelagan nature, which remind Latufui greatly of her home islands. The other humans aboard are a lofty Thekh, and Hugo von Trachtenberg, a German in very high regard of himself, of that feckless type who think themselves gentleman adventurers but are little more than grandiose fraudsters. Nevertheless, he speaks Krid (as truly as any Terrene can) and acts as translator between princess and captain. It is a Venerian truth universally recognized that two unaccompanied women travelers must be in need of a male protector. The dreary hours Herr von Trachtenberg fills with his notion of gay chitchat! And in the evenings, the interminable games of Barrington. Von Trachtenberg claims to have gambled the game profession-ally in the cloud casinos: I let him win enough for the sensation to go to his head, then take him game after game. Ten times champion of the County Kildare mixed bridge championships is more than enough to beat his hide at Barrington. Still he does not get the message—yes, I am a wealthy widow, but I have no interest in jejune Prussians. Thus I retire to my cabin to begin my studies for the *crescite dolium* cut.

Has this world a more splendid sight than the harbor of Yez Tok? It is a city most perpendicular, of pillars and towers, masts and spires. The tall funnels of the ships, bright with the heraldry of the Krid maritime families, blend with god-poles and lighthouse and customs towers and cranes of the harbor, which in turn yield to the tower houses and campaniles of the Bourse, the whole rising to merge with the trees of the Ishtarian Littoral Forest—pierced here and there by the comical roofs of the estancias of the Thent *zavars* and the gilded figures of the star gods on their minarets. That forest also rises, a cloth of green, to break into the rocky palisades of the Exx Palisades. And there—oh how thrilling!—glimpsed through mountain passes unimaginably high, a glittering glimpse of the snows of the alti-plano. Snow. Cold. Bliss!

It is only now, after reams of purple prose, that I realize what I was trying to say of Yez Tok: simply, it is city as botany—stems and trunks, boles and bracts, root and branch!

And out there, in the city-that-is-a-forest, is the man who will guide me farther in my brother's footsteps: Mr. Daniel Okiring.

Plate 4: *V crescite dolium:* the Gourd of Plenty. A ubiquitous climbing plant of the Ishtari littoral, the Gourd of Plenty is so well adapted to urban environments that it would be considered a weed, but for the gourds, which contains a nectar prized as a delicacy among the coastal Thents. It is toxic to both Krid and humans.

The papercut bears a note on the true scale, written in gold ink.

The Hunter's Tale

Have you seen a janthar? Really seen a janthar? Bloody magnificent, in the same way that a hurricane or an exploding volcano is magnificent. Magnificent and appalling. The films can never capture the sense of scale. Imagine a house, with fangs. And tusks. And spines. A house that can hit forty miles per hour. The films can never get the sheer sense of mass and speed—or the elegance and grace—that something so huge can be so nimble, so agile! And what the films can never, ever capture is the smell. They smell of curry. Vindaloo curry. Venerian body chemistry. But that's why you never, ever eat curry on *asjan*. Out in the Stalva, the grass is tall enough to hide even a janthar. The smell is the only warning you get. You catch a whiff of vindaloo, you run.

You always run. When you hunt janthar, there will always be a moment when it turns, and the janthar hunts you. You run. If you're lucky, you'll draw it on to the gun line. If not . . . The 'thones of the Stalva have been hunting them this way for centuries. Coming-of-age thing. Like my own Maasai people. They give you a spear and point you in the general direction of a lion. Yes, I've killed a lion. I've also killed janthar—and run from even more.

The 'thones have a word for it: the pnem. The fool who runs.

That's how I met your brother. He applied to be a pnem for Okiring *Asjans*. Claimed experience over at Hunderewe with Costa's hunting company. I didn't need to call Costa to know he was a bullshitter. But I liked the fellow— he had charm and didn't take himself too seriously. I knew he'd never last five minutes as a pnem. Took him on as a camp steward. They like the personal service, the hunting types. If you can afford to fly yourself and your friends on a jolly to Venus, you expect to have someone to wipe your arse for you. Charm works on these bastards. He'd wheedle his way into their affections and get them drinking. They'd invite him and before you knew it he was getting their life-stories—and a lot more besides—out of them. He was a careful cove too—he'd always stay one drink behind them and be up early and sharp-eyed as a hawk the next morning. Bring them their bed tea. Fluff up their pillows. Always came back with the fattest tip. I knew what he was doing, but he did it so well—I'd taken him on, hadn't I? So, an aristocrat. Why am I not surprised? Within three trips, I'd made him Maître de la Chasse. Heard he'd made and lost one fortune already . . . is that true? A jewel thief? Why am I not surprised by that either?

The Thirtieth Earl of Mar fancied himself as a sporting type. Booked a three-month Grand *Asjan;* he and five friends, shooting their way up the Great Littoral to the Stalva. Wives, husbands, lovers, personal servants, twenty Thent *asjanis* and a caravan of forty *graapa* to carry their bags and baggage. They had one *graap* just for the champagne—they'd shipped every last drop of it from Earth. Made so much noise we cleared the forest for ten miles around. Bloody brutes—we'd set up hides at water holes so they could blast away from point-blank range. That's not hunting. Every day they'd send a dozen bearers back with hides and trophies. I'm surprised there was anything left, the amount of metal they pumped into those poor beasts. The stench of rot . . . God! The sky was black with carrion avios.

Your brother excelled himself: suave, in control, charming, witty, the soul of attention. Oh, most attentive. Especially to the Lady Mar . . . She was no kack-hand with the guns, but I think she tired of the boys-club antics of the gents. Or maybe it was just the sheer relentless slaughter. Either way, she increasingly remained in camp. Where your brother attended to her. Aristocrats—they sniff each other out.

So Arthur poled the Lady Mar while we blasted our bloody, brutal, bestial way up onto the High Stalva. Nothing would do the thirtieth earl but to go after janthar. Three out of five *asjanis* never even come across a janthar. Ten percent of hunters who go for janthar don't come back. Only ten percent! He liked those odds.

Twenty-five sleeps we were up there, while Great Day turned to Great Evening. I wasn't staying for night on the Stalva. It's not just a different season, it's a different world. Things come out of sleep, out of dens, out of the ground. No, not for all the fortune of the earls of Mar would I spend night on the Stalva.

By then, we had abandoned the main camp. We carried bare rations, sleeping out beside our mounts with one ear tuned to the radio. Then the call came: janthar sign! An *asjani* had seen a fresh path through a speargrass meadow five miles to the north of us. In a moment, we were mounted and tearing through the High Stalva. The earl rode like a madman, whipping his *graap* to reckless speed. Damn fool: of all the Stalva's many grasslands, the tall pike-grass meadows were the most dangerous. A janthar could be right next to you and you wouldn't see it. And the pike grass disorients, reflects sounds, turns you around. There was no advising the Earl of Mar and his chums, though. His wife hung back—she claimed her mount had picked up a little lameness. Why did I not say something when Arthur went back to accompany the Lady Mar! But my concern was how to get everyone out of the pike grass alive.

Then the earl stabbed his shock goad into the flank of his *graap*, and before I could do anything he was off. My radio crackled—form a gun line! The mad fool was going to run the janthar himself. Aristocrats! Your pardon, ma'am. Moments later, his *graap* came crashing back through the pike grass to find its herd mates. My only hope was to form a gun line and hope—and pray—that he would lead the janthar right into our cross fire. It takes a lot of ordnance to stop a janthar. And in this kind of tall-grass terrain, where you can hardly see your hand in front of your face, I had to set the firing positions just right so the idiots wouldn't blow each other to bits.

I got them into some semblance of position. I held the center—the *lakoo*. Your brother and the Lady Mar I ordered to take *jeft* and *garoon*—the last two positions of the left wing of the gun line. Finally, I got them all to radio silence. The 'thones teach you how to be still, and how to listen, and how to know what is safe and what is death. Silence, then a sustained crashing. My spotter called me, but I did not need her to tell me: that was the sound of death. I could only hope that the earl remembered to run in a straight line, and not to trip over anything, and that the gun line would fire in time . . . a hundred hopes. A hundred ways to die.

Most terrifying sound in the world, a janthar in full pursuit! It sounds like it's coming from everywhere at once. I yelled to the gun line, *Steady there, steady. Hold your fire!* Then I smelled it. Clear, sharp: unmistakable. Curry. I put up the cry: *Vindaloo! Vindaloo!* And there was the mad earl, breaking out of the cane. Madman! What was he thinking! He was in the wrong place, headed in the wrong direction. The only ones who could cover him were Arthur and Lady Mar. And there, behind him: the janthar. Bigger than any I had ever seen. The Mother of All Janthar. The Queen of the High Stalva. I froze. We all froze. We might as well try to kill a mountain. I yelled to Arthur and Lady Mar. Shoot! Shoot now! Nothing. Shoot for the love of all the stars! Nothing. Shoot! Why didn't they shoot?

The 'thones found the Thirtieth Earl of Mar spread over a hundred yards.

They hadn't shot because they weren't there. They were at it like dogs— your brother and the Lady Mar, back where they had left the party. They hadn't even heard the janthar.

Strange woman, the Lady Mar. Her face barely moved when she learned of her husband's terrible death. Like it was no surprise to her. Of course, she became immensely rich when the will went through. There was no question of your brother's ever working for me again. Shame. I liked him. But I can't help thinking that he was as much used as user in that sordid little affair. Did the Lady of Mar murder her husband? Too much left to chance. Yet it was a very convenient accident. And I can't help but think that the thirtieth earl knew what his lady was up to; and a surfeit of cuckoldry drove him to prove he was a man.

The janthar haunted the highlands for years. Became a legend. Every aristo idiot on the Inner Worlds who fancied himself a Great Terrene Hunter went after it. None of them ever got it though it claimed five more lives. The Human-Slayer of the Selva. In the end it stumbled into a 'thone clutch trap and died on a pungi stake, eaten away by gangrene. So we all pass. No final run, no gun line, no trophies.

Your brother—as I said, I liked him though I never trusted him. He left when the scandal broke—went up-country, over the Stalva into the Palisade country. I heard a rumor he'd joined a mercenary *javrost* unit, fighting up on the altiplano.

Botany, is it? Safer business than Big Game.

Plate 5: *V trifex aculeatum:* Stannage's Bird-Eating Trifid. Native of the Great Littoral Forest of Ishtaria. Carnivorous in its habits; it lures smaller, nectar-feeding avios with its sweet exudate, then stings them to death with its whiplike style and sticky, poisoned stigma.

Cutpaper, inks, folded tissue.

The princess is brushing her hair. This she does every night, whether in Tonga, or Ireland, on Earth, or aboard a space-crosser, or on Venus. The ritual is invariable. She kneels, unpins, and uncoils her tight bun and lets her hair fall to its natural length, which is to the waist. Then she takes two silver-backed brushes, and, with great and vigorous strokes, brushes her hair from the crown of her head to the tips. One hundred strokes, which she counts in a Tongan rhyme that I very much love to hear.

When she is done, she cleans the brushes, returns them to the baize-lined case, then takes a bottle of coconut oil and works it through her hair. The air is suffused with the sweet smell of coconut. It reminds me so much of the whin flowers of home, in the spring. She works patiently and painstakingly, and when she has finished, she rolls her hair back into its bun and pins it. A simple, dedicated, repetitive task, but it moves me almost to tears.

Her beautiful hair! How dearly I love my friend Latufui!

We are sleeping at a hohvandha, a Thent roadside inn, on the Grand North Road in Canton Hoa in the Great Littoral Forest. Tree branches scratch at my window shutters. The heat, the humidity, the animal noise are all overpowering. We are far from the cooling breezes of the Vestal Sea. I wilt, though Latufui relishes the warmth. The arboreal creatures of this forest are deeper-voiced than in Ireland; bellings and honkings and deep booms. How I wish we could spend the night here—Great Night—for my Carfax tells me that the Ishtarian Littoral Forest contains this world's greatest concentration of luminous creatures—fungi, plants, animals, and those peculiarly Venerian phyla in between. It is almost as bright as day. I have made some daytime studies of the Star Flower—no Venerian Botanica can be complete without it—but for it to succeed, I must hope that there is a supply of luminous paint at Loogaza, where we embark for the crossing of the Stalva.

My dear Latufui has finished now and closed away her brushes in their green baize-lined box. So faithful and true a friend! We met in Nuku'alofa on the Tongan leg of my Botanica of the South Pacific. The king, her father, had issued the invitation—he was a keen collector—and at the reception I was introduced to his very large family, including Latufui, and was immediately charmed by her sense, dignity, and vivacity. She invited me to tea the following day—a very grand affair—where she confessed that as a minor princess, her only hope of fulfilment was in marrying well—an institution in which she had no interest. I replied that I had visited the South Pacific as a time apart from Lord Rathangan—it had been clear for some years that he had no interest in me (nor I in him). We were two noble ladies of compatible needs and temperaments, and there and then we became firmest friends and inseparable companions. When Patrick shot himself and Rathangan passed into my possession, it was only natural that the princess move in with me.

I cannot conceive of life without Latufui; yet I am deeply ashamed that I have not been totally honest in my motivations for this Venerian expedition. Why can I not trust? Oh secrets! Oh simulations!

V stellafloris noctecandentis: the Venerian Starflower. Its name is the same in Thent, Thekh, and Krid. Now a popular Terrestrial garden

plant, where it is known as glow berry, though the name is a misnomer. Its appearance is a bunch of night-luminous white berries,
though the berries are in fact globular bracts, with the bioluminous
flower at the center. Selective strains of this flower traditionally provide illumination in Venerian settlements during the Great Night.

Paper, luminous paint (not reproduced). The original papercut
is mildly radioactive.

By high train to Camahoo.

We have our own carriage. It is of aged gothar wood, still fragrant and
spicy. The hammocks do not suit me at all. Indeed, the whole train has a
rocking, swaying lollop that makes me seasick. In the caravanserai at Loogaza,
the contraption looked both ridiculous and impractical. But here, in the high
grass, its ingenuity reveals itself. The twenty-foot-high wheels carry us high
above the grass, though I am in fear of grass fires—the steam tractor at the
head of the train does throw off the most ferocious pother of soot and embers.

I am quite content to remain in my carriage and work on my Stalva-grass
study—I think this may be most sculptural. The swaying makes for many a
slip with the scissor, but I think I have caught the feathery, almost downy
nature of the flower heads. Of a maritime people, the princess is at home in
this rolling ocean of grass and spends much of her time on the observation
balcony, watching the patterns the wind draws across the grasslands.

It was there that she fell into conversation with the Honorable Cormac de
Buitlear, a fellow Irishman. Inevitably, he ingratiated himself and within minutes was taking tea in our carriage. The Inner Worlds are infested with young
men claiming to be the junior sons of minor Irish gentry, but a few minutes' gentle questioning revealed not only that he was indeed the Honorable
Cormac—of the Bagenalstown De Buitlears—but a relative, close enough to
know of my husband's demise, and the scandal of the Blue Empress.

Our conversation went like this.

> HIMSELF: The Grangegorman Hydes. My father used to knock
> around with your elder brother—what was he called?
> MYSELF: Richard.
> HIMSELF: The younger brother—wasn't he a bit of a black sheep?
> I remember there was this tremendous scandal. Some jewel—a
> sapphire as big as a thrush's egg. Yes—that was the expression
> they used in the papers. A thrush's egg. What was it called?
> MYSELF: The Blue Empress.

> HIMSELF: Yes! That was it. Your grandfather was presented it by some Martian princess. Services rendered.
>
> MYSELF: He helped her escape across the Tharsis steppe in the revolution of '11, then organized the White Brigades to help her regain the Jasper Throne.
>
> HIMSELF: Your brother, not the old boy. You woke up one morning to find the stone gone and him vanished. Stolen.

I could see that Princess Latufui found the Honorable Cormac's bluntness distressing, but if one claims the privileges of a noble family, one must also claim the shames.

> MYSELF: It was never proved that Arthur stole the Blue Empress.
>
> HIMSELF: No, no. But you know how tongues wag in the country. And his disappearance was, you must admit, *timely*. How long ago was that now? God, I must have been a wee gossoon.
>
> MYSELF: Fifteen years.
>
> HIMSELF: Fifteen years! And not a word? Do you know if he's even alive?
>
> MYSELF: We believe he fled to the Inner Worlds. Every few years we hear of a sighting, but most of them are so contrary, we dismiss them. He made his choice. As for the Blue Empress: broken up and sold long ago, I don't doubt.
>
> HIMSELF: And here I find you on a jaunt across one of the Inner Worlds.
>
> MYSELF: I am creating a new album of papercuts. The Botanica Veneris.
>
> HIMSELF: Of course. If I might make so bold, Lady Rathangan: the Blue Empress: do you believe Arthur took it?

And I made him no verbal answer but gave the smallest shake of my head.

Princess Latufui had been restless all this evening—the time before sleep, that is: Great Evening was still many Terrene days off. Can we ever truly adapt to the monstrous Venerian calendar? Arthur has been on this world for fifteen years—has he drifted not just to another world, but another clock, another calendar? I worked on my Stalva-grass cut—I find that curving the leaf-bearing nodes gives the necessary three-dimensionality—but my heart was not in it. Latufui sipped at tea and fumbled at stitching and pushed newspapers around until eventually she threw open the cabin door in frustration and demanded that I join her on the balcony.

The rolling travel of the high train made me grip the rail for dear life, but the high plain was as sharp and fresh as if starched, and there, a long line on the horizon beyond the belching smokestack and pumping pistons of the tractor, were the Palisades of Exx: a grey wall from one horizon to the other. Clouds hid the peaks, like a curtain lowered from the sky.

Dark against the grey mountains, I saw the spires of the observatories of Camahoo. This was the Thent homeland; and I was apprehensive, for among those towers and minarets is a *hoondahvi*, a Thent opium den, owned by the person who might be able to tell me the next part of my brother's story—a story increasingly disturbing and dark. A person who is not human.

"Ida, dear friend. There is a thing I must ask you."

"Anything, dear Latufui."

"I must tell you, it is not a thing that can be asked softly."

My heart turned over in my chest. I knew what Latufui would ask.

"Ida: have you come to this world to look for your brother?"

She did me the courtesy of a direct question. No preamble, no preliminary sifting through her doubts and evidences. I owed it a direct answer.

"Yes," I said. "I have come to find Arthur."

"I thought so."

"For how long?"

"Since Ledekh-Olkoi. Ah, I cannot say the words right. When you went to get papers and gum and returned empty-handed."

"I went to see a Mr. Stafford Grimes. I had information that he had met my brother soon after his arrival on this world. He directed me to Mr. Okiring, a retired asjan-hunter in Yez Tok."

"And Cama-oo? Is this another link in the chain?"

"It is. But the Botanica is no sham. I have an obligation to my backers—you know the state of my finances as well as I, Latufui. The late Count Rathangan was a profligate man. He ran the estate into the ground."

"I could wish you had trusted me. All those weeks of planning and organizing. The maps, the itineraries, the tickets, the transplanetary calls to agents and factors. I was so excited! A journey to another world! But for you, there was always something else. None of that was the whole truth. None of it was honest."

"Oh, my dear Latufui. . . ." But how could I say that I had not told her because I feared what Arthur might have become. Fears that seemed to be borne out by every ruined life that had touched his. What would I find? Did anything remain of the wild, carefree boy I remembered chasing old Bunty the dog across the summer lawns of Grangegorman? Would I recognize him? Worse, would he listen to me? "There is a wrong to right. An old debt to be canceled. It's a family thing."

"I live in your house but not in your family," Princess Latufui said. Her words were barbed with truth. They tore me. "We would not do that in Tonga. Your ways are different. And I thought I was more than a companion."

"Oh, my dear Latufui." I took her hands in mine. "My dear dear Latufui. Your are far far more to me than a companion. You are my life. But you of all people should understand my family. We are on another world, but we are not so far from Rathangan, I think. I am seeking Arthur, and I do not know what I will find, but I promise you, what he says to me, I will tell to you. Everything."

Now she laid her hands over mine, and there we stood, cupping hands on the balcony rail, watching the needle spires of Camahoo rise from the grass spears of the Stalva.

> *V vallumque foenum:* Stalva Pike Grass. Another non-Terrene that is finding favor in Terrestrial ornamental gardens. Earth never receives sufficient sunlight for it to attain its full Stalva height. *Yetten* in the Stalva Thent dialect.
>
> Card, onionskin paper, corrugated paper, paint. This papercut is unique in that it unfolds into three parts. The original, in the Chester Beatty Library in Dublin, is always displayed unfolded.

The Mercenary's Tale

In the name of the Leader of the Starry Skies and the Ever-Circling Spiritual Family, welcome to my *hoondahvi.* May *apsas* speak; may *gavanda* sing, may the *thoo* impart their secrets!

I understand completely that you have not come to drink. But the greeting is standard. We pride ourself on being the most traditional *hoondahvi* in Exxaa Canton.

Is the music annoying? No? Most Terrenes find it aggravating. It's an essential part of the *hoondahvi* experience, I am afraid.

Your brother, yes. How could I forget him? I owe him my life.

He fought like a man who hated fighting. Up on the altiplano, when we smashed open the potteries and set the Porcelain Towns afire up and down the Valley of the Kilns, there were those who blazed with love and joy at the slaughter and those whose faces were so dark it was as if their souls were clogged with soot. Your brother was one of those. Human expressions are hard for us to read—your faces are wood, like masks. But I saw his face and knew that he loathed what he did. That was what made him the best of *javrosts*. I am an old career soldier; I have seen many many come to our band. The ones in love with violence: unless they can take discipline, we turn them away. But when a mercenary hates what he does for his silver, there must be a greater darkness driving him. There is a thing they hate more than the violence they do.

Are you sure the music is tolerable? Our harmonies and chord patterns apparently create unpleasant electrical resonance in the human brain. Like small seizures. We find it most reassuring. Like the rhythm of the kittening womb.

Your brother came to us in the dawn of Great Day 6817. He could ride a *graap*, bivouac, cook, and was handy with both bolt and blade. We never ask questions of our *javrosts*—in time they answer them all themselves—but rumors blow on the wind like *thagoon* down. He was a minor aristocrat, he was a gambler; he was a thief, he was a murderer; he was a seducer, he was a traitor. Nothing to disqualify him. Sufficient to recommend him.

In Old Days the Duke of Yoo disputed mightily with her neighbor the Duke of Hetteten over who rightly ruled the altiplano and its profitable potteries. From time immemorial, it had been a place beyond: independently minded and stubborn of spirit, with little respect for gods or dukes. Wars were fought down generations, laying waste to fames and fortunes, and when in the end, the House of Yoo prevailed, the peoples of the plateau had forgotten they ever had lords and mistresses and debts of fealty. It is a law of earth and stars alike that people should be well governed, obedient, and quiet in their ways, so the Duke of Yoo embarked on a campaign of civil discipline. Her house corps had been decimated in the Porcelain Wars, so House Yoo hired mercenaries. Among them, my former unit, Gellet's *Javrosts*.

They speak of us still, up on the plateau. We are the monsters of their Great Nights, the haunters of their children's dreams. We are legend. We are Gellet's *Javrosts*. We are the new demons.

For one Great Day and Great Night, we ran free. We torched the topless star shrines of Javapanda and watched them burn like chimneys. We smashed the funerary jars and trampled the bones of the illustrious dead of Toohren. We overturned the houses of the holy, burned elders and kits in their homes. We lassoed rebels and dragged them behind our *graapa*, round and round the village, until all that remained was a bloody rope. We forced whole communities from their homes, driving them across the altiplano until the snow heaped their bodies. And Arthur was at my side. We were not friends—there is too much history on this world for human and Thent ever to be that. He was my *badoon*. You do not have a concept for it, let alone a word. A passionate colleague. A brother who is not related. A fellow devotee. . . .

We killed and we killed and we killed. And in our wake came the Duke of Yoo's soldiers—restoring order, rebuilding towns, offering defense against the murderous renegades. It was all strategy. The Duke of Yoo knew the plateauneers would never love her, but she could be their savior. Therefore, a campaign of final outrages was planned. Such vileness! We were ordered to Glehenta, a pottery town at the head of Valley of the Kilns. There we would enter the *glotoonas*—the birthing creches—and slaughter every infant down to the last kit. We rode, Arthur at my side, and though human emotions are strange and distant to me, I knew them well enough to read the storm in his heart. Night snow was falling as we entered Glehenta, lit by ten thousand starflowers. The people locked their doors and cowered from us. Through the heart of town we rode; past the great conical kilns, to the *glotoonas*. Matres flung themselves before our *graapa*—we rode them down. Arthur's face was darker than the Great Midnight. He broke formation and rode up to Gellet himself. I went to him. I saw words between your brother and our commander. I did not hear them. Then Arthur drew his blasket and in a single shot blew the entire top of Gellet's body to ash. In the fracas, I shot down three of our troop; then we were racing through the glowing streets, our hooves clattering on the porcelain cobbles, the erstwhile Gellet's *Javrosts* behind us.

And so we saved them. For the Duke of Yoo had arranged it so that her Ducal Guard would fall upon us even as we attacked, annihilate us, and achieve two notable victories: presenting themselves as the saviors of Glehenta and destroying any evidence of their scheme. Your brother and I sprung the trap. But we did not know until leagues and months later, far from the altiplano. At the foot of the Ten Thousand Stairs, we parted—we thought it safer. We never saw each other again though I heard he had gone back up the stairs, to the Pelerines. And if you do find him, please don't tell him what became of me. This is a shameful place.

And I am ashamed that I have told you such dark and bloody truths about your brother. But at the end, he was honorable. He was right. That he saved the guilty—an unintended consequence. Our lives are made up of such.

Certainly, we can continue outside on the *hoondahvi* porch. I did warn you that the music was irritating to human sensibilities.

V lucerna vesperum: Schaefferia: the Evening Candle. A solitary tree of the foothills of the Exx Palisades of Ishtaria, the Schaefferia is noted for its many upright, luminous blossoms, which flower in Venerian Great Evening and Great Dawn.

Only the blossoms are reproduced. Card, folded and cut tissue, luminous paint (not reproduced). The original is also slightly radioactive.

A cog railway runs from Camahoo Terminus to the Convent of the Starry Pelerines. The Starsview Special takes pilgrims to see the stars and planets. Our carriage is small, luxurious, intricate, and ingenious in that typically Thent fashion, and terribly tedious. The track has been constructed in a helix inside Awk Mountain, so our journey consists of interminable, noisy spells inside the tunnel, punctuated by brief, blinding moments of clarity as we emerge onto the open face of the mountain. Not for the vertiginous!

Thus, hour upon hour, we spiral our way up Mount Awk.

Princess Latufui and I play endless games of Moon Whist, but our minds are not in it. My forebodings have darkened after my conversation with the Thent *hoondahvi* owner in Camahoo. The princess is troubled by my anxiety. Finally, she can bear it no more.

"Tell me about the Blue Empress. Tell me everything."

I grew up with two injunctions in case of fire: save the dogs and the Blue Empress. For almost all my life, the jewel was a ghost stone—present but unseen, haunting Grangegorman and the lives it held. I have a memory from earliest childhood of seeing the stone—never touching it—but I do not trust the memory. Imaginings too easily become memories, memories imaginings.

We are not free in so many things, we of the landed class. Richard would inherit, Arthur would make a way in the worlds, and I would marry as well as I could—land to land. The Barony of Rathangan was considered one of the most desirable in Kildare, despite Patrick's seeming determination to drag it to the bankruptcy court. A match was made, and he was charming and bold; a fine sportsman and a very handsome man. It was an equal match: snide comments from both halves of the county. The Blue Empress was part of my treasure—on the strict understanding that it remain in the custody of my lawyers. Patrick argued—and it was there that I first got an inkling of his true character—and the wedding was off the wedding was on the wedding was off the wedding was on again and the banns posted. A viewing was arranged, for his people to itemize and value the Hyde treasure. For the first time in long memory, the Blue Empress was taken from its safe and displayed to human view. Blue as the wide Atlantic it was, and as boundless and clear. You could lose yourself forever in the light inside that gem. And yes, it was the size of a thrush's egg.

And then the moment that all the stories agree on: the lights failed. Not so unusual at Grangegorman—the same grandfather who brought back the Blue Empress installed the hydro plant—and when they came back on again; the sapphire was gone: baize and case and everything.

We called upon the honor of all present, ladies and gentlemen alike. The lights would be put out for five minutes, and when they were switched back on, the Blue Empress would be back in the Hyde treasury. It was not. Our people demanded we call the police, Patrick's people, mindful of their client's attraction to scandal, were less insistent. We would make a further appeal to honor: if the Blue Empress was not back by morning, then we would call the guards.

Not only was the Blue Empress still missing, so was Arthur.

We called the Garda Siochana. The last we heard was that Arthur had left for the Inner Worlds.

The wedding went ahead. It would have been a greater scandal to call it off. We were two families alike in notoriety. Patrick could not let it go: he went to his grave believing that Arthur and I had conspired to keep the Blue Empress out of his hands. I have no doubt that Patrick would have found a way of forcing me to sign over possession of the gem to him and would have sold it. Wastrel.

As for the Blue Empress: I feel I am very near to Arthur now. One cannot run forever. We will meet, and the truth will be told.

Then light flooded our carriage as the train emerged from the tunnel onto the final ramp and there, before us, its spires and domes dusted with snow blown from the high peaks, was the Convent of the Starry Pelerines.

> *V aquilonis vitis visionum:* the Northern Littoral, or Ghost Vine. A common climber of the forests of the southern slopes of the Ishtari altiplano, domesticated and widely grown in Thent garden terraces. Its white, trumpet-shaped flowers are attractive, but the plant is revered for its berries. When crushed, the infused liquor known as *pula* creates powerful auditory hallucinations in Venerian physiology and forms the basis of the Thent mystical *hoondahvi* cult. In Terrenes, it produces a strong euphoria and a sense of omnipotence.
>
> Alkaloid-infused paper. Ida Granville-Hyde used Thent Ghost-Vine liquor to tint and infuse the paper in this cut. It is reported to be still mildly hallucinogenic.

The Pilgrim's Tale

You'll come out onto the Belvedere? It's supposed to be off-limits to Terrenes—technically blasphemy—sacred space and all that—but the pelerines turn a blind eye. Do excuse the cough . . . ghastly, isn't it? Sounds like a bag of bloody loose change. I don't suppose the cold air does much for my dear old alveoli, but at this stage it's all a matter of damn.

That's Gloaming Peak there. You won't see it until the cloud clears. Every Great Evening, every Great Dawn, for a few Earth-days at a time, the cloud breaks. It goes up, oh so much farther than you could ever imagine. You look up, and up, and up—and beyond it, you see the stars. That's why the pelerines came here. Such a sensible religion. The stars are gods. One star, one god. Simple. No faith, no heaven, no punishment, no sin. Just look up and wonder. The Blue Pearl: that's what they call our Earth. I wonder if that's why they care for us. Because we're descended from divinity? If only they knew! They really are very kind.

Excuse me. Bloody marvelous stuff, this Thent brew. I'm in no pain at all. I find it quite reassuring that I shall slip from this too too rancid flesh swaddled in a blanket of beatific thoughts and analgesic glow. They're very kind, the pelerines. Very kind.

Now, look to your right. There. Do you see? That staircase, cut into the rock, winding up up up. The Ten Thousand Stairs. That's the old way to the altiplano. Everything went up and down those steps: people, animals, goods, palanquins and stick-stick men, traders and pilgrims and armies. Your brother. I watched him go, from this very belvedere. Three years ago, or was it five? You never really get used to the Great Day. Time blurs.

We were tremendous friends, the way that addicts are. You wouldn't have come this far without realizing some truths about your brother. Our degradation unites us. Dear thing. How we'd set the world to rights, over flask after flask of this stuff! He realized the truth of this place early on. It's the way to the stars. God's waiting room. And we, this choir of shambling wrecks, wander through it, dazzled by our glimpses of the stars. But he was a dear friend, a dear dear friend. Dear Arthur.

We're all darkened souls here, but he was haunted. Things done and things left undone, like the prayer book says. My father was a vicar—can't you tell? Arthur never spoke completely about his time with the *javrosts*. He hinted—I think he wanted to tell me, very much, but was afraid of giving me his nightmares. That old saw about a problem shared being a problem halved? Damnable lie. A problem shared is a problem doubled. But I would find him up here all times of the

Great Day and Night, watching the staircase and the caravans and stick convoys going up and down. Altiplano porcelain, he'd say. Finest in all the worlds. So fine you can read the Bible through it. Every cup, every plate, every vase and bowl, was portered down those stairs on the shoulders of a stickman. You know he served up on the altiplano, in the Duke of Yoo's Pacification. I wasn't here then, but Aggers was, and he said you could see the smoke going up—endless plumes of smoke, so thick the sky didn't clear and the pelerines went for a whole Great Day without seeing the stars. All Arthur would say about it was, that'll make some fine china. That's what made porcelain from the Valley of the Kilns so fine: bones—the bones of the dead, ground up into powder. He would never drink from a Valley cup—he said it was drinking from a skull.

Here's another thing about addicts—you never get rid of it. All you do is replace one addiction with another. The best you can hope for is that it's a better addiction. Some become god addicts, some throw themselves into worthy deeds, or self-improvement, or fine thoughts, or helping others, God help us all. Me, my lovely little vice is sloth—I really am an idle little bugger. It's so easy, letting the seasons slip away; slothful days and indolent nights, coughing my life up one chunk at a time. For Arthur, it was the visions. Arthur saw wonders and horrors, angels and demons, hopes and fears. True visions—the things that drive men to glory or death. Visionary visions. It lay up on the altiplano, beyond the twists and turns of the Ten Thousand Steps. I could never comprehend what it was, but it drove him. Devoured him. Ate his sleep, ate his appetite, ate his body and his soul and his sanity.

It was worse in the Great Night. . . . Everything's worse in the Great Night. The snow would come swirling down the staircase and he saw things in it— faces—heard voices. The faces and voices of the people who had died, up there on the altiplano. He had to follow them, go up, into the Valley of the Kilns, where he would ask the people to forgive him—or kill him.

And he went. I couldn't stop him—I didn't want to stop him. Can you understand that? I watched him from this very belvedere. The pelerines are not our warders, any of us is free to leave at any time, though I've never seen anyone leave but Arthur. He left in the evening, with the lilac light catching Gloaming Peak. He never looked back. Not a glance to me. I watched him climb the steps to that bend there. That's where I lost sight of him. I never saw or heard of him again. But stories come down the stairs with the stick-men and they make their way even to this little aerie, stories of a seer—a visionary. I look and I imagine I see smoke rising, up there on the altiplano.

It's a pity you won't be here to see the clouds break around the Gloaming, or look at the stars.

V genetric nives: Mother-of-snows (direct translation from Thent). Ground-civer hi-alpine of the Exx Palisades. The plant forms extensive carpets of thousands of minute white blossoms.

The most intricate papercut in the *Botanica Veneris*. Each floret is three millimeters in diameter. Paper, ink, gouache.

A high-stepping spider-car took me up the Ten Thousand Steps, past caravans of stickmen, spines bent, shoulders warped beneath brutal loads of finest porcelain.

The twelve cuts of the *Botanica Veneris* I have given to the princess, along with descriptions and botanical notes. She would not let me leave, clung to me, wracked with great sobs of loss and fear. It was dangerous; a sullen land with Great Night coming. I could not convince her of my reason for heading up the stairs alone, for they did not convince even me. The one, true reason I could not tell her. Oh, I have been despicable to her! My dearest friend, my love. But worse even than that, false.

She stood watching my spider-car climb the steps until a curve in the staircase took me out of her sight. Must the currency of truth always be falsehood?

Now I think of her spreading her long hair out, and brushing it, firmly, directly, beautifully, and the pen falls from my fingers. . . .

Egayhazy is a closed city; hunched, hiding, tight. Its streets are narrow, its buildings lean toward one another; their gables so festooned with starflower that it looks like a perpetual festival. Nothing could be further from the truth: Egayhazy is an angry city, aggressive and cowed: sullen. I keep my Ledbekh-Teltai in my bag. But the anger is not directed at me, though from the story I heard at the Camahoo *hoondahvi*, my fellow humans on this world have not graced our species. It is the anger of a country under occupation. On walls and doors, the proclamations of the Duke of Yoo are plastered layer upon layer: her pennant, emblazoned with the four white hands of House Yoo, flies from public buildings, the radio-station mast, tower tops, and the gallows. Her *Javrosts* patrol streets so narrow that their *graapa* can barely squeeze through them. At their passage, the citizens of Egayhazy flash jagged glares, mutter altiplano oaths. And there is another sigil: an eight-petaled flower; a blue so deep it seems almost to shine. I see it stenciled hastily on walls and doors and the occupation-force posters. I see it in little badges sewn to the quilted jackets of the Egayhazians; and in tiny glass jars in low-set windows. In the market of Yent, I witnessed *Javrosts* overturn and smash a vegetable stall that dared to offer a few posies of this blue bloom.

The staff at my hotel were suspicious when they saw me working up some sketches from memory of this blue flower of dissent. I explained my work and showed some photographs and asked, what was this flower? A common plant of the high altiplano, they said. It grows up under the breath of the high snow; small and tough and stubborn. It's most remarkable feature is that it blooms when no other flower does—in the dead of the Great Night. The Midnight Glory was one name though it had another, newer, which entered common use since the occupation: the Blue Empress.

I knew there and then that I had found Arthur.

A pall of sulfurous smoke hangs permanently over the Valley of Kilns, lit with hellish tints from the glow of the kilns below. A major ceramics center on a high, treeless plateau? How are the kilns fueled? Volcanic vents do the firing, but they turn this long defile in the flank of Mount Tooloowera into a little hell of clay, bones, smashed porcelain, sand, slag, and throat-searing sulfur. Glehenta is the last of the Porcelain Towns, wedged into the head of the valley, where the river Iddis still carries a memory of freshness and cleanliness. The pottery houses, like upturned vases, lean toward one another like companionable women.

And there is the house to which my questions guided me: as my informants described; not the greatest but perhaps the meanest; not the foremost but perhaps the most prominent, tucked away in an alley. From its roof flies a flag, and my breath caught: not the Four White Hands of Yoo—never that, but neither the Blue Empress. The smoggy wind tugged at the hand-and-dagger of the Hydes of Grangegorman.

Swift action: to hesitate would be to falter and fail, to turn and walk away, back down the Valley of the Kilns and the Ten Thousand Steps. I rattle the ceramic chimes. From inside, a huff and sigh. Then a voice: worn ragged, stretched and tired, but unmistakable.

"Come on in. I've been expecting you."

> *V crepitant movebitvolutans:* Wescott's Wandering Star. A wind-mobile vine, native of the Ishtaria altiplano, that grows into a tight spherical web of vines which, in the Venerian Great Day, becomes detached from an atrophied root stock and rolls cross-country, carried on the wind. A central calyx contains woody nuts that produce a pleasant rattling sound as the Wandering Star is in motion.

Cut paper, painted, layed, and gummed. Perhaps the most intricate of the Venerian papercuts.

The Seer's Story

Tea?

I have it sent up from Camahoo when the stickmen make the return trip. Proper tea. Irish breakfast. It's very hard to get the water hot enough at this altitude, but it's my little ritual. I should have asked you to bring some. I've known you were looking for me from the moment you set out from Loogaza. You think anyone can wander blithely into Glehenta?

Tea.

You look well. The years have been kind to you. I look like shit. Don't deny it. I know it. I have an excuse. I'm dying, you know. The liquor of the vine—it takes as much as it gives. And this world is hard on humans. The Great Days— you never completely adjust—and the climate: if it's not the thin air up here, it's the molds and fungi and spores down there. And the ultraviolet. It dries you out, withers you up. The town healer must have frozen twenty melanomas off me. No, I'm dying. Rotten inside. A leather bag of mush and bones. But you look very well, Ida. So, Patrick shot himself? Fifteen years too late, say I. He could have spared all of us . . . enough of that. But I'm glad you're happy. I'm glad you have someone who cares, to treat you the way you should be treated.

I am the Merciful One, the Seer, the Prophet of the Blue Pearl, the Earth Man, and I am dying.

I walked down that same street you walked down. I didn't ride, I walked, right through the center of town. I didn't know what to expect. Silence. A mob. Stones. Bullets. To walk right through and out the other side without a door opening to me. I almost did. At the very last house, the door opened and an old man came out and stood in front of me so that I could not pass. "I know you." He pointed at me. "You came the night of the *Javrosts*." I was certain then that I would die, and that seemed not so bad a thing to me. "You were the merciful one, the one who spared our young." And he went into the house and brought me a porcelain cup of water and I drank it down, and here I remain. The Merciful One.

They have decided that I am to lead them to glory, or, more likely, to death. It's justice, I suppose. I have visions, you see—*pula* flashbacks. It works differently on Terrenes than Thents. Oh, they're hardheaded enough not to believe in divine inspiration or any of that rubbish. They need a figurehead—the repentant mercenary is a good role, and the odd bit of mumbo jumbo from the inside of my addled head doesn't go amiss.

Is your tea all right? It's very hard to get the water hot enough this high. Have I said that before? Ignore me—the flashbacks. Did I tell you I'm dying? But it's good to see you; oh, how long is it?

And Richard? The children? And Grangegorman? And is Ireland . . . of course. What I would give for an eyeful of green, for a glimpse of summer sun, a blue sky.

So, I have been a con man and a lover, a soldier and an addict, and now I end my time as a revolutionary. It is surprisingly easy. The Group of Seven Altiplano Peoples' Liberation Army do the work: I release gnomic pronouncements that run like grass fire from here to Egayhazy. I did come up with the Blue Empress motif: the Midnight Glory: blooming in the dark, under the breath of the high snows. Apt. They're not the most poetic of people, these potters. We drove the Duke of Yoo from the Valley of the Kilns and the Ishtar Plain: she is resisted everywhere, but she will not relinquish her claim on the altiplano so lightly. You've been in Egayhazy—you've seen the forces she's moving up here. Armies are mustering, and my agents report 'rigibles coming through the passes in the Palisades. An assault will come. The Duke has an alliance with House Shorth—some agreement to divide the altiplano up between them. We're outnumbered. Outmaneuvered and outsupplied, and we have nowhere to run. They'll be at each other's throats within a Great Day, but that's a matter of damn for us. The Duke may spare the kilns—they're the source of wealth. Matter of damn to me. I'll not see it, one way or other. You should leave, Ida. *Pula* and local wars—never get sucked into them.

Ah. Unh. Another flashback. They're getting briefer, but more intense.

Ida, you are in danger. Leave before night—they'll attack in the night. I have to stay. The Merciful One, the Seer, the Prophet of the Blue Pearl, can't abandon his people. But it was good, so good of you to come. This is a terrible place. I should never have come here. The best traps are the slowest. In you walk, through all the places and all the lives and all the years, never thinking that you are already in the trap, then you go to turn around, and it has closed behind you. Ida, go as soon as you can . . . go right now. You should never have come. But . . . oh, how I hate the thought of dying up here on this terrible plain! To see Ireland again. . . .

V volanti musco: Altiplano Air-moss. The papercut shows part of a symbiotic lighter-than-air creature of the Ishtari altiplano. The plant part consists of curtains of extremely light hanging moss that gather water from the air and low clouds. The animal part is not reproduced.

Shredded paper, gum.

He came to the door of his porcelain house, leaning heavily on a stick, a handkerchief pressed to mouth and nose against the volcanic fumes. I had tried to plead with him to leave, but whatever else he has become, he is a Hyde of Grangegorman, and stubborn as an old donkey. There is a wish for death in him; something old and strangling and relentless with the gentlest eyes.

"I have something for you," I said, and I gave him the box without ceremony.

His eyebrows rose when he opened it.

"Ah."

"I stole the Blue Empress."

"I know."

"I had to keep it out of Patrick's hands. He would have broken and wasted it, like he broke and wasted everything." Then my slow mind, so intent on saying this confession right, that I had practiced on the space-crosser, and in every room and every mode of conveyance on my journey across this world, flower to flower, story to story: my middle-aged mind tripped over Arthur's two words. "You knew?"

"All along."

"You never thought that maybe Richard, maybe Father, or Mammy, or one of the staff had taken it?"

"I had no doubt that it was you, for those very reasons you said. I chose to keep your secret, and I have."

"Arthur, Patrick is dead, Rathangan is mine. You can come home now."

"Ah, if it were so easy!"

"I have a great forgiveness to ask from you, Arthur."

"No need. I did it freely. And do you know what, I don't regret what I did. I was notorious—the Honorable Arthur Hyde, jewel thief and scoundrel. That has currency out in the worlds. It speaks reams that none of the people I used it on asked to see the jewel, or the fortune I presumably had earned from selling it. Not one. Everything I have done, I have done on reputation alone. It's an achievement. No, I won't go home, Ida. Don't ask me to. Don't raise that phantom before me. Fields of green and soft Kildare mornings. I'm valued here. The people are very kind. I'm accepted. I have virtues. I'm not the minor son of Irish gentry with no land and the arse hanging out of his pants. I am the Merciful One, the Prophet of the Blue Pearl."

"Arthur, I want you to have the jewel."

He recoiled as if I had offered him a scorpion.

"I will not have it. I will not touch it. It's an ill-favored thing. Unlucky. There are no sapphires on this world. You can never touch the Blue Pearl. Take it back to the place it came from."

For a moment, I wondered if he was suffering from another one of his hallucinating seizures. His eyes, his voice were firm.

"You should go, Ida. Leave me. This is my place now. People have tremendous ideas of family—loyalty and undying love and affection: tremendous expectations and ideals that drive them across worlds to confess and receive forgiveness. Families are whatever works. Thank you for coming. I'm sorry I wasn't what you wanted me to be. I forgive you—though as I said there is nothing to forgive. There. Does that make us a family now? The Duke of Yoo is coming, Ida. Be away from here before that. Go. The townspeople will help you."

And with a wave of his handkerchief, he turned and closed his door to me.

I wrote that last over a bowl of altiplano mate at the stickmen's caravanserai in Yelta, the last town in the Valley of the Kilns. I recalled every word, clearly and precisely. Then I had an idea; as clear and precise as my recall of that sad, unresolved conversation with Arthur. I turned to my valise of papers, took out my scissors and a sheet of the deepest indigo and carefully, from memory, began to cut. The stickmen watched curiously, then with wonder. The clean precision of the scissors, so fine and intricate, the difficulty and accuracy of the cut, absorbed me entirely. Doubts fell from me: Why had I come to this world? Why had I ventured alone into this noisome valley? Why had Arthur's casual acceptance of what I had done, the act that shaped both his life and mine, so disappointed me? What had I expected from him? Snip went the scissors, fine curls of indigo paper fell from them onto the table. It had always been the scissors I turned to when the ways of men grew too much. It was a simple cut. I had the heart of it right away, no false starts, no new beginnings. Pure and simple. My onlookers hummed in appreciation. Then I folded the cut into my diary, gathered up my valises, and went out to the waiting spider-car. The eternal clouds seem lower today, like a storm front rolling in. Evening is coming.

—

I write quickly, briefly.

Those are no clouds. Those are the 'rigibles of the Duke of Yoo. The way is shut. Armies are camped across the altiplano. Thousands of soldiers and javrosts. I am trapped here. What am I to do? If I retreat to Glehenta, I will meet the same fate as Arthur and the Valley people—if they even allow me to do that. They might think that I was trying to carry a warning. I might be captured as a spy. I do not want to imagine how the Duke of Yoo treats spies. I do not imagine my Terrene identity will protect me. And the sister of the Seer, the Blue Empress! Do I hide in Yelta and hope that they will pass me by? But how could I live with myself knowing that I had abandoned Arthur?

There is no way forward, no way back, no way around.

I am an aristocrat. A minor one, but of stock. I understand the rules of class, and breeding. The Duke is vastly more powerful than I, but we are of a class. I can speak with her, gentry to gentry. We can communicate as equals.

I must persuade her to call off the attack.

Impossible! A middle-aged Irish widow, armed only with a pair of scissors. What can she do? Kill an army with gum and tissue? The death of a thousand papercuts?

Perhaps I could buy her off. A prize beyond prize: a jewel from the stars, from their goddess itself. Arthur said that sapphires are unknown on this world. A stone beyond compare.

I am writing as fast as I am thinking now.

I must go and face the Duke of Yoo, female to female. I am of Ireland, a citizen of no mean nation. We confront the powerful, we defeat empires. I will go to her and name myself and I shall offer her the Blue Empress. The true Blue Empress. Beyond that, I cannot say. But I must do it and do it now.

I cannot make the driver of my spider-car take me into the camp of the enemy. I have asked her to leave me and make her own way back to Yelta. I am writing this with a stub of pencil. I am alone on the high altiplano. Above the shield wall, the cloud layer is breaking up. Enormous shafts of dazzling light spread across the high plain. Two mounted figures have broken from the line and ride toward me. I am afraid—and yet I am calm. I take the Blue Empress from its box and grasp it tight in my gloved hand. Hard to write now. No more diary. They are here.

V. Gloria medianocte: the Midnight Glory, or Blue Empress.
    Card, paper, ink.

Rich Larson was born in West Africa, has studied in Rhode Island and worked in Spain, and at twenty-three now writes from Edmonton, Alberta. His short work has been nominated for the Theodore Sturgeon Award and appears in multiple Year's Best anthologies, as well as in magazines such as *Asimov's, Analog, Clarkesworld, F&SF, Interzone, Strange Horizons, Lightspeed,* and *Apex.* Find him online at richwlarson.tumblr.com.

MESHED

Rich Larson

In the dusked-down gym, Oxford Diallo is making holo after holo his ever-loving bitch, shredding through them with spins, shimmies, quick-silver crossovers. He's a sinewy scarecrow, nearly seven foot already, but handles the ball so damn shifty you'd swear he has gecko implants done up in those supersized hands. Even with the Nike antioxygen mask clamped to his face, the kid is barely breathing hard.

"He's eighteen on November thirtieth, right?" I ask, cross-checking my Google retinal but still not quite believing it. I'm sick as anyone of hearing about the next Giannis Antetokounmpo, the next Thon Maker, but Oxford Diallo looks legit, frighteningly legit.

Diallo senior nods. Oxford's pa is not one for words; that much I already gleaned from the silent autocab ride from hotel to gym. Movie star cheek-bones, hard sharp eyes. The stubble on his head has a swatch of gray coming in. He's not as tall as his son, which is like saying, I don't know, the Empire State Building is not as tall as Taipei 101. They're both really fucking tall, and the elder's got more heft to him, especially with the puffy orange fisherman's coat he has on. I guess he's fresh enough from Senegal that the climate-controlled gym feels cold to him.

On the floor, Oxford moves to a shooting drill, loping between LED-lit circles, catching and firing the ball in rhythm. High release, smooth snap of the wrist. The nylon net goes hiss hiss hiss. He makes a dozen in a row, and when he finally misses it jolts me, like a highlight compilation has somehow gone wrong. That's how good the stroke is.

"Form looks solid," I say, because I don't think his pa would understand if I told him watching his son shoot jumpers is like freebasing liquid poetry.

"He works hard," Diallo senior allows. "Many shots. Every day." His retinal blinks ice blue. "Excuse me, Victor." He picks a small plastic case off the bleacher and heads for the lockers. Normally I'd think it's some kind of bit, leaving me alone to contemplate in silence, but he's been doing it like clockwork since I picked him and his son up from the terminal at SeaTac. Some kind of lung condition. It's not hereditary, so I didn't bother remembering the name of it.

I'm already sold, I've been sold for the past half hour, but Oxford starts to slam anyways. He launches the ball high for an alley-oop, hunts down the bounce and plucks it out of the air, lofting up, hanging hard like gravity's got the day off. He swipes it right-to-left behind his back and flushes it with his offhand in one mercury-slick motion.

"Fuck," I breathe. "We have got to get this kid meshed."

I mean, seeing it is one thing. Being able to feel it via nervecast, feel that impossible airtime and liquid power, have the rim float towards you in first person while your muscles twitch and flex, is going to be something else entirely.

After a few more goes at the rack, Oxford sees me waving and jaunts over, looping the ball between his lanky legs on repeat. He takes after his pa facially but his eyes aren't as sharp yet, and when the antioxygen mask peels free with a sweat-suction pop, he's got a big white Cheshire grin that would never be able to fit into Diallo senior's mouth.

"Oxford, my man," I say. "How do you like the shoes?"

He curls his toes in the factory-fresh Nikes, flexing the porous canvas. The new thing is the impact gel, which is supposed to tell when you're coming down hard and cradle the ankle, mitigate sprains and all that. But they also happen to look bomb as fuck, lime green with DayGlo orange slashes. I told my girlfriend, Wendee, I'm getting her a pair for her birthday; she told me she'd rather get herpes.

"I like them well," Oxford says reverently, but I can tell his vocabulary is letting him down. The look in his eyes says bomb as fuck.

"Better make some room in your closet," I say. "Because we're going to get you geared up to here. All the merch you can handle. Anything you want."

"You want to sign me," Oxford grins.

"Oxford, I want you to eat, breathe, and shit Nike for the foreseeable future," I tell him, straight up. "I would say you're going to be a star, but stars are too small. You are going to be the goddamn sun about which the league revolves in a few years."

Oxford pounds the ball thoughtfully behind his back, under his shinbones. "The sun is a star. Also."

"And a smartass, too," I say. "Fanfeeds are going to love you." I start tugging the contract together in my retinal, putting the bank request through. Sometimes the number of zeroes my company trusts me to wield still floors me. "We'll want your mesh done for Summit, which might take some doing. Technically nerve mesh shouldn't go in until eighteen, but technically it also has health-monitoring functionality, so with parental consent we should be able to bully in early. I'll do up a list of clinics for your pa—"

I stop short when I realize the grin has dropped off Oxford's face and down some chasm where it might be irretrievable.

"No," he says, shaking his head.

"No what?"

His eyes go hard and sharp. "No mesh."

What do you mean he's not getting meshed? my boss pings me, plus a not-unusual torrent of anger/confusion emotes that makes my teeth ache.

"I mean he doesn't want it," I say, sticking my hands under the tap. "He says he won't get the mesh, period."

I'm in the bathroom, because I couldn't think up a better excuse. The mirror is scrolling me an advertisement for skin rejuvenation, dicing up my face and projecting a version sans stress lines. The water gushes out hot.

Do they even know what it is? Did you explain?

"They know what a nerve mesh is," I say indignantly. "They're from Senegal, not the moon." I slap some water on my cheeks, because that always helps in the movies, then muss and unmuss my hair. The mirror suggests I try a new Lock'n'Load Old Spice sculpting gel. "But yeah," I mutter. "I, uh, I did explain."

Once Oxford's pa got back to the bleachers, I gave both of them the whole wiki, you know, subcutaneous nodes designed to capture and transmit biofeedback, used to monitor injuries and fatigue and muscle movement, and also nervecast physical sensation and first-person visual to spectators. If we get our way, with a little swoosh in the bottom left corner.

It's not something I usually have to sell people on. Most kids, even ones from the most urban of situations, have saved up enough for at least one classic nervecast of Maker sinking the game-winner for Seattle in the '33 Finals, or Dray Cardeno dunking all over three defenders back when he was still with the Phoenix Phantoms. Most kids dream about getting their mesh how they dream about getting their face on billboards and releasing their own signature shoes.

The Diallos listened real intent, real polite, and when I was finished Oxford just shook his head, and his pa put a hand on his shoulder and told me that his son's decision was final, and if Nike wasn't willing to flex on the nerve mesh, another sponsor would. At which point I spilled some damage control, got both of them to agree to dinner, and bailed to the bathroom for a check-in with my boss.

It's a zero-risk procedure now, for fuck's sakes. You can do it with an autosurgeon. Change his mind. A procession of eye rolling and then glaring emotes, all puffing and red-cheeked.

"What if we just put a pin in the mesh thing and sign him anyways?" I say. "We can't let this one get away. You saw the workout feed. We sign him unmeshed, let things simmer, work it into the contract later on as an amendment."

If he's playing at HoopSumm, he needs a mesh. That's the coming out party. How the fuck are we supposed to market him without a mesh? Skeptical emote, one eyebrow sky-high. *I thought you could handle this one solo, Vic. Thought you wanted that recommendation for promo. Am I wrong?*

"No," I say quick. "I mean, you're not wrong." I yank a paper towel off the dispenser and work it into a big wad with my wet hands. I never elect biofeedback when chatting someone with the power to get me fired; if I did there would be some serious middle-finger emotes mobbing his way.

Figure out if it's him or the dad who's the problem. Then use the one to get to the other. It's not brain surgery. There's a chortling emote for the pun, then he axes the chat.

I'm left there shredding the damp paper towel into little bits, thinking about the promotion that I do want, that I absolutely do want. I'd finally be making more than my old man, and Wendee would be happy for me for at least a week, and maybe during that blissed-out week I would get up the balls to ask her to move in.

But first, I have to get the Diallos to sign off on a nerve mesh. I'm not exactly bursting with ideas. That is, not until I go to toss the towel in the recycler and see a rumpled napkin inked with bright red blood sitting on top. Then I remember Oxford's pa and his little plastic case. I shove it all down and head back to the gym, only pausing to order a tube of that new hair gel.

I take them to a slick new brick-and-glass AI-owned bar, because taking them up the Space Needle would be too obvious. A little holohost springs up at the entry, flashes my retinal for available funds, and takes us straight to private dining. We pass a huge transparent pillar full of chilled wine, which I notice Oxford's pa look at sideways. More important is Oxford himself staring at the shiny black immersion pods set into the back of the bar. I send them a subtle ping to start scrolling ad banners for some fresh League nervecasts while we settle in around the table.

"Fully automated," I say, as the waiter rolls up to start dispensing bread baskets, arms all clicking and whirring. "Not bad, right?"

Oxford's pa nods his head, looking weirdly amused.

"They have AI cafés in Dakar," Oxford informs me, scrolling through the tabletop menu. "Since last year."

He's already put in an order for scallops, so I guess it's too late to head for the Space Needle. Instead I ping the kitchens for oysters and a few bottles of whatever wine has the highest alcohol content, which turns out to be something called General Washington. I pull up a wiki about vintages to give Oxford's pa some background, seeing how I can barely tell the difference between a white and a red.

"To the Diallos," I say, once me and him have our glasses filled and Oxford is nursing a Coke.

"Cheers," Oxford beams.

We make some chatter about the length of the flight, about the stereotype that it always rains in Seattle but how really it's mostly just cloudy. My mouth is more or less on autopilot because I'm watching for Oxford to peer over at the immersion pods. When I catch him at it the third time, I give him a nod.

"Have a go, man," I say. "Company tab. We'll grab you when the food is here." Oxford grins and lopes off without any further convincing, leaving me with Diallo senior. I lean over and top off his wine glass. "You started off playing in the African leagues, isn't that right, Mr. Diallo?"

He takes a drink and makes an approving glance at the bottle. "Yes," he says. "Then Greece."

"You must have been a terror back then," I say. "To drag Trikala all the way to the A1 finals."

Oxford's pa shrugs, but looks nearly pleased.

"I watched a few highlight reels," I say modestly. "Part of the job, isn't it, checking out the pedigree." I swish my wine back and forth and take a big gulp. "Oxford gets it from somewhere."

"From more than me or his mother," Diallo senior says. "From who knows where. Maybe God."

But he's glad enough to talk about the stint in Greece for a while, about how he was nearly picked up by Cordoba in the Liga ACB before the bronchiectasis reared its head and suddenly he couldn't run how he used to. I ping the kitchens to hold the food.

When the bottle is gone and Oxford's pa is finally slumping a bit in his chair, eyes a bit shiny, I spring the question. "Why doesn't your boy want a mesh?" I say.

Oxford's pa flicks his gaze over to the immersion pod where his son is jacked in. "His grandfather had a mesh," he says. "My wife's father. He was a soldier."

I kind of startle at that. I mean, I know, in theory, that the nerve mesh technology was military before it went commercial—so was Velcro—but I never thought about it getting use over in fucking West Africa.

"They used them to track troop movements," Oxford's pa continues. "And to monitor the health of the soldiers. To monitor their anxiety."

"Ours do that, too," I say. "Mental health of our players is a top priority."

"They did more than that." Diallo senior empties his glass with a last gulp, then sets it down and looks over at the second bottle. "They wired them for remote override of the central nervous system. You have heard of puppeteering, yes?"

I shake my head. I already know I'm not going to like whatever it is.

Oxford's pa opens the new wine bottle with his big spidery hands, looking pensive. "It means a soldier cannot break ranks or desert," he says. "A soldier cannot turn down an order to execute six prisoners taking up too much space in the convoy. Someone else, someone far away, will pull their finger to pull the trigger." He sloshes wine into his glass and tops mine off, gesturing with his other hand. "A soldier cannot be interrogated, because someone far away will lock their jaws shut, or, if the interrogation is very painful, unplug their brainstem."

He mimes yanking a cord with two fingers, and I feel suddenly sick, and not from the wine. "That's fucking awful," I say. "Christ."

"Not our invention," Diallo senior says.

"But that's nothing like what we do with ours," I say. "We don't control anything. Not a thing. If you could help your son to understand that—"

"Not a thing," Diallo senior echoes. He snorts. "You think knowing a million people are going to be watching out of your eyes does not control what you do?"

"If you're talking about off-court fanfeeds, those are entirely optional," I say, but I'm not sure that's what he's talking about. "The fans love them, of course," I add. "But it's not contractual."

"Oxford does not want you inside his body," Diallo senior says. "He does not want you behind his eyes. He does not want the mesh."

Then his retinal blinks blue, and it's a good thing, because I don't have a good response. He excuses himself to the washroom with his kit, weaving just slightly on his way, which leaves me sitting with a full wine glass and the mental image of some mutilated soldier having his brain shut down by committee.

But that's nothing like our mesh.

I nab Oxford out of the immersion pod while his pa's still in the washroom. He climbs out looking all groggy, craning his head to see where the scallops are at.

"What'd you think?" I say. "You like the nervecast?"

Oxford nods, almost reverently. "I crossed up Ash Limner," he says.

"That could be you in there, you know," I say, tapping the pod. "People would be paying to be you in there."

Oxford gives the pod a look with just a bit of longing in it.

"Everyone has a mesh," I say. "Ash Limner is meshed. Dray Cardeno is meshed. Why not Oxford Diallo, huh?"

Oxford chews his lip. "I promised," he says.

"To your grandfather?" I ask.

He looks surprised. "Yes."

"But this mesh is different, Oxford," I say. "We don't call the shots. You call the shots. We're just along for the ride."

Oxford frowns. "He said the mesh is a net you never get untangled from."

"You said you liked the nervecast," I say. "That's kind of hypocritical of you, don't you think? You enjoying someone else's nervecast when you won't get a mesh for yourself?"

"No," Oxford says simply. "They chose."

"They chose, yeah, of course," I say. "It's always a choice. But they made the right choice. Man, you have a gift. Your dad said it himself. You have a gift from God." I put my hand on the pod again. "You owe it to the world to make the most of that gift. I'm never going to know what it's like to slam how you do. I could barely dirty-dunk back in high school. Ninety-nine point ninety-nine percent of people are never going to know what it's like. Unless you let us."

I can sense him wavering. He's looking down at the pod, looking at his reflection in the shiny black mirror of it. I feel guilty in my gut, but I push right through, because this is important, getting this deal, and he'll thank me later.

"You owe it to us," I say. "Your dad's in the washroom. You know what he's doing in there?"

Oxford looks up, startled. Nods.

"Hacking up blood," I say. "He's never going to run again. Not how he used to. You don't think he'd like a chance to feel that again? To hit the break? To get out for that big dunk in transition, pound up the hardwood, slice right to the rack, drop the bomb like *wham*." I clap my hands together and Oxford flinches a bit. "You owe it, man," I say. "You owe it to your dad. He got you here, didn't he? He got you all this way."

And that's when Diallo senior comes out of the washroom, and I couldn't have done it any better if I choreographed it myself, because he staggers a bit against the wall and looks suddenly old, suddenly tired. Oxford looks at him, looks scared as hell. Maybe realizing, for the first time, that his pa won't be around forever.

I reach as high as I can and put my hand on his shoulder. "You know the right call, yeah?"

He hesitates, then slowly nods, and I want to bite off my tongue but I tell myself it's worth it. Tell myself the both of them will thank me later.

Supper is quiet. Oxford is obviously still thinking about what I said, stealing odd glances over at his pa, and his pa is trying to figure out what's going on without actually asking. It's a relief for everyone, I think, when the oysters are finished and we head back outside.

The Seattle sky's gone dark and the air is a bit nippy. Oxford's pa pulls on a pair of gloves while we wait for the autocab. When it pulls up, Oxford announces he's not ready to head back to the hotel yet. He wants to shoot.

"Yeah, alright," I say. "Can head back to the gym. Got it rented for the whole day."

"No," Oxford says. "Somewhere outside."

So we end up doing loops through the downtown until GPS finds an outdoor court at some Catholic school ten minutes away. There's no one else there when we show up, and the court has one of those weird rubbery surfaces, but Oxford doesn't seem to mind. He zips off his trackies and digs his ball out of his duffel.

His pa keeps the gloves on to feed him shots, moving him around the arc, hitting him with nice crisp passes right in the shooting pocket. You can tell that this whole thing, this whole tableau, with him under the net and Oxford catching, shooting, catching, shooting, is something they've done a million times on a million nights. The bright white floodlights make them into long black silhouettes. Neither of them talk, but little puffs of steam come out of Oxford's mouth as he moves.

I watch from the chain-link fence, leaning back on it. Oxford's form is still smooth levers and pistons, but when I get a glimpse of his face I can see he is not smiling how he smiled in the gym. I manage to lock eyes with him, and I give him a nod, then give him some privacy by walking down to the other end of the court. I hear him start talking to his pa in what my audio implant tells me is Serer.

I'm thinking the contract is as good as signed, and I'm about to tell as much to my boss when I hear the ball slam into the chain-link fence, sending ripples all down the length. I turn to see Oxford's pa shrugging off his orange jacket, face tight and livid mad. He looks right at me, the sort of look you give something stuck to the bottom of your bomb-as-fuck shoe, then turns to his son.

"You think I cannot remember what it feels like to run?" he says. "You pity me?"

Oxford shakes his head desperately, saying something in Serer again, but his pa is not listening.

"We will play, then," he says, and I get that he's talking in English so I'll understand. "You beat me, you can get the mesh surgery. Yes?"

"I did not want. . . . " Oxford trails off. He stares at me, confused, then at his pa, hurt.

"It will be easy," Diallo senior says. "I am old. I have bad lungs." He scoops the ball off the pavement and fires it into Oxford's chest. His son smothers it with his big hands but still has to take a step back, maybe more from the surprise than from the impact.

Oxford puts it on the floor and reluctantly starts his dribble. "Okay," he says, biting at his lips again. "Okay."

But he sleepwalks forward and his pa slaps the ball away, way quicker than I would have thought possible. Diallo senior bullies his son back into the post, hard dribble, fake to the right and then a short sharp jump hook up over his left shoulder. It's in the net before Oxford can even leave his feet.

They're playing make it take it, or at least Oxford's pa is. He gets the ball again and bangs right down to another post-up, putting an elbow into Oxford's chest. Oxford stumbles. The same jump hook, machine precision, up and in. The cords swish.

"I thought you want it now," Diallo senior says. "I thought you want your mesh."

Oxford looks stricken, but he's not looking over at me anymore. He's zeroed in. The next time his pa goes for the hook, he's ready for it, floating up like an astronaut and slapping the shot away hard. Diallo senior collects it in the shadows, brings it back, but the next time down on the block goes no better. Oxford pokes the ball away and dribbles it back to the arc, near enough to me that I can hear a sobbing whine in his throat. I remember that he's really still a kid, all seven feet of him, and then he drills the three-pointer with his pa's hand right in his face.

And after that it's an execution. It's Oxford darting in again and again breathing short angry breaths, sometimes stopping and popping the pull-up jumper, sometimes yanking it all the way to the rack. He's almost crying. I don't know if they're playing to sevens, or what, but I know the game is over when Oxford slips his pa on a spin and climbs up and under from the other side of the net, enough space to scoop in the finger roll nice and easy, but instead his arm seems to jack out another foot at least, impossibly long, and he slams it home hard enough that the backboard shivers. He comes down with a howl ripped out of his belly, and the landing almost bowls his pa over, sends him back staggering.

Diallo senior gathers himself. Slow. He goes to pick up the ball, but suddenly his grimace turns to a cough and he doubles over. The rusty wracking sound is loud in the cold air and goes on forever. Oxford stands there frozen, panting how he never panted in the gym, staring at his pa, and I stand there frozen staring at both of them. Then Diallo senior spits up blood in a ragged parabola on the sticky blue court, and his son breaks the frieze. He stumbles over, wraps his arms around him.

A call from my boss blinks onto my retinal, accompanied by a sample from one of the latest blip-hop hits. It jangles back and forth across my vision while I stand there like a statue. Finally, I cancel the call and take a breath.

"You don't have to sign right away," I say.

Oxford and his pa both look up, remembering I'm there. I shouldn't be.

"You can think about it," I stammer, ashamed like I've never been. "More. About the contract."

I want to tell them to forget the contract. Forget the mesh. We'll make you famous without it. But instead I skulk away, out through the cold metal gate, leaving the Diallos huddled there under the floodlight, breathing a single cloud of steam.

Alastair Reynolds is the bestselling author of over a dozen novels. He has received the British Science Fiction Award for his novel *Chasm City*, as well as the Seiun and Sidewise awards, and was shortlisted for the Hugo and Arthur C. Clarke awards. He has a Ph.D in Astronomy and worked for the European Space Agency before he left to write full time. His short fiction has been appearing in *Interzone, Asimov's,* and elsewhere since 1990. Alastair's latest novel is *The Medusa Chronicles*, co-written with Stephen Baxter.

After spending many years in the Netherlands, he has now returned to Wales.

A MURMURATION

Alastair Reynolds

What we call the "hut" is a couple of insulated portable cabins, with a few smaller sheds containing generators, fuel, wind turbine parts and so on. The main cabin contains a chemical toilet, a wash basin, basic cooking facilities and a set of bunk-beds. The second cabin holds our desks, computer equipment and supply stores. Two or three of us can share the hut at a time, but there is not normally a need for more than one to keep an eye on the experiment. Resources being tight, lately we tend to come out on our own.

In all honesty, I prefer it this way. Birds draw out the solitude in us. They repay patience and silence—long hours of a kind of alert, anticipatory stillness. The days begin to blur into each other; weekends and weekdays becoming arbitrary distinctions. I find myself easily losing track of the calendar, birds and weather becoming my only temporal markers. I watch the migration patterns, record the nuances of altering plumage, study the changeful skies. I could not be happier.

There is just one thing to spoil my contentment, but even that, I am confident, will soon be behind me.

I *will* finish the paper.

It sounds easy, put like that. A vow. A recommitment, a redoubling of my own efforts. One last push.

It started easily enough—the usual set of objections, no real hint of the trouble to come. Very few papers ever go through without some amendments, so none of us were bothered that there were a few issues that needed addressing. But when we had fixed those, the anonymous referee came back with requests for more changes.

We took care of those, but still the referee wanted more of us. This kept going on. Just when we think we have addressed all possible doubts, the referee somehow manages to find something new to quibble with. I do my best to be stoic, reminding myself that the referee is just another scientist doing her job, that they too are under similar pressures, and that I should not feel under any personal attack.

But I only have to glance at their comments.

The authors are inconsistent in their handling of the normalisation terms for the correlation function of the velocity modulus. I am not convinced that their treatment of the smoothed Dirac delta-function is rigorous across the quoted integral.

My blood boils. I entertain a momentary fantasy of meeting the referee out here, on some lonely strip of marshland, of swerving violently and running them into a ditch.

Asking, as I watch them gag on muddy water: "Rigorous enough for you now?"

The basis of our experiment is a ring of twenty tripods, arranged in a two kilometre circle. The hut is on one side of the circle, the wind turbine offset a short distance from the other side. During the day I check all the tripods, picking the least waterlogged path in the 4WD.

Each unit carries a pair of stereometric digital cameras. The lenses need to be kept clean, the power and electronic connections verified. The cameras should be aimed into the middle of the perimeter, and elevated sufficiently to catch the murmuration's epicentre. The cameras are meant to be steerable, but not all of the motors work properly now.

Beneath each camera is a grey digital control box. The boxes contain microprocessor boards, emergency batteries, and the rectangles of their internal ethernet modules, flickering with yellow LEDs. The boxes are supposedly weatherproof but the rain usually finds a way into them. Like the motors, there have been some failures of the circuit boards.

About one in five of the stations have more equipment. On these units we also included laser/radar rangefinders and Doppler velocity recorders. These in turn require extra processors and batteries in the control boxes, which is yet more to go wrong. The effort is worth it, though.

The equipment allows us to track the instantaneous vectors of anything up to two hundred and fifty thousand birds, perhaps even half a million, in a single compact flock. Our spatial/temporal resolution is sufficient to determine wing movements down to the level of specific feather groups. At the same time we also gather data on the attentional shifts implied by eye and head tracking of individual birds.

The human eye sees a blurring of identities, birds becoming the indistinguishable, amorphous elements of some larger whole. The cameras and computers see through all of that. I know the science, I know the algorithms, I know our data-carrying capacity. All the same, I am still quietly astonished that we can do this.

When the cameras are checked, which can take anywhere between three and six hours, I have one final inspection to perform. I drive to the wind turbine, and make a visual inspection of the high grey tower and the swooping blades. More often than not there is nothing to be done. The blades turn, the power flows, our electrical and computer systems work as they are meant to.

The rest is down to the birds.

It's odd, really, but there are times when I find even the hut a little too closed-in and oppressive for my tastes. Sometimes I just stop the 4WD out here, wind the window down, and watch the light change over the marsh. I like it best when the day is overcast, the clouds sagging low over the trees and bushes of the marsh, their greyness relieved only by a bold supercilial swipe of pale yellow above the horizon. Birds come and go, and but it's too early for the roosting. I watch herons, curlew, reed warblers—sometimes even the slow, methodical patrol of our resident marsh harrier. She quarters the ground with the ruthless precision of a surveillance drone.

Beyond the birds, the only constancy is the regular swoosh of the turbine blades.

It's a good time to catch up on work or reading.

I pull laser-printed pages from the unruly nest of the glove compartment, along with tissues, cough sweets, empty medicine packets, a scuffed CD without a case. I rest a stiff-backed road atlas on the steering wheel, so that I can write on the pages.

I've already marked up certain problematic passages in yellow highlighter. Now I use a finer pen to scribble more detailed notes in the margins. Eventually I'll condense these notes into a short email to the journal editor. In turn they'll forward them on to the author of the paper I am refereeing.

This is how it works. I'm engaged in a struggle with my own anonymous referee, half-convinced that they've got it in for me, while at the same time trying to be just as nit-picking and difficult for this other author. Doubtless they feel just as irritated by me. But from my end, I know that there's nothing personal in it. I just want the work to be as good as it can be, the arguments as lucid, the analysis as rigorous. So what if I know the lead author, and don't particularly care for her? I can rise above that.

I hold one of the sheets up to the yellowing sky, so that the band of light pushes through the highlit yellow passages. I read back my own scrawl in the margins:

Sloppy handling of the synthetic correlation function—doesn't inspire confidence in rest of analysis.

Am I being too harsh with them?

Perhaps. But then we've all been through this mill.

Starlings gather, arriving from all directions, concentrating in the air above the copse of trees and bushes near the middle of the study area. They come in small numbers, as individuals or in flocks of a few dozen, before falling into the greater mass. There is no exact threshold at which the concentration of birds becomes a recognisable murmuration, but it needs at least a few thousand before the form begins to emerge as a distinct phenomenon in its own right, with its swooping, gyring, folding cohesiveness—a kind of living membrane in the sky.

Meanwhile, our instruments record. One hundred parametric data points per bird per millisecond, on average, or upwards of fifty gigabytes of data for the whole murmuration. Since the murmuration may persist for several tens of minutes, our total data cube for the whole observation may contain more than thirty terabytes of data, and a petabyte is not exceptional. We use some of the same data-handling and compression routines as the particle physicists in CERN, with their need to track millions of microscopic interaction events. They are tracking tiny bundles of energy, mass, spin and charge. We are tracking warm, feathery bodies with hearts and wings and twitchy central nervous systems!

All of it is physics, though, whether you are studying starlings or quarks.

On my workstation I sift through slices of the data with tracker-wheels and mouse glides.

I graph up a diagram of the murmuration at a moment in time, from an arbitrary viewing angle. It is a smear-shaped mass of tiny dots, like a pixelated thumbprint. On the edges of the murmuration the birds are easily distinguishable. Closer to the core the dots crowd over each other, forming gradients of increasing concentration, the birds packing together with an almost Escher-like density. Confronted with those black folds and ridges, it is hard not to think of the birds as blending together, clotting into a suspended, gravity-defying whole.

I mouse click and each dot becomes a line. Now the smear is a bristly mass, like the pattern formed by iron filings in the presence of a magnetic field. These are the instantaneous vectors for each bird—the direction and speed in which they are moving.

We know from previous studies that each starling has a direct influence on—and is in turn influenced by—about seven neighbours. We can verify this with the vector plots, tracking the change in direction of a particular bird, and then noting the immediate response of its neighbours. But if that were the limit of the bird's influence, the murmuration would be sluggish to respond to an outside factor, such as the arrival of a sparrowhawk.

In fact the entity responds as a whole, dividing and twisting to outfox the intruder. It turns out that there is a correlation distance much greater than the separation between immediate neighbours. Indeed, that correlation between distant birds may be as wide as the entire murmuration. It is as if they are bound together by invisible threads, each feeling the tug of the other—a kind of rubbery net, stretching and compressing.

In fact, the murmuration may contain several distinct "domains" of influence, where the flight patterns of groups of birds are highly correlated. In the plot on my workstation, these show up as sub-smears of strongly aligned vectors. They come and go as the murmuration proceeds, blending and dissipating—crowds within the larger crowd.

This is where the focus of our recent research lies. What causes these domains to form? What causes them to break up? Can we trace correlation patterns between the domains, or are they causally distinct? How sharp are the boundaries—how permeable?

This paper, the one that is bouncing back and forth between us and the referee, was only intended to set out the elements of our methodology—demonstrating that we had the physical and mathematical tools to study the murmuration at any granularity we chose. Beyond that, we had plans to produce a series of papers which would build on this preliminary work with increasingly complex experiments. So far we have been no more than passive observers. But if we have any claim to understand the murmuration, then we should be able to predict its response to an external stimulus.

I am starting to sense an impasse. Can we honestly go through this all over again with our next publication, and the one after? The thought of that leaves me drained. We have the tools for the next phase of our work, so why not push ahead with the follow-up study, and fold the results of that back into the present paper? Steal a march on our competitors, and dazzle our referee with the sheer effortless audacity of our work?

I think so.

The next day I set up the sparrowhawk.

I need hardly add that it is not a real sparrowhawk. Designed for us by our colleagues at the robotics laboratory, it is a clever, swift-moving drone. It has wings and a tail and its flight characteristics are similar to those of a real bird. It has synthetic feathers, a plastic bill, large glassy eyes containing swivel-mounted cameras. To the human eye, it looks a little crude and toy-like—surely too caricatured to pass muster. But the sparrowhawk's visual cues have been exaggerated very carefully. From a starling's point of view, it is maximally effective, maximally terrifying. It lights up all the right fear responses.

Come the roost, I set down a folding deck chair, balance the laptop in my lap, stub my gloved fingers onto the scuffed old keyboard, with half the letters worn away, and I watch the spectacle. The sparrowhawk whirrs from the roof of the 4WD, soars into the air, darts forward almost too quickly for my own eyes to track.

It picks a spot in the murmuration and arcs in like a guided missile.

The murmuration cleaves, twists, recombines.

The sparrowhawk executes a hairpin turn and returns for the attack. It skewers through the core of the flock, jackknifes its scissor wings, zigzags back. It makes a low electric hum. Some birds scatter from the periphery, but the murmuration as a whole turns out to be doggedly persistent, recognising on some collective level that the sparrowhawk cannot do it any real damage, only picking off its individual units in trifling numbers.

The sparrowhawk maintains its bloodless attack. The murmuration pulses, distends, contracts, its fluctuations on the edge of chaos, like a fibrillating heart. I think of the sparrowhawk as a surgeon, drawing a scalpel through a vital organ, but the tissue healing faster than the blade can cut.

Never mind—the point is not to do harm, but to study the threat response. And by the time the sparrowhawk's batteries start to fade, I know that our data haul will be prodigious.

I can barely sleep with anticipation.

—

But overnight, there's a power-outage. The computers crash, the data crunching fails. We run on the emergency generator for a little while, then the batteries. Come morning I drive out in the 4WD, open the little door at the base of the tower, and climb the clattery metal ladder up the inside. There are battery-operated lights, but no windows. The ladder goes up through platforms, each a little landing, before swapping over the other side. Heights are not my thing, but it's just about within my capabilities to go all the way to the top without getting seriously sweaty palms or stomach butterflies.

At the top, I come out inside the housing of the turbine. It's a rectangular enclosure about the size of our generator shed. I can just about stand up in it, moving around the heavy electrical machinery occupying most of the interior space. At one end, a thick shaft goes out through the housing to connect to the blades.

The turbine is complicated, but fortunately only a few things tend to go wrong with it. There are electrical components, similar to fuses, which tend to burn out more often than they should. We keep a supply of them up in the housing, knowing how likely it is that they will need swapping out. I am actually slightly glad to see that it is one of the fuses that has gone, because at least there is no mystery about what needs to be done. I have fixed them so many times, I could do it in my sleep.

I open the spares box. Only three left in it, and I take one of them out now. I swap the fuse, then reset the safety switches. After a few moments, the blades unlock and begin to grind back into motion. The electrical gauges twitch, showing that power is being sent back to our equipment. Not much wind today, but we only need a few kilowatts.

Job done.

I think of starting down, but having overcome my qualms to get this high, I cannot resist the opportunity to poke my head out of the top. At the back of the electrical gear is a small ladder which leads to an access hatch in the roof of the housing.

I go up the short steps of the ladder, undo the catches, and heave open the access hatch.

My knees wobble a bit. I push my head through the hatch, like a tank commander. I look around. There's a rubberised walkway on top, and a set of low handrails, so in theory I could go all the way out and stand on top of the housing. But I've never done that, and I doubt that I would ever have the nerve.

Still with only my head jutting out, I look back at the hut, a huddle of pale rectangles. The perimeter circle is hard to trace from this elevation, but eventually I glimpse the spaced-out sentinels of the tripods, with the scratchy traces of my own wheel tracks between them. Then I pivot around and try to pick out the causeway. Telegraph poles offer a hint of its direction. But it's harder to follow than I expect, seeming to abandon itself in a confusion of marsh and bog. I squint to the horizon, looking for a trace of its continuation.

Strange how some things are clearer to the eye at ground level than they are from the air.

Birds must know this in their bones.

The next day, the computers up and running again, I squeeze our data until it bleeds science. With the vector tracking, we can trace the response to the sparrowhawk across all possible interaction lengths. Remarkable to see how effectively the 'news' of the sparrowhawk's arrival is disseminated through that vast assemblage of birds.

Because there is no centralised order, the murmuration is best considered as a scale-free network. The internet is like that, and so is the human brain. Scale-free networks are robust against directed attacks. There is no single hub which is critical to the function of the whole, but rather a tangle of distributed pathways, no one of which is indispensable. On the other hand, the scale-free paradigm does not preclude the existence of those vector domains I mentioned earlier. Just as the internet has its top-level domains, so the brain has its hierarchies, its functional modules.

Would it be a leap too far to start thinking of the murmuration as hosting some level of modular organisation?

I jot down some speculative notes. No harm in sleeping on them. In the meantime, though, I write up the sparrowhawk results in as dry and unexciting manner as I can manage, downplaying any of the intellectual thrill I feel. Passive voice all the way. *The sparrowhawk was prepared for remote control. Standard reduction methods were used in the data analysis. The murmuration was observed from twenty spatially separated viewing positions—see Fig. 3.*

The way to do science is never to sound excited by it, never to sound involved, never to sound as if this is something done by people, with lives and loves and all the usual hopes and fears.

I send the latest version of the paper back to the journal, and cross my fingers.

—

I open the glove compartment and take out the latest version of the paper. I skim it quickly, then go back through some of the more problematic passages with the yellow highlighter, before adding more detailed notes in the margin. My initial optimism quickly turns to dismay. Why in hell have they opened up this whole other can of worms? I squint at an entire new section of the paper, hardly believing my eyes.

Sparrowhawks? Robot sparrowhawks? And pages of graphs and histograms and paragraphs of analysis, all springing from work which was not even fore-shadowed in the original paper?

What are they thinking?

I'm furious at this. Furious with the journal editor, for not spotting this late addition before it was forwarded to me. Furious with the authors, for adding to our mutual workload. Furious for their presumption, that I will presum-ably be sufficiently distracted by this to overlook the existing flaws—like a magpie distracted by something shiny? (Except that's a myth; corvids are not attracted to shiny things at all.)

Furious above all else that they are prepared to squander this good and original science, to slip it into this paper like a lazy afterthought, as a kind of intellectual bribe.

No, this must not stand.

I put the 4WD back into gear. I must settle my thoughts before firing back an intemperate response. But really, I'm enraged. They think they know who I am, I'm sure. I imagine encountering them out here, running them down, feeling the bounce of my wheels over their bodies. I'd stop the 4WD, get out, walk slowly back. Savour the squelch of my boots on the marshy ground.

Their whimpering, their broken-boned pleas.

"You think this is how we do science, do you?" I'd ask them, entirely rhe-torically. "You think it is a kind of game, a kind of bluff? Well, the joke's on you. I'm recommending your paper be rejected."

And then I would walk away, ignoring their noises, get back into the 4WD, drive off. At night their cries would still come in across the marsh. I wouldn't let myself be troubled by that. They brought this on themselves, after all.

But that sparrowhawk, I'll admit, *was beautiful.*

I go out to the walk-in traps and collect the overnight haul. There are almost always some birds in the snares, and almost always some starlings. It is how we ring them, bring them in for study, assess their overall genetic fitness.

Generally they are none the worse for having been caught up in the nets overnight.

I collect ten adult specimens, let the others go, and take the ten back to the hut.

A firm in Germany has made the digital polarising masks for us. They are elegant little contraptions, similar in design to the hoods fitted around captive birds of prey. These are smaller, though, optimised to be worn by starlings, and to offer no significant resistance to normal flight. Each hood is actually a marvel of miniature electronic engineering. Bulging out from either side are two glassy hemispheres.

In its neutral mode, the bird has an unrestricted view of its surroundings. Each hemisphere, though, is divided into digitally-controlled facets. These can be selectively darkened via wireless computer signals, effectively blocking out an area of the starling's vision.

The consequence of this—the point of the masks—is that we can control the birds' collision-avoidance response remotely. By making a given bird think it is about to be struck by another bird, we can cause it to fly in any direction we choose.

Again, it is asking too much of human reflexes to control a bird at such a level. But the computers can do it elegantly and repeatably. Each of our ten hooded starlings then becomes a remote-controlled agent, under our direct operation. Like the robot sparrowhawk, we can steer our agents into the murmuration. The distinction is that the hooded starlings do not trigger a threat response from their seven neighbours; they are absorbed into the whole, accepted and assimilated.

But they *can* influence the other birds. And by careful control of our hooded agents, we can initiate global changes in the entire murmuration. We can instigate domains, break them up, make them coalesce. Anything that happens under the influence of natural factors, we can now bring about at our will.

By we, of course, I mean I.

Old habits die hard. Science is always done in the 'we', even when the work is borne on a single pair of shoulders. But frankly, I am starting to doubt the commitment of my fellow researchers. There is always a division of labour in any collaborative enterprise, and sometimes that division can seem unfair. If the brunt of the work is my responsibility, though, I fail to see why I should not receive the lion's share of the credit.

As I wait for the murmuration to form, I make some deft amendments to the list of the authors, striking out a name here, a name there.

Feathers will fly, of course.

—

Ten birds might not seem much but these birds are like precision instruments, guided with digital finesse. To begin with, we—I—restrict myself to only minor interventions.

I make the murmuration split into two distinct elements, then recombine.

Suitably encouraged, I quarter it like a flag. I pull it apart into four rippling sheets of birds, with arcs of clear air between them. The edges are improbably straight, as if the birds are glassed-in, boxed by invisible planes. But that is the power of incredibly delicate control processes, of stimulus and feedback operations happening much too swiftly for human perception. If an edge starts losing coherence, the computer makes a tiny adjustment to one or more of the control starlings and the order is reestablished. This happens many times a second, at the speed of avian reactions.

They have always lived in a faster world than us. They live a hundred days in one of our hours. To them we are slow, lumbering, ogrelike beings, pinned to the ground by the stonelike mass of our bodies. We envy them; they pity us.

I push forward. I carve geometries out of the murmuration. I fold it into a torus, then a ribbon, then a Möbius strip. I do not need to know how to make these shapes, only to instruct the laptop in my desires. It works out the rest, and becomes more adept as it goes along.

I make the murmuration spell out letters, then I coax those letters into lumpy, smeared-out words. I spell my name in birds. They banner around me like the slogans towed by light aircraft. I laugh even as I feel that I have crossed some line, some invisible threshold between pristine science and sordid exploitation.

But I carry on anyway. I am starting to think about those domains, those hints of modular organisation.

How far could I push this, if I were so determined?

Angry exchanges of emails. Editor not happy with this latest change of direction. Much to-ing and fro-ing. Questions over the change in the listed authors—deemed most unorthodox. Accusations of unprofessionalism. If we were in a room together, the three of us, we might get somewhere. Or we might end up throwing textbooks.

Is this a travesty of the way science ought to be done, or is it science at its shining best—as loaded with passion and conviction as any other human enterprise? No one would doubt that poets squabble, that a work of great literature might take some toll on its creator, that art forges enemies as readily as allies. Why do we hold science to a colder, more emotionless set of standards? If we care at all about the truth, should we not celebrate this anger, this clashing of viewpoints?

It means that something vital is at stake.

Hard in the spitting crucible of all this to remember that every one of us was drawn to this discipline because of a love of birds.

But that is science.

My proposition is simple. The domains are controllable. I can cause them to form, contain the shape and extent of their boundaries, determine the interaction of their vector groups with the surrounding elements. I can move the domains around with the flock. I can blend one domain into another, merging them like a pair of colliding galaxies. Depending on their vector properties, I can choose whether that act results in the destruction of both domains or the formation of a larger one.

I sense the possibility of being able to execute a kind of Boolean algebra.

If the domains behave in a controllable and repeatable way, and I can determine their states—their aggregate vector sums—then I can treat them as inputs in a series of logic operations.

The thought thrills me. I cannot wait for the coming of dusk.

With the laptop reprogrammed, I quickly satisfy myself that the elements of my Boolean experiment are indeed workable. I create the simplest class of logic gate, an AND gate. I classify the input domain states as either being 0 or 1, and after some trials I achieve a reliable "truth table" of outputs, with my gate only spitting out a "1" if the two inputs share that value.

I push on. I create OR and NOT gates, a "not AND," or NAND gate, a NOR gate, an XOR and XNOR gate. Each is trickier than the last, each requires defter control of the domains and vector states. To make things easier—at the burden of a high computational load on the computer and the ethernet network—I retrieve more birds from the snares, fitting them with additional digital hoods.

Now I can create finer domains, stringing them together like the modules in an electrical circuit.

I begin to "wire up" the flock. I assign gates to perform logical operations, but also to store data. Again, I need only tell the laptop what I want it to do— it takes care of the computational heavy-lifting. All I know is what my eyes tell me. The murmuration has grown knotted and clotted, dense with domain boundaries and threaded with the thick synapses of internal data corridors. It swoops and billows over me, a circuit board of birds.

The astonishing thing is that on the level of individual starlings, they sense no strangeness—no inkling that they are participating in anything but a normal murmuration. The complexity is emergent, operating on a scale that the birds simply cannot sense, cannot share. They are cells in a larger organism.

I lash together a Perl script, a simple text-to-logic program on the laptop, enabling me to send natural language queries to the flock.

IS ONE AND ONE TWO?

There is a process of calculation. The circuit shuffles. I glean the flow of information along its processing channels—the physical movement of birds and their larger domain boundaries.

The answer returns. The laptop takes the Boolean configuration and converts it back into natural language.

>>YES.

I try another query.

IS ONE AND ZERO ZERO?

A swoop, a billow, a constant busy shuffling of birds.

>>NO.

I smile. Maybe a fluke.

IS ONE AND ZERO ONE?

>>YES.

I am elated.

Over the next thirty minutes, I run through question after question. The birds answer unfailingly. They are computing, and doing so with the utmost machinelike reliability.

>>YES YES NO YES YES NO NO NO.

I am doing algebra with starlings.

But as the gloom gathers, as the dusk deepens, something troubles me.

In all my interventions to date, one thing has remained true. The murmuration eventually dissipates. The roosting instinct overpowers the flocking instinct, and the birds cascade down into the trees. It happens very quickly, a kind of runaway escalation. Whenever I have witnessed it, I am always saddened, for it is the end of the show, but I am also awed by what is another demonstration of marvellous collective action.

And then the skies are clear again, until the birds lift at dawn. This is what should happen.

But now the murmuration will not break up.

Some birds leave it, maybe a third, but a core remains. I hammer at the laptop—more puzzled than worried at first. I try to disrupt the logic flow, randomise the data, dismantle the knotty Boolean architecture. But the pattern remains obstinately present. The sky darkens, until only the cameras and rangefinders are able to track the birds, and then with difficulty.

But I can still hear them up there—a warm but unseen presence, like a halo of dark matter hovering over me.

I think it's time to recuse myself from refereeing this paper.

After all the time and work I've invested in the process, it's hardly a decision I take lightly. But there is a difference between acting as a gatekeeper and a psychiatrist. I'm afraid that recent developments have given me cause for concern.

We all work under some degree of stress. Science is not a carefree playground. It's an arena where reputations crash as readily as they soar. Commit some error of analysis, read too much into noise, claim a premature discovery, and you may as well tie your own academic noose. Forget those keynote lectures. Forget those expenses-paid conference invitations. You'll be tarnished—dead in the water.

I've felt the pressure myself. I know what solitude and overwork can do to your objectivity. All the same, there are limits. I should have sensed that things were not going well long before they reached this latest development.

I explain to the journal editor that I'm no longer in a position to offer a balanced opinion on the worth of this work. Frankly, I'm not even sure it still qualifies as science.

I'm stuffing the paper back into the glove compartment when it meets some obstruction, some object lodged at the back. I push my fingers into the mess and meet a stiff, sharp-edged rectangle about the size of a credit card.

For a moment there's a tingle of recognition.

I pull out the offending object, study it under the 4WD's dome light. It's a piece of grey foil printed with the name and logo of a pharmaceutical company. The foil contains six blisters. All but one of the blisters have been popped and emptied of their contents.

The sixth still holds a small yellow pill.

I wonder what it does?

I sleep badly, but dare to hope that the murmuration will have gone by morning—broken up or drifted away elsewhere. But when I wake, I find it still present.

If anything, it has grown. I run a number count and find that it has been absorbing birds, sucking them into itself. More than half a million now. Enslaved to the murmuration, the individual birds will eventually exhaust themselves and drop out of the sky. But the whole does not care, any more than I concern myself with the loss of a few skin cells. As long as there are fresh starlings to be fed into the machine, it will persist.

I drive the 4WD out again, set up the laptop, try increasingly desperate and random measures to make the pattern terminate itself.

Nothing works.

But the supply of new birds is not inexhaustible. Sooner or later, if they keep coming, it will churn its way through all the starlings in the country. Long before that happens, though, the wrongness of this thing will have become known to others beside myself. They will know that I had something to do with it. They will admire me at first, for my cleverness. After that, they will start blaming me.

I want it to end. Here. Now.

So.

Desperate measures. The wind is stiff today, the bushes and trees buckling over. Even the birds struggle to hold their formation, although the will of the murmuration forces itself through.

I make it move. I can still do that.

I steer the murmuration in the direction of the wind turbine. The blades swoop around at the limit of their speed: if it were any windier, the automatic brakes would lock the turbine into immobility. The edge of the flock begins to enter the meat slicer. I hear its helicopter whoosh, the cyclic chop of its great rotors. The blades knock the birds out of the sky in their hundreds, an instant bludgeoning execution. They tumble out of formation, dead before they hit the ground.

This is merciful, I tell myself. Better than being trapped in the murmuration.

But my control slackens. The domains are resisting, slipping out of my grip. The ensemble won't allow itself to be destroyed by the wind turbine.

It knows what I have tried to do.

It knows that I am trying to murder it.

On my laptop the Perl script says:

>>NO. NO. NO.

The pill leaves a bitter but familiar aftertaste. With a clarity of mind I haven't known—or don't remember knowing—in quite some time, I make my way once more to the top of the turbine tower. It's odd that I feel this compulsion, since my fear of heights hasn't abated, and for once there's nothing wrong with the turbine, beyond some fresh dark smears on the still-turning blades.

In the housing, I ease around the humming core of the generator and its whirring shaft. The dials are all still registering power—enough for my needs, at any rate. We're still down to those last few replacement fuses, but there's no need to swap one of them at the moment.

I climb the little ladder and poke my head out through the roof hatch.

Steeling myself, pushing my fear aside, I put my elbows on the rim and lever my body up through the hatch. Finally I'm sitting on the rim, with my legs and feet still dangling back into the housing. The wind is hard and cold up here, a relentless solid force, but with the enclosing handrails there's no real chance of me falling. All the same, it takes my last reserves of determination to rise from the hatch, pushing myself up until I am standing on the rubberised decking. The handrails seem too low now, and the gaps between the uprights too widely spaced. With each swoop of the blades, the housing moves under me. My knees wobble. My stomach flutters and sweat pools in the palms of my gloved hands.

But I will not fall. That's not why I've come to the top of the turbine.

Once more I survey my little world from this lofty vantage. The hut, the instruments, the parked vehicle. The low sky. The boggy tracks of my daily routine.

The harder gleam of the causeway, arrowing away.

But it never gets anywhere. The causeway vanishes into bog and then the bog opens up into the silver mirror of a larger expanse of open water. I squint, trying to pick up the causeway's continuation beyond the flooded area. There, maybe. A scratch of iron-grey, arrowing on toward the horizon. But dark shapes bordering that scratch. Cars, vans—all stopped. Some of them tipped over or emptied like skulls. Burnt out.

I might be imagining it.

Beyond the marsh, beyond the enclosing water, nothing that hints at civilisation. The telegraph poles run some distance, then sag into the water—their lines cut or submerged.

I realise now that I've been here a lot longer than weeks. I know also that I don't need to worry about being a scientist any more. That's the least of anyone's concerns. Being a scientist is just something I used to do, a long time ago.

I wish I could hold onto this. I wish I could remember that the paper doesn't matter, that the journal doesn't matter, that nothing matters. That the only thing left to worry about is holding on, keeping things at bay. But unless I'm mistaken that was the last of my medication.

Finally the wind and the swaying overcome my will. I start down the tower, back to the ground.

At the 4WD I stand and watch the birds. That clarity hasn't completely left me, that knowledge of what I am and what has become of me. I can feel it leaking out of my head as if there are drainage holes in the base of my skull. For the moment, though, there's still enough of it there. I know what happened.

But the murmuration still contains troubling structure—sharp edges, block knots of density, shifting domains and restless connections. Symmetries and geometries. Did I cause all of that to come into being, or is this now the way of things? Is it a kind of equivalence, order emerging in the natural world, while order is eclipsed in ours? Have I been trying to communicate with the murmuration, or is it the other way around? Which of us is the observer, which the phenomenon?

If I tried to kill it, will it find it in itself to forgive me?

I try to hold onto these questions. They seem hugely important to me now. But one pill was never going to hold the dusk at bay.

In the morning I feel much better about things now. Finally, I think I can see a way through—a fresh approach, a new chance of publication. It will mean going back to the start of the process, but sometimes you have no choice— you just have to cut your losses.

I draft a letter to the editor. Although it pains me to do it, I feel that we have no option but to request a new referee. Things have gone on long enough with this old one. Frankly the whole exchange was in danger of getting too personal. We all know that the anonymous part counts for very little these days, and in all honesty professional feelings were starting to get in the way. I had a suspicion about their identity, and of course mine was all too visible to them. We had history. Too much bad blood, too much accumulated recrimination and mistrust. At least this way we will be off to a clean start again.

I read it over, make a few alterations, then send the letter. It might be misplaced optimism, but this time I am quietly confident of success.

I look forward to hearing from the editor.

RECOMMENDED READING

"Ruins" by Eleanor Arnason, *Old Venus*
"A Stopped Clock" by Madeline Ashby, *War Stories from the Future*
"City of Ash" by Paolo Bacigalupi, *Matter* (July 2015)
"My Last Bringback" by John Barnes, *Meeting Infinity*
"The Heart's Filthy Lesson" by Elizabeth Bear, *Old Venus*
"The Machine Starts" by Greg Bear, *Future Visions*
"It Takes More Muscles to Frown" by Ned Beauman, *Twelve Tomorrows 2016*
"Twelve and Tag" by Gregory Norman Bossert, *Asimov's* (March 2015)
"Ratcatcher" by Tobias S. Buckell, *Xenowealth*
"Evangelist" by Adam-Troy Castro, *Analog* (November 2015)
"The Great Silence" by Ted Chiang, *e-flux Journal* (56th Venice Biennale)
"勢孤取和 (Influence Isolated, Make Peace)" by John Chu, *Lightspeed* (June 2015)
"The Vital Abyss" by James S.A. Corey, Orbit Books
"The Citadel of Weeping Pearls" by Aliette de Bodard, *Asimov's* (October/November 2015)
"Taste the Whip" by Andy Dudak, *Diabolical Plots* (March 2015)
"The Four Thousand, the Eight Hundred" by Greg Egan, *Asimov's* (December 2015)
"The New Mother" by E. J. Fischer, *Asimov's* (April/May 2015)
"Liminal Grid" by Jaymee Goh, *Strange Horizons* (November 9, 2015)

"The Light Brigade" by Kameron Hurley, Patreon

"The 1st Annual Lunar Biathlon" by Rachael Jones, *Crossed Genres* (October 2015)

"The Last Hunt" by Vylar Kaftan, *Asimov's* (September 2015)

"Consolation" by John Kessel, *Twelve Tomorrows 2016*

"Machine Learning" by Nancy Kress, *Future Visions*

"Gamer's End" by Yoon Ha Lee, *Press Start to Play*

"My Father's Crab" by Bruce McAllister, *Analog* (October 2015)

"The Falls: A Luna Story" by Ian McDonald, *Meeting Infinity*

"Little Sisters" by Vonda McIntyre, Book View Cafe

"When Your Child Strays from God" by Sam J. Miller, *Clarkesworld* (July 2015)

"Plural" by Lia Swope Mitchell, *Cosmos* (February/March 2015)

"The Molenstraat Music Festival" by Sean Monaghan, *Asimov's* (September 2015)

"Binti" by Nnedi Okorafor, *Tor.com* (August 17, 2015)

"Our Lady of the Open Road" by Sarah Pinsker, *Asimov's* (June 2015)

"Today's Smarthouse in Love" by Sarah Pinsker, *The Magazine of Fantasy & Science Fiction* (May/June 2015)

"The City of Your Soul" by Robert Reed, *The Magazine of Fantasy & Science Fiction* (November/December 2015)

"Slow Bullets" by Alastair Reynolds, Tachyon Publications

"The Three Resurrections of Jessica Churchill" by Kelly Robson, *Clarkesworld* (February 2015)

"Inhuman Garbage" by Kristine Kathryn Rusch, *Asimov's* (March 2015)

"The Museum of Modern Warfare" by Kristine Kathryn Rusch, *Analog* (December 2015)

"I Had No Head and My Eyes Were Floating Way up in the Air" by Clifford D. Simak, *I Am Crying All Inside and Other Stories: The Complete Short Fiction of Clifford D. Simak*

"The Reluctant Jew" by Rachel Swirsky, *Jews vs Aliens*

"Planet Lion" by Catherynne M. Valente, *Uncanny* (May/June 2015)

"The Internet of Things Your Mother Never Told You" by Jo Lindsay Walton, *Twelve Tomorrows 2016*

"On the Night of the Robo-Bulls and Zombie Dancers" by Nick Wolven, *Asimov's* (February 2015)

"Ether" by Zhang Ran, *Clarkesworld* (January 2015)

PERMISSIONS

ABOUT THE EDITOR

Neil Clarke is the editor of *Clarkesworld* and *Forever Magazine,* owner of Wyrm Publishing, and a three-time Hugo Award Nominee for Best Editor (short form). He currently lives in New Jersey with his wife and two children. You can find him online at neil-clarke.com.